JACK HIGGINS

Three Complete Novels

Also by Jack Higgins

JACK HIGGINS

Three Complete Novels

Eye of the Storm

Thunder Point

On Dangerous Ground

G. P. Putnam's Sons   New York

G. P. Putnam's Sons
Publishers Since 1838
a member of
Penguin Putnam Inc.
375 Hudson Street
New York, NY 10014

Library of Congress Cataloging-in-Publication Data

Higgins, Jack, date.
[Novels. Selections]
Three complete novels / Jack Higgins.
p. cm.
Contents: Eye of the storm—Thunder point—On dangerous ground.
ISBN 0-399-14727-6
1. Adventure stories, English. 2. Spy stories, English. I. Title.

PR6058.I343 A6   2001   00–051840
823'914—dc21

Printed in the United States of America

1   3   5   7   9   10   8   6   4   2

Book design by Meighan Cavanaugh

Contents

Eye of the Storm

The winds of heaven are blowing. Implement all that is on the table. May God be with you.

—Coded message,
Iraq radio, Baghdad
January 1991

The mortar attack on Number Ten Downing Street when the War Cabinet was meeting at 10:00 A.M. on Thursday, 7 February 1991, is now a matter of history. It has never been satisfactorily explained. Perhaps it went something like this. . . .

ONE

It was just before dark as Dillon emerged from the alley and paused on the corner. Rain drifted across the Seine in a flurry of snow, sleet mixed with it and it was cold, even for January in Paris. He wore a reefer coat, peaked cap, jeans and boots, just another sailor off one of the barges working the river, which he very definitely was not.

He lit a cigarette in cupped hands and stayed there for a moment in the shadows, looking across the cobbled square at the lights of the small café on the other side. After a while, he dropped the cigarette, thrust his hands deep in his pockets and started across.

In the darkness of the entrance two men waited, watching his progress. One of them whispered, "That must be him."

He made a move. The other held him back. "No, wait till he's inside."

Dillon, his senses sharpened by years of entirely the wrong kind of living, was aware of them, but gave no sign. He paused at the entrance, slipped his left hand under the reefer coat to check that the Walther PPK was securely tucked into the waistband of his jeans against the small of his back, then he opened the door and went in.

It was typical of the sort of place to be found on that part of the river: half a dozen tables with chairs, a zinc-topped bar, bottles lined against a cracked mirror behind it. The entrance to the rear was masked by a bead curtain.

The barman, a very old man with a gray moustache, wore an alpaca coat, the sleeves frayed at the cuffs and there was no collar to his shirt. He put down the magazine he was reading and got up from the stool.

"Monsieur?"

Dillon unbuttoned his reefer coat and put his cap on the bar, a small man, no more than five feet five with fair hair and eyes that seemed to the barman to be of no particular color at all except for the fact that they were the coldest the old man had ever looked into. He shivered, unaccountably afraid, and then Dillon smiled. The change was astonishing, suddenly nothing but warmth there and immense charm. His French, when he spoke, was perfect.

"Would there be such a thing as half a bottle of champagne in the house?"

The old man stared at him in astonishment. "Champagne? You must be joking, monsieur. I have two kinds of wine only. One is red and the other white."

He placed a bottle of each on the bar. It was stuff of such poor quality that the bottles had screw tops instead of corks.

"All right," Dillon said. "The white it is. Give me a glass."

He put his cap back on, went and sat at a table against the wall from where he could see both the entrance and the curtained doorway. He got the bottle open, poured some of the wine into the glass and tried it.

He said to the barman, "And what vintage would this be, last week's?"

"Monsieur?" The old man looked bewildered.

"Never mind." Dillon lit another cigarette, sat back and waited.

The man who stood closest to the curtain peering through was in his mid-fifties, of medium height with a slightly decadent look to his face, the fur collar of his dark overcoat turned up against the cold. He looked like a prosperous businessman right down to the gold Rolex on his left wrist, which in a way he was as a senior commercial attaché at the Soviet Embassy in Paris. He was also a colonel in the KGB, one Josef Makeev.

The younger, dark-haired man in the expensive vicuña overcoat who peered over his shoulder was called Michael Aroun. He whispered in French, "This is ridiculous. He can't be our man. He looks like nothing."

"A serious mistake many people have made, Michael," Makeev said. "Now wait and see."

The bell tinkled as the outer door swung open, rain blowing in, and the two men entered who had been waiting in the doorway as Dillon crossed the square. One of them was over six feet tall, bearded, an ugly scar running into the right eye. The other was much smaller, and they were dressed in reefer coats and denims. They looked exactly what they were, trouble.

They stood at the bar and the old man looked worried. "No trouble," the younger one said. "We only want a drink."

The big man turned and looked at Dillon. "It seems as if we've got one right here." He crossed to the table, picked up Dillon's glass and drank from it. "Our friend doesn't mind, do you?"

Without getting out of his chair Dillon raised his left foot and stamped downwards against the bearded man's kneecap. The man went down with a choked cry, grabbing at the table, and Dillon stood. The bearded man tried to pull himself up and sank into one of the chairs. His friend took a hand from his pocket, springing the blade of a gutting knife, and Dillon's left hand came up holding the Walther PPK.

"On the bar. Christ, you never learn, people like you, do you? Now get this piece of dung on his feet and out of here while I'm still in a good mood. You'll need the casualty department of the nearest hospital, by the way. I seem to have dislodged his kneecap."

The small man went to his friend and struggled to get him on his feet. They stood there for a moment, the bearded man's face twisted in agony. Dillon went and opened the door, the rain pouring relentlessly down outside.

As they lurched past him, he said, "Have a good night," and closed the door.

Still holding the Walther in his left hand, he lit a cigarette using a match from the stand on the bar and smiled at the old barman, who looked terrified. "Don't worry, Dad, not your problem." Then he leaned against the bar and called in English, "All right, Makeev, I know you're there, so let's be having you."

The curtain parted and Makeev and Aroun stepped through.

"My dear Sean, it's good to see you again."

"And aren't you the wonder of the world?" Dillon said, just the trace of an Ulster accent in his voice. "One minute trying to stitch me up, the next all sweetness and light."

"It was necessary, Sean," Makeev said. "I needed to make a point to my friend here. Let me introduce you."

"No need," Dillon told him. "I've seen his picture often enough. If it's not on the financial pages, it's usually in the society magazines. Michael Aroun, isn't it? The man with all the money in the world."

"Not quite all, Mr. Dillon." Aroun put a hand out.

Dillon ignored it. "We'll skip the courtesies, my old son, while you tell whoever is standing on the other side of that curtain to come out."

"Rashid, do as he says," Aroun called, and said to Dillon, "It's only my aide."

The young man who stepped through had a dark, watchful face, and wore a leather car coat, the collar turned up, his hands thrust deep in the pockets.

Dillon knew a professional when he saw one. "Plain view." He motioned with the Walther. Rashid actually smiled and took his hands from his pockets. "Good," Dillon said. "I'll be on my way, then."

He turned and got the door open. Makeev said, "Sean, be reasonable. We only want to talk. A job, Sean."

"Sorry, Makeev, but I don't like the way you do business."

"Not even for a million, Mr. Dillon?" Michael Aroun said.

Dillon paused and turned to look at him calmly, then smiled, again with enormous charm. "Would that be in pounds or dollars, Mr. Aroun?" he asked and walked out into the rain.

As the door banged Aroun said, "We've lost him."

"Not at all," Makeev said. "A strange one this, believe me." He turned to Rashid. "You have your portable phone?"

"Yes, Colonel."

"Good. Get after him. Stick to him like glue. When he settles, phone me. We'll be at Avenue Victor Hugo."

Rashid didn't say a word, simply went. Aroun took out his wallet and extracted a thousand-franc note, which he placed on the bar. He said to the barman, who was looking totally bewildered, "We're very grateful," then turned and followed Makeev out.

As he slid behind the wheel of the black Mercedes saloon, he said to the Russian, "He never even hesitated back there."

"A remarkable man, Sean Dillon," Makeev said as they drove away. "He first picked up a gun for the IRA in nineteen seventy-one. Twenty years, Michael, twenty years and he hasn't seen the inside of a cell once. He was involved in the Mountbatten business. Then he became too hot for his own people to handle so he moved to Europe. As I told you, he's worked for everyone. The PLO, the Red Brigade in Germany in the old days. The Basque national movement, the ETA. He killed a Spanish general for them."

"And the KGB?"

"But of course. He's worked for us on many occasions. We always use the best and Sean Dillon is exactly that. He speaks English and Irish, not that that bothers you, fluent French and German, reasonable Arabic, Italian and Russian."

"And no one has ever caught him in twenty years. How could anyone be that lucky?"

"Because he has the most extraordinary gift for acting, my friend. A genius, you might say. As a young boy, his father took him from Belfast to

London to live, where he was awarded a scholarship to the Royal Academy of Dramatic Art. He even worked for the National Theatre when he was nineteen or twenty. I have never known anyone who can change personality and appearance so much just by body language. Makeup seldom enters into it, although I admit that it helps when he wants. He's a legend that the security services of most countries keep quiet about because they can't put a face to him, so they don't know what they're looking for."

"What about the British? After all, they must be the experts where the IRA are concerned."

"No, not even the British. As I said, he's never been arrested, not once, and unlike many of his IRA friends, he never courted media publicity. I doubt if there's a photo of him anywhere except for the odd boyhood snap."

"What about when he was an actor?"

"Perhaps, but that was twenty years ago, Michael."

"And you think he might undertake this business if I offer him enough money?"

"No, money alone has never been enough for this man. It always has to be the job itself where Dillon is concerned. How can I put it? How interesting it is. This is a man to whom acting was everything. What we are offering him is a new part. The Theatre of the Street perhaps, but still acting." He smiled as the Mercedes joined the traffic moving around the Arc de Triomphe. "Let's wait and see. Wait until we hear from Rashid."

At that moment, Captain Ali Rashid was by the Seine at the end of a small pier jutting out into the river. The rain was falling very heavily, still plenty of sleet in it. The floodlights were on at Notre Dame and the effect was of something seen partially through a net curtain. He watched Dillon turn along the narrow pier to the building on stilts at the far end, waited until he went in and followed him.

The place was quite old and built of wood, barges and boats of various kinds moored all around. The sign over the door said *Le Chat Noir*. He peered through the window cautiously. There was a bar and several tables just like the other place. The only difference was that people were eating. There was even a man sitting on a stool against the wall playing an accordion. All very Parisian. Dillon was standing at the bar speaking to a young woman.

Rashid moved back, walked to the end of the pier, paused by the rail in the shelter of a small terrace and dialed the number of Aroun's house in the Avenue Victor Hugo on his portable phone.

There was a slight click as the Walther was cocked and Dillon rammed the muzzle rather painfully into Rashid's right ear. "Now then, son, a few answers," he demanded. "Who are you?"

"My name is Rashid," the young man said. "Ali Rashid."

"What are you then? PLO?"

"No, Mr. Dillon. I'm a captain in the Iraqi Army, assigned to protect Mr. Aroun."

"And Makeev and the KGB?"

"Let's just say he's on our side."

"The way things are going in the Gulf, you need somebody on your side, my old son." There was the faint sound of a voice from the portable phone. "Go on, answer him."

Makeev said, "Rashid, where is he?"

"Right here, outside a café on the river near Notre Dame," Rashid told him. "With the muzzle of his Walther well into my ear."

"Put him on," Makeev ordered.

Rashid handed the phone to Dillon, who said, "Now then, you old sod."

"A million, Sean. Pounds if you prefer that currency."

"And what would I have to be doing for all that money?"

"The job of a lifetime. Let Rashid bring you round here and we'll discuss it."

"I don't think so," Dillon said. "I think what I'd really like is for you to get your arse into gear and come and pick us up yourself."

"Of course," Makeev said. "Where are you?"

"The left bank opposite Notre Dame. A little pub on a pier called *Le Chat Noir*. We'll be waiting."

He slipped the Walther into his pocket and handed the phone to Rashid who said, "He's coming, then?"

"Of course he is." Dillon smiled. "Now let's you and me go inside and have ourselves a drink in comfort."

In the sitting room on the first floor of the house in Avenue Victor Hugo overlooking the Bois de Boulogne, Josef Makeev put down the phone and moved to the couch where his overcoat was.

"Was that Rashid?" Aroun demanded.

"Yes. He's with Dillon now at a place on the river. I'm going to get them."

"I'll come with you."

Makeev pulled on his coat. "No need, Michael. You hold the fort. We won't be long."

He went out. Aroun took a cigarette from a silver box and lit it, then he turned on the television. He was halfway into the news. There was direct coverage from Baghdad, Tornado fighter bombers of the British Royal Air Force attacking at low level. It made him bitterly angry. He switched off, poured himself a brandy and went and sat by the window.

Michael Aroun was forty years of age and a remarkable man by any standards. Born in Baghdad of a French mother and an Iraqi father who was an army officer, he'd had a maternal grandmother who was American. Through her, his mother had inherited ten million dollars and a number of oil leases in Texas.

She had died the year Aroun had graduated from Harvard law school leaving everything to her son because his father, retired as a general from the Iraqi army, was happy to spend his later years at the old family house in Baghdad with his books.

Like most great businessmen, Aroun had no academic training in the field. He knew nothing of financial planning or business administration. His favorite saying, one much quoted, was: When I need a new accountant, I buy a new accountant.

His friendship with Saddam Hussein had been a natural development from the fact that the Iraqi President had been greatly supported in his early days in politics by Aroun's father, who was also an important member of the Baath Party. It had placed Aroun in a privileged position as regards the development of his country's oilfields, brought him riches beyond calculation.

After the first billion you stopped counting, another favorite saying. And now he was faced with disaster. Not only the promised riches of the Kuwait oilfields snatched from him, but that portion of his wealth which stemmed from Iraq dried up, finished as a result of the Coalition's massive air-strikes that had devastated his country since the seventeenth of January.

He was no fool. He knew that the game was over, should probably have never started, and that Saddam Hussein's dream was already finished. As a businessman he played the percentages and that didn't offer Iraq too much of a chance in the ground war that must eventually come.

He was far from ruined in personal terms. He had oil interests still in the USA, and the fact that he was a French as well as an Iraqi citizen gave Washington a problem. Then there was his shipping empire and vast quantities of real estate in various capital cities around the world. But that wasn't the point. He was angry when he switched on the television and saw what was happening in Baghdad each night, for, surprising in one so self-centered, he was a patriot. There was also the fact, infinitely more important, that his father had been killed in a bombing raid on the third night of the air war.

And there was a great secret in his life, for in August, shortly after the invasion of Kuwait by Iraqi forces, Aroun had been sent for by Saddam Hussein himself. Sitting here by the French window, a glass of brandy in one hand, rain slanting across the terrace, he gazed out across the Bois de Boulogne in the evening light and remembered that meeting.

There was an air-raid practice in progress as he was driven in an army Land-Rover through the streets of Baghdad, darkness everywhere. The driver was a young intelligence captain named Rashid, whom he had met before, one of the new breed, trained by the British at Sandhurst. Aroun gave him an English cigarette and took one himself.

"What do you think, will they make some sort of move?"

"The Americans and Brits?" Rashid was being careful. "Who knows? They're certainly reacting. President Bush seems to be taking a hard line."

"No, you're mistaken," Aroun said. "I've met the man face-to-face twice now at White House functions. He's what our American friends call a nice guy. There's no steel there at all."

Rashid shrugged. "I'm a simple man, Mr. Aroun, a soldier, and perhaps I see things simply. Here is a man, a Navy combat pilot at twenty, who saw a great deal of active service, who was shot down over the Sea of Japan and survived to be awarded the Distinguished Flying Cross. I would not underestimate such a man."

Aroun frowned. "Come on, my friend, the Americans aren't going to come halfway round the world with an army to protect one little Arab state."

"Isn't that exactly what the British did in the Falklands War?" Rashid reminded him. "They never expected such a reaction in Argentina. Of course they had Thatcher's determination behind them, the Brits, I mean."

"Damned woman," Aroun said and leaned back as they went in through the gate of the presidential palace, feeling suddenly depressed.

He followed Rashid along corridors of marble splendor, the young officer leading the way, a torch in one hand. It was a strange, rather eerie experience, following that small pool of light on the floor, their footfalls echoing. There was a sentry on each side of the ornate door they finally halted before. Rashid opened it and they went in.

Saddam Hussein was alone, sitting in uniform at a large desk, the only light a shaded lamp. He was writing, slowly and carefully, looked up and smiled, putting down his pen.

"Michael." He came round the desk and embraced Aroun like a brother. "Your father? He is well?"

"In excellent health, my President."

"Give him my respects. You look well, Michael. Paris suits you." He smiled again. "Smoke if you want. I know you like to. The doctors have unfortunately had to tell me to cut it out or else."

He sat down behind the desk again and Aroun sat opposite, aware of

Rashid against the wall in the darkness. "Paris was fine, but my place is here now in these difficult times."

Saddam Hussein shook his head. "Not true, Michael. I have soldiers in plenty, but few men such as you. You are rich, famous, accepted at the highest levels of society and government anywhere in the world. More than that, because of your beloved mother of blessed memory, you are not just an Iraqi, but also a French citizen. No, Michael, I want you in Paris."

"But why, my President?" Aroun asked.

"Because one day I may require you to do a service for me and for your country that only you could perform."

Aroun said, "You can rely on me totally, you know that."

Saddam Hussein got up and paced to the nearest window, opened the shutters and stepped on to the terrace. The all-clear sounded mournfully across the city and lights began to appear here and there.

"I still hope our friends in America and Britain stay in their own backyard, but if not . . ." He shrugged. "Then we may have to fight them in *their* own backyard. Remember, Michael, as the Prophet instructs us in the Koran, there is more truth in one sword than ten thousand words." He paused and then carried on, still looking out across the city. "One sniper in the darkness, Michael, British SAS or Israeli, it doesn't really matter, but what a coup—the death of Saddam Hussein."

"God forbid it," Michael Aroun said.

Saddam turned to him. "As God wills, Michael, in all things, but you see my point? The same would apply to Bush or the Thatcher woman. The proof that my arm reaches everywhere. The ultimate coup." He turned. "Would you be capable of arranging such a thing, if necessary?"

Aroun had never felt so excited in his life. "I think so, my President. All things are possible, especially when sufficient money is involved. It would be my gift to you."

"Good." Saddam nodded. "You will return to Paris immediately. Captain Rashid will accompany you. He will have details of certain codes we will be using in radio broadcasts, that sort of thing. The day may never come, Michael, but if it does, . . ." He shrugged. "We have friends in the right places." He turned to Rashid. "That KGB colonel at the Soviet Embassy in Paris?"

"Colonel Josef Makeev, my President."

"Yes," Saddam Hussein said to Aroun. "Like many of his kind not happy with the changes now taking place in Moscow. He will assist in any way he can. He's already expressed his willingness." He embraced Aroun, again like a brother. "Now go. I have work to do."

The lights had still not come on in the palace and Aroun stumbled out into the darkness of the corridor, following the beam of Rashid's torch.

Since his return to Paris he had got to know Makeev well, keeping their acquaintance, by design, purely on a social level, meeting mainly at various embassy functions. And Saddam Hussein had been right. The Russian was very definitely on their side, only too willing to do anything that would cause problems for the United States or Great Britain.

The news from home, of course, had been bad. The buildup of such a gigantic army. Who could have expected it? And then in the early hours of the seventeenth of January the air war had begun. One bad thing after another and the ground attack still to come.

He poured himself another brandy, remembering his despairing rage at the news of his father's death. He'd never been religious by inclination, but he'd found a mosque in a Paris side street to pray in. Not that it had done any good. The feeling of impotence was like a living thing inside him, and then came the morning when Ali Rashid had rushed into the great ornate sitting room, a notepad in one hand, his face pale and excited.

"It's come, Mr. Aroun. The signal we've been waiting for. I just heard it on the radio transmitter from Baghdad."

The winds of heaven are blowing. Implement all that is on the table. May God be with you.

Aroun had gazed at it in wonder, his hand trembling as he held the notepad, and his voice was hoarse when he said, "The President was right. The day has come."

"Exactly," Rashid said. "Implement all that is on the table. We're in business. I'll get in touch with Makeev and arrange a meeting as soon as possible."

Dillon stood at the French windows and peered out across the Avenue Victor Hugo to the Bois de Boulogne. He was whistling softly to himself, a strange, eerie little tune.

"Now this must be what the house agents call a favored location."

"May I offer you a drink, Mr. Dillon?"

"A glass of champagne wouldn't come amiss."

"Have you a preference?" Aroun asked.

"Ah, the man who has everything," Dillon said. "All right, Krug would be fine, but non-vintage. I prefer the grape mix."

"A man of taste, I see." Aroun nodded to Rashid, who opened a side door and went out.

Dillon, unbuttoning his reefer coat, took out a cigarette and lit it. "So, you need my services this old fox tells me." He nodded at Makeev, who lounged against the fireplace warming himself. "The job of a lifetime, he said, and for a million pounds. Now what would I have to do for all that?"

Rashid entered quickly with the Krug in a bucket, three glasses on a tray. He put them on the table and started to open the bottle.

Aroun said, "I'm not sure, but it would have to be something very special. Something to show the world that Saddam Hussein can strike anywhere."

"He needs something, the poor old sod," Dillon said cheerfully. "Things aren't going too well." As Rashid finished filling three glasses, the Irishman added, "And what's your trouble, son? Aren't you joining us?"

Rashid smiled and Aroun said, "In spite of Winchester and Sandhurst, Mr. Dillon, Captain Rashid remains a very *Muslim* Muslim. He does not touch alcohol."

"Well here's to you." Dillon raised his glass. "I respect a man with principles."

"This would need to be big, Sean, no point in anything small. We're not talking about blowing up five British Army paratroopers in Belfast," Makeev said.

"Oh, it's Bush you want, is it?" Dillon smiled. "The President of the United States flat on his back with a bullet in him?"

"Would that be so crazy?" Aroun demanded.

"It would be this time, son," Dillon told him. "George Bush has not just taken on Saddam Hussein, he's taken on the Arabs as a people. Oh, that's total rubbish, of course, but it's the way a lot of Arab fanatics see it. Groups like Hizbollah, the PLO or the wild cards like the Wrath of Allah people. The sort who would happily strap a bomb to their waist and detonate it while the President reached out to shake just another hand in the crowd. I know these people. I know how their minds tick. I've helped train Hizbollah people in Beirut. I've worked for the PLO."

"What you are saying is nobody can get near Bush at the moment?"

"Read your papers. Anybody who looks even slightly Arab is keeping off the streets these days in New York and Washington."

"But you, Mr. Dillon, do not look Arab to the slightest degree," Aroun said. "For one thing you have fair hair."

"So did Lawrence of Arabia and he used to pass himself off as an Arab." Dillon shook his head. "President Bush has the finest security in the world, believe me. A ring of steel, and in present circumstances he's going to stay home while this whole Gulf thing works through, mark my words."

"What about their Secretary of State, James Baker?" Aroun said. "He's been indulging in shuttle diplomacy throughout Europe."

"Yes, but knowing when, that's the problem. You'll know he's been in

London or Paris when he's already left and they show him on television. No, you can forget the Americans on this one."

There was silence and Aroun looked glum. Makeev was the first to speak. "Give me, then, the benefit of your professional expertise, Sean. Where does one find the weakest security, as regards national leaders?"

Dillon laughed out loud. "Oh, I think your man here can answer that, Winchester and Sandhurst."

Rashid smiled. "He's right. The British are probably the best in the world at covert operations. The success of their Special Air Service Regiment speaks for itself, but in other areas. . . ." He shook his head.

"Their first problem is bureaucracy," Dillon told them. "The British Security Service operates in two main sections. What most people still call MI5 and MI6. MI5 or DI5, to be pedantic, specializes in counterespionage in Great Britain. The other lot operates abroad. Then you have Special Branch at Scotland Yard who have to be brought into the act to make any actual arrests. The Yard also has an antiterrorist squad. Then there's army intelligence units galore. All life is there and they're all at each other's throats and that, gentlemen, is when mistakes begin to creep in."

Rashid poured some more champagne into his glass. "And you are saying that makes for bad security with their leaders? The Queen, for example?"

"Come on," Dillon said. "It's not all that many years ago that the Queen woke up in Buckingham Palace and found an intruder sitting on the bed. How long ago, six years, since the IRA almost got Margaret Thatcher and the entire British Cabinet at a Brighton hotel during the Tory Party Conference?" He put down his glass and lit another cigarette. "The Brits are very old-fashioned. They like a policeman to wear a uniform so they know who he is and they don't like being told what to do, and that applies to Cabinet Ministers who think nothing of strolling through the streets from their houses in Westminster to Parliament."

"Fortunate for the rest of us," Makeev said.

"Exactly," Dillon said. "They even have to go softly—softly on terrorists—up to a degree anyway, not like French Intelligence. Jesus, if the lads in Action Service got their hands on me they'd have me spread out and my bollocks wired up for electricity before I knew what was happening. Mind you, even they are prone to the occasional error."

"What do you mean?" Makeev demanded.

"Have you got a copy of the evening paper handy?"

"Certainly, I've been reading it," Aroun said. "Ali, on my desk."

Rashid returned with a copy of *Paris Soir*. Dillon said, "Page two. Read it out. You'll find it interesting."

He helped himself to more champagne while Rashid read the item aloud. "Mrs. Margaret Thatcher, until recently Prime Minister of Britain, is staying overnight at Choisy as a guest of President Mitterrand. They are to have further talks in the morning. She leaves at two o'clock for an airforce emergency field at Valenton, where an RAF plane returns her to England."

"Incredible, isn't it, that they could have allowed such a press release, but I guarantee the main London newspapers will carry that story also."

There was a heavy silence and then Aroun said, "You're not suggesting . . . ?"

Dillon said to Rashid. "You must have some road maps handy. Get them."

Rashid went out quickly. Makeev said, "Good God, Sean, not even you . . ."

"Why not?" Dillon asked calmly and turned to Aroun. "I mean, you want something big, a major coup? Would Margaret Thatcher do, or are we just playing games here?"

Before Aroun could reply, Rashid came back with two or three road maps. He opened one out on the table and they looked at it, all except Makeev, who stayed by the fire.

"There we are, Choisy," Rashid said. "Thirty miles from Paris, and here is the air-force field at Valenton only seven miles away."

"Have you got a map of larger scale?"

"Yes." Rashid unfolded one of the others.

"Good," Dillon said. "It's perfectly clear that only one country road links Choisy to Valenton and here, about three miles before the airfield, there's a railway crossing. Perfect."

"For what?" Aroun demanded.

"An ambush. Look, I know how these things operate. There'll be one car, two at the most, and an escort. Maybe half a dozen CRS police on motorbikes."

"My God!" Aroun whispered.

"Yes, well. He's got very little to do with it. It could work. Fast, very simple. What the Brits call a piece of cake."

Aroun turned in appeal to Makeev, who shrugged. "He means it, Michael. You said this was what you wanted, so make up your mind."

Aroun took a deep breath and turned back to Dillon. "All right."

"Good," Dillon said calmly. He reached for a pad and pencil on the table and wrote on it quickly. "Those are the details of my numbered bank account in Zurich. You'll transfer one million pounds to it first thing in the morning."

"In advance?" Rashid said. "Isn't that expecting rather a lot?"

"No, my old son, it's you people who are expecting rather a lot, and the rules have changed. On successful completion, I'll expect a further million."

"Now look here," Rashid started, but Aroun held up a hand.

"Fine, Mr. Dillon, and cheap at the price. Now what can we do for you?"

"I need operating money. I presume a man like you keeps large supplies of the filthy stuff around the house?"

"Very large," Aroun smiled. "How much?"

"Can you manage dollars? Say twenty thousand?"

"Of course." Aroun nodded to Rashid, who went to the far end of the room, swung a large oil painting to one side disclosing a wall safe, which he started to open.

Makeev said, "And what can I do?"

"The old warehouse in rue de Helier, the one we've used before. You've still got a key?"

"Of course."

"Good. I've got most things I need stored there, but for this job I'd like a light machine gun. A tripod job. A Heckler & Koch or an M60. Anything like that will do." He looked at his watch. "Eight o'clock. I'd like it there by ten. All right?"

"Of course," Makeev said again.

Rashid came back with a small briefcase. "Twenty thousand. Hundred dollar bills, I'm afraid."

"Is there any way they could be traced?" Dillon asked.

"Impossible," Aroun told him.

"Good. And I'll take the maps."

He walked to the door, opened it and started down the curving staircase to the hall. Aroun, Rashid and Makeev followed him.

"But is this all, Mr. Dillon?" Aroun said. "Is there nothing more we can do for you? Won't you need help?"

"When I do, it comes from the criminal classes," Dillon said. "Honest crooks who do things for cash are usually more reliable than politically motivated zealots. Not always, but most of the time. Don't worry, you'll hear from me, one way or another. I'll be on my way, then."

Rashid got the door open. Rain and sleet drifted in and Dillon pulled on his cap. "A dirty old night for it."

"One thing, Mr. Dillon," Rashid said. "What happens if things go wrong? I mean, you'll have your million in advance and we'll . . ."

"Have nothing? Don't give it a thought, me old son. I'll provide an alternative target. There's always the new British Prime Minister, this John Major. I presume his head on a plate would serve your boss back in Baghdad just as well."

He smiled once, then stepped out into the rain and pulled the door shut behind him.

TWO

Dillon paused outside *Le Chat Noir* on the end of the small pier for the second time that night. It was almost deserted, a young man and woman at a corner table holding hands, a bottle of wine between them. The accordion was playing softly and the musician talked to the man behind the bar at the same time. They were the Jobert brothers, gangsters of the second rank in the Paris underworld. Their activities had been severely curtailed since Pierre, the one behind the bar, had lost his left leg in a car crash after an armed robbery three years previously.

As the door opened and Dillon entered, the other brother, Gaston, stopped playing. "Ah, Monsieur Rocard. Back already."

"Gaston." Dillon shook hands and turned to the barman. "Pierre."

"See, I still remember that little tune of yours, the Irish one." Gaston played a few notes on the accordion.

"Good," Dillon said. "A true artist."

Behind them the young couple got up and left. Pierre produced half a bottle of champagne from the bar fridge. "Champagne as usual, I presume, my friend? Nothing special, but we are poor men here."

"You'll have me crying all over the bar," Dillon said.

"And what may we do for you?" Pierre enquired.

"Oh, I just want to put a little business your way." Dillon nodded at the door. "It might be an idea if you closed."

Gaston put his accordion on the bar, went and bolted the door and pulled down the blind. He returned and sat on his stool. "Well, my friend?"

"This could be a big payday for you boys." Dillon opened the briefcase, took out one of the road maps and disclosed the stacks of hundred dollar bills. "Twenty thousand American. Ten now and ten on successful completion."

"My God!" Gaston said in awe, but Pierre looked grim.

"And what would be expected for all this money?"

Dillon had always found it paid to stick as close to the truth as possible, and he spread the road map out across the bar.

"I've been hired by the Union Corse," he said, naming the most feared criminal organization in France, "to take care of a little problem. A matter of what you might term business rivalry."

"Ah, I see," Pierre said. "And you are to eliminate the problem?"

"Exactly. The men concerned will be passing along this road here toward Valenton shortly after two o'clock tomorrow. I intend to take them out here at the railway crossing."

"And how will this be accomplished?" Gaston asked.

"A very simple ambush. You two are still in the transport business, aren't you? Stolen cars, trucks?"

"You should know. You've bought from us on enough occasions," Pierre told him.

"A couple of vans, that's not too much to expect, is it?"

"And then what?"

"We'll take a drive down to this place tonight." He glanced at his watch. "Eleven o'clock from here. It'll only take an hour."

Pierre shook his head. "Look, this could be heavy. I'm getting too old for gunplay."

"Wonderful," Dillon said. "How many did you kill when you were with the OAS?"

"I was younger then."

"Well, it comes to us all, I suppose. No gunplay. You two will be in and out so quickly you won't know what's happening. A piece of cake." He took several stacks of hundred dollar bills from the briefcase and put them on the bar counter. "Ten thousand. Do we deal?"

And greed, as usual, won the day as Pierre ran his hands over the money. "Yes, my friend, I think we do."

"Good. I'll be back at eleven, then." Dillon closed his briefcase, Gaston went and unlocked the door for him and the Irishman left.

Gaston closed the door and turned. "What do you think?"

Pierre poured two cognacs. "I think our friend Rocard is a very big liar."

"But also a very dangerous man," Gaston said. "So what do we do?"

"Wait and see." Pierre raised his glass. "*Salut.*"

Dillon walked all the way to the warehouse in rue de Helier, twisting from one street to another, melting into the darkness occasionally to check that he wasn't being followed. He had learned a long time ago that the problem with all revolutionary political groups was that they were riddled with factions and informers, a great truth where the IRA was concerned. Because of that, as he had indicated to Aroun, he preferred to use professional criminals whenever possible when help was needed. Honest crooks who do things for cash, that was the phrase he'd used. Unfortunately it didn't always hold true and there had been something in big Pierre's manner.

There was a small Judas gate set in the larger double doors of the warehouse. He unlocked it and stepped inside. There were two cars, a Renault saloon and a Ford Escort, and a police BMW motorcycle covered with a sheet. He checked that it was all right, then moved up the wooden stairs to the flat in the loft above. It was not his only home. He also had a barge on the river, but it was useful on occasions.

On the table in the small living room there was a canvas holdall with a note on top that simply said, *As ordered.* He smiled and unzipped it. Inside was a Kalashnikov PK machine gun, the latest model. Its tripod was folded, the barrel off for easy handling, and there was a large box of belt cartridges, a similar box beside it. He opened a drawer in the sideboard, took out a folded sheet and put it in the holdall. He zipped it up again, checked the Walther in his waistband and went down the stairs, the holdall in one hand.

He locked the Judas and went along the street, excitement taking control as it always did. It was the best feeling in the world when the game was in play. He turned into the main street and a few minutes later, hailed a cab and told the driver to take him to *Le Chat Noir.*

They drove out of Paris in Renault vans, exactly the same except for the fact that one was black and the other white. Gaston led the way, Dillon beside him in the passenger seat, and Pierre followed. It was very cold; snow mixed with the rain, although it wasn't sticking. They talked very little, Dillon lying back in the seat eyes closed so that the Frenchman thought he was asleep.

Not far from Choisy, the van skidded and Gaston said, "Christ almighty," and wrestled with the wheel.

Dillon said, "Easy, the wrong time to go in a ditch. Where are we?"

"Just past the turning to Choisy. Not long now." Dillon sat up. The snow was covering the hedgerows but not the road. Gaston said, "Its a pig of a night. Just look at it."

"Think of all those lovely dollar bills," Dillon told him. "That should get you through."

It stopped snowing, the sky cleared showing a half-moon, and below them at the bottom of the hill was the red light of the railway crossing. There was an old, disused building of some sort at one side, its windows boarded up, a stretch of cobbles in front of it lightly powdered with snow.

"Pull in here," Dillon said.

Gaston did as he was told and braked to a halt, switching off the motor. Pierre came up in the white Renault, got down from behind the wheel awkwardly because of the false leg and joined them.

Dillon stood looking at the crossing a few yards away and nodded. "Perfect. Give me the keys."

Gaston did as he was told. The Irishman unlocked the rear door, disclosing the holdall. He unzipped it as they watched, took out the Kalashnikov, put the barrel in place expertly, then positioned it so that it pointed to the rear. He filled the ammunition box, threading the cartridge belt in place.

"That looks a real bastard," Pierre said.

"Seven-point-two-millimeter cartridges mixed with tracer and armor piercing," Dillon said. "It's a killer all right. Kalashnikov. I've seen one of these take a Land-Rover full of British paratroopers to pieces."

"Really," Pierre said, and as Gaston was about to speak, he put a warning hand on his arm. "What's in the other box?"

"More ammunition."

Dillon took out the sheet from the holdall, covered the machine gun, then locked the door. He got behind the driving wheel, started the engine and moved the van a few yards, positioned it so that the tail pointed on an angle toward the crossing. He got out and locked the door and clouds scudded across the moon and the rain started again, more snow in it now.

"So, you leave this here?" Pierre said. "What if someone checks it?"

"What if they do?" Dillon knelt down at the off side rear tire, took a knife from his pocket, sprang the blade and poked at the rim of the wheel. There was a hiss of air and the tire went down rapidly.

Gaston nodded. "Clever. Anyone gets curious, they'll just think a breakdown."

"But what about us?" Pierre demanded. "What do you expect?"

"Simple. Gaston turns up with the white Renault just after two this afternoon. You block the road at the crossing, not the railway track, just the road, get out, lock the door and leave it. Then get the hell out of there." He turned to Pierre. "You follow in a car, pick him up and straight back to Paris."

"But what about you?" the big man demanded.

"I'll be already here, waiting in the van. I'll make my own way. Back to Paris now. You can drop me at *Le Chat Noir* and that's an end of it. You won't see me again."

"And the rest of the money?" Pierre demanded as he got behind the Renault's wheel and Gaston and Dillon joined him.

"You'll get it, don't worry," Dillon said. "I always keep my word, just as I expect others to keep theirs. A matter of honor, my friend. Now let's get moving."

He closed his eyes again, leaned back. Pierre glanced at his brother, switched on the engine and drove away.

It was just on half past one when they reached *Le Chat Noir*. There was a lock-up garage opposite the pub. Gaston opened the doors and Pierre drove in.

"I'll be off then," Dillon said.

"You're not coming in?" the big man asked. "Then Gaston can run you home."

Dillon smiled. "No one's ever taken me home in my life."

He walked away, turning into a side street, and Pierre said to his brother, "After him and don't lose him."

"But why?" Gaston demanded.

"Because I want to know where he's staying, that's why. It stinks, this thing, Gaston, like bad fish stinks, so get moving."

Dillon moved rapidly from street to street, following his usual pattern, but Gaston, a thief since childhood and an expert in such matters, managed to stay on his trail, never too close. Dillon had intended returning to the warehouse in rue de Helier, but pausing on the corner of an alley to light a cigarette, he glanced back and could have sworn he saw a movement. He was right, for it was Gaston ducking into a doorway out of sight.

For Dillon, even the suspicion was enough. He'd had a feeling about Pierre all night, a bad feeling. He turned left, worked his way back to the river and walked along the pavement and past a row of trucks, their windshields covered with snow. He came to a small hotel, the cheapest sort of place, the kind used by prostitutes or truckers stopping overnight and went in.

The desk clerk was very old and wore an overcoat and scarf against the cold. His eyes were wet. He put down his book and rubbed them. "Monsieur?"

"I brought a load in from Dijon a couple of hours ago. Intended to drive back tonight, but the damn truck's giving trouble. I need a bed."

"Thirty francs, monsieur."

"You're kidding," Dillon said. "I'll be out of here at the crack of dawn."

The old man shrugged. "All right, you can have number eighteen on the second landing for twenty, but the bed hasn't been changed."

"When does that happen, once a month?" Dillon took the key, gave him his twenty francs and went upstairs.

The room was as disgusting as he expected even in the diffused light from the landing. He closed the door, moved carefully through the darkness and looked out cautiously. There was a movement under a tree on the river side of the road. Gaston Jobert stepped out and hurried away along the pavement.

"Oh, dear," Dillon whispered, then lit a cigarette and went and lay on the bed and thought about it, staring up at the ceiling.

Pierre, sitting at the bar of *Le Chat Noir* waiting for his brother's return, was leafing through *Paris Soir* for want of something better to do when he noticed the item on Margaret Thatcher's meeting with Mitterrand. His stomach churned and he read the item again with horror. It was at that moment the door opened and Gaston hurried in.

"What a night. I'm frozen to the bone. Give me a cognac."

"Here." Pierre poured some into a glass. "And you can read this interesting tidbit in *Paris Soir* while you're drinking."

Gaston did as he was told and suddenly choked on the cognac. "My God, she's staying at Choisy."

"And leaves from that old air-force field at Valenton. Leaves Choisy at two o'clock. How long to get to that railway crossing? Ten minutes?"

"Oh, God, no," Gaston said. "We're done for. This is out of our league, Pierre. If this takes place, we'll have every cop in France on the streets."

"But it isn't going to. I knew that bastard was bad news. Always something funny about him. You managed to follow him?"

"Yes, he doubled around the streets for a while, then ended up at that fleapit old François runs just along the river. I saw him through the window booking in." He shivered. "But what are we going to do?" He was almost sobbing. "This is the end, Pierre. They'll lock us up and throw away the key."

"No they won't," Pierre told him. "Not if we stop him, they won't. They'll be too grateful. Who knows, there might even be a reward in it. Now what's Inspector Savary's home number?"

"He'll be in bed."

"Of course he will, you idiot, nicely tucked up with his old lady where all good detectives should be. We'll just have to wake him up."

Inspector Jules Savary came awake cursing as the phone rang at his bedside. He was on his own, for his wife was spending a week in Lyons at her mother's. He'd had a long night. Two armed robberies and a sexual assault on a woman. He'd only just managed to get to sleep.

He picked up the phone. "Savary here."

"It's me, Inspector, Pierre Jobert."

Savary glanced at the bedside clock. "For Christ's sake, Jobert, it's two-thirty in the morning."

"I know, Inspector, but I've got something special for you."

"You always have, so it can wait till the morning."

"I don't think so, Inspector. I'm offering to make you the most famous cop in France. The pinch of a lifetime."

"Pull the other one," Savary said.

"Margaret Thatcher. She's staying at Choisy tonight, leaves for Valenton at two? I can tell you all about the man who's going to see she never gets there."

Jules Savary had never come awake so fast. "Where are you, *Le Chat Noir?*"

"Yes," Jobert told him.

"Half an hour." Savary slammed down the phone, leapt out of bed and started to dress.

It was at exactly the same moment that Dillon decided to move on. The fact that Gaston had followed him didn't necessarily mean anything more than the fact that the brothers were anxious to know more about him. On the other hand . . .

He left, locking the door, found the back stairs and descended cautiously. There was a door at the bottom that opened easily enough and gave access to a yard at the rear. An alley brought him to the main road. He crossed, walked along a line of parked trucks, chose one about fifty yards from the hotel, but giving him a good view. He got his knife out, worked away at the top of the passenger window. After a while it gave so that he could get his fingers in and exert pressure. A minute later he was inside. Better not to smoke, so he sat back, collar up, hands in pockets, and waited. It was half past three when the four unmarked cars eased up to the hotel. Eight men got out, none in uniform, which was interesting.

"Action Service, or I miss my guess," Dillon said softly.

Gaston Jobert got out of the rear car and stood talking to them for a moment, then they all moved into the hotel. Dillon wasn't angry, just pleased that he'd got it right. He left the truck, crossed the road to the shelter of the nearest alley and started to walk to the warehouse in rue de Helier.

The French secret service, notorious for years as the SDECE, has had its name changed to Direction Générale de la Sécurité Extérieure, DGSE, under the Mitterrand government in an attempt to improve the image of a shady and ruthless organization with a reputation for stopping at nothing. Having said that, measured by results, few intelligence organizations in the world are so efficient.

The service, as in the old days, was still divided into five sections and many departments, the most famous, or infamous, depending on your point of view, being Section 5, more commonly known as Action Service, the department responsible for the smashing of the OAS.

Colonel Max Hernu had been involved in all that, had hunted the OAS down as ruthlessly as anyone, in spite of having served as a paratrooper in both Indochina and Algeria. He was sixty-one years of age, an elegant, white-haired man who now sat at his desk in the office on the first floor of DGSE's headquarters on the Boulevard Mortier. It was just before five o'clock and Hernu, wearing horn-rimmed reading glasses, studied the report in front of him. He had been staying the night at his country cottage forty miles out of Paris and had only just arrived. Inspector Savary watched respectfully.

Hernu removed his glasses. "I loathe this time of the morning. Takes me back to Dien Bien Phu and the waiting for the end. Pour me another coffee, will you?"

Savary took his cup, went to the electric pot on the stand and poured the coffee, strong and black. "What do you think, sir?"

"These Jobert brothers, you believe they're telling us everything?"

"Absolutely, sir, I've known them for years. Big Pierre was OAS, which he thinks gives him class, but they're second-rate hoods really. They do well in stolen cars."

"So this would be out of their league?"

"Very definitely. They've admitted to me that they've sold this man Rocard cars in the past."

"Of the hot variety?"

"Yes, sir."

"Of course they are telling the truth. The ten thousand dollars speak for them there. But this man Rocard, you're an experienced copper, Inspector. How many years on the street?"

"Fifteen, sir."

"Give me your opinion."

"His physical description is interesting because according to the Jobert boys, there isn't one. He's small, no more than one sixty-five. No discernible color to the eyes, fair hair. Gaston says the first time they met him he thought he was a nothing, and then he apparently half-killed some guy twice his size in the bar in about five seconds flat."

"Go on." Hernu lit a cigarette.

"Pierre says his French is too perfect."

"What does he mean by that?"

"He doesn't know. It's just that he always felt that there was something wrong."

"That he wasn't French?"

"Exactly. Two facts of interest there. He's always whistling a funny little tune. Gaston picked it up because he plays accordion. He says Rocard told him once that it was Irish."

"Now that is interesting."

"A further point. When he was assembling the machine gun in the back of the Renault at Valenton he told the boys it was a Kalashnikov. Not just bullets. Tracer, armor piercing, the lot. He said he'd seen one take out a Land-Rover full of British paratroopers. Pierre didn't like to ask him where."

"So, you smell IRA here, Inspector? And what have you done about it?"

"Got your people to get the picture books out, Colonel. The Joberts are looking through them right now."

"Excellent." Hernu got up and this time refilled his coffee cup himself. "What do you make of the hotel business. Do you think he's been alerted?"

"Perhaps, but not necessarily," Savary said. "I mean, what have we got here, sir? A real pro out to make the hit of a lifetime. Maybe he was just being extra careful, just to make sure he wasn't followed to his real destination. I mean, I wouldn't trust the Joberts an inch, so why should he?"

He shrugged and Max Hernu said shrewdly, "There's more. Spit it out."

"I got a bad feeling about this guy, Colonel. I think he's special. I think he may have used the hotel thing because he suspected that Gaston might follow him, but then he'd want to know why. Was it the Joberts just being curious, or was there more to it?"

"So you think he could have been up the street watching our people arrive?"

"Very possibly. On the other hand, maybe he didn't know Gaston was tailing him. Maybe the hotel thing was a usual precaution. An old resistance trick from the war."

Hernu nodded. "Right, let's see if they've finished. Have them in."

Savary went out and returned with the Jobert brothers. They stood there looking worried, and Hernu said, "Well?"

"No luck, Colonel, he wasn't in any of the books."

"All right," Hernu said. "Wait downstairs. You'll be taken home. We'll collect you again later."

"But what for, Colonel?" Pierre asked.

"So that your brother can go to Valenton in the Renault and you can follow in the car just like Rocard told you. Now get out." They hurriedly left, and Hernu said to Savary, "We'll see Mrs. Thatcher is spirited to safety by another route, but a pity to disappoint our friend Rocard."

"If he turns up, Colonel."

"You never know, he just might. You've done well, Inspector. I think I'll have to requisition you for Section Five. Would you mind?"

Would he mind? Savary almost choked with emotion, "An honor, sir . . ."

"Good. Go and get a shower then and some breakfast. I'll see you later."

"And you, Colonel?"

"Me, Inspector?" Hernu laughed and looked at his watch. "Five-fifteen. I'm going to ring British Intelligence in London. Disturb the sleep of a very old friend of mine. If anyone can help us with our mystery man it should be he."

The Directorate General of the British Security Service occupies a large white and red brick building not far from the Hilton Hotel in Park Lane, although many of its departments are housed in various locations throughout London. The special number that Max Hernu rang was of a Section known as Group Four, located on the third floor of the Ministry of Defence. It had been set up in 1972 to handle matters concerning terrorism and subversion in the British Isles. It was responsible only to the Prime Minister. It had been administered by only one man since its inception, Brigadier Charles Ferguson. He was asleep in his flat in Cavendish Square when the telephone beside his bed awakened him.

"Ferguson," he said, immediately wide awake, knowing it had to be important.

"Paris, Brigadier," an anonymous voice said. "Priority one. Colonel Hernu."

"Put him through and scramble."

Ferguson sat up, a large, untidy man of sixty-five with rumpled gray hair and a double chin.

"Charles?" Hernu said in English.

"My dear Max. What brings you on the line at such a disgusting hour? You're lucky I'm still on the phone. The powers that be are trying to make me redundant along with Group Four."

"What nonsense."

"I know, but the Director General was never happy with my freebooter status all these years. What can I do for you?"

"Mrs. Thatcher is overnighting at Choisy. We've details of a plot to hit her on the way to the airfield at Valenton tomorrow."

"Good God!"

"All taken care of. The lady will now take a different route home. We're still hoping the man concerned will show up, though I doubt it. We'll be waiting though, this afternoon."

"Who is it? Anyone we know?"

"From what our informants say, we suspect he's Irish, though his French is good enough to pass as a native. The thing is, the people involved have looked through all our IRA pictures with no success."

"Have you a description?"

Hernu gave it to him. "Not much to go on, I'm afraid."

"I'll have a computer check done and get back to you. Tell me the story." Which Hernu did. When he was finished, Ferguson said, "You've lost him, old chap. I'll bet you dinner on it at the Savoy Grill next time you're over."

"I've a feeling about this one. I think he's special," Hernu said.

"And yet not on your books, and we always keep you up to date."

"I know," Hernu said. "And you're the expert on the IRA, so what do we do?"

"You're wrong there," Ferguson said. "The greatest expert on the IRA is right there in Paris, Martin Brosnan, our Irish-American friend. After all, he carried a gun for them till nineteen seventy-five. I heard he was a professor of Political Philosophy at the Sorbonne."

"You're right," Hernu said. "I'd forgotten about him."

"Very respectable these days. Writes books and lives rather well on all that money his mother left him when she died in Boston five years ago. If you've a mystery on your hands, he might be the man to solve it."

"Thanks for the suggestion," Hernu said. "But first we'll see what happens at Valenton. I'll be in touch."

Ferguson put down the phone, pressed a button on the wall and got out of bed. A moment later the door opened and his manservant, an ex-Gurkha, came in putting a dressing gown over his pyjamas.

"Emergency, Kim. I'll ring Captain Tanner and tell her to get round here, then I'll have a bath. Breakfast when she arrives."

The Gurkha withdrew. Ferguson picked up the phone and dialed a number. "Mary? Ferguson here. Something big. I want you at Cavendish Square within the hour. Oh, better wear your uniform. We've got that thing at the Ministry of Defence at eleven. You always impress them in full war paint."

He put the phone down and went into the bathroom feeling wide-awake and extremely cheerful.

It was six-thirty when the taxi picked up Mary Tanner on the steps of her Lowndes Square flat. The driver was impressed, but then most people were. She wore the uniform of a captain in the Women's Royal Army Corps, the wings of an Army Air Corps pilot on her left breast. Below them were the ribbon of the George Medal, a gallantry award of considerable distinction, and campaign ribbons for Ireland and for service with the United Nations peacekeeping force in Cyprus.

She was a small girl, black hair cropped short, twenty-nine years of age and a lot of service under the belt. A doctor's daughter who'd taken an English degree at London University, tried teaching and hated it. After that came the army. A great deal of her service had been with the Military Police. Cyprus for a while, but three tours of duty in Ulster. It had been the affair in Derry that had earned her the George Medal and left her with the scar on her left cheek, which had brought her to Ferguson's attention. She'd been his aide for two years now.

She paid off the taxi, hurried up the stairs to the flat on the first floor and let herself in with her own key. Ferguson was sitting on the sofa beside the fireplace in the elegant drawing room, a napkin under his chin, while Kim served his poached eggs.

"Just in time," he said. "What would you like?"

"Tea, please. Earl Grey, Kim, and toast and honey."

"Got to watch our figure."

"Rather early in the day for sexist cracks, even for you, Brigadier. Now what have we got?"

He told her while he ate and Kim brought her tea and toast and she sat opposite, listening.

When he finished she said, "This Brosnan, I've never heard of him."

"Before your time, my love. He must be about forty-five now. You'll find a file on him in my study. He was born in Boston. One of those filthy rich American families. Very high society. His mother was a Dubliner. He did all the right things, went to Princeton, took his degree, then went and spoiled it all by volunteering for Vietnam and as an enlisted man. I believe that was nineteen sixty-six. Airborne Rangers. He was discharged a sergeant and heavily decorated."

"So what makes him so special?"

"He could have avoided Vietnam by staying at university, but he didn't. He also enlisted in the ranks. Quite something for someone with his social standing."

"You're just an old snob. What happened to him after that?"

"He went to Trinity College, Dublin, to work on a doctorate. He's a Protestant, by the way, but his mother was a devout Catholic. In August sixty-nine, he was visiting an uncle on his mother's side, a priest in Belfast. Remember what happened? How it all started?"

"Orange mobs burning Catholics out?" she said.

"And the police not doing too much about it. The mob burned down Brosnan's uncle's church and started on the Falls Road. A handful of old IRA hands with a few rifles and handguns held them off, and when one of them was shot, Brosnan picked up his rifle. Instinctive, I suppose. I mean Vietnam and all that."

"And from then on he was committed?"

"Very much so. You've got to remember that in those early days, there were plenty of men like him in the movement. Believers in Irish freedom and all that sort of thing."

"Sorry, sir, I've seen too much blood on the streets of Derry to go for that one."

"Yes, well I'm not trying to whitewash him. He's killed a few in his time, but always up front, I'll say that for him. He became quite famous. There was a French war photographer called Anne-Marie Audin. He saved her life in Vietnam after a helicopter crash. Quite a romantic story. She turned up in Belfast and Brosnan took her underground for a week. She got a series out of it for *Life* magazine. The gallant Irish struggle. You know the sort of thing."

"What happened after that?"

"In nineteen seventy-five he went to France to negotiate an arms deal. As it turned out, it was a setup and the police were waiting. Unfortunately he shot one of them dead. They gave him life. He escaped from prison in seventy-nine, at my instigation, I might add."

"But why?"

"Someone else before your time, a terrorist called Frank Barry. Started off in Ulster with a splinter group called the Sons of Erin, then joined the European terrorist circuit, an evil genius if ever there was one. Tried to get Lord Carrington on a trip to France when he was Foreign Secretary. The French hushed it up, but the Prime Minister was furious. Gave me direct orders to hunt Barry down whatever the cost."

"Oh, I see now. You needed Brosnan to do that?"

"Set a thief to catch a thief and so forth, and he got him for us."

"And afterwards?"

"He went back to Ireland and took that doctorate."

"And this Anne-Marie Audin, did they marry?"

"Not to my knowledge, but she did him a bigger favor than that. Her family is one of the oldest in France and enormously powerful politically and he had been awarded the Legion of Honour for saving her in Vietnam. Anyway, her pressure behind the scenes bore fruit five years ago. President Mitterrand granted him a pardon. Wiped the slate clean."

"Which is how he's at the Sorbonne now? He must be the only professor they've had who shot a policeman dead."

"Actually one or two after the war had done just that when serving with the Resistance."

"Does the leopard ever change its spots?" she asked.

"O, ye of little faith. As I say, you'll find his file in the study if you want to know more." He passed her a piece of paper. "That's the description of the mystery man. Not much to go on, but run it through the computer anyway."

She went out.

Kim entered with a copy of the *Times*. Ferguson read the headlines briefly, then turned to page two where his attention was immediately caught by the same item concerning Mrs. Thatcher's visit to France that had appeared in *Paris Soir*.

"Well, Max," he said softly, "I wish you luck," and he poured himself another cup of coffee.

THREE

It was much warmer in Paris later that morning, most of the snow clearing by lunchtime. It was clear in the countryside too, only a bit here and there on the hedgerows as Dillon moved toward Valenton, keeping to the back roads. He was riding the BMW motorcycle from the garage and was dressed as a CRS policeman: helmet, goggles, a MAT49 machine gun slung across the front of the dark uniform raincoat.

Madness to have come, of course, but he couldn't resist the free show. He pulled off a narrow country lane by a farm gate after consulting his map, followed a track through a small wood on foot and came to a low stonewall on a hill. Way below some two hundred yards on was the railway crossing, the black Renault still parked where he had left it. There wasn't a soul about. Perhaps fifteen minutes later, a train passed through.

He checked his watch. Two-fifteen. He focused his Zeiss glasses on the scene below again and then the white Renault came down the road, half turning to block the crossing. There was a Peugeot behind it, Pierre at the wheel, and he was already reversing, turning the car as Gaston ran toward him. It was an old model, painted scarlet and cream.

"Very pretty," Dillon said softly, as the Peugeot disappeared up the road.

"Now for the cavalry," he said and lit a cigarette.

It was perhaps ten minutes later that a large truck came down the road and braked to a halt, unable to progress farther. It had high canvas sides on which was emblazoned *Steiner Electronics*.

"Electronics my arse," Dillon said.

A heavy machine gun opened up from inside the truck, firing through the side, raking the Renault. As the firing stopped, Dillon took a black plastic electronic detonator from his pocket, switched it on and pulled out the aerial.

A dozen men in black overalls and riot helmets, all clutching machine carbines, jumped out. As they approached the Renault, Dillon pressed the detonator. The self-destruct charge in the second black box, the one he had told Pierre contained extra ammunition, exploded instantly, the vehicle disintegrating, parts of the paneling lifting into the air in slow motion. There were several men on the ground, others running for cover.

"There you are, chew on that, gentlemen," Dillon said.

He walked back through the wood, pushed the BMW off its stand, swung a leg over and drove away.

He opened the door of the warehouse on rue de Helier, got back on the BMW, rode inside and parked it. As he turned to close the door, Makeev called from above, "It went wrong, I presume?"

Dillon took off his helmet. "I'm afraid so. The Jobert brothers turned me in."

As he went up the stairs Makeev said. "The disguise, I like that. A policeman is just a policeman to people. Nothing to describe."

"Exactly. I worked for a great Irishman called Frank Barry for a while years ago. Ever heard of him?"

"Certainly. A veritable Carlos."

"He was better than Carlos. Got knocked off in seventy-nine. I don't know who by. He used the CRS copper on a motorcycle a lot. Postmen are good too. No one ever notices a postman."

He followed the Russian into the sitting room. "Tell me," Makeev said.

Dillon brought him up to date. "It was a chance using those two and it went wrong, that's all there is to it."

"Now what?"

"As I said last night, I'll provide an alternative target. I mean, all that lovely money. I've got to think of my old age."

"Nonsense, Sean, you don't give a damn about your old age. It's the game that excites you."

"You could be right." Dillon lit a cigarette. "I know one thing. I don't like to be beaten. I'll think of something for you and I'll pay my debts."

"The Joberts? Are they worth it?"

"Oh, yes," Dillon said. "A matter of honor, Josef."

Makeev sighed. "I'll go and see Aroun, give him the bad news. I'll be in touch."

"Here or at the barge." Dillon smiled. "Don't worry, Josef. I've never failed yet, not when I set my mind to a thing."

Makeev went down the stairs. His footsteps echoed across the warehouse, the Judas gate banged behind him. Dillon turned and went back into the long room, whistling softly.

But I don't understand," Aroun said. "There hasn't been a word on television."

"And there won't be." Makeev turned from the French windows overlooking the Avenue Victor Hugo. "The affair never happened, that is the way the French will handle it. The idea that Mrs. Thatcher could have in any way been at risk on French soil would be considered a national affront."

Aroun was pale with anger. "He failed, this man of yours. A great deal of talk, Makeev, but nothing at the end of it. A good thing I didn't transfer that million to his Zurich account this morning."

"But you agreed," Makeev said. "In any case, he may ring at any time to check the money has been deposited."

"My dear Makeev, I have five hundred million dollars on deposit at that bank. Faced with the possibility of me transferring my business, the managing director was more than willing to agree to a small deception when Rashid spoke to him this morning. When Dillon phones to check on the situation, the deposit will be confirmed."

"This is a highly dangerous man you are dealing with," Makeev said. "If he found out . . ."

"Who's going to tell him? Certainly not you, and he'll get paid in the end, but only if he produces a result."

Rashid poured him a cup of coffee and said to Makeev, "He promised an alternative target, mentioned the British Prime Minister. What does he intend?"

"He'll be in touch when he's decided," Makeev said.

"Talk." Aroun walked to the window and stood sipping his coffee. "All talk."

"No, Michael," Josef Makeev told him. "You could not be more mistaken."

Martin Brosnan's apartment was by the river on the Quai de Montebello opposite the Île de la Cité and had one of the finest views of Notre Dame in Paris. It was within decent walking distance of the Sorbonne, which suited him perfectly.

It was just after four as he walked toward it, a tall man with broad shoulders in an old-fashioned trenchcoat, dark hair that still had no gray in it, in spite of his forty-five years, and was far too long, giving him the look of some sixteenth-century bravo. Martin Aodh Brosnan. The Aodh was Gaelic for Hugh and his Irishness showed in the high cheekbones and gray eyes.

It was getting colder again and he shivered as he turned the corner into Quai de Montebello and hurried along to the apartment block. He owned it all, as it happened, which gave him the apartment on the corner of the first floor, the most favored location. Scaffolding ran up the corner of the building to the fourth floor where some sort of building work was taking place.

As he was about to go up the steps to the ornate entrance, a voice called, "Martin?"

He glanced up and saw Anne-Marie Audin leaning over the balustrade of the terrace. "Where in the hell did you spring from?" he asked in astonishment.

"Cuba. I just got in."

He went up the stairs two at a time and she had the door open as he got there. He lifted her up in his arms in an enormous hug and carried her back into the hall. "How marvelous to see you. Why Cuba?"

She kissed him and helped him off with the trenchcoat. "Oh, I had a rather juicy assignment for *Time* magazine. Come in the kitchen. I'll make your tea."

A standing joke for years, the tea. Surprising in an American, but he couldn't stand coffee. He lit a cigarette and sat at the table and watched her move around the kitchen, her short hair as dark as his own, this supremely elegant woman who was the same age as himself and looked twelve years younger.

"You look marvelous," he told her as she brought the tea. He sampled it and nodded in approval. "That's grand. Just the way you learned to make it back in South Armagh in nineteen seventy-one with me and Liam Devlin showing you the hard way how the IRA worked."

"How is the old rogue?"

"Still living in Kilrea outside Dublin. Gives the odd lecture at Trinity College. Claims to be seventy, but that's a wicked lie."

"He'll never grow old, that one."

"Yes, you really do look marvelous," Brosnan said. "Why didn't we get married?"

It was a ritual question he had asked for years, a joke now. There was a time when they had been lovers, but for some years now, just friends. Not that it was by any means the usual relationship. He would have died for her, almost had in a Vietnam swamp the first time they had met.

"Now that we've got that over, tell me about the new book," she said.

"A philosophy of terrorism," he told her. "Very boring. Not many people will buy a copy."

"A pity," she said, "coming from such an expert in the field."

"Doesn't really matter," he said. "Knowing the reasons still won't make people act any differently."

"Cynic. Come on, let's have a real drink." She opened the fridge and took out a bottle of Krug.

"Non-vintage?"

"What else?"

They went into the magnificent long drawing room. There was an ornate gold mirror over the marble fireplace, plants everywhere, a grand piano, comfortable, untidy sofas and a great many books. She had left the French windows to the balcony standing ajar. Brosnan went to close them as she opened the Krug at the sideboard and got two glasses. At the same moment, the bell sounded outside.

When Brosnan opened the door he found Max Hernu and Jules Savary standing there, the Jobert brothers behind them.

"Professor Brosnan?" Hernu said. "I am Colonel Max Hernu."

"I know very well who you are," Brosnan said. "Action Service, isn't it? What's all this? My wicked past catching up with me?"

"Not quite, but we do need your assistance. This is Inspector Savary and these two are Gaston and Pierre Jobert."

"You'd better come in, then," Brosnan said, interested in spite of himself.

The Jobert brothers stayed in the hall, on Hernu's orders, when he and Savary followed Brosnan into the drawing room. Anne-Marie turned, frowning slightly, and Brosnan made the introductions.

"A great pleasure." Hernu kissed her hand. "I'm a longtime admirer."

"Martin?" she looked worried now. "You're not getting involved in anything?"

"Of course not," he assured her. "Now what can I do for you, Colonel?"

"A matter of national security, Professor. I hesitate to mention the fact, but Mademoiselle Audin is a photojournalist of some distinction."

She smiled. "Total discretion, you have my word, Colonel."

"We're here because Brigadier Charles Ferguson in London suggested it."

"That old devil? And why should he suggest you see me?"

"Because you are an expert in matters relating to the IRA, Professor. Let me explain."

Which he did, covering the whole affair as rapidly as possible. "You see, Professor," he said as he concluded, "the Jobert brothers have combed our IRA picture books without finding him, and Ferguson has had no success with the brief description we were able to give."

"You've got a real problem."

"My friend, this man is not just anybody. He must be special to attempt such a thing, but we know nothing more than that we think he's Irish and he speaks fluent French."

"So what do you want me to do?"

"Speak to the Joberts."

Brosnan glanced at Anne-Marie, then shrugged. "All right, wheel them in."

He sat on the edge of the table drinking champagne while they stood before him, awkward in such circumstances. "How old is he?"

"Difficult, monsieur," Pierre said. "He changes from one minute to the next. It's like he's more than one person. I'd say late thirties."

"And description?"

"Small with fair hair."

"He looks like nothing," Gaston put in. "We thought he was a no-no and then he half-killed some big ape in our café one night."

"All right. He's small, fair-haired, late thirties and he can handle himself. What makes you think he's Irish?"

"When he was assembling the Kalashnikov he made a crack about seeing one take out a Land-Rover full of English paratroopers."

"Is that all?"

Pierre frowned. Brosnan took the bottle of Krug from the bucket and Gaston said, "No, there's something else. He's always whistling a funny sort of tune. A bit eerie. I managed to follow it on my accordion. He said it was Irish."

Brosnan's face had gone quite still. He stood there, holding the bottle in one hand, a glass in the other.

"And he likes that stuff, monsieur," Pierre said.

"Champagne?" Brosnan asked.

"Well, yes, any champagne is better than nothing, but Krug is his favorite."

"Like this, non-vintage?"

"Yes, monsieur. He told us he preferred the grape mix," Pierre said.

"The bastard always did."

Anne-Marie put a hand on Brosnan's arm. "You know him, Martin?"

"Almost certainly. Could you pick that tune out on the piano?" he asked Gaston.

"I'll try, monsieur."

He lifted the lid, tried the keyboard gently, then played the beginning of the tune with one finger.

"That's enough." Brosnan turned to Hernu and Savary. "An old Irish folk song, 'The Lark in the Clear Air,' and you've got trouble, gentlemen, because the man you're looking for is Sean Dillon."

"Dillon?" Hernu said. "Of course. The man of a thousand faces, someone once called him."

"A slight exaggeration," Brosnan said, "but it will do."

They sent the Jobert brothers home and Brosnan and Anne-Marie sat on a sofa opposite Hernu and Savary. The inspector made notes as the American talked.

"His mother died in childbirth. I think that was nineteen fifty-two. His father was an electrician. Went to work in London, so Dillon went to school there. He had an incredible talent for acting, a genius really. He can change before your eyes, hunch his shoulders, put on fifteen years. It's astonishing."

"So you knew him well?" Hernu asked.

"In Belfast in the bad old days, but before that he won a scholarship to the Royal Academy of Dramatic Art. Only stayed a year. They couldn't teach him anything. He did one or two things at the National Theatre. Nothing much. He was very young, remember. Then in nineteen seventy-one his father, who'd returned home to Belfast, was killed by a British Army patrol. Caught in crossfire. An accident."

"And Dillon took it hard?"

"You could say that. He offered himself to the Provisional IRA. They liked him. He had brains, an aptitude for languages. They sent him to Libya to one of those terrorist training camps for a couple of months. A fast course in weaponry. That's all it took. He never looked back. God knows how many he's killed."

"So, he still operates for the IRA?"

Brosnan shook his head. "Not for years. Oh, he still counts himself as a soldier, but he thinks the leadership are a bunch of old women, and they couldn't handle him. He'd have killed the Pope if he'd thought it was needed. He was too happy to do things that were counterproductive. The word is that he was involved in the Mountbatten affair."

"And since those days?" Hernu asked.

"Beirut, Palestine. He's done a lot for the PLO. Most terrorist groups have used his services." Brosnan shook his head. "You're going to have trouble here."

"Why exactly?"

"The fact that he used a couple of crooks like the Joberts. He always does that. All right, it didn't work this time, but he knows the weakness of all revolutionary movements. That they're ridden with either hotheads or informers. You called him the faceless man, and that's right because I doubt if you'll find a photo of him in any file, and frankly, it wouldn't matter if you did."

"Why does he do it?" Anne-Marie asked. "Not for any political ends?"

"Because he likes it," Brosnan said, "because he's hooked. He's an actor, remember. This is for real and he's good at it."

"I get the impression that you don't care for him very much," Hernu said. "In personal terms, I mean."

"Well, he tried to kill me and a good friend of mine a long time ago," Brosnan told him. "Does that answer your question?"

"It's certainly reason enough." Hernu got up and Savary joined him. "We must be going. I want to get all this to Brigadier Ferguson as soon as possible."

"Fine," Brosnan said.

"We may count on your help in this thing, I hope, Professor?"

Brosnan glanced at Anne-Marie, whose face was set. "Look," he said, "I don't mind talking to you again if that will help, but I don't want to be personally involved. You know what I was, Colonel. Whatever happens I won't go back to anything like that. I made someone a promise a long time ago."

"I understand perfectly, Professor." Hernu turned to Anne-Marie. "Mademoiselle, a distinct pleasure."

"I'll see you out," she said and led the way.

When she returned Brosnan had the French windows open and was standing looking across the river smoking a cigarette. He put an arm around her. "All right?"

"Oh, yes," she said. "Perfect," and laid her head against his chest.

At that precise moment Ferguson was sitting by the fire in the Cavendish Place flat when the phone rang. Mary Tanner answered it in the study. After a while she came out. "That was Downing Street. The Prime Minister wants to see you."

"When?"

"Now, sir."

Ferguson got up and removed his reading glasses. "Call the car. You come with me and wait."

She picked up the phone, spoke briefly, then put it down. "What do you think it's about, Brigadier?"

"I'm not sure. My imminent retirement or your return to more mundane duties. Or this business in France. He'll have been told all about it by now. Anyway, let's go and see," and he led the way out.

They were checked through the Security gates at the end of Downing Street. Mary Tanner stayed in the car while Ferguson was admitted through the most famous door in the world. It was rather quiet compared to the last time he'd been there, a Christmas party given by Mrs. Thatcher for the staff in the Pillared Room. Cleaners, typists, office workers. Typical of her, that. The other side of the Iron Lady.

He regretted her departure, that was a fact, and sighed as he followed a young aide up the main staircase lined with replicas of portraits of all those great men of history. Peel, Wellington, Disraeli and many more. They reached the corridor; the young man knocked on the door and opened it.

"Brigadier Ferguson, Prime Minister."

The last time Ferguson had been in that study it had been a woman's room, the feminine touches unmistakably there, but things were different now, a little more austere in a subtle way, he was aware of that. Darkness was falling fast outside and John Major was checking some sort of report, the pen in his hand moving with considerable speed.

"Sorry about this. It will only take a moment," he said.

It was the courtesy that astounded Ferguson, the sheer basic good manners that one didn't experience too often from heads of government. Major signed the report, put it on one side and sat back, a pleasant, gray-haired man in horn-rimmed glasses, the youngest Prime Minister of the twentieth century. Almost unknown to the general public on his succession to Margaret Thatcher and yet his handling of the crisis in the Gulf had already marked him out as a leader of genuine stature.

"Please sit down, Brigadier, I'm on a tight schedule, so I'll get right to the point. The business affecting Mrs. Thatcher in France. Obviously very disturbing."

"Indeed so, Prime Minister. Thank God it all turned out as it did."

"Yes, but that seems to have been a matter of luck more than anything else. I've spoken to President Mitterrand and he's agreed that in all our interests and especially with the present situation in the Gulf there will be a total security clamp-down."

"What about the press, Prime Minister?"

"Nothing will reach the press, Brigadier," John Major told him. "I understand the French failed to catch the individual concerned?"

"I'm afraid that is so according to my latest information, but Colonel Hernu of Action Service is keeping in close touch."

"I've spoken to Mrs. Thatcher and it was she who alerted me to your presence, Brigadier. As I understand it, the intelligence section known as Group Four was set up in 1972, responsible only to the Prime Minister, its purpose to handle specific cases of terrorism and subversion?"

"That is correct."

"Which means you will have served five Prime Ministers if we include myself."

"Actually, Prime Minister, that's not quite accurate," Ferguson said. "We do have a problem at the moment."

"Oh, I know all about that. The usual security people have never liked your existence, Brigadier, too much like the Prime Minister's private army. That's why they thought a changeover at Number Ten was a good time to get rid of you."

"I'm afraid so, Prime Minister."

"Well it wasn't and it isn't. I've spoken to the Director General of Security Services. It's taken care of."

"I couldn't be more delighted."

"Good. Your first task quite obviously is to run down whoever was behind this French affair. If he's IRA, then he's our business, wouldn't you agree?"

"Absolutely."

"Good. I'll let you go and get on with it then. Keep me informed of every significant development on an eyes-only basis."

"Of course, Prime Minister."

The door behind opened as if by magic, the aide appeared to usher Ferguson out. The Prime Minister was already working over another sheaf of papers as the door closed and Ferguson was led downstairs.

As the limousine drove away, Mary Tanner reached forward to close the screen. "What happened? What was it about?"

"Oh, the French business." Ferguson sounded curiously remote. "You know, he's really got something about him, this one."

"Oh, come off it, sir," Mary said. "I mean, don't you honestly think we could do with a change, after all these years of Tory government?"

"Wonderful spokesperson for the workers you make," he said. "Your dear old dad, God rest him, was a professor of Surgery at Oxford, your mother owns half of Herefordshire. That flat of yours in Lowndes Square, a million, would you say? Why is it the children of the rich are always so depressingly left-wing while still insisting on dining at the Savoy?"

"A gross exaggeration."

"Seriously, my dear, I've worked for Labour as well as Conservative Prime Ministers. The color of the politician doesn't matter. The Marquess of Salisbury when he was Prime Minister, Gladstone, Disraeli, had very similar problems to those we have today. Fenians, anarchists, bombs in London, only dynamite instead of Semtex, and how many attempts were there on Queen Victoria's life?" He gazed out at the Whitehall traffic as they moved toward the Ministry of Defence. "Nothing changes."

"All right, end of lecture, but what happened?" she demanded.

"Oh, we're back in business, that's what happened," he said. "I'm afraid we'll have to cancel your transfer back to the Military Police."

"Damn you!" she cried, and flung her arms around his neck.

Ferguson's office on the third floor of the Ministry of Defence was on a corner at the rear overlooking Horse Guards Avenue with a view of the Victoria Embankment and the river at the far end. He had hardly got settled behind his desk when Mary hurried in.

"Coded fax from Hernu. I've put it through the machine. You're not going to like it one little bit."

It contained the gist of Hernu's meeting with Martin Brosnan, the facts on Sean Dillon—everything.

"Dear God," Ferguson said. "Couldn't be worse. He's like a ghost, this Dillon chap. Does he exist or doesn't he? As bad as Carlos in international terrorist terms, but totally unknown to the media or the general public and nothing to go on."

"But we do have one thing, sir."

"What's that?"

"Brosnan."

"True, but will he help?" Ferguson got up and moved to the window. "I tried to get Martin to do something for me the other year. He wouldn't touch it with a bargepole." He turned and smiled. "It's the girlfriend, you see, Anne-Marie Audin. She has a horror of him becoming what he once was."

"Yes, I can understand that."

"But never mind. We'd better get a report on their latest developments to the Prime Minister. Let's keep it brief."

She produced a pen and took notes as he dictated. "Anything else, sir?" she asked when he had finished.

"I don't think so. Get it typed. One copy for the file, the other for the P.M. Send it straight round to Number Ten by messenger. Eyes only."

Mary did a rough type of the report herself, then went along the corridor to the typing and copying room. There was one on each floor and the clerks all had full security clearance. The copier was clattering as she went in. The man standing in front of it was in his mid-fifties, white hair, steel-rimmed army glasses, his shirt sleeves rolled up.

"Hello, Gordon," she said. "A priority one here. Your very best typing. One copy for the personal file. You'll do it straight away?"

"Of course, Captain Tanner." He glanced at it briefly. "Fifteen minutes. I'll bring it along."

She went out and he sat down at his typewriter, taking a deep breath to steady himself as he read the words. *For the Eyes of the Prime Minister only*. Gordon Brown had served in the Intelligence Corps for twenty-five years, reaching the rank of Warrant Officer. A worthy, if unspectacular career, culminating in the award of an M.B.E. and the offer of employment at the Ministry of Defence on his retirement from the Army. And everything had been fine until the death of his wife from cancer the previous year. They were childless, which left him alone in a cold world at fifty-five years of age, and then something miraculous happened.

There were invitation cards flying around at the Ministry all the time to receptions at the various embassies in London. He often helped himself to one. It was just something to do, and at an art display at the German Embassy he'd met Tania Novikova, a secretary-typist at the Soviet Embassy.

They'd got on so well together. She was thirty and not particularly pretty, but when she'd taken him to bed on their second meeting at his flat in Camden it was like a revelation. Brown had never known sex like it, was hooked instantly. And then it had started. The questions about his job, anything and everything about what went on at the Ministry of Defence. Then there was a cooling off. He didn't see her and was distracted, almost out of his mind. He'd phoned her at her flat. She was cold at first, distant, and then she'd asked him if he'd been doing anything interesting.

He knew then what was happening but didn't care. There was a series of reports passing through on British Army changes in view of political changes in Russia. It was easy to run off spare copies. When he took them round to her flat, it was just as it had been and she took him to heights of pleasure such as he had never known.

From then on he would do anything, providing copies of everything that might interest her. *For the Eyes of the Prime Minister only*. How grateful would she be for that? He finished typing, ran off two extra copies, one for himself. He had a file of them now in one of his bedroom drawers. The other was for Tania Novikova, who was, of course, not a secretary-typist at the Soviet Embassy as she had informed Brown, but a captain in the KGB.

Gaston opened the door of the lock-up garage opposite *Le Chat Noir* and Pierre got behind the wheel of the old cream and red Peugeot. His brother got in the rear seat and they drove away.

"I've been thinking," Gaston said. "I mean, what if they don't get him? He could come looking for us, Pierre."

"Nonsense," Pierre told him. "He's long gone, Gaston. What kind of fool would hang around after what's happened? No, light me a cigarette and shut up. We'll have a nice dinner and go on to the Zanzibar afterwards. They've still got those Swedish sisters stripping."

It was just before eight, the streets at that place quiet and deserted, people inside because of the extreme cold. They came to a small square and as they started to cross it a CRS man on his motorcycle came up behind them, flashing his lights.

"There's a cop on our tail," Gaston said.

He pulled up alongside, anonymous in his helmet and goggles, and waved them down.

"A message from Savary, I suppose," Pierre said and pulled over to the pavement.

"Maybe they've got him," Gaston said excitedly.

The CRS man halted behind them, pushed his bike up on its stand and approached. Gaston got the rear door open and leaned out. "Have they caught the bastard?"

Dillon took a Walther with a Carswell silencer from inside the flap of his raincoat and shot him twice in the heart. He pushed up his goggles and turned. Pierre crossed himself. "It's you."

"Yes, Pierre. A matter of honor."

The Walther coughed twice more, Dillon pushed it back inside his raincoat, got on the BMW and drove away. It started to snow a little, the square very quiet. It was perhaps half an hour later that a policeman on foot patrol, caped against the cold, found them.

Tania Novikova's flat was just off the Bayswater Road not far from the Soviet Embassy. She'd had a hard day, had intended an early night. It was just before ten-thirty when her doorbell rang. She was toweling herself down after a nice, relaxing bath. She pulled on a robe, and went downstairs.

Gordon Brown's evening shift had finished at ten. He couldn't wait to get to her and had had the usual difficulty parking his Ford Escort. He stood at the door, ringing the bell impatiently, hugely excited. When she opened the door and saw who it was, she was immediately angry and drew him inside.

"I told you never to come here, Gordon, under any circumstances."

"But this is special," he pleaded. "Look what I've brought you."

In the living room she took the large envelope from him, opened it and slipped out the report. *For the Eyes of the Prime Minister only*. Her excitement was intense as she read through it. Incredible that this fool could have delivered her such a coup. His arms were around her waist, sliding up to her breasts and she was aware of his excitement.

"It's good stuff, isn't it?" he demanded.

"Excellent, Gordon. You *have* been a good boy."

"Really?" His grip tightened. "I can stay over then?"

"Oh, Gordon, it's such a pity. I'm on the night shift."

"Please, darling." He was shaking like a leaf. "Just a few minutes then."

She had to keep him happy, she knew that, put the report on the table and took him by the hand. "Quarter of an hour, Gordon, that's all, and then you'll have to go," and she led him into the bedroom.

After she'd got rid of him, she dressed hurriedly, debating what to do. She was a hard, committed Communist. That was how she had been raised and how she would die. More than that, she served the KGB with total loyalty. It had nurtured her, educated her, given her whatever status she had in their world. For a young woman, she was surprisingly old-fashioned. Had no time for Gorbachev or the Glasnost fools who surrounded him. Unfortunately, many in the KGB did support him, and one of those was her boss at the London Embassy, Colonel Yuri Gatov.

What would his attitude be to such a report, she wondered as she let herself out into the street and started to walk? What would Gorbachev's attitude be to the failed attempt to assassinate Mrs. Thatcher? Probably the same outrage the British Prime Minister must feel, and if Gorbachev felt that way, so would Colonel Gatov. So, what to do?

It came to her then as she walked along the frosty pavement of the Bayswater Road, that there was someone who might very well be interested and not only because he thought as she did, but because he was himself right in the center of all the action—Paris. Her old boss, Colonel Josef Makeev. That was it. Makeev would know how best to use such information. She turned into Kensington Palace Gardens and went into the Soviet Embassy.

By chance, Makeev was working late in his office that night when his secretary looked in and said, "A call from London on the scrambler. Captain Novikova."

Makeev picked up the red phone. "Tania," he said, a certain affection in his voice, for they had been lovers during the three years she'd worked for him in Paris. "What can I do for you?"

"I understand there was an incident affecting Empire over there earlier today?" she said.

It was an old KGB coded phrase, current for years, always used when referring to assassination attempts of any kind at high government level where Britain was concerned.

Makeev was immediately alert. "That's correct. The usual kind of it-didn't-happen affair."

"Have you an interest?"

"Very much so."

"There's a coded fax on the way. I'll stand by in my office if you want to talk."

Tania Novikova put down the phone. She had her own fax coding machine at a second desk. She went to it, tapping the required details out quickly, checking on the screen to see that she had got it right. She added Makeev's personal number, inserted the report and waited. A few moments later, she got a message received okay signal. She got up, lit a cigarette and went and stood by the window, waiting.

The jumbled message was received in the radio and coding room at the Paris Embassy. Makeev stood waiting impatiently for it to come through. The operator handed it to him and the colonel inserted it into the decoder and tapped in his personal key. He couldn't wait to see the contents, was reading it as he went along the corridor, as excited as Tania Novikova when he saw the line *For the Eyes of the Prime Minister only*. He sat behind his desk and read it through again. He thought about it for a while, then reached for the red phone.

You've done well, Tania. This one was my baby."

"I'm so pleased."

"Does Gatov know about this?"

"No, Colonel."

"Good, let's keep it that way."

"Is there anything else I can do?"

"Very much so. Cultivate your contact. Let me have anything else on the instant. There could be more for you. I have a friend coming to London. The particular friend you've been reading about."

"I'll wait to hear."

She put down the phone, totally elated, and went along to the canteen.

In Paris, Makeev sat there for a moment, frowning, then he picked up the phone and rang Dillon. There was a slight delay before the Irishman answered.

"Who is it?"

"Josef, Sean, I'm on my way there. Utmost importance."

Makeev put down the phone, got his overcoat and went out.

FOUR

Brosnan had taken Anne-Marie to the cinema that evening and afterwards to a small restaurant in Montmartre called *La Place Anglaise*. It was an old favorite because, and in spite of the name, one of the specialities of the house was Irish stew. It wasn't particularly busy, and they had just finished the main course when Max Hernu appeared, Savary standing behind him.

"Snow in London, snow in Brussels and snow in Paris," Hernu brushed it from his sleeve and opened his coat.

"Do I deduce from your appearance here that you've had me followed?" Brosnan asked.

"Not at all, Professor. We called at your apartment, where the porter told us you had gone to the cinema. He was also kind enough to mention three or four restaurants he thought you might be at. This is the second."

"Then you'd better sit down and have a cognac and some coffee," Anne-Marie told him. "You both look frozen."

They took off their coats and Brosnan nodded to the headwaiter, who hurried over and took the order.

"I'm sorry, mademoiselle, to spoil your evening, but this is most important," Hernu said. "An unfortunate development."

Brosnan lit a cigarette. "Tell us the worst."

It was Savary who answered. "About two hours ago the bodies of the Jobert brothers were found by a beat policeman in their car in a small square not far from *Le Chat Noir*."

"Murdered, is that what you are saying?" Anne-Marie put in.

"Oh, yes, mademoiselle," he said. "Shot to death."

"Two each in the heart?" Brosnan said.

"Why, yes, Professor, the pathologist was able to tell us that at the start of his examination. We didn't stay for the rest. How did you know?"

"Dillon, without a doubt. It's a real pro's trick, Colonel, you should know that. Never one shot, always two in case the other man manages to get one off at you as a reflex."

Hernu stirred his coffee. "Did you expect this, Professor?"

"Oh, yes. He'd have come looking for them sooner or later. A strange man. He always keeps his word, never goes back on a contract, and he expects the same from those he deals with. What he calls a matter of honor. At least he did in the old days."

"Can I ask you something?" Savary said. "I've been on the street fifteen years. I've known killers in plenty and not just the gangsters who see it as part of the job, but the poor sod who's killed his wife because she's been unfaithful. Dillon seems something else. I mean, his father was killed by British soldiers so he joined the IRA. I can see that, but everything that's happened since. Twenty years of it. All those hits and not even in his own country. Why?"

"I'm not a psychiatrist," Brosnan said. "They'd give you all the fancy names starting with psychopath and working down. I knew men like him in the army in Vietnam in Special Forces and good men, some of them, but once they started, the killing, I mean, it seemed to take over like a drug. They became driven men. The next stage was always to kill when it wasn't necessary. To do it without emotion. Back there in Nam it was as if people had become, how can I put it, just things."

"And this, you think, happened to Dillon?" Hernu asked.

"It happened to me, Colonel," Martin Brosnan said bleakly.

There was silence. Finally, Hernu said, "We must catch him, Professor."

"I know."

"Then you'll join us in hunting him down?"

Anne-Marie put a hand on his arm, dismay on her face, and she turned to the two men, a kind of desperate anger there. "That's your job, not Martin's."

"It's all right," Martin soothed her. "Don't worry." He said to Hernu, "Any advice I can give, any information that might help, but no personal involvement. I'm sorry, Colonel, that's the way it has to be."

Savary said. "You told us he tried to kill you once. You and a friend."

"That was in seventy-four. He and I both worked for this friend of mine, a man named Devlin, Liam Devlin. He was what you might call an old-fashioned revolutionary. Thought you could still fight it out like the old days, an undercover army against the troops. A bit like the Resistance in France during the war. He didn't like bombs, soft target bits, that kind of stuff."

"What happened?" the Inspector asked.

"Dillon disobeyed orders and the bomb that was meant for the police patrol killed half a dozen children. Devlin and I went after him. He tried to take us out."

"Without success, obviously?"

"Well, we weren't exactly kids off the street." His voice had changed in a subtle way. Harder, more cynical. "Left me with a groove in one shoulder and I gave him one in the arm himself. That was when he first dropped out of sight into Europe."

"And you didn't see him again?"

"I was in prison for over four years from nineteen seventy-five, Inspector. Belle Isle. You're forgetting your history. He worked with a man called Frank Barry for a while, another refugee from the IRA who turned up on the European scene. A really bad one, Barry. Do you remember him?"

"I do, indeed, Professor," Hernu said. "As I recall, he tried to assassinate Lord Carrington, the British Foreign Secretary, on a visit to France in nineteen seventy-nine in very similar circumstances to this recent affair."

"Dillon was probably doing a copy-cat of that operation. He worshipped Barry."

"Whom you killed, on behalf of British Intelligence, I understand?"

Anne-Marie said, "Excuse me."

She got up and walked down to the powder room. Hernu said, "We've upset her."

"She worries about me, Colonel, worries that some circumstances might put a gun in my hand again and send me sliding all the way back."

"Yes, I can see that, my friend." Hernu got up and buttoned his coat. "We've taken up enough of your time. My apologies to Mademoiselle Audin."

Savary said, "Your lectures at the Sorbonne, Professor, the students must love you. I bet you get a full house."

"Always," Brosnan said.

He watched them go and Anne-Marie returned. "Sorry about that, my love," he told her.

"Not your fault." She looked tired. "I think I'll go home."

"You're not coming back to my place?"

"Not tonight. Tomorrow, perhaps."

The headwaiter brought the bill, which Brosnan signed, then helped them into their coats and ushered them to the door. Outside, snow sprinkled the cobbles. She shivered and turned to Brosnan. "You changed, Martin, back there when you were talking to them. You started to become the other man again."

"Really?" he said and knew that it was true.

"I'll get a taxi."

"Let me come with you?"

"No, I'd rather not."

He watched her go down the street, then turned and went the other way. Wondering about Dillon, where he was and what he was doing.

Dillon's barge was moored in a small basin on the Quai St-Bernard. There were mainly motor cruisers there, pleasure craft with canvas hoods over them for the winter. The interior was surprisingly luxurious, a stateroom lined with mahogany, two comfortable sofas, a television. His sleeping quarters were in a cabin beyond with a divan bed and a small shower-room adjacent. The kitchen was on the other side of the passageway, small, but very modern. Everything a good cook could want. He was in there now, waiting for the kettle to boil when he heard the footfalls on deck. He opened a drawer, took out a Walther, cocked it and slipped it into his waistband at the rear. Then he went out.

Makeev came down the companionway and entered the stateroom. He shook snow from his overcoat and took it off. "What a night. Filthy weather."

"Worse in Moscow," Dillon told him. "Coffee?"

"Why not."

Makeev helped himself to a cognac from a bottle on the sideboard and the Irishman came back with a china mug in each hand. "Well, what's happened?"

"First of all, my sources tell me the Jobert brothers have turned up very dead, indeed. Was that wise?"

"To use an immortal phrase from one of those old James Cagney movies, they had it coming. Now what else has happened?"

"Oh, an old friend from your dim past has surfaced. One Martin Brosnan."

"Holy Mother of God!" Dillon seemed transfixed for a moment. "Martin? Martin Brosnan? Where in the hell did he turn up from?"

"He's living right here in Paris, just up the river from you on Quai de Montebello, the block on the corner opposite Notre Dame. Very ornate entrance. Within walking distance of here. You can't miss it. Has scaffolding on the front. Some sort of building work going on."

"All very detailed." Dillon took a bottle of Bushmills from the cupboard and poured one. "Why?"

"I've had a look on my way here."

"What's all this got to do with me?"

So Makeev told him—Max Hernu, Savary, Tania Novikova in London, everything. "So," he said as he finished, "at least we know what our friends are up to."

"This Novikova girl could be very useful to me," Dillon said. "Will she play things our way?"

"No question. She worked for me for some years. A very clever young woman. Like me, she isn't happy with present changes back home. Her boss is a different matter. Colonel Yuri Gatov. All for change. One of those."

"Yes, she could be important," Dillon said.

"Do I take it this means you want to go to London?"

"When I know, I'll let you know."

"And Brosnan?"

"I could pass him on the street and he wouldn't recognize me."

"You're sure?"

"Josef, I could pass you and you wouldn't recognize me. You've never really seen me change, have you? Have you come in your car?"

"Of course not. Taxi. I hope I can get one back."

"I'll get my coat and walk some of the way with you."

He went out and Makeev buttoned his coat and poured another brandy. There was a slight sound behind him and when he turned, Dillon stood there in cap and reefer coat hunched over in some strange way. Even the shape of his face seemed different. He looked fifteen years older. The change in body language was incredible.

"My God, it's amazing," Makeev said.

Dillon straightened up and grinned, "Josef, my old son, if I'd stuck to the stage I'd have been a theatrical knight by now. Come on, let's get going."

The snow was only a light powdering on the ground, barges passed on the river, and Notre Dame, floodlit, floated in the night. They reached the Quai de Montebello without seeing a taxi.

Makeev said, "Here we are, Brosnan's place. He owns the block. It seems his mother left him rather well off."

"Is that a fact?"

Dillon looked across at the scaffolding and Makeev said, "Apartment Four, the one on the corner on the first floor."

"Does he live alone?"

"Not married. Has a woman friend, Anne-Marie Audin . . ."

"The war photographer? I saw her once back in seventy-one in Belfast. Brosnan and Liam Devlin, my boss at the time, were giving her a privileged look at the IRA."

"Did you meet her?"

"Not personally. Do they live together?"

"Apparently not." A taxi came out of a side-turning and moved toward them and Makeev raised an arm. "We'll speak tomorrow."

The taxi drove off and Dillon was about to turn away when Brosnan came round the corner. Dillon recognized him instantly.

"Now then, Martin, you old bastard," he said softly.

Brosnan went up the steps and inside. Dillon turned, smiling, and walked away, whistling to himself softly.

At his flat in Cavendish Square Ferguson was just getting ready to go to bed when the phone rang. Hernu said, "Bad news. He's knocked off the Jobert brothers."

"Dear me," Ferguson said. "He doesn't mess about, does he?"

"I've been to see Brosnan to ask him to come in with us on this. I'm afraid he's refused. Offered to give us his advice and so on, but he won't become actively involved."

"Nonsense," Ferguson said. "We can't have that. When the ship is sinking it's all hands to the pumps, and this ship is sinking very fast indeed."

"What do you suggest?"

"I think it might be an idea if I came over to see him. I'm not sure of the time. I've things to arrange. Possibly the afternoon. We'll let you know."

"Excellent. I couldn't be more pleased."

Ferguson sat there thinking about it for a while and then he phoned Mary Tanner at her flat. "I suppose like me, you'd hoped for a relatively quiet night after your early rise this morning?" he said.

"It had crossed my mind. Has something happened?"

He brought her up to date. "I think it might be an idea to go over tomorrow, have a chat with Hernu, then speak to Brosnan. He must be made to realize how serious this is."

"Do you want me to come?"

"Naturally. I can't even make sense of a menu over there, whereas we all know that one of the benefits of your rather expensive education is fluency in the French language. Get in touch with the transport officer at the Ministry and tell him I want the Lear jet standing by tomorrow."

"I'll handle it. Anything else?"

"No, I'll see you at the office in the morning, and don't forget your passport."

Ferguson put down the phone, got into bed and switched off the light.

Back on the barge, Dillon boiled the kettle, then poured a little Bushmill's whisky into a mug, added some lemon juice, sugar and the boiling water and went back into the stateroom, sipping the hot toddy. *My God, Martin*

Brosnan after all these years. His mind went back to the old days with the American and Liam Devlin, his old commander. Devlin, the living legend of the IRA. Wild, exciting days, taking on the might of the British Army, face-to-face. Nothing would ever be the same as that.

There was a stack of London newspapers on the table. He'd brought them all at the Gare de Lyon newsstand earlier. There was the *Daily Mail*, the *Express*, the *Times*, and the *Telegraph*. It was the political sections that interested him most and all the stories were similar. The Gulf crisis, the air strikes on Baghdad, speculation on when the land war would start. And photos, of course. Prime Minister John Major outside Number Ten Downing Street. The British press was wonderful. There were discussions about security, speculation as to possible Arab terrorist attacks and articles that even included maps and street plans of the immediate area around Downing Street. And more photos of the Prime Minister and cabinet ministers arriving for the daily meetings of the War Cabinet. London, that was where the action was, no doubt about it. He put the papers away neatly, finished his toddy and went to bed.

One of the first things Ferguson did on reaching his office was to dictate a further brief report to the Prime Minister bringing him up to date and informing him of the Paris trip. Mary took the draft along to the copy room. The duty clerk just coming to the end of the night shift was a woman, a Mrs. Alice Johnson, a war widow whose husband had been killed in the Falklands. She got on with the typing of the report instantly, had just finished putting it through the copier when Gordon Brown entered. He was on a split shift. Three hours from ten until one and six until ten in the evening. He put his briefcase down and took off his jacket.

"You go whenever you like, Alice. Anything special?"

"Just this report for Captain Tanner. It's a Number Ten job. I said I'd take it along."

"I'll take it for you," Brown said. "You get going."

She passed him both copies of the report and started to clear her desk. No chance to make an extra copy, but at least he could read it, which he did as he went along the corridor to Mary Tanner's office. She was sitting at her desk when he went in.

"That report you wanted, Captain Tanner. Shall I arrange a messenger?"

"No, thanks, Gordon. I'll see to it."

"Anything else, Captain?"

"No, I'm just clearing the desk. Brigadier Ferguson and I are going to Paris." She glanced at her watch. "I'll have to get moving. We're due out of Gatwick at eleven."

"Well, I hope you enjoy yourself."

When he went back to the copy room Alice Johnson was still there. "I say, Alice," he said, "would you mind hanging on for a little while? Only something's come up. I'll make it up to you."

"That's all right," she said. "You get off."

He put on his coat, hurried downstairs to the canteen and went into one of the public telephone booths. Tania Novikova was only at the flat because of the lateness of the hour when she had left the Embassy the previous night. "I've told you not to ring me here. I'll ring you," she told him.

"I must see you. I'm free at one."

"Impossible."

"I've seen another report. The same business."

"I see. Have you got a copy?"

"No, that wasn't possible, but I've read it."

"What did it say?"

"I'll tell you at lunchtime."

She realized then that control on her part, severe control, was necessary. Her voice was cold and hard when she said, "Don't waste my time, Gordon, I'm busy. I think I'd better bring this conversation to an end. I may give you a ring sometime, but then I may not."

He panicked instantly. "No, let me tell you. There wasn't much. Just that the two French criminals involved had been murdered, they presumed by the man Dillon. Oh, and Brigadier Ferguson and Captain Tanner are flying over to Paris in the Lear jet at noon."

"Why?"

"They're hoping to persuade this man Martin Brosnan to help them."

"Good," she said. "You've done well, Gordon. I'll see you tonight at your flat. Six o'clock and bring your work schedule for the next couple of weeks." She rang off.

Brown went upstairs, full of elation.

Ferguson and Mary Tanner had an excellent flight and touched down at Charles de Gaulle airport just after one. By two o'clock they were being ushered into Hernu's office at DGSE headquarters on Boulevard Mortier.

He embraced Ferguson briefly. "Charles, you old rogue, it's far too long."

"Now, then, none of your funny French ways," Ferguson told him. "You'll be kissing me on both cheeks next. Mary Tanner, my aide."

She was wearing a rather nice Armani trouser suit of dark brown and a pair of exquisite ankle boots by Manolo Blahnik. Diamond stud earrings and a small gold Rolex divers' watch completed the picture. For a girl who was not supposed to be particularly pretty, she looked stunning. Hernu, who knew class when he saw it, kissed her hand. "Captain Tanner, your reputation precedes you."

"Only in the nicest way, I hope," she replied in fluent French.

"Good," Ferguson said. "So now we've got all that stuff over, let's get down to brass tacks. What about Brosnan?"

"I have spoken to him this morning and he's agreed to see us at his apartment at three. Time for a late lunch. We have excellent canteen facilities here. Everyone mixes in from the Director downwards." He opened the door. "Just follow me. It may not be quite the best food in Paris, but it's certainly the cheapest."

In the stateroom at the barge, Dillon was pouring a glass of Krug and studying a large-scale map of London. Around him, pinned to the mahogany walls, were articles and reports from all the newspapers specifically referring to affairs at Number Ten, the Gulf War and how well John Major was doing. There were photos of the youngest Prime Minister of the century, several of them. In fact, the eyes seemed to follow him about. It was as if Major was watching him.

"And I've got my eye on you, too, fella," Dillon said softly.

The things that intrigued him were the constant daily meetings of the British War Cabinet at Number Ten. All those bastards, all together in the same spot. What a target. Brighton all over again, and that affair had come close to taking out the entire British Government. But Number Ten as a target? That didn't seem possible. Fortress Thatcher it had been dubbed by some after that redoubtable lady's security improvements. There were footsteps on the deck overhead. He opened a drawer in the table casually revealing a Smith & Wesson .38 revolver, closed it again as Makeev came in.

"I could have telephoned, but I thought I'd speak to you personally," the Russian said.

"What now?"

"I've brought you some photos we've had taken of Brosnan as he is now. Oh, and that's the girlfriend, Anne-Marie Audin."

"Good. Anything else?"

"I've heard from Tania Novikova again. It seems Brigadier Ferguson and his aide, a Captain Mary Tanner, have flown over. They were due out of Gatwick at eleven." He glanced at his watch. "I'd say they'll be with Hernu right now."

"To what end?"

"The real purpose of the trip is to see Brosnan. Try and persuade him to help actively in the search for you."

"Really?" Dillon smiled coldly. "Martin's becoming a serious inconvenience. I might have to do something about that."

Makeev nodded at the clippings on the walls. "Your own private gallery?"

"I'm just getting to know the man," Dillon said. "Do you want a drink?"

"No, thanks." Suddenly Makeev felt uncomfortable. "I've things to do. I'll be in touch."

He went up the companionway. Dillon poured himself a little more champagne, sipped a little, then stopped, walked into the kitchen and poured the whole bottle down the sink. Conspicuous waste, but he felt like it. He went back into the stateroom, lit a cigarette and looked at the clippings again, but all he could think about was Martin Brosnan. He picked up the photos Makeev had brought and pinned them up beside the clippings.

Anne-Marie was in the kitchen at the Quai de Montebello, Brosnan going over a lecture at the table, when the doorbell rang. She hurried out, wiping her hands on a cloth.

"That will be them," she said. "I'll get it. Now don't forget your promise."

She touched the back of his neck briefly and went out. There was a sound of voices in the hall and she returned with Ferguson, Hernu and Mary Tanner.

"I'll make some coffee," Anne-Marie said and went into the kitchen.

"My dear Martin." Ferguson held out his hand. "It's been too long."

"Amazing," Brosnan said. "We only ever meet when you want something."

"Someone you haven't met, my aide, Captain Mary Tanner."

Brosnan looked her over quickly, the small, dark girl with the scar on the left cheek, and liked what he saw. "Couldn't you find a better class of work than what this old sod has to offer?" he demanded.

Odd that she should feel slightly breathless faced with this forty-five-year-old man with the ridiculously long hair and the face that had seen rather too much of the worst of life.

"There's a recession on. You have to take what's going these days," she said, her hand light in his.

"Right. We've had the cabaret act, so let's get down to business," Ferguson said. Hernu went to the window, Ferguson and Mary took the sofa opposite Brosnan.

"Max tells me he spoke to you last night after the murder of the Jobert brothers?"

Anne-Marie came in with coffee on a tray. Brosnan said, "That's right."

"He tells me you've refused to help us?"

"That's putting it a bit strongly. What I said was that I'd do anything I could except become actively involved myself, and if you've come to attempt to change my mind, you're wasting your time."

Anne-Marie poured coffee. Ferguson said, "You agree with him, Miss Audin?"

"Martin slipped out of that life a long time ago, Brigadier," she said carefully. "I would not care to see him step back in for whatever reason."

"But surely you can see that a man like Dillon must be stopped?"

"Then others must do the stopping. Why Martin, for God's sake?" She was distressed now and angry. "It's your job, people like you. This sort of thing is how you make your living."

Max Hernu came across and picked up a cup of coffee. "But Professor Brosnan is in a special position as regards this business, you must see that, mademoiselle. He knew Dillon intimately, worked with him for years. He could be of great help to us."

"I don't want to see him with a gun in his hand," she said, "and that's what it would come down to. Once his foot is on that road again, it can only have one end."

She was very distressed, turned and went through into the kitchen. Mary Tanner went after her and closed the door. Anne-Marie was leaning against the sink, arms folded as if holding herself in, agony on her face.

"They don't see, do they? They don't understand what I mean."

"I do," Mary said simply. "I understand exactly what you mean," and as Anne-Marie started to sob quietly, went and put her arms around her.

Brosnan opened the French windows and stood on the terrace by the scaffolding taking in lungfuls of cold air. Ferguson joined him. "I'm sorry for the distress we've caused her."

"No, you're not, you only see the end in view. You always did."

"He's a bad one, Martin."

"I know," Brosnan nodded. "A real can of worms the little bastard has opened this time. I must get a smoke."

He went inside. Hernu was sitting by the fire. Brosnan found a packet of cigarettes, hesitated, then opened the kitchen door. Anne-Marie and Mary were sitting opposite each other, holding hands across the table.

Mary turned. "She'll be fine. Just leave us for a while."

Brosnan went back to the terrace. He lit a cigarette and leaned against the balustrade. "She seems quite a lady, that aide of yours. That scar on her left cheek. Shrapnel. What's her story?"

"She was doing a tour of duty as a lieutenant with the Military Police in Londonderry. Some IRA chap was delivering a car bomb when the engine failed. He left it at the curb and did a runner. Unfortunately, it was outside an old folks' home. Mary was driving past in a Land-Rover when a civilian alerted her. She got in the car, released the brake and managed to freewheel down the hill on to some wasteland. It exploded as she made a run for it."

"Good God!"

"Yes, I'd agree, on that occasion. When she came out of hospital she received a severe reprimand for breaking standing orders and the George Medal for the gallantry of her action. I took her on after that."

"A lot of still waters there." Brosnan sighed and tossed his cigarette out into space as Mary Tanner joined them.

"She's gone to lie down in the bedroom."

"All right," Brosnan said. "Let's go back in." They went and sat down again and he lit another cigarette. "Let's get this over with. What did you want to say?"

Ferguson turned to Mary. "Your turn, my dear."

"I've been through the files, checked out everything the computer can tell us." She opened her brown handbag and took out a photo. "The only likeness of Dillon we can find. It's from a group photo taken at RADA twenty years ago. We had an expert in the department blow it up."

There was a lack of definition, the texture grainy and the face was totally anonymous. Just another young boy.

Brosnan gave it back. "Useless. I didn't even recognize him myself."

"Oh, it's him all right. The man on his right became quite successful on television. He's dead now."

"Not through Dillon?"

"Oh, no, stomach cancer, but he was approached by one of our people back in nineteen eighty-one and confirmed that it was Dillon standing next to him in the photo."

"The only likeness we have," Ferguson said. "And no bloody use at all."

"Did you know that he took a pilot's license, and a commercial one at that?" Mary said.

"No, I never knew that," Brosnan said.

"According to one of our informants, he did it in Lebanon some years ago."

"Why were your people on his case in eighty-one?" Brosnan asked.

"Yes, well, that's interesting," she told him. "You told Colonel Hernu that he'd quarreled with the IRA, had dropped out and joined the international terrorist circuit."

"That's right."

"It seems they took him back in nineteen eighty-one. They were having trouble with their active service units in England. Too many arrests, that kind of thing. Through an informer in Ulster we heard that he was operating in London for a time. There were at least three or four incidents attributed to him. Two car bombs and the murder of a police informant in Ulster who'd been relocated with his family in Maida Vale."

"And we didn't come within spitting distance of catching him," Ferguson said.

"Well, you wouldn't," Brosnan told him. "Let me go over it again. He's an actor of genius. He really can change before your eyes, just by use of body language. You'd have to see it to believe it. Imagine what he can do with makeup, hair-coloring changes. He's only five feet five, remember. I've seen him dress as a woman and fool soldiers on foot patrol in Belfast."

Mary Tanner was leaning forward intently. "Go on," she said softly.

"You want to know another reason why you've never caught him? He works out a series of aliases. Changes hair color, uses whatever tricks of makeup are necessary, then takes his photo. That's what goes on his false passport or identity papers. He keeps a collection, then when he needs to move, makes himself into the man on the photo."

"Ingenious," Hernu said.

"Exactly, so no hope of any help from television or newspaper publicity of the have-you-seen-this-man type. Wherever he goes, he slips under the surface. If he was working in London and needed anything at all—help, weapons, whatever—he'd simply pretend to be an ordinary criminal and use the underworld."

"You mean he wouldn't go near any kind of IRA contact at all?" Mary said.

"I doubt it. Maybe someone who'd been in very deep cover for years, someone he could really trust, and people like that are thin on the ground."

"There is a point in all this which no one has touched on," Hernu said. "Who is he working for?"

"Well it certainly isn't the IRA," Mary said. "We did an instant computer check and we have links with both the RUC computer and British Army Intelligence at Lisburn. Not a smell from anyone about the attempt on Mrs. Thatcher."

"Oh, I believe that," Brosnan said. "Although you can never be sure."

"There are the Iraqis, of course," Ferguson said. "Saddam would dearly love to blow everyone up at the moment."

"True, but don't forget Hizbollah, PLO, Wrath of Allah and a few others in between. He's worked for them all," Brosnan reminded him.

"Yes," Ferguson said. "And checking our sources through that lot would take time and I don't think we've got it."

"You think he'll try again?" Mary asked.

"Nothing concrete, my dear, but I've been in this business a lifetime.

I always go by my instincts, and this time my instincts tell me there's more to it."

"Well, I can't help you there. I've done all I can." Brosnan stood up.

"All you're prepared to, you mean?" Ferguson said.

They moved into the hall and Brosnan opened the door. "I suppose you'll be going back to London?"

"Oh, I don't know. I thought we might stay over and sample the delights of Paris. I haven't stayed at the Ritz since the refurbishment."

Mary Tanner said, "That will give the expenses a bashing." She held out her hand. "Goodbye, Professor Brosnan, it was nice to be able to put a face to the name."

"And you," he said. "Colonel," he nodded to Hernu and closed the door.

When he went into the drawing room Anne-Marie came in from the bedroom. Her face was drawn and pale. "Did you come to any decision?" she asked.

"I gave you my word. I've helped them all I can. Now they've gone, and that's an end to it."

She opened the table drawer. Inside there was an assortment of pens, envelopes, writing paper, stamps. There was also a Browning High Power 9-millimeter pistol, one of the most deadly hand-guns in the world, preferred by the SAS above all others.

She didn't say a word, simply closed the drawer and looked at him calmly. "I'll make some tea," she said and went into the kitchen.

In the limousine Hernu said, "You've lost him. He won't do any more."

"I wouldn't be too sure of that. We'll discuss it over dinner at the Ritz later. You'll join us, I hope? Eight o'clock all right?"

"Delighted," Hernu said. "Group Four must be rather more generous with its expenses than my own poor department."

"Oh, it's all on dear Mary here," Ferguson said. "Flashed this wonderful piece of plastic at me the other day which American Express had sent her. The Platinum Card. Can you believe that, Colonel?"

"Damn you!" Mary said.

Hernu lay back and laughed helplessly.

Tania Novikova came out of the bathroom of Gordon Brown's Camden flat combing her hair. He pulled on a dressing gown.

"You've got to go?" he said.

"I must. Come into the living room." She pulled on her coat and turned to face him. "No more coming to the Bayswater flat, no more telephones. The work schedule you showed me. All split shifts for the next month. Why?"

"They're not popular, especially for people with families. That isn't a problem for me, so I agreed to do it for the moment. And it pays more."

"So, you usually finish at one o'clock and start again at six in the evening?"

"Yes."

"You have an answering machine, the kind where you can phone home and get your messages?"

"Yes."

"Good. We can keep in touch that way."

She started for the door and he caught her arm. "But when will I see you?"

"Difficult at the moment, Gordon, we must be careful. If you've nothing better to do, always come home between shifts. I'll do what I can."

He kissed her hungrily. "Darling."

She pushed him away. "I must go now, Gordon."

She opened the door, went downstairs and let herself out of the street entrance. It was still very cold and she pulled up her collar.

"My God, the things I do for Mother Russia," she said. She went down to the corner and hailed a cab.

FIVE

It was colder than ever in the evening, a front from Siberia sweeping across Europe, too cold for snow even. In the apartment, just before seven, Brosnan put some more logs on the fire.

Anne-Marie, lying full-length on the sofa, stirred and sat up. "So we stay in to eat?"

"I think so," he said. "A vile night."

"Good. I'll see what I can do in the kitchen."

He put on the television news program. More air strikes against Baghdad, but still no sign of a land war. He switched the set off and Anne-Marie emerged from the kitchen and picked up her coat from the chair where she had left it.

"Your fridge, as usual, is almost empty. Unless you wish me to concoct a meal based on some rather stale cheese, one egg and half a carton of milk, I'll have to go round the corner to the delicatessen."

"I'll come with you."

"Nonsense," she said. "Why should we both suffer? I'll see you soon."

She blew him a kiss and went out. Brosnan went and opened the French windows. He stood on the terrace, shivering, and lit a cigarette, watching for her. A moment later, she emerged from the front door and started along the pavement.

"Goodbye, my love," he called dramatically. "Parting is such sweet sorrow."

"Idiot!" she called back. "Go back in before you catch pneumonia."

She moved away, careful on the frozen pavement, and disappeared round the corner.

At that moment, the phone rang. Brosnan turned and hurried in, leaving the French windows open.

Dillon had an early meal at a small café he often frequented. He was on foot and his route back to the barge took him past Brosnan's apartment block. He paused on the other side of the road, cold in spite of the reefer coat and the knitted cap pulled down over his ears. He stood there, swinging his arms vigorosly, looking up at the lighted windows of the apartment.

When Anne-Marie came out of the entrance, he recognized her instantly and stepped back into the shadows. The street was silent, no traffic movement at all, and when Brosnan leaned over the balustrade and called down to her, Dillon heard every word he said. It gave him a totally false impression. That she was leaving for the evening. As she disappeared round the corner, he crossed the road quickly. He checked the Walther in his waistband at the rear, had a quick glance each way to see that no one was about, then started to climb the scaffolding.

It was Mary Tanner on the phone. "Brigadier Ferguson wondered whether we could see you again in the morning before going back?"

"It won't do you any good," Brosnan told her.

"Is that a yes or a no?"

"All right," he said reluctantly. "If you must."

"I understand," she said, "I really do. Has Anne-Marie recovered?"

"A tough lady, that one," he said. "She's covered more wars than we've had hot dinners. That's why I've always found her attitude about such things where I'm concerned, strange."

"Oh, dear," she said. "You men can really be incredibly stupid on occasions. She loves you, Professor, it's as simple as that. I'll see you in the morning."

Brosnan put the phone down. There was a draught of cold air, the fire flared up. He turned and found Sean Dillon standing in the open French windows, the Walther in his left hand.

"God bless all here," he said.

The delicatessen in the side street, as with so many such places these days, was run by an Indian, a Mr. Patel. He was most assiduous where Anne-Marie was concerned, carrying the basket for her as they went round the shelves. Delicious French bread sticks, milk, eggs, Brie cheese, a beautiful quiche.

"Baked by my wife with her own hands," Mr. Patel assured her. "Two minutes in the microwave and a perfect meal."

She laughed. "Then all we need is a very large tin of caviar and some smoked salmon to complement it."

He packed the things carefully for her. "I'll put them on Professor Brosnan's account as usual."

"Thank you," she said.

He opened the door for her. "A pleasure, mademoiselle."

She started back along the frosty pavement feeling suddenly unaccountably cheerful.

Jesus, Martin, and the years have been good to you." Dillon pulled the glove off his right hand with his teeth and found a pack of cigarettes in his pocket. Brosnan, a yard from the table drawer and the Browning High Power, made a cautious move. "Naughty." Dillon gestured with the Walther. "Sit on the arm of the sofa and put your hands behind your head."

Brosnan did as he was told. "You're enjoying yourself, Sean."

"I am so. How's that old sod Liam Devlin these days?"

"Alive and well. Still in Kilrea outside Dublin, but then you know that."

"And that's a fact."

"The job at Valenton, Mrs. Thatcher," Brosnan said. "Very sloppy, Sean. I mean, to go with a couple of bums like the Joberts. You really must be losing your touch."

"You think so?"

"Presumably it was a big payday?"

"Very big," Dillon said.

"I hope you got your money in advance."

"Very funny." Dillon was beginning to get annoyed.

"One thing does intrigue me," Brosnan said. "What you want with me after all these years?"

"Oh, I know all about you," Dillon said. "How they're pumping you for information about me. Hernu, the Action Service colonel, that old bastard Ferguson and this girl sidekick of his, this Captain Tanner. Nothing I don't know. I've got the right friends, you see, Martin, the kind of people who can access anything."

"Really, and were they happy when you failed with Mrs. Thatcher?"

"Just a tryout, that, just a perhaps. I've promised them an alternative target. You know how this game works."

"I certainly do, and one thing I do know is that the IRA doesn't pay for hits. Never has."

"Who said I was working for the IRA?" Dillon grinned. "Plenty of other people with enough reason to hit the Brits these days."

Brosnan saw it then, or thought he did. "Baghdad?"

"Sorry, Martin, you can go to your Maker puzzling over that one for all eternity."

Brosnan said, "Just indulge me. A big hit for Saddam. I mean, the war stinks. He needs something badly."

"Christ, you always did run on."

"President Bush stays back in Washington, so that leaves the Brits. You fail on the best known woman in the world, so what's next? The Prime Minister?"

"Where you're going it doesn't matter, son."

"But I'm right, aren't I?"

"Damn you, Brosnan, you always were the clever bastard!" Dillon exploded angrily.

"You'll never get away with it," Brosnan said.

"You think so? I'll just have to prove you wrong, then."

"As I said, you must be losing your touch, Sean. This bungled attempt to get Mrs. Thatcher. Reminds me of a job dear old Frank Barry pulled back in seventy-nine when he tried to hit the British Foreign Secretary, Lord Carrington, when he was passing through Saint-Étienne. I'm rather surprised you used the same ground plan, but then you always did think Barry was special, didn't you?"

"He was the best."

"And at the end of things, very dead," Brosnan said.

"Yes, well, whoever got him must have given it to him in the back," Dillon said.

"Not true," Brosnan told him. "We were face-to-face as I recall."

"You killed Frank Barry?" Dillon whispered.

"Well, somebody had to," Brosnan said. "It's what usually happens to mad dogs. I was working for Ferguson, by the way."

"You bastard." Dillon raised the Walther, took careful aim and the door opened and Anne-Marie walked in with the shopping bags.

Dillon swung toward her. Brosnan called, "Look out!" and went down and Dillon fired twice at the sofa.

Anne-Marie screamed, not in terror, but in fury, dropped her bags and rushed at him. Dillon tried to fend her off, staggered back through the French windows. Inside, Brosnan crawled toward the table and reached for the drawer. Anne-Marie scratched at Dillon's face. He cursed, pushing her away from him. She fell against the balustrade and went over backwards.

Brosnan had the drawer open now, knocked the lamp on the table sideways, plunging the room into darkness, and reached for the Browning. Dillon fired three times very fast and ducked for the door. Brosnan fired twice, too late. The door banged. He got to his feet, ran to the terrace and looked over. Anne-Marie lay on the pavement below. He turned and ran through the drawing room into the hall, got the door open and went downstairs two at a time. It was snowing when he went out on the steps. Of Dillon there was no sign, but the night porter was kneeling beside Anne-Marie.

He looked up. "There was a man, Professor, with a gun. He ran across the road."

"Never mind." Brosnan sat down and cradled her in his arms. "An ambulance, and hurry."

The snow was falling quite fast now. He held her close and waited.

Ferguson, Mary and Max Hernu were having a thoroughly enjoyable time in the magnificent dining room at the Ritz. They were already on their second bottle of Louis Roederer Crystal champagne and the brigadier was in excellent form.

"Who was it who said that when a man tires of champagne, he's tired of life?" he demanded.

"He must certainly have been a Frenchman," Hernu told him.

"Very probably, but I think the time has come when we should toast the provider of this feast." He raised his glass. "To you, Mary, my love."

She was about to respond when she saw, in the mirror on the wall, Inspector Savary at the entrance speaking to the headwaiter. "I think you're being paged, Colonel," she told Hernu.

He glanced round. "What's happened now?" He got up, threaded his way through the tables and approached Savary. They talked for a few moments, glancing toward the table.

Mary said, "I don't know about you, sir, but I get a bad feeling."

Before he could reply, Hernu came back to them, his face grave. "I'm afraid I've got some rather ugly news."

"Dillon?" Ferguson asked.

"He paid a call on Brosnan a short while ago."

"What happened?" Ferguson demanded. "Is Brosnan all right?"

"Oh, yes. There was some gun play. Dillon got away." He sighed heavily. "But Mademoiselle Audin is at the Hôpital St-Louis. From what Savary tells me, it doesn't look good."

Brosnan was in the waiting room on the second floor when they arrived, pacing up and down smoking a cigarette. His eyes were wild, such a rage there as Mary Tanner had never seen.

She was the first to reach him. "I'm so sorry."

Ferguson said, "What happened?"

Briefly, coldly, Brosnan told them. As he finished, a tall, graying man in surgeon's robes came in. Brosnan turned to him quickly. "How is she,

Henri?" He said to the others, "Professor Henri Dubois, a colleague of mine at the Sorbonne."

"Not good, my friend," Dubois told him. "The injuries to the left leg and spine are bad enough, but even more worrying is the skull fracture. They're just preparing her for surgery now. I'll operate straight away."

He went out. Hernu put an arm around Brosnan's shoulders. "Let's go and get some coffee, my friend. I think it's going to be a long night."

"But I only drink tea," Brosnan said, his face bone white, his eyes dark. "Never could stomach coffee. Isn't that the funniest thing you ever heard?"

There was a small café for visitors on the ground floor. Not many customers at that time of night. Savary had gone off to handle the police side of the business; the others sat at a table in the corner.

Ferguson said, "I know you've got other things on your mind, but is there anything you can tell us? Anything he said to you?"

"Oh, yes—plenty. He's working for somebody and definitely not the IRA. He's being paid for this one and from the way he boasted, it's big money."

"Any idea who?"

"When I suggested Saddam Hussein he got angry. My guess is you wouldn't have to look much further. An interesting point. He knew about all of you."

"All of us?" Hernu said. "You're sure?"

"Oh, yes, he boasted about that." He turned to Ferguson. "Even knew about you and Captain Tanner being in town to pump me for information, that's how he put it. He said he had the right friends." He frowned, trying to remember the phrase exactly. "The kind of people who can access any-thing."

"Did he, indeed." Ferguson glanced at Hernu. "Rather worrying, that."

"And you've got another problem. He spoke of the Thatcher affair as being just a tryout, that he had an alternative target."

"Go on," Ferguson said.

"I managed to get him to lose his temper by needling him about what a botch-up the Valenton thing was. I think you'll find he intends to have a crack at the British Prime Minister."

Mary said, "Are you certain?"

"Oh, yes." He nodded. "I baited him about that, told him he'd never get away with it. He lost his temper. Said he'd just have to prove me wrong."

Ferguson looked at Hernu and sighed. "So now we know. I'd better go along to the Embassy and alert all our people in London."

"I'll do the same here," Hernu said. "After all, he has to leave the country some time. We'll alert all airports and ferries. The usual thing, but discreetly, of course."

They got up and Brosnan said, "You're wasting your time. You won't get him, not in any usual way. You don't even know what you're looking for."

"Perhaps, Martin," Ferguson said. "But we'll just have to do our best, won't we?"

Mary Tanner followed them to the door. "Look, if you don't need me, Brigadier, I'd like to stay."

"Of course, my dear. I'll see you later."

She went to the counter and got two cups of tea. "The French are wonderful," she said. "They always think we're crazy to want milk in our tea."

"Takes all sorts," he said and offered her a cigarette. "Ferguson told me how you got that scar."

"Souvenir of old Ireland." She shrugged.

He was desperately trying to think of something to say. "What about your family? Do they live in London?"

"My father was a professor of surgery at Oxford. He died some time ago. Cancer. My mother's still alive. Has an estate in Herefordshire."

"Brothers and sisters?"

"I had one brother. Ten years older than me. He was shot dead in Belfast in nineteen eighty. Sniper got him from the Divis Flats. He was a Marine Commando Captain."

"I'm sorry."

"A long time ago."

"It can't make you particularly well disposed toward a man like me."

"Ferguson explained to me how you became involved with the IRA after Vietnam."

"Just another bloody Yank sticking his nose in, is that what you think?" He sighed. "It seemed the right thing to do at the time, it really did, and don't let's pretend. I was up to my neck in it for five long and bloody years."

"And how do you see it now?"

"Ireland?" he laughed harshly. "The way I feel I'd see it sink into the sea with pleasure." He got up. "Come on, let's stretch our legs," and he led the way out.

Dillon was in the kitchen in the barge heating the kettle when the phone rang. Makeev said, "She's in the Hôpital St-Louis. We've had to be discreet in our inquiries, but from what my informant can ascertain, she's on the critical list."

"Sod it," Dillon said. "If only she'd kept her hands to herself."

"This could cause a devil of a fuss. I'd better come and see you."

"I'll be here."

Dillon poured hot water into a basin, then he went into the bathroom. First he took off his shirt, then he got a briefcase from the cupboard under the sink. It was exactly as Brosnan had forecast. Inside he had a range of passports, all of himself suitably disguised. There was also a first-class makeup kit.

Over the years he had traveled backwards and forwards to England many times, frequently through Jersey in the Channel Islands. Jersey was British soil. Once there, a British citizen didn't need a passport for the flight to the English mainland. So, a French tourist holidaying in Jersey. He selected a passport in the name of Henri Jacaud, a car salesman from Rennes.

To go with it, he found a Jersey driving license in the name of Peter Hilton with an address in the Island's main town of Saint Helier. Jersey driving licenses, unlike the usual British mainland variety, carry a photo. It was always useful to have positive identification on you, he'd learned that years ago. Nothing better than for people to be able to check the face with a photo, and the photos on the driving license and on the French passport were identical. That was the whole point.

He dissolved some black hair dye into the warm water and started to brush it into his fair hair. Amazing what a difference it made, just changing the hair color. He blow-dried it and brilliantined it back in place, then he selected, from a range in his case, a pair of horn-rimmed spectacles, slightly tinted. He closed his eyes, thinking about the role, and when he opened them again, Henri Jacaud stared out of the mirror. It was quite extraordinary. He closed the case, put it back in the cupboard, pulled on his shirt and went into the stateroom carrying the passport and the driving license.

At that precise moment Makeev came down the companionway. "Good God!" he said. "For a moment I thought it was someone else."

"But it is," Dillon said. "Henri Jacaud, car salesman from Rennes on his way to Jersey for a winter break. Hydrofoil from Saint-Malo." He held up the driving license. "Who is also Jersey resident Peter Hilton, accountant in Saint Helier."

"You don't need a passport to get to London?"

"Not if you're a Jersey resident; it's British territory. The driving license just puts a face to me. Always makes people feel happier. Makes them feel they know who you are, even the police."

"What happened tonight, Sean? What really happened?"

"I decided the time had come to take care of Brosnan. Come on, Josef, he knows me too damned well. Knows me in a way no one else does and that could be dangerous."

"I can see that. A clever one, the professor."

"There's more to it than that, Josef. He understands how I make my moves, how I think. He's the same kind of animal as I am. We inhabited the same world, and people don't change. No matter how much he thinks he has, he's still the same underneath, the same man who was the most feared enforcer the IRA had in the old days."

"So you decided to eliminate him?"

"It was an impulse. I was passing his place, saw the woman leaving. He called to her. The way it sounded I thought she was gone for the night, so I took a chance and went up the scaffolding."

"What happened?"

"Oh, I had the drop on him."

"But didn't kill him?"

Dillon laughed, went out to the kitchen and returned with a bottle of Krug and two glasses. As he uncorked it he said, "Come on, Josef, face-to-face after all those years. There were things to be said."

"You didn't tell him who you were working for?"

"Of course not," Dillon lied cheerfully and poured the champagne. "What do you take me for?"

He toasted Makeev, who said, "I mean, if he knew you had an alternative target, that you intended to go for Major . . ." He shrugged. "That would mean that Ferguson would know. It would render your task in London impossible. Aroun, I'm sure, would want to abort the whole business."

"Well he doesn't know." Dillon drank some more champagne. "So Aroun can rest easy. After all, I want that second million. I checked with Zurich, by the way. The first million has been deposited."

Makeev shifted uncomfortably. "Of course. So, when do you intend to leave?"

"Tomorrow or the next day. I'll see. Meanwhile something you can organize for me. This Tania Novikova in London. I'll need her help."

"No problem."

"First, my father had a second cousin, a Belfast man living in London called Danny Fahy."

"IRA?"

"Yes, but not active. A deep cover man. Brilliant with his hands. Worked in light engineering. Could turn his hand to anything. I used him in nineteen eighty-one when I was doing a few jobs for the organization in London. In those days he lived at number ten Tithe Street in Kilburn. I want Novikova to trace him."

"Anything else?"

"Yes, I'll need somewhere to stay. She can organize that for me, too. She doesn't live in the Embassy I suppose?"

"No, she has a flat off the Bayswater Road."

"I wouldn't want to stay there, not on a regular basis. She could be under surveillance. Special Branch at Scotland Yard have a habit of doing that with employees of the Soviet Embassy, isn't that so?"

"Oh, it's not like the old days." Makeev smiled. "Thanks to that fool Gorbachev, we're all supposed to be friends these days."

"I'd still prefer to stay somewhere else. I'll contact her at her flat, no more than that."

"There is one problem," Makeev said. "As regards hardware, explosives, weapons, anything like that you might need. I'm afraid she won't be able to help you there. A handgun perhaps, but no more. As I mentioned when I first told you about her, her boss, Colonel Yuri Gatov, the commander of KGB station in London, is a Gorbachev man, and very well disposed to our British friends."

"That's all right," Dillon said. "I have my own contacts for that kind of thing, but I will need more working capital. If I am checked going through Customs on the Jersey to London flight, I couldn't afford to be caught with large sums of money in my briefcase."

"I'm sure Aroun can fix that for you."

"That's all right, then. I'd like to see him again before I go. Tomorrow morning, I think. Arrange that, will you?"

"All right." Makeev fastened his coat. "I'll keep you posted on the situation at the hospital." He reached the bottom of the companionway and turned. "There is one thing. Say you managed to pull this thing off. It would lead to the most ferocious manhunt. How would you intend to get out of England?"

Dillon smiled. "That's exactly what I'm going to give some thought to now. I'll see you in the morning."

Makeev went up the companionway. Dillon poured another glass of Krug, lit a cigarette and sat at the table, looking at the clippings on the walls. He reached for the pile of newspapers and sorted through them and finally found what he wanted. An old copy of the magazine *Paris Match* from the previous year. Michael Aroun was featured on the front cover. Inside was a seven-page feature about his life-style and habits. Dillon lit a cigarette and started going through it.

It was one o'clock in the morning and Mary Tanner was sitting alone in the waiting room when Professor Henri Dubois came in. He was very tired, shoulders bowed, and he sank wearily into a chair and lit a cigarette.

"Where is Martin?" he asked her.

"It seems Anne-Marie's only close relative is her grandfather. Martin is trying to contact him. Do you know him?"

"Who doesn't, mademoiselle? One of the richest and most powerful industrialists in France. Very old. Eighty-eight, I believe. He was once a patient of mine. He had a stroke last year. I don't think Martin will get very far there. He lives on the family estate, Château Vercors. It's about twenty miles outside Paris."

Brosnan came in, looking incredibly weary, but when he saw Dubois he said eagerly, "How is she?"

"I won't pretend, my friend. She'd not good. Not good at all. I've done everything that I possibly can. Now we wait."

"Can I see her?"

"Leave it for a while. I'll let you know."

"You'll stay?"

"Oh, yes. I'll grab a couple of hours' sleep on my office couch. How did you get on with Pierre Audin?"

"I didn't. Had to deal with his secretary, Fournier. The old man's confined to a wheelchair now. Doesn't know the time of day."

Dubois sighed. "I suspected as much. I'll see you later."

When he'd gone, Mary said, "You could do with some sleep yourself."

He managed a dark smile. "The way I feel now, I don't think I could ever sleep again. All my fault, in a way." There was despair on his face.

"How can you say that?

"Who I am, or to put it another way, what I was. If it hadn't been for that, none of this would have happened."

"You can't talk like that," she said. "Life doesn't work like that."

The phone on the table rang and she answered it, spoke for a few brief moments, then put it down. "Just Ferguson checking." She put a hand on his shoulder. "Come on, lie down on the couch. Just close your eyes. I'll be here. I'll wake you the moment there's word."

Reluctantly, he lay back and did as he was told and surprisingly did fall into a dark, dreamless sleep. Mary Tanner sat there, brooding, listening to his quiet breathing.

It was just after three when Dubois came in. As if sensing his presence, Brosnan came awake with a start and sat up. "What is it?"

"She's regained consciousness."

"Can I see her?" Brosnan got up.

"Yes, of course." As Brosnan made for the door, Dubois put a hand on his arm. "Martin, it's not good. I think you should prepare for the worst."

"No." Brosnan almost choked. "It's not possible."

He ran along the corridor, opened the door of her room and went in. There was a young nurse sitting beside her. Anne-Marie was very pale, her head so swathed in bandages that she looked like a young nun.

"I'll wait outside, monsieur," the nurse said and left.

Brosnan sat down. He reached for her hand and Anne-Marie opened her eyes. She stared vacantly at him and then recognition dawned and she smiled.

"Martin, is that you?"

"Who else?" He kissed her hand.

Behind them, the door clicked open slightly as Dubois peered in.

"Your hair. Too long. Ridiculously too long." She put up a hand to touch it. "In Vietnam, in the swamp, when the Vietcong were going to shoot me. You came out of the reeds like some medieval warrior. Your hair was too long then and you wore a headband."

She closed her eyes and Brosnan said, "Rest now, don't try to talk."

"But I must." She opened them again. "Let him go, Martin. Give me your promise. It's not worth it. I don't want you going back to what you were." She grabbed at his hand with surprising strength. "Promise me."

"My word on it," he said.

She lay back, staring up at the ceiling. "My lovely wild Irish boy. Always loved you, Martin, no one else."

Her eyes closed gently, the monitoring machine beside the bed changed its tone. Henry Dubois was in the room in a second. "Outside, Martin—wait."

He pushed Brosnan out and closed the door. Mary was standing in the corridor. "Martin?" she said.

He stared at her vacantly and then the door opened and Dubois appeared. "I'm so sorry, my friend. I'm afraid she's gone."

On the barge, Dillon came awake instantly when the phone rang. Makeev said, "She's dead, I'm afraid."

"That's a shame," Dillon said. "It was never intended."

"What now?" Makeev asked.

"I think I'll leave this afternoon. A good idea in the circumstances. What about Aroun?"

"He'll see us at eleven o'clock."

"Good. Does he know what's happened?"

"No."

"Let's keep it that way. I'll meet you outside the place just before eleven."

He replaced the phone, propped himself up against the pillows. Anne-Marie Audin. A pity about that. He'd never gone in for killing women. An informer once in Derry, but she deserved it. An accident this time, but it smacked of bad luck and that made him feel uneasy. He stubbed out his cigarette and tried to go to sleep again.

It was just after ten when Mary Tanner admitted Ferguson and Hernu to Brosnan's apartment. "How is he?" Ferguson asked.

"He's kept himself busy. Anne-Marie's grandfather is not well, so Martin's been making all the necessary funeral arrangements with his secretary."

"So soon?" Ferguson said.

"Tomorrow, in the family plot at Vercors."

She led the way in. Brosnan was standing at the window staring out. He turned to meet them, hands in pockets, his face pale and drawn. "Well?" he demanded.

"Nothing to report," Hernu told him. "We've notified all ports and airports, discreetly, of course." He hesitated. "We feel it would be better not to go public on this, Professor. Mademoiselle Audin's unfortunate death, I mean."

Brosnan seemed curiously indifferent. "You won't get him. London's the place to look and sooner rather than later. Probably on his way now, and for London you'll need me."

"You mean you'll help us? You'll come in on this thing?" Ferguson said.

"Yes."

Brosnan lit a cigarette, opened the French windows and stood on the terrace, Mary joined him. "But you can't, Martin, you told me that you promised Anne-Marie."

"I lied," he said calmly. "Just to make her going easier. There's nothing out there. Only darkness."

His face was rock hard, the eyes bleak. It was the face of a stranger. "Oh, my God," she whispered.

"I'll have him," Brosnan said. "If it's the last thing I do on this earth, I'll see him dead."

SIX

It was just before eleven when Makeev drew up before Michael Aroun's apartment in Avenue Victor Hugo. His chauffeur drew in beside the curb and as he switched off the engine, the door opened and Dillon climbed into the rear seat.

"You'd better not be wearing designer shoes," he said. "Slush everywhere."

He smiled and Makeev reached over to close the partition. "You seem in good form, considering the situation."

"And why shouldn't I be? I just wanted to make sure you hadn't told Aroun about the Audin woman."

"No, of course not."

"Good." Dillon smiled. "I wouldn't like anything to spoil things. Now let's go and see him."

Rashid opened the door to them. A maid took their coats. Aroun was waiting in the magnificent drawing room. "Valenton, Mr. Dillon. A considerable disappointment."

Dillon said, "Nothing's ever perfect in this life, you should know that. I promised you an alternative target and I intend to go for it."

"The British Prime Minister?" Rashid asked.

"That's right." Dillon nodded. "I'm leaving for London later today. I thought we'd have a chat before I go."

Rashid glanced at Aroun, who said, "Of course, Mr. Dillon. Now, how can we help you?"

"First, I'm going to need operating money again. Thirty thousand dollars. I want you to arrange that from someone in London. Cash, naturally. Colonel Makeev can finalize details."

"No problem," Aroun said.

"Secondly, there's the question of how I get the hell out of England after the successful conclusion of the venture."

"You sound full of confidence, Mr. Dillon," Rashid told him.

"Well, you have to travel hopefully, son," Dillon said. "The thing with any major hit, as I've discovered during the years, is not so much achieving it as moving on with a whole skin afterwards. I mean, if I get the British Prime Minister for you, the major problem for me is getting out of England, and that's where you come in, Mr. Aroun."

The maid entered with coffee on a tray. Aroun waited while she laid the cups out on a table and poured. As she withdrew he said, "Please explain."

"One of my minor talents is flying. I share that with you, I understand. According to an old *Paris Match* article I was reading, you bought an estate in Normandy called Château Saint Denis about twenty miles south of Cherbourg on the coast?"

"That's correct."

"The article mentioned how much you loved the place, how remote and unspoiled it was. A time capsule from the eighteenth century."

"Exactly what are we getting at here, Mr. Dillon?" Rashid demanded.

"It also said it had its own landing strip and that it wasn't unknown for Mr. Aroun to fly down there from Paris when he feels like it, piloting his own plane."

"Quite true," Aroun said.

"Good. This is how it will go, then. When I'm close to, how shall we put it, the final end of things, I'll let you know. You'll fly down to this Saint Denis place. I'll fly out from England and join you there after the job is done. You can arrange my onwards transportation."

"But how?" Rashid demanded. "Where will you find a plane?"

"Plenty of flying clubs, old son, and planes to hire. I'll simply fly off the map. Disappear, put it any way you like. As a pilot yourself you must know that one of the biggest headaches the authorities have is the vast amount of uncontrolled airspace. Once I land at Saint Denis, you can torch the bloody thing up." He looked from Rashid to Aroun. "Are we agreed?"

It was Aroun who said, "Absolutely, and if there is anything else we can do."

"Makeev will let you know. I'll be going now." Dillon turned to the door.

Outside, he stood on the pavement beside Makeev's car, the snow falling lightly. "That's it, then. We shan't be seeing each other, not for a while anyway."

Makeev passed him an envelope. "Tania's home address and telephone number." He glanced at his watch. "I couldn't get her earlier this morning. I left a message to say I wanted to speak to her at noon."

"Fine," Dillon said. "I'll speak to you from Saint-Malo before I get the Hydrofoil for Jersey, just to make sure everything is all right."

"I'll drop you off," Makeev told him.

"No, thanks. I feel like the exercise." Dillon held out his hand. "To our next merry meeting."

"Good luck, Sean."

Dillon smiled. "Oh, you always need that as well," and he turned and walked away.

Makeev spoke to Tania on the scrambler at noon. "I have a friend calling to see you," he said. "Possibly late this evening. The one we've spoken of."

"I'll take care of him, Colonel."

"You've never handled a more important business transaction," he said, "believe me. He'll need alternative accommodation, by the way. Make it convenient to your own place."

"Of course."

"And I want you to put a trace out on this man."

He gave her Danny Fahy's details. When he was finished, she said, "There should be no problem. Anything else?"

"Yes, he likes Walthers. Take care, my dear, I'll be in touch."

When Mary Tanner went into the suite at the Ritz, Ferguson was having afternoon tea by the window.

"Ah, there you are," he said. "Wondered what was keeping you. We've got to get moving."

"To where?" she demanded.

"Back to London."

She took a deep breath. "Not me, Brigadier, I'm staying."

"Staying?" he said.

"For the funeral at Château Vercors at eleven o'clock tomorrow morning. After all, he's going to do what you want him to. Don't we owe him some support?"

Ferguson put up a hand defensively. "All right, you've made your point. However, I need to go back to London now. You can stay if you want and follow tomorrow afternoon. I'll arrange for the Lear jet to pick you up, both of you. Will that suffice?"

"I don't see why not." She smiled brightly and reached for the teapot. "Another cup, Brigadier?"

Sean Dillon caught the express to Rennes and changed trains for Saint-Malo at three o'clock. There wasn't much tourist traffic, the wrong time of the year for that, and the atrocious weather all over Europe had killed whatever there was. There couldn't have been more than twenty passengers on the Hydrofoil to Jersey. He disembarked in Saint Helier just before six o'clock on the Albert Quay and caught a cab to the airport.

He knew he was in trouble before he arrived, for the closer they got, the thicker the fog was. It was an old story in Jersey, but not the end of the world. He confirmed that both evening flights to London were canceled, went out of the airport building, caught another taxi and told the driver to take him to a convenient hotel.

It was thirty minutes later that he phoned Makeev in Paris. "Sorry I didn't have a chance to phone from Saint-Malo. The train was late. I might have missed the Hydrofoil. Did you contact Novikova?"

"Oh, yes," Makeev told him. "Everything is in order. Looking forward to meeting you. Where are you?"

"A place called Hotel L'Horizon in Jersey. There was fog at the airport. I'm hoping to get out in the morning."

"I'm sure you will. Stay in touch."

"I'll do that."

Dillon put down the phone, then he put on his jacket and went downstairs to the bar. He'd heard somewhere that the hotel's grill was a quite exceptional restaurant. After a while he was approached by a handsome, energetic Italian who introduced himself as the headwaiter, Augusto. Dillon took a menu from him gratefully, ordered a bottle of Krug and relaxed.

It was at roughly the same time that the doorbell sounded at Brosnan's apartment on the Quai de Montebello. When he opened the door, a large glass of Scotch in one hand, Mary Tanner stood there.

"Hello," he said. "This is unexpected."

She took the glass of Scotch and emptied it into the potted plant that stood by the door. "That won't do you any good at all."

"If you say so. What do you want?"

"I thought you'd be alone. I didn't think that was a good idea. Ferguson spoke to you before he left?"

"Yes, he said you were staying over. Suggested we followed him tomorrow afternoon."

"Yes, well, that doesn't take care of tonight. I expect you haven't eaten a thing all day, so I suggest we go out for a meal, and don't start saying no."

"I wouldn't dream of it, Captain." He saluted.

"Don't fool around. There must be somewhere close by that you like."

"There is indeed. Let me get a coat and I'll be right with you."

It was a typical little side-street bistro, simple and unpretentious, booths to give privacy and cooking smells from the kitchen that were out of this world. Brosnan ordered champagne.

"Krug?" she said when the bottle came.

"They know me here."

"Always champagne with you?"

"I was shot in the stomach years ago. It gave me problems. The doctors said no spirits under any circumstances, no red wine. Champagne was okay. Did you notice the name of this place?"

"La Belle Aurore."

"Same as the café in Casablanca. Humphrey Bogart? Ingrid Bergman?" He raised his glass. "Here's looking at you, kid."

They sat there in companionable silence for a while and then she said, "Can we talk business?"

"Why not? What do you have in mind?"

"What happens next? I mean, Dillon just fades into the woodwork, you said that yourself. How on earth do you hope to find him?"

"One weakness," Brosnan said. "He won't go near any IRA contacts for fear of betrayal. That leaves him with only one choice. The usual one he makes. The underworld. Anything he needs—weaponry, explosives, even physical help—he'll go to the obvious place and you know where that is?"

"The East End of London?"

"Yes, just about as romantic as Little Italy in New York or the Bronx. The Kray brothers, the nearest thing England ever had to cinema gangsters, the Richardson gang. Do you know much about the East End?"

"I thought all that was history?"

"Not at all. A lot of the big men, the governors as they call them, have gone legitimate to a certain degree, but all the old-fashioned crimes—hold-ups, banks, security vans—are committed by roughly the same group. All family men, who just look upon it as business, but they'll shoot you if you get in the way."

"How nice."

"Everyone knows who they are, including the police. It's in that fraternity Dillon will look for help."

"Forgive me," she said. "But that must be rather a close-knit community."

"You're absolutely right, but as it happens, I've got what you might call the entrée."

"And how on earth do you have that?"

He poured her another glass of champagne. "Back in Vietnam in nineteen sixty-eight, during my wild and foolish youth, I was a paratrooper, Airborne Rangers. I formed part of a Special Forces detachment to operate in Cambodia, entirely illegally, I might add. It was recruited from all branches of the services. People with specialist qualifications. We even had a few Marines and that's how I met Harry Flood."

"Harry Flood?" she said and frowned. "For some reason, that name's familiar."

"Could be. I'll explain. Harry's the same age as me. Born in Brooklyn. His mother died when he was born. He grew up with his father, who died when Harry was eighteen. He joined the Marines for something to do, went to, Nam, which is where I met him." He laughed. "I'll never forget the first time. Up to our necks in a stinking swamp in the Mekong Delta."

"He sounds quite interesting."

"Oh, that and more. Silver Star, Navy Cross. In sixty-nine when I was getting out, Harry still had a year of his enlistment to do. They posted him to London. Embassy Guard duty. He was a sergeant then and that's when it happened."

"What did?"

"He met a girl at the old Lyceum Ballroom one night, a girl called Jean Dark. Just a nice, pretty twenty-year-old in a cotton frock, only there was one difference. The Dark family were gangsters, what they call in the East End real villains. Her old man had his own little empire down by the river, was in his own way as famous as the Kray brothers. He died later that year."

"What happened?" She was totally fascinated.

"Jean's mother tried to take over. Ma Dark, everyone called her. There were differences. Rival gangs. That sort of thing. Harry and Jean got married, he took his papers in London, stayed on and just got sucked in. Sorted the rivals out and so on."

"You mean he became a gangster?"

"Not to put too fine a point on it, yes, but more than that, much more. He became one of the biggest governors in the East End of London."

"My God, now I remember. He has all those casinos. He's the man doing all that riverside development on the Thames."

"That's right. Jean died of cancer about five or six years ago. Her mother died ages before that. He just carried on."

"Is he British now?"

"No, never gave up his American nationality. The authorities could never toss him out because he has no criminal record. Never served a single day in jail."

"And he's still a gangster?"

"That depends on your definition of the term. There's plenty he got away with, or his people did, in the old days. What you might call old-fashioned crime."

"Oh, you mean nothing nasty like drugs or prostitution? Just armed robbery, protection, that sort of thing?"

"Don't be bitter. He has the casinos, business interests in electronics and property development. He owns half of Wapping. Nearly all the river frontage. He's extremely legitimate."

"And still a gangster?"

"Let's say, he's still the governor to a lot of East Enders. The Yank, that's what they call him. You'll like him."

"Will I?" She looked surprised. "And when are we going to meet?"

"As soon as I can arrange it. Anything that moves in the East End and Harry or his people know about it. If anyone can help me catch Sean Dillon, he can." The waiter appeared and placed bowls of French onion soup before them. "Good," he said. "Now let's eat, I'm starving."

Harry Flood crouched in one corner of the pit, arms folded to conserve his body heat. He was naked to the waist, barefoot, clad only in a pair of camouflage pants. The pit was only a few feet square and rain poured down relentlessly through the bamboo grid high above his head. Sometimes the Vietcong would peer down at him, visitors being shown the Yankee dog who squatted in his own foulness, although he'd long since grown used to the stench.

It seemed as if he'd been there for ever and time no longer had any meaning. He had never felt such total despair. It was raining faster now, pouring over the edge of the pit in a kind of waterfall, the water rising rapidly. He was on his feet and yet suddenly it was up to his chest and he was struggling. It poured over his head relentlessly, and he no longer had a footing and struggled and kicked to keep afloat, fighting for breath, clawing at the side of the pit. Suddenly a hand grabbed his, a strong hand, and it pulled him up through the water and he started to breathe again.

He came awake with a start and sat upright. He'd had that dream for years on and off ever since Vietnam, and that was a hell of a long time ago. It usually ended with him drowning. The hand pulling him out was something new.

He reached for his watch. It was almost ten. He always had a nap early evening before visiting one of the clubs later, but this time he'd overslept. He put his watch on, hurried into the bathroom, and had a quick shower. There was gray in his black hair now, he noticed that as he shaved.

"Comes to us all, Harry," he said softly and smiled.

In fact he smiled most of the time, although anyone who observed closely would have noticed a certain world-weariness to it. The smile of a man who had found life, on the whole, disappointing. He was handsome enough in a rather hard way, muscular, with good shoulders. In fact not bad for forty-six, which he usually told himself at least once a day, if only for encouragement. He dressed in a black silk shirt buttoned at the neck without a tie and a loose fitting Armani suit in dark brown raw silk. He checked his appearance in the mirror.

"Here we go again, baby," he said and went out.

His apartment was enormous, part of a warehouse development on Cable Wharf. The brick walls of the sitting room were painted white, the wooden floor lacquered, Indian rugs scattered everywhere. Comfortable sofas, a bar, bottles of every conceivable kind ranged behind. Only for guests. He never drank alcohol. There was a large desk in front of the rear wall and the wall itself was lined with books.

He opened the French windows and went on to the balcony overlooking the river. It was very cold. Tower Bridge was to his right, the Tower of London just beyond it, floodlit. A ship passed down from the Pool of London in front of him, its lights clear in the darkness so that he could see crew members working on deck. It always gave him a lift and he took a great lungful of that cold air.

The door opened at the far end of the sitting room and Mordecai Fletcher came in. He was six feet tall with iron-gray hair and a clipped moustache and wore a well-cut, double-breasted blazer and a Guards tie. The edge was rather taken off his conventional appearance by the scar tissue round the eyes and the flattened nose that had been broken more than once.

"You're up," he said flatly.

"Isn't that what it looks like?" Flood asked.

Mordecai had been his strong right arm for the best part of fifteen years, a useful heavy-weight boxer who'd had the sense to get out of the ring before his brains were scrambled. He went behind the bar, poured a Perrier water, added ice and lemon and brought it over.

Flood took it without thanking him. "God, how I love this old river. Anything come up?"

"Your accountant called. Some papers to sign on that market development. I told him to leave them in the morning."

"Was that all?"

"Maurice was on the phone from the *Embassy*. He says Jack Harvey was in for a bite to eat with that bitch of a niece of his."

"Myra?" Flood nodded. "Anything happen?"

"Maurice said Harvey asked if you'd be in later. Said he'd come back and have a go at the tables." He hesitated. "You know what the bastard's after, Harry, and you've been avoiding him."

"We aren't selling, Mordecai, and we certainly aren't going into partnership. Jack Harvey's the worst hood in the East End. He makes the Kray brothers look like kindergarten stuff."

"I thought that was you, Harry."

"I never did drugs, Mordecai, didn't run girls, you know that. Okay, I was a right villain for a few years, we both were." He walked into the sitting room to the desk and picked up the photo in its silver frame that always stood there. "When Jean was dying, for all those lousy months." He shook his head. "Nothing seemed important, and you know the promise she made me give her toward the end. To get out."

Mordecai closed the window. "I know, Harry. She was a woman and a half, Jean."

"That's why I made us legitimate, and wasn't I right? You know what the firm's net worth is? Nearly fifty million. Fifty million." He grinned. "So let Jack Harvey and others like him keep dirtying their hands if they want."

"Yes, but to most people in the East End you're still the Governor, Harry, you're still the Yank."

"I'm not complaining." Flood opened a cupboard and took out a dark overcoat. "There's times when it helps a deal along, I know that. Now let's get moving. Who's driving tonight?"

"Charlie Salter."

"Good."

Mordecai hesitated. "Shall I carry a shooter, Harry?"

"For God's sake, Mordecai, we're legit now, I keep telling you."

"But Jack Harvey isn't, that's the trouble."

"Leave Jack Harvey to me."

They went down in the old original freight elevator to the warehouse where the black Mercedes saloon waited, Charlie Salter leaning against it reading a paper, a small, wiry man in a gray chauffeur's uniform. He folded the paper quickly and got the rear door open.

"Where to, Harry?"

"The *Embassy*, and drive carefully. A lot of frost around tonight and I'll have the paper."

Salter got behind the wheel and Mordecai got in beside him and reached for the electronic door control. The warehouse doors opened and they turned onto the wharf. Flood opened the paper, leaned back and started catching up on how the Gulf War was progressing.

The *Embassy Club* was only half a mile away, just off Wapping High Street. It had only been open six months, another of Harry Flood's developments of old warehouse property. The car park was up a side street at the rear and was already quite full. There was an old Negro in charge who sat in a small hut.

"Kept your place free, Mr. Flood," he said, coming out.

Flood got out of the car with Mordecai and took out his wallet as Salter went off to park. He extracted a five-pound note and gave it to the old man. "Don't go crazy, Freddy."

"With this?" The old man smiled. "Wouldn't even buy me a woman at the back of the pub these days. Inflation's a terrible thing, Mr. Flood."

Flood and Mordecai were laughing as they went up the side street, and Salter caught up with them as they turned the corner and reached the entrance. Inside it was warm and luxurious, black and white tiles on the floor, oak paneling, oil paintings. As the cloakroom girl took their coats, a small man in evening dress hurried to meet them. His accent was unmistakeably French.

"Ah, Mr. Flood, a great pleasure. Will you be dining?"

"I should think so, Maurice. We'll just have a look round first. Any sign of Harvey?"

"Not yet."

They went down the steps into the main dining room. The club atmosphere continued, paneled walls, paintings, table booths with leather seats. The place was almost full, waiters working busily. A trio played on a small dais in one corner and there was a dance floor, though not large.

Maurice threaded his way through the tables by the floor and opened a door in quilted leather that led to the casino part of the premises. It was just as crowded in there, people jostling each other at the roulette wheel, the chairs occupied at most of the tables.

"We losing much?" Flood asked Maurice.

"Swings and roundabouts, Mr. Flood. It all balances out as usual."

"Plenty of punters, anyway."

"And not an Arab in sight," Mordecai said.

"They're keeping their heads down," Maurice told him. "What with the Gulf business."

"Wouldn't you?" Flood grinned. "Come on, let's go and eat."

He had his own booth in a corner to one side of the band, overlooking the floor. He ordered smoked salmon and scrambled eggs and more Perrier water. He took a Camel cigarette from an old silver case. English cigarettes were something he'd never been able to come to terms with. Mordecai gave him a light and leaned against the wall. Flood sat there, brooding, surveying the scene, experiencing one of those dark moments when you wondered what life was all about and Charlie Salter came down the steps from the entrance and hurried through the tables.

"Jack Harvey and Myra—just in," he said.

Harvey was fifty years of age, of medium height and overweight, a fact that the navy blue Barathea suit failed to hide, in spite of having been cut in Savile Row. He was balding, hardly any hair there at all, and he had the fleshy, decadent face of the wrong sort of Roman emperor.

His niece, Myra, was thirty and looked younger, her jet-black hair caught up in a bun and held in place by a diamond comb. There was little makeup on her face except for the lips and they were blood red. She wore a sequined jacket and black miniskirt by Gianni Versace and very high-heeled black shoes, for she was only a little over five feet tall. She looked immensely attractive, men turning to stare at her. She was also her uncle's right hand, had a degree in business studies from London University and was just as ruthless and unscrupulous as he was.

Flood didn't get up, just sat there waiting. "Harry, my old son," Harvey said and sat down. "Don't mind if we join you, do you?"

Myra leaned down and kissed Flood on the cheek. "Like my new perfume, Harry? Cost a fortune, but Jack says it's like an aphrodisiac, the smell's so good."

"That's a big word for you, isn't it?" Flood said.

She sat on his other side and Harvey took out a cigar. He clipped it and looked up at Mordecai. "Come on, where's your bleeding lighter, then?"

Mordecai took out his lighter and flicked it without a change of expression, and Myra said, "Any chance of a drink? We know you don't, Harry, but think about the rest of us poor sods."

Her voice had a slight cockney accent, not too much, and it had its own attraction. She put a hand on his knee and Flood said, "Champagne cocktail, isn't that what you like?"

"It'll do to be going on with."

"Not me, can't drink that kind of piss," Harvey said. "Scotch and water. A big one."

Maurice, who had been hovering, spoke to a waiter, then whispered in Flood's ear, "Your scrambled eggs, Mr. Flood."

"I'll have them now," Flood told him.

Maurice turned away and a moment later a waiter appeared with a silver salver. He removed the dome and put the plate in front of Flood, who got to work straight away.

Harvey said, "I've never seen you eat a decent meal yet, Harry. What's wrong with you?"

"Nothing, really," Flood told him. "Food doesn't mean much to me, Jack. When I was a kid in Vietnam, the Vietcong had me prisoner for a while. I learned you could get by on very little. Later on I was shot in the gut. Lost eighteen inches of my intestines."

"You'll have to show me your scar sometime," Myra said.

"There's always a silver lining. If I hadn't been shot, the Marine Corps wouldn't have posted me to that nice soft job as a guard at the London Embassy."

"And you wouldn't have met Jean," Harvey said. "I remember the year you married her, Harry, the year her old dad died. Sam Dark." He shook his head. "He was like an uncrowned king in the East End after the Krays got put inside. And Jean." He shook his head again. "What a goer. The boys were queuing up for her. There was even a Guards officer, a lord." He turned to Myra. "Straight up."

"And instead she married me," Flood said.

"Could have done worse, Harry. I mean, you helped her keep things going a treat, especially after her mum died, we all know that."

Flood pushed his plate away and wiped his mouth with a napkin. "Compliments night is it, Jack? Now what have you really come for?"

"You know what I want, Harry, I want in. The casinos, four of them now, and how many clubs, Myra?"

"Six," she said.

"And all this development on the river," Harvey went on. "You've got to share the cake."

"There's only one trouble with that, Jack," Flood told him. "I'm a legitimate businessman, have been for a long time, whereas you . . ." He shook his head. "Once a crook, always a crook."

"You Yank bastard," Harvey said. "You can't talk to me like that."

"I just did, Jack."

"We're in, Harry, whether you like it or not."

"Try me," Flood said.

Salter had drifted across the room and leaned against the wall beside Mordecai. The big man whispered to him and Salter moved away.

Myra said, "He means it, Harry, so be reasonable. All we're asking for is a piece of the action."

"You come in with me, you're into computers, building development, clubs and gambling," Flood told her. "Which means I'm in with you into pimps, whores, drugs and protection. I shower three times a day, sweetness, and it still wouldn't make me feel clean."

"You Yank bastard!" She raised her hand and he grabbed her wrist.

Harvey stood up. "Let it go, Myra, let it go. Come on. I'll be seeing you, Harry."

"I hope not," Flood told him.

They went out and Mordecai leaned down. "He's a disgusting piece of slime. Always turned my stomach, him and his boyfriends."

"Takes all sorts," Flood said. "Don't let your prejudices show, Mordecai, and get me a cup of coffee."

The swine," Jack Harvey said as he and Myra walked along the pavement toward the car park. "I'll see him in hell, talking to me that way."

"I told you we were wasting our time," she said.

"Right." He eased his gloves over his big hands. "Have to show him we mean business then, won't we?"

A dark van was parked at the end of the street. As they approached, the side lights were turned on. The young man who leaned out from behind the wheel was about twenty-five, hard and dangerous-looking in a black leather bomber jacket and flat cap.

"Mr. Harvey," he said.

"Good boy, Billy, right on time." Harvey turned to his niece. "I don't think you've met Billy Watson, Myra."

"No, I don't think I have," she said looking him over.

"How many have you got in the back?" Harvey demanded.

"Four, Mr. Harvey. I heard this Mordecai Fletcher was a bit of an animal." He picked up a baseball bat. "This should cool him."

"No shooters, like I told you?"

"Yes, Mr. Harvey."

"Flesh on flesh, that's all it needs, and maybe a couple of broken legs. Get on with it. He'll have to come out sooner or later."

Harvey and Myra continued along the pavement. "Five?" she said. "You think that's enough?"

"Enough?" he laughed harshly. "Who does he think he is, Sam Dark? Now he was a man, but this bloody Yank . . . They'll cripple him. Put him on sticks for six months. They're hard boys, Myra."

"Really?" she said.

"Now come on and let's get out of this bleeding cold," and he turned into the car park.

It was an hour later that Harry Flood got ready to leave. As the cloak-room girl helped him on with his coat, he said to Mordecai, "Where's Charlie?"

"Oh, I gave him the nod a couple of minutes ago. He went ahead to get the car warmed up. I mean it's spawn of the north time out there, Harry, we'll have the bleeding Thames freezing over next."

Flood laughed and they went down the steps and started along the pavement. When it happened, it was very quick, the rear doors of the van parked on the other side of the road swinging open, the men inside rushing out and crossing the road on the run. They all carried baseball bats. The first to reach them swung hard. Mordecai ducked inside, blocked the blow and pitched him over his hip down the steps of the basement area behind.

The other four paused and circled, bats ready. "That won't do you any good," Billy Watson said. "It's leg-breaking time."

There was a shot behind them, loud in the frosty air and then another. As they turned, Charlie Salter moved out of the darkness reloading a sawed-off shotgun. "Now drop 'em," he said. "Unless you want to be jam all over the pavement."

They did as they were told and stood there waiting for what was to come. Mordecai moved close and looked them over, then he grabbed the nearest one by the hair. "Who are you working for, sonny?"

"I don't know, mister."

Mordecai turned him and ran him up against the railings, holding his face just above the spikes. "I said who are you working for?"

The youth cracked instantly. "Jack Harvey. It was just a wages job. It was Billy who pulled us in."

Billy said, "You bastard. I'll get you for that."

Mordecai glanced at Flood, who nodded. The big man said to Billy, "You stay. The rest of you, piss off."

They turned and ran for it. Billy Watson stood looking at them, his face wild. Salter said, "He needs a good slapping, this one."

Billy suddenly picked up one of the baseball bats and raised it defensively. "All right, let's be having you. Harry Flood—big man. No bloody good on your own are you, mate?"

Mordecai took a step forward and Flood said, "No," and moved in himself. "All right, son."

Billy swung, Flood swayed to one side, found the right wrist, twisting. Billy cried out and dropped the baseball bat and in the same moment, the American half-turned, striking him hard across the face with his elbow, sending him down on one knee.

Mordecai picked up the baseball bat. "No, he's got the point, let's get going," Flood said.

He lit a cigarette as they went along the street. Mordecai said, "What about Harvey? You going to stitch him up?"

"I'll think about it," Flood said, and they moved across to the car park.

Billy Watson got himself together, held onto the railings for a while. It was snowing a little as he turned and limped across the road to the van. As he went round to the driver's side, Myra Harvey stepped out of the entrance of a narrow alley, holding the collar of her fur coat up around her neck.

"Well that didn't go too well, did it?"

"Miss Harvey," he croaked. "I thought you'd gone."

"After my uncle dropped me off, I got a taxi back. I wanted to see the fun."

"Here," he said. "Are you telling me you expected it to go like it did?"

"I'm afraid so, sunshine. My uncle gets it wrong sometimes. Lets his emotions get the better of him. You really think five young punks like you could walk all over Harry Flood?" She opened the driver's door and pushed him in. "Go on, get over. I'll drive."

She climbed behind the wheel, the fur coat opened, and the miniskirt went about as high as it could.

As she switched on, Billy said, "But where are we going?"

"Back to my place. What you need is a nice hot bath, sunshine." Her left hand squeezed his thigh hard and she drove away.

SEVEN

The flight from Jersey got into Heathrow Terminal One just after eleven the following morning. It took half an hour for Dillon's case to come through and he sat smoking and reading the paper while he waited. The war news was good for the coalition forces. A few pilots down in Iraq, but the airstrikes were having a terrible effect.

His case came and he walked through. There was a rush of customers, as several planes had come in at around the same time. Customs didn't seem to be stopping anyone that morning, not that they'd have found anything on him. His suitcase contained a change of clothes and toilet articles, no more, and there were only a couple of newspapers in the briefcase. He also had two thousand dollars in his wallet, which was in twenty hundred-dollar bills. Nothing wrong with that. He'd destroyed the French passport at the hotel in Jersey. No turning back now. When he went back to France it would be very definitely a different route, and until then the Jersey driving license in the name of Peter Hilton was all the identification he needed.

He took the escalator to the upper concourse and joined the queue at one of the bank counters, changing five hundred dollars for sterling. He repeated the exercise at three other banks, then went downstairs to get a taxi, whistling softly to himself.

He told the driver to drop him at Paddington Station, where he left the suitcase in a locker. He phoned Tania Novikova on the number Makeev had given him, just on the chance she was at home, and got her answering machine. He didn't bother to leave a message, but went out and hailed a cab and told the driver to take him to Covent Garden.

In his tinted glasses, striped tie and navy blue Burberry trenchcoat he looked thoroughly respectable.

The driver said, "Terrible weather, guv. I reckon we're going to see some real heavy snow soon."

"I shouldn't be surprised." Dillon's accent was impeccable public school English.

"You live in London, guv?"

"No, just in town for a few days on business. I've been abroad for some time," Dillon said glibly. "New York. Haven't been in London for years."

"A lot of changes. Not like it used to be."

"So I believe. I was reading the other day that you can't take a walk up Downing Street anymore."

"That's right, guv. Mrs. Thatcher had a new security system installed, gates at the end of the street."

"Really?" Dillon said. "I'd like to see that."

"We'll go that way if you like. I can take you down to Whitehall, then cut back to Covent Garden."

"Suits me."

Dillon sat back, lit a cigarette and watched. They moved down White-hall from Trafalgar Square past Horse Guards with the two Household Cav-alrymen on mounted duty, wearing greatcoats against the cold, sabers drawn.

"Must be bleeding cold for the horses," the cabby said and then added, "Here we are, guv, Downing Street." He slowed a little. "Can't stop. If you do, the coppers come up and ask you what you're doing."

Dillon looked across at the end of the street. "So those are the famous gates?"

"Thatcher's folly, some twerps call it, but if you ask me, she was usually right. The bloody IRA have pulled off enough stunts in London during the past few years. I'd shoot the lot of them, I would. If I drop you in Long Acre, will that do, guv?"

"Fine," Dillon told him and sat back, thinking about those rather mag-nificent gates at the end of Downing Street.

The taxi pulled into the curb and Dillon gave him a ten-pound note. "Keep it," he said, turned and walked briskly away along Langley Street. The whole Covent Garden area was as busy as usual, people dressed for the extreme cold, more like Moscow than London. Dillon went with the throng and finally found what he wanted in an alley near Neal's Yard, a small theatrical shop, the window full of old costume masks and makeup. A bell tinkled when he went in. The man who appeared through a curtain at the rear was about seventy, with snow-white hair and a round, fleshy face.

"And what can I do for you?" he asked.

"Some makeup, I think. What have you got in boxes?"

"Some very good kits here," the old boy said. He took one down and opened it on the counter. "They use these at the National Theatre. In the business, are you?"

"Amateur, that's all, I'm afraid, church players." Dillon checked the contents of the box. "Excellent. I'll take an extra lipstick, bright red, some black hair dye and also some solvent."

"You are going to town. Clayton's my name, by the way. I'll give you my card in case you ever need anything else." He got the required items and put them inside the make-up box and closed it. "Thirty quid for cash and don't forget, anything you need . . ."

"I won't," Dillon said and went out whistling.

In the village of Vercors it was snowing as the cortege drove down from the chateau. In spite of the weather, villagers lined the street, men with their caps off, as Anne-Marie Audin went to her final rest. There were only three cars behind the hearse, old Pierre Audin and his secretary in the first, a number of servants in the other. Brosnan and Mary Tanner, with Max Hernu following, walked up through the tombstones and paused as the old man was lifted from the car into his wheel-chair. He was pushed inside, the rest followed.

It was very old, a typical village church, white-washed walls, the Stations of the Cross, and it was cold, very cold. In fact Brosnan had never felt so cold and sat there, shaking slightly, hardly aware of what was being said, rising and kneeling obediently with everyone else. It was only when the service ended and they stood as the pallbearers carried the coffin down the aisle that he realized that Mary Tanner was holding his hand.

They walked through the graveyard to the family mausoleum. It was the size of a small chapel, built in gray granite and marble with a steep Gothic roof. The oaken doors stood open. The priest paused to give the final benediction, the coffin was taken inside. The secretary turned the wheelchair and pushed it down the path past them, the old man huddled over, a rug across his knees.

"I feel so sorry for him," Mary said.

"No need, he doesn't know what time of day it is," Brosnan told her.

"That's not always true."

She walked to the car, and put a hand on the old man's shoulder as he sat there in his wheelchair. Then she returned.

"So, my friends, back to Paris," Hernu said.

"And then London," Brosnan said.

Mary took his arm as they walked toward the car. "Tomorrow, Martin, tomorrow morning will be soon enough, and I won't take no for an answer."

"All right," he said. "Tomorrow it is," and he got in the rear of the car and leaned back, suddenly drained, and closed his eyes, Mary sitting beside him as Hernu drove away.

It was just after six when Tania Novikova heard the doorbell. She went downstairs and opened the door. Dillon stood there, suitcase in one hand, briefcase in the other. "Josef sends his regards."

She was amazed. Since Makeev had spoken to her she had accessed KGB files in London to discover as much about Dillon as she could and had been astonished at his record. She had expected some kind of dark hero. Instead, she had a small man in a trenchcoat with tinted glasses and a college tie.

"You are Sean Dillon?" she said.

"As ever was."

"You'd better come in."

Women had never been of great importance to Dillon. They were there to satisfy a need on occasions, but he had never felt the slightest emotional involvement with one. Following Tania Novikova up the stairs, he was aware that she had a good figure and that the black trouser suit became her. Her hair was caught up at the nape of the neck in a velvet bow, but, when she turned to him in the full light of her sitting room, he realized that she was really rather plain.

"You had a good trip?" she asked.

"All right. I was delayed in Jersey last night because of fog."

"Would you like a drink?"

"Tea would be fine."

She opened a drawer, produced a Walther, two spare clips and a Carswell silencer. "Your preferred weapon according to Josef."

"Definitely."

"Also, I thought this might come in useful." She handed him a small bundle. "They say it can stop a .45 bullet at point-blank range. Nylon and titanium."

Dillon unfolded it. Nothing like as bulky as a flak jacket, it was designed like a small waistcoat and fastened with Velcro tabs.

"Excellent," he said and put it in his briefcase together with the Walther and the silencer. He unbuttoned his trenchcoat, lit a cigarette and stood in the kitchen door and watched her make the tea. "You're very convenient for the Soviet Embassy here?"

"Oh, yes, walking distance." She brought the tea out on a tray. "I've fixed you up with a room in a small hotel just round the corner in the Bayswater Road. It's the sort of place commercial travelers overnight at."

"Fine." He sipped his tea. "To business. What about Fahy?"

"No luck so far. He moved from Kilburn a few years ago to a house in Finchley. Only stayed there a year and moved again. That's where I've drawn a blank. But I'll find him, I've got someone on his case."

"You must. It's essential. Does KGB's London station still have a forgery department?"

"Of course."

"Good." He took out his Jersey driving license. "I want a private pilot's license in the same name and address. You'll need a photo." He slipped a finger inside the plastic cover of the license and pulled out a couple of identical prints. "Always useful to have a few of these."

She took one of them. "Peter Hilton, Jersey. Can I ask why this is necessary?"

"Because when the right time comes, time to get the hell out of it, I want to fly, and they won't hire a plane to you unless you have a license issued by the Civil Aviation Authority." He helped himself to some more tea. "Tell your expert I want full instrument rating and twin-engine."

"I'll write that down." She opened her handbag, took out an envelope, slipped the photo inside and made a note on the cover. "Is there anything else?"

"Yes, I'd like full details of the present security system at Number Ten Downing Street."

She caught her breath. "Am I to take it that is your target?"

"Not as such. The man inside, but that's a different thing. The Prime Minister's daily schedule, how easy is it to access that?"

"It depends what you want. There are always fixed points in the day. Question time in the House of Commons, for example. Of course, things are different because of the Gulf. The War Cabinet meets every morning at ten o'clock."

"At Downing Street?"

"Oh, yes, in the Cabinet room. But he has other appointments during the day. Only yesterday he did a broadcast on British Forces Network to the troops in the Gulf."

"Was that from BBC?"

"No, they have their own headquarters at Bridge House. That's near Paddington Station and not too far from here."

"Interesting. I wonder what his security was like."

"Not much, believe me. A few detectives, no more than that. The British are crazy."

"A damn good job they are. This informant of yours, the one who got you all the information on Ferguson. Tell me about him." Which she did, and when she was finished he nodded. "You've got him well and truly by the cobblers then?"

"I think you could say that."

"Let's keep it that way." He got up and buttoned his coat. "I'd better go and book in at this hotel."

"Have you eaten?" she asked.

"No."

"I have a suggestion. Just along from the hotel is an excellent Italian restaurant, *Luigi's*. One of those little family-owned places. You get settled in at the hotel and I'll walk along to the Embassy. I'll check on what we have on the Downing Street defences and see if anything's turned up on Fahy."

"And the flying license?"

"I'll put that in hand."

"Twenty-four hours."

"All right."

She got a coat and scarf, went downstairs with him and they left together. The pavements were frosty and she carried his briefcase for him and held on to his arm until they reached the hotel.

"I'll see you in an hour," she said and moved on.

It was the sort of place which had been a thriving pub and hotel in late Victorian times. The present owners had done their best with it and that wasn't very much. The dining room to the left of the foyer was totally uninviting, no more than half a dozen people eating there. The desk clerk was an old man with a face like a skull who wore a faded brown uniform. He moved with infinite slowness, booking Dillon in and gave him his key. Guests were obviously expected to carry their own cases.

The room was exactly what he'd expected. Twin beds, cheap coverings, a shower room, a television with a slot for coins and a kettle, a little basket beside it containing sachets of coffee, teabags and powdered milk. Still, it wouldn't be for long and he opened his suitcase and unpacked.

Among Jack Harvey's interests was a funeral business in Whitechapel. It was a sizeable establishment and did well, for, as he liked to joke, the dead were always with us. It was an imposing, three-storeyed Victorian building which he'd had renovated. Myra had the top floor as a penthouse and took an interest in the running of the place. Harvey had an office on the first floor.

Harvey told his driver to wait, went up the steps and rang the bell. The night porter answered.

"My niece in?" Harvey demanded.

"I believe so, Mr. Harvey."

Harvey moved through the main shop with coffins on display and along the passage with the little Chapels of Rest on each side where relatives could view the bodies. He went up two flights of stairs and rang the bell on Myra's door.

She was ready for him, alerted by a discreet call from the porter, let him wait for a moment, then opened the door. "Uncle Jack."

He brushed past her. She was wearing a gold sequined minidress, black stockings and shoes. "You going out or something?" he demanded.

"A disco, actually."

"Well, never mind that now. You saw the accountants? Is there any way I can get at Flood legally? Any problems with leases? Anything?"

"Not a chance," Myra said. "We've gone through the lot with a fine-tooth comb. There's nothing."

"Right, then I'll just have to get him the hard way."

"That didn't exactly work last night, did it?"

"I used rubbish, that's why, a bunch of young jerks who didn't deserve the time of day."

"So what do you intend?"

"I'll think of something." As he turned to the door, he heard a movement in the bedroom. "Here, who's in there." He flung the door open and revealed Billy Watson standing there, looking hunted. "Jesus!" Harvey said to Myra. "Disgusting. All you can ever think of is a bit of the other."

"At least we do it the right way," she told him.

"Screw you!" he said.

"No, he'll do that."

Harvey stormed downstairs. Billy said, "You don't give a monkey's for anyone, do you?"

"Billy, love, this is the house of the dead," she said and picked up her fur coat and handbag. "They're lying in their coffins downstairs and we're alive. Simple as that, so make the most of it. Now, let's get going."

Dillon was sitting in a small booth in the corner at *Luigi's* drinking the only champagne available, a very reasonable Bollinger non-vintage, when Tania came in. Old Luigi greeted her personally and as a favored customer and she sat down.

"Champagne?" Dillon asked.

"Why not." She looked up at Luigi. "We'll order later."

"One thing that hasn't been mentioned is my operating money. Thirty thousand dollars. Aroun was to arrange that," Dillon said.

"It's taken care of. The man in question will be in touch with me tomorrow. Some accountant of Aroun's in London."

"Okay, so what have you got for me?" he asked.

"Nothing on Fahy yet. I've set the wheels in motion as regards the flying license."

"And Number Ten?"

"I've had a look at the file. The public always had a right of way along Downing Street. The IRA coming so close to blowing up the whole cabinet at the Tory Party Conference in Brighton the other year made for a change in thinking about security. The bombing campaign in London and attacks on individuals accelerated things."

"So?"

"Well, the public used to be able to stand at the opposite side of the road from Number Ten watching the great and the good arrive and depart, but no longer. In December eighty-nine, Mrs. Thatcher ordered new security measures. In effect the place is now a fortress. The steel railings are ten feet high. The gates, by the way, are neo-Victorian, a nice touch that, from the Iron Lady."

"Yes, I saw them today."

Luigi hovered anxiously and they broke off and ordered minestrone, veal chops, sauté potatoes and a green salad.

Tania carried on: "There were accusations in some quarters that she'd become the victim of paranoid delusions. Nonsense, of course. That lady has never been deluded about anything in her life. Anyway, on the other side of the gates there's a steel screen designed to come up fast if an unauthorized vehicle tries to get through."

"And the building itself?"

"The windows have specially strengthened glass and that includes the Georgian windows. Oh, and the net curtains are definitely a miracle of modern science. They're blast-proof."

"You certainly have the facts."

"Incredibly, everything I've told you has been reported in either a British newspaper or magazine. The British press puts its own right to publish above every other consideration. They just refuse to face up to security implications. On file at the clippings library of any major British newspaper you'll find details of the interior of Number Ten or the Prime Minister's country home, Chequers, or even Buckingham Palace."

"What about getting in as ancillary staff?"

"That used to be a real loophole. Most catering for functions is done by outside firms, and some of the cleaning, but they're very tough about security clearance for these people. There are always slipups, of course. There was a plumber working on the Chancellor of the Exchequer's home at Number Eleven who opened a door and found himself wandering about Number Ten trying to get out."

"It sounds like a French farce."

"Only recently staff from one of the outside firms employed to offer cleaning services of one kind or another, staff who had security clearance, were found to be operating under false identities. Some of them had clearance for the Home Office and other Ministries."

"Yes, but all you're saying is mistakes occur."

"That's right." She hesitated. "Have you anything particular in mind?"

"You mean potshots with a sniper's rifle from a rooftop two hundred yards away as he comes out of the door? I don't think so. No, I really have no firm idea at the moment, but I'll come up with something. I always do." The waiter brought their soup. Dillon said, "Now that smells good enough to eat. Let's do just that."

Afterwards, he walked her round to her door. It was snowing just a little and very cold. He said, "Must remind you of home, this weather?"

"Home?" She looked blank for a moment then laughed. "Moscow, you mean?" She shrugged. "It's been a long time. Would you like to come up?"

"No, thanks. It's late and I could do with the sleep. I'll stay at the hotel tomorrow morning. Let's say till noon. From what I saw I don't think I could stand the thought of lunch there. I'll be back after two, so you'll know where I'll be."

"Fine," she said.

"I'll say good night, then."

She closed the door, Dillon turned and walked away. It was only after he rounded the corner into the Bayswater Road that Gordon Brown moved out of the shadows of a doorway opposite and looked up at Tania's window. The light came on. He stayed there for a while longer, then turned and walked away.

In Paris the following morning the temperature went up three or four degrees and it started to thaw. Mary and Hernu in the colonel's black Citroën picked Brosnan up just before noon. He was waiting for them in the entrance of the Quai de Montebello apartment block. He wore his trenchcoat, and a tweed cap and carried a suitcase. The driver put the case in the trunk and Brosnan got in the rear with the other two.

"Any news?" he asked.

"Not a thing," the colonel told him.

"Like I said, he's probably there already. What about Ferguson?"

Mary glanced at her watch. "He's due to see the Prime Minister now, to alert him as to the seriousness of this whole business."

"About all he can do," Brosnan said. "That and spread the word to the other branches of the security services."

"And how would you handle it, my friends?" Hernu asked.

"We know he worked in London for the IRA in nineteen eighty-one. As I told Mary, he must have used underworld contacts to supply his needs. He always does and it will be the same this time. That's why I must see my old friend Harry Flood."

"Ah, yes, the redoubtable Mr. Flood. Captain Turner was telling me about him, but what if he can't help?"

"There's another way. I have a friend in Ireland just outside Dublin at Kilrea, Liam Devlin. There's nothing he doesn't know about IRA history in the last few years and who did what. It's a thought." He lit a cigarette and leaned back. "But I'll get the bastard, one way or another. I'll get him."

The driver took them to the end of the Charles de Gaulle terminal where the private planes parked. The Lear was waiting on the tarmac. There was no formality. Everything had been arranged. The driver took their cases across to where the second pilot waited.

Hernu said, "Captain, if I may presume." He kissed Mary lightly on both cheeks. "And you, my friend." He held out his hand. "Always remember that when you set out on a journey with revenge at the end of it, it is necessary to first dig two graves."

"Philosophy now?" Brosnan said. "And at your time of life? Goodbye, Colonel."

They strapped themselves into their seats, the second pilot pulled up the stairs, locked the door and went and joined his companion in the cockpit.

"Hernu is right, you know," Mary said.

"I know he is," Brosnan answered. "But there's nothing I can do about that."

"I understand, believe me, I do," she said as the plane rolled forward.

When Ferguson was shown into the study at Number Ten, the Prime Minister was standing at the window drinking a cup of tea. He turned and smiled. "The cup that refreshes, Brigadier."

"They always say it was tea that got us through the war, Prime Minister."

"Well as long as it gets me through my present schedule. We've a meeting of the War Cabinet at ten every morning, as you know, and all the other pressing matters to do with the Gulf."

"And the day-to-day running of the country," Ferguson said.

"Yes, well we do our best. No one ever said politics was easy, Brigadier." He put down the cup. "I've read your latest report. You think it likely the man Dillon is here somewhere in London?"

"From what he said to Brosnan, I think we must assume that, Prime Minister."

"You've alerted all branches of the security services?"

"Of course, but we can't put a face to him, you see. Oh, there's the description. Small, fair haired and so on, but as Brosnan says, he'll look entirely different by now."

"It's been suggested to me that perhaps some press coverage might be useful."

Ferguson said, "Well, it's a thought, but I doubt it would achieve anything. What could they say? In furtherance of an enquiry the police would like to contact a man named Sean Dillon who isn't called that anymore? As regards a description, we don't know what he looks like and if we did, he wouldn't look like that anyway."

"My goodness, you carried that off beautifully, Brigadier." The Prime Minister roared with laughter.

"Of course there could be more lurid headlines. IRA jackal stalks the Prime Minister."

"No, I'm not having any of that nonsense," the Prime Minister said firmly. "By the way, as regards the suggestion that Saddam Hussein might be behind this affair, I must tell you your other colleagues in the Intelligence Services disagree. They are firmly of the opinion this is an IRA matter, and I must tell you that is how they are pursuing it."

"Well, if Special Branch think they'll find him by visiting Irish pubs in Kilburn, that's their privilege."

There was a knock at the door, an aide came in. "We're due at the Savoy in fifteen minutes, Prime Minister."

John Major smiled with great charm. "Another of those interminable luncheons, Brigadier. Prawn cocktail to start . . ."

"And chicken salad to follow," Ferguson said.

"Find him, Brigadier," the Prime Minister told him. "Find him for me," and the aide showed Ferguson out.

Tania, with good news for Dillon, knew there was no point in calling at the hotel before two, so she went to her flat. As she was looking for her key in her handbag Gordon Brown crossed the road.

"I was hoping I might catch you," he said.

"For God's sake, Gordon, you must be crazy."

"And what happens when something important comes up and you need to know? Can't wait for you to get in touch. It might be too late, so I'd better come in, hadn't I?"

"You can't. I'm due back at the Embassy in thirty minutes. I'll have a drink with you, that's all."

She turned and walked down to the pub on the corner before he could argue. They sat in a corner of the snug pub which was empty, aware of the noise from the main bar. Brown had a beer and Tania a vodka and lime.

"What have you got for me?" she asked.

"Shouldn't the question be the other way about?" She got up at once and he put a hand on her arm. "I'm sorry. Don't go."

"Then behave yourself." She sat down again. "Now get on with it."

"Ferguson had a meeting with the Prime Minister just before twelve. He was back in the office at twelve-thirty before I finished the first half of my shift. He dictated a report to Alice Johnson, she's one of the confidential typists who works with me. The report was for the file."

"Did you get a copy?"

"No, but I did the same as last time. Took it along to his office for her and read it on the way. Captain Tanner stayed in Paris with Brosnan for the funeral of a French woman."

"Anne-Marie Audin?" she prompted him.

"They're flying in today. Brosnan has promised full cooperation. Oh, all the other branches of the Intelligence Services have been notified about Dillon. No newspaper coverage on the P.M.'s instructions. The impression I got was he's told Ferguson to get on with it."

"Good," she said. "Very good, but you must stay on the case, Gordon. I have to go."

She started to get up and he caught her wrist. "I saw you last night, about eleven it was, coming back to your flat with a man."

"You were watching my flat?"

"I often do on my way home."

Her anger was very real, but she restrained it. "Then if you were there you'll know that the gentleman in question, a colleague from the Embassy, didn't come in. He simply escorted me home. Now let me go, Gordon."

She pulled free and walked out and Brown, thoroughly depressed, went to the bar and ordered another beer.

When she knocked on the door of Dillon's room just after two, he opened it at once. She brushed past him and went inside.

"You look pleased with yourself," he said.

"I should be."

Dillon lit a cigarette. "Go on, tell me."

"First, I've had words with my mole at Group Four. Ferguson's just been to see the Prime Minister. They believe you're here and all branches of Intelligence have been notified. Brosnan and the Tanner woman are coming in from Paris. Brosnan's offered full cooperation."

"And Ferguson?"

"The Prime Minister said no press publicity. Just told him to go all out to get you."

"It's nice to be wanted."

"Second." She opened her handbag and took out a passport-style booklet. "One pilot's license as issued by the Civil Aviation Authority to one Peter Hilton."

"That's bloody marvelous," Dillon said and took it from her.

"Yes, the man who does this kind of thing pulled out all the stops. I told him all your requirements. He said he'd give you a commercial license. Apparently you're also an instructor."

Dillon checked his photo and rifled through the pages. "Excellent. Couldn't be better."

"And that's not the end," she said. "You wanted to know the whereabouts of one Daniel Maurice Fahy?"

"You've found him?"

"That's right, but he doesn't live in London. I've brought you a road map." She unfolded it. "He has a farm here at a place called Cadge End in Sussex. It's twenty-five to thirty miles from London. You take the road through Dorking toward Horsham, then head into the wilds."

"How do you know all this?"

"The operative I put on the job managed to trace him late yesterday afternoon. By the time he'd looked the place over, then dropped into the pub in the local village to make a few enquiries, it was very late. He didn't get back to London until after midnight. I got his report this morning."

"And?"

"He says the farm is very out of the way near a river called the Arun. Marsh country. The village is called Doxley. The farm is a mile south of it. There's a signpost."

"He is efficient, your man."

"Well, he's young and trying to prove himself. From what he heard in the pub, Fahy runs a few sheep and dabbles in agricultural machinery."

Dillon nodded. "That makes sense."

"One thing that might come as a surprise. He has a girl staying with him, his grandniece, it seems. My man saw her."

"And what did he say?"

"That she came into the pub for some bottles of beer. About twenty. Angel, they called her, Angel Fahy. He said she looked like a peasant."

"Wonderful." He got up and reached for his jacket. "I must get down there right away. Do you have a car?"

"Yes, but it's only a Mini. Easier parking in London."

"No problem. As you said, thirty miles at the most. I can borrow it, then?"

"Of course. It's in the garage at the end of my street. I'll show you."

He put on his trenchcoat, opened the briefcase, took out the Walther, rammed a clip in the bolt and put it in his left-hand pocket. The silencer he put in the right. "Just in case," he said, and they went out.

The car was in fact a Mini-Cooper, which meant performance, jet black with a gold trim. "Excellent," he said. "I'll get moving."

He got behind the wheel and she said, "What's so important about Fahy?"

"He's an engineer who can turn his hand to anything, a bomb maker of genius, and he's been in deep cover for years. He helped me when I last operated here in eighty-one, helped me a lot. It also helps that he was my father's second cousin. I knew him when I was a kid over here. You haven't mentioned the cash from Aroun, by the way."

"I've to pick it up this evening at six. All very dramatic. A Mercedes stops at the corner of Brancaster Street and Town Drive. That's not far from here. I say, 'It's cold, even for this time of the year,' and the driver hands me a briefcase."

"God help us, he must have been seeing too much television," Dillon said. "I'll be in touch," and he drove away.

Ferguson had stopped off at his office at the Ministry of Defence after Downing Street to bring the report on the Dillon affair file up to date and clear his desk generally. As always, he preferred to work at the flat, so he returned to Cavendish Square, had Kim prepare him a late lunch of scrambled eggs and bacon, and was browsing through his *Times* when the doorbell rang. A moment later Kim showed in Mary Tanner and Brosnan.

"My dear Martin." Ferguson got up and shook hands. "So here we are again."

"So it would seem," Brosnan said.

"Everything go off all right at the funeral?" Ferguson asked.

"As funerals go, it went," Brosnan said harshly and lit a cigarette. "So where are we? What's happening?"

"I've seen the Prime Minister again. There's to be no press publicity."

"I agree with him there," Brosnan said. "It would be pointless."

"All relevant intelligence agencies, plus Special Branch, of course, have been notified. They'll do what they can."

"Which isn't very much," Brosnan said.

"Another point," Mary put in. "I know he's threatened the Prime Minister, but we don't have a clue what he intends or when. He could be up to something this very evening for all we know."

Brosnan shook his head. "No, I think there'll be more to it than that. These things take time. I should know."

"So where will you start?" Ferguson asked.

"With my old friend Harry Flood. When Dillon was here in eighty-one he probably used underworld contacts to supply his needs. Harry may be able to dig something out."

"And if not?"

"Then I'll borrow that Lear jet of yours again, fly to Dublin and have words with Liam Devlin."

"Ah, yes," Ferguson said. "Who better?"

"When Dillon went to London in nineteen eighty-one he must have been under someone's orders. If Devlin could find out who, that could be a lead to all sorts."

"Sounds logical to me. So you'll see Flood tonight?"

"I think so."

"Where are you staying?"

"With me," Mary said.

"At Lowndes Square?" Ferguson's eyebrows went up. "Really?"

"Come on, Brigadier, don't be an old fuddy-duddy. I've got four bedrooms remember, each with its own bathroom, and Professor Brosnan can have one with a lock on the inside of his door."

Brosnan laughed. "Come on, let's get out of here. See you later, Brigadier."

They used Ferguson's car. She closed the sliding window between them and the driver and said, "Don't you think you'd better ring your friend, let him know you'd like to see him?"

"I suppose so. I'll need to check his number."

She took a notebook from her handbag. "I have it here. It's ex-directory. There you go. Cable Wharf. That's in Wapping."

"Very efficient."

"And here's a phone."

She handed him the car phone. "You do like to be in charge," he said and dialed the number.

It was Mordecai Fletcher who answered. Brosnan said, "Harry Flood, please."

"Who wants him?"

"Martin Brosnan."

"The Professor? This is Mordecai. We haven't heard from you for what—three or four years? Christ, but he's going to be pleased."

A moment later a voice said, "Martin?"

"Harry?"

"I don't believe it. You've come back to haunt me, you bastard."

EIGHT

For Dillon in the Mini-Cooper, the run from London went easily enough. Although there was a light covering of snow on the fields and hedgerows, the roads were perfectly clear and not particularly busy. He was in Dorking within half an hour. He passed straight through and continued toward Horsham, finally pulling into a petrol station about five miles outside.

As the attendant was topping up the tank Dillon got his road map out. "Place called Doxley, you know it?"

"Half a mile up the road on your right a signpost says Grimethorpe. That's the airfield, but before you get there you'll see a sign to Doxley."

"So it's not far from here?"

"Three miles maybe, but it might as well be the end of the world." The attendant chuckled as he took the notes Dillon gave him. "Not much there, mister."

"Thought I'd take a look. Friend told me there might be a weekend cottage going."

"If there is, I haven't heard of it."

Dillon drove away, came to the Grimethorpe sign within a few minutes, followed the narrow road and found the Doxley sign as the garage man had indicated. The road was even narrower, high banks blocking the view until he came to the brow of a small hill and looked across a desolate landscape, powdered with snow. There was the occasional small wood, a scattering of hedged fields and then flat marshland drifting toward a river, which had to be the Arun. Beside it, perhaps a mile away, he saw houses, twelve or fifteen, with red pantiled roofs, and there was a small church, obviously Doxley. He started down the hill to the wooded valley below and as he came to it, saw a five-barred gate standing open and a decaying wooden sign with the legend Cadge End Farm.

The track led through the wood and brought him almost at once to a farm complex. There were a few chickens running here and there, a house and two large barns linked to it so that the whole enclosed a courtyard. It looked incredibly rundown, as if nothing had been done to it for years, but then, as Dillon knew, many country people preferred to live like that. He got out of the Mini and crossed to the front door, knocked and tried to open it. It was locked. He turned and went to the first barn. Its old wooden doors stood open. There was a Morris van in there and a Ford car jacked up on bricks, no wheels, agricultural implements all over the place.

Dillon took out a cigarette. As he lit it in cupped hands, a voice behind said, "Who are you? What do you want?"

He turned and found a girl in the doorway. She wore baggy trousers tucked into a pair of rubber boots, a heavy roll-neck sweater under an old anorak and a knitted beret like a Tam o' Shanter, the kind of thing you found in fishing villages on the West Coast of Ireland. She was holding a doublebarreled shotgun threateningly. As he took a step toward her, she thumbed back the hammer.

"You stay there." The Irish accent was very pronounced.

"You'll be the one they call Angel Fahy?" he said.

"Angela, if it's any of your business."

Tania's man had been right. She did look like a little peasant. Broad cheekbone, upturned nose and a kind of fierceness there. "Would you really shoot with that thing?"

"If I had to."

"A pity that, and me only wanting to meet my father's cousin, once removed, Danny Fahy."

She frowned. "And who in the hell might you be, mister?"

"Dillon's the name. Sean Dillon."

She laughed harshly. "That's a damn lie. You're not even Irish and Sean Dillon is dead, everyone knows that."

Dillon dropped into the hard distinctive accent of Belfast. "To steal a great man's line, girl dear, all I can say is, reports of my death have been greatly exaggerated."

The gun went slack in her hands. "Mother Mary, are you Sean Dillon?"

"As ever was. Appearances can be deceiving."

"Oh, God," she said. "Uncle Danny talks about you all the time, but it was always like stories, nothing real to it at all and here you are."

"Where is he?"

"He did a repair on a car for the landlord of the local pub, took it down there an hour ago. Said he'd walk back, but he'll be there a while yet drinking, I shouldn't wonder."

"At this time? Isn't the pub closed until evening?"

"That might be the law, Mr. Dillon, but not in Doxley. They never close."

"Let's go and get him, then."

She left the shotgun on a bench and got into the Mini beside him. As they drove away, he said, "What's your story then?"

"I was raised on a farm in Galway. My da was Danny's nephew, Michael. He died six years ago when I was fourteen. After a year, my mother married again."

"Let me guess," Dillon said. "You didn't like your stepfather and he didn't like you?"

"Something like that. Uncle Danny came over for my father's funeral, so I'd met him and liked him. When things got too heavy, I left home and came here. He was great about it. Wrote to my mother and she agreed I could stay. Glad to get rid of me."

There was no self-pity at all and Dillon warmed to her. "They always say some good comes out of everything."

"I've been working it out," she said. "If you're Danny's second cousin and I'm his great-niece, then you and I are blood related, isn't that a fact?"

Dillon laughed. "In a manner of speaking."

She looked ecstatic as she leaned back. "Me, Angel Fahy, related to the greatest gunman the Provisional IRA ever had."

"Well, now, there would be some who would argue about that," he said as they reached the village and pulled up outside the pub.

It was a small, desolate sort of place, no more than fifteen rather dilapidated cottages and a Norman church with a tower and an overgrown graveyard. The pub was called the *Green Man* and even Dillon had to duck to enter the door. The ceiling was very low and beamed. The floor was constructed of heavy stone flags worn with the years, the walls were whitewashed. The man behind the bar in his shirt sleeves was at least eighty.

He glanced up and Angel said, "Is he here, Mr. Dalton?"

"By the fire, having a beer," the old man said.

A fire burned in a wide stone hearth and there was a wooden bench and a table in front of it. Danny Fahy sat there reading the paper, a glass in front of him. He was sixty-five, with an untidy, grizzled beard, and wore a cloth cap and an old Harris Tweed suit.

Angel said, "I've brought someone to see you, Uncle Danny."

He looked up at her and then at Dillon, puzzlement on his face. "And what can I do for you, sir?"

Dillon removed his glasses. "God bless all here!" he said in his Belfast accent. "And particularly you, you old bastard."

Fahy turned very pale, the shock was so intense. "God save us, is that you, Sean, and me thinking you were in your box long ago?"

"Well, I'm not and I'm here." Dillon took a five-pound note from his wallet and gave it to Angel. "A couple of whiskies, Irish for preference."

She went back to the bar and Dillon turned. Danny Fahy actually had tears in his eyes and he flung his arms around him. "Dear God, Sean, but I can't tell you how good it is to see you."

The sitting room at the farm was untidy and cluttered, the furniture very old. Dillon sat on a sofa while Fahy built up the fire. Angel was in the kitchen cooking a meal. It was open to the sitting room and Dillon could see her moving around.

"And how's life been treating you, Sean?" Fahy stuffed a pipe and lit it. "Ten years since you raised Cain in London town. By God, boy, you gave the Brits something to think about."

"I couldn't have done it without you, Danny."

"Great days. And what happened after?"

"Europe, the Middle East. I kept on the move. Did a lot for the PLO. Even learned to fly."

"Is that a fact?"

Angel came and put plates of bacon and eggs on the table. "Get it while it's hot." She returned with a tray laden with teapot and milk, three mugs and a plate piled high with bread and butter. "I'm sorry there's nothing fancier, but we weren't expecting company."

"It looks good to me," Dillon told her and tucked in.

"So now you're here, Sean, and dressed like an English gentleman." Fahy turned to Angel. "Didn't I tell you the actor this man was? They never could put a glove on him in all these years, not once."

She nodded eagerly, smiling at Dillon, and her personality had changed with the excitement. "Are you on a job now, Mr. Dillon, for the IRA, I mean?"

"It would be a cold day in hell before I put myself on the line for that bunch of old washerwomen," Dillon said.

"But you are working on something, Sean?" Fahy said. "I can tell. Come on, let's in on it."

Dillon lit a cigarette. "What if I told you I was working for the Arabs, Danny, for Saddam Hussein himself?"

"Jesus, Sean, and why not? And what is it he wants you to do?"

"He wants something now—a coup. Something big. America's too far away. That leaves the Brits."

"What could be better?" Fahy's eyes were gleaming.

"Thatcher was in France the other day seeing Mitterrand. I had plans for her on the way to her plane. Perfect setup, quiet country road, and then someone I trusted let me down."

"And isn't that always the way?" Fahy said. "So you're looking for another target Who, Sean?"

"I was thinking of John Major."

"The new Prime Minister?" Angel said in awe. "You wouldn't dare."

"Sure and why wouldn't he? Didn't the boys nearly get the whole bloody British Government at Brighton," Danny Fahy told her. "Go on, Sean, what's your plan?"

"I haven't got one, Danny, that's the trouble, but there would be a payday for this like you wouldn't believe."

"And that's as good a reason to make it work as any. So you've come to Uncle Danny looking for help?" Fahy went to a cupboard, came back with a bottle of Bushmills and two glasses and filled them. "Have you any ideas at all?"

"Not yet, Danny. Do you still work for the Movement?"

"Stay in deep cover, that was the order from Belfast so many years ago I've forgotten. Since then not a word, and me bored out of my socks, so I moved down here. It suits me. I like the countryside here, I like the people. They keep to themselves. I've built up a fair business repairing agricultural machinery and I run a few sheep. We're happy here, Angel and me."

"And still bored out of your socks. Do you remember Martin Brosnan, by the way?"

"I do so. You were bad friends with that one."

"I had a run-in with him in Paris recently. He'll probably turn up in London looking for me. He'll be working for Brit intelligence."

"The bastard." Fahy frowned as he refilled his pipe. "Didn't I hear some fanciful talk of how Brosnan got into Ten Downing Street as a waiter years ago and didn't do anything about it?"

"I heard that story, too. A flight of fancy and no one would get in these days as a waiter or anything else. You know they've blocked the street off? The place is a fortress. No way in there, Danny."

"Oh, there's always a way, Sean. I was reading in a magazine the other day how a lot of French Resistance people in the Second World War were held at some Gestapo headquarters. Their cells were on the ground floor, the Gestapo on the first floor. The RAF had a fella in a Mosquito fly in at fifty feet and drop a bomb that bounced off the street and went in through the first-floor window, killing all the bloody Gestapo so the fellas downstairs got away."

"What in the hell are you trying to say to me?" Dillon demanded.

"That I'm a great believer in the power of the bomb and the science of ballistics. You can make a bomb go anywhere if you know what you're doing."

"What is this?" Dillon demanded.

Angel said. "Go on, show him, Uncle Danny."

"Show me what?" Dillon said.

Danny Fahy got up, putting another match to his pipe. "Come on, then," and he turned and went to the door.

Fahy opened the door of the second barn and led the way in. It was enormous, oak beams rearing up to a steeply pitched roof. There was a loft stuffed with hay and reached by a ladder. There were various items of farm machinery including a tractor. There was also a fairly new Land-Rover, and an old BSA 500cc motorcycle in fine condition, up on its stand.

"This is a beauty," Dillon said in genuine admiration.

"Bought it second-hand last year. Thought I'd renovate it to make a profit, but now I'm finished, I can't bear to let it go. It's as good as a BMW." There was another vehicle in the shadows of the rear and Fahy switched on a light and a white Ford Transit van stood revealed.

"So?" Dillon said. "What's so special?"

"You wait, Mr. Dillon," Angel told him. "This is really something."

Fahy said, "Not what it seems."

There was an excited look on his face, a kind of pride as he opened the sliding door. Inside there was a battery of metal pipes, three in all, bolted to the floor, pointing up to the roof at an angle.

"Mortars, Sean, just like the lads have been using in Ulster."

Dillon said, "You mean this thing works?"

"Hell, no, I've no explosives. It would work, that's all I can say."

"Explain it to me."

"I've welded a steel platform to the floor, that's to stand the recoil, and I've also welded the tubing together. That's standard cast-iron stuff available anywhere. The electric timers are dead simple. Stuff you can buy at any do-it-yourself shop."

"How would it work?"

"Once switched on it would give you a minute to get out of the van and run for it. The roof is cut out. That's just stretched polythene covering the hole. You can see I've sprayed it the same color. It gives the mortars a clean exit. I've even worked out an extra little device linked to the timer that will self-destruct the van after it's fired the mortars."

"And where would they be?"

"Over here." Fahy walked to a workbench. "Standard oxygen cylinders." There were several stacked together, the bottom plates removed.

"And what would you need for those, Semtex?" Dillon asked, naming the Czechoslovakian explosive so popular with terrorists everywhere.

"I'd say about twelve pounds in each would do nicely, but that's not easily come by over here."

Dillon lit a cigarette and walked around the van, his face blank. "You're a bad boy, Danny. The Movement told you to stay in deep cover."

"Like I told you, how many years ago was that?" Fahy demanded. "A man would go crazy."

"So you found yourself something to do?"

"It was easy, Sean. You know I was in the light engineering for years."

Dillon stood looking at it. Angel said, "What do you think?"

"I think he's done a good job."

"As good as anything they've done in Ulster," Fahy said.

"Maybe, but whenever they've been used, they've never been too strong on accuracy."

"They worked like a dream in that attack on Newry police station six years ago. Killed nine coppers."

"What about all the other times they couldn't hit a barn door? Someone even blew himself up with one of these things in Portadown. A bit hit-and-miss."

"Not the way I'd do it. I can plot the target on a large-scale map, have a look at the area on foot beforehand, line the van up and that's it. Mind you, I've been thinking that some sort of fin welded on to the oxygen cylinders would help steady them in flight. A nice big curve and then down, and the whole world blows up. All the security in the world wouldn't help. I mean, what good are gates if you go over them?"

"You're talking Downing Street now?" Dillon said.

"And why not?"

"They meet at ten o'clock every morning in the Cabinet Room. What they call the War Cabinet. You'd not only get the Prime Minister, you'd get virtually the whole government."

Fahy crossed himself. "Holy Mother of God, it would be the hit of a lifetime."

"They'd make up songs about you, Danny," Dillon told him. "They'd be singing about Danny Fahy in bars all over Ireland fifty years from now."

Fahy slammed a clenched fist into his palm. "All hot air, Sean, no meaning to it without the Semtex, and like I said, that stuff's impossible to get your hands on over here."

"Don't be too sure, Danny," Dillon said. "There might be a source. Now let's go and have a Bushmills and sort this out."

Fahy had a large-scale map of London spread across the table and examined it with a magnifying glass. "Here would be the place," he said. "Horse Guards Avenue, running up from the Victoria Embankment at the side of the Ministry of Defence."

"Yes." Dillon nodded.

"If we left the Ford on the corner with Whitehall, then as long as I had a predetermined sighting, to get my direction, I reckon the mortar bombs would go over those roofs in a bloody great curve and land smack on Ten Downing Street!" He put his pencil down beside the ruler. "I'd like to have a look, mind you."

"And so you will," Dillon said.

"Would it work, Mr. Dillon?" Angel demanded.

"Oh, yes," he said. "I think it really could. Ten o'clock in the morning, the whole bloody War Cabinet." He started to laugh. "It's beautiful, Danny, beautiful." He grabbed the other man's arm. "You'll come in with me on this?"

"Of course I will."

"Good," Dillon said. "Big, big money, Danny. I'll set you up for your old age. Total luxury. Spain, Greece, anywhere you want to go." Fahy rolled up the map and Dillon said, "I'll stay overnight. We'll go up to London tomorrow and have a look." He smiled and lit another cigarette. "It's looking good, Danny. Really good. Now tell me about this airfield near here at Grimethorpe."

"A real broken-down sort of a place. It's only three miles from here. What would you want with Grimethorpe?"

"I told you I learned to fly in the Middle East. A good way of getting out of places fast. Now what's the situation at this Grimethorpe place?"

"It goes way back into the past. A flying club in the thirties. Then the RAF used it as a feeder station during the Battle of Britain, so they built three hangars. Someone tried it as a flying club a few years ago. There's a tarmac runway. Anyway, it failed. A fella called Bill Grant turned up three years ago. He has two planes there, that's all I know. His firm is called Grant's Air Taxis. I heard recently he was in trouble. His two mechanics had left. Business was bad." He smiled. "There's a recession on, Sean, and it even affects the rich."

"Does he live on the premises?"

"Yes," Angel said. "He did have a girlfriend, but she moved on."

"I think I'd like to meet him," Dillon said. "Maybe you could show me, Angel?"

"Of course."

"Good, but first I'd like to make a phone call."

He rang Tania Novikova at her flat. She answered at once. "It's me," he said.

"Has it gone well?"

"Unbelievable. I'll tell you tomorrow. Did you pick up the money?"

"Oh, yes, no problem."

"Good. I'll be at the hotel at noon. I'm overnighting here. See you then," and he rang off.

Brosnan and Mary Tanner went up in the freight elevator with Charlie Salter and found Mordecai waiting for them. He pumped Brosnan's hand up and down. "It's great to see you, Professor. I can't tell you how great. Harry's been on hot bricks."

"This is Mary Tanner," Brosnan said. "You'd better be nice. She's an Army captain."

"Well, this is a pleasure, miss." Mordecai shook her hand. "I did my National Service in the Grenadier Guards, but lance-corporal was all I managed."

He led them into the sitting room. Harry Flood was seated at the desk going over some accounts. He glanced up and jumped to his feet. "Martin." He rushed round the desk and embraced Brosnan, laughing in delight.

Brosnan said, "Mary Tanner. She's Army, Harry, a real hotshot, so watch your step. I'm working for Brigadier Charles Ferguson of British Intelligence and she's his aide."

"Then I'll behave." Flood took her hand. "Now come over here and let's have a drink and you tell me what all this is about, Martin."

They sat in the sofa complex in the corner and Brosnan covered everything in finest detail. Mordecai leaned against the wall listening, no expression on his face.

When Brosnan was finished, Flood said, "So what do you want from me, Martin?"

"He always works the underworld, Harry, that's where he gets everything he needs. Not only physical help, but explosives, weaponry. He'll work the same way now, I know he will."

"So what you want to know is who he'd go to?"

"Exactly."

Flood looked up at Mordecai. "What do you think?"

"I don't know, Harry. I mean there are plenty of legit arms dealers, but what you need is someone who's willing to supply the IRA."

"Any ideas?" Flood asked.

"Not really, guv. I mean, most of your real East End villains love Maggie Thatcher and wear Union Jack underpants. They don't go for Irish geezers letting off bombs at Harrods. We could make enquiries, of course."

"Then do that," Flood said. "Put the word out now, but discreetly."

Mordecai went out and Harry Flood reached for the champagne bottle. "You're still not drinking?" Brosnan said.

"Not me, old buddy, but no reason you shouldn't. You can fill me in with the events of recent years, and then we'll go along to the *Embassy*, one of my more respectable clubs, and have something to eat."

At around the same time, Sean Dillon and Angel Fahy were driving along the dark country road from Cadge End to Grimethorpe. The lights of the car picked out light snow and frost on the hedgerows.

"It's beautiful, isn't it?" she said.

"I suppose so."

"I like it here, the countryside and all that. I like Uncle Danny, too. He's been really good to me."

"That makes sense. You were raised in the country back there in Galway."

"It wasn't the same. It was poor land there. It was hard work to make any kind of a living and it showed in the people, my mother, for instance. It was as if they'd been to war and lost and there was nothing to look forward to."

"You've got a way with the words, girl," he told her.

"My English teacher used to say that. She said if I worked hard and studied I could do anything."

"Well that must have been a comfort."

"It didn't do me any good. My stepfather just saw me as an unpaid farm laborer. That's why I left."

The lights picked out a sign that said Grimethorpe airfield, the paint-work peeling. Dillon turned into a narrow tarmac road that was badly poth_oled. A few moments later, they came to the airfield. There were three hangars, an old control tower, a couple of Nissen huts, a light at the windows of one of them. A jeep was parked there and Dillon pulled in beside it. As they got out, the door of the Nissen hut opened and a man stood there.

"Who is it?"

"It's me, Mr. Grant, Angel Fahy. I've brought someone to see you."

Grant, like most pilots, was small and wiry. He looked to be in his mid-forties, wore jeans and an old flying jacket of the kind used by American aircrew in the Second World War. "You'd better come in, then."

The interior of the Nissen hut was warm, heated by a coke-burning stove, the pipe going up through the roof. Grant obviously used it as a living room. There was a table with the remains of a meal on it, an old easy chair by the stove facing a television set in the corner. Beneath the windows on the other side there was a long, sloping desk with a few charts.

Angel said, "This is a friend of my uncle's."

"Hilton," Dillon said. "Peter Hilton."

Grant put his hand out, looking wary. "Bill Grant. I don't owe you money, do I?"

"Not to my knowledge." Dillon was back in his public-school role.

"Well, that makes a nice change. What can I do for you?"

"I want a charter in the next few days. Just wanted to check if you might be able to do something before I tried anywhere else."

"Well, that depends."

"On what? You do have a plane, I take it?"

"I've got two. The only problem is how long the bank lets me hang onto them. Do you want to have a look?"

"Why not?"

They went out, crossed the apron to the end hangar, and he opened a Judas so they could step through. He reached to one side, found a switch and lights came on. There were two planes there, side by side, both twin engines.

Dillon walked up to the nearest. "I know this baby, a Cessna Conquest. What's the other?"

"Navajo Chieftain."

"If things are as tricky as you say, what about fuel?"

"I always keep my planes juiced up, Mr. Hilton, always full tanks. I'm too old a hand to do otherwise. You never know when a job might come up." He smiled ruefully. "Mind you, I'll be honest. What with the recession, there aren't too many people looking for charters these days. Where would you like me to take you?"

"Actually I was thinking of going for a spin myself one day," Dillon said. "I'm not sure when."

"You're certified, then?" Grant looked dubious.

"Oh, yes, fully." Dillon took out his pilot's license and passed it across.

Grant examined it quickly and handed it back. "You could handle either of these two, but I'd rather come myself, just to make sure."

"No problem," Dillon said smoothly. "It's the West Country I was thinking of. Cornwall. There's an airfield at Land's End."

"I know it well. Grass runway."

"I've got friends near there. I'd probably want to stay overnight."

"That's fine by me." Grant switched off the lights and they walked back to the Nissen hut. "What line are you in, Mr. Hilton?"

"Oh, finance, accountancy, that sort of thing," Dillon said.

"Have you any idea when you might want to go? I should point out that kind of charter's going to be expensive. Around two thousand five hundred pounds. With half a dozen passengers that's not so bad, but on your own . . ."

"That's fine," Dillon said.

"Then there would be my overnight expenses. A hotel and so on."

"No problem." Dillon took ten fifty-pound notes from his wallet and put them on the table. "There's five hundred down. It's a definite booking for some time in the next four or five days. I'll phone you here to let you know when."

Grant's face brightened as he picked up the bank notes. "That's fine. Can I get you a coffee or something before you go?"

"Why not?" Dillon said.

Grant went into the kitchen at the far end of the Nissen hut. They heard him filling a kettle. Dillon put a finger to his lips, made a face at Angel and crossed to the charts on the desk. He went through them quickly, found the one for the general English Channel area and the French coast. Angel stood beside him watching as he traced his finger along the Normandy coast. He found Cherbourg and moved south. There it was, Saint-Denis, with the landing strip clearly marked, and he pushed the charts back together. Grant in the kitchen had been watching through the half-open door. As the kettle boiled, he quickly made coffee in three mugs and took them in.

"Is this weather giving you much trouble?" Dillon said. "The snow?"

"It will if it really starts to stick," Grant said. "It could make it difficult for that grass runway at Land's End."

"We'll just have to keep our fingers crossed." Dillon put down his mug. "We'd better be getting back."

Grant went to the door to see them off. They got in the Mini and drove away. He waved, closed the door and went to the desk and examined the charts. It was the third or fourth down, he was sure of that. *General English Channel area and the French coast.*

He frowned and said softly, "And what's your game, mister, I wonder?"

As they drove back through the dark country lanes Angel said, "Not Land's End at all, Mr. Dillon, it's that Saint-Denis place in Normandy, that's where you want to fly to."

"Our secret," he said and put his left hand on hers, still steering. "Can I ask you to promise me one thing?"

"Anything, Mr. Dillon."

"Let's keep it to ourselves, just for now. I don't want Danny to know. You do drive, do you?"

"Drive? Of course I do. I take the sheep to market in the Morris van myself."

"Tell me, how would you like a trip up to London tomorrow morning with me, you and Danny?"

"I'd like it fine."

"Good, that's all right, then."

As they carried on through the night her eyes were shining.

NINE

It was a cold, crisp morning, winter on every hand, but the roads were clear as Dillon drove up to London, Angel and Danny Fahy following in the Morris van. Angel was driving, and more than competently. He could see her in his rearview mirror and she stayed right on his tail all the way into London until they came to the Bayswater Road. There was a plan already half-formed in his mind and he got out of the Mini-Cooper, parked it at the curb and opened the doors of Tania's garage.

As Angel and Danny drew up behind him he said, "Put the Morris inside." Angel did as she was told. When she and Danny Fahy came out, Dillon closed the doors and said, "You'll remember the street and the garage, if you lose me, that is?"

"Don't be silly, Mr. Dillon, of course I will," Angel said.

"Good. It's important. Now get in the Mini. We're going for a little run round."

Harry Flood was sitting at the desk in his apartment at Cable Wharf checking the casino accounts from the night before when Charlie Salter brought in coffee on a tray. The phone rang and the small man picked it up. He handed it to Flood.

"The Professor."

"Martin, how goes it?" Flood said. "I enjoyed last night. The Tanner lady is something special."

"Is there any news? Have you managed to come up with anything?" Brosnan asked.

"Not yet, Martin, just a minute." Flood put a hand over the receiver and said to Salter, "Where's Mordecai?"

"Doing the rounds, Harry, just like you asked him, putting the word out discreetly."

Flood returned to Brosnan. "Sorry, old buddy, we're doing everything we can, but it's going to take time."

"Which we don't really have," Brosnan said. "All right, Harry, I know you're doing your best. I'll stay in touch."

He was standing at Mary Tanner's desk in the living room of her Lowndes Square flat. He put the phone down, walked to the window and lit a cigarette.

"Anything?" she asked and crossed the room to join him.

"I'm afraid not. As Harry has just said it takes time. I was a fool to think anything else."

"Just try and be patient, Martin." She put a hand on his arm.

"But I can't," he said. "I've got this feeling and it's hard to explain. It's like being in a storm and waiting for that bloody great thunderclap you know is going to come. I know Dillon, Mary. He's moving fast on this. I'm certain of it."

"So what would you like to do?"

"Will Ferguson be at Cavendish Square this morning?"

"Yes."

"Then let's go to see him."

Dillon parked the Mini-Cooper near Covent Garden. An enquiry in a book-shop nearby led them to a shop not too far away specializing in maps and charts of every description. Dillon worked his way through the large-scale Ordnance Survey maps of Central London until he found the one covering the general area of Whitehall.

"Would you look at the detail in that thing?" Fahy whispered. "You could measure the size of the garden at Number Ten to half an inch."

Dillon purchased the map, which the assistant rolled up tightly and inserted into a protective cardboard tube. He paid for it and they walked back to the car.

"Now what?" Danny asked.

"We'll take a run round. Have a look at the situation."

"That suits me."

Angel sat in the rear, her uncle beside Dillon as they drove down toward the river and turned into Horse Guards Avenue. Dillon paused slightly on the corner before turning into Whitehall and moving toward Downing Street.

"Plenty of coppers around," Danny said.

"That's to make sure people don't park." A car had drawn in to the curb on their left and as they pulled out to pass, they saw that the driver was consulting a map.

"Tourist, I expect," Angel said.

"And look what's happening," Dillon told her.

She turned and saw two policemen converging on the car. A quiet word, it started up and moved away.

Angel said, "They don't waste time."

"Downing Street," Dillon announced a moment later.

"Would you look at those gates?" Danny said in wonder. "I like the Gothic touch. Sure and they've done a good job there."

Dillon moved with the traffic round Parliament Square and went back up Whitehall toward Trafalgar Square. "We're going back to Bayswater," he said. "Notice the route I've chosen."

He moved out of the traffic of Trafalgar Square through Admiralty Arch along the Mall, round the Queen Victoria Monument, past Buckingham Palace and along Constitution Hill, eventually reaching Marble Arch by way of Park Lane and turning into the Bayswater Road.

"And that's simple enough," Danny Fahy said.

"Good," Dillon said. "Then let's go and get a nice cup of tea at my truly awful hotel."

Ferguson said, "You're getting too restless, Martin."

"It's the waiting," Brosnan told him. "Flood's doing his best, I know that, but I don't think time is on our side."

Ferguson turned from the window and sipped a little of the cup of tea he was holding. "So what would you like to do?"

Brosnan hesitated, glanced at Mary and said, "I'd like to go and see Liam Devlin in Kilrea. He might have some ideas."

"Something he was never short of." Ferguson turned to Mary. "What do you think?"

"I think it makes sense, sir. After all, a trip to Dublin's no big deal. An hour and a quarter from Heathrow on either Aer Lingus or B.A."

"And Liam's place at Kilrea is only half an hour from the city," Brosnan said.

"All right," Ferguson said. "You've made your point, both of you, but make it Gatwick and the Lear jet, just in case anything comes up and you need to get back here in a hurry."

"Thank you, sir," Mary said.

As they reached the door, Ferguson added, "I'll give the old rogue a call, just to let him know you're on your way," and he reached for the phone.

As they went downstairs Brosnan said, "Thank God. At least I feel we're doing something."

"And I get to meet the great Liam Devlin at long last," Mary said and led the way out to the limousine.

In the small café at the hotel, Dillon, Angel and Fahy sat at a corner table drinking tea. Fahy had the Ordnance Survey map partially open on his knee. "It's extraordinary. The things they give away. Every detail."

"Could it be done, Danny?"

"Oh, yes, no trouble. You remember that corner, Horse Guards Avenue and Whitehall? That would be the place, slightly on an angle. I can see it in my mind's eye. I can plot the distance from that corner to Number Ten exactly from this map."

"You're sure you'd clear the buildings in between?" Dillon said.

"Oh, yes. I've said before, Sean, ballistics is a matter of science."

"But you can't stop there," Angel said. "We saw what happened to that man in the car. The police were on him in seconds."

Dillon turned to Fahy. "Danny?"

"Well, that's all you would need. Everything pre-timed, Angel. Press the right switch to activate the circuit, get out of the van and the mortars start firing within a minute. No policeman could act fast enough to stop it."

"But what would happen to you?" she demanded.

It was Dillon who answered. "Just listen to this. We drive up from Cadge End one morning early, you, Danny, in the Ford transit, and Angel and me in the Morris van. We'll have that BSA motorcycle in the back of that. Angel will park the Morris, like today, in the garage at the end of the road. We'll have a duckboard in the back so I can run the BSA out."

"And you'll follow me, is that it?"

"I'll be right up your tail. When we reach the corner of Horse Guards Avenue and Whitehall, you set your switch, get out of the Ford and jump straight on my pillion and we'll be away. The War Cabinet meets every morning at ten. With luck we could get the lot."

"Jesus, Sean, they'd never know what hit them."

"Straight back to Bayswater to Angel waiting in the garage with the Morris, put the BSA in the back and away we go. We'll be in Cadge End while they're still trying to put the fires out."

"It's brilliant, Mr. Dillon," Angel told him.

"Except for one thing," Fahy said. "Without the bloody explosives, we don't have any bloody bombs."

"You leave that to me," Dillon said. "I'll get your explosives for you." He stood up. "But I've got things to do. You two go back to Cadge End and wait. I'll be in touch."

"And when would that be, Sean?"

"Soon—very soon," and Dillon smiled as they went out.

Tania was knocking at his door precisely at noon. He opened it and said, "You've got it?"

She had a briefcase in her right hand, opened it on the table to reveal the thirty thousand dollars he'd asked for.

"Good," he said. "I'll just need ten thousand to be going on with."

"What will you do with the rest?"

"I'll hand it in at the desk. They can keep your briefcase in the hotel safe."

"You've worked something out, I can tell." She looked excited. "What happened at this Cadge End place?"

So he told her and in detail, the entire plan. "What do you think?" he asked when he'd finished.

"Incredible. The coup of a lifetime. But what about the explosives? You'd need Semtex."

"That's all right. When I was operating in London in eighty-one I used to deal with a man who had access to Semtex." He laughed. "In fact he had access to everything."

"And who is this man? How can you be sure he's still around?"

"A crook named Jack Harvey and he's around all right. I looked him up."

"But I don't understand."

"Amongst other things he has a funeral business in Whitechapel. I looked it up in the Yellow Pages and it's still there. By the way, your Mini, I can still use it?"

"Of course."

"Good. I'll park it somewhere in the street. I want that garage free."

He picked up his coat. "Come on, we'll go and have a bite to eat and then I'll go and see him."

You've read the file on Devlin, I suppose?" Brosnan asked Mary Tanner as they drove through the center of Dublin and crossed the River Liffey by St. George's Quay and moved on out of the other side of the city, driven by a chauffeur in a limousine from the Embassy.

"Yes," she said. "But is it all true? The story about his involvement with the German attempt to get Churchill in the war?"

"Oh, yes."

"The same man who helped you break out of that French prison in nineteen seventy-nine?"

"That's Devlin."

"But, Martin, you said he claimed to be seventy. He must be older than that."

"A few years is a minor detail where Liam Devlin is concerned. Let's put it this way, you're about to meet the most extraordinary man you've ever met in your life. Scholar, poet and gunman for the IRA."

"The last part is no recommendation to me," she said.

"I know," he told her. "But never make the mistake of lumping Devlin in with the kind of rubbish the IRA employs these days."

He retreated into himself, suddenly sombre, and the car continued out into the Irish countryside, leaving the city behind.

Kilrea Cottage, the place was called, on the outskirts of the village next to a convent. It was a period piece, single-storeyed with Gothic-looking gables and lead windows on either side of the porch. They sheltered in there from the light rain while Brosnan tugged an old-fashioned bell pull. There was the sound of footsteps, the door opened.

"Cead míle fáilte," Liam Devlin said in Irish. "A hundred thousand welcomes," and he flung his arms around Brosnan.

The interior of the house was very Victorian. Most of the furniture was mahogany, the wallpaper was a William Morris replica, but the paintings on the walls, all Atkinson Grimshaws, were real.

Liam Devlin came in from the kitchen with tea things on a tray. "My housekeeper comes mornings only. One of the good sisters from the convent next door. They need the money."

Mary Tanner was totally astonished. She'd expected an old man and found herself faced with this ageless creature in black silk Italian shirt, black pullover, gray slacks in the latest fashionable cut. There was still considerable color in hair that had once been black and the face was pale, but she sensed that had always been so. The blue eyes were extraordinary, as was that perpetual ironic smile with which he seemed to laugh at himself as much as at the world.

"So, you work for Ferguson, girl?" he said to Mary as he poured the tea.

"That's right."

"That business in Derry the other year when you moved that car with the bomb. That was quite something."

She felt herself flushing. "No big deal, Mr. Devlin, it just seemed like the right thing to do at the time."

"Oh, we can all see that on occasions; it's the doing that counts." He turned to Brosnan. "Anne-Marie. A bad business, son."

"I want him, Liam," Brosnan said.

"For yourself or for the general cause?" Devlin shook his head. "Push the personal thing to one side, Martin, or you'll make mistakes, and that's something you can't afford to do with Sean Dillon."

"Yes, I know," Brosnan said. "I know."

"So, he intends to take a crack at this John Major fella, the new Prime Minister?" Devlin said.

"And how do you think he's likely to do that, Mr. Devlin?" Mary asked.

"Well, from what I hear about security at Ten Downing Street these days, I wouldn't rate his chances of getting in very high." He looked at Brosnan and grinned. "Mind you, Mary, my love, I remember a young fella of my acquaintance called Martin Brosnan who got into Number Ten posing as a waiter at a party not ten years ago. Left a rose on the Prime Minister's desk. Of course, the office was held by a woman then."

Brosnan said, "All in the past, Liam, what about now?"

"Oh, he'll work as he always has, using contacts in the underworld."

"Not the IRA?"

"I doubt whether the IRA has any connection with this whatsoever."

"But they did last time he worked in London ten years ago."

"So?"

"I was wondering. If we knew who recruited him that time, it could help."

"I see what you mean, give you some sort of lead as to who he worked with in London?"

"All right, not much of a chance, but the only one we've got, Liam."

"There's still your friend Flood in London."

"I know, and he'll pull out all the stops, but that takes time and we don't have much to spare."

Devlin nodded. "Right, son, you leave it with me and I'll see what I can do." He glanced at his watch. "One o'clock. We'll have a sandwich and perhaps a Bushmills together, and I suggest you go to your Lear jet and hare back to London. I'll be in touch, believe me, the minute I have something."

Dillon parked round the corner from Jack Harvey's funeral business in Whitechapel and walked, the briefcase in one hand. Everything was beautifully discreet, down to the bell push that summoned the day porter to open the door.

"Mr. Harvey," Dillon lied cheerfully. "He's expecting me."

"Down the hall past the Chapels of Rest and up the stairs. His office is on the first floor. What was the name, sir?"

"Hilton." Dillon looked around at the coffins on display, the flowers. "Not much happening."

"Trade, you mean." The porter shrugged. "That all comes in the back way."

"I see."

Dillon moved down the hall, pausing to glance into one of the Chapels of Rest, taking in the banked flowers, the candles. He stepped in and looked down at the body of a middle-aged man neatly dressed in a dark suit, hands folded, the face touched with makeup.

"Poor sod," Dillon said and went out.

At the reception desk, the porter picked up a phone. "Miss Myra? A visitor. A Mr. Hilton, says he has an appointment."

Dillon opened the door to Harvey's outer office and moved in. There were no office furnishings, just a couple of potted plants and several easy chairs. The door to the inner office opened and Myra entered. She wore skin-tight black trews, black boots and a scarlet, three-quarter length caftan. She looked very striking.

"Mr. Hilton?"

"That's right."

"I'm Myra Harvey. You said you had an appointment with my uncle."

"Did I?"

She looked him over in a casual way and behind him the door opened and Billy Watson came in. The whole thing was obviously prearranged. He leaned against the door, suitably menacing in a black suit, arms folded.

"Now what's your game?" she said.

"That's for Mr. Harvey."

"Throw him out, Billy," she said and turned to the door.

Billy put one rough hand on Dillon's shoulder. Dillon's foot went all the way down the right leg, stamping on the instep; he pivoted and struck sideways with clenched fist, the knuckles on the back of the hand connecting with Billy's temple. Billy cried out in pain and fell back into one of the chairs.

"He's not very good, is he?" Dillon said.

He opened his briefcase and took out ten one-hundred-dollar bills with a rubber band round them and threw them at Myra. She missed the catch and had to bend to pick them up. "Would you look at that," she said. "And brand new."

"Yes, new money always smells so good," Dillon said. "Now tell Jack an old friend would like to see him with more of the same."

She stood there looking at him for a moment, eyes narrowed, then she turned and opened the door to Harvey's office. Billy tried to get up and Dillon said, "I wouldn't advise it."

Billy subsided as the door opened and Myra appeared. "All right, he'll see you."

The room was surprisingly businesslike with walls paneled in oak, a green carpet in Georgian silk and a gas fire that almost looked real, burning in a steel basket on the hearth. Harvey sat behind a massive oak desk smoking a cigar.

He had the thousand dollars in front of him and looked Dillon over calmly. "My time's limited, so don't muck me about, son." He picked up the bank notes. "More of the same?"

"That's right."

"I don't know you. You told Myra you were an old friend, but I've never seen you before."

"A long time ago, Jack, ten years to be precise. I looked different then. I was over from Belfast on a job. We did business together, you and me. You did well out of it as I recall. All those lovely dollars raised by IRA sympathizers in America."

Harvey said. "Coogan. Michael Coogan."

Dillon took off his glasses. "As ever was, Jack."

Harry nodded slowly and said to his niece. "Myra, an old friend, Mr. Coogan from Belfast."

"I see," she said. "One of those."

Dillon lit a cigarette, sat down, the briefcase on the floor beside him and Harvey said, "You went through London like bloody Attila the Hun last time. I should have charged you more for all that stuff."

"You gave me a price, I paid it," Dillon said. "What could be fairer?"

"And what is it this time?"

"I need a little Semtex, Jack. I could manage with forty pounds, but that's the bottom line. Fifty would be better."

"You don't want much, do you? That stuff's like gold. Very strict government controls."

"Bollocks," Dillon said. "It passes from Czechoslovakia to Italy, Greece, onwards to Libya. It's everywhere, Jack, you know it and I know it, so don't waste my time. Twenty thousand dollars." He opened the briefcase on his knee and tossed the rest of the ten thousand packet by packet across the desk. "Ten now and ten on delivery."

The Walther with the Carswell silencer screwed on the end of the barrel lay ready in the briefcase. He waited, the lid up, and then Harvey smiled. "All right, but it'll cost you thirty."

Dillon closed the briefcase. "No can do, Jack. Twenty-five I can manage, but no more."

Harvey nodded. "All right. When do you want it?"

"Twenty-four hours."

"I think I can manage that. Where can we reach you?"

"You've got it wrong way round, Jack. I contact you."

Dillon stood up and Harvey said affably, "Anything else we can do for you?"

"Actually there is," Dillon said. "Sign of goodwill, you might say. I could do with a spare handgun."

"Be my guest, my old son." Harvey pushed his chair back and opened the second drawer down on his right hand. "Take your pick."

There was a Smith & Wesson .38 revolver, a Czech Cesca and an Italian Beretta, which was the one Dillon selected. He checked the clip and slipped the gun in his pocket. "This will do nicely."

"Lady's gun," Harvey said, "but that's your business. We'll be seeing you, then, tomorrow."

Myra opened the door. Dillon said, "A pleasure, Miss Harvey," and he brushed past Billy and walked out.

Billy said, "I'd like to break that little bastard's legs."

Myra patted his cheek. "Never mind, sunshine, on your two feet you're useless. It's in the horizontal position you come into your own. Now go and play with your motorbike or something," and she went back in her uncle's office.

Dillon paused at the bottom of the stairs and slipped the Beretta inside the briefcase. The only thing better than one gun was two. It always gave you an ace in the hole and he walked back to the Mini-Cooper briskly.

Myra said, "I wouldn't trust him an inch, that one."

"A hard little bastard," Harvey said. "When he was here for the IRA in nineteen eighty-one, I supplied him with arms, explosives, everything. You were at college then, not in the business, so you probably don't remember."

"Is Coogan his real name?"

"Course not." He nodded. "Yes, hell on wheels. I was having a lot of hassle in those days from George Montoya down in Bermondsey, the one they called Spanish George. Coogan knocked him off for me one night, him and his brother, outside a bar called the *Flamenco*. Did it for free."

"Really?" Myra said. "So where do we get him Semtex?"

He laughed, opened the top drawer and took out a bunch of keys. "I'll show you." He led the way out and along the corridor and unlocked a door. "Something even you didn't know, darling."

The room was lined with shelves of box files. He put his hand on the middle shelf of the rear wall and it swung open. He reached for a switch and turned on a light, revealing a treasure house of weapons of every description.

"My God!" she said.

"Whatever you want, it's here," he said. "Hand guns, AK assault rifles, M15s." He chuckled. "And Semtex." There were three cardboard boxes on a table. "Fifty pounds in each of those."

"But why did you tell him it might take time?"

"Keep him dangling." He led the way out and closed things up. "Might screw a few more bob out of him."

As they went back into his office she said, "What do you think he's up to?"

"I couldn't care less. Anyway, why should you worry? You suddenly turned into a bleeding patriot or something?"

"It isn't that, I'm just curious."

He clipped another cigar. "Mind you, I have had a thought. Very convenient if I got the little bugger to knock off Harry Flood for me," and he started to laugh.

It was just after six and Ferguson was just about to leave his office at the Ministry of Defence when his phone rang. It was Devlin. "Now then, you old sod, I've news for you."

"Get on with it then," Ferguson said.

"Dillon's control in eighty-one in Belfast was a man called Tommy McGuire. Remember him?"

"I do indeed. Wasn't he shot a few years ago? Some sort of IRA feud?"

"That was the story, but he's still around up there using another identity."

"And what would that be?"

"I've still to find that out. People to see in Belfast. I'm driving up there tonight. I take it, by the way, that involving myself in this way makes me an official agent of Group Four? I mean I wouldn't like to end up in prison, not at my age."

"You'll be covered fully, you have my word on it. Now what do you want us to do?"

"I was thinking that if Brosnan and your Captain Tanner wanted to be in on the action, they could fly over in the morning in that Lear jet of yours, to Belfast, that is, and wait for me at the Europa Hotel, in the bar. Tell Brosnan to identify himself to the head porter. I'll be in touch probably around noon."

"I'll see to it," Ferguson said.

"Just one more thing. Don't you think you and I are getting just a little geriatric for this sort of game?"

"You speak for yourself," Ferguson said and put the phone down.

He sat thinking about it, then phoned through for a secretary. He also called Mary Tanner at the Lowndes Square flat. As he was talking to her,

Alice Johnson came in with her notepad and pencil. Ferguson waved her down and carried on speaking to Mary.

"So, early start in the morning. Gatwick again, I think. You'll be there in an hour in the Lear. Are you dining out tonight?"

"Henry Flood suggested the River Room at the Savoy, he likes the dance band."

"Sounds like fun."

"Would you like to join us, sir?"

"Actually, I would," Ferguson said.

"We'll see you then. Eight o'clock."

Ferguson put down the phone and turned to Alice Johnson. "A brief note, Eyes of the Prime Minister only, the special file." He quickly dictated a report that brought everything up to date, including his conversation with Devlin. "One copy for the P.M. and alert a messenger. Usual copy for me and the file. Hurry it up and bring them along for my signature. I want to get away."

She went down to the office quickly. Gordon Brown was standing at the copier as she sat behind the typewriter. "I thought he'd gone?" he said.

"So did I, but he's just given me an extra. Another Eyes of the Prime Minister only."

"Really."

She started to type furiously, was finished in two minutes. She stood up. "He'll have to hang on. I need to go to the toilet."

"I'll do the copying for you."

"Thanks, Gordon."

She went out and along the corridor, was opening the toilet door when she realized she'd left her handbag on the desk. She turned and hurried back to the office. The door was partially open and she could see Gordon standing at the copier reading a copy of the report. To her astonishment, he folded it, slipped it in his inside pocket and hurriedly did another.

Alice was totally thrown, had no idea what to do. She went back along the corridor to the toilet, went in and tried to pull herself together. After a while she went back.

The report and a file copy were on her desk. "All done," Gordon Brown said. "And I've requested a messenger."

She managed a light smile. "I'll get them signed."

"Right, I'm just going down to the canteen. I'll see you later."

Alice went along the corridor, knocked on Ferguson's door and went in. He was at his desk writing and looked up. "Oh, good. I'll sign those and you can get the P.M.'s copy off to Downing Street straight away." She was trembling now and he frowned. "My dear Mrs. Johnson, what is it?"

So she told him.

He sat there, grim-faced, and as she finished, reached for the telephone. "Special Branch, Detective Inspector Lane for Brigadier Ferguson, Group Four. Top Priority, no delay. My office now."

He put the phone down. "Now this is what you do. Go back to the office and behave as if nothing had happened."

"But he isn't there, Brigadier, he went to the canteen."

"Really?" Ferguson said. "Now why would he do that?"

When Tania heard Gordon Brown's voice she was immediately angry. "I've told you about this, Gordon."

"Yes, but it's urgent."

"Where are you?"

"In the canteen at the Ministry. I've got another report."

"Is it important?"

"Very."

"Read it to me."

"No, I'll bring it round after I come off shift at ten."

"I'll see you at your place, Gordon, I promise, but I want to know what you've got now and if you refuse, then don't bother to call again."

"No, that's all right, I'll read it."

Which he did and when he was finished she said, "Good boy, Gordon, I'll see you later."

He put the phone down and turned, folding the copy of the report. The door to the phone box was jerked open and Ferguson plucked the report from his fingers.

TEN

Dillon was in his room at the hotel when Tania called him. "I've got rather hot news," she said. "The hunt for a lead on you is moving to Belfast."

"Tell me," he said.

Which she did. When she was finished, she said, "Does any of this make any sense?"

"Yes," he said. "The McGuire fella was a big name with the Provos in those days."

"And he's dead, is he, or is he still around?"

"Devlin's right about that. His death was reported, supposedly because of in-fighting in the Movement, but it was just a ruse to help him drop out of sight."

"If they found him, could it give you problems?"

"Maybe, but not if I found him first."

"And how could you do that?"

"I know his half-brother, a fella called Macey. He would know where he is."

"But that would mean a trip to Belfast yourself."

"That would be no big deal. An hour and a quarter by British Airways. I don't know what time the last plane tonight gets in. I'd have to check."

"Just a minute, I've got a B.A. Worldwide Timetable here," she said and opened her desk drawer. She found it and looked at the Belfast schedule. "The last plane is eight-thirty. You'll never make it. It's quarter to seven now. It's murder getting out to Heathrow in the evening traffic and this weather will make it worse. Probably at least an hour or maybe an hour and a half."

"I know," Dillon said. "What about the morning?"

"Same time, eight-thirty."

"I'll just have to get up early."

"Is it wise?"

"Is anything in this life? I'll handle it, don't worry. I'll be in touch."

He put the phone down, thought about it for a while, then called British Airways and booked a seat on the morning flight with an open return. He lit a cigarette and walked to the window. Was it wise, she'd said, and he tried to remember what Tommy McGuire had known about him in eighty-one. Nothing about Danny Fahy, that was certain, because Fahy wasn't supposed to be involved that time. That had been personal. But Jack Harvey was another matter. After all, it had been McGuire who'd put him onto Harvey as an arms supplier in the first place.

He pulled on his jacket, got his trenchcoat from the wardrobe and went out. Five minutes later he was hailing a cab on the corner. He got in and told the driver to take him to Covent Garden.

Gordon Brown sat on the other side of Ferguson's desk in the half-light. He had never been so frightened in his life. "I didn't mean any harm, Brigadier, I swear it."

"Then why did you take a copy of the report?"

"It was just a whim. Stupid, I know, but I was so intrigued with it being for the Prime Minister."

"You realize what you've done, Gordon, a man of your service? All those years in the Army? This could mean your pension."

Detective Inspector Lane of Special Branch was in his late thirties and in his crumpled tweed suit and glasses looked like a schoolmaster. He said, "I'm going to ask you again, Mr. Brown." He leaned on the end of the desk. "Have you ever taken copies like this before?"

"Absolutely not, I swear it."

"You've never been asked by another person to do such a thing?"

Gordon managed to look suitably shocked. "Good heavens, Inspector, that would be treason. I was a Sergeant-Major in the Intelligence Corps."

"Yes, Mr. Brown, we know all that," Lane said.

The internal phone went and Ferguson lifted it. It was Lane's sergeant, Mackie. "I'm outside, Brigadier, just back from the flat in Camden. I think you and the Inspector should come out."

"Thank you." Ferguson put the phone down. "Right, I think we'll give you time to think things over, Gordon. Inspector?"

He nodded to Lane, got up and moved to the door and Lane followed him. Mackie was standing in the anteroom still in trilby and raincoat, a plastic bag in one hand.

"You found something, Sergeant?" Lane asked.

"You could call it that, sir." Mackie took a cardboard file from his plastic bag and opened it. "A rather interesting collection."

The copies of the reports were neatly stacked in order, the latest ones for the Prime Minister's attention on top.

Lane said, "Christ, Brigadier, he's been at it for a while."

"So it would seem," Ferguson said. "But to what purpose?"

"You mean he's working for someone, sir?"

"Without a doubt. The present operation I'm engaged on is most delicate. There was an attack on a man working for me in Paris. A woman died. We wondered how the villain of the piece knew about them, if you follow me. Now we know. Details of these reports were passed on to a third party. They must have been."

Lane nodded. "Then we'll have to work on him some more."

"No, we don't have the time. Let's try another way. Let's just let him go. He's a simple man. I think he'd do the simple thing."

"Right, sir." Lane turned to Mackie. "If you lose him, you'll be back pounding the pavement in Brixton, and so will I, because I'm coming with you."

They hurried out and Ferguson opened the door and went back in the office. He sat down behind the desk. "A sad business, Gordon."

"What's going to happen to me, Brigadier?"

"I'll have to think about it." Ferguson picked up the copy of the report. "Such an incredibly stupid thing to do." He sighed. "Go home, Gordon, go home. I'll see you in the morning."

Gordon Brown couldn't believe his luck. He got the door open somehow and left, hurrying down the corridor to the staff cloakroom. The narrowest escape of his life. It could have meant the end of everything. Not only his career and pension, but prison. But that was it: no more and Tania would have to accept that. He went downstairs to the car park, pulling on his coat, found his car and was turning into Whitehall a few moments later, Mackie and Lane hard on his tail in the Sergeant's unmarked Ford Capri.

Dillon knew that late-night shopping was the thing in the Covent Garden area. There were still plenty of people around in spite of the winter cold and he hurried along until he came to the theatrical shop, Clayton's, near Neal's Yard. The lights were on in the window, the door opened to his touch, the bell tinkling.

Clayton came through the bead curtain and smiled. "Oh, it's you. What can I do for you?"

"Wigs," Dillon told him.

"A nice selection over here." He was right. There was everything— short, long, permed, blonde, redhead. Dillon selected one that was shoulder-length and gray.

"I see," Clayton said. "The granny look?"

"Something like that. What about costume? I don't mean anything fancy. Second-hand?"

"In here."

Clayton went through the bead curtain and Dillon followed him. There was rack upon rack of clothes and a jumbled heap in the corner. He worked very quickly, sorting through, selected a long brown skirt with an elastic waist and a shabby raincoat that almost came down to his ankles.

Clayton said, "What are you going to play, Old Mother Riley or a bag lady?"

"You'd be surprised." Dillon had seen a pair of jeans on top of the jumble in the corner. He picked them up and searched through a pile of shoes beside them, selecting a pair of runners that had seen better days.

"These will do," he said. "Oh, and this," and he picked an old head-scarf from a stand. "Stick 'em all in a couple of plastic bags. How much?"

Clayton started to pack them. "By rights I should thank you for taking them away, but we've all got to live. Ten quid to you."

Dillon paid him and picked up the bags. "Thanks a lot."

Clayton opened the door for him. "Have a good show, luv, give 'em hell."

"Oh, I will," Dillon said and he hurried down to the corner, hailed a cab and told the driver to take him back to the hotel.

When Tania Novikova went down to answer the bell and opened the door to find Gordon Brown there, she knew, by instinct, that something was wrong.

"What's this, Gordon? I told you I'd come round to your place."

"I must see you, Tania, it's essential. Something terrible has happened!"

"Calm down," she said. "Just take it easy. Come upstairs and tell me all about it."

Lane and Mackie were parked at the end of the street and the Inspector was already on the car phone to Ferguson, giving him the address.

"Sergeant Mackie's done a quick check at the door, sir. The card says a Miss Tania Novikova."

"Oh, dear," Ferguson said.

"You know her, sir?"

"Supposedly a secretary at the Soviet Embassy, Inspector. In fact she's a captain in the KGB."

"That means she's one of Colonel Yuri Gatov's people, sir. He runs London Station."

"I'm not so sure. Gatov is a Gorbachev man and very pro-West. On the other hand, I always understood the Novikova woman to be to the right of Genghis Khan. I'd be surprised if Gatov knew about this."

"Are you going to notify him, sir?"

"Not yet. Let's see what she's got to say first. It's information we're after."

"Shall we go in, sir?"

"No, wait for me. I'll be with you in twenty minutes."

Tania peered cautiously through a chink in the curtains. She saw Mackie standing by his car at the end of the street and it was enough. She could smell policemen anywhere in the world, Moscow, Paris, London—it was always the same.

"Tell me again, Gordon, exactly what happened."

Gordon Brown did as he was told and she sat there listening patiently. She nodded when he'd finished. "We were lucky, Gordon, very lucky. Go and make us a cup of coffee in the kitchen. I've got a couple of phone calls to make." She squeezed his hand. "Afterwards we'll have a very special time together."

"Really?" His face brightened and he went out.

She picked up the phone and called Makeev at his Paris apartment. It rang for quite a time and she was about to put it down when it was picked up at the other end.

"Josef, it's Tania."

"I was in the shower," he said. "I'm dripping all over the carpet."

"I've only got seconds, Josef. I just wanted to say goodbye. I'm blown. My mole was exposed. They'll be kicking in the door any minute."

"My God!" he said. "And Dillon?"

"He's safe. All systems go. What that man has planned will set the world on fire."

"But you, Tania?"

"Don't worry, I won't let them take me. Goodbye, Josef."

She put the phone down, lit a cigarette, then called the hotel and asked for Dillon's room. He answered at once.

"It's Tania," she said. "We've got trouble."

He was quite calm. "How bad?"

"They rumbled my mole, let him go, and the poor idiot came straight here. I smell Special Branch at the end of the street."

"I see. What are you going to do?"

"Don't worry, I won't be around to tell them anything. One thing: They'll know that Gordon gave me the contents of tonight's report. He was in the telephone booth in the Ministry canteen when Ferguson arrested him."

"I see."

"Promise me one thing," she said.

"What's that?"

"Blow them away, all of them." The doorbell rang. She said, "I've got to go. Luck, Dillon."

As she put down the phone, Gordon Brown came in with the coffee. "Was that the door?"

"Yes. Be an angel, Gordon, and see who it is."

He opened the door and started downstairs. Tania took a deep breath. Dying wasn't difficult. The cause she believed in had always been the most important thing in her life. She stubbed out her cigarette, opened a drawer in the desk, took out a Makarov pistol and shot herself through the right temple.

Gordon Brown, halfway down the stairs, turned and bounded up, bursting into the room. At the sight of her lying there beside the desk, the pistol still in her right hand, he let out a terrible cry and fell on his knees.

"Tania, my darling," he moaned.

And then he knew what he must do as he heard something heavy crash against the door below. He pried the Makarov from her hand and as he raised it, his own hand was trembling. He took a deep breath to steady himself and pulled the trigger in the same moment that the front door burst open and Lane and Mackie started upstairs, Ferguson behind them.

There was a small crowd at the end of the street exhibiting the usual public curiosity. Dillon joined in, his collar up, hands in pockets. It started to snow slightly as they opened the rear doors of the ambulance. He watched as the two blanket-covered stretchers were loaded. The ambulance drove away. Ferguson stood on the pavement for a few moments talking to Lane and Mackie. Dillon recognized the Brigadier straight away, had been shown his photo many years previously. Lane and Mackie were obviously policemen.

After a while, Ferguson got in his car and was driven away, Mackie went into the flat and Lane also drove away. The stratagem was obvious: For Mackie to wait just in case someone turned up. One thing was certain. Tania Novikova was dead and so was the boyfriend, and Dillon knew that thanks to her sacrifice, he was safe.

He went back to the hotel and phoned Makeev at his flat in Paris. "I've got bad news, Josef."

"Tania?"

"How did you know?"

"She phoned. What's happened?"

"She was blown or rather her mole was. She killed herself, Josef, rather than get taken. A dedicated lady."

"And the mole? The boyfriend?"

"Did the same. I've just seen the bodies carted out to an ambulance. Ferguson was there."

"How will this affect you?"

"In no way. I'm off to Belfast in the morning to cut off the only chance of a lead they have."

"And then?"

"I'll amaze you, Josef, and your Arab friend. How does the entire British War Cabinet sound to you?"

"Dear God, you can't be serious?"

"Oh, but I am. I'll be in touch very soon now."

He replaced the phone, put on his jacket and went down to the bar, whistling.

Ferguson was sitting in a booth in the lounge bar of the pub opposite Kensington Park Gardens and the Soviet Embassy, waiting for Colonel Yuri Gatov. The Russian, when he appeared, looked agitated, a tall, white-haired man in a camel overcoat. He saw Ferguson and hurried over.

"Charles, I can't believe it. Tania Novikova dead. Why?"

"Yuri, you and I have known each other for better than twenty-five years, often as adversaries, but I'll take a chance on you now, a chance that you really do want to see change in our time and an end to East-West conflict."

"But I do, you know that."

"Unfortunately, not everyone in the KGB would agree with you and Tania Novikova was one."

"She was a hardliner, true, but what are you saying, Charles?"

So Ferguson told him—Dillon, the attempt on Mrs. Thatcher, Gordon Brown, Brosnan, everything.

Gatov said. "This IRA wild card intends to attempt the life of the Prime Minister, that's what you're telling me, and Tania was involved?"

"Oh, very directly."

"But, Charles, I knew nothing, I swear."

"And I believe you, old chap, but she must have had a link with someone. I mean she managed to convey vital information to Dillon in Paris. That's how he knew about Brosnan and so on."

"Paris," Gatov said. "That's a thought. Did you know she was in Paris for three years before transferring to London? And you know who's head of Paris Station for the KGB?"

"Of course, Josef Makeev," Ferguson said.

"Anything but a Gorbachev man. Very much of the old guard."

"It would explain a great deal," Ferguson said. "But we'll never prove it."

"True." Gatov nodded. "But I'll give him a call anyway, just to worry him."

Makeev had not strayed far from the phone and picked it up the moment it rang.

"Makeev here."

"Josef? Yuri Gatov. I'm phoning from London."

"Yuri. What a surprise," Makeev said, immediately wary.

"I've got some distressing news, Josef. Tania, Tania Novikova."

"What about her?"

"She committed suicide earlier this evening along with some boyfriend of hers, a clerk at the Ministry of Defence."

"Good heavens." Makeev tried to sound convincing.

"He was feeding her classified information. I've just had a session with Charles Ferguson of Group Four. You know Charles?"

"Of course."

"I was quite shocked. I must tell you I had no knowledge of Tania's activities. She worked for you for three years, Josef, so you know her as well as anyone. Have you any thoughts on the matter?"

"None, I'm afraid."

"Ah, well, if you can think of anything, let me know."

Makeev poured himself a Scotch and went and looked out into the frostbound Paris street. For a wild moment he'd had an impulse to phone Michael Aroun, but what would be the point, and Tania had sounded so certain. Set the world on fire, that had been her phrase.

He raised his glass. "To you, Dillon," he said softly. "Let's see if you can do it."

It was almost eleven in the River Room at the Savoy, the band still playing, and Harry Flood, Brosnan and Mary were thinking of breaking up the party when Ferguson appeared at last.

"If ever I've needed a drink I need one now. A Scotch, and a very large one."

Flood called a waiter and gave the order and Mary said, "What on earth's happened?"

Ferguson gave them a quick résumé of the night's events. When he was finished, Brosnan said, "It explains a great deal, but the infuriating thing is it gets us no closer to Dillon."

"One point I must make," Ferguson said. "When I arrested Brown in the canteen at the Ministry he was on the phone and he had the report in his hand. I believe it likely he was speaking to the Novikova woman then."

"I see what you're getting at," Mary said. "You think she, in her turn, may have transmitted the information to Dillon?"

"Possibly," Ferguson said.

"So what are you suggesting?" Brosnan asked. "That Dillon would go to Belfast, too?"

"Perhaps," Ferguson said. "If it was important enough."

"We'll just have to take our chances, then." Brosnan turned to Mary. "Early start tomorrow. We'd better get moving."

As they walked through the lounge to the entrance, Brosnan and Ferguson went ahead and stood talking. Mary said to Flood, "You think a lot of him, don't you?"

"Martin?" He nodded. "The Vietcong had me in a pit for weeks. When the rains came, it used to fill up with water and I'd have to stand all night so I didn't drown. Leeches, worms, you name it, and then one day, when it was as bad as it could be, a hand reached down and pulled me out, and it was Martin in a headband, hair to his shoulders and his face painted like an Apache Indian. He's special people."

Mary looked across at Brosnan. "Yes," she said. "I suppose that just about sums him up."

Dillon ordered a taxi to pick him up at six o'clock from the hotel. He was waiting for it on the steps, his case in one hand when it arrived, a briefcase in the other. He was wearing his trenchcoat, suit, striped tie and glasses to fit the Peter Hilton persona, carried the Jersey driving license and the flying license as proof of identity. In the case was a toilet bag and the items he had obtained from Clayton at Covent Garden, all neatly folded. He'd included a towel from the hotel, socks and underpants. It all looked terribly normal and the wig could be easily explained.

The run to Heathrow was fast at that time in the morning. He went and picked up his ticket at the booking desk, then put his case through and got his seat assignment. He wasn't carrying a gun. No possible way he could do that, not with the kind of maximum security that operated on the Belfast planes.

He got a selection of newspapers, went up to the gallery restaurant and ordered a full English breakfast, then he started to work his way through the papers, checking on how the war in the Gulf was doing.

At Gatwick, there was a light powdering of snow at the side of the runway as the Lear jet lifted off. As they leveled off, Mary said, "How do you feel?"

"I'm not sure," Brosnan said. "It's been a long time since I was in Belfast. Liam Devlin, Anne-Marie. So long ago."

"And Sean Dillon?"

"Don't worry, I wasn't forgetting him, I could never do that."

He turned and stared far out into the distance as the Lear jet lifted up out of the clouds and turned north-west.

Although Dillon wasn't aware of it, Brosnan and Mary had already landed and were on their way to the Europa Hotel when his flight touched down at Aldergrove airport outside Belfast. There was a half-hour wait for the baggage, and when he got his case, he made for the green line and followed a stream of people through. Customs officers stopped some, but he wasn't one of them, and within five minutes he was outside and into a taxi.

"English, are you?" the driver asked.

Dillon slipped straight into his Belfast accent. "And what makes you think that?"

"Jesus, I'm sorry," the driver said. "Anywhere special?"

"I'd like a hotel in the Falls Road," Dillon said. "Somewhere near Craig Street."

"You won't get much round there."

"Scenes of my youth," Dillon told him. "I've been working in London for years. Just in town for business overnight. Thought I'd like to see the old haunts."

"Suit yourself. There's the Deepdene, but it's not much, I'm telling you."

A Saracen armored car passed then, and as they turned into a main road, they saw an Army patrol. "Nothing changes," Dillon said.

"Sure and most of those lads weren't even born when the whole thing started," the driver told him. "I mean, what are we in for? Another Hundred Years' War?"

"God knows," Dillon said piously and opened his paper.

The driver was right. The Deepdene wasn't much. A tall Victorian building in a mean side street off the Falls Road. He paid off the driver, went in and found himself in a shabby hall with a worn carpet. When he tapped the bell on the desk, a stout, motherly woman emerged.

"Can I help you, dear?"

"A room," he said. "Just the one night."

"That's fine." She pushed a register at him and took a key down. "Number nine on the first floor."

"Shall I pay now?"

"Sure and there's no need for that. Don't I know a gentleman when I see one?"

He went up the stairs, found the door and unlocked it. The room was as shabby as he'd expected, a single brass bedstead, a wardrobe. He put his case on the table and went out again, locking the door, then went the other way along the corridor and found the back stairs. He opened the door at the bottom into an untidy backyard. The lane beyond backed onto incredibly derelict houses, but it didn't depress him in the slightest. This was an area he knew like the back of his hand, a place where he'd led the British Army one hell of a dance in his day. He moved along the alley, a smile on his face, remembering, and turned into the Falls Road.

ELEVEN

I remember them opening this place in seventy-one," Brosnan said to Mary. He was standing at the window of the sixth-floor room of the Europa Hotel in Great Victoria Street next to the railway station. "For a while it was a prime target for IRA bombers, the kind who'd rather blow up anything rather than nothing."

"Not you, of course."

There was a slight, sarcastic edge which he ignored. "Certainly not. Devlin and I appreciated the bar too much. We came in all the time."

She laughed in astonishment. "What nonsense. Are you seriously asking me to believe that with the British Army chasing you all over Belfast you and Devlin sat in the Europa's bar?"

"Also the restaurant on occasion. Come on, I'll show you. Better take our coats, just in case we get a message while we're down there."

As they were descending in the lift, she said, "You're not armed, are you?"

"No."

"Good, I'd rather keep it that way."

"How about you?"

"Yes," she said calmly. "But that's different. I'm a serving officer of Crown Forces in an Active Service zone."

"What are you carrying?"

She opened her handbag and gave him a brief glimpse of the weapon. It was not much larger than the inside of her hand, a small automatic.

"What is it?" he asked.

"Rather rare. An old Colt .25. I picked it up in Africa."

"Hardly an elephant gun."

"No, but it does the job." She smiled bleakly. "As long as you can shoot, that is."

The lift doors parted and they went across the lounge.

Dillon walked briskly along the Falls Road. Nothing had changed, nothing at all. It was just like the old days. He twice saw RUC patrols backed up by soldiers and once, two armored troop carriers went by, but no one paid any attention. He finally found what he wanted in Craig Street about a mile from the hotel. It was a small, double-fronted shop with steel shutters on the windows. The three brass balls of a pawnbroker hung over the entrance with the sign Patrick Macey.

Dillon opened the door and walked into musty silence. The dimly lit shop was crammed with a variety of items. Television sets, video recorders, clocks. There was even a gas cooker and a stuffed bear in one corner.

There was a mesh screen running along the counter and the man who sat on a stool behind it was working on a watch, a jeweler's magnifying glass in one eye. He glanced up, a wasted-looking individual in his sixties, his face gray and pallid.

"And what can I do for you?"

Dillon said, "Nothing ever changes, Patrick. This place still smells exactly the same."

Macey took the magnifying glass from his eye and frowned. "Do I know you?"

"And why wouldn't you, Patrick? Remember that hot night in June of seventy-two when we set fire to that Orangeman, Stewart's, warehouse and shot him and his two nephews as they ran out. Let me see, there were the three of us." Dillon put a cigarette in his mouth and lit it carefully. "There was you and your half-brother, Tommy McGuire, and me."

"Holy Mother of God, Sean Dillon, is that you?" Macey said.

"As ever was, Patrick."

"Jesus, Sean, I never thought to see you in Belfast city again. I thought you were . . ."

He paused and Dillon said, "Thought I was where, Patrick?"

"London," Patrick Macey said. "Somewhere like that," he added lamely.

"And where would you have got that idea from?" Dillon went to the door, locking it and pulled down the blind.

"What are you doing?" Macey demanded in alarm.

"I just want a nice private talk, Patrick, me old son."

"No, Sean, none of that. I'm not involved with the IRA, not anymore."

"You know what they say, Patrick, once in, never out. How is Tommy these days, by the way?"

"Ah, Sean, I'd have thought you'd know. Poor Tommy's been dead these five years. Shot by one of his own. A stupid row between the Provos and one of the splinter groups. INLA were suspected."

"Is that a fact?" Dillon nodded. "Do you see any of the other old hands these days? Liam Devlin, for instance?"

And he had him there, for Macey was unable to keep the look of alarm from his face. "Liam? I haven't seen him since the seventies."

"Really?" Dillon lifted the flap at the end of the counter and walked round. "It's a terrible liar you are." He slapped him across the face. "Now get in there," and pushed him through the curtain that led to the office at the rear.

Macey was terrified. "I don't know a thing."

"About what? I haven't asked you anything yet, but I'm going to tell you a few things. Tommy McGuire isn't dead. He's living somewhere else in this fair city under another name and you're going to tell me where. Secondly, Liam Devlin has been to see you. Now I'm right on both counts, aren't I?" Macey was frozen with fear, terrified, and Dillon slapped him again. "Aren't I?"

The other man broke then. "Please, Sean, please. It's my heart. I could have an attack."

"You will if you don't speak up, I promise you."

"All right. Devlin was here a little earlier this morning enquiring about Tommy."

"And shall I tell you what he said?"

"Please, Sean." Macey was shaking. "I'm ill."

"He said that bad old Sean Dillon was on the loose in London town and that he wanted to help run him down and who could be a better source of information than Dillon's old chum, Tommy McGuire. Am I right?"

Macey nodded. "Yes."

"Good, now we're getting somewhere." Dillon lit another cigarette and nodded at the large, old-fashioned safe in the corner. "Is that where the guns are?"

"What guns, Sean?"

"Come on, don't muck me about. You've been dealing in handguns for years. Get it open."

Macey took a key from his desk drawer, went and opened the safe. Dillon pulled him to one side. There were several weapons in there. An old Webley, a couple of Smith & Wesson revolvers. The one that really caught his eyes was an American Army Colt .45 automatic. He hefted it in his hand and checked the magazine.

"Wonderful, Patrick. I knew I could depend on you." He put the gun on the desk and sat down opposite Macey. "So what happened?"

Macey's face was very strange in color now. "I don't feel well."

"You'll feel better when you've told me. Get on with it."

"Tommy lives on his own about half a mile from here in Canal Street. He's done up the old warehouse at the end. Calls himself Kelly, George Kelly."

"I know that area well, every stick and stone."

"Devlin asked for Tommy's phone number and called him there and then. He said it was essential to see him. That it was to do with you. Tommy agreed to see him at two o'clock."

"Fine," Dillon said. "See how easy it was? Now I can call on him myself before Devlin does and discuss old times, only I won't bother to phone. I think I'll surprise him. Much more fun."

"You'll never get in to see him," Macey said. "You can only get in at the front, all the other doors are welded. He's been paranoid for years. Terrified someone's going to knock him off. You'd never get in the front door. It's all TV security cameras and that kind of stuff."

"There's always a way," Dillon said.

"There always was for you." Macey tore at his shirt collar, choking. "Pills," he moaned and got the drawer in front of him open. The bottle he took fell from his hands.

He lay back on the chair and Dillon got up and went round and picked up the bottle. "Trouble is, Patrick, the moment I go out of the door you'll be on the phone to Tommy and that wouldn't do, would it?"

He walked across to the fireplace and dropped the pill bottle into the gleaming coals. There was a crash behind him and he turned to find Macey had tumbled from the chair to the floor. Dillon stood over him for a moment. Macey's face was very suffused with purple now and his legs were jerking. Suddenly, he gave a great gasp like air escaping, his head turned to one side and he went completely still.

Dillon put the Colt in his pocket, went through the shop and opened the door, locking it with the Yale, leaving the blind down. A moment later he turned the corner into the Falls Road and walked back toward the hotel as fast as he could.

He laid the contents of the case on the bed in the shabby hotel room, then he undressed. First of all he put on the jeans, the old runners and a heavy jumper. Then came the wig. He sat in front of the mirror at the small dressing table, combing the gray hair until it looked wild and unkempt. He tied the headscarf over it and studied himself. Then he pulled on the skirt that reached his ankles. The old raincoat that was far too large completed the outfit.

He stood in front of the wardrobe examining himself in the mirror. He closed his eyes, thinking the role, and when he opened them again it wasn't Dillon anymore, it was a decrepit, broken, bag lady.

He hardly needed any makeup, just a foundation to give him the sallow look and the slash of scarlet lipstick for the mouth. All wrong, of course, but totally right for the character. He took a half bottle of whisky from a pouch in the brief case and poured some into his cupped hands, rubbing it over his face, then he splashed some more over the front of the raincoat. He put the Colt, a couple of newspapers and the whisky bottle into a plastic bag and was ready to leave.

He glanced in the mirror at that strange, nightmarish old woman. "Showtime," he whispered and let himself out.

All was quiet as he went down the backstairs and went out into the yard. He closed the door behind him carefully and crossed to the door which led to the alley. As he reached it, the hotel door opened behind him.

A voice called, "Here, what do you think you're doing?"

Dillon turned and saw a kitchen porter in a soiled white apron putting a cardboard box in the dustbin.

"Go fuck yourself," Dillon croaked.

"Go on, get out of it, you old bag!" the porter shouted.

Dillon closed the door behind him. "Ten out of ten, Sean," he said softly and went up the alley.

He turned into the Falls Road and started to shuffle along the pavement, acting so strangely that people stepped out of the way to avoid him.

It was almost one and Brosnan and Mary Tanner at the bar of the Europa were thinking about lunch when a young porter approached. "Mr. Brosnan?"

"That's right."

"Your taxi is here, sir."

"Taxi?" Mary said. "But we didn't order one."

"Yes we did," Brosnan said.

He helped her on with her coat and they followed the young porter through the foyer, down the steps at the front entrance to the black cab waiting at the curb. Brosnan gave the porter a pound and they got in. The driver on the other side of the glass wore a tweed cap and an old reefer coat. Mary Tanner pulled the sliding glass partition to one side.

"I presume you know where we're going?" she said.

"Oh, I certainly do, my love." Liam Devlin smiled at her over his shoulder, moved into gear and drove away.

It was just after one-thirty when Devlin turned the taxi into Canal Street. "That's the place at the end," he said. "We'll park in the yard at the side." They got out and moved back into the street and approached the entrance. "Be on your best behavior, we're on television," he said and reached to a bell push beside the massive, iron-bound door.

"Not very homelike," Mary commented.

"Yes, well, with Tommy McGuire's background he needs a fortress rather than a cozy semidetached on some desirable estate." Devlin turned to Brosnan. "Are you carrying, son?"

"No," Brosnan said. "But she is. You are, I suppose?"

"Call it my innate caution or perhaps the wicked habits of a lifetime."

A voice sounded through the box beside the door. "Is that you, Devlin?"

"And who else, you stupid bugger. I've got Martin Brosnan with me and a lady friend of his and we're freezing in this damn cold, so get the door open."

"You're early. You said two o'clock."

They could hear steps on the other side and then the door opened to reveal a tall, cadaverous man in his mid-sixties. He wore a heavy Arran pullover and baggy jeans and carried a Sterling sub-machine gun.

Devlin brushed past him, leading the way in. "What do you intend to do with that thing, start another war?"

McGuire closed the door and barred it. "Only if I have to." He looked them over suspiciously. "Martin?" He held out a hand. "It's been a long time. As for you, you old sod," he said to Devlin, "whatever's keeping you out of your grave you should bottle it. We'd make a fortune." He looked Mary over. "And who might you be?"

"A friend," Devlin told him. "So let's get on with it."

"All right, this way."

The interior of the warehouse was totally bare except for a van parked to one side. A steel staircase led to a landing high above with what had once been glass-fronted offices. McGuire went first and turned into the first office on the landing. There was a desk and a bank of television equipment, one screen showing the street, another the entrance. He put the Sterling on the desk.

Devlin said, "You live here?"

"Upstairs. I've turned what used to be the storage loft into a flat. Now let's get on with it, Devlin. What is it you want? You mentioned Sean Dillon."

"He's on the loose again," Brosnan said.

"I thought he must have come to a bad end. I mean, it's been so long." McGuire lit a cigarette. "Anyway, what's it to do with me?"

"He tried to knock off Martin here in Paris. Killed his girlfriend instead."

"Jesus!" McGuire said.

"Now he's on the loose in London and I want him," Brosnan told him.

McGuire looked at Mary again. "And where does she fit in?"

"I'm a captain in the British Army," she said crisply. "Tanner's the name."

"For God's sake, Devlin, what is this?" McGuire demanded.

"It's all right," Devlin told him. "She hasn't come to arrest you, although we all know that if Tommy McGuire was still in the land of the living he'd draw about twenty-five years."

"You bastard!" McGuire said.

"Be sensible," Devlin told him. "Just answer a few questions and you can go back to being George Kelly again."

McGuire put a hand up defensively. "All right, I get the point. What do you want to know?"

"Nineteen eighty-one, the London bombing campaign," Brosnan said. "You were Dillon's control."

McGuire glanced at Mary. "That's right."

"We know Dillon would have experienced the usual problems as regards weapons and explosives, Mr. McGuire," Mary said. "And I've been given to understand he always favors underworld contacts in that sort of situation. Is that so?"

"Yes, he usually worked in that way," McGuire said reluctantly and sat down.

"Have you any idea who he used in London in nineteen eighty-one?" Mary persisted.

McGuire looked hunted. "How would I know? It could have been anybody."

Devlin said, "You lying bastard, you know something, I can tell you do." His right hand came out of the pocket of the reefer holding an old Luger pistol and he touched McGuire between the eyes. "Quick now, tell us or I'll . . ."

McGuire pushed the gun to one side. "All right, Devlin, you win." He lit another cigarette. "He dealt with a man in London called Jack Harvey, a big operator, a real gangster."

"There, that wasn't so hard, was it?" Devlin said.

There was a thunderous knocking on the door below and they all looked at the television screen to see an old bag lady on the front step. Her voice came clearly through the speaker. "The lovely man you are, Mr. Kelly. Could you spare a poor soul a quid?"

McGuire said into the microphone, "Piss off, you old bag."

"Oh, Jesus, Mr. Kelly, I'll die here on your step in this terrible cold, so I will for the whole world to see."

McGuire got up. "I'll go and get rid of her. I'll only be a minute."

He hurried down the stairs and extracted a five-pound note from an old wallet as he approached the door. He got it open and held it out. "Take this and clear off."

Dillon's hand came up out of the plastic shopping bag holding the Colt. "A fiver, Tommy boy. You're getting generous in your old age. Inside."

He pushed him through and closed the door. McGuire was terrified. "Look, what is this?"

"Nemesis," Dillon said. "You pay for your sins in this life, Tommy, we all do. Remember that night in seventy-two, you, me and Patrick when we shot the Stewarts as they ran out of the fire?"

"Dillon?" McGuire whispered. "It's you?" He started to turn and raised his voice. "Devlin!" he called.

Dillon shot him twice in the back breaking his spine, driving him on his face. As he got the door open behind him, Devlin appeared on the landing, the Luger in his hand, already firing. Dillon fired three times rapidly, shattering the office window, then was outside, slamming the door behind him.

As he started up the street, two stripped-down Land-Rovers, four soldiers in each, turned out of the main road, attracted by the sound of the firing and came toward him. The worst kind of luck, but Dillon didn't hesitate. As he came to a drain in the gutter, he pretended to slip and dropped the Colt through the bars.

As he got up someone called, "Stay where you are."

They were paratroopers in camouflage uniforms, flak jackets and red berets, each man with his rifle ready and Dillon gave them the performance of his life. He staggered forward, moaning and crying and clutching at the young lieutenant in charge.

"Jesus, sir, there's terrible things going on back there in that warehouse. There's me sheltering from the cold and these fellas come on and start shooting each other."

The young officer smelled the whisky and pushed him away. "Check what's in the carrier, Sergeant."

The Sergeant rifled through. "Bottle of hooch and some newspapers, sir."

"Right, go and wait over there." The officer pushed Dillon along the pavement behind the patrol and got a loudhailer from one of the Land-Rovers. "You inside," he called. "Throw your weapons out through the door, then follow them with your hands up. Two minutes or we'll come in to get you."

All members of the patrol were in a readiness posture, intent only on the entrance. Dillon eased back into the courtyard, turned and hurried past Devlin's taxi, finding what he was seeking in seconds, a manhole cover. He got it up and went down a steel ladder, pulling the cover behind him. It had been a way in which he had evaded the British Army on many occasions in the old days and he knew the system in the Falls Road area perfectly.

The tunnel was small and very dark. He crawled along it, aware of the sound of rushing water, and came out on the sloping side of a larger tunnel, the main sewer. There were outlets to the canal that ran down to Belfast Lough, he knew that. He pulled off the skirt and the wig and threw them in the water using the headscarf to wipe his lips and face vigorously, then he hurried along the side until he came to another steel ladder. He started up toward the rays of light beaming in through the holes in the cast iron, waited a moment, then eased it up. He was on a cobbled pathway beside the Canal, the backs of decaying, boarded-up houses on the other side. He put the manhole back in place and made for the Falls Road as fast as possible.

In the warehouse, the young officer stood beside McGuire's body and examined Mary Tanner's ID card. "It's perfectly genuine," she said. "You can check."

"And these two?"

"They're with me. Look, Lieutenant, you'll get a full explanation from my boss. That's Brigadier Charles Ferguson at the Ministry of Defence."

"All right, Captain," he said defensively. "I'm only doing my job. It's not like the old days here, you know. We have the RUC on our backs. Every death has to be investigated fully, otherwise there's the devil to pay."

The sergeant came in. "The Colonel's on the wire, boss."

"Fine," the young lieutenant said and went out.

Brosnan said to Devlin, "Do you think it was Dillon?"

"A hell of a coincidence if it wasn't. A bag woman?" Devlin shook his head. "Who'd have thought it?"

"Only Dillon would be capable."

"Are you trying to say he came over from London specially?" Mary demanded.

"He knew what we were about thanks to Gordon Brown, and how long is the scheduled flight from London to Belfast?" Brosnan asked. "An hour and a quarter?"

"Which means he's got to go back," she said.

"Perhaps," Liam Devlin nodded. "But nothing's absolute in this life, girl, you'll learn that, and you're dealing with a man who's kept out of police hands for twenty years or more, all over Europe."

"Well it's time we got the bastard." She looked down at McGuire. "Not too nice, is it?"

"The violence, the killing. Drink with the devil and this is what it comes down to," Devlin told her.

Dillon went in through the back door of the hotel at exactly two-fifteen and hurried up to his room. He stripped off the jeans and jumper, put them in the case and shoved them up into a cupboard above the wardrobe. He washed his face quickly, then dressed in white shirt and tie, dark suit and blue Burberry. He was out of the room and descending the back stairs, briefcase in hand, within five minutes of having entered. He went up the alley, turned into the Falls Road and started to walk briskly. Within five minutes he managed to hail a taxi and told the driver to take him to the airport.

The officer in charge of Army Intelligence for the Belfast city area was a Colonel McLeod and he was not the least bit pleased with the situation with which he was confronted.

"It really isn't good enough, Captain Tanner," he said. "We can't have you people coming in here like cowboys and acting on your own initiative." He turned to look at Devlin and Brosnan. "And with people of very dubious background into the bargain. There is a delicate situation here these days and we do have the Royal Ulster Constabulary to placate. They see this as their turf."

"Yes, well, that's as may be," Mary told him. "But your sergeant outside was kind enough to check on flights to London for me. There's one at four-thirty and another at six-thirty. Don't you think it would be a good idea to check out the passengers rather thoroughly?"

"We're not entirely stupid, Captain, I've already put that in hand, but I'm sure I don't need to remind you that we are not an army of occupation. There is no such thing as martial law here. It's impossible for me to close down the airport, I don't have the authority. All I can do is notify the police and airport security in the usual way and as you've been at pains to explain, where this man Dillon is concerned, we don't have much to tell them." His phone went. He picked it up and said, "Brigadier Ferguson? Sorry to bother you, sir. Colonel McLeod, Belfast HQ. We appear to have a problem."

But Dillon, at the airport, had no intention of returning on the London flight. Perhaps he could get away with it, but madness to try when there were other alternatives. It was just after three as he searched the departure board. He'd just missed the Manchester flight, but there was a flight to Glasgow due out at three-fifteen and it was delayed.

He crossed to the booking desk. "I was hoping to catch the Glasgow flight," he told the young woman booking clerk, "but got here too late. Now I see it's delayed."

She punched details up on her screen. "Yes, half-hour delay, sir, and there's plenty of space. Would you like to try for it?"

"I certainly would," he said gratefully and got the money from his wallet as she made out the ticket.

There was no trouble with security and the contents of his briefcase were innocuous enough. Passengers had already been called and he boarded the plane and sat in a seat at the rear. Very satisfactory. Only one thing had gone wrong. Devlin, Brosnan and the woman had got to McGuire first. A pity, that, because it raised the question of what he'd told them. Harvey, for example. He'd have to move fast there, just in case.

He smiled charmingly when the stewardess asked him if he'd like a drink. "A cup of tea would be just fine," he said and took a newspaper from his briefcase.

McLeod had Brosnan, Mary and Devlin taken up to the airport, and they arrived just before the passengers were called for the four-thirty London flight. An RUC police inspector took them through to the departure lounge.

"Only thirty passengers, as you can see, and we've checked them all thoroughly."

"I've an idea we're on a wild-goose chase," McLeod said.

The passengers were called and Brosnan and Devlin stood by the door and looked each person over as they went through. When they'd passed, Devlin said, "The old nun, Martin, you didn't think like doing a strip search?"

McLeod said impatiently, "Oh, for God's sake, let's get moving."

"An angry man," Devlin said as the colonel went ahead. "They must have laid the cane on something fierce at his public school. It's back to London for you two, then?"

"Yes, we'd better get on with it," Brosnan said.

"And you, Mr. Devlin?" Mary asked. "Will you be all right?"

"Ah, Ferguson, to be fair, secured me a clean bill of health years ago for services rendered to Brit Intelligence. I'll be fine." He kissed her on the cheek. "A real pleasure, my love."

"And for me."

"Watch out for the boy here. Dillon's the original tricky one."

They had reached the concourse. He smiled and suddenly was gone, disappeared into the crowd.

Brosnan took a deep breath. "Right, then, London. Let's get moving," and he took her arm and moved through the throng.

The flight to Glasgow was only forty-five minutes. Dillon landed at four-thirty. There was a shuttle-service plane to London at five-fifteen. He got a ticket at the desk, hurried through to the departure lounge, where the first thing he did was phone Danny Fahy at Cadge End. It was Angel who answered.

"Put your Uncle Danny on, it's Dillon," he told her.

Danny said, "Is that you, Sean?"

"As ever was. I'm in Glasgow waiting for a plane. I'll be arriving at Heathrow Terminal One at six-thirty. Can you come and meet me? You'll just have time."

"No problem, Sean. I'll bring Angel for the company."

"That's fine and, Danny, be prepared to work through the night. Tomorrow could be the big one."

"Jesus, Sean—" but Dillon put the phone down before Fahy could say anything more.

Next, he phoned Harvey's office at the undertaker's in Whitechapel. It was Myra who answered.

"This is Peter Hilton here, we met yesterday. I'd like a word with your uncle."

"He isn't here. He's gone up to Manchester for a function. Won't be back until tomorrow morning."

"That's no good to me," Dillon said. "He promised me my stuff in twenty-four hours."

"Oh, it's here," Myra said. "But I'd expect cash on delivery."

"You've got it." He looked at his watch and allowed for the time it would take to drive from Heathrow to Bayswater to get the money. "I'll be there about seven forty-five."

"I'll be waiting."

As Dillon put the phone down, the flight was called and he joined the crowd of passengers hurrying through.

Myra, standing by the fire in her uncle's office, came to a decision. She got the key of the secret room from his desk drawer and then went out to the head of the stairs.

"Billy, are you down there?"

He came up a moment later. "Here I am."

"Been in the coffin room again, have you? Come on, I need you." She went along the corridor to the end door, opened it and pulled back the false wall. She indicated one of the boxes of Semtex. "Take that to the office."

When she rejoined him, he'd put the box on the desk. "A right bloody weight. What is it?"

"It's money, Billy, that's all that concerns you. Now listen and listen good. That small guy, the one who roughed you up yesterday."

"What about him?"

"He's turning up here at seven forty-five to pay me a lot of money for what's in that box."

"So?"

"I want you waiting outside from seven-thirty in those nice black leathers of yours with your BMW handy. When he leaves, you follow him, Billy, to bloody Cardiff if necessary." She patted his face. "And if you lose him, sunshine, don't bother coming back."

It was snowing lightly at Heathrow as Dillon came through at Terminal One. Angel was waiting for him and waved excitedly.

"Glasgow," she said. "What were you doing there?"

"Finding out what Scotsmen wear under their kilts."

She laughed and hung onto his arm. "Terrible, you are."

They went out through the snow and joined Fahy in the Morris van. "Good to see you, Sean. Where to?"

"My hotel in Bayswater," Dillon said. "I want to book out."

"You're moving in with us?" Angel asked.

"Yes," Dillon nodded, "but I've a present to pick up for Danny first at an undertaker's in Whitechapel."

"And what would that be, Sean?" Fahy demanded.

"Oh, about fifty pounds of Semtex."

The van swerved and skidded slightly, Fahy fighting to control it. "Holy Mother of God!" he said.

At the undertaker's, the night porter admitted Dillon at the front entrance.

"Mr. Hilton, is it? Miss Myra's expecting you, sir."

"I know where to go."

Dillon went up the stairs, along the corridor and opened the door of the outer office. Myra was waiting for him. "Come in," she said.

She was wearing a black trouser suit and smoking a cigarette. She went and sat behind the desk and tapped the carton with one hand. "There it is. Where's the money?"

Dillon put the briefcase on top of the carton and opened it. He took out fifteen thousand, packet by packet, and dropped it in front of her. That left five thousand dollars in the briefcase, the Walther with the Carswell silencer and the Beretta. He closed the case and smiled.

"Nice to do business with you."

He placed the briefcase on top of the carton and picked it up and she went to open the door for him.

"What are you going to do with that, blow up the Houses of Parliament?"

"That was Guy Fawkes," he said and moved along the passage and went downstairs.

The pavement was frosty as he walked along the street and turned the corner to the van. Billy, waiting anxiously in the shadows, manhandled his BMW up the street past the parked cars until he could see Dillon stop at the Morris van. Angel got the back door open and Dillon put the carton inside. She closed it and they went round and got in beside Fahy.

"Is that it, Sean?"

"That's it, Danny, a fifty-pound box of Semtex with the factory stamp on it all the way from Prague. Now, let's get out of here, we've got a long night ahead of us."

Fahy drove through a couple of side streets and turned onto the main road, and as he joined the traffic stream, Billy went after him on the BMW.

TWELVE

For technical reasons the Lear jet had not been able to get a flight slot out of Aldergrove Airport until five-thirty. It was a quarter-to-seven when Brosnan and Mary landed at Gatwick and a Ministry limousine was waiting. Mary checked on the car phone and found Ferguson at the Cavendish Square flat. He was standing by the fire warming himself when Kim showed them in.

"Beastly weather and a lot more snow on the way, I fear." He sipped some of his tea. "Well, at least you're in one piece, my dear, it must have been an enlivening exprience."

"That's one way of describing it."

"You're absolutely certain it was Dillon?"

"Well, let's put it this way," Brosnan said, "if it wasn't, it was one hell of a coincidence that some one decided to choose that moment to shoot Tommy McGuire. And then there's the bag lady act. Typical Dillon."

"Yes, quite remarkable."

"Admittedly he wasn't on the London plane, sir, coming back," Mary said.

"You mean you *think* he wasn't on the plane," Ferguson corrected her. "For all I know the damned man might have passed himself off as the pilot. He seems capable of anything."

"There is another plane due out to London at eight-thirty, sir. Colonel McLeod said he'd have it thoroughly checked."

"A waste of time." Ferguson turned to Brosnan. "I suspect you agree, Martin?"

"I'm afraid so."

"Now, let's go over the whole thing again. Tell me everything that happened."

When Mary was finished, Ferguson said, "I checked the flight schedules out of Aldergrove a little while ago. There were planes available to Manchester, Birmingham, Glasgow. There was even a flight to Paris at six-thirty. No big deal to fly back to London from there. He'd be here tomorrow."

"And there's always the sea trip," Brosnan reminded him. "The ferry from Larne to Stranraer in Scotland and a fast train from there to London."

"Plus the fact that he could have crossed the Irish border, gone to Dublin and proceeded from there in a dozen different ways," Mary said, "which doesn't get us anywhere."

"The interesting thing is the reason behind his trip," Ferguson said. "He didn't know of your intention to seek out McGuire until last night when Brown revealed the contents of that report to Novikova, and yet he went rushing off to Belfast at the earliest opportunity. Now why would that be?"

"To shut McGuire's mouth," Mary said. "It's an interesting point that our meeting with McGuire was arranged for two o'clock, but we were nearly half an hour early. If we hadn't been, Dillon would have got to him first."

"Even so, he still can't be certain what McGuire told you, if anything."

"But the point was, sir, that Dillon *knew* McGuire had something on him, that's why he went to such trouble to get to him, and it was obviously the information that this man Jack Harvey was his arms supplier in the London campaign of eighty-one."

"Yes, well, when you spoke to me at Aldergrove before you left I ran a check. Detective Inspector Lane of Special Branch tells me that Harvey is a known gangster and on a big scale. Drugs, prostitution, the usual things. The police have been after him for years with little success. Unfortunately, he is now also a very established businessman. Property, clubs, betting shops and so forth."

"What are you trying to say, sir?" Mary asked.

"That it isn't as easy as you might think. We can't just pull Harvey in for questioning because a dead man accused him of something that happened ten years ago. Be sensible, my dear. He'd sit still, keep his mouth shut and a team of the best lawyers in London would have him out on the pavement in record time."

"In other words it would be laughed out of court?" Brosnan said.

"Exactly." Ferguson sighed. "I've always had a great deal of sympathy for the idea that where the criminal classes are concerned, the only way we're going to get any justice is to take all the lawyers out into the nearest square and shoot them."

Brosnan peered out of the window at the lightly falling snow. "There is another way."

"I presume you're referring to your friend Flood?" Ferguson smiled tightly. "Nothing at all to stop you seeking his advice, but I'm sure you'll stay within the bounds of legality."

"Oh, we will, Brigadier, I promise you." Brosnan picked up his coat. "Come on, Mary, let's go and see Harry."

Following the Morris wasn't too much of a problem for Billy on his BMW. The snow was only lying on the sides of the road and the tarmac was wet. There was plenty of traffic all the way out of London and through Dorking. There wasn't quite as much on the Horsham road but still enough to give him cover.

He was lucky when the Morris turned at the Grimethorpe sign because it had stopped snowing and the sky had cleared exposing a half-moon. Billy switched off his headlamp and followed the lights of the Morris at a distance, anonymous in the darkness. When it turned at the Doxley sign, he followed cautiously, pausing on the brow of the hill, watching the lights move in through the farm gate.

He switched off his engine and coasted down the hill, pulling in by the gate and the wooden sign that said Cadge End Farm. He walked along the track through the trees and could see into the lighted interior of the barn across the yard. Dillon, Fahy and Angel were standing beside the Morris. Dillon turned, came out and crossed the yard.

Billy beat a hasty retreat, got back on the BMW and rolled on down the hill, only switching on again when he was some distance from the farm. Five minutes later he was on the main road and returning to London.

In the sitting room Dillon called Makeev at the Paris apartment. "It's me," he said.

"I've been worried," Makeev told him. "What with Tania . . ."

"Tania took her own way out," Dillon said. "I told you. It was her way of making sure they didn't get anything out of her."

"And this business you mentioned, the Belfast trip?"

"Taken care of. It's all systems go, Josef."

"When?"

"The War Cabinet meets at ten o'clock in the morning at Downing Street. That's when we'll hit."

"But how?"

"You can read about it in the papers. The important thing now is for you to tell Michael Aroun to fly down to his Saint-Denis place in the morning. I hope to be flying in sometime in the afternoon."

"As quickly as that?"

"Well I won't be hanging about, will I? What about you, Josef?"

"I should think I might well make the flight from Paris to Saint-Denis with Aroun and Rashid myself."

"Good. Till our next merry meeting, then, and remind Aroun about that second million."

Dillon put the phone down, lit a cigarette, then picked up the phone again and called Grimethorpe airfield. After a while he got an answer.

"Bill Grant here." He sounded slightly drunk.

"Peter Hilton, Mr. Grant."

"Oh, yes," Grant said, "and what can I do for you?"

"That trip I wanted to make to Land's End, tomorrow, I think."

"What time?"

"If you could be ready from noon onwards. Is that all right?"

"As long as the snow holds off. Much more and we could be in trouble."

Grant put the phone down slowly, reached for the bottle of Scotch whisky at his hand and poured a generous measure, then opened the table drawer. There was an old Webley service revolver in there and a box of .38 cartridges. He loaded the weapon, then put it back in the drawer.

"Right, Mr. Hilton, we'll just have to see what you're about, won't we?" and he swallowed the whisky down.

Do I know Jack Harvey?" Harry Flood started to laugh, sitting there behind his desk, and looked up at Mordecai Fletcher. "Do I know him, Mordecai?"

The big man smiled at Brosnan and Mary who were standing there, still with their coats on. "Yes, I think you could say we know Mr. Harvey rather well."

"Sit down, for God's sake, and tell me what happened in Belfast," Flood said.

Which they did, Mary giving him a rapid account of the entire affair. When she was finished, she said, "Do you think it's possible that Harvey was Dillon's weapons supplier in eighty-one?"

"Nothing would surprise me about Jack Harvey. He and his niece, Myra, run a tight little empire that includes every kind of criminal activity. Women, drugs, protection, big-scale armed robbery, you name it, but arms for the IRA?" He looked up at Mordecai. "What do you think?"

"He'd dig up his granny's corpse and sell it if he thought there was a profit in it," the big man said.

"Very apt." Flood turned to Mary. "There's your answer."

"Fine," Brosnan said, "and if Dillon used Harvey in eighty-one, the chances are he's using him again."

Flood said, "The police would never get anywhere with Harvey on the basis of your story, you must know that. He'd walk."

"I should imagine the Professor was thinking of a more subtle approach, like beating it out of the bastard," Mordecai said and slammed a fist into his palm.

Mary turned to Brosnan who shrugged. "What else would you suggest? Nobody's going to get anywhere with a man like Harvey by being nice."

"I have an idea," Harry Flood said. "Harvey's been putting a lot of pressure on me lately to form a partnership. What if I tell him I'd like to have a meeting to discuss things?"

"Fine," Brosnan said, "but as soon as possible. We can't hang around on this, Harry."

Myra was sitting at her uncle's desk going through club accounts when Flood called her.

"Harry," she said, "what a nice surprise."

"I was hoping for a word with Jack."

"Not possible, Harry, he's in Manchester at some sporting club function at the Midland."

"When is he due back?"

"First thing. He's got some business later in the morning, so he's getting up early and catching the seven-thirty breakfast shuttle from Manchester."

"So he should be with you about nine?"

"More like nine-thirty with the morning traffic into London. Look, what is this, Harry?"

"I've been thinking, Myra, maybe I've been stupid. About a partnership, I mean. Jack might have a point. There's a lot we could do if we got together."

"Well, I'm sure he'll be pleased to hear that," Myra said.

"I'll see you then, nine-thirty sharp in the morning with my accountant," Flood told her and rang off.

Myra sat there looking at the phone for a while, then she picked it up, rang the Midland in Manchester and asked for her uncle. Jack Harvey, champagne and more than one brandy inside him, was in excellent humor when he picked up the phone at the hotel's front desk.

"Myra, my love, what's up? A fire or something or a sudden rush of bodies?"

"Even more interesting. Harry Flood's been on the phone."

She told him what had happened and Harvey sobered up instantly. "So he wants to meet at nine-thirty?"

"That's right. What do you think?"

"I think it's a load of cobblers. Why should he suddenly change his mind just like that? No, I don't like it."

"Shall I phone him back and cancel?"

"No, not at all, I'll meet him. We'll just take precautions, that's all."

"Listen," she said, "Hilton, or whatever his bloody name is, called and told me he wanted his stuff. He came round, paid cash and went on his way. Is that all right?"

"Good girl. Now as regards Flood, all I'm saying is be ready to give him the proper reception, just in case. Know what I mean?"

"I think so, Jack," she said. "I think so."

Harry Flood said, "We'll meet outside the Harvey Funeral Emporium just before half-nine in the morning, then. I'll bring Mordecai and you can play my accountant," he told Brosnan.

"What about me?" Mary demanded.

"We'll see."

Brosnan got up and went and stood at the French windows looking at the river. "I wish I knew what the bastard was doing right now," he said.

"Tomorrow, Martin," Flood told him. "All things come to him who waits."

It was around midnight when Billy parked the BMW in the yard at the rear of the Whitechapel premises and went in. He climbed the stairs wearily to Myra's apartment. She heard him coming, got her door open and stood there, light flowing through her short nightdress.

"Hello, sunshine, you made it," she said to Billy.

"I'm bloody frozen," Billy told her.

She got him inside, sat him down and started to unzip his leathers. "Where did he go?"

He reached for a bottle of brandy, poured a large one and got it down. "Only an hour out of London, Myra, but the back of bloody beyond."

He told her everything, Dorking, the Horsham Road, Grimethorpe, Doxley and Cadge End Farm.

"Brilliant, sunshine. What you need is a nice hot bath."

She went into the bathroom and turned on the taps. When she went back into the living room Billy was asleep on the couch, legs sprawled. "Oh, dear," she said, got a blanket to cover him, then went to bed.

When Makeev knocked on the door at Avenue Victor Hugo it was opened by Rashid. "You've news for us?" the young Iraqi asked.

"He seems certain." Makeev disengaged himself. "I only tell you what he has told me."

Aroun turned and stood looking down at the fire, then said to Rashid, "We'll leave at nine from Charles de Gaulle in the Citation. We'll be there in not much more than an hour."

"At your orders," Rashid said.

"You can phone old Alphonse at the Château now. I want him out of there at breakfast time. He can take a few days off. I don't want him around."

Rashid nodded and went out to the study. Makeev said, "Alphonse?"

"The caretaker. At this time of the year he's on his own unless I tell him to bring the servants in from the local village. They're all on retainers."

Makeev said, "I'd like to come with you if that's all right."

"Of course, Josef." Aroun poured two more glasses of cognac. "God forgive me, I know I drink when I should not, but on this occasion." He raised his glass. "To Dillon, and may all go as he intends."

It was one o'clock in the morning and Fahy was working on one of the oxygen cylinders on the bench when Dillon entered the barn.

"How's it going?"

"Fine," Fahy said. "Nearly finished. This one and one to go. How's the weather?"

Dillon walked to the open door. "It's stopped snowing, but more's expected. I checked on the teletext on your television."

Fahy carried the cylinder to the Ford Transit, got inside and fitted it into one of the tubes with great care while Dillon watched. Angel came in with a jug and two mugs in one hand. "Coffee?" she asked.

"Lovely." Her uncle held a mug while she filled it and then did the same for Dillon.

Dillon said, "I've been thinking. The garage where I wanted you to wait with the van, Angel, I'm not sure that's such a good idea now."

Fahy paused, a spanner in his hand and looked up. "Why not?"

"It was where the Russian woman, my contact, kept her car. The police will probably know that. If they're keeping an eye on her flat they may well be checking the garage, too."

"So what do you suggest?"

"Remember where I was staying, the hotel on the Bayswater Road? There's a supermarket next door with a big parking area at the rear. We'll use that. It won't make much of a difference," he said to Angel. "I'll show you when we get there."

"Anything you say, Mr. Dillon." She stayed watching as Fahy finished the fitting of his improvised mortar bomb and moved back to the bench. "I was thinking, Mr. Dillon, this place in France, this Saint-Denis?"

"What about it?"

"You'll be flying straight off there afterwards?"

"That's right."

She said carefully, "Where does that leave us?"

Fahy paused to wipe his hands. "She's got a point, Sean."

"You'll be fine, the both of you," Dillon said. "This is a clean one, Danny, the cleanest I ever pulled. Not a link with you or this place. If it works tomorrow, and it will, we'll be back here by eleven-thirty at the outside and that will be the end of it."

"If you say so," Fahy said.

"But I do, Danny, and if it's the money you're worried about, don't. You'll get your share. The man I'm working for can arrange financial payments anywhere. You can have it here if you want or Europe if that's better."

"Sure and the money was never the big thing, Sean," Fahy said. "You know that. It's just that if there's a chance of something going wrong, any kind of chance." He shrugged. "It's Angel I'm thinking about."

"No need. If there was any risk I'd be the first to say come with me, but there won't be." Dillon put his arm about the girl. "You're excited, aren't you?"

"Me stomach's turning over something dreadful, Mr. Dillon."

"Go to bed." He pushed her toward the door. "We'll be leaving at eight."

"I won't sleep a wink."

"Try. Now go on, that's an order."

She went out reluctantly. Dillon lit another cigarette and turned back to Fahy. "Is there anything I can do?"

"Not a thing, another half hour should do it. Go and put your head down yourself, Sean. As for me, I'm as bad as Angel. I don't think I could. I've found some old biker's leathers for you, by the way," Fahy added. "They're over there by the BSA."

There was a jacket and leather trousers and boots. They'd all seen considerable service and Dillon smiled. "Takes me back to my youth. I'll go and try them on."

Fahy paused and ran a hand over his eyes as if tired. "Look, Sean, does it have to be tomorrow?"

"Is there a problem?"

"I told you I wanted to weld some fins on to the oxygen cylinders to give more stability in flight. I haven't time to do that now." He threw his spanner down on the bench. "It's all too rushed, Sean."

"Blame Martin Brosnan and his friends, not me, Danny," Dillon told him. "They're breathing down my neck. Nearly had me in Belfast. God knows when they might turn up again. No, Danny, it's now or never."

He turned and went out and Fahy picked up his spanner reluctantly and went back to work.

The leathers weren't bad at all and Dillon stood in front of the wardrobe mirror as he zipped up the jacket. "Would you look at that?" he said softly. "Eighteen years old again when the world was young and anything seemed possible."

He unzipped the jacket again, took it off, then opened his briefcase and unfolded the bulletproof waistcoat Tania had given him at their first meeting. He pulled it snugly into place, fastened the Velcro tabs, then put his jacket on again.

He sat on the edge of the bed, took the Walther out of the briefcase, examined it and screwed the Carswell silencer in place. Next he checked the Beretta and put it on the bedside locker close to hand. He put the briefcase in the wardrobe, then switched off the light and lay on the bed, looking up at the ceiling through the darkness.

He never felt emotional, not about anything, and it was exactly the same now, on the eve of the greatest coup of his life. "You're making history with this one, Sean," he said softly. "History."

He closed his eyes and after a while, slept.

It snowed again during the night and just after seven, Fahy walked along the track to check the road. He walked back and found Dillon standing at the farmhouse door eating a bacon sandwich, a mug of tea in his hand.

"I don't know how you can," Fahy told him. "I couldn't eat a thing. I'd bring it straight up."

"Are you scared, Danny?"

"To death."

"That's good. It sharpens you up, gives you that edge that can make all the difference."

They crossed to the barn and stood beside the Ford Transit. "Well, she's as ready as she ever will be," Fahy said.

Dillon put a hand on his shoulder. "You've done wonders, Danny, wonders."

Angel appeared behind them. She was dressed, ready to go, in her old trousers and boots, anorak and sweater and the Tam o' Shanter. "Are we moving?"

"Soon," Dillon said. "We'll get the BSA into the Morris now."

They opened the rear doors of the Morris, put the duckboard on the incline and ran the bike up inside. Dillon lifted it up on its stand and Fahy shoved the duckboard in. He passed a crash helmet through. "That's for you. I'll have one for myself in the Ford." He hesitated. "Are you carrying, Sean?"

Dillon took the Beretta from inside his black leather jacket. "What about you?"

"Jesus, Sean, I always hated guns, you know that."

Dillon slipped the Beretta back in place and zipped up his jacket. He closed the van doors and turned. "Everybody happy?"

"Are we ready for off then?" Angel asked.

Dillon checked his watch. "Not yet. I said we'd leave at eight. We don't want to be too early. Time for another cup of tea."

They went across to the farmhouse and Angel put the kettle on in the kitchen. Dillon lit a cigarette and leaned against the sink watching. "Don't you have any nerves at all?" she asked him. "I can feel my heart thumping."

Fahy called, "Come and see this, Sean."

Dillon went in the living room. The television was on in the corner and the morning show was dealing with the snow which had fallen over London overnight. Trees in the city squares, statues, monuments, were all covered, and many of the pavements.

"Not good," Fahy said.

"Stop worrying, the roads themselves are clear," Dillon said as Angel came in with a tray. "A nice cup of tea, Danny, with plenty of sugar for energy and we'll be on our way."

At the Lowndes Square flat Brosnan was boiling eggs in the kitchen and watching the toast when the phone went. He heard Mary answer it. After a while she looked in. "Harry's on the phone; he'd like a word."

Brosnan took the phone. "How goes it?"

"Okay, old buddy, just checking you were leaving soon."

"How are we going to handle things?"

"We'll just have to play it by ear, but I also think we'll have to play rough."

"I agree," Brosnan said.

"I'm right in assuming that would give Mary a problem?"

"I'm afraid so."

"Then she definitely can't go in. Leave it to me. I'll handle it when we get there. See you soon."

Brosnan put the phone down and went back to the kitchen where Mary had put out the eggs and toast and was pouring tea. "What did he have to say?" she asked.

"Nothing special. He was just wondering what the best approach would be."

"And I suppose you think that would be to batter Harvey over the head with a very large club?"

"Something like that."

"Why not thumbscrews, Martin?"

"Why not, indeed?" He reached for the toast. "If that's what it takes."

The early morning traffic on the Horsham road to Dorking and onwards to London was slower than usual because of the weather. Angel and Dillon led the way in the Morris, Fahy close behind in the Ford Transit. The girl was obviously tense, her knuckles white as she gripped the wheel too tightly, but she drove extremely well. Epsom then Kingston and on toward the river, crossing the Thames at Putney Bridge. It was already nine-fifteen as they moved along the Bayswater Road toward the hotel.

"Over there," Dillon said. "There's the supermarket. The entrance to the car park is down the side." She turned in, changing to the lowest gear, crawling along as she went into the car park, which was already quite full. "There at the far end," Dillon said, "just the spot."

There was a huge trailer parked there, protected by a plastic sheet that was itself covered by snow. She parked on the other side of it and Fahy stopped nearby. Dillon jumped out, pulling on his crash helmet, went round and opened the doors. He put the duckboard in the right position, got inside and eased the BSA out, Angel helping. As he threw a leg over the seat she shoved the duckboard back inside the van and closed the doors. Dillon switched on and the BSA responded sweetly, roaring into life. He glanced at his watch. It was nine-twenty. He pulled the machine up on its stand and went over to Fahy in the Ford.

"Remember, the timing is crucial and we can't go round and round in circles at Whitehall, somebody might get suspicious. If we're too early, try and delay things on the Victoria Embankment. Pretend you've broken down and I'll stop as if I'm assisting, but from the Embankment up Horse Guards Avenue to the corner with Whitehall will only a take a minute, remember that."

"Jesus, Sean." Fahy looked terrified.

"Easy, Danny, easy," Dillon said. "It'll be fine, you'll see. Now get moving."

He swung a leg over the BSA again and Angel said, "I prayed for you last night, Mr. Dillon."

"Well, that's all right, then. See you soon," and he rode away and joined up behind the Ford.

THIRTEEN

Harry Flood and Mordecai were waiting in the Mercedes, Salter at the wheel, when a taxi drew up outside the undertaker's in White chapel and Brosnan and Mary got out. They picked their way carefully through the snow on the pavement and Flood opened the door for them to get in.

He glanced at his watch. "Just coming up to nine-thirty. We might as well go straight in."

He took a Walther from his breast pocket and checked the slider. "You want something, Martin?" he asked.

Brosnan nodded. "It's a thought."

Mordecai opened the glove compartment, took out a Browning and passed it over the seat. "That suit you, Professor?"

Mary said, "For God's sake, anybody would think you were trying to start the Third World War."

"Or prevent it starting," Brosnan said. "Have you ever thought of that?"

"Let's move," Flood said. Brosnan followed him out and Mordecai emerged from the other side. As Mary tried to follow, Flood said, "Not this time, lover. I told Myra I'd be bringing my accountant, which takes care of Martin, and Mordecai goes everywhere with me. That's all they're expecting."

"Now look here," she said. "I'm the case officer on this, the official representative of the Ministry."

"Well, bully for you. Take care of her, Charlie," Flood told Salter and he turned to the entrance where Mordecai was already ringing the bell.

The porter who admitted them smiled obsequiously. "Morning, Mr. Flood. Mr. Harvey presents his compliments and wonders whether you'd mind stepping into the waiting room for a few moments. He's only just arrived from Heathrow."

"That's fine," Flood said and followed him through.

The waiting room was suitably subdued, with dark leather chairs, rust-colored walls and carpet. The lighting was mainly provided by fake candles, and music suitable to the establishment played softly over a speaker system.

"What do you think?" Brosnan asked.

"I think he's just in from Heathrow," Flood said. "Don't worry."

Mordecai peered out through the entrance and across to one of the Chapels of Rest. "Flowers, that's what I find funny about these places. I always associate death with flowers."

"I'll remember that when your turn comes to go," Flood said. " 'No flowers by request.' "

It was approximately nine-forty as the Ford Transit pulled into a lay-by on the Victoria Embankment, and Fahy's hands were sweating. In the rear mirror, he saw Dillon pull the BSA up on its stand and walk toward him. He leaned in the window.

"Are you okay?"

"Fine, Sean."

"We'll stay here for as long as we can get away with it. Fifteen minutes would be ideal. If a traffic warden comes, just pull away and I'll follow you. We'll drive along the Embankment for half a mile, turn and come back."

"Right, Sean." Fahy's teeth were chattering.

Dillon took out a packet of cigarettes, put two in his mouth, lit them and passed one to Fahy. "Just to show you what a romantic fool I am," and he started to laugh.

When Harry Flood, Brosnan and Mordecai went into the outer office, Myra was waiting for them. She was wearing the black trouser suit and boots and carried a sheaf of documents in one hand.

"You look very businesslike, Myra," Flood told her.

"So I should, Harry, the amount of work I do around here." She kissed him on the cheek and nodded to Mordecai. "Hello, muscles." Then she looked Brosnan over. "And this is?"

"My new accountant, Mr. Smith."

"Really?" She nodded. "Jack's waiting." She opened the door and led the way into the office.

The fire burned brightly in the grate; it was warm and comfortable. Harvey sat behind the desk smoking his usual cigar. Billy was over to the left sitting on the arm of the sofa, his raincoat casually draped across his knee.

"Jack," Harry Flood said. "Nice to see you."

"Is that so?" Harvey looked Brosnan over. "Who's this?"

"Harry's new accountant, Uncle Jack." Myra moved round the desk and stood beside him. "This is Mr. Smith."

Harvey shook his head. "I've never seen an accountant that looked like Mr. Smith, have you, Myra?" He turned back to Flood. "My time's valuable, Harry, what do you want?"

"Dillon," Harry Flood said. "Sean Dillon."

"Dillon?" Harvey looked totally mystified. "And who the Christ is Dillon?"

"Small man," Brosnan said. "Irish, although he can pass as anything he wants. You sold him guns and explosives in nineteen eighty-one."

"Very naughty of you, that, Jack," Harry Flood said. "He blew up large parts of London and now we think he's at it again."

"And where else would he go for his equipment except his old chum, Jack Harvey?" Brosnan said. "I mean, that's logical, isn't it?"

Myra's grip tightened on her uncle's shoulder and Harvey, his face flushed, said, "Billy!"

Flood put up a hand. "I'd just like to say that if that's a sawed-off he's got under the coat, I hope it's cocked."

Billy fired instantly through the raincoat, catching Mordecai in the left thigh as the big man drew his pistol. Flood's Walther came out of his pocket in one smooth motion and he hit Billy in the chest, sending him back over the sofa, the other barrel discharging, some of the shot catching Flood in the left arm.

Jack Harvey had the desk drawer open, his hand came up clutching a Smith & Wesson and Brosnan shot him very deliberately through the shoulder. There was chaos for a moment, the room full of smoke and the stench of cordite.

Myra leaned over her uncle, who sank back into the chair, moaning. Her face was set and angry. "You bastards!" she said.

Flood turned to Mordecai. "You okay?"

"I will be when Dr. Aziz has finished with me, Harry. The little bastard was quick."

Flood, still holding the Walther, clutched his left arm, blood seeping between his fingers. He glanced at Brosnan. "Okay, let's finish this."

He took two paces to the desk and raised the Walther directly at Harvey. "I'll give it to you right between the eyes if you don't tell us what we want to know. What about Sean Dillon?"

"Screw you!" Jack Harvey said.

Flood lowered the Walther for a moment and then took deliberate aim and Myra screamed. "No, for God's sake, leave him alone. The man you want calls himself Peter Hilton. He was the one Uncle Jack dealt with in eighty-one. He used another name then. Michael Coogan."

"And more recently?"

"He bought fifty pounds of Semtex. Picked it up last night and paid cash. I had Billy follow him home on his BMW."

"And where would that be?"

"Here." She picked a sheet of paper up from the desk. "I'd written it all down for Jack."

Flood looked it over and passed it to Brosnan, managing a smile in spite of the pain. "Cadge End Farm, Martin. Sounds promising. Let's get out of here."

He walked to the door and Mordecai limped out ahead of him, dripping blood. Myra had crossed to Billy, who started to groan loudly. She turned and said harshly, "I'll get you for this, the lot of you."

"No, you won't, Myra," Harry Flood told her. "If you're sensible you'll put it all down to experience and give your personal doctor a call," and he turned and went out followed by Brosnan.

It was just before ten as they got into the Mercedes. Charlie Salter said, "Jesus, Harry, we're getting blood all over the carpets."

"Just drive, Charlie, you know where to go."

Mary looked grim. "What happened in there?"

"This happened." Brosnan held up the sheet of paper with the directions to Cadge End Farm.

"My God," Mary said as she read it. "I'd better call the Brigadier."

"No, you don't," Flood said. "I figure this is our baby, considering the trouble we've gone to and the wear and tear; wouldn't you agree, Martin?"

"Definitely."

"So, the first thing we do is call at the quiet little nursing home in Wapping run by my good friend Dr. Aziz so he can take care of Mordecai and see to my arm. After that, Cadge End."

As Fahy turned out of the traffic on the Victoria Embankment into Horse Guards Avenue past the Ministry of Defence building he was sweating in spite of the cold. The road itself was clear and wet from the constant traffic, but there was snow on the pavements and the trees and the buildings on either hand. He could see Dillon in his rear-view mirror, a sinister figure in his black leathers on the BSA, and then it was the moment of truth and everything seemed to happen at once.

He pulled in at the junction of Horse Guards Avenue and Whitehall on the angle he'd worked out. On the other side of the road at Horse Guards Parade there were two troopers of the Household Cavalry, mounted as usual, with drawn sabres.

Some distance away, a policeman turned and saw the van. Fahy turned off the engine, switched on the timers and pulled on his crash helmet. As he got out and locked the door the policeman called to him and hurried forward. Dillon swerved in on the BSA, Fahy swung a leg over the pillion seat and they were away, sliding past the astonished policeman in a half-circle and moving fast up toward Trafalgar Square. As Dillon joined the traffic around the square, the first explosion sounded. There was another, perhaps two, and then it all seemed to become one with the greater explosion of the Ford Transit self-destructing.

Dillon kept on going, not too fast, through Admiralty Arch and along the Mall. He was at Marble Arch and turning along the Bayswater Road within ten minutes and rode into the car park of the supermarket soon after. As soon as she saw them, Angel was out of the van. She got the doors open and put the duckboard in place. Dillon and Fahy shoved the bike inside and slammed the doors.

"Did it work?" Angel demanded. "Did everything go all right?"

"Just leave it for now. Get in and drive," Dillon told her. She did as she was told and he and Fahy got in beside her. A minute later and they were turning into the Bayswater Road. "Just go back the way we came and not too fast," Dillon said.

Fahy switched on the radio, fiddling his way through the various BBC stations. "Nothing," he said. "Bloody music and chat."

"Leave it on," Dillon told him. "And just be patient. You'll hear all about it soon enough."

He lit a cigarette and sat back, whistling softly.

In the small theater at the nursing home just off Wapping High Street, Mordecai Fletcher lay on the operating table while Dr. Aziz, a gray-haired Indian in round steel spectacles, examined his thigh.

"Harry, my friend, I thought you'd given this kind of thing up," he said. "But here we are again like a bad Saturday night in Bombay."

Flood was sitting in a chair, jacket off, while a young Indian nurse attended to his arm. She had cut the shirt sleeve off and was swabbing the wound. Brosnan and Mary stood watching.

Flood said to Aziz, "How is he?"

"He'll have to stay in for two or three days. I can only get some of this shot out under anaesthetic, and an artery is severed. Now let's look at you."

He held Flood's arm and probed gently with a pair of small pincers. The nurse held an enamel bowl. Aziz dropped one piece of shot in it, then two. Flood winced with pain. The Indian found another. "That could be it, Harry, but we'll need an X ray."

"Just bandage it up for now and give me a sling," Flood said. "I'll be back later."

"If that's what you want."

He bandaged the arm skillfully, assisted by the nurse, then opened a cupboard and found a pack of morphine ampules. He jabbed one in Flood's arm.

"Just like Vietnam, Harry," Brosnan said.

"It will help with the pain," Aziz told Flood, as the nurse eased him into his jacket. "I'd advise you to be back no later than this evening, though."

The nurse fastened a sling behind Flood's neck. As she put his overcoat across his shoulders, the door burst open and Charlie Salter came in. "All hell's broken loose, just heard it on the radio. Mortar attack on Ten Downing Street."

"Oh, my God!" Mary Tanner said.

Flood showed her through the door and she turned to Brosnan. "Come on, Martin, at least we know where the bastard's gone."

The War Cabinet had been larger than usual that morning, fifteen including the Prime Minister. It had just begun its meeting in the Cabinet Room at the back of Number Ten Downing Street when the first mortar, curving in a great arc of some two hundred yards from the Ford Transit van at the corner of Horse Guards Avenue and Whitehall, landed. There was a huge explosion, so loud that it was clearly audible in the office of Brigadier Charles Ferguson at the Ministry of Defence overlooking Horse Guards Avenue.

"Christ!" Ferguson said, and like most people in the Ministry, rushed to the nearest window.

At Downing Street in the Cabinet Room the specially strengthened windows cracked, but most of the blast was absorbed by the special blast-proof net curtains. The first bomb left a crater in the garden, uprooting a cherry tree. The other two landed further off-target in Mountbatten Green, where some outside broadcast vehicles were parked. Only one of those exploded, but at the same moment, the van blew up as Fahy's self destruct device went into action. There was surprisingly little panic in the Cabinet Room. Everyone crouched, some seeking the protection of the table. There was a draught of cold air from shattered windows, voices in the distance.

The Prime Minister stood up and actually managed a smile. With incredible calm he said, "Gentlemen, I think we had better start again somewhere else," and he led the way out of the room.

Mary and Brosnan were in the back of the Mercedes, Harry Flood in the passenger seat beside Charlie Salter, who was making the best time he could through heavy traffic.

Mary said, "Look, I need to speak to Brigadier Ferguson. It's essential."

They were crossing Putney Bridge. Flood turned and looked at Brosnan, who nodded. "Okay," Flood said. "Do what you like."

She used her car phone, ringing the Ministry of Defence, but Ferguson wasn't there. There was some confusion as to his whereabouts. She left the car phone number with the control room and put the phone down.

"He'll be running round half-demented like everyone else," Brosnan said and lit a cigarette.

Flood said to Salter, "Okay, Charlie, Epsom, then Dorking and the Horsham Road beyond that, and step on it."

The BBC newsflash which came over the radio in the Morris van was delivered in the usual calm and unemotional way. There had been a bomb attack on Number Ten Downing Street at approximately ten A.M. The building had sustained some damage, but the Prime Minister and members of the War Cabinet meeting together at that time were all safe.

The van swerved as Angel sobbed. "Oh, God, no!"

Dillon put a hand on the wheel. "Steady girl," he said calmly. "Just stick to your driving."

Fahy looked as if he was going to be sick. "If I'd had time to put those fins on the cylinders it would have made all the difference. You were in too much of a hurry, Sean. You let Brosnan rattle you and that was fatal."

"Maybe it was," Dillon said, "but at the end of the day all that matters is we missed."

He took out a cigarette, lit it and suddenly started to laugh helplessly.

Aroun had left Paris at nine-thirty, flying the Citation jet himself, Rashid having the rating qualifying him as the second pilot necessary under flight regulations. Makeev, in the cabin behind them, was reading the morning paper when Aroun called in to the control tower at Maupertus Airport at Cherbourg to clear for his landing on the private strip at Saint-Denis.

The controller gave him his clearance and then said, "We've just had a newsflash. Bomb attack on the British Cabinet at Downing Street in London."

"What happened?" Aroun demanded.

"That's all they're saying at the moment."

Aroun smiled excitedly at Rashid, who'd also heard the message. "Take over and handle the landing." He scrambled back to the cabin and sat opposite Makeev. "Newsflash just in. Bomb attack on Ten Downing Street."

Makeev threw down his paper. "What happened?"

"That's all for the moment." Aroun looked up to heaven, spreading his hands. "Praise be to God."

Ferguson was standing beside the outside broadcast vans at Mountbatten Green with Detective Inspector Lane and Sergeant Mackie. It was snowing slightly and a police forensic team were making a careful inspection of Fahy's third mortar bomb, the one which hadn't exploded.

"A bad business, sir," Lane said. "To use an old-fashioned phrase, right at the heart of Empire. I mean, how can they get away with this kind of thing?"

"Because we're a democracy, Inspector, because people have to get on with their lives, and that means we can't turn London into some Eastern-European style armed fortress."

A young constable came across with a mobile phone and whispered to Mackie. The sergeant said, "Excuse me, Brigadier, it's urgent. Your office has been trying to contact you. Captain Tanner's been on the line."

"Give it to me." Ferguson took the phone. "Ferguson here. I see. Give me the number." He gestured to Mackie who took out pad and pencil and wrote it down as Ferguson dictated it.

The Mercedes was passing through Dorking when the phone went. Mary picked it up at once. "Brigadier?"

"What's going on?" he demanded.

"The mortar attack on Number Ten. It has to be Dillon. We found out he picked up fifty pounds of Semtex in London last night, supplied by Jack Harvey."

"Where are you now?"

"Just leaving Dorking, sir, taking the Horsham Road, Martin and me and Harry Flood. We've got an address for Dillon."

"Give it to me." He nodded to Mackie again and repeated it aloud so the sergeant could write it down.

Mary said, "The road's not good, sir, with the snow, but we should be at this Cadge End place in half an hour."

"Fine. Nothing rash, Mary, my love, but don't let the bastard get away. We'll get backup to you as soon as possible. I'll be in my car, so you've got the phone number."

"All right, sir."

She put the phone down and Flood turned. "Okay?"

"Backup on the way, but we're not to let him get away."

Brosnan took the Browning from his pocket and checked it. "He won't," he said grimly. "Not this time."

Ferguson quietly filled in Lane on what had happened. "What do you think Harvey will be up to, Inspector?"

"Receiving treatment from some bent doctor in a nice little private nursing home somewhere, sir."

"Right, have that checked out and if it's as you say, don't interfere. Just have them watched, but this Cadge End place is where we go and fast. Now go and organize the cars."

Lane and Mackie hurried away and as Ferguson made to follow them the Prime Minister appeared round the corner of the building. He was wearing a dark overcoat, the Home Secretary and several aides with him. He saw Ferguson and came over.

"Dillon's work, Brigadier?"

"I believe so, Prime Minister."

"Rather close." He smiled. "Too close for comfort. A remarkable man, this Dillon."

"Not for much longer, Prime Minister, I've just had an address for him at last."

"Then don't let me detain you, Brigadier. Carry on, by all means."

Ferguson turned and hurried away.

The track through the trees at Cadge End was covered with more snow since they had left. Angel bumped along it to the farmyard and turned into the barn. She switched off and it seemed terribly quiet.

Fahy said, "Now what?"

"A nice cup of tea, I think." Dillon got out, went round and opened the van doors and pulled out the duckboard. "Help me, Danny." They got the BSA out, and he lifted it up on its stand. "Performed brilliantly. You did a good job there, Danny."

Angel had gone ahead and as they followed her, Fahy said, "You haven't a nerve in your body, have you, Sean?"

"I could never see the point."

"Well, I have, Sean, and what I need isn't bloody tea, it's whisky."

He went in the living room and Dillon went up to his bedroom. He found an old holdall and packed it quickly with his suit, trenchcoat, shirts, shoes and general bits and pieces. He checked his wallet. About four hundred pounds left in there. He opened his briefcase, which held the five thousand dollars remaining from his expense money and the Walther with the Carswell silencer on the end. He cocked the gun, leaving it ready for action, put it back in the briefcase together with the Jersey driving license and the pilot's license. He unzipped his jacket, took out the Beretta and checked it, then he slipped it into the waistband of his leather trousers at the rear, tucking the butt under the jacket.

When he went downstairs carrying the holdall and briefcase Fahy was standing looking at the television set. There were shots of Whitehall in the snow, Downing Street and Mountbatten Green.

"They just had the Prime Minister on inspecting the damage. Looked as if he didn't have a worry in the world."

"Yes, his luck is good," Dillon said.

Angel came in and handed him a cup of tea. "What happens now, Mr. Dillon?"

"You know very well what happens, Angel. I fly off into the wild blue yonder."

"To that Saint-Denis place?"

"That's right."

"Okay for you, Sean, and us left here to carry the can," Fahy said.

"And what can would that be?"

"You know what I mean."

"Nobody has any kind of a line on you, Danny. You're safe till Doomsday. I'm the one the buggers are after. Brosnan and his girlfriend, and Brigadier Ferguson, I'm the one they'll put this down to."

Fahy turned away and Angel said, "Can't we go with you, Mr. Dillon?"

He put down his cup and put his hands on her shoulders. "There's no need, Angel. I'm the one running, not you or Danny. They don't even know you exist."

He went across to the phone, picked it up and rang Grimethorpe airfield. Grant answered straight away. "Yes, who is it?"

"Peter Hilton, old boy." Dillon reverted to his public-school persona. "Okay for my flight? Not too much snow?"

"It's clear down at the other end in the West Country," Grant said. "Might be tricky taking off here, though. When were you thinking of going?"

"I'll be round in half an hour. That all right?" Dillon asked.

"I'll expect you."

As Dillon put the phone down, Angel cried, "No, Uncle Danny."

Dillon turned and found Fahy standing in the doorway with a shotgun in both hands. "But it's not all right with me, Sean," and he thumbed back the hammers.

"Danny boy," Dillon spread his hands. "Don't do this."

"We're going with you, Sean, and that's an end to it."

"Is it your money you're worried about, Danny? Didn't I tell you the man I'm working for can arrange payments anywhere?"

Fahy was trembling now, the shotgun shaking in his hand. "No, it's not the money." He broke a little then. "I'm frightened, Sean. Jesus, when I saw that on the television. If I'm caught, I'll spend the rest of my life in jail. I'm too old, Sean."

"Then why did you come in with me in the first place?"

"I wish I knew. Sitting here, all these years, bored out of my mind. The van, the mortars, it was just something to do, a fantasy, and then you turned up and made it real."

"I see," Dillon said.

Fahy raised the shotgun. "So that's it, Sean. If we don't go, you don't go."

Dillon's hand at his back found the butt of the Beretta, his arm swung and he shot Fahy twice in the heart sending him staggering out into the hall. He hit the wall on the other side and slid down.

Angel screamed, ran out and knelt beside him. She stood up slowly, staring at Dillon. "You've killed him."

"He didn't give me any choice."

She turned, grabbed at the front door, and Dillon went after her. She dashed across the yard into one of the barns and disappeared. Dillon moved inside the entrance and stood there listening. There was a rustling somewhere in the loft and straw dust floated down.

"Angel, listen to me. I'll take you with me."

"No, you won't. You'll kill me like me Uncle Danny. You're a bloody murderer." Her voice was muffled.

For a moment, he extended his left arm pointing the Beretta up to the loft. "And what did you expect? What did you think it was all about?"

There was silence. He turned, hurried across to the house, stepped over Fahy's body. He put the Beretta back in his waistband at the rear, picked up his briefcase and the holdall containing his clothes, went back to the barn and put them on the passenger seat of the Morris.

He tried once more. "Come with me, Angel. I'd never harm you, I swear it." There was no reply. "To hell with you, then," he said, got behind the wheel and drove away along the track.

It was some time later, when everything was very quiet, that Angel came down the ladder and crossed to the house. She sat beside her uncle's body, back against the wall, a vacant look on her face and didn't move, not even when she heard the sound of a car driving into the courtyard outside.

FOURTEEN

The runway at Grimethorpe was completely covered with snow. The hangar doors were closed and there was no sign of either of the planes. Smoke was drifting up from the iron stovepipe, the only sign of life as Dillon drove up to the huts and the old tower and braked to a halt. He got out with his holdall and briefcase and walked to the door. When he went in, Bill Grant was standing by the stove drinking coffee.

"Ah, there you are, old man. Place looked deserted," Dillon said. "I was beginning to worry."

"No need." Grant, who was wearing old black flying overalls and leather flying jacket, reached for a bottle of Scotch and poured some into his mug of coffee.

Dillon put down his holdall, but still carried the briefcase in his right hand. "I say, is that wise, old chap?" he asked in his most public-school voice.

"I never was particularly wise, old chap." Grant seemed to be mocking him now. "That's how I ended up in a dump like this."

He crossed to his desk and sat down behind it. Dillon saw that there was a chart on the desk, the English Channel area, the Normandy coast, the Cherbourg approaches, the chart Dillon had checked out with Angel that first night.

"Look, I'd really like to get going, old chap," he said. "If it's the rest of the fee you're worried about I can pay cash." He held up the briefcase. "I'm sure you've no objection to American dollars."

"No, but I do have an objection to being taken for a fool." Grant indicated the chart. "Land's End my arse. I saw you checking this out the other night with the girl. English Channel and French coast. What I'd like to know is what you're trying to get me into."

"You're really being very silly," Dillon said.

Grant pulled open a drawer in the desk and took out his old Webley revolver. "We'll see, shall we? Now just put the briefcase on the desk and stand back while I see what we've got."

"Certainly, old chap, no need for violence." Dillon stepped close and put the briefcase on the desk. At the same moment he pulled the Beretta from his waistband at the rear, reached across the table and shot Grant at point-blank range.

Grant went backwards over the chair. Dillon put the Beretta back in place, folded the chart, put it under his arm, picked up his holdall and briefcase and went out, trudging through the snow to the hangar. He went in through the Judas, unbolted the great sliding door inside so that the two aircraft stood revealed. He chose the Cessna Conquest for no better reason than that it was the nearest. The stairs to the door were down. He threw the holdall and the briefcase inside, went up, pulling the door behind him.

He settled in the left-hand pilot's seat and sat there studying the chart. Approximately a hundred and forty miles to the airstrip at Saint-Denis. Unless he encountered problems with headwinds, in a plane like this he should do it in forty-five minutes. No flight plan filed, of course, so he would be a bogey on somebody's radar screen, but that didn't matter. If he went straight out to sea over Brighton, he would be lost in mid-Channel before anyone knew what was going on. There was a question of the approach to Saint-Denis, but if he hit the coast at six hundred feet, with any luck he would be below the radar screen operated at Maupertus Airport at Cherbourg.

He put the chart on the other seat where he could see it and switched on, firing first the port engine, then the starboard. He took the Conquest out of the hangar and paused to make a thorough cockpit check. As Grant had boasted, the fuel tanks were full. Dillon strapped himself in and taxied across the apron and down to the end of the runway.

He turned into the wind and started forward. He was immediately aware of the drag from the snow, boosted power and gave it everything he could, easing back the column. The Conquest lifted and started to climb. He banked to turn toward his heading for Brighton and saw a black limousine down below moving out of the trees toward the hangars.

"Well I don't know who the hell you are," he said softly, "but if it's me you're after you're too late," and he turned the Conquest in a great curve and started for the coast.

Angel sat at the kitchen table, holding the mug of coffee Mary had given her. Brosnan and Harry Flood, his arm in the sling, stood listening and Charlie Salter leaned on the door.

"It was Dillon and your uncle at Downing Street, is that what you're saying?" Mary asked.

Angel nodded. "I drove the Morris with Mr. Dillon's motorbike in it. He followed Uncle Danny, he was in the Ford Transit." She looked dazed. "I drove them back from Bayswater and Uncle Danny was afraid, afraid of what might happen."

"And Dillon?" Mary asked.

"He was flying away from the airfield up the road, Grimethorpe. He made arrangements with Mr. Grant who runs the place. Said he wanted to go to Land's End, but he didn't."

She sat clutching the mug, staring into space. Brosnan said gently. "Where did he want to go, Angel, do you know?"

"He showed me on the chart. It was in France. It was down along the coast from Cherbourg. There was a landing strip marked. A place called Saint-Denis."

"You're sure?" Brosnan said.

"Oh, yes. Uncle Danny asked him to take us too, but he wouldn't, then Uncle Danny got upset. He came in with the shotgun and then . . ." She started to sob.

Mary put her arms around her. "It's all right now, it's all right."

Brosnan said, "Was there anything else?"

"I don't think so." Angel still looked dazed. "He offered Uncle Danny money. He said the man he was working for could arrange payments any-where in the world."

"Did he say who the man was?" Brosnan asked.

"No, he never did." She brightened. "He did say something about work-ing for the Arabs the first time he came."

Mary glanced at Brosnan. "Iraq?"

"I always did think that was a possibility."

"Right, let's get going," Flood said. "Check out this Grimethorpe place. You stay here with the kid, Charlie," he said to Salter, "until the cavalry arrives. We'll take the Mercedes," and he turned and led the way out.

In the Great Hall at Saint-Denis, Rashid, Aroun and Makeev stood drinking champagne, waiting for the television news.

"A day for rejoicing in Baghdad," Aroun said. "The people will know now how strong their President is."

The screen filled with the announcer who spoke briefly, then the pictures followed. Whitehall in the snow, the Household Cavalry guards, the rear of Ten Downing Street, curtains hanging from smashed windows, Mountbatten Green and the Prime Minister inspecting the damage. The three men stood in shocked silence.

It was Aroun who spoke first. "He has failed," he whispered. "All for nothing. A few broken windows, a hole in the garden."

"The attempt was made," Makeev protested. "The most sensational attack on the British Government ever mounted, and at the seat of power."

"Who gives a damn?" Aroun tossed his champagne glass into the fireplace. "We needed a result and he hasn't given us one. He failed with the Thatcher woman and he failed with the British Prime Minister. In spite of all your big talk, Josef, nothing but failure."

He sat down in one of the high-backed chairs at the dining table, and Rashid said, "A good thing we didn't pay him his million pounds."

"True," Aroun said, "but the money is the least of it. It's my personal position with the President which is at stake."

"So what are we going to do?" Makeev demanded.

"Do?" Aroun looked up at Rashid. "We're going to give our friend Dillon a very warm reception on a cold day, isn't that so, Ali?"

"At your orders, Mr. Aroun," Rashid said.

"And you, Josef, you're with us in this?" Aroun demanded.

"Of course," Makeev said because there was little else he could say. "Of course." When he poured another glass of champagne, his hands were shaking.

As the Mercedes came out of the trees at Grimethorpe, the Conquest banked and flew away. Brosnan was driving, Mary beside him, Harry Flood in the back.

Mary leaned out of the window. "Do you think that's him?"

"Could be," Brosnan said. "We'll soon find out."

They drove past the open hangar with the Navajo Chieftain inside and stopped at the huts. It was Brosnan, first through the door, who found Grant. "Over here," he said.

Mary and Flood joined him. "So it *was* Dillon in that plane," she commented.

"Obviously," Brosnan said grimly.

"Which means the bastard's slipped the lot of us," Flood said.

"Don't be too sure," Mary told him. "There was another plane in that hangar," and she turned and ran out.

"What goes on?" Flood demanded as he followed Brosnan out.

"Amongst other things, the lady happens to be an Army Air Corps pilot," Brosnan said.

When they reached the hangar, the Airstair door of the Navajo was open and Mary was inside in the cockpit. She got up and came out. "Full tanks."

"You want to follow him?" Brosnan demanded.

"Why not? With any luck we'll be right up his tail." She looked fierce and determined, opened her handbag and took out her cellnet phone. "I'm not having this man get away with what he's done. He needs putting down once and for all."

She moved outside, pulled up the aerial on her phone and dialed the number of Ferguson's car.

The limousine, leading a convoy of six unmarked Special Branch cars, was just entering Dorking when Ferguson received her call. Detective Inspector Lane was sitting beside him, Sergeant Mackie in front beside the driver.

Ferguson listened to what Mary had to say and made his decision. "I totally agree. You must follow Dillon at your soonest to this Saint-Denis place. What do you require from me?"

"Speak to Colonel Hernu at Service Five. Ask him to discover who owns the airstrip at Saint-Denis so we know what we're getting into. He'll want to come himself, obviously, but that will take time. Ask him to deal with the authorities at Maupertus Airport at Cherbourg. They can act as a link for us when I get close to the French coast."

"I'll see to that at once, and you take down this radio frequency." He gave her the details quickly. "That will link you directly to me at the Ministry of Defence. If I'm not back in London they'll patch you through."

"Right, sir."

"And Mary, my love," he said, "take care. Do take care."

"I'll do my best, sir." She closed her cellnet phone, put it in her handbag and went back into the hangar.

"Are we on our way, then?" Brosnan asked.

"He's going to talk to Max Hernu in Paris. He'll arrange a link for us with Maupertus Airport at Cherbourg to let us know what we're getting into." She smiled tightly. "So let's get going. It would be a shame to get there and find he'd moved on."

She climbed up into the Navajo and moved into the cockpit. Harry Flood went next and settled himself into one of the cabin seats. Brosnan followed, pulled up the Airstair door, then went and settled in the co-pilot's seat beside her. Mary switched on first one engine, then the other, completed her cockpit check, then took the Navajo outside. It had started to snow, a slight wind whipping it across the runway in a curtain as she taxied to the far end and turned.

"Ready?" she asked.

Brosnan nodded. She boosted power, the Navajo roared along the runway and lifted up into the gray sky as she pulled back the control column.

Max Hernu was sitting at his desk in his office at DGSE headquarters going through some papers with Inspector Savary when Ferguson was put through to him. "Charles, exciting times in London this morning."

"Don't laugh, old friend, because the whole mess could well land in your lap," Ferguson said. "Number one, there's a private airstrip at a place called Saint-Denis down the coast from Cherbourg. Who owns it?"

Hernu put a hand over the phone and said to Savary, "Check the computer. Who owns a private airstrip at Saint-Denis on the Normandy coast?" Savary rushed out and Hernu continued. "Tell me what all this is about, Charles."

Which Ferguson did. When he was finished, he said, "We've got to get this bastard this time, Max, finish him off for good."

"I agree, my friend." Savary hurried in with a piece of paper and passed it to Hernu who read it and whistled. "The airstrip in question is part of the Château Saint-Denis estate which is owned by Michael Aroun."

"The Iraqi billionaire?" Ferguson laughed harshly. "All is explained. Will you arrange clearance for Mary Tanner with Cherbourg and also see that she has that information?"

"Of course, my friend. I'll also arrange a plane at once and get down there myself with a Service Five team."

"Good hunting to all of us," Charles Ferguson said and rang off.

There was a great deal of low cloud over the Normandy coast. Dillon, still a few miles out to sea, came out of it at about a thousand feet and went lower, approaching the coastline at about five hundred feet over a turbulent whitecapped sea.

The trip had gone like a dream, no trouble at all. Navigation had always been his strong point, and he came in off the sea and saw Château Saint-Denis perched on the edge of the cliffs, the airstrip a few hundred yards beyond. There was some snow, but not as much as there had been in England. There was a small prefabricated hangar, the Citation jet parked outside. He made a single pass over the house, turned into the wind and dropped his flaps for a perfect landing.

Aroun and Makeev were sitting by the fire in the Great Hall when they heard the sound of the plane overhead. Rashid hurried in and opened the

French windows. They joined him on the snow-covered terrace, Aroun holding a pair of binoculars. Three hundred yards away on the airstrip, the Cessna Conquest landed and taxied toward the hangar, turning to line itself up beside the Citation.

"So, he's here," Aroun said.

He focused the binoculars on the plane, saw the door open and Dillon appear. He passed the binoculars to Rashid who had a look, then handed them to Makeev.

"I'll go down and pick him up in the Land-Rover," Rashid said.

"No you won't." Aroun shook his head. "Let the bastard walk through the snow, a suitable welcome, and when he gets here, we'll be waiting for him."

Dillon left the holdall and the briefcase just inside the Conquest when he climbed down. He walked across to the Citation and lit a cigarette, looking it over. It was a plane he'd flown many times in the Middle East, a personal favorite. He finished the cigarette and lit another. It was bitterly cold and very quiet, fifteen minutes and still no sign of any transport.

"So that's the way it is?" he said softly and walked back to the Conquest.

He opened the briefcase, checked the Walther and the Carswell silencer and eased the Beretta at he small of his back, then he picked up the hold-all in one hand, the briefcase in the other, crossed the runway and followed the track through the trees.

Fifty miles out to sea, Mary identified herself to the tower at Maupertus Airport. She got a reply instantly.

"We've been expecting you."

"Am I clear to land at Saint-Denis airstrip?" she asked.

"Things are closing in rapidly. We had a thousand feet only twenty minutes ago. It's six hundred now at the most. Advise you try here."

Brosnan heard all this on the other headphones and turned to her in alarm. "We can't do that, not now."

She said to Maupertus, "It's most urgent that I see for myself."

"We have a message for you from Colonel Hernu."

"Read it," she said.

"The Saint-Denis airstrip is part of Château Saint-Denis and owned by Mr. Michael Aroun."

"Thank you," she said calmly. "Out." She turned to Brosnan. "You heard that? Michael Aroun."

"One of the wealthiest men in the world," Brosnan said, "and Iraqi."

"It all fits," she said.

He unbuckled his seatbelt. "I'll go and tell Harry."

Dillon trudged through the snow toward the terrace at the front of the house and the three men watched him come. Aroun said, "You know what to do, Josef."

"Of course." Makeev took a Makarov automatic from his pocket, made sure it was ready for action and put it back.

"Go and admit him, Ali," Aroun told Rashid.

Rashid went out. Aroun went to the sofa by the fire and picked up a newspaper. When he went to the table to sit down, he placed the newspaper in front of him, took a Smith & Wesson revolver from his pocket and slipped it under.

Rashid opened the door as Dillon came up the snow-covered steps. "Mr. Dillon," the young captain said. "So you made it?"

"I'd have appreciated a lift," Dillon told him.

"Mr. Aroun is waiting inside. Let me take your luggage."

Dillon put the case down and held on to the briefcase. "I'll keep this," he smiled. "What's left of the cash."

He followed Rashid across the enormous stretch of black and white tiles and entered the Great Hall where Aroun waited at the table. "Come in, Mr. Dillon," the Iraqi said.

"God bless all here," Dillon told him, walked across to the table and stood there, the briefcase in his right hand.

"You didn't do too well," Aroun said.

Dillon shrugged. "You win some, you lose some."

"I was promised great things. You were going to set the world on fire."

"Another time perhaps." Dillon put the briefcase on the table.

"Another time." Aroun's face was suddenly contorted with rage. "Another time? Let me tell you what you have done. You have not only failed me, you have failed Saddam Hussein, President of my country. I pledged my word to him, my word, and because of your failure, my honor is in shreds."

"What do you want me to do, say I'm sorry?"

Rashid was sitting on the edge of the table, swinging a leg. He said to Aroun. "In the circumstances, a wise decision not to pay this man."

Dillon said, "What's he talking about?"

"The million in advance that you instructed me to deposit in Zurich."

"I spoke to the manager. He confirmed it had been placed in my account," Dillon said.

"On my instructions, you fool. I have millions on deposit at that bank. I only had to threaten to transfer it elsewhere to bring him to heel."

"You shouldn't have done that," Dillon said calmly. "I always keep my word, Mr. Aroun. I expect others to keep theirs. A matter of honor."

"Honor? You talk to me of honor." Aroun laughed out loud. "What do you think of that, Josef?"

Makeev, who had been standing behind the door, stepped out, the Makarov in his hand. Dillon half-turned and the Russian said, "Easy, Sean, easy."

"Aren't I always, Josef?" Dillon said.

"Hands on head, Mr. Dillon," Rashid told him. Dillon complied. Rashid unzipped the biker's jacket, checked for a weapon and found nothing. His hands went round Dillon's waist and discovered the Beretta. "Very tricky," he said and put it on the table.

"Can I have a cigarette?" Dillon put a hand in his pocket and Aroun threw the newspaper aside and picked up the Smith & Wesson. Dillon produced a cigarette pack. "All right?" He put one in his mouth and Rashid gave him a light. The Irishman stood there, the cigarette dangling from the corner of his mouth. "What happens now? Does Josef blow me away?"

"No, I reserve that pleasure for myself," Aroun said.

"Mr. Aroun, let's be reasonable." Dillon flicked the catches on his briefcase and started to open it. "I'll give you back what's left of the operating money and we'll call it quits. How's that?"

"You think money can make this right?" Aroun asked.

"Not really," Dillon said and took the Walther with the Carswell silencer from the briefcase and shot him between the eyes. Aroun went over, his chair toppling, and Dillon, turning, dropped to one knee and hit Makeev twice as the Russian got off one wild shot.

Dillon was up and turning, the Walther extended, and Rashid held his hands at shoulder height. "No need for that, Mr. Dillon, I could be useful."

"You're damn right you could be," Dillon said.

There was a sudden roaring of an aircraft passing overhead. Dillon grabbed Rashid by the shoulder and pushed him to the French windows. "Open them," he ordered.

"All right." Rashid did as he was told and they went out on the terrace from where they could see the Navajo landing in spite of the mist rolling in.

"Now who might that be?" Dillon asked. "Friends of yours?"

"We weren't expecting anyone, I swear it," Rashid said.

Dillon shoved him back in and put the end of the Carswell silencer to the side of his neck. "Aroun had a nice private safe hidden safely away in the apartment at Avenue Victor Hugo in Paris. Don't tell me he didn't have the same here."

Rashid didn't hesitate. "It's in the study, I'll show you."

"Of course you will," Dillon said and shoved him toward the door.

Mary taxied the Navajo along the strip and lined it up to the Conquest and the Citation. She killed the engine. Brosnan was already into the cabin and had the door open. He went down quickly and turned to give Flood a hand. Mary followed. It was very quiet, wind lifting the snow in a flurry.

"The Citation?" Mary said. "It can't be Hernu, there hasn't been enough time."

"It must be Aroun's," Brosnan told her.

Flood pointed to where Dillon's footsteps, clearly visible in the snow, led toward the track to the wood, the château standing proudly on the other side. "That's our way," he said and started forward, Brosnan and Mary following.

FIFTEEN

The study was surprisingly small and paneled in bleached oak, the usual oil paintings of past aristocrats on the walls. There was an antique desk with a chair, an empty fireplace, a television with a fax machine and shelves lined with books on one wall.

"Hurry it up," Dillon said and he sat on the end of the desk and lit a cigarette.

Rashid went to the fireplace and put his hand to the paneling on the right-hand side. There was obviously a hidden spring. A panel opened outwards revealing a small safe. Rashid twirled the dial in the center backwards and forwards, then tried the handle. The safe refused to open.

Dillon said, "You'll have to do better."

"Just give me time." Rashid was sweating. "I must have got the combination wrong. Let me try again."

He tried, pausing only to wipe sweat from his eyes with his left hand, and then there was a click that even Dillon heard.

"That's it," Rashid said.

"Good," Dillon told him. "Let's get on with it." He extended his left arm, the Walther pointing at Rashid's back.

Rashid opened the safe, reached inside and turned, a Browning in his hand. Dillon shot him in the shoulder spinning him around and shot him again in the back. The young Iraqi bounced off the wall, fell to the floor and rolled on his face.

Dillon stood over him for a moment. "You never learn, you people," he said softly.

He looked inside the safe. There were neat stacks of hundred-dollar bills, French francs, English fifty-pound notes. He went back to the Great Hall and got his briefcase. When he came back he opened it on the desk and filled it with as much money as he could from the safe, whistling softly to himself. When the briefcase could hold no more he snapped it shut. It was at that moment he heard the front door open.

Brosnan led the way up the snow-covered steps, the Browning Mordecai had given him in his right hand. He hesitated for a moment and then tried the front door. It opened to his touch.

"Careful," Flood said.

Brosnan peered in cautiously, taking in the vast expanse of black and white tiles, the curving stairway. "Quiet as the grave. I'm going in."

As he started forward, Flood said to Mary, "Stay here for the moment," and went after him.

The double doors to the Great Hall stood fully open and Brosnan saw Makeev's body at once. He paused, then moved inside, the Browning ready. "He's been here, all right. I wonder who this is?"

"Another on the far side of the table," Flood told him.

They walked round and Brosnan dropped to one knee and turned the body over. "Well, well," Harry Flood said, "even I know who that is. It's Michael Aroun."

Mary moved into the entrance hall, closing the door behind her, and watched the two men go into the Great Hall. There was a slight eerie creaking on her left and she turned and saw the open door to the study. She took the Colt .25 from her handbag and went forward.

As she approached the door, the desk came into view and she also saw Rashid's body on the floor beside it. She took a quick step inside in a kind of reflex action and Dillon moved from behind the door, tore the Colt from her hand and slipped it into a pocket.

"Well, now," he said, "isn't this an unexpected pleasure?" and he rammed the Walther into her side.

But why would he kill him?" Flood asked Brosnan. "I don't understand that."

"Because the bastard cheated me. Because he wouldn't pay his debts."

They turned and found Mary at the door, Dillon behind her, the Walther in his left hand, the briefcase in the other. Brosnan raised the Browning. Dillon said, "On the floor and kick it over, Martin, or she dies. You know I mean it."

Brosnan put the Browning down carefully then kicked it across the parquet floor.

"Good," Dillon said. "That's much better." He pushed Mary toward them and sent the Browning sliding into the outer hall with the toe of his boot.

"Aroun we recognize, but as a matter of interest, who was this one?" Brosnan indicated Makeev.

"Colonel Josef Makeev, KGB, Paris Station. He was the fella that got me into this. A hardliner who didn't like Gorbachev or what he's been trying to do."

"There's another body in the study," Mary told Brosnan.

"An Iraqi Intelligence captain named Ali Rashid, Aroun's minder," Dillon said.

"Gun for sale, is that what it's come down to, Sean?" Brosnan nodded to Aroun. "Why did you really kill him?"

"I told you, because he wouldn't pay his debts. A matter of honor, Martin. I always keep my word, you know that. He didn't. How in the hell did you find me?"

"A lady called Myra Harvey had you followed last night. That led us to Cadge End. You're getting careless, Sean."

"So it would seem. If it's any consolation to you, the only reason we didn't blow the entire British War Cabinet to hell was because you and your friends got too close. That pushed me into doing things in a hurry, always fatal. Danny wanted to fit stabilizing fins on those oxygen cylinders that we used as mortar bombs. It would have made all the difference as regards their accuracy, but there wasn't time, thanks to you."

"I'm delighted to hear it," Brosnan said.

"And how did you find me here?"

"That poor, wretched young woman told us," Mary said.

"Angel? I'm sorry about her. A nice kid."

"And Danny Fahy and Grant at the airfield? You're sorry about them, too?" Brosnan demanded.

"They shouldn't have joined."

"Belfast and the Tommy McGuire shooting, it was you?" Mary said.

"One of my better performances."

"And you didn't come back on the London train," she added. "Am I right?"

"I flew to Glasgow, then got the shuttle to London from there."

"So what happens now?" Brosnan asked.

"To me?" Dillon held up the briefcase. "I've got a rather large sum in cash that was in Aroun's safe in here and a choice of airplanes. The world's my oyster. Anywhere, but Iraq."

"And us?" Harry Flood looked ill, his face drawn with pain and he eased his left arm in the sling.

"Yes, what about us?" Mary demanded. "You've killed everyone else, what's three more?"

"But I don't have any choice," Dillon said patiently.

"No, but I do, you bastard."

Harry Flood's right hand slipped inside the sling, pulled out the Walther he had been concealing in there and shot him twice in the heart. Dillon staggered back against the paneling, dropping his briefcase and slid to the floor, turning over in a kind of convulsion. Suddenly he was still and lay there, facedown, the Walther with the Carswell silencer still clutched in his left hand.

Ferguson was in his car and halfway back to London when Mary called him using the phone in Aroun's study.

"We got him, sir," she said simply when he replied.

"Tell me about it."

So she did, Michael Aroun, Makeev, Ali Rashid, everything. When she was finished, she said, "So that's it, sir."

"So it would appear. I'm on my way back to London, just passed through Epsom. I left Detective Inspector Lane to clear things up at Cadge End."

"What now, Brigadier?"

"Get back on your plane and leave at once. French territory, remember. I'll speak to Hernu now. He'll take care of it. Now go and get your plane. Contact me in mid-flight and I'll give you landing arrangements."

The moment she was off the line he phoned Hernu's office at DGSE's headquarters. It was Savary who answered. "Ferguson here, have you got an arrival time for Colonel Hernu at Saint-Denis?"

"The weather isn't too good down there, Brigadier. They're landing at Maupertus Airport at Cherbourg and will proceed onwards by road."

"Well what he's going to find there rivals the last act of Macbeth," Ferguson said, "so let me explain and you can forward the information."

Visibility was no more than a hundred yards at the airstrip, mist drifting in from the sea as Mary Tanner taxied the Navajo to the end of the runway, Brosnan sitting beside her. Flood leaned over from his seat to peer into the cockpit.

"Are you sure we can make it?" he asked.

"It's landing in this stuff that's the problem, not taking off," she said and took the Navajo forward into the gray wall. She pulled the column back and started to climb and gradually left the mist behind and turned out to sea, leveling at nine thousand feet. After a while she put on the automatic pilot and sat back.

"You all right?" Brosnan asked.

"Fine. Slightly drained, that's all. He was so—so elemental. I can't believe he's gone."

"He's gone all right," Flood said cheerfully, a half-bottle of Scotch in one hand, a plastic cup held awkwardly in the other, for he had discovered the Navajo's bar box.

"I thought you never drank?" Brosnan said.

"Special occasion." Flood raised his cup. "Here's to Dillon. May he roast in hell."

Dillon was aware of voices, the front door closing. When he surfaced it was like coming back from death to life. The pain in his chest was excruciating, but that was hardly surprising. The shock effect of being hit at such close quarters was considerable. He examined the two ragged holes in his biker's jacket and unzipped it, putting the Walther on the floor. The bullets Flood had fired at him were embedded in the Titanium and nylon vest Tania had given him that first night. He unfastened the Velcro tabs, pulled the vest away and threw it down, then he picked up the Walther and stood.

He'd been genuinely unconscious for a while, but that was a common experience when shot at close quarters and wearing any kind of body armor. He went to the drinks cabinet and poured a brandy, looking round the room at the bodies, his briefcase still on the floor where he had dropped it, and when he heard the roar of the Navajo's engine starting up, he saw it all. Everything was being left to the French, which was logical. It was their patch, after all, and that probably meant Hernu and the boys from Action Service were on their way.

Time to go, but how? He poured another brandy and thought about it. There was Michael Aroun's Citation jet, but where could he fly without leaving some sort of trail? No, the best answer, as usual, was Paris. He'd always been able to fade into the woodwork there. There was the barge and the apartment over the warehouse at Rue de Helier. Everything he would ever need.

He finished the brandy, picked up the briefcase and hesitated, looking down at the Titanium waistcoat with the two rounds embedded in it. He smiled and said softly, "You can chew on that, Martin."

He pulled the French windows wide and stood on the terrace for a moment, breathing deeply on the cold air, then he went down the steps to the lawn and walked quickly across to the trees, whistling softly.

Mary tuned her radio to the frequency Ferguson had given her. She was picked up by the radio room at the Ministry of Defence immediately, a sophisticated scrambling device was brought into operation and then she was patched through to him.

"Well out over the Channel, sir, heading for home."

"We'll make that Gatwick," he said. "They'll be expecting you. Hernu has just phoned me from his car on the way to Saint-Denis. Exactly as I thought. The French don't want this kind of mess on their patch. Aroun, Rashid and Makeev died in a car crash, Dillon goes straight into a pauper's grave. No name, just a number. Similar sort of thing at our end over that chap Grant."

"But how, sir?"

"One of our doctors has already been alerted to certify him as having died of a heart attack. We've had our own establishment to handle this sort of thing since the Second World War. Quiet street in North London. Has its own crematorium. Grant will be five pounds of gray ash by tomorrow. No autopsy."

"But Jack Harvey?"

"That's slightly different. He and young Billy Watson are still with us, in bed at a private nursing home in Hampstead. Special Branch are keeping an eye on them."

"Do I get the impression that we're not going to do anything?"

"No need. Harvey doesn't want to do twenty years in prison for working with the IRA. He and his motley crew will keep their mouths shut. So, by the way, will the KGB."

"And Angel?"

"I thought she might come and stay with you for a while. I'm sure you can handle her, my dear. The woman's touch and all that." There was a pause and then he said, "Don't you see, Mary, it never happened, not any of it."

"That's it, then, sir?"

"That's it, Mary. See you soon."

Brosnan said, "What did the old sod have to say?"

So she told them. When she was finished, Flood laughed out loud. "So it never happened? That's marvelous."

Mary said, "What now, Martin?"

"God knows." He leaned back and closed his eyes.

She turned to Harry Flood who toasted her and emptied his cup. "Don't ask me," he said.

She sighed, switched off the auto pilot, took control of the plane herself and flew onwards toward the English coast.

Ferguson, writing quickly, completed his report and closed the file. He got up and walked to the window. It was snowing again as he looked out to the left toward the junction of Horse Guards Avenue and Whitehall where it had all happened. He was tired, more tired than he had been in a long time, but there was still one thing to do. He turned back to his desk, was reaching for the scrambler phone when it rang.

Hernu said, "Charles, I'm at Saint-Denis and we've got trouble."

"Tell me," Ferguson said and already his stomach was hollow.

"Three bodies only. Makeev, Rashid and Michael Aroun."

"And Dillon?"

"No sign, just a very fancy bulletproof vest on the floor with two Walther rounds embedded in it."

"Oh, my God," Ferguson said, "the bastard's still out there."

"I'm afraid so, Charles. I'll put the word out to the police, of course, and all the usual agencies, but I can't say I'm particularly hopeful."

"Why would you be?" Ferguson asked. "We haven't succeeded in putting a hand on Dillon in twenty years, so why should it be any different now?" He took a deep breath. "All right, Max, I'll be in touch."

He went back to the window and stood looking out at the falling snow. No point in calling the Navajo. Mary, Brosnan and Flood would hear the bad news soon enough, but there was still one thing to be done. He turned reluctantly to his desk, picked up the scrambler, pausing for only a moment before phoning Downing Street and asking to speak to the Prime Minister.

It was toward evening, snow falling heavily as Pierre Savigny, a farmer from the village of St. Just outside Bayeux, drove carefully along the main road toward Caen in his old Citroën truck. He almost didn't see the man in biker's leathers who stepped into the road, an arm raised.

The Citroën skidded to a halt and Dillon opened the passenger door and smiled. "Sorry about that," he said in his impeccable French, "but I've been walking for quite a while."

"And where would you be going on a filthy evening like this?" Savigny asked, as Dillon climbed into the passenger seat.

"Caen. I'm hoping to catch the night train to Paris. My motorbike broke down. I had to leave it in a garage in Bayeux."

"Then you're in luck, my friend," Savigny said. "I'm on my way to Caen now. Potatoes for tomorrow's market." He moved into gear and drove away.

"Excellent." Dillon put a cigarette in his mouth, flicked his lighter and sat there, the briefcase on his knees.

"You're a tourist then, monsieur?" Savigny asked as he increased speed.

Sean Dillon smiled softly. "Not really," he said. "Just passing through," and he leaned back in the seat and closed his eyes.

Thunder Point

For my daughter Hannah

Whether Reichsleiter Martin Bormann, Head of the Nazi Party Chancellery and Secretary to Adolf Hitler, the most powerful man in Germany after the Führer, actually escaped from the Führer Bunker in Berlin in the early hours of May 2, 1945, or died trying to cross the Weidendammer Bridge has always been a matter of conjecture, Josef Stalin believed him to be alive; Jacob Glas, Bormann's chauffeur, swore that he saw him in Munich after the war; and Eichmann told the Israelis he was still alive in 1960. Simon Wiesenthal, the greatest Nazi hunter of them all, always insisted he was alive, and then there was a Spaniard who had served in the German SS who insisted that Bormann had left Norway in a U-boat bound for South America at the very end of the war . . .

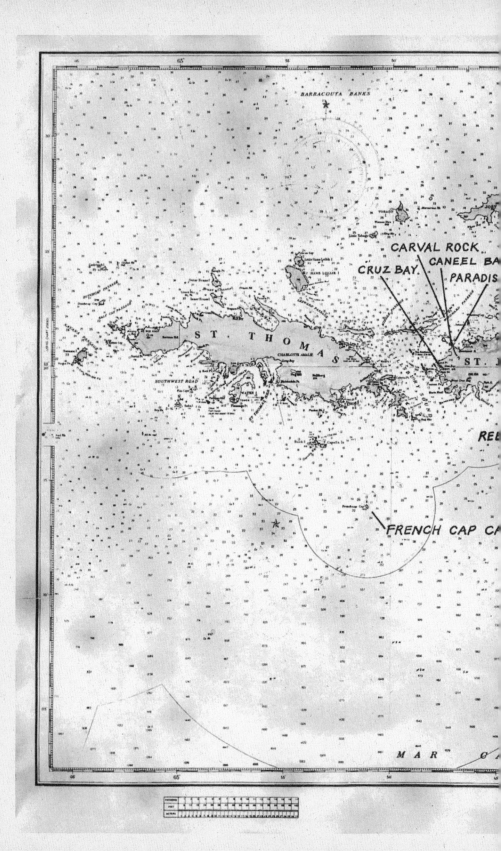

CARVAL ROCK.

CANEEL BA

CRUZ BAY.

PARADIS

ST. THOMAS

CHARLOTTE AMALIE

SOUTHWEST ROAD

BARRACOUTA BANKS

ST.

REE

FRENCH CAP CA

MAR   CA

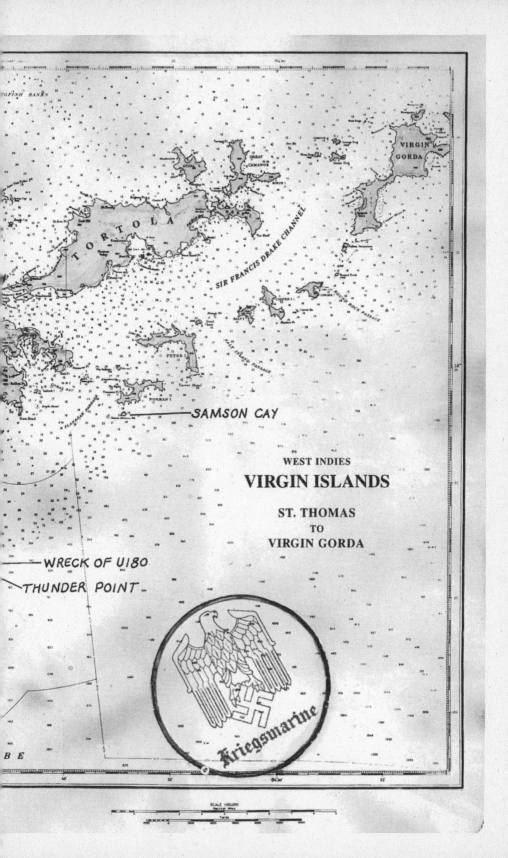

VIRGIN
GORDA

TORTOLA

SIR FRANCIS DRAKE CHANNEL

PETER

SAMSON CAY

WEST INDIES
VIRGIN ISLANDS

ST. THOMAS
TO
VIRGIN GORDA

WRECK OF U180

THUNDER POINT

Kriegsmarine

SCALE 1:100,000

Prologue

The city seemed to be on fire, a kind of hell on earth, the ground shaking as shells exploded, and as dawn came, smoke drifted in a black pall. In the eastern half of Berlin, the Russians were already formally in control, and refugees, carrying what they could of their belongings, moved along Wilhelmstrasse close to the Reich Chancellery in the desperate hope of somehow reaching the West and the Americans.

Berlin was doomed, everyone knew that, and the panic was dreadful to see. Close by the Chancellery, a group of SS was stopping everyone they saw in uniform. Unless such individuals could account for themselves, they were immediately accused of desertion in the face of the enemy and hung from the nearest lamp post or tree. A shell screamed in, fired at random by Russian artillery. There were cries of alarm and people scattered.

The Chancellery itself was battered and defaced by the bombardment, particularly at the rear, but deep in the earth protected by thirty meters of concrete, the Führer and his staff still worked on in a subterranean world that was totally self-supporting, still in touch by radio and radio-telephone with the outside world.

The rear of the Reich Chancellery was also damaged, pock-marked by shell fire, and the once lovely gardens were a wilderness of uprooted trees and the occasional shell hole. One blessing: there was little air activity, low cloud and driving rain having cleared the sky of aircraft for the moment.

The man who walked in that ruined garden on his own seemed curiously indifferent to what was happening, didn't even flinch when another shell landed on the far side of the Chancellery. As the rain increased in force, he simply turned up his collar, lit a cigarette and held it in cupped hand as he continued to walk.

He was not very tall, with heavy shoulders and a coarse face. In a crowd of laborers or dock workers, he would have faded into the background, nothing special, not memorable to the slightest degree. Everything about him was nondescript, from the shabby ankle-length greatcoat to the battered peaked cap.

A nobody of any importance, that would have been the conclusion, and yet this man was Reichsleiter Martin Bormann, Head of the Nazi Party Chancellery and Secretary to the Führer, the most powerful man in Germany after Hitler himself. The vast majority of the German people had never even heard of him, and even fewer would have recognized him if they saw him. But then he had organized his life that way, deliberately choosing to be an anonymous figure wielding his power only from the shadows.

But that was all over, everything was finished, and this was the final end of things. The Russians could be here at any moment. He'd tried to persuade Hitler to leave for Bavaria, but the Führer had refused, had insisted, as he had publicly declared for days, that he would commit suicide.

An SS Corporal came out of the Bunker entrance and hurried toward him. He gave the Nazi salute. "Herr Reichsleiter, the Führer is asking for you."

"Where is he?"

"In his study."

"Good, I'll come at once." As they walked toward the entrance several shells landed on the far side of the Chancellery again, debris lifting into the air. Bormann said, "Tanks?"

"I'm afraid so, Herr Reichsleiter, less than half a mile away now."

The SS Corporal was young and tough, a seasoned veteran. Bormann clapped him on the shoulder. "You know what they say? Everything comes to he who waits."

He started to laugh, and the young corporal laughed with him as they started down the concrete steps.

When Bormann knocked on the study door and went in the Führer was seated behind the desk, examining some maps with a magnifying glass. He glanced up.

"Ah, Bormann, there you are. Come in. We don't have much time."

"I suppose not, my Führer," Bormann said uncertainly, unsure of what was meant.

"They'll be here soon, Bormann, the damned Russians, but they won't find me waiting. Stalin would like nothing better than to exhibit me in a cage."

"That can never be, my Führer."

"Of course not. I shall commit suicide, and my wife will accompany me on that dark journey."

He was referring to his mistress, Eva Braun, whom he had finally married at midnight on the twenty-eighth.

"I had hoped that even now you would reconsider whether or not to make a break for Bavaria," Bormann told him, but more for something to say than anything else.

"No, my mind is made up, but you, my old friend, you have work to do."

Hitler stood up and shuffled round the table, the man who only three years previously had controlled Europe from the Urals in the east to the English Channel. Now, his cheeks were sunken, his jacket appeared too large, and when he took Bormann's hands, his own shook with palsy. And yet the power was there still and Bormann was moved.

"Anything, my Führer."

"I knew I could depend on you. The Kamaradenwerk, Action for Comrades." Hitler shuffled back to his chair. "That is your task, Bormann, to see that the National Socialism survives. We have hundreds of millions in Switzerland and elsewhere in the world in gold in numbered accounts, but you have details of those."

"Yes, my Führer."

Hitler reached under his desk and produced a rather strange-looking briefcase, dull silver in appearance. Bormann noted the Kriegsmarine insignia etched in the top right-hand corner.

Hitler flicked it open. "The keys are inside along with a number of items which will prove useful to you over the years." He held up a buff envelope. "Details of similar accounts in various South American countries and the United States. We have friends in all those places only waiting to hear from you."

"Anything else, my Führer?"

Hitler held up a large file. "I call this the Blue Book. It contains the names of many members of the British establishment, both in the ranks of the aristocracy and Parliament, who are friendly to our cause. A number of our American friends are there also. And last, but not least," he passed another envelope across. "Open it."

The paper was of such quality that it was almost like parchment. It had been written in English in July 1940, in Estoril in Portugal, and was addressed to the Führer. The signature at the bottom was that of his Royal

Highness the Duke of Windsor. It was in English and the content was quite simple. He was agreeing to take over the throne of Great Britain in the event of a successful invasion.

"The Windsor Protocol," Hitler said simply.

"Can this be true?" Bormann asked in astonishment.

"Himmler himself vouched for it. He had the Duke approached by his agents in Portugal at the time."

Or said that he had, Bormann told himself. That devious little animal had always been capable of anything. He replaced the document in its envelope and handed it to the Führer, who replaced it and the other items in the briefcase. "This is standard issue to the U-boat captains at the moment. Completely self-sealing, water- and fireproof." The Führer pushed it across to Bormann. "Yours now." He gazed in space for a moment in reverie. "What a swine Himmler is to try and make a separate peace with the Allies, and now I hear that Mussolini and his girlfriend were murdered by partisans in northern Italy, strung up by their ankles."

"A mad world." Bormann waited for a moment, then said, "One point, my Führer, how do I leave? We are now surrounded here."

Hitler came back to life. "Quite simple. You will fly out using the East-West Avenue. As you know, Field Marshal Ritter von Greim and Hannah Reitsch got away in an Arado just after midnight yesterday. I spoke personally to the Commander of the Luftwaffe Base at Rechlin." He glanced at a paper on his desk. "A young man, a Captain Neumann, volunteered to fly in a Feiseler Storch during the night. He arrived safely and is now waiting your orders."

"But where, my Führer?" Bormann asked.

"In that huge garage at Goebbels' house near the Brandenburg Gate. From there he will fly you to Rechlin and refuel for the onward flight to Bergen in Norway."

"Bergen?" Bormann asked.

"From where you will proceed by submarine to South America, Venezuela to be precise. You'll be expected. One stop on the way. You'll be expected there too, but all the details are in here." He handed him an envelope. "You'll also find my personal signed authorization in there giving you full powers in my name and several false passports."

"So, I leave tonight?" Bormann asked.

"No, you leave within the next hour," Hitler said calmly. "Because of the driving rain and low clouds there is no air cover at the moment. Captain Neumann thinks he could achieve total surprise, and I agree. I have every confidence you will succeed."

There could be no arguing with that and Bormann nodded. "Of course, my Führer."

"Then there only remains one more thing," Hitler said. "You'll find someone in the bedroom. Bring him in."

The man Bormann found in there wore the uniform of a Lieutenant General in the SS. There was something familiar about him and Bormann felt acutely uncomfortable for some reason.

"My Führer," the man said and gave Hitler a Nazi salute.

"Note the resemblance, Bormann?" Hitler asked.

It was then that Bormann realized why he'd felt so strange. It was true, the General did have a look of him. Not perfect, but it was undeniably there.

"General Strasser will stay here in your place," Hitler said. "When the general breakout occurs he will leave with the others. He can stay out of the way until then. In the confusion and darkness of leaving it's hardly likely anyone will notice. They'll be too concerned with saving their own skins." He turned to Strasser. "You will do this for your Führer?"

"With all my heart," Strasser said.

"Good, then you will now exchange uniforms. You may use my bedroom." He came round the desk and took both of Bormann's hands in his. "I prefer to say goodbye now, old friend. We will not meet again."

Cynical as he was by nature, Bormann felt incredibly moved. "I will succeed, my Führer, my word on it."

"I know you will."

Hitler shuffled out, the door closed behind him and Bormann turned to Strasser. "Right, let's get started."

Precisely half an hour later Bormann left the Bunker by the exit into Hermann Goering Strasse. He wore a heavy leather military overcoat over his SS uniform and carried a military holdall, which held the briefcase and a change of civilian clothes. In one pocket he carried a silenced Mauser pistol, and a Schmeisser machine pistol was slung across his chest. He moved along the edge of the Tiergarten, aware of people everywhere, mainly refugees, crossed by the Brandenburg Gate, and arrived at Goebbels' house quite quickly. Like most properties in the area it had suffered damage, but the vast garage building seemed intact. The sliding doors were closed, but there was a small Judas gate, which Bormann opened cautiously.

It was dark in there and a voice called, "Stay where you are, hands high."

Lights were switched on and Bormann found a young man in the uniform of a Captain in the Luftwaffe and a flying jacket standing by the wall, a pistol in his hand. The small Feiseler Storch spotter plane stood in the center of the empty garage.

"Captain Neumann?"

"General Strasser?" The young man looked relieved and holstered his pistol. "Thank God, I've been expecting Ivans ever since I got here."

"You have orders?"

"Of course. Rechlin to refuel and then Bergen. A distinct pleasure, actually."

"Do you think we stand a chance of getting away?"

"There's nothing up there to shoot us down at the moment. Filthy weather. Only ground fire to worry about." He grinned. "Is your luck good, General?"

"Always."

"Excellent. I'll start up, you get in and we'll taxi across the road to the Brandenburg Gate. From there I'll take off toward the Victory Column. They won't be expecting that because the wind is in the wrong direction."

"Isn't that dangerous?" Bormann asked.

"Absolutely." Neumann climbed up into the cabin and started the engine.

There was broken glass and rubble in the street and the Storch bumped its way along, passing many astonished refugees, moved across the Brandenburg Gate and turned toward the Victory Column in the distance. The rain was driving down.

Neumann said, "Here we go," and boosted power.

The Storch roared down the center of the road, here and there people fleeing before it, and suddenly they were airborne and turning to starboard to avoid the Victory Column. Bormann was not even aware of any ground fire.

"You must live right, Herr Reichsleiter," the young pilot said.

Bormann turned to him sharply. "What did you call me?"

"I'm sorry if I've said the wrong thing," Neumann said. "But I met you at an award ceremony once in Berlin."

Bormann decided to leave it for the moment. "Don't worry about it." He looked down at the flames and smoke below as Berlin burned, the Russian artillery keeping up a constant bombardment. "Truly a scene from hell."

"Twilight of the Gods, Reichsleiter," Neumann said. "All we need is Wagner to provide suitable music," and he took the Storch up into the safety of the dark clouds.

It was the second part of the journey which was particularly arduous, cutting across the east coast of Denmark and then up across the Skagerrak, refueling at a small Luftwaffe base at Kristiansand for the final run. It was pitch-dark when they reached Bergen and cold, very cold, a little sleet mixed with the rain as they landed. Neumann had contacted the base half an hour earlier to notify their arrival. There were lights in the control tower and the buildings, a poor blackout. The German occupying forces in Norway knew that the end was near, that there was no possibility of an Allied invasion. It simply wasn't necessary. An aircraftsman with a torch in each hand guided them to a parking place, then walked away. Bormann could see a Kubelwagen driving toward them. It stopped on the other side of the parked aircraft of which there were several.

Neumann switched off. "So, we made it, Herr Reichsleiter. Rather different from Berlin."

"You did well," Bormann said. "You're a fine pilot."

"Let me get your bag for you."

Bormann got down to the ground and Neumann passed him the bag. Bormann said, "Such a pity you recognized me," and he took the silenced Mauser from his greatcoat pocket and shot him through the head.

The man standing beside the Kubelwagen was a naval officer and wore the white-topped cap affected by U-boat Commanders. He was smoking a cigarette and he dropped it to the ground and stamped on it as Bormann approached.

"General Strasser?"

"That's right," Bormann told him.

"Korvettenkapitän Paul Friemel." Friemel gave him a half-salute. "Commanding U180."

Bormann tossed his bag into the rear of the Kubelwagen and eased himself into the passenger seat. As the other man got behind the wheel, the Reichsleiter said, "Are you ready for sea?"

"Absolutely, General."

"Good, then we'll leave at once."

"At your orders, General," Friemel said and drove away.

Bormann took a deep breath, he could smell the sea on the wind. Strange, but instead of feeling tired he was full of energy and he lit a cigarette and leaned back, looking up at the stars and remembering Berlin only as a bad dream.

1992

ONE

Just before midnight it started to rain as Dillon pulled in the Mercedes at the side of the road, switched on the interior light and checked his map. Klagenfurt was twenty miles behind, which meant that the Yugoslavian border must be very close now. There was a road sign a few yards further on and he took a torch from the glove compartment, got out of the car and walked toward it, whistling softly, a small man, no more than five feet four or five with hair so fair that it was almost white. He wore an old black leather flying jacket with a white scarf at his throat and dark blue jeans. The sign showed Fehring to the right and five kilometers further on. He showed no emotion, simply took a cigarette from a silver case, lit it with an old-fashioned Zippo lighter and returned to the car.

It was raining very heavily now, the road badly surfaced, mountains rising to his right, and he switched on the radio and listened to a little night music, occasionally whistling the tune until he came to gates on the left and slowed to read the sign. It badly needed a fresh coat of paint, but the inscription was clear enough. Fehring Aero Club. He turned in through the gates and followed a track, lurching over potholes until he saw the airfield below.

He switched off his lights and paused. It seemed a poor sort of place, a couple of hangars, three huts and a rickety excuse for a control tower, but there was light streaming out from one of the hangars and from the windows of the end hut. He moved into neutral, eased off the brake and let the Mercedes run down the hill silently, coming to a halt on the far side of the runway from the hangars. He sat there thinking about things for a moment, then took a Walther PPK and black leather gloves from the attaché case on the seat next to him. He checked the Walther, slipped it into his waistband at the rear, then pulled on the gloves as he started across the runway in the rain.

The hangar was old and smelled of damp as if not used in years, but the airplane that stood there in the dim light looked well enough, a Cessna 441 Conquest with twin turboprop engines. A mechanic in overalls had the cowling on the port engine open and stood on a ladder working on it. The cabin door was open, the stairs down and two men loaded boxes inside.

As they emerged, one of them called in German, "We're finished, Doctor Wegner."

A bearded man emerged from the small office in one corner of the hangar. He wore a hunting jacket, the fur collar turned up against the cold.

"All right, you can go." As they walked away he said to the mechanic, "Any problems, Tomic?"

"No big deal, Herr Doctor, just fine-tuning."

"Which won't mean a thing unless this damn man Dillon turns up." As Wegner turned, a young man came in, the woollen cap and reefer coat he wore beaded with rain.

"He'll be here," Wegner told him. "I was told he could never resist a challenge, this one."

"A mercenary," the young man said. "That's what we've come down to. The kind of man who kills people for money."

"There are children dying over there," Wegner said, "and they need what's on that plane. To achieve that I'd deal with the Devil himself."

"Which you'll probably have to."

"Not kind," Dillon called in excellent German. "Not kind at all," and he stepped out of the darkness at the end of the hangar.

The young man put a hand in his pocket and Dillon's Walther appeared fast. "Plain view, son, plain view."

Dillon walked forward, swung the young man round and extracted a Mauser from his right-hand pocket. "Would you look at that now? You can't trust a soul these days."

Wegner said in English, "Mr. Dillon? Mr. Sean Dillon?"

"So they tell me." Dillon slipped the Mauser into his hip pocket, took out his silver case one-handed, still holding the Walther, and managed to extract a cigarette. "And who might you be, me old son?" His speech had the hard, distinctive edge to it that was found only in Ulster and not in the Republic of Ireland.

"I am Dr. Hans Wegner of International Drug Relief, and this is Klaus Schmidt from our office in Vienna. He arranged the plane for us."

"Did he now? That's something to be said in his favor." Dillon took the Mauser from his hip pocket and handed it back. "Doing good is all very fine, but playing with guns when you don't know how is a mug's game."

The young man flushed deeply, took the Mauser and put it in his pocket, and Wegner said mildly, "Herr Schmidt has made the run by road twice with medical supplies."

"Then why not this time?" Dillon asked, slipping the Walther back in his waistband.

"Because that part of Croatia is disputed territory now," Schmidt said. "There's heavy fighting between Serbs and Moslems and Croats."

"I see," Dillon said. "So I'm to manage by air what you can't by road?"

"Mr. Dillon, it's a hundred and twenty miles to Sabac from here and the airstrip is still open. Believe it or not, but the phone system still works quite well over there. I'm given to understand that this plane is capable of more than three hundred miles an hour. That means you could be there in twenty minutes or so."

Dillon laughed out loud. "Would you listen to the man? It's plain to see you don't know the first thing about flying a plane." He saw that the mechanic high on his ladder was smiling. "Ah, so you speak English, old son."

"A little."

"Tomic is a Croatian," Dr. Wegner said.

Dillon looked up. "What do you think?"

Tomic said, "I was in the airforce for seven years. I know Sabac. It's an emergency strip, but a sound asphalt runway."

"And the flight?"

"Well, if you're just some private pilot out here to do a bit of good in this wicked world you won't last twenty miles."

Dillon said softly, "Let's just say I've seldom done a good thing in my life and I'm not that kind of pilot. What's the terrain like?"

"Mountainous in parts, heavily forested, and the weather forecast stinks, I checked it myself earlier, but it's not only that, it's the airforce, they still patrol the area regularly."

"Mig fighters?" Dillon asked.

"That's right." Tomic slapped the wing of the Conquest with one hand. "A nice airplane, but no match for a Mig." He shook his head. "But maybe you've got a death wish."

"That's enough, Tomic," Wegner said angrily.

"Oh, it's been said before." Dillon laughed. "But let's get on. I'd better look at the charts."

As they moved toward the office Wegner said, "Our people in Vienna did make it plain. Your services are purely voluntary. We need all the money we can raise for the drugs and medical supplies."

"Understood," Dillon said.

They went into the office where a number of charts were spread across the desk. Dillon started to examine them.

"When would you leave?" Wegner asked.

"Just before dawn," Dillon told him. "Best time of all and least active. I hope the rain keeps up."

Schmidt, genuinely curious, said, "Why would you do this? I don't understand. A man like you." He seemed suddenly awkward. "I mean, we know something of your background."

"Do you now?" Dillon said. "Well, as the good doctor said, I find it hard to resist a challenge."

"And for this you would risk your life?"

"Ah, sure and I was forgetting." Dillon looked up and smiled and an astonishing change came to his face, nothing but warmth and great charm there. "I should also mention that I'm the last of the world's great adventurers. Now leave me be like a good lad and let me see where I'm going."

He leaned over the charts and started to examine them intently.

Just before five the rain was as relentless as ever, the darkness as impenetrable, as Dillon stood in the entrance of the hangar and peered out. Wegner and Schmidt approached him.

The older man said, "Can you really take off in weather like this?"

"The problem is landing, not taking off." Dillon called to Tomic, "How are things?"

Tomic emerged from the cabin, jumped to the ground and came toward them wiping his hands on a rag. "Everything in perfect working order."

Dillon offered him a cigarette and glanced out. "And this?"

Tomic peered up into the darkness. "It'll get worse before it gets better, and you'll find ground mist over there, especially over the forest, mark my words."

"Ah, well, better get on with it as the thief said to the hangman." Dillon crossed to the Conquest.

He went up the steps and examined the interior. All the seats had been removed and it was stacked with long, olive-green boxes. Each one was stenciled in English: Royal Army Medical Corps.

Schmidt, who had joined him, said, "As you can see, we get our supplies from unusual sources."

"You can say that again. What's in these?"

"See for yourself." Schmidt unclipped the nearest one, removed a sheet of oiled paper to reveal box after box of morphine ampoules. "Over there, Mr. Dillon, they sometimes have to hold children down when they operate on them because of the lack of any kind of anesthetic. These prove a highly satisfactory substitute."

"Point taken," Dillon said. "Now close it up and I'll get moving."

Schmidt did as he was told, then jumped to the ground. As Dillon pulled up the steps Wegner said, "God go with you, Mr. Dillon."

"There's always that chance," Dillon said. "It's probably the first time I've done anything he'd approve of," and he closed the door and clamped it in place.

He settled into the left-hand pilot's seat, fired the port engine and after that the starboard. The chart was next to him on the other seat, but he had already pretty well committed it to memory. He paused on the apron outside the hangar, rain streaming from his windscreen, did a thorough cockpit check, then strapped in and taxied to the end of the runway, turning into the wind. He glanced across to the three men standing in the hangar entrance, raised a thumb, then started forward, his engine roar deepening as he boosted power. Within a second or two he had disappeared, the sound of the engines already fading.

Wegner ran a hand over his face. "God, but I'm tired." He turned to Tomic. "Has he a chance?"

Tomic shrugged. "Quite a man, that one. Who knows?"

Schmidt said, "Let's get some coffee. We're going to have a long wait."

Tomic said, "I'll join you in a minute. I just want to clear my tools away."

They crossed toward the end hut. He watched them go, waited until they'd gone inside before turning and swiftly crossing to the office. He picked up the telephone and dialed a lengthy series of numbers. As the good doctor had said, the telephone system still worked surprisingly well over there.

When a voice answered he spoke in Serbo-Croatian. "This is Tomic, get me Major Branko."

There was an instant response. "Branko here."

"Tomic. I'm at the airfield at Fehring and I've got traffic for you. Cessna Conquest just left, destination Sabac. Here is his radio frequency."

"Is the pilot anyone we know?"

"Name of Dillon—Sean Dillon. Irish, I believe. Small man, very fair hair, late thirties I'd say. Doesn't look much. Nice smile, but the eyes tell a different story."

"I'll have him checked out through Central Intelligence, but you've done well, Tomic. We'll give him a warm welcome."

The phone clicked and Tomic replaced the receiver. He took out a packet of the vile Macedonian cigarettes he affected and lit one. Pity about Dillon. He'd rather liked the Irishman, but that was life and he started to put his tools away methodically.

And Dillon was already in trouble, not only thick cloud and the constant driving rain, but even at a thousand feet a swirling mist that gave only an intermittent view of pine forest below.

"And what in the hell are you doing here, old son?" he asked softly. "What are you trying to prove?"

He got a cigarette out of his case, lit it and a voice spoke in his earphones in heavily accented English. "Good morning, Mr. Dillon, welcome to Yugoslavia."

The plane took station to starboard not too far away, the red stars on its fuselage clear enough, a Mig 21, the old Fishbed, probably the Soviet jet most widely distributed to its allies. Outdated now, but not as far as Dillon was concerned.

The Mig pilot spoke again. "Course one-two-four, Mr. Dillon. We'll come to a rather picturesque castle at the edge of the forest, Kivo it's called, intelligence headquarters for this area. There's an airstrip there and they're expecting you. They might even arrange a full English breakfast."

"Irish," Dillon said cheerfully. "A full Irish breakfast, and who am I to refuse an offer like that? One-two-four it is."

He turned onto the new course, climbing to two thousand feet as the weather cleared a little, whistling softly to himself. A Serbian prison did not commend itself, not if the stories reaching Western Europe were even partly true, but in the circumstances, he didn't seem to have any choice and then, a couple of miles away on the edge of the forest beside a river he saw Kivo, a fairytale castle of towers and battlements surrounded by a moat, the airstrip clear beside it.

"What do you think?" the Mig pilot asked. "Nice, isn't it?"

"Straight out of a story by the Brothers Grimm," Dillon answered. "All we need is the ogre."

"Oh, we have that too, Mr. Dillon. Now put down nice and easy and I'll say goodbye."

Dillon looked down into the interior of the castle, noticed soldiers moving toward the edge of the airstrip preceded by a jeep and sighed. He said into his mike, "I'd like to say it's been a good life, but then there are those difficult days, like this morning for instance. I mean, why did I even get out of bed?"

He heaved the control column right back and boosted power, climbing fast, and the Mig pilot reacted angrily. "Dillon, do as you're told or I'll blast you out of the sky."

Dillon ignored him, leveling out at five thousand, searching the sky for any sign, and the Mig, already on his tail, came up behind and fired. The Conquest staggered as cannon shell tore through both wings.

"Dillon—don't be a fool!" the pilot cried.

"Ah, but then I always was."

Dillon went down fast, leveling at two thousand feet over the edge of the forest, aware of vehicles moving from the direction of the castle. The Mig came in again firing his machine guns now and the Conquest's windscreen disintegrated, wind and rain roaring in. Dillon sat there, hands firm on the control column, blood on his face from a glass splinter.

"Now then," he said into his mike. "Let's see how good you are."

He dropped the nose and went straight down, the pine forest waiting for him below, and the Mig went after him, firing again. The Conquest bucked, the port engine dying as Dillon leveled out at four hundred feet, and behind him the Mig, no time to pull out at the speed it was doing, plowed into the forest and fireballed.

Dillon, trimming as best he could for flying on one engine, lost power and dropped lower. There was a clearing up ahead and to his left. He tried to bank toward it, was already losing height as he clipped the tops of the pine trees. He cut power instantly and braced himself for the crash. In the end, it was the pine trees which saved him, retarding his progress so much that by the time he hit the clearing for a belly landing, he wasn't actually going all that fast.

The Conquest bounced twice, and came to a shuddering halt. Dillon released his straps, scrambled out of his seat and had the door open in an instant. He was out headfirst, rolling over in the rain, and on his feet and running, his right ankle twisting so that he fell on his face again. He scrambled up and limped away as fast as he could, but the Conquest didn't burst into flame, it simply crouched there in the rain as if tired.

There was thick black smoke above the trees from the burning Mig and then soldiers appeared on the other side of the clearing. A jeep moved out of the trees behind them, top down, and Dillon could see an officer standing up in it wearing a winter campaign coat, Russian-style, with a fur collar. More soldiers appeared, some of them with Dobermans, all barking loudly and straining against their leashes.

It was enough. Dillon turned to hobble into the trees and his leg gave out on him. A voice on a loudhailer called in English, "Oh, come now, Mr. Dillon, be sensible, you don't want me to set the dogs on you."

Dillon paused, balanced on one foot, then he turned and hobbled to the nearest tree and leaned against it. He took a cigarette from his silver case, the last one, and lit it. The smoke tasted good as it bit at the back of his throat and he waited for them.

They stood in a semicircle, soldiers in baggy tunics, guns covering him, the dogs howling against being restrained. The jeep rolled to a halt and the officer, a Major from his shoulder boards, stood up and looked down at him, a good-looking man of about thirty with a dark, saturnine face.

"So, Mr. Dillon, you made it in one piece," he said in faultless Public School English. "I congratulate you. My name, by the way, is Branko— John Branko. My mother was English, is, I should say. Lives in Hampstead."

"Is that a fact." Dillon smiled. "A desperate bunch of rascals you've got here, Major, but *Cead míle fáilte* anyway."

"And what would that mean, Mr. Dillon?"

"Oh, that's Irish for a hundred thousand welcomes."

"What a charming sentiment." Branko turned and spoke in Serbo-Croatian to the large, brutal-looking Sergeant who sat behind him clutching an AK assault rifle. The Sergeant smiled, jumped to the ground and advanced on Dillon.

Major Branko said, "Allow me to introduce you to my Sergeant Zekan. I've just told him to offer you a hundred thousand welcomes to Yugoslavia, or Serbia as we prefer to say now."

Dillon knew what was coming, but there wasn't a thing he could do. The butt of the AK caught him in the left side, driving the wind from him as he keeled over. The Sergeant lifted a knee in his face. The last thing Dillon remembered was the dogs barking, the laughter, and then there was only darkness.

When Sergeant Zekan took Dillon along the corridor, someone screamed in the distance and there was the sound of heavy blows. Dillon hesitated but the Sergeant showed no emotion, simply put a hand between the Irishman's shoulder blades and pushed him toward a flight of stone steps and urged him up. There was an oaken door at the top banded with iron. Zekan opened it and pushed him through.

The room inside was oak beamed with granite walls, tapestries hanging here and there. A log fire burned in an open hearth and two of the Dobermans sprawled in front of it. Branko sat behind a large desk reading a file and drinking from a crystal glass, a bottle in an ice bucket beside him. He glanced up and smiled, then took the bottle from the ice bucket and filled another glass.

"Krug champagne, Mr. Dillon, your preferred choice, I understand."

"Is there anything you don't know about me?" Dillon asked.

"Not much." Branko lifted the file, then dropped it on the desk. "The intelligence organizations of most countries have the useful habit of frequently co-operating with each other even when their countries don't. Do sit down and have a drink. You'll feel better."

Dillon took the chair opposite and accepted the glass that Zekan handed him. He emptied it in one go and Branko smiled, took a cigarette from a packet of Rothmans and tossed it across.

"Help yourself." He reached out and refilled Dillon's glass. "I much prefer the non-vintage, don't you?"

"It's the grape mix," Dillon said and lit the cigarette.

"Sorry about that little touch of violence back there," Branko told him. "Just a show for my boys. After all, you did cost us that Mig and it takes two years to train the pilots. I should know, I'm one myself."

"Really?" Dillon said.

"Yes, Cranwell, courtesy of your British Royal Air Force."

"Not mine," Dillon told him.

"But you were born in Ulster, I understand. Belfast, is that not so, and Belfast, as I understand it, is part of Great Britain and not the Republic of Ireland."

"A debatable point," Dillon said. "Let's say I'm Irish and leave it at that." He swallowed some more champagne. "Who dropped me in it? Wegner or Schmidt?" He frowned. "No, of course not. Just a couple of do-gooders. Tomic. It would be Tomic, am I right?"

"A good Serb." Branko poured a little more champagne. "How on earth did you get into this, a man like you?"

"You mean you don't know?"

"I'll be honest, Mr. Dillon. I knew you were coming, but no more than that."

"I was in Vienna for a few days to sample a little opera. I'm partial to Mozart. Bumped into a man I'd had dealings with over the years in the bar during the first interval. Told me he'd been approached by this organization who needed a little help, but were short on money."

"Ah, I see now." Branko nodded. "A good deed in a naughty world as Shakespeare put it? All those poor little children crying out for help? The cruel Serbs."

"God help me, Major, but you have a way with the words."

"A sea change for a man like you I would have thought." Branko opened the file. "Sean Dillon, born Belfast, went to live in London when you were a boy, father a widower. A student of the Royal Academy of Dramatic Art at eighteen, even acted with the National Theatre. Your father returned to Belfast in 1971 and was killed by British paratroopers."

"You *are* well informed."

"You joined the Provisional IRA, trained in Libya courtesy of Colonel Qaddafi and never looked back." Branko turned a page. "You finally broke with the IRA. Some disagreement as to strategy."

"Bunch of old women." Dillon reached across and helped himself to more Krug.

"Beirut, the PLO, even the KGB. You really do believe in spreading your services around." Branko laughed suddenly in a kind of amazement. "The underwater attack on those two Palestinian gunboats in Beirut in 1990. You were responsible for that? But that was for the Israelis."

"I charge very reasonable rates," Dillon said.

"Fluent German, Spanish and French, oh, and Irish."

"We mustn't forget that."

"Reasonable Arabic, Italian and Russian." Branko closed the file. "Is it true you were responsible for the mortar attack on No. 10 Downing Street during the Gulf War when the British Prime Minister, John Major, was meeting with the War Cabinet?"

"Now do I look as if I'd do a thing like that?"

Branko leaned back and looked at him seriously. "How do you see yourself, my friend, gun for hire like one of those old Westerns, riding into town to clean things up single-handed?"

"To be honest, Major, I never think about it."

"And yet you took on a job like this present affair for a bunch of well-meaning amateurs and for no pay?"

"We all make mistakes."

"You certainly did, my friend. Those boxes on the plane. Morphine ampoules on top, Stinger missiles underneath."

"Jesus." Dillon laughed helplessly. "Now who would have thought it."

"They say you have a genius for acting, that you can change yourself totally, become another person with a look, a gesture."

"No, I think that was Laurence Olivier." Dillon smiled.

"And in twenty years, you've never seen the inside of a cell."

"True."

"Not any longer, my friend." Branko opened a drawer, took out a two-hundred pack of Rothmans cigarettes and tossed them across. "You're going to need those." He glanced at Zekan and said in Serbo-Croatian, "Take him to his cell."

Dillon felt the Sergeant's hand on his shoulder pulling him up and propelling him to the door. As Zekan opened it Branko said, "One more thing, Mr. Dillon. The firing squad operates most mornings here. Try not to let it put you off."

"Ah, yes," Dillon said. "Ethnic cleansing, isn't that what you call it?"

"The reason is much simpler than that. We just get short of space. Sleep well."

They went up a flight of stone steps, Zekan pushing Dillon ahead of him. He pulled him to a halt outside an oak door on the passageway at the top, took out a key and unlocked it. He inclined his head and stood to one side and Dillon entered. The room was quite large. There was an army cot in one corner, a table and chair, books on a shelf and, incredibly, an old toilet and in a cubicle in one corner. Dillon went to the window and peered through bars to the courtyard eighty feet below and the pine forest in the near distance.

He turned. "This must be one of your better rooms. What's the catch?" Then realized he was wasting his time, for the Sergeant had no English.

As if perfectly understanding him Zekan smiled, showing bad teeth, took Dillon's silver case and Zippo lighter from a pocket and laid them carefully on the table. He withdrew, closing the door, and the key rattled in the lock.

Dillon went to the window and tried the bars, but they seemed firm. Too far down anyway. He opened one of the packs of Rothmans and lit one. One thing was certain. Branko was being excessively kind and there had to be a reason for that. He went and lay on the bed, smoking his cigarette, staring up at the ceiling and thinking about it.

In 1972, aware of the growing problem of terrorism and its effect on so many aspects of life at both political and national level, the British Prime Minister of the day ordered the setting up of a small elite intelligence unit, known simply by the code name Group Four. It was to handle all matters concerning terrorism and subversion in the British Isles. Known rather bitterly in more conventional intelligence circles as the Prime Minister's private army, it owed allegiance to that office alone.

Brigadier Charles Ferguson had headed Group Four since its inception, had served a number of Prime Ministers, both Conservative and Labour, and had no political allegiance whatsoever. He had an office on the third floor of the Ministry of Defence overlooking Horse Guards Avenue, and was still working at his desk at nine o'clock that night when there was a knock at the door.

"Come in," Ferguson said, stood up and walked to the window, a large, rather untidy-looking man with a double chin and untidy gray hair who wore a baggy suit and a Guards tie.

As he peered out at the rain toward Victoria Embankment and the Thames, the door opened behind him. The man who entered was in his late thirties, wore a tweed suit and glasses. He could have been a clerk, or even a schoolmaster, but Detective Inspector Jack Lane was neither of these things. He was a cop. Not an ordinary one, but a cop all the same, and after some negotiating, Ferguson had succeeded in borrowing him from Special Branch at Scotland Yard to act as his personal assistant.

"Got something for me, Jack?" Ferguson's voice was ever so slightly plummy.

"Mainly routine, Brigadier. The word is that the Director General of the Security Services is still unhappy at the Prime Minister's refusal to do away with Group Four's special status."

"Good God, don't they ever give up, those people? I've agreed to keep them informed on a need-to-know basis and to liaise with Simon Carter, the Deputy Director, and that damned MP, the one with the fancy title. Extra Minister at the Home Office."

"Sir Francis Pamer, sir."

"Yes, well that's all the cooperation they're going to get out of me. Anything else?"

Lane smiled. "Actually, I've saved the best bit till last. Dillon—Sean Dillon?"

Ferguson turned. "What about him?"

"Had a signal from our contacts in Yugoslavia. Dillon crashed in a light plane this morning, supposedly flying in medical supplies only they turned out to be Stinger missiles. They're holding him in that castle at Kivo. It's all here."

He passed a sheet of paper across and Ferguson put on half-moon spectacles and studied it. He nodded in satisfaction. "Twenty years and the bastard never saw the inside of a prison cell."

"Well, he's in one now, sir. I've got his record here if you want to look at it."

"And why would I want to do that? No use to anyone now. You know what the Serbs are like, Jack. Might as well stick it in the dead-letter file. Oh, you can go home now."

"Good night, sir."

Lane went out and Ferguson crossed to his drinks cabinet and poured a large Scotch. "Here's to you, Dillon," he said softly. "And you can chew on that, you bastard."

He swallowed the whisky down, returned to his desk and started to work again.

TWO

East of Puerto Rico in the Caribbean are the Virgin Islands, partly British like Tortola and Virgin Gorda. Across the water are St. Croix, St. Thomas and St. John, proudly American since 1917 when the United States purchased them from the Danish government for twenty-five million dollars.

St. John is reputed to have been discovered by Columbus on his second voyage to the New World in 1493 and without a doubt is probably the most idyllic island in the entire Caribbean, but not that night as a tropical storm, the tail end of Hurricane Able, swept in across the old town of Cruz Bay, stirring the boats at anchor in the harbor, driving rain across the roof tops, the sky exploding into thunder.

To Bob Carney, fast asleep in the house at Chocolate Hole on the other side of Great Cruz Bay, it was the sound of distant guns. He stirred in his sleep, and suddenly it was the same old dream, the mortars landing everywhere, shaking the ground, the screams of the wounded and dying. He'd lost his helmet, flung himself to the ground, arms protecting his head, was not even aware of being hit, only afterwards, as the attack faded and he sat up. There was pain then in both arms and legs from shrapnel wounds, blood on his hands. And then, as the smoke cleared, he became aware of another Marine sitting against a tree, both legs gone above the knees. He was shaking, had a hand outstretched as if begging for help, and Carney cried out in horror and sat bolt upright in bed, awake now.

The same lousy old dream, Vietnam, and that was a long time ago. He switched on the bedside lamp and checked his watch. It was only two-thirty. He sighed and stood up, stretching for a moment, then padded through the dark house to the kitchen, switched on the light and got a beer from the icebox.

He was very tanned, the blond hair faded, both from regular exposure to sea and sun. Around five foot eight, he had an athlete's body, not surprising in a man who had been a ship's captain and was now a master diver by profession. Forty-four years of age, but most people would have taken seven or eight years off that.

He went through the living room and opened a window to the veranda. Rain dripped from the roof and out to sea lightning crackled. He drank a little more of his beer, then put the can down and closed the window. Better to try and get a little more sleep. He was taking a party of recreational scuba divers out from Caneel Bay at nine-thirty, which meant that as usual he needed his wits about him, plus all his considerable expertise.

As he went through the living room he paused to pick up a framed photo of his wife, Karye, and his two young children, the boy Walker and his daughter, little Wallis. They'd departed for Florida only the previous day for a vacation with their grandparents, which left him a bachelor for the next month. He smiled wryly, knowing just how much he'd miss them, and went back to bed.

At the same moment in his house on the edge of Cruz Bay at Gallows Point, Henry Baker sat in his study reading in the light of a single desk lamp. He had the door to the veranda open because he liked the rain and the smell of the sea. It excited him, took him back to the days of his youth and his two years' service in the Navy during the Korean War. He'd made full Lieutenant, had even been decorated with the Bronze Star, could have made a career of it. In fact they'd wanted him to, but there was the family publishing business to consider, responsibilities and the girl he'd promised to marry.

It hadn't been a bad life considering. No children, but he and his wife had been content until cancer took her at fifty. From then on he'd really lost interest in the business, had been happy to accept the right kind of deal for a takeover, which had left him very rich and totally rootless at fifty-eight.

It was a visit to St. John which had been the saving of him. He'd stayed at Caneel Bay, the fabulous Rock Resort on its private peninsula north of Cruz Bay. It was there that he'd been introduced to scuba diving by Bob Carney and it had become an obsession. He'd sold his house in the Hamptons, moved to St. John and bought the present place. His life at sixty-three was totally satisfactory and worthwhile, although Jenny had had something to do with that as well.

He reached for her photo. Jenny Grant, twenty-five, face very calm, wide eyes above high cheekbones, short dark hair, and there was still a wariness in those eyes as if she expected the worst, which was hardly surprising when Baker recalled their first meeting in Miami when she'd tried to proposition him in a car park, her body shaking from the lack of the drugs she'd needed.

When she'd collapsed, he'd taken her to the hospital himself, had personally guaranteed the necessary financing to put her through a drug rehabilitation unit, had held her hand all the way because there was no one else. It was the usual story. She was an orphan raised by an aunt who'd thrown her out at sixteen. A fair voice had enabled her to make some kind of living singing in saloons and cocktail lounges, and then the wrong man, bad company, and the slide had begun.

He'd brought her back to St. John to see what the sea and sun could do. The arrangement had worked perfectly and on a strictly platonic basis. He was the father she had never known, she was the daughter he had been denied. He'd invested in a cafe and bar for her on the Cruz Bay waterfront called Jenny's Place. It had proved a great success. Life couldn't be better and he always waited up for her. It was at that moment he heard the jeep drive up outside, there was the sound of the porch door and she came in laughing, a raincoat over her shoulder. She threw it on a chair and leaned down and kissed his cheek.

"My God, it's like a monsoon out there."

"It'll clear by morning, you'll see." He took her hand. "Good night?"

"Very." She nodded. "A few tourists in from Caneel and the Hyatt. Gosh, but I'm bushed."

"I'd get to bed if I were you, it's almost three o'clock."

"Sure you don't mind?"

"Of course not. I may go diving in the morning, but I should be back before noon. If I miss you, I'll come down to the cafe for lunch."

"I wish you wouldn't dive on your own."

"Jenny, I'm a recreational diver, no decompression needed because I work within the limits exactly as Bob Carney taught me, and I never dive without my Marathon diving computer, you know that."

"I also know that whenever you dive there's always a chance of some kind of decompression sickness."

"True, but very small." He squeezed her hand. "Now stop worrying and go to bed."

She kissed him on the top of his head and went out. He returned to his book, carrying it across to the couch by the window, stretching out comfortably. He didn't seem to need so much sleep these days, one of the penalties of growing old, he imagined, but after a while his eyes started to close and sleep he did, the book sliding to the floor.

He came awake with a start, light beaming in through the venetian blinds. He lay there for a moment, then checked his watch. It was a little after five and he got up and went out on to the veranda. It was already dawn, light breaking on the horizon, but strangely still, and the sea was extraordinarily calm, something to do with the hurricane having passed. Perfect for diving, absolutely perfect.

He felt cheerful and excited at the same time, hurried into the kitchen, put the kettle on and made a stack of cheese sandwiches while it boiled. He filled a thermos with coffee, put it in a holdall with the sandwiches and took his old reefer coat down from behind the door.

He left the jeep for Jenny and walked down to the harbor. It was still very quiet, not too many people about, a dog barking in the distance. He dropped into his inflatable dinghy at the dock, cast off and started the outboard motor, threaded his way out through numerous boats until he came to his own, the *Rhoda*, named after his wife, a thirty-five-foot Sport Fisherman with a flying bridge.

He scrambled aboard, tying the inflatable on a long line, and checked the deck. He had four air tanks standing upright in their holders; he'd put them in the day before himself. He opened the lid of the deck locker and checked his equipment. There was a rubber and nylon diving suit which he seldom used, preferring the lighter, three-quarter-length one in orange and blue. Fins, mask, plus a spare because the lenses were correctional according to his eye prescription, two buoyancy jackets, gloves, air regulators and his Marathon computer.

"Carney training," he said softly, "never leave anything to chance."

He went round to the prow and unhitched from the buoy, then went up the ladder to the flying bridge and started the engines. They roared into life and he took the *Rhoda* out of harbor toward the open sea with conscious pleasure.

There were all his favorite dives to choose from, the Cow & Calf, Carval Rock, Congo, or there was Eagle Shoal if he wanted a longer trip. He'd confronted a lemon shark there only the previous week, but the sea was so calm he just headed straight out. There was always Frenchman's Cap to the south and west and maybe eight or nine miles, a great dive, but he just kept going, heading due south, pushing the *Rhoda* up to fifteen knots, pouring himself some coffee and breaking out the sandwiches. The sun was up now, the sea the most perfect blue, the peaks of the islands all around, a breathtakingly beautiful sight. Nothing could be better.

"My God," he said softly, "it's a damn privilege to be here. What in hell was I doing with my life all those years?"

He lapsed into a kind of reverie, brooding about things, and it was a good thirty minutes later that he suddenly snapped out of it and checked on his position.

"Christ," he said, "I must be twelve miles out."

Which was close to the edge of things and that awesome place where everything simply dropped away and it was two thousand feet to the bottom, except for Thunder Point and that, he knew, was somewhere close. But no one ever dived there, the most dangerous reef in the entire region. Even Carney didn't dive there. Strong currents, a nightmare world of fissures and channels. Carney had told him that years before an old diver had described it to him. A hundred and eighty feet on one side, then the ridge of the reef at around seventy, and two thousand feet on the other. The old boy had hit bad trouble, had only just made it to the surface, had never tried again. Few people even knew where it was anyway, and the sea out there was generally so turbulent that that in itself was enough to keep anyone away, but not today. It was a millpond. Baker had never seen anything like it. A sudden excitement surged in him and he switched on his fathometer, seeking the bottom, throttling back the engines, and then he saw it, the yellow ridged lines on the black screen.

He killed the engine and drifted, checking the depth reading until he was certain he was above the ridge of the reef at seventy feet, then scrambled round to the prow and dropped the anchor. After a while, he felt it bite satisfactorily and worked his way round to the deck. He felt incredibly cheerful as he stripped, pulled on the orange and blue nylon diving suit, then quickly assembled his gear, clamping a tank to his inflatable. He strapped the computer to the line of his air pressure gauge, then eased himself into the jacket, taking the weight of the tank, strapping the Velcro wrappers firmly across his waist and hooking a net diving bag to his weight belt as he always did with a spotlight inside in case he came across anything interesting. He pulled on a pair of diving gloves, then sat with his feet on the platform at the stern and pulled on his fins. He spat on his mask, rinsed it, adjusted it to his face, then simply stood up and stepped into the water.

It was incredibly clear and blue. He swam round to the anchor rope, paused, then started down, following the line. The sensation of floating in space was, as always, amazing, a silent, private world, sunlight at first, but fading as he descended.

The reef where the anchor was hooked was a forest of coral and sea grass, fish of every conceivable description, and suddenly a barracuda that was at least five feet long swerved across his vision and paused, turning toward him threateningly, which didn't bother Baker in the slightest, because barracuda were seldom a threat to anyone.

He checked his dive computer. It not only indicated the depth he was at, but told him how long he was safe there and constantly altered its reading according to any change in depth he made during the dive. He was at this point at seventy feet and he turned and headed over to the left-hand side, where the reef slid down to a hundred and eighty. He went over the edge, then changed his mind and went up again. It was amazing how much an extra ten or fifteen feet reduced your bottom time.

There was a reasonably strong current; he could feel it pushing him to one side. He imagined what it must be like when conditions were bad, but he was damned if that was going to stop him having a look at the big drop. The edge of the reef over there was very clearly defined. He paused, holding on to a coral head and peered over, looking down the cliff face into a great blue vault that stretched into infinity. He went over, descended to eighty feet and started to work his way along.

It was interesting. He noted a considerable amount of coral damage, large sections having obviously been torn away, recently, presumably the result of the hurricane although they were on a fault line here and earth tremors were also common. Some distance ahead, there was a very obvious section where what looked like an entire overhang had gone revealing a wide ledge below, and there was something there, perched on the ledge yet part of it hanging over. Baker paused for a moment, then approached cautiously.

It was then that he received not only the greatest thrill of his diving career but the greatest shock of a long life. The object which was pressed on the ledge and partly sticking out over two thousand feet of water was a submarine.

During his naval service Baker had done a training course in a submarine when based in the Philippines. No big deal, just part of general training, but he remembered the lectures, the training films they'd had to watch, mainly Second World War stuff, and he recognized what he was looking at instantly. It was a type VII U-boat, by far the most common craft of its kind used by the German Kriegsmarine, the configuration was unmistakable. The conning tower was encrusted with marine growth, but when he approached he could still discern the number on the side—180. The attack and control room periscopes were still intact and there was a snorkel. He recalled having heard that the Germans had gradually introduced that as the war progressed, a device that enabled the boat to proceed under water much faster because it was able to use the power of its diesel engines. Approximately two-thirds of it rested stern first on the ledge and the prow jutted out into space.

He glanced up aware of a school of horse-eyed jacks overhead mixed with silversides, then descended to the top of the conning tower and hung on to the bridge rail. Aft was the high gun platform with its 20mm cannon and forward and below him was the deck gun, encrusted, as was most of the surface, with sponge and coral of many colors.

The boat had become a habitat as with all wrecks, fish everywhere, yellow-tail snappers, angel and parrot fish and sergeant-majors and many others. He checked his computer. On the bridge he was at a depth of seventy-five feet and he had only twenty minutes at the most before the need to surface.

He drifted away a little distance to look the U-boat over. Obviously the overhang, which had recently been dislodged, had provided a kind of canopy for the wreck for years, protecting it from view, and at a site which was seldom visited, it had been enough. That U-boats had worked the area during the Second World War was common knowledge. He'd known one old sailor who'd always insisted that crews would come ashore on St. John by night in search of fresh fruit and water, although Baker had always found that one hard to swallow.

He swung over to the starboard side and saw what the trouble had been instantly, a large, ragged gash about fifteen feet long in the hull below the conning tower. The poor bastards must have gone down like a stone. He descended, holding on to a jagged, coral-encrusted edge, and peered into the control room. It was dark and gloomy in there, silverfish in clouds, and he got the spotlight from his dive bag and shone it inside. The periscope shafts were clearly visible, again encrusted like everything else, but the rest was a confusion of twisted metal, wires and pipes. He checked his computer, saw that he had fifteen minutes, hesitated, then went inside.

Both the aft and forward water-tight doors were closed, but that was standard practice when things got bad. He tried the unlocking wheel on the forward hatch, but it was immovable and hopelessly corroded. There were some oxygen bottles, even a belt of some kind of ammunition, and the most pathetic thing of all, a few human bones in the sediment of the floor. Amazing that there was any trace at all after so many years.

Suddenly he felt cold. It was as if he was an intruder who shouldn't be here. He turned to go and his light picked out a handle in the corner, very like a suitcase handle. He reached for it, the sediment stirred and he found himself clutching a small briefcase in some kind of metal, encrusted like everything else. It was enough and he went out through the gash in the hull, drifted up over the edge of the reef and went for the anchor.

He made it with five minutes to spare. Stupid bastard, he told himself, taking such a chance, and he ascended just by the book, one foot per second, one hand sliding up the line, the briefcase in the other, leaving the line at twenty feet to swim under the boat and surface at the stern.

He pushed the briefcase on board, then wriggled out of his equipment, which was always the worst part. You're getting old, Henry, he told himself as he scrambled up the ladder and turned to heave his buoyancy jacket and tank on board.

He schooled himself to do everything as normal, stowing away the tank and the equipment following his usual routine. He toweled himself dry, changed into jeans and a fresh denim shirt, all the time ignoring the brief-case. He opened his thermos and poured some coffee, then went and sat in one of the swivel chairs in the stern, drinking and staring at the briefcase encrusted with coral.

The encrusting was superficial more than anything else. He got a wire brush from his tool kit and applied it vigorously and realized at once that the case was made of aluminum. As the surface cleared, the Eagle and Swastika of the German Kriegsmarine was revealed etched into the top right-hand corner. It was secured by two clips and there was a lock. The clips came up easily enough, but the lid remained obstinately down, obviously locked, which left him little choice. He found a large screwdriver, forced it in just above the lock and was able to prize open the lid within a few moments. The inside was totally dry, the contents a few photos and several letters bound together by a rubber band. There was also a large diary in red Moroccan leather stamped with a Kriegsmarine insignia in gold.

The photos were of a young woman and two little girls. There was a date on the back of one of them at the start of a handwritten paragraph in German, August 8, 1944. The rest made no sense to him as he didn't speak the language. There was also a faded snap of a man in Kriegsmarine uniform. He looked about thirty and wore a number of medals, including the Knight's Cross at his throat. Someone special, a real ace from the look of him.

The diary was also in German. The first entry was April 30, 1945, and he recognized the name, Bergen, knew that was a port in Norway. On the flyleaf was an entry he did understand. Korvettenkapitän Paul Friemel, U180, obviously the captain and owner of this diary.

Baker flicked through the pages, totally frustrated at being unable to decipher any of it. There were some twenty-seven entries, sometimes a page for each day, sometimes more. On some occasions there was a notation to indicate position, and he had little difficulty in seeing from those entries that the voyage had taken the submarine into the Atlantic and south to the Caribbean.

The strange thing was the fact that the final entry was dated May 28, 1945, and that didn't make too much sense. Henry Baker had been sixteen years of age when the war in Europe had ended, and he recalled the events of those days with surprising clarity. The Russians had reached Berlin and reduced it to hell on earth, and Adolf Hitler, holed up in the Führer Bunker at the Reich Chancellery, had committed suicide on May the 1st at 10:30 P.M. along with his wife of a few hours only, Eva Braun. That was the effective end of the Third Reich and capitulation had soon followed. If that were so, what in the hell was U180 doing in the Virgin Islands with a final log entry dated May 28?

If only he could speak German, and the further frustrating thing was that he didn't know a soul in St. John who did. On the other hand, if he did, would he want to share such a secret? One thing was certain: If news of the submarine and its whereabouts got out, the place would be invaded within days.

He flicked through the pages again, paused suddenly and turned back a page. A name jumped out at him. *Reichsleiter Martin Bormann*. Baker's excitement was intense. Martin Bormann, Head of the Nazi Party Chancellery and Secretary to the Führer. Had he escaped from the Bunker at the end, or had he died trying to escape from Berlin? How many books had been written about that?

He turned the page idly and another name came out at him: the *Duke of Windsor*. Baker sat staring at the page, his throat dry, and then he very carefully closed the diary and put it back in the case with the letter and photos. He closed the lid, put the case in the wheelhouse and started the engines. Then he went and hauled in the anchor.

Whatever it was, it was heavy, had to be. He had a U-boat that had gone down in the Virgin Islands three weeks after the end of the war in Europe, a private diary kept by the captain which mentioned the most powerful man in Nazi Germany after Hitler, and the Duke of Windsor.

"My God, what have I got into?" he murmured.

He could go to the authorities, of course, the Coast Guard, for example, but it had been his find, that was the trouble, and he was reluctant to relinquish that. But what in the hell to do next, and then it came to him and he laughed out loud.

"Garth Travers, of course," and he pushed up to full throttle and hurried back to St. John.

In 1951 as a Lieutenant in the U.S. Navy, Baker had been assigned as liaison officer to the British Royal Navy destroyer *Persephone*, which was when he had first met Garth Travers, a gunnery officer. Travers was on the fast track, had taken a degree in history at Oxford University, and the two young officers had made a firm friendship, cemented by five hours in the water one dark night off the Korean coast, which they'd spent hanging on to each other after a landing craft on which they'd been making a night drop with Royal Marine Commandos had hit a mine.

And Travers had gone on to great things, had retired a Rear Admiral. Since then he'd written several books on naval aspects of the Second World War, had translated a standard work on the Kriegsmarine from the German which Baker's publishing house had published in the last year he'd been in the business. Travers was the man, no doubt about it.

He was close inshore to St. John now and saw another Sport Fisherman bearing down on him and he recognized the *Sea Raider*, Bob Carney's boat. It slowed, turning toward him, and Baker slowed too. There were four people in the stern dressed for diving, three women and a man. Bob Carney was on the flying bridge.

"Morning, Henry," he called. "Out early. Where you been?"

"French Cap." Baker didn't like lying to a friend but had no choice.

"Conditions good?"

"Excellent, millpond out there."

"Fine." Carney smiled and waved. "Take care, Henry."

The *Sea Raider* moved away and Baker pushed up to full power and headed for Cruz Bay.

When he reached the house, he knew at once that Jenny wasn't there because the jeep had gone. He checked his watch. Ten o'clock. Something must have come up to take her out. He went into the kitchen, got a beer from the icebox and went to his study, carrying the briefcase in one hand. He placed it on the desk, pulled his phone file across and leafed through it one-handed while he drank the beer. He found what he was looking for soon enough and checked his watch again. Ten after ten, which meant ten after three in the afternoon in London. He picked up the telephone and dialed.

In London it was raining, drumming against the windows of the house in Lord North Street where Rear Admiral Garth Travers sat in a chair by the fire in his book-lined study enjoying a cup of tea and reading the *Times*. When the phone rang, he made a face, but got up and went to the desk.

"Who am I talking to?"

"Garth? It's Henry—Henry Baker."

Travers sat down behind the desk. "Good God, Henry, you old sod. Are you in London?"

"No, I'm calling from St. John."

"Sounds as if you're in the next room."

"Garth, I've got a problem, I thought you might be able to help. I've found a U-boat."

"You've what?"

"An honest-to-God U-boat, out here in the Virgins, on a reef about eighty feet down. One-eighty was the number on the conning tower. It's a type seven."

Travers' own excitement was extreme. "I'm not going to ask you if you've been drinking. But why on earth has no one discovered it before?"

"Garth, there are hundreds of wrecks in these waters; we don't know the half of it. This is in a bad place, very dangerous. No one goes there. It's half on a ledge which was protected by an overhang, or I miss my guess. There's a lot of fresh damage to the cliff face. We've just had a hurricane."

"So what condition is she in?"

"There was a gash in the hull and I managed to get in the control room. I found a briefcase in there, a watertight job in aluminum."

"With a Kriegsmarine insignia engraved in the top right-hand corner?"

"That's right!"

"Standard issue, fireproof and waterproof, all that sort of thing. What did you say the number was, one-eighty? Hang on a minute and I'll look it up. I've got a book on one of my shelves that lists every U-boat commissioned by the Kriegsmarine during the War and what happened to them."

"Okay."

Baker waited patiently until Travers returned. "We've got a problem, old son, you're certain this was a type seven?"

"Absolutely."

"Well the problem is that one-eighty was a type nine, dispatched to Japan from France in August forty-four with technical supplies. She went down in the Bay of Biscay."

"Is that so?" Baker said. "Well how does this grab you? I found the personal diary of a Korvettenkapitän Paul Friemel in that briefcase and the final entry is dated May twenty-eighth, nineteen forty-five."

"But V.E. day in Europe was May the eighth," Travers said.

"Exactly, so what have we got here? A German submarine with a false number that goes down in the Virgins three weeks after the end of the bloody war."

"It certainly is intriguing," Travers said.

"You haven't heard the best bit, old buddy. Remember all those stories about Martin Bormann having escaped from Berlin?"

"Of course I do."

"Well I can't read German, but I sure can read his name and it's right here in the diary, and another little bombshell for you. So is the Duke of Windsor's."

Travers loosened his tie and took a deep breath. "Henry, old son, I must see that diary."

"Yes, that's what I thought," Baker said. "There's the British Airways overnight flight leaving Antigua around eight this evening our time. I should be able to make it. Last time I used it we got into London Gatwick at nine o'clock in the morning. Maybe you could give me a late breakfast."

"I'll be looking forward to that," Travers said and replaced the receiver.

The Professional Association of Diving Instructors, of which Henry was a certificated member, has strict regulations about flying after diving. He checked his book of rules and discovered that he should wait at least four hours after a single no-decompression dive at eighty feet. That gave him plenty of leeway, especially if he didn't fly down to Antigua until the afternoon, which was exactly what he intended.

First he rang British Airways in San Juan. Yes, they had space in the first-class cabin on BA flight 252 leaving Antigua at 20.10 hours. He made the booking and gave them one of his Gold Card numbers. Next he rang Carib Aviation in Antigua, an air-taxi firm he'd used before. Yes, they were happy to accept the charter. They'd send up one of their Partenavias early afternoon to St. Thomas. If they left for the return trip to Antigua at four-thirty, they'd be there by six at the latest.

He sat back, thinking about it. He'd book a water taxi across to Charlotte Amalie, the main town on St. Thomas. Forty minutes, that's all it would take, fifteen at the most by taxi to the airport. Plenty of time to pack and get himself ready, but first he had to see Jenny.

The waterfront was bustling when he walked down into Cruz Bay this time. It was a picturesque little town, totally charming and ever so slightly run-down in the way of most Caribbean ports. Baker had fallen in love with the place the first time he'd seen it. It was everything you'd hope for. He used to joke that all it needed was Humphrey Bogart in a sailor's cap and denims running a boat from the harbor on mysterious missions.

Jenny's Place was slightly back from the road just before Mongoose Junction. There were steps up to the veranda, a neon sign above the door. Inside it was cool and shaded, two large fans revolving in the low ceiling. There were several booths against the walls, a scattering of marble-topped tables across a floor of black and white tiles. There were high stools at the long mahogany bar, bottles on glass shelves against the mirrored wall behind. A large, handsome black man with graying hair was polishing glasses, Billy Jones, the barman. He had the scar tissue around the eyes and the slightly flattened nose of a professional fighter. His wife, Mary, was manager.

He grinned. "Hi there, Mr. Henry, you looking for Jenny?"

"That's right."

"Went down the front with Mary to choose the fish for tonight. They shouldn't be too long. Can I get you something?"

"Just a coffee, Billy, I'll have it outside."

He sat in a cane chair on the veranda, drinking the coffee and thinking about things, was so much within himself that he didn't notice the two women approach until the last minute.

"You're back, Henry."

He looked up and found Jenny and Mary Jones coming up the steps. Mary wished him good morning and went inside and Jenny sat on the rail, her figure very slim in tee-shirt and blue jeans.

She frowned. "Is something wrong?"

"I've got to go to London," he told her.

"To London? When?"

"This afternoon."

Her frown deepened and she came and sat beside him. "What is it, Henry?"

"Something happened when I was diving this morning, something extraordinary. I found a wreck about eighty or ninety feet down."

"You damn fool." She was angry now. "Diving at that kind of depth on your own and at your age. Where was this?"

Although not a serious diver, she did go down occasionally and knew most of the sites. He hesitated. It was not only that he knew she would be thoroughly angry to know that he'd dived a place like Thunder Point and it certainly wasn't that he didn't trust her. He just wanted to keep the location of the submarine to himself for the moment, certainly until he'd seen Garth Travers.

"All I can tell you, Jenny, is that I found a German U-boat from nineteen forty-five."

Her eyes widened. "My God!"

"I managed to get inside. There was a briefcase, an aluminum thing. Watertight. I found the Captain's diary inside. It's in German, which I can't read, but there were a couple of names I recognized."

"Such as?"

"Martin Bormann and the Duke of Windsor."

She looked slightly dazed. "Henry, what's going on here?"

"That's what I'd like to know." He took her hand. "Remember that English friend of mine, Rear Admiral Travers?"

"The one you served in the Korean War with? Of course, you introduced me to him the year before last when we were in Miami and he was passing through."

"I phoned him earlier. He's got all sorts of records on the German Kriegsmarine. He checked on the boat for me. One-eighty, that's what's painted on the conning tower, but one-eighty was a different type boat and it went down in the Bay of Biscay in nineteen forty-four."

She shook her head in bewilderment. "But what does it all mean?"

"There were stories for years about Bormann, dozens of books, all saying he didn't die in Berlin at the end of the War, that he survived. People had sightings of him in South America, or so they said."

"And the Duke of Windsor?"

"God knows." He shook his head. "All I know is this could be important and I found the damn boat, Jenny, me, Henry Baker. Christ, I don't know what's in the diary, but maybe it changes history."

He got up and walked to the rail, gripping it with both hands. She had never seen him so excited, got up herself and put a hand on his shoulder. "Want me to come with you?"

"Hell no, there's no need for that."

"Billy and Mary could run things here."

He shook his head. "I'll be back in a few days. Four at the most."

"Fine." She managed a smile. "Then we'd better get back to the house and I'll help you pack."

His flight in the Carib Aviation Partenavia was uneventful except for strong headwinds that held them back a little so that the landing was later than he'd anticipated, around six-thirty. By the time he'd passed through customs, collected his luggage and proceeded to the British Airways desk, it was seven o'clock. He went through security into the departure lounge and the flight was called ten minutes later.

The service in British Airways First Class was as superb as usual. He had carried Korvettenkapitän Friemel's case through with him and he accepted a glass of champagne from the stewardess, opened the case and browsed through it for a while, not just the diary, but the photos and the letters. Strange, because he didn't understand a word. It was the photo of the Kriegsmarine officer that really intrigued him, presumably Friemel himself, the face of the enemy, only Baker didn't feel like that, but then seamen of all nations, even in war, tended to have a high regard for each other. It was the sea, after all, which was the common enemy.

He closed the case and put it in the locker overhead when takeoff was announced and spent his time reading one or two of the London newspapers which were in plentiful supply. The meal was served soon after takeoff, and after it had been cleared away the stewardess reminded him that each seat had its own small video screen and offered him a brochure which included a lengthy list of videos available.

Baker browsed through it. It would at least help pass the time, and then he shivered a little as if someone had passed over his grave. There was a film there he'd heard about, a German film, *Das Boot*, in English, *The Boat*, from all accounts a harrowing story of life in a U-boat at the worst time in the War.

Against his better judgment he ordered it and asked for a large Scotch. The cabin crew went round pulling down the window blinds so that those who wished to might sleep. Baker inserted the video, put on the earphones and sat there, in the semidarkness, watching. He called for another Scotch after twenty minutes and kept watching. It was one of the most disturbing films of its kind he had ever seen.

An hour was enough. He switched off, tilted his seat back and lay there, staring through the darkness thinking about Korvettenkapitän Paul Friemel and U180 and that final ending on Thunder Point, wondering what had gone wrong. After a while, he slept.

THREE

It was ten o'clock when the doorbell rang at the house in Lord North Street. Garth Travers answered the door himself and found Henry Baker standing there in the rain, the briefcase in one hand, his overnight case in the other. He had no raincoat and the collar of his jacket was turned up.

"My dear chap," Travers said. "For God's sake, come in before you drown." He turned as he closed the door. "You'll stay here of course?"

"If that suits, old buddy."

"It's good to hear that description of me again," Travers told him. "I'll show you to your room later. Let's get you some breakfast. My housekeeper's day off, so you'll get it Navy style."

"Coffee would be fine for the moment," Baker said.

They went to the large, comfortable kitchen and Travers put the kettle on. Baker placed the briefcase on the table. "There it is."

"Fascinating." Travers examined the Kriegsmarine insignia on the case, then glanced up. "May I?"

"That's why I'm here."

Travers opened the case. He examined the letters quickly. "These must be keepsakes, dated at various times in nineteen forty-three and -four. All from his wife from the looks of things." He turned to the photos. "Knight's Cross holder? Must have been quite a boy." He looked at the photos of the woman and the two little girls and read the handwritten paragraph on the back of one of them. "Oh dear."

"What is it?" Baker asked.

"It reads, 'my dear wife Lottie and my daughters, Ilse and Marie, killed in a bombing raid on Hamburg, August the eighth, nineteen forty-four.' "

"Dear God!" Baker said.

"I can check up on him easily enough. I have a book listing all holders of the Knight's Cross. It was the Germans' highest award for valor. You make the coffee and I'll get it."

Travers went out and Baker found cups, a tin of instant milk in the icebox, had just finished when Travers returned with the book in question. He sat down opposite Baker and reached for his coffee.

"Here we are, Paul Friemel, Korvettenkapitän, joined the German Navy as an officer cadet after two years studying medicine at Heidelberg." Travers nodded. "Outstanding record in U-boats. Knight's Cross in July forty-four for sinking an Italian cruiser. They were on our side by then, of course. After that he was assigned to shore duties at Kiel." He made a face. "Oh dear, mystery piles on mystery. It says here he was killed in a bombing raid on Kiel in April, nineteen forty-five."

"Like hell he was," Baker said.

"Exactly." Travers opened the diary and glanced at the first page. "Beautiful handwriting and perfectly legible." He riffled the pages. "Some of the entries are quite short. Can't be more than thirty pages at the most."

"Your German is fluent as I recall," Baker said.

"Like a native, old boy; my maternal grandmother was from Munich. I'll tell you what I'll do, an instant translation into my word processor. Should take no more than an hour and a half. You get yourself some breakfast. Ham and eggs in the refrigerator, sorry, icebox to you, bread bin over there. Join me in the study when you're ready."

He went out and Baker, relaxed now that everything was in hand, busied himself making breakfast, aware that he was hungry. He sat at the table to eat it, reading Travers' copy of that morning's London *Times* while he did so. It was perhaps an hour later that he cleared everything away and went into the study.

Travers sat at the word processor, watching the screen, his fingers rippling over the keyboard, the diary open and standing on a small lectern on his right-hand side. There was a curiously intent look on his face.

Baker said cheerfully, "How's it going?"

"Not now, old boy, please."

Baker shrugged, sat by the fire and picked up a magazine. It was quiet, only the sound of the word processor except when Travers suddenly said, "My God!" and then a few minutes after that, "No, I can't believe it."

"For heaven's sake, what is it, Garth?" Baker demanded.

"In a minute, old boy, almost through."

Baker sat there on tenterhooks, and after a while Travers sat back with a sigh. "Finished. I'll run it through the copier."

"Does it have anything interesting to say?"

"Interesting?" Travers laughed harshly. "That's putting it mildly. First of all I must make the point that it isn't the official ship's log; it's essentially a private account of the peculiar circumstances surrounding his final voyage. Maybe he was trying to cover himself in some way, who knows, but it's pretty sensational. The thing is, what are we going to do about it?"

"What on earth do you mean?"

"Read it for yourself. I'll go and make some more coffee," Travers said as the copier stopped. He shuffled the sheets together and handed them to Baker, who settled himself in the chair by the fire and started to read.

Bergen, Norway, 30 April 1945. I, Paul Friemel, start this account, more because of the strangeness of the task I am to perform than anything else. We left Kiel two days ago in this present boat designated U180. My command is in fact a craft that was damaged by bombing while under construction at Kiel in nineteen forty-three. We are to my certain knowledge carrying the number of a dead ship. My orders from Grand Admiral Doenitz are explicit. My passenger will arrive this evening from Berlin, although I find this hard to swallow. He will carry a direct order in the Führer's own hand. I will learn our destination from him.

There was a gap here in the diary and then a further entry for the evening of the same day.

I received orders to proceed to the airstrip where a Feiseler Storch landed. After a few minutes an officer in the uniform of an SS General appeared and asked if I was Korvettenkapitän Friemel. He in no way identified himself, although at that stage I felt that I had seen him before. When we reached the dock, he took me to one side before boarding and presented me with a sealed envelope. When I opened it I found it contained the order from the Führer himself, which had been mentioned in Grand Admiral Doenitz's personal order to me. It ran as follows:

From the leader and Chancellor of the State. Reichsleiter Martin Bormann acts with my authority on a matter of the utmost importance and essential to the continuance of the Third Reich. You will place yourself under his direct authority, at all times remembering your solemn oath as an officer of the Kriegsmarine to your Führer, and will accept his command and authority as he sees fit and in all situations.

I recall now, having seen Bormann once at a State function in Berlin in 1942. Few people would recognize the man, for of all our leaders, I would conclude he is the least known. He is smaller than I would have thought, rough featured with overlong arms. Frankly, if seen in working clothes, one would imagine him a docker or laborer. The Reichsleiter enquired as to whether I accepted his authority which, having little option, I have agreed to do. He instructed me that as regards my officers and the crew, he was to be known as General Strasser.

1 May. Although the officers' area is the most spacious on board, it only caters for three with one bunk lashed up. I have taken this for myself and given the Reichsleiter the Commanding Officer's compartment on the port side and aft of what passes for a wardroom in this boat. It is the one private place we have, though only a felt curtain separates his quarters from the wardroom. As we left Bergen on the evening tide, the Reichsleiter joined me on the bridge and informed me that our destination was Venezuela.

2 May 1945. As the boat has been fitted with a snorkel I am able to contemplate a voyage entirely underwater, though I fear this may not be possible in the heavy weather of the North Atlantic. I have laid a course underwater by way of the Iceland-Faroes narrows and once we have broken into the Atlantic will review the situation.

3 May 1945. Have received by radio from Bergen the astonishing news that the Führer has died on the 1st of May fighting valiantly at the head of our forces in Berlin, in an attempt to deny the Russians victory. I conveyed the melancholy news to the Reichsleiter, who accepted it with what I thought to be astonishing calm. He then instructed me to pass the news to the crew, stressing that the war would continue. An hour later we received word over the radio that Grand Admiral Doenitz had set up a provisional government in Schleswig-Holstein. I doubt that it can last long with the Russians in Berlin and the Americans and British across the Rhine.

Baker was more than fascinated by this time and quickly passed through several pages which at that stage were mainly concerned with the ship's progress.

5 May. We received an order from U-boat command that all sub-marines at sea must observe a cease-fire from this morning at 08.00 hours. The order is to return to harbor. I discussed this with the Reichsleiter in his quarters, who pointed out that he had the Führer's authority to continue still and asked me if I queried it. I found this difficult to answer and he suggested that I consider the situation for a day or two.

8 May 1945. We received this evening by radio the message I have been expecting. Total capitulation to the enemy. Germany has gone down to defeat. I again met with the Reichsleiter in his quarters and while discussing the situation received a ciphered message from Bergen instructing me to return or to continue the voyage as ordered. The Reichsleiter seized upon this and demanded my obedience, insisting on his right to speak to the crew over the intercom. He disclosed his identity and the matter of his authority from the Führer. He pointed out that there was nothing left for any of us in Germany and that there were friends waiting in Venezuela. A new life for those who wanted it, the possibility for a return to Germany for those who wanted that. It was difficult to argue with his reasoning and, on the whole, my crew and officers accepted it.

12 May 1945. Continued south and this day received general signal from Canadian Navy in Nova Scotia to any U-boat still at sea, demanding we report exact situation, surface and proceed under black flag. Failure to do so apparently condemning us to be considered as pirate and liable to immediate attack. The Reichsleiter showed little concern at this news.

15 May 1945. The snorkel device is in essence an air pipe raised above the surface when we run at periscope depth. In this way we may run on our diesel engines underwater without using up our batteries. I have discovered considerable problems with the device, for if the sea is rough, and nothing is rougher than the Atlantic, the ball cock closes. When this happens, the engines still draw in air, which means an instant fall in pressure in the boat and this gives the crew huge problems. We have had three cases of ruptured eardrums, but proceeding with the aid of the snorkel does make it difficult for us to be detected from the air.

17 May 1945. So far into the Atlantic are we now that I feel our risk of detection from the air to be minimal and decided from today to proceed on the surface. We carve through the Atlantic's heavy seas, continually awash, and our chances of encountering anyone in these latitudes are slim.

20 May 1945. The Reichsleiter has kept himself to himself for much of the trip except for eating with the officers, preferring to remain on his bunk and read. Today he asked if he could accompany me when I was taking my watch. He arrived on the bridge in foul weather gear when we were barreling through fifteen- and twenty-foot waves and thoroughly enjoyed the experience.

21 May 1945. An extraordinary night for me. The Reichsleiter appeared at dinner obviously the worse for drink. Later he invited me to his quarters where he produced a bottle of Scotch whisky from one of his cases and insisted I join him. He drank freely, talking a great deal about the Führer and the final days in the Bunker in Berlin. When I asked him how he had escaped, he told me they had used the East-West Avenue in the center of Berlin as a runway for light aircraft. At this stage he had finished the whisky, pulled out one of his duffel bags from under the bunk and opened it. He took out an aluminium Kriegsmarine captain's briefcase like my own and put it on the bunk, then found a fresh bottle of whisky.

By now he was very drunk and told me of his last meeting with the Führer, who had charged him with a sacred duty to continue the future of the Third Reich. He said an organization called the Odessa Line had been set up years before by the SS to provide an escape line, in the event of temporary defeat, for those officers of SS and other units essential to the continuance of the struggle.

Then he moved on to the Kamaradenwerk, Action for Comrades, an organization set up to continue National Socialist ideas after the war. There were hundreds of millions salted away in Switzerland, South America and other places and friends in every country at the highest level of government. He took his aluminium case from the bunk, opened it and produced a file. He called it the Blue Book. He said it listed many members of the English aristocracy, many members of the English Parliament, who had secretly supported the Führer during the nineteen-thirties and also many Americans. He then took a paper from a buff envelope and unfolded it before me. He told me it was the Windsor Protocol, a secret agreement with the Führer signed by the Duke of Windsor while resident at Estoril in Portugal in 1940 after the fall of France. In it he agreed to ascend the throne of England again after a successful German invasion. I asked him *what value such a document could be and how could he be sure it was genuine. He became extremely angry and told me that, in any event, there were those on his Blue Book list who would do anything to avoid exposure and that his own future was taken care of. I asked him at that point if he was certain and he laughed and said you could always trust an English gentleman. At this point he became so drunk that I had to assist him on to the bunk. He fell asleep instantly and I examined the contents of the briefcase. The names in his Blue Book list meant nothing to me, but the Windsor Protocol looked genuine enough. The only other thing in the briefcase was a list of numbered bank accounts and the Führer order and I closed it and placed it under the bunk with his other luggage.*

Baker stopped at this point, put the diary down, got up and walked to the window as Garth Travers entered.

Travers said, "Here's the coffee. Thought I'd leave you to get on with it. Have you finished?"

"Just read what Bormann told him on the twenty-first of May."

"The best is yet to come, old boy, I'll be back," and Travers went out again.

25 May 1945. 500 miles north of Puerto Rico. I envisage using the Anegada Passage through the Leeward Islands into the Caribbean Sea with a clear run to the Venezuelan coast from there.

26 May 1945. The Reichsleiter called me to his quarters and informed me that it was necessary to make a stop before reaching our destination and requested to see the chart for the Virgin Islands. The island he indicated is a small one, Samson Cay, south-east of St. John in the American Virgin Islands, but in British sovereign waters being a few miles south of Norman Island in the British Virgin Islands. He gave me no indication of his reason for wishing to stop there.

27 May 1945. Surfaced off the coast of Samson Cay at 21.00 hours. A dark night with a quarter moon. Some lights observed on shore. The Reichsleiter requested that he be put ashore in one of the inflatables, and I arranged for Petty Officer Schroeder to take him. Before leaving he called me to his quarters and told me that he was expecting to meet friends on shore, but as a precaution against something going wrong he was not taking anything of importance with him. He particularly indicated the briefcase which he left on the bunk and gave me a sealed envelope which he said would give me details of my destination in Venezuela if anything went wrong and the name of the man I was to hand the briefcase to. He told me to send Schroeder back for him at 02.00 hours and that if he was not on the beach I was to fear the worst and depart. He wore civilian clothes and left his uniform.

Travers came back in at that moment. "Still at it?"

"I'm on the final entry."

The Admiral went to the drinks cabinet and poured Scotch into two glasses. "Drink that," he said, passing one to Baker. "You're going to need it."

28 May 1945. Midnight. I have just been on the bridge and noticed an incredible stillness to everything, quite unnatural and like nothing I have experienced before. Lightning on the far horizon and distant thunder. The waters here in the lagoon are shallow and give me concern. I write this at the chart table while waiting for the radio officer to check for weather reports.

There was a gap here and then a couple of lines scrawled hurriedly.

Radio report from St. Thomas indicates hurricane approaching fast. We must make for deep water and go down to ride it out. The Reichsleiter must take his chance.

"Only the poor buggers didn't ride it out," Travers said. "The hurricane caught them when they were still vulnerable. Must have ripped her side open on the reef where you found her."

"I'm afraid so," Baker said. "Then I presume the current must have driven her in on that ledge under the overhang."

"Where she remained all these years. Strange no one ever discovered her before."

"Not really," Baker said. "It's a bad place. No one goes there. It's too far out for people who dive for fun and it's very dangerous. Another thing. If the recent hurricane hadn't broken away the overhang, I might well have missed it myself."

"You haven't actually given me the location yet," Travers remonstrated.

"Yes, well, that's my business," Baker said.

Travers smiled. "I understand, old boy, I understand, but I really must point out that this is a very hot potato."

"What on earth are you getting at?"

"Number one, we'd appear to have positive proof after all the rumor and speculation for nearly fifty years, that Martin Bormann escaped from Berlin."

"So?" Baker said.

"More than that! There's the Blue Book list of Hitler's sympathizers here in England, not only the nobility but Members of Parliament plus the names of a few of your fellow countrymen. Worse than that, this Windsor Protocol."

"What do you mean?" Baker asked.

"According to the diary, Bormann kept them in a similar survival case to this." He tapped the aluminium briefcase. "And he left it on the bunk in the Commanding Officer's quarters. Now just consider this. According to Friemel's final entry he was in the control room at the chart table, entering the diary when he got that final radio report about the hurricane. He shoves the diary in his briefcase and locks it, only a second to do that, then gets on with the emergency. That would explain why you found the briefcase in the control room."

"I'll buy that," Baker agreed.

"No, you're missing the real point, which is that the case survived."

"So what are you getting at?"

"These things were built for survival, which means it's almost certain Bormann's is still in the Commanding Officer's quarters with the Blue Book, the Windsor Protocol and Hitler's personal order concerning Bormann. Even after all these years the facts contained in those documents would cause a hell of a stink, Henry, especially the Windsor thing."

"I wouldn't want to cause that kind of trouble," Baker told him.

"I believe you, I know you well enough for that, but what if someone else found that submarine?"

"I told you, no one goes there."

"You also told me you thought an overhang had been torn off revealing it. I mean, somebody *could* dive there, Henry, just like you did."

"The conditions were unusually calm," Baker said. "It's a bad place, Garth, no one goes there, I know, believe me. Another thing, the Commanding Officer's compartment is forward and aft of the wardroom, on the port side, that's what Friemel said in the diary."

"That's right. I was shown over a type VII U-boat. The Navy had one or two they took over after the War. The captain's cabin, so-called, is across from the radio and sound rooms. Quick access to the control room. That was the point."

"Yes, well my point is that you can't get in there. The forward watertight hatch is closed fast."

"Well you'd expect that. If they were in trouble, he'd have ordered every watertight hatch in the boat closed. Standard procedure."

"I tried to move the wheel. Corroded like hell. The door is solid. No way of getting in there."

"There's always a way, Henry, you know that." Travers sat there frowning for a moment, then said, "Look, I'd like to show the diary to a friend of mine."

"Who are we talking about?"

"Brigadier Charles Ferguson. We've known each other for years. He might have some ideas."

"What makes him so special?"

"He works on the intelligence side of things. Runs a highly specialized anti-terrorist unit responsible only to the Prime Minister, and that's privileged information, by the way."

"I wouldn't have thought this was exactly his field," Baker said.

"Just let me show him the diary, old boy," Travers said soothingly. "See what he thinks."

"Okay," Baker said. "But the location stays my little secret."

"Of course. You can come with me if you want."

"No, I think I'll have a bath and maybe go for a walk. I always feel like hell after a long jet flight. I could see this Brigadier Ferguson later if you think it necessary."

"Just as you like," Travers said. "I'll leave you to it. You know where everything is."

Baker went out and Travers looked up Ferguson's personal phone number at the Ministry of Defence and was speaking to him at once. "Charles, Garth Travers here."

"My dear old boy, haven't seen you in ages."

Travers came directly to the point. "I think you should see me at your soonest moment, Charles. A rather astonishing document has come into my hands."

Ferguson remained as urbane as ever. "Really? Well we must do something about that. You've been to my flat in Cavendish Square?"

"Of course I have."

"I'll see you there in thirty minutes."

Ferguson sat on the sofa beside the fireplace in his elegant drawing room and Travers sat opposite. The door opened and Ferguson's manservant Kim, an ex-Ghurka Corporal, entered, immaculate in snow-white jacket and served tea. He withdrew silently and Ferguson reached for his cup of tea and continued reading. Finally he put the cup down and leaned back.

"Quite bizarre, isn't it?"

"You believe it then?"

"The diary? Good God, yes. I mean you obviously vouch for your friend Baker. He isn't a hoaxer or anything?"

"Certainly not. We were lieutenants together in Korea. Saved my life. He was chairman of a highly respected publishing house in New York until a few years ago. He's also a multi-millionaire."

"And he won't tell you the location?"

"Oh, that's understandable enough. He's like a boy again. He's made this astonishing discovery." Travers smiled. "He'll tell us eventually. So what do you think? I know it's not really in your line."

"But that's where you're wrong, Garth. I think it's very much in my line, because I work for the Prime Minister and I think he should see this."

"There is one point," Travers said. "If Bormann landed on this Samson Cay place, there had to be a reason. I mean, who in the hell was he meeting?"

"Perhaps he was to be picked up by somebody, a fast boat and a passage by night, you know the sort of thing. I mean, he probably left the briefcase on board as a precaution until he knew everything was all right, but we can find out easily enough. I'll get my assistant, Detective Inspector Lane, on to it. Regular bloodhound." He slipped the papers comprising the diary back into their envelope. "Give me a moment. I'm going to send my driver round with this to Downing Street. Eyes of the Prime Minister only, then I'll see how soon he can see us. I'll be back."

He went out to his study and Travers poured another cup of tea. It was cold and he walked restlessly across to the window and looked outside. It was still raining, a thoroughly miserable day. As he turned, Ferguson came back.

"Can't see us until two o'clock, but I spoke to him personally and he's going to have a quick look when the package arrives. You and I, old son, are going to have an early luncheon at the Garrick. I've told Lane we'll be there in case he gets a quick result on Samson Cay."

"Umbrella weather," Travers said. "How I loathe it."

"Large gin and tonic will work wonders, old boy." Ferguson ushered him out.

They had steak and kidney pie at the Garrick, sitting opposite each other at the long table in the dining room, and coffee in the bar afterwards, which was where Jack Lane found them.

"Ah, there you are, Jack, got anything for me?" Ferguson demanded.

"Nothing very exciting, sir. Samson Cay is owned by an American hotel group called Samson Holdings. They have hotels in Las Vegas, Los Angeles and three in Florida, but Samson Cay would appear to be their flagship. I've got you a brochure. Strictly a millionaire's hideaway!"

He passed it across and they examined it. There were the usual pictures of white beaches, palm trees, cottages in an idyllic setting.

"Garden of Eden according to this," Ferguson said. "They even have a landing strip for light aircraft, I see."

"And a casino, sir."

"Can't be too big as casinos go," Travers pointed out. "They only cater for a hundred people."

"Isn't the numbers that count, old boy," Ferguson said. "It's the amount of cash across the table. What about during the War, Jack?"

"There was always a hotel of some sort. In those days it was owned by an American family called Herbert, who were also in the hotel business. Remember Samson Cay is in the British Virgin Islands, which means it comes under the control of Tortola as regards the law, customs and so forth. I spoke to their public record office. According to their files the hotel stayed empty during the War. The occasional fishermen from Tortola, a couple caretaking the property and that's all."

"Doesn't help but thanks, Jack, you've done a good job."

"It might help if I knew what it was about, sir."

"Later, Jack, later. Off you go and make Britain a safer place to live in." Lane departed with a grin, and Ferguson turned to Travers.

"Right, old boy, Downing Street awaits."

The Prime Minister was sitting behind his desk in his study when an aide showed them in. He stood up and came round the desk to shake hands. "Brigadier."

"Prime Minister," Ferguson said. "May I introduce Rear Admiral Travers?"

"Of course. Do sit down, gentlemen." He went and sat behind his desk again. "An incredible business this."

"An understatement, Prime Minister," Ferguson replied.

"You were quite right to bring it to my attention. The royal aspect is what concerns me most." The phone rang. He picked it up, listened, then said, "Send them up." As he replaced the receiver he said, "I know you've had your problems with the Security Services, Brigadier, but I feel this to be one of those cases where we should honor our agreement to keep them informed about anything of mutual interest. You recall you agreed to liaise with the Deputy Director, Simon Carter, and Sir Francis Pamer?"

"I did indeed, Prime Minister."

"I called both of them in immediately after reading the diary. They've been downstairs having a look at it themselves. They're on their way up."

A moment later the door opened and the aide ushered in the two men. Simon Carter was fifty, a small man with hair already snow-white. Never a field agent, he was an ex-academic, one of the faceless men who controlled Britain's intelligence system. Sir Francis Pamer was forty-seven, tall and elegant in a blue flannel suit. He wore a Guards tie, thanks to three years as a subaltern in the Grenadiers, and had a slight smile permanently fixed to the corner of his mouth in a way that Ferguson found intensely irritating.

They all shook hands and sat down. "Well, gentlemen?" the Prime Minister said.

"Always assuming it isn't a hoax," Pamer said. "A fascinating story."

"It would explain many aspects of the Bormann legend," Simon Carter put in. "Arthur Axmann, the Hitler Youth leader, said he saw Bormann's body lying in the road near the Lehrter Station in Berlin, that was after the breakout from the Bunker."

"It would seem now that what he saw was someone who looked like Bormann," Travers said.

"So it would appear," Carter agreed. "That Bormann was on this U-boat and survived would explain the numerous reports over the years of sightings of him in South America."

"Simon Wiesenthal, the Nazi hunter, always thought him alive," Pamer said. "Before Eichmann was executed, he told the Israelis that Bormann was alive. Why would a man faced with death lie?"

"All well and good, gentlemen," the Prime Minister told them, "but frankly, I think the question of whether Martin Bormann survived the war or not purely of academic interest. It would change history a little and the newspapers would get some mileage out of it."

"And a damn sight more out of this Blue Book list that's mentioned. Members of Parliament and the nobility." Carter shuddered. "The mind boggles."

"My dear Simon," Pamer told him. "There were an awful lot of people around before the War who found aspects of Hitler's message rather attractive. There are also names in that list with a Washington base."

"Yes, well their children and grandchildren wouldn't thank you to have their names mentioned, and what in the hell was Bormann doing at this Samson Cay?"

"There's a resort there now, one of those rich man's hideaways," Ferguson said. "During the War there was a hotel, but it was closed for the duration. We checked with public records in Tortola. Owned by an American family called Herbert."

"What do you think Bormann was after there?" Pamer asked.

"One can only guess, but my theory runs something like this," Ferguson said. "He probably intended to let U180 proceed to Venezuela on its own.

I would hazard a guess that he was to be picked up by someone and Samson Cay was the rendezvous. He left the briefcase as a precaution in case anything went wrong. After all, he did give Friemel instructions about its disposal if anything happened to him."

"A pretty scandal, I agree, gentlemen, the whole thing, but imagine the furor it would cause if it became known that the Duke of Windsor had signed an agreement with Hitler," the Prime Minister said.

"Personally I feel it more than likely that this so-called Windsor Protocol would prove fraudulent," Pamer told him.

"That's as may be, but the papers would have a field day, and, frankly, the Royal Family have had more than their share of scandal in this past year or so," the Prime Minister replied.

There was silence and Ferguson said gently, "Are you suggesting that we attempt to recover Bormann's briefcase before anyone else does, Prime Minister?"

"Yes, that would seem the sensible thing to do. Do you think you might handle that, Brigadier?"

It was Simon Carter who protested, "Sir, I must remind you that this U-boat lies in American territorial waters."

"Well I don't think we need to bring our American cousins into this," Ferguson said. "They would have total rights to the wreck and the contents. Imagine what they'd get for the Windsor Protocol at auction."

Carter tried again. "I really must protest, Prime Minister. Group Four's brief is to combat terrorism and subversion."

The Prime Minister raised a hand. "Exactly, and I can think of few things more subversive to the interests of the nation than the publication of this Windsor Protocol. Brigadier, you will devise a plan, do whatever is necessary and as soon as possible. Keep me informed and also the Deputy Director and Sir Francis."

"So the matter is entirely in my hands?" Ferguson asked.

"Total authority. Just do what you have to." The Prime Minister got up. "And now you really must excuse me, gentlemen. I have a tight schedule."

The four men walked down to the security gates where Downing Street met Whitehall and paused at the pavement.

Carter said, "Damn you, Ferguson, you always get your way, but see you keep us informed. Come on, Francis," and he strode away.

Francis Pamer smiled. "Don't take it to heart, Brigadier, it's just that he hates you. Good hunting," and he hurried after Carter.

Travers and Ferguson walked along Whitehall looking for a taxi and Travers said, "Why does Carter dislike you so?"

"Because I succeeded too often where he's failed and because I'm outside the system and only answerable to the Prime Minister and Carter can't stand that."

"Pamer seems a decent enough sort."

"So I've heard."

"He's married, I suppose?"

"As a matter of fact, no. Apparently much in demand by the ladies. One of the oldest baronetcies in England. I believe he's the twelfth or thirteenth. Has a wonderful house in Hampshire. His mother lives there."

"So what is his connection with intelligence matters?"

"The Prime Minister has made him a junior minister at the Home Office. Extra Minister I believe his title is. A kind of roving trouble shooter. As long as he and Carter keep out of my hair I'll be well pleased."

"And Henry Baker—do you think he'll tell you where U180 is lying?"

"Of course he will, he'll have to." Ferguson saw a taxi and waved it down. "Come on, let's get moving and we'll confront him now."

After his bath, Baker had lain on his bed for a moment, a towel about his waist and, tired from the amount of traveling he'd done, fell fast asleep. When he finally awakened and checked his watch it was shortly after two o'clock. He dressed quickly and went downstairs.

There was no sign of Travers and when he opened the front door it was still raining hard. In spite of that, he decided to go for a walk as much to clear his head as anything else. He helped himself to an old trenchcoat from the cloakroom and an umbrella and went down the steps. He felt good, but then rain always made him feel that way and he was still excited about the way things were going. He turned toward Millbank and paused, looking across to Victoria Tower Gardens and the Thames.

In St. John, for obscure reasons, people drive on the left-hand side of the road as in England, and yet on that rainy afternoon in London, Henry Baker did what most Americans would do before crossing the road. He looked left and stepped straight into the path of a London Transport bus coming from the right. Westminster Hospital being close by, an ambulance was there in minutes, not that it mattered, for he was dead by the time they reached the Casualty Department.

FOUR

In St. John it was just after ten o'clock in the morning as Jenny Grant walked along the waterfront to the cafe and went up the steps and entered the bar. Billy was sweeping the floor and he looked up and grinned.

"A fine, soft day, you heard from Mr. Henry yet?"

"Five hours time difference." She glanced at her watch. "Just after three o'clock in the afternoon there, Billy. There's time."

Mary Jones appeared at the end of the bar. "Telephone call for you in the office. London, England."

Jenny smiled instantly. "Henry?"

"No, some woman. You take it, honey, and I'll get you a cup of coffee."

Jenny brushed past her and went into the office, and Mary poured a little water into the coffee percolator. There was a sharp cry from inside the office. Billy and Mary glanced at each other in alarm, then hurried in.

Jenny sat behind the desk looking dazed, clutching the phone in one hand, and Mary said, "What is it, honey? Tell Mary."

"It's a policewoman ringing me from Scotland Yard in London," Jenny whispered. "Henry's dead. He was killed in a road accident."

She started to cry helplessly and Mary took the phone from her. "Hello, are you still there?"

"Yes," a neutral voice replied. "I'm sorry if the other lady was upset. There's no easy way to do this."

"Sure, honey, you got your job to do."

"Could you find out where he was staying in London?"

"Hang on." Mary turned to Jenny. "She wants to know the address he was staying at over there."

So Jenny told her.

It was just before five and Travers, in response to a telephone call from Ferguson asking him to meet him, waited in the foyer of the mortuary in the Cromwell Road. The Brigadier came bustling in a few minutes later.

"Sorry to keep you, Garth, but I want to expedite things. There has to be an autopsy for the coroner's inquest and we can't have that unless he's formally identified."

"I've spoken to the young woman who lives with him, Jenny Grant. She's badly shocked but intends to fly over as soon as possible. Should be here tomorrow."

"Yes, well, I don't want to hang about." Ferguson took a folded paper from his inside breast pocket. "I've got a court order from a Judge in chambers here which authorizes Rear Admiral Garth Travers to make formal identification, so let's get on with it."

A uniformed attendant appeared at that moment. "Is one of you gentlemen Brigadier Ferguson?"

"That's me," Ferguson told him.

"Professor Manning is waiting. This way, sir."

The post-mortem room was lit by fluorescent lighting that bounced off the white-lined walls. There were four stainless-steel operating tables. Baker's body lay on the nearest one, his head on a block. A tall, thin man in surgeon's overalls stood waiting, flanked by two mortuary technicians. Travers noted with distaste that they all wore green rubber boots.

"Hello, Sam, thanks for coming in," Ferguson said. "This is Garth Travers."

Manning shook hands. "Could we get on, Charles? I have tickets for Covent Garden."

"Of course, old boy." Ferguson took out a pen and laid the form on the end of the operating table. "Do you, Rear Admiral Travers, formally identify this man as Henry Baker, an American citizen of St. John in the American Virgin Islands?"

"I do."

"Sign here." Travers did so and Ferguson handed the form to Manning. "There you go, Sam, we'll leave you to it," and he nodded to Travers and led the way out.

Ferguson closed the glass partition in his Daimler so the driver couldn't hear what was being said.

"A hell of a shock," Travers said. "It hasn't sunk in yet."

"Leaves us in rather an interesting situation," Ferguson commented.

"In what way?"

"The location of U180. Has it died with him?"

"Of course," Travers said. "I was forgetting."

"On the other hand, perhaps the Grant girl knows. I mean she lived with him and all that."

"Not that kind of relationship," Travers told him. "Purely platonic. I met her just the once. I was passing through Miami and they happened to be there. Lovely young woman."

"Well let's hope this paragon of all the virtues has the answer to our problem," Ferguson said.

"And if not?"

"Then I'll just have to think of something."

"I wonder what Carter will make of all this."

Ferguson groaned. "I suppose I'd better bring him up to date. Keep the sod happy," and he reached for his car phone and dialed Inspector Lane.

At precisely the same time Francis Pamer, having made a very fast trip indeed from London in his Porsche Cabriolet to his country home at Hatherley Court in Hampshire, was mounting the grand staircase to his mother's apartment on the first floor. The house had been in the family for five hundred years and he always visited it with conscious pleasure, but not now. There were more important things on his mind.

When he tapped on the door of the bedroom and entered he found his mother propped up in the magnificent four-poster bed, a uniformed nurse sitting beside her. She was eighty-five and very old and frail and lay there with her eyes closed.

The nurse stood up. "Sir Francis. We weren't expecting you."

"I know. How is she?"

"Not good, sir. Doctor was here earlier. He said it could be next week or three months from now."

He nodded. "You have a break. I want to have a little chat with her." The nurse went out and Pamer sat on the bed and took his mother's hand. She opened her eyes. "How are you, darling?" he asked.

"Why, Francis, what a lovely surprise." Her voice was very faded.

"I had some business not too far away, Mother, so I thought I'd call in."

"That was nice of you, dear."

Pamer got up, lit a cigarette and walked to the fire. "I was talking about Samson Cay today."

"Oh, are you thinking of taking a holiday, dear? If you go and that nice Mr. Santiago is there, do give him my regards."

"Of course. I'm right, aren't I? It was your mother who brought Samson Cay into the family?"

"Yes, dear, her father, George Herbert, gave it to her as a wedding present."

"Tell me about the War again, Mother," he said. "And Samson Cay."

"Well, the hotel was empty for most of the War. It was small then, of course, just a little colonial-style place."

"And when did you go there? You never really talked about that and I was too young to remember."

"March nineteen forty-five. You were born in July, the previous year, and those terrible German rockets kept hitting London, V1s and V2s. Your father was out of the army then and serving in Mr. Churchill's government as a Junior Minister, just like you, dear. He was worried about the attacks on London continuing so he arranged passage on a boat to Puerto Rico for you and me. We carried on to Samson Cay from there. Now I remember. It was the beginning of April when we got there. We went over from Tortola by boat. There was an old man and his wife. Black people. Very nice. Jackson, that was it. May and Joseph."

Her voice faded and he went and sat on the bed and took her hand again. "Did anyone visit, Mother? Can you remember that?"

"Visit?" She opened her eyes. "Only Mr. Strasser. Such a nice man. Your father told me he might be coming. He just appeared one night. He said he'd been dropped off in a fishing boat from Tortola and then the hurricane came. It happened the same night. Terrible. We were in the cellar for two days. I held you all the time, but Mr. Strasser was very good. Such a kind man."

"Then what happened?"

"He stayed with us for quite a while. Until June, I think, and then your father arrived."

"And Strasser?"

"He left after that. He had business in South America, and the war in Europe was over, of course, so we came back to England. Mr. Churchill had lost the election and your father wasn't in Parliament anymore, so we lived down here, darling. The farms were a great disappointment."

She was wandering a little. Pamer said, "You once told me my father served with Sir Oswald Mosley in the First World War in the trenches."

"That's true dear, they were great friends."

"Remember Mosley's black shirts, Mother, the British Fascist Party? Did Father have any connection with that?"

"Good heavens no. Poor Oswald. He often spent the weekend here. They arrested him at the beginning of the War. Said he was pro-German. Ridiculous. He was such a gentleman." The voice trailed away and then strengthened. "Such a difficult time we had. Goodness knows how we managed to keep you at Eton. How lucky we all were when your father met Mr. Santiago. What wonderful things they did together at Samson Cay. Some people say it's the finest resort in the Caribbean now. I'd love to visit again, I really would."

Her eyes closed and Pamer went and put her hands under the cover. "You sleep now, Mother, it will do you good."

He closed the door gently, went downstairs to the library, got himself a Scotch and sat by the fire thinking about it all. The contents of the diary had shocked him beyond measure and it was a miracle that he had managed to keep his composure in front of Carter, but the truth was plain now. His father, a British Member of Parliament, a serving officer, a member of government, had had connections with the Nazi Party, one of those who had eagerly looked forward to a German invasion in 1940. The involvement must have been considerable. The whole business with Martin Bormann and Samson Cay proved that.

Francis Pamer's blood ran cold and he went and got another Scotch and wandered around the room looking at the portraits of his ancestors. Five hundred years, one of the oldest families in England, and he was a Junior Minister now, had every prospect of further advancement, but if Ferguson managed to arrange the recovery of Bormann's briefcase from the U-boat he was finished. No reason to doubt that his father's name would be on the Blue Book list of Nazi sympathizers. The scandal would finish him. Not only would he have to say goodbye to any chance of a high position in government, he would have to resign his Parliamentary seat at the very least. Then there would be the clubs. He shuddered. It didn't bear thinking about, but what to do?

The answer was astonishingly simple. Max—Max Santiago. Max would know. He hurried to the study, looked up the number of the Samson Cay resort, phoned through and asked for Carlos Prieto, the general manager.

"Carlos? Francis Pamer here."

"Sir Francis. What a pleasure. What can I do for you? Are you coming to see us soon?"

"I hope so, Carlos. Listen, I need to speak to Señor Santiago urgently. Would you know where he is?"

"Certainly. Staying at the Ritz in Paris. Business, I understand, then he returns to Puerto Rico in three days."

"Bless you, Carlos." Pamer had never felt such relief.

He asked the operator to get him the Ritz in Paris and checked his watch. Five-thirty. He waited impatiently until he heard the receptionist at the Ritz in his ear and asked for Santiago at once.

"Be there, Max, be there," he murmured.

A voice said in French, "Santiago here. Who is this?"

"Thank God. Max, this is Francis. I must see you. Something's happened, something bad. I need your help."

"Calm yourself, Francis, calm yourself. Where are you?"

"Hatherley Court."

"You could be at Gatwick by six-thirty your time?"

"I think so."

"Good. I'll have a charter waiting for you. We can have dinner and you can tell me all about it."

The phone clicked and he was gone. Pamer got his passport from the desk and a wad of traveler's checks, then he went upstairs, opened his mother's door and peered in. She was sleeping. He closed the door gently and went downstairs.

The phone sounded in his study. He hurried in to answer it and found Simon Carter on the line. "There you are. Been chasing you all over the place. Baker's dead. Just heard from Ferguson."

"Good God," Pamer said and then had a thought. "Doesn't that mean the location of U180 died with him?"

"Well he certainly didn't tell Travers, but apparently his girlfriend is flying over tomorrow, a Jenny Grant. Ferguson is hoping that she knows. Anyway, I'll keep you in touch."

Pamer went out, frowning, and the nurse entered the hall from the kitchen area. "Leaving, Sir Francis?"

"Urgent Government business, Nellie, give her my love."

He let himself out, got in the Porsche and drove away.

At Garth Travers' in Lord North Street the Admiral and Ferguson finished searching Baker's suitcase. "You didn't really expect to find the location of that damned reef hidden amongst his clothes, did you?" Travers asked.

"Stranger things have happened," Ferguson said, "believe me." They went into the study. The aluminium briefcase was on the desk. "This is it, is it?"

"Yes," Travers told him.

"Let's have a look."

The Admiral opened it. Ferguson examined the letter, the photos and glanced through the diary. "You copied this on your word processor here I presume?"

"Oh, yes, I typed the translation straight out of the top of my head."

"So the disk is still in the machine?"

"Yes."

"Get it out, there's a good chap, and stick it in the case, also any copy you have."

"I say, Charles, that's a bit thick after all I've done and anyway, it was Baker's property in the legal sense of the word."

"Not any more it isn't."

Grumbling, Travers did as he was told. "Now what happens?"

"Nothing much. I'll see this young woman tomorrow and see what she has to say."

"And then?"

"I don't really know, but frankly, it won't concern you from here on in."

"I thought you'd say that."

Ferguson slapped him on the shoulder. "Never mind, meet me in the Piano Bar at the Dorchester at eight. We'll have a drink."

He let himself out of the front door, turned down the steps and got into the rear of the waiting Daimler.

As the Citation jet lifted off the runway at Gatwick, Francis Pamer got himself a Scotch from the bar box thinking about Max Santiago. Cuban, he knew that, one of the landed families chased out by Castro in nineteen fifty-nine. The Max bit came from his mother, who was German. That he had money was obvious, because when he had struck the deal with old Joseph Pamer to develop Samson Cay Resort in nineteen seventy, he already controlled a number of hotels. How old would he be now, sixty-seven or-eight? All Francis Pamer knew for sure was that he had always been a little afraid of him, but that didn't matter. Santiago would know what to do and that was all that was important. He finished his Scotch and settled back to read the *Financial Times* until the Citation landed at Le Bourget Airport in Paris half an hour later.

Santiago was standing on the terrace of his magnificent suite at the Ritz, an impressively tall man in a dark suit and tie, his hair still quite black in spite of his age. He had a calm, imperious face, the look of a man who was used to getting his own way, and dark, watchful eyes.

He turned as the room waiter showed Pamer in. "My dear Francis, what a joy to see you." He held out a hand. "A glass of champagne, you need it, I can tell." His English was faultless.

"You can say that again," Pamer said and accepted the crystal glass gratefully.

"Now come and sit down and tell me what the trouble is."

They sat on either side of the fire. Pamer said, "I don't know where to begin."

"Why, at the beginning, naturally."

So Pamer did just that.

When he was finished, Santiago sat there for a while without saying a word. Pamer said, "What do you think?"

"Unfortunate to say the least."

"I know. I mean, if this business ever got out, Bormann on the island, my mother, my father."

"Oh, your mother didn't have the slightest idea who Bormann was," Santiago said. "Your father did, of course."

"I beg your pardon?" Pamer was stunned.

"Your father, dear old Joseph, was a Fascist all his life, Francis, and so was my father, and a great friend of General Franco. People like that were, how shall I put it, connected? Your father had very heavy links with Nazi Germany before the War, but then so did many members of the English establishment, and why not? What sensible person wanted to see a bunch of Communists take over? Look what they have done to my own Cuba."

"Are you saying you knew my father had this connection with Martin Bormann?"

"Of course. My own father, in Cuba at that time, was also involved. Let me explain, Francis. The Kamaradenwerk, Action for Comrades, the organization set up to take care of the movement in the event of defeat in Europe, was, still is, a worldwide network. Your father and my father were just two cogs in the machine."

"I don't believe it."

"Francis, how do you think your father was able to hang on to Hatherley Court? Your education at Eton, your three years in the Grenadier Guards, where did the money come from? Your father didn't even have his salary as an M.P. after he lost his seat."

"To the bloody Labour Party," Pamer said bitterly.

"Of course, but over the years he was allowed to, shall we say, assist with certain business dealings. When my own family left Cuba because of that animal Castro, there were funds made available to us in the United States. I built up the hotel chain, was able to indulge in certain illegal but lucrative forms of traffic."

Pamer had always suspected some kind of drug involvement and his blood ran cold. "Look, I don't want to know about that."

"You do like spending the money though, Francis." Santiago smiled for the first time. "The development of Samson Cay suited us very well. A wonderful cover, a playground for the very rich, and behind that facade, perfect for the conducting of certain kinds of business."

"And what if someone investigated it?"

"Why should they? Samson Holdings is, as the name implies, a holding company. It's like a Russian doll, Francis, one company inside another, and the name of Pamer appears on none of the boards and you'd have to go some way back to find the name of Santiago."

"But it was my grandmother's family who originally owned it."

"The Herbert people? That was a long time ago, Francis. Look, your mother's name was Vail, her mother's maiden name was Herbert I admit, but I doubt that any connection would be made. You mentioned that Ferguson had checked with Public Records in Tortola, who told him the hotel was unoccupied during the War."

"Yes, I wonder how they made the mistake?"

"Quite simple. A clerk nearly forty years later looks in the file and sees a notation that the hotel was unoccupied for the duration, which it was, Francis. Your mother didn't turn up with you until April forty-five, only four or five weeks before the end of the War. In any case it's of no consequence. I'll have my people check the Records Office in Tortola. If there's anything there we'll remove it."

"You can do that?" Pamer said aghast.

"I can do anything, Francis. Now, this Rear Admiral Travers, what's his address?"

"Lord North Street."

"Good. I'll get someone to pay him a call, although I shouldn't imagine he has the diary in his possession any longer or the translation from the sound of Ferguson."

"They'll be careful, your people," Pamer said. "I mean we don't want a scandal."

"That's exactly what you will have if we don't get in first on this thing. I'll get one of my people to check out this young woman, what was her name?"

"Jenny Grant."

"I'll have flights checked to see when she's arriving. Simple enough. She'll be on either the Puerto Rico or Antigua flight."

"And then what?"

Santiago smiled. "Why, we'll have to hope that she'll be able to tell us something, won't we?"

Pamer felt sick. "Look, Max, they won't hurt her or anything?"

"Poor old Francis, what a thoroughly spineless creature you are." Santiago propelled him to the door and opened it. "Wait for me in the bar. I have telephone calls to make, then we'll have dinner."

He pushed him out into the corridor and closed the door.

The Piano Bar at the Dorchester was busy when Garth Travers went in and there was no sign of Ferguson. He was greeted warmly by one of the waiters, for it was one of his favorite watering holes. A corner table was found and he ordered a gin and tonic and relaxed. Ferguson arrived fifteen minutes later and joined him.

"Got to do better than that," the Brigadier told him and ordered two glasses of champagne. "I love this place." He looked up at the mirrored ceiling. "Quite extraordinary, and that chap at the piano plays our kind of music, doesn't he?"

"Which is another way of saying we're getting on," Travers said. "You're in a good mood. Anything happened?"

"Yes, Lane did a check through British Airways at Gatwick. She's on Flight 252 departing Antigua at twenty-ten hours their time, arriving at Gatwick at five past nine in the morning."

"Poor girl," Travers said.

"Will you ask her to stay with you?"

"Of course."

"I thought you might." Ferguson nodded. "Under the circumstances I think it would be better if you picked her up. My driver will have the Daimler at your place at seven-thirty. I know it's early, but you know what the traffic is like."

"That's fine by me. Do you want me to bring her straight to you?"

"Oh, no, give her a chance to settle. She'll be tired after her flight. I can see her later." Ferguson hesitated. "There's a strong possibility that she'll want to see the body."

"Is it still at the mortuary?"

"No, at a firm of undertakers we use on department matters. Cox and Son, in the Cromwell Road. If she asks to go, take her there, there's a good chap."

He waved to a waiter and ordered two more glasses of champagne, and Travers said, "What about the U-boat, the diary, all that stuff? Do I say anything to her?"

"No, leave that to me." Ferguson smiled. "Now drink up and I'll buy you dinner."

And in Antigua, when she went up the steps to the first-class compartment, Jenny Grant felt as if she were moving in slow motion. The stewardess who greeted her cheerfully had the instinct that comes from training and experience that told her something was wrong. She took her to her seat and helped her get settled.

"Would you like a drink? Champagne, coffee?"

"Actually I could do with a brandy. A large one," Jenny told her.

The stewardess was back with it in a moment. There was concern on her face now. "Look, is there something wrong? Can I help?"

"Not really," Jenny said. "I've just lost the best friend I ever had to a road accident in London, that's why I'm going over."

The young woman nodded sympathetically. "There's no one sitting next to you, only six in the cabin this trip, nobody to bother you." She squeezed Jenny's shoulder. "Anything you need, just let me know."

"I'll probably try to sleep through the whole trip."

"Probably the best thing for you."

The stewardess went away and Jenny leaned back, drinking her brandy and thinking about Henry, all the kindness, all the support. He'd saved her life, that was the truth of it, and the strange thing was that try as she might, for some reason she couldn't remember his face clearly and tears welled up in her eyes, slow and bitter.

The Daimler arrived just before seven-thirty. Travers left a note for his housekeeper, Mrs. Mishra, an Indian lady whose husband kept a corner store not too far away, explaining the situation, hurried down the steps to Ferguson's limousine and was driven away, passing a British Telecom van parked at the end of the street. The van started up, moved along the street and parked outside Travers' house.

A telephone engineer in official overalls got out with a toolbox in one hand. He had the name Smith printed on his left-hand breast pocket. He went along the flagged path leading to the back of the house and the rear courtyard. He went up the steps to the kitchen door, punched a gloved hand through the glass pane, reached in and opened it. A moment later he was also opening the front door and another Telecom engineer got out of the van and joined him. The name on his overalls pocket was Johnson.

Once inside they worked their way methodically through the Admiral's study, searching every drawer, pulling the books from the shelves, checking for signs of a safe and finding none.

Finally, Smith said, "Waste of time. It isn't here. Go and get the van open."

He unplugged the Admiral's word processor and followed Johnson out, putting it in the back of the van. They went back inside and Johnson said, "What else?"

"See if there's a television or video in the living room, then take this typewriter."

Johnson did as he was told. When he returned to the living room Smith was screwing the head of the telephone back into place.

"You're tapping the phone?"

"Why not? We might hear something to our advantage."

"Is that smart? I mean, the kind of people we're dealing with, Intelligence people, they're not rubbish."

"Look, to all intents and purposes this is just another hit-and-run burglary," Smith told him. "Anyway, Mr. Santiago wants a result on this one and you don't screw around with him, believe me. Now let's get moving."

Mrs. Mishra, the Admiral's housekeeper, didn't normally arrive until nine o'clock, but the fact that she'd had the previous day off meant there was laundry to take care of so she had decided to make an early start. As she turned the corner of Lord North Street and walked toward the house, an overcoat over her sari against the early morning chill, she saw the two men come out of the house.

She hurried forward. "Is there a problem?"

They turned toward her. Smith said urbanely, "Not that I know of. Who are you, love?"

"Mrs. Mishra, the housekeeper."

"Problem with one of the telephones. We've taken care of it. You'll find everything's fine now."

They got in the van, Johnson behind the wheel, and drove away. Johnson said, "Unfortunate that."

"No big deal. She's Indian, isn't she? We're just another couple of white faces to her."

Smith lit a cigarette and leaned back, enjoying the view of the river as they turned into Millbank.

Mrs. Mishra didn't notice anything was amiss because the study door was half-closed. She went into the kitchen, put her bag on the table and saw the Admiral's note. As she was reading it she became aware of a draft, turned and saw the broken pane in the door.

"Oh my God!" she said in horror.

She quickly went back along the passage and checked the living room, noticed the absence of the television and video at once. The state of the study confirmed her worst fears and she immediately picked up the phone and dialed 999 for the police emergency service.

Travers recognized Jenny Grant at once as she emerged into the arrival hall at Gatwick pushing her suitcase on a trolley. She wore a three-quarter-length tweed coat over a white blouse and jeans and she looked tired and strained, dark circles under her eyes.

"Jenny?" he said as he approached. "Do you remember me? Garth Travers?"

"Of course I do, Admiral." She tried a smile and failed miserably.

He put his hands lightly on her shoulders. "You look bushed, my dear. Come on, let's get out of here. I've got a car waiting. Let me take your case."

The driver put the case in the boot of the Daimler and Travers joined her in the rear. As they drove away he said, "I expect you to stay with me, naturally, if that's all right?"

"You're very kind. Will you do something for me?" She was almost pleading. "Will you tell me exactly what happened?"

"From what witnesses have told the police he simply looked the wrong way and stepped in front of a bus."

"What a bloody stupid way to go." There was a kind of anger in her voice now. "I mean, here we had a sixty-three-year-old man who insisted on diving every day, sometimes to a hundred and thirty feet in hazardous conditions, and he has to die in such a stupid and trivial way."

"I know. Life's a bit of a bad joke sometimes. Would you care for a cigarette?"

"As a matter of fact, I would. I gave up six months ago, started again on the plane coming over last night." She took one from the packet he offered and accepted a light. "There's something else I'd like, and before we do anything else."

"What's that?"

"To see him," she said simply.

"I thought you might," Garth Travers said. "That's where we're going now."

The undertaker's was a pleasant enough place, considering what it was. The waiting room was panelled and banked with flowers. An old man in black suit and a tie entered. "May I help you?"

"Mr. Cox? I'm Admiral Travers and this is Miss Grant. You were expecting us, I believe?"

"Of course." His voice was a whisper. "If you would come this way."

There were several rooms off a rear corridor with sliding doors open revealing coffins standing on trestles and flowers everywhere, the smell quite overpowering. Mr. Cox led the way into the end one. The coffin was quite simple, made of mahogany.

"As I had no instructions I had to do the best I could," Cox said. "The fittings are gold plastic as I assumed cremation would be the intention."

He slid back the lid and eased the gauze from the face. Henry Baker looked very calm in death, eyes closed, face pale. Jenny put a hand to his face, slightly dislodging the gauze.

Cox carefully rearranged the gauze. "I wouldn't, miss."

She was bewildered for a moment and Travers said, "There was an autopsy, my dear, had to be, it's a court requirement. They'll be holding a coroner's inquest, you see. Day after tomorrow."

She nodded. "It doesn't matter, he's gone now. Can we leave, please?"

In the car he gave her another cigarette. "Are you all right?"

"Absolutely." She smiled suddenly. "He was a smashing fella, Admiral, isn't that what they say in England? The dearest, kindest man I ever knew." She took a deep breath. "Where to now?"

"My house in Lord North Street. You'd probably like a bath, rest up a little and so on."

"Yes, that would be nice."

She leaned back and closed her eyes.

The surprise at Lord North Street was the police car. The front door stood open and Travers hurried up the steps, Jenny behind him. He went into the hall and found the chaos in his study instantly, followed the sounds of voices and found Mrs. Mishra and a young policewoman in the kitchen.

"Oh, Admiral," Mrs. Mishra said as he entered. "Such a terrible thing. They have stolen many things. The television, your word processor and typewriter. The study is such a mess, but I saw their names on their overalls."

"Admiral Travers?" the policewoman said. "Typical daytime robbery, I'm afraid, sir. They gained access through that door."

She indicated the hole in the glass. Travers said, "The bloody swine."

"They were in a Telecom van," Mrs. Mishra said. "Telephone engineers. I saw them leave. Imagine such a thing."

"That's a common ploy during the day, sir," the policewoman said, "to pass themselves off as some kind of workmen."

"I don't suppose there's much chance of catching them either?" Travers inquired.

"I doubt it, sir, I really do. Now if I could have full details about what's missing."

"Yes, of course, just give me a moment." He turned to Jenny. "Sorry about this. Mrs. Mishra, this is Miss Grant. She'll be staying for a while. Tell the driver to take her case up and show her to her room."

"Of course, Admiral."

Mrs. Mishra ushered Jenny out and Travers said to the policewoman, "There's a chance there could be more to this than meets the eye, officer. I'll just make a phone call and I'll be with you directly."

Smith and Johnson," Ferguson said. "That's a good one."

"Seems like a run-of-the-mill daytime robbery, sir," Lane said. "All the usual hallmarks. They only took the kind of portable items that convert to quick cash. The television, video and the rest."

"Rather sophisticated, I would have thought, having their very own Telecom van."

"Probably stolen, sir. We'll run a check."

"Rather fortunate I relieved Travers of the diary and the translation software he'd made from it if they were looking for something more important than television sets."

"You really think it could have been that, sir?"

"All I know is that I learned a long time ago to suspect coincidence, Jack. I mean, how often does Garth Travers leave the house at seven-thirty in the morning? They must have seen him go."

"And you think taking the run-of-the-mill kind of stuff was just a blind?"

"Perhaps."

"But how would they know about the existence of the diary, sir?"

"Yes, well that is the interesting point." Ferguson frowned. "I've had a thought, Jack. Go to Lord North Street. Get one of your old friends from Special Branch, someone who specializes in bugging devices, to do a sweep."

"You really think . . . ?"

"I don't think anything, Jack, I'm merely considering all the options. Now on your way."

Lane went out and Ferguson picked up the phone and rang Lord North Street and spoke to Travers. "How's your guest?"

"Fine. Bearing up remarkably well."

Ferguson looked at his watch. "Bring her to my place in Cavendish Square at about twelve-thirty. We might as well get on with it, but don't say a word. Leave it all to me."

"You can rely on me."

Travers put the phone down and went into the living room, where Jenny sat by the fire drinking coffee. "Sorry about all this," he said, "a hell of an introduction."

"Not your fault."

He sat down. "We'll go out soon for a spot of lunch, but I'd like to introduce you to an old friend of mine, Brigadier Charles Ferguson."

She was an astute young woman and sensed something at once. "Did he know Henry?"

"Not directly."

"But this is something to do with Henry?"

He reached across and patted her hand. "All in good time, my dear, just trust me."

Santiago was still at his suite at the Ritz when the man who called himself Smith phoned through from London. "Not a thing, guv, certainly nothing like you described."

"Hardly surprising, but it was worth checking," Santiago said. "A nice clean job, I trust."

"Sure, guv, just made it look run-of-the-mill. I tapped the phone, just in case you wanted to listen in."

"You did what?" Santiago was coldly angry. "I told you, these are Intelligence people involved in this one, the kind of people who check everything."

"Sorry, guv, I thought I was doing the right thing."

"Never mind, it's too late now. Just drop any other commissions you have at the moment and wait to hear from me," and Santiago put the phone down.

In the living room at Cavendish Square Jenny sat beside the fire opposite Ferguson and Travers stood by the window.

"So you see, Miss Grant," Ferguson said, "there will have to be a coroner's inquest, which is set for the day after tomorrow."

"And I can have the body then?"

"Well that is really a matter for the next of kin."

She opened her handbag and took out a paper, which she unfolded and passed to him. "Henry took up serious diving a year or so ago."

"Rather old for that, I should have thought," Ferguson said.

"Yes, well he had a near-miss one day. Ran out of air at fifty feet. Oh, he made it to the surface okay, but he immediately went to his lawyer and had him draw up a power of attorney in my name."

Ferguson looked it over. "That seems straightforward enough. I'll see that it's passed to the coroner." He reached down at the side of the sofa and produced Friemel's aluminium briefcase. "Have you seen this before?"

She looked puzzled. "No."

"Or this?" He opened it and took out the diary.

"No, never." She frowned. "What is this?"

Ferguson said, "Did Mr. Baker tell you why he was coming to London?"

She looked at him, then turned to glance at Travers, then she turned back. "Why do you think he came here, Brigadier?"

"Because he discovered the wreck of a German submarine somewhere off St. John, Miss Grant. Did he tell you about that?"

Jenny Grant took a deep breath. "Yes, Brigadier, he did tell me. He said he'd been diving and that he'd discovered a submarine and a briefcase."

"This case," he said, "with this diary inside. What else did he tell you?"

"Well, it was in German, which he didn't understand, but he did recognize the name Martin Bormann and . . ." Here she paused.

Ferguson said gently, "And . . . ?"

"The Duke of Windsor," she said lamely. "Look, I know it sounds crazy but . . ."

"Not crazy at all, my dear. And where did Mr. Baker find this U-boat?"

"I've no idea. He wouldn't tell me."

There was a pause while Ferguson glanced at Travers. He sighed. "You are absolutely certain of that, Miss Grant?"

"Of course I am. He said he didn't want to tell me for the time being. He was very excited about his find." She paused, frowning. "Look, what are you trying to tell me, Brigadier? What's going on here? Does this have something to do with Henry's death?"

"No, not at all," he said soothingly and nodded to Travers.

The Admiral said, "Jenny, poor old Henry's death was a complete accident. We have plenty of witnesses. He stepped into the path of a London Transport bus. The driver was a sixty-year-old Cockney who won the Military Medal for Gallantry in the Korean War in nineteen fifty-two as an infantry private. Just an accident, Jenny."

"So, you've no idea where the U-boat lies?" Ferguson asked again.

"Is it important?"

"Yes, it could be."

She shrugged. "I honestly don't know. If you want my opinion, it would have to be somewhere far out."

"Far out? What do you mean?"

"Most of the dive sites that tourists use from St. Thomas and St. John are within reasonable distance. There are plenty of wrecks around, but the idea that a German U-boat had remained undiscovered since the end of the war," she shook her head, "that's nonsense. It could only happen if it was somewhere remote and far out."

"Further out to sea."

"That's right."

"And you've no idea where?"

"No, I'm not much of a diver, I'm afraid. You'd need to go to an expert."

"And is there such a person?"

"Oh, sure, Bob Carney."

Ferguson picked up his pen and made a note. "Bob Carney? And who might he be?"

"He has the watersports concession at Caneel Bay Resort. I mean, he spends most of his time teaching tourists to dive, but he's a real diver and quite famous. He was in the oil fields in the Gulf of Mexico, salvage work, all that stuff. They've done magazine articles about him."

"Really?" Ferguson said. "He's the best diver in the Virgin Islands then?"

"In the whole Caribbean, Brigadier," she said.

"Really." Ferguson glanced at Travers and stood up. "Good. Many thanks for your cooperation, Miss Grant. I appreciate this is not a good time, but you must eat. Perhaps you'll allow me to take you and Admiral Travers out for a meal tonight."

She hesitated and then said, "That's kind of you."

"Not at all. I'll send my car to pick you up at seven-thirty." He ushered them to the outside door. "Take care." He nodded to the Admiral. "I'll be in touch, Garth."

He was having a cup of tea and thinking about things half an hour later when Lane arrived. The Inspector dropped a hard, black metal bug on the coffee table. "You were right, sir, this little bastard was in the living room telephone."

"So," Ferguson said, picking it up. "The plot thickens."

"Look, sir, Baker knew about the diary because he found it, the girl knew because he told her, the Admiral knew, you know, the P.M. had a copy, the Deputy Director of the Intelligence Services knew, Sir Francis Pamer knew." He paused.

"You're missing yourself out, Jack."

"Yes, sir, but who the hell was it who knew who would go to the trouble of knocking off Admiral Travers' pad?"

"There you go again, Jack, police jargon." Ferguson sighed. "It's like a spider's web. There are lots of lines of communication between all those people you mention. God knows how many."

"So what are you going to do, sir? I mean, we don't even know where the bloody U-boat is. On top of that, we've all sorts of dirty work going on underneath things. Burglary, illegal phone-tapping."

"You're right, Jack, the whole thing assumes a totally new dimension."

"It might be better to bring Intelligence in on it, sir."

"Hardly, although when you get back to the office, you may phone

Simon Carter and Sir Francis and tell them the girl says she doesn't know the site."

"But then what, sir?"

"I'm not sure. We'll have to send someone out there to find out for us."

"Someone who knows about diving, sir?"

"That's a thought, but if there is skulduggery afoot, someone who's just as big a villain as the opposition." Ferguson paused. "Correction, someone who is worse."

"Sir?" Lane looked bewildered.

Ferguson suddenly started to laugh helplessly. "My dear Jack, isn't life delicious on occasions? I spend simply ages getting someone I positively detest banged up, the cell door locked tight, and suddenly discover he's exactly what I need in the present situation."

"I don't understand, sir."

"You will, Jack. Ever been to Yugoslavia?"

"No, sir."

"Good, a new experience for you. We'll leave at dawn. Have them get the Learjet ready. Tell Admiral Travers I'll have to postpone dinner with him and the young lady."

"And the destination, sir?"

"The air strip at Kivo Castle, Jack. Tell them to clear it with the Serbian High Command. I don't think they'll have a problem."

FIVE

Dillon was dozing on his bed at Kivo when the sound of a plane circling overhead awoke him. He lay there for a moment listening, aware of the change in the engine note that indicated a landing was being made. A jet by the sound of it. He went to the barred window and peered out. It was raining hard and as he looked out across the walls he saw a Learjet come in out of low cloud and make an approach to the airstrip. It landed perfectly, then taxied forward so that he could see there were no markings. It disappeared from view and he went and got a cigarette, wondering who it could be.

A shouted command drifted up and there was a crackle of rifle fire. He went back to the window, but he could only see part of the courtyard below. One or two soldiers appeared and laughter drifted up, presumably the General clearing out the cells again, and he wondered how many poor bastards had ended up against the wall this time. There was more laughter and then an army truck crossed his line of vision and disappeared.

"You're in a mess this time, my old son," he murmured softly. "A hell of a bloody mess," and he went and lay on the bed, finishing his cigarette and thinking about it.

In Paris, Santiago was about to leave his suite for a lunch appointment when the phone rang. It was Francis Pamer. "I tried to catch you earlier, but you were out," Pamer told him.

"Business, Francis, that's why I'm here. What have you got for me?"

"Carter had a word with me. He spoke to Ferguson. He said the girl doesn't know the location of the U-boat. He said that she knew about it, that Baker had told her about his discovery before he left, but that he hadn't told her where the damned thing is."

"Does Ferguson believe her?"

"Apparently," Pamer told him. "At least that was the impression Carter got."

"And what's Ferguson up to now?"

"I don't know. He just told Carter that he'd keep him posted."

"What about the girl? Where is she staying?" Santiago asked him.

"With Admiral Travers at Lord North Street. There's the coroner's inquest tomorrow. Once that's over Ferguson's agreed she can have the body."

"I see," Santiago said.

"What do you think, Max?"

"About the girl, you mean? I don't know. She could be telling the truth. On the other hand, she could be lying and there's only one way to find that out."

"What do you mean?"

"Why, by asking her, Francis, in the proper way, of course. A little persuasion, gentle or otherwise, works wonders."

"For God's sake, Max," Pamer began and Santiago cut him off.

"Just do what's necessary, keep me posted as regards Ferguson's plans and I'll have the girl taken care of. I had intended to return to Puerto Rico tomorrow, but I'll hang on for another day or two here. In the meantime, I'll speak to my people in San Juan, tell them to get the *Maria Blanco* ready for sea. The moment we know for definite that Ferguson intends some sort of operation in the Virgins, I'll sail down to Samson Cay and use it as a base."

Pamer said, "Christ, Max, I don't know whether I'm coming or going with this thing. If it comes out, I'm finished."

"But it won't, Francis, because I'll see that it doesn't. I've always anticipated seeing you in the Cabinet. Very useful to have a friend who's a British Cabinet Minister. I've no intention of allowing that not to happen, so don't worry."

Santiago put the phone down, thought about it for a moment, then picked it up again and rang his house in San Juan on the island of Puerto Rico.

Dillon was reading a book, head propped up against the pillow, when the key rattled in the lock, the door opened and Major Branko entered. "Ah, there you are," he said.

Dillon didn't bother getting up. "And where else would I be?"

"That sounds a trifle bitter," Branko told him. "After all, you're still with us. Cause for a certain amount of gratitude, I should have thought."

"What do you want?" Dillon asked.

"I've brought someone to see you, hardly an old friend, but I'd listen to what he has to say if I were you."

He stood to one side. Dillon swung his legs to the floor, was starting to get up and Ferguson entered the room followed by Jack Lane.

"Holy Mother of God!" Dillon said and Branko went out and closed the door behind him.

Dear me, Dillon, but you are up the creek without a paddle, aren't you?" Ferguson dusted the only chair with his hat and sat. "We've never actually made it face to face before, but I imagine you know who I am?"

"Brigadier Charles bloody Ferguson," Dillon said. "Head of Group Four."

"And this is Detective Inspector Jack Lane, my assistant, on loan from Special Branch at Scotland Yard so he doesn't like you."

Lane's face was like stone. He leaned against the wall, arms folded, and Dillon said, "Is that a fact?"

"Look at him, Jack," Ferguson said. "The great Sean Dillon, soldier of the IRA in his day, master assassin, better than Carlos the Jackal, some say."

"I am looking at him, sir, and all I see is just another killer."

"Ah, but this one is special, Jack, the man of a thousand faces. Could have been another Olivier if he hadn't taken to the gun. He can change before your very eyes. Mind you, he cocked up his attempt to blow up the Prime Minister and the War Cabinet at Number Ten during the Gulf War as nobody knows better than you, Jack. By God, you gave us a hard time on that one, Dillon."

"A pleasure."

"But you're behind walls now," Lane said.

Ferguson nodded. "Twenty years, Jack, twenty years without getting his collar felt once and where does he end up?" He looked around the room. "You must have been out of your mind, Dillon. Medical supplies for the sick and the dying? You?"

"We all have our off days."

"Stinger missiles as well so you didn't even check your cargo properly. You must be losing your touch."

"All right, the show's over," Dillon told him. "What do you want?"

Ferguson got up and went to the window. "They've been shooting Croatians down there in the courtyard. We heard them as we drove over from the airstrip. They were clearing the bodies away in a truck as we drove in." He turned. "It'll be your turn one of these fine mornings, Dillon. Unless you're sensible, of course."

Dillon got a cigarette from one of the Rothmans packets and lit it with his Zippo. "You mean I have a choice?" he asked calmly.

"You could say that." Ferguson sat down again. "You shoot guns rather well, Dillon, fly a plane, speak a number of languages, but the thing I'm interested in at the moment was that underwater job you did for the Israelis. It was you, wasn't it, who blew up those PLO boats off Beirut?"

"Do you tell me?" Dillon said, sounding very Irish.

"Oh, for God's sake, sir, let's leave the bastard to rot," Lane said.

"Come on, man, don't be stupid. Was it you, or wasn't it?" Ferguson demanded.

"As ever was," Dillon told him.

"Good. Now here's the situation. I have a job that requires a man of your peculiar talents."

"A crook he means," Lane put in.

Ferguson ignored him. "I'm not sure exactly what's going on at the moment, but it could demand a man who can handle himself if things get rough. What I am certain of is that it would require, at the right moment, considerable diving skills."

"And where would all this take place?"

"The American Virgin Islands." Ferguson stood up. "The choice is yours, Dillon. You can stay here and be shot or you can leave now and fly back to London in the Learjet we have at the airstrip with the Inspector and me."

"And what will Major Branko have to say about it?"

"No problem there. Nice boy. His mother lives in Hampstead. He's had enough of this Yugoslavian mess, and who can blame him. I'm going to arrange political asylum for him in England."

Dillon said, "Is there nothing you can't do?"

"Not that I can think of."

Dillon hesitated. "I'm a wanted man over there in the UK, you know that."

"Slate wiped clean, my word on it, which disgusts Inspector Lane here, but that's the way it is. Of course it also means you'll have to do exactly as you're told."

"Of course." Dillon picked up his flying jacket and pulled it on. "Yours to command."

"I thought you'd see sense. Now let's get out of this disgusting place," and Ferguson rapped on the door with his Malacca cane.

Dillon finished the diary and closed it. Lane was dozing, his head on a pillow, and the Irishman passed the diary to Ferguson, who sat on the other side of the aisle, but facing him.

"Very interesting," Dillon said.

"Is that all you've got to say?"

The Irishman reached for the bar box, found a miniature of Scotch, poured it into one of the plastic cups provided and added water. "What do you expect me to say? All right, Henry Baker's death was unfortunate, but he died happy, by God. Finding U180 must have been the biggest thing that ever happened to him."

"You think so?"

"Every diver's dream, Brigadier, to find a wreck that's never been discovered before, preferably stuffed with Spanish doubloons, but if you can't have that, the wreck on its own will do."

"Really."

"You've never dived?" Dillon laughed. "A silly question. It's another world down there, a special feeling, nothing quite like it." He swallowed some of his whisky. "So this woman you mentioned, this Jenny Grant, she says he didn't tell her where the U-boat is located?"

"That's right."

"Do you believe her?"

Ferguson sighed. "I'm afraid I do. Normally I don't believe in anyone, but there's something about her, something special."

"Falling for a pretty face in your old age," Dillon said. "Always a mistake that."

"Don't be stupid, Dillon," the Brigadier replied sharply. "She's a nice girl and there's something about her, that's all I mean. You can judge for yourself. We'll have dinner with Garth Travers and her this evening."

"All right." Dillon nodded. "So if she doesn't know where the damn thing is, what do you expect me to do?"

"Go to the Virgin Islands and find it, that's what I expect you to do, Dillon. It's no great hardship, I assure you. I visited St. John a few years back. Lovely spot."

"For a holiday?"

"You won't be on holiday, only pretending. You'll earn your keep."

"Brigadier," Dillon said patiently, "the sea is a hell of a big place. Have you any idea how difficult it is to locate a ship down there on the bottom? Even in Caribbean waters with good visibility, you could miss seeing it at a hundred yards."

"You'll think of something, you always do, Dillon, isn't that your special talent?"

"Jesus, but you have the most touching faith in me. All right, let's get down to brass tacks. Baker's death? Are you sure that was an accident?"

"Absolutely no question. There were witnesses. He simply looked the wrong way and stepped into the path of the bus. The driver, I might add, is beyond reproach."

"All right, so what about the burglary at this Admiral Travers' house, the bug in the telephone?"

Ferguson nodded. "A smell of stinking fish there. All the hallmarks of an opportunistic housebreaking, but the bug says otherwise."

"Who would it be?"

"God knows, Dillon, but all my instincts tell me there's someone out there and they're up to no good."

"But what?" Dillon said. "That's the point."

"I'm sure you'll come up with an answer."

"So when do you want me to go out to the Virgins?"

"I'm not sure. Two or three days, we'll see." Ferguson eased a pillow behind his head.

"And where do I stay while I'm hanging around in London?" Dillon enquired.

"I'll arrange for you to stay with Admiral Travers in Lord North Street. For the moment, you can earn your keep by keeping an eye on the girl," Ferguson told him. "Now shut up, there's a good chap, I need a spot of shut-eye."

He folded his arms and closed his eyes. Dillon finished his Scotch and leaned back thinking about it.

Ferguson murmured, "Oh, Dillon, just one thing."

"And what would that be?"

"Dr. Wegner and that young fool Klaus Schmidt, the people you dealt with at Fehring? Well-intentioned amateurs, but the man you bumped into in Vienna who put you in touch with them, Farben? He was acting for me. I got him to set you up, then got someone who works for me to shop you to the Serbs."

"Believe it or not, Brigadier, but something of the sort had occurred to me. I presume the Stinger missiles were your idea?"

"Wanted to see you behind bars, you see," Ferguson said. "If I couldn't get you one way . . ." He shrugged. "Mind you, this present business has got nothing to do with it. Lucky for you the situation arose."

"Or you'd have left me to rot."

"Not really. They'd have shot you sooner or later."

"Ah, well, what does it matter now?" Dillon said. "You might say it's all come out in the wash when you think about it," and he closed his eyes and dozed himself.

At Lord North Street, just before six, it was still raining as Dillon sat at the kitchen table and watched Jenny Grant make the tea. He had only just been introduced, for Ferguson was closeted in the study with Travers.

She turned and smiled. "Would you like some toast or anything?"

"Not really. Would you mind if I smoked?"

"Not at all." She busied herself with the tea things. "You're Irish, but you sound different."

"North of Ireland," he said. "What you would call Ulster and others the six counties."

"IRA country?"

"That's right," he told her calmly.

She poured the tea. "And what exactly are you doing here, Mr. Dillon? Would I be correct in assuming the Brigadier wants you to keep an eye on me?"

"And why would you think that?"

She sat opposite and sipped some of her tea. "Because you look like that kind of man."

"And how would you be knowing that sort of person, Miss Grant?"

"Jenny," she said, "and I used to know all sorts of men, Mr. Dillon, and they were usually the wrong kind." She brooded for a moment. "But Henry saved me from all that." She looked up and her eyes glistened. "And now he's gone."

"Another cup?" He reached for the pot. "And what do you do in St. John?"

She took a deep breath and tried hard. "I have a cafe and bar called Jenny's Place. You must visit some time."

"You know what?" Dillon smiled. "I might just take you up on that," and he drank some more of his tea.

In the study Travers was aghast. "Good heavens, Charles, IRA? I'm truly shocked."

"You can be shocked as much as you like, Garth, but I need the little bugger. I hate to admit it, but he's very, very good. I intend to send him out to St. John once I've got things sorted. In the meantime he can stay here and act as your minder, just in case anything untoward happens."

"All right," Travers said reluctantly.

"If the girl asks I've told him to tell her he's a diver I've brought in to help with this thing."

"Do you think she'll believe that? I find her rather a smart young woman."

"I don't see why not. He *is* a diver amongst other things." Ferguson got up. "By the way, you had a man from my department earlier who replaced the bug in your phone and gave you a cellular telephone, didn't he?"

"That's right."

Ferguson led the way out and they went in the kitchen, where Jenny and Dillon sat at the table. Ferguson said, "Right, you two, I'm off. We'll all meet for dinner at eight. The River Room at the Savoy, I think." He turned to Dillon. "That suit you?"

Dillon said, "A jacket-and-tie job, that, and here's me with only the clothes I'm standing up in."

"All right, Dillon, you can go shopping tomorrow," Ferguson said wearily and turned to Travers. "Good thing you're as small as he is, Garth. You can fix him up with a blazer, I'm sure. See you later."

The front door banged behind him and Dillon smiled. "Always in a hurry, that man."

Travers said reluctantly, "All right, you'd better come with me and I'll show you where you're sleeping and find you something to wear."

He led the way out and Dillon winked at Jenny and followed him.

Not too far away the fake telephone engineer who had called himself Smith turned into an alley where an old van was parked and knocked on the rear door. It was opened by Johnson and Smith joined him inside. There were various items of recording equipment and a receiver.

"Anything?" Smith asked.

"Not a thing. It's been on all day. Housekeeper ordering groceries, asking for a repair man for the washing machine. The Admiral phoned the London Library to order a book and the Army and Navy club about a function next month. Bit of a bore, the whole thing. What about you?"

"I was watching the house a short while ago and Ferguson turned up."

"You sure?"

"Oh, yes, definitely him. The photos on the file Mr. Santiago has supplied are very good. He had a guy with him."

"Any ideas?"

"No. Small, very fair hair, black leather flying jacket. He stayed, Ferguson left."

"So what do we do now?"

"Leave the recorder on. I can do a sweep in the morning and listen to anything interesting. I'll watch the house while you take some time off. If they go out, I'll follow and speak to you on the car phone."

"Okay," Johnson said. "I'll catch up with you later."

They got out of the van, he locked it and they went their separate ways.

Ferguson hadn't arrived when the Admiral, Dillon and Jenny reached the Savoy and went to the River Room. The table had been ordered, however, and the headwaiter led them to it.

"I suppose we might as well have a drink," Travers said.

Dillon turned to the wine waiter. "Bottle of Krug, non-vintage." He smiled amiably at Travers. "I prefer the grape mix."

"Do you, indeed?" the Admiral said stiffly.

"Yes." Dillon offered Jenny a cigarette. She was wearing a simple white blouse and black skirt. "You're looking rather nice." His voice had changed, and for the moment he was the perfect English gentleman, public-school accent and all.

"Are you ever the same for five minutes together?" she asked.

"Jesus, and wouldn't that be a bore? Let's dance." He reached for her hand and led her to the floor.

"You know you're not looking too bad yourself," she said.

"Well the blazer fits, but I find the Navy tie a bit incongruous."

"Ah, I see it now, you don't like institutions?"

"Not totally true. The first time I came to the River Room, I belonged to a famous institution, the Royal Academy of Dramatic Art."

"You're kidding me?" she said.

"No, I was a student there for one year only and I was offered a job with the National Theatre. I played Lyngstrand in Ibsen's 'Lady From the Sea,' the one who was coughing his guts up all the time."

"And after that?"

"Oh, there were family commitments. I had to go home to Ireland."

"What a shame. What have you been doing lately?"

He told the truth for once. "I've been flying medical supplies into Yugoslavia."

"Oh, you're a pilot."

"Some of the time. I've been a lot of things. Butcher, baker, candlestick maker. Diver."

"A diver?" She showed her surprise. "Really? You're not having me on?"

"No, why should I?"

She leaned back as they circled the floor. "You know, I get a funny feeling about you."

"What do you mean?"

"Well, it may sound crazy, but if someone asked me to speculate about you, for some totally illogical reason I'd say you were a soldier."

Dillon's smile was slightly lopsided. "Now what gave me away?"

"I'm right then." She was delighted with herself. "You were once a soldier."

"I suppose you could put it that way."

The music stopped, he took her back to the table and excused himself. "I'm just going to see what cigarettes they have in the bar."

As he went away, the Admiral said, "Look, my dear, no sense in getting too involved with him, you know, not your sort."

"Oh, don't be an old snob, Admiral." She lit a cigarette. "He seems perfectly nice to me. He's just been flying medical supplies into Yugoslavia and he used to be a soldier."

Travers snorted and came right out with it. "Soldier of the bloody IRA."

She frowned. "You can't be serious."

"Infamous character," Travers said. "Worse than Carlos. They've been after him for years all over the place. Only reason he's here is because Charles has done a deal with him. He's going to help out with this thing, go to St. John, find the submarine and so on. Apparently the damned man's also a diver."

"I can't believe it."

As Dillon came out of the bar, he met Ferguson arriving and they came down to the table together.

"You're looking well, my dear," Ferguson said to Jenny. "The coroner's inquest is at ten-thirty tomorrow, by the way. No need for you to go as Garth here made the formal identification."

"But I'd prefer to be there," she said.

"Very well, if that's what you'd like."

"How soon after that can we arrange cremation?"

"That *is* what you want?"

"His ashes, yes," she said calmly. "I'm not expecting a service. Henry was an atheist."

"Really." Ferguson shrugged. "Well, if you're happy to use our people, they could do it virtually straightaway."

"Tomorrow afternoon?"

"I suppose so."

"Good. If you would arrange that I'd be grateful. If you're ordering I'd like caviar to start, a steak medium rare and a salad on the side."

"Would you now?" Ferguson said.

"It's called celebrating life." She reached for Dillon's hand. "And I'd like to dance again." She smiled. "It's not often I get the chance to do the foxtrot with an IRA gunman."

There were no more than five or six people in the small oak-paneled court in Westminster the following morning. Jenny sat at the front bench with Travers and Ferguson, and Dillon stood at the back near the Court usher, once more in his flying jacket. There was a brief pause while one of the people sitting at the front approached the bench and received some sort of warrant from the Clerk of the Court. As he went out, Smith and Johnson came into the court and sat on a bench on the other side of the aisle from Dillon. They were both respectably dressed in jacket and tie, but one look was enough for Dillon. Twenty years of entirely the wrong kind of living had given him an instinct for such things.

The Clerk of the Court got things started. "Rise for her Majesty's Coroner."

The Coroner was old with very white hair and wore a gray suit. Jenny was surprised. She'd expected robes. He opened the file before him. "This is an unusual case and I have taken note of the facts placed before me and have decided that in consequence the presence of a jury is not necessary. Is Brigadier Charles Ferguson in court?"

Ferguson stood up. "Yes, sir."

"I see you have served a D notice in this matter on behalf of the Ministry of Defence and this court accepts that there must be reasons for doing so affecting National Security. I accept the order and will have it entered into these proceedings. I will also, at this point, make it clear to any member of the press present that it is an offense punishable by a term of imprisonment to report details of any case covered by a D notice."

"Thank you, sir." Ferguson sat down.

"As the witnesses' statements given to the police in this unfortunate matter seem perfectly straightforward, I only need official identification of the deceased to be able to close these proceedings."

The Clerk of the Court nodded to Travers, who got up and went to the stand. The Coroner glanced at his papers. "You are Rear Admiral Garth Travers?"

"I am, sir."

"And your relationship with the deceased?"

"A close friend of many years on vacation from St. John in the American Virgin Islands, staying with me at my house in Lord North Street."

"And you made the official identification?" Travers nodded. "Is Miss Jennifer Grant in court?" She stood awkwardly and he said, "I have a power of attorney here in your name. You wish to claim the body?"

"I do, sir."

"So be it and so ordered. My Clerk will issue the necessary warrant. You have the sympathy of the court, Miss Grant."

"Thank you."

As she sat, the Clerk called, "Rise for Her Majesty's Coroner."

They all did so and the Coroner went out. Travers turned to Jenny. "All right, my dear?"

"Fine," she said, but her face was pale.

"Let's go," he said. "Charles is just getting the warrant. He'll catch us up."

They passed Dillon and went out. Smith and Johnson got up and filed out with the other people while Ferguson busied himself with the Clerk of the Court.

It was sunny outside and yet Jenny shivered slightly and drew her collar about her throat. "It's cold."

"You could probably do with a hot drink," Travers said, concerned.

Dillon was standing on the top step as Ferguson joined him. Smith and Johnson had paused a little distance away by the bus stop for Smith to take out a cigarette and Johnson was lighting it for him.

Dillon said to Ferguson, "Do you know those two?"

"Why, should I?" the Brigadier asked.

At that moment a bus stopped, Smith and Johnson and a couple of other people boarded it and it pulled away. "Brigadier, I've lasted all these years by trusting my instincts and they tell me we've got a couple of bad guys there. What were they doing at the inquest anyway?"

"Perhaps you're right, Dillon. On the other hand, there are many people who view Court proceedings of any sort as free entertainment."

"Is that a fact now?"

The Daimler drew in to the pavement at the bottom of the steps and Jack Lane got out and joined them. "Everything go off all right, sir?"

"Yes, Jack." Ferguson handed him the Court order. "Give that to old Cox. Tell him we'd like the cremation carried out this afternoon." He glanced at Jenny. "Three o'clock suit you?"

She nodded, paler than ever now. "No problem."

Ferguson turned to Lane. "You heard. There were a couple of men in Court, by the way. Dillon had his doubts about them."

"How could he tell?" Lane asked, ignoring the Irishman. "Were they wearing black hats?"

"Jesus, would you listen to the man?" Dillon said. "Such wit in him."

Lane scowled, took an envelope from his pocket and held it out to Ferguson. "As you ordered, sir."

"Give it to him then."

Lane pushed it into Dillon's hand. "A damn sight more than you deserve."

"What have we got here then?" Dillon started to open the envelope.

"You need clothes, don't you?" Ferguson said. "There's a charge card for you in there and a thousand pounds."

Dillon took the rather handsome piece of plastic out. It was an American Express Platinum Card in his own name. "Sweet Joseph and Mary, isn't this going a little over the top, even for you, Brigadier?"

"Don't let it go to your head. It's all part of a new persona I'm creating for you. You'll be told at the right time."

"Good," Dillon said. "Then I'll be on my way. I'll get spending."

"And don't forget a couple of suitcases, Dillon," Ferguson said. "You're going to need them. Lightweight clothing, it's hot out there at this time of year, and if it's not too much trouble, try and look like a gentleman."

"Wait for me," Jenny called and turned to the other two men. "I'll go with Dillon. Nothing else to do and it will help me kill time. I'll see you back at the house, Admiral."

She went down the steps and hurried after Dillon. "What do you think?" Travers asked.

"Oh, she has depths, that girl, she'll make out," Ferguson said. "Now let's get moving," and he led the way down to the car.

As the Daimler was driving along Whitehall toward the Ministry of Defence, the car phone sounded. Lane, sitting on the pull-down seat, his back to the chauffeur, answered, then glanced up at Ferguson, a hand over the receiver.

"The Deputy Director, Brigadier. He says he'd like an updating on how things are going. Wonders whether you could meet him and Sir Francis at Parliament. Afternoon tea on the Terrace."

"The cremation is at three," Ferguson said.

"You don't need to be there," Travers told him. "I'll see to it."

"But I'd like to be there," Ferguson said. "It's the civilized thing to do. The girl needs our support." He said to Lane, "Four-thirty to five. Best I can do."

Lane confirmed the appointment and Travers said, "Very decent of you, Charles."

"Me, decent?" Ferguson looked positively wicked. "I'll take Dillon along and introduce him. Just imagine, Sean Dillon, the Carlos of our times, on the Terrace of the Houses of Parliament. I can't wait to see Simon Carter's face," and he started to laugh helplessly.

Dillon and Jenny made for Harrods. "Try and look like a gentleman, that's what the man said," he reminded her. "What do you suggest?"

"A decent suit for general purposes, gray flannel perhaps and a blazer. A nice loose linen jacket and slacks, it really does get hot in St. John at this time of the year, really hot."

"I'm yours to command," he assured her.

They ended up in the bar upstairs with two suitcases filled with his purchases. "Strange having to buy an entire wardrobe," she said. "Socks, shirts, underwear. What on earth happened to you?"

"Let's say I had to leave where I was in a hurry." He called over a waiter and ordered two glasses of champagne and smoked salmon sandwiches.

"You like your champagne," she said.

Dillon smiled. "As a great man once said, there are only two things that never let you down in this life. Champagne and scrambled eggs."

"That's ridiculous, scrambled eggs go off very quickly. Anyway, what about people? Can't you rely on them?"

"I never had much of a chance of finding out. My mother died giving birth to me and I was her first, so no brothers or sisters. Then I was an actor. Few friends there. Your average actor would shoot his dear old granny if he thought it would get him the part."

"You haven't mentioned your father. Is he still around?"

"No, he was killed back in seventy-one in Belfast. He got caught in the cross-fire of a firefight. Shot dead by a British army patrol."

"So you joined the IRA?"

"Something like that."

"Guns and bombs, you thought that would be an answer?"

"There was a great Irishman called Michael Collins who led the fight for Irish freedom back in the early twenties. His favorite saying was something Lenin once said: 'The purpose of terrorism is to terrorize, it's the only way a small country can hope to take on a great nation and have any chance of winning.' "

"There's got to be a better way," she said. "People are fundamentally decent. Take Henry. I was a tramp, Dillon, drugged up to my eyeballs and working the streets in Miami. Any man could have me as long as the price was right and then along came Henry Baker, a decent and kindly man. He saw me through the drug unit, helped me rehabilitate, took me to St. John to share his house, set me up in business." She was close to tears. "And he never asked me for a thing, Dillon, never laid a hand on me. Isn't that the strangest thing?"

A life spent mainly on the move and one step ahead of trouble had left Dillon with little time for women. They were there on occasions to satisfy an urge, but no more than that and he'd never pretended otherwise, but now, sitting there opposite Jenny Grant, he felt a kind of warmth and sympathy that was new to him.

Jesus, Sean, don't go falling for her, now there's a good lad, he thought, but reached over and put a hand on one of hers. "It will pass, girl, dear, everything does, the one sure thing in this wicked old life. Now have a sandwich, it'll do you good."

The crematorium was in Hampstead, a red brick building, reasonably functional looking but surrounded by rather pleasant parkland. There were poplar trees, beds of roses and other flowers of every description. The Daimler arrived with Dillon sitting up front beside the chauffeur, and Ferguson,

Travers and the girl in the rear. Old Mr. Cox was waiting for them at the top of the steps, discreetly dressed in black.

"As you've asked for no kind of service I've already had the coffin taken in," he said to Ferguson. "Presumably the young lady would like a final look?"

"Thank you," Jenny said.

She followed him, Travers with a hand on her arm, and Ferguson and Dillon brought up the rear. The chapel was very plain, a few rows of chairs, a lectern, a cross on the wall. The coffin stood on a velvet-draped dais pointing at a curtained section of the wall. Music played faintly from some hidden tape recorder, dreary anodyne stuff. It was all very depressing.

"Would you care to see the deceased again?" Mr. Cox asked Jenny.

"No, thank you. I just wanted to say goodbye. Let him go now."

She was totally dry-eyed as Cox pressed a button on a box in the wall and the coffin rolled forward, parting the curtains, and disappeared.

"What's through there?" she asked.

"The furnace room." Cox seemed embarrassed. "The ovens."

"When can I have the ashes?"

"Later this afternoon. What would your needs be in that direction? Of course some people prefer to strew the ashes in our beautiful garden, but we do have a columbarium where the urn may be displayed with a suitable plaque."

"No, I'll take them with me."

"That won't be possible at the moment. It takes time, I'm afraid."

Travers said, "Perhaps you could have the ashes delivered to my house in Lord North Street in a suitable receptacle." He was embarrassed.

Cox said, "Of course." He turned to Jenny. "I presume you'll be flying back to the Caribbean, Miss Grant? We do provide a suitable container."

"Thank you. Can we go now?" she asked Ferguson.

Travers and Jenny got into the Daimler and Dillon paused at the top of the steps. There was a car parked close to the entrance to the drive and Smith was standing beside it, looking across at them. Dillon recognized him instantly, but in the same moment, Smith got in the car and it shot away.

As Ferguson emerged from the chapel Dillon said, "One of those two men I saw at the inquest was standing over there a moment ago. Just driven away."

"Really? Did you get the number?"

"Didn't have a chance to see it, the angle the car was at. Blue Renault, I think. You don't seem too worried."

"Why should I be, I've got you, haven't I? Now get in the car, there's a good chap." As they drove away he patted Jenny's hand. "Are you all right, my dear?"

"Yes, I'm fine, don't worry."

"I've been thinking," Ferguson told her. "If Henry didn't tell you the exact location of the submarine, can you think of anyone else he might have spoken to?"

"No," she said firmly. "If he didn't tell me, then he didn't tell anyone."

"No other diver maybe, I mean, he must have friends who dive as well, or another diver who might be able to help."

"Well there's always Bob Carney," she said, "the diver I told you about. He knows the Virgin Isles like the back of his hand."

"So, if anybody could help it would most likely be he?" Ferguson asked.

"I suppose so, but I wouldn't count on it. There's a lot of water out there."

The Daimler turned into Lord North Street and stopped. Travers got out first and reached a hand to Jenny. Ferguson said, "Dillon and I have work to do. We'll see you later."

Dillon turned in surprise. "What's this?"

"I've an appointment to meet the Deputy Director of the Security Services, Simon Carter, and a Junior Minister called Sir Francis Pamer on the Terrace at the Houses of Parliament. I'm supposed to keep them informed of my plans and I thought it might be amusing to take you along. After all, Dillon, Simon Carter's been trying to get his hands on you for years."

"Holy Mother of God," Dillon said, "but you're a wicked man, Brigadier."

Ferguson picked up the car phone and dialed Lane at the Ministry of Defence. "Jack, American called Bob Carney, resident St. John, presently a diver. Everything you can get. The CIA should help."

He put the phone down and Dillon said, "And what are you up to now, you old fox?"

But Ferguson made no reply, simply folded his hands across his stomach and closed his eyes.

SIX

The House of Commons has sometimes been referred to as the most exclusive club in London, mainly because of the amenities which, together with the upper chamber, the House of Lords, include twenty-six restaurants and bars each providing subsidized food and drinks.

There is always a queue waiting to get in, supervised by policemen, composed not only of tourists, but of constituents with appointments to see their Members of Parliament and everyone has to take their turn, no matter who, which explained why Ferguson and Dillon waited in line, moving forward slowly.

"At least you look respectable," Ferguson said, taking in Dillon's double-breasted blazer and gray flannels.

"Thanks to your Amex card," Dillon told him. "They treated me like a millionaire in Harrods."

"Really?" Ferguson said dryly. "You do realize that's a Guard's Brigade tie you're wearing?"

"Sure and I didn't want to let you down, Brigadier. Wasn't the Grenadiers your regiment?"

"Cheeky bastard!" Ferguson said as he reached the security checkpoint.

It was manned not by the security guards usually found at such places, but by very large policemen whose efficiency was in no doubt. Ferguson stated his business and produced his security card.

"Wonderful," Dillon said. "They all looked about seven feet tall, just like coppers used to do."

They came to the Central Lobby where people with an appointment to see their MP waited. It was extremely busy and Ferguson moved on, through a further corridor and down more stairs, finally leading the way out through an entrance on to the Terrace overlooking the Thames.

Once again, there were lots of people about, some with a glass in their hand enjoying a drink, Westminster Bridge to the left, the Embankment on the far side of the river. A row of tall, rather Victorian-looking lamps ran along the parapet. The synthetic carpetlike covering on the ground was green, but further along it changed to red, a distinct line marking the difference.

"Why the change in color?" Dillon asked.

"Everything in the Commons is green," Ferguson said. "The carpets, the leather of the chairs. Red for the House of Lords. That part of the Terrace up there is the Lords'."

"Jesus, but you English do love your class distinction, Brigadier."

As Dillon lit a cigarette with his Zippo, Ferguson said, "Here they are now. Behave yourself, there's a good chap."

"I'll do my best," Dillon said as Simon Carter and Sir Francis Pamer approached.

"There you are, Charles," Carter said. "We were looking for you."

"People all over the place," Pamer said. "Like a damned souk these days. Now what's happening, Brigadier? Where are we at with this business?"

"Well let's go and sit down and I'll tell you. Dillon here's going to handle things at the sharp end."

"All right," Pamer said. "What do you fancy, afternoon tea?"

"A drink would be more to my taste," Ferguson told him. "And I'm pressed for time."

Pamer led the way along to the Terrace bar and they found seats in the corner. He and Carter ordered gin and tonics, Ferguson Scotch. Dillon smiled with total charm at the waiter. "I'll have an Irish and water, Bushmills if you have it."

He had deliberately stressed his Ulster accent and Carter was frowning. "Dillon, did you say? I don't think we've met before."

"No," Dillon said amiably, "although not for want of trying on your part, Mr. Carter. Sean Dillon."

Carter's face was very pale now and he turned to Ferguson. "Is this some sort of practical joke?"

"Not that I'm aware of."

Carter shut up as the waiter brought the drinks and as soon as he had gone, continued. "Sean Dillon? Is he who I think he is?"

"As ever was," Dillon told him.

Carter ignored him. "And you'd bring a damned scoundrel like this, here to this particular place, Ferguson? A man that the Intelligence services have hunted for years."

"That may be," Ferguson said calmly. "But he's working for Group Four now, all taken care of under my authority, so let's get on with it, shall we?"

"Ferguson, you go too far." Carter was seething.

"Yes, I'm told that often, but to business. To give you a résumé of what's happened. There was a burglary at Lord North Street, which may or may not have been genuine. However, we did discover a bug in the telephone which could indicate some kind of opposition. Have you any agents working the case?" he asked Carter.

"Certainly not. I'd have told you."

"Interesting. When we were at the inquest on Baker this morning Dillon noticed two men who gave him pause for thought. He noticed one of them again later when we were at the crematorium."

Carter frowned. "But who could it be?"

"God knows, but it's another reason for having Dillon on the job. The girl still insists she doesn't know the site of the submarine."

"Do you believe her?" Pamer put in.

"I do," Dillon said. "She's not the sort to lie."

"And you would know, of course," Carter said acidly.

Dillon shrugged. "Why should she lie about it? What would be the point?"

"But she must know something," Pamer said. "At the very least she must have some sort of a clue."

"Who knows?" Ferguson said. "But at this stage of the game we must proceed on the assumption that she doesn't."

"So what happens next?" Carter demanded.

"Dillon will proceed to St. John and take it from there. The girl mentioned a diver, a man named Carney, Bob Carney, who was a close friend of Baker. Apparently he knows the area like the back of his hand. The girl can make a suitable introduction, persuade him to help."

"But there's no guarantee he can find the damned thing," Pamer said.

"We'll just have to see, won't we?" Ferguson looked at his watch. "We'll have to go."

He stood and led the way outside. They paused by the wall on the edge of the Terrace. Carter said, "So that's it then?"

"Yes," Ferguson told him. "Dillon and the girl will probably leave for St. John tomorrow or the day after."

"Well I can't say I like it."

"No one is asking you to." Ferguson nodded to Dillon. "Let's get moving."

He moved away and Dillon smiled at the two of them with all his considerable charm. "It's been a sincere sensation, but one thing, Mr. Carter." He leaned over the parapet and looked down at the brown water of the Thames. "Only fifteen feet, I'd say, maybe less when the tide's up. All that security at the front door and nothing here. I'd think about that if I were you."

"Two-knot current out there," Pamer said. "Not that I can swim myself. Never could. Should be enough to keep the wolves at bay."

Dillon walked away and Carter said, "It makes my skin crawl to think of that little swine walking around here, a free man. Ferguson must be crazy."

Pamer said, "Yes, I see your point, but what do you think about the girl? Do you believe her?"

"I'm not sure," Carter said. "And Dillon has a point. Why would she lie?"

"So we're no further forward?"

"I wouldn't say that. She knows the area, she knew Baker intimately, the kind of places he went to and so on. Even if she doesn't know the actual location she may be able to work it out with this Carney fellow to help her, the diver."

"And Dillon, of course."

"Yes, well, I prefer to forget about him and under the circumstances, what I could do with is another drink," and Carter turned and led the way into the bar.

At his suite in Paris Max Santiago listened patiently while Pamer gave him details of the meeting on the Terrace.

"Astonishing," he said when Pamer had finished. "If this Dillon is the kind of man you describe, he would be a formidable opponent."

"But what about the girl?"

"I don't know, Francis, we'll have to see. I'll be in touch."

He put the phone down momentarily, picked it up again and rang Smith in London and when he answered, told him exactly what he wanted him to do.

It was just after six and Dillon was in the study reading the evening paper by the fire when the doorbell sounded. He went and opened it and found old Mr. Cox standing there, a hearse parked at the curb. He was holding a cardboard box in his hands.

"Is Miss Grant at home?"

"Yes, I'll get her for you," Dillon told him.

"No need." Cox handed him the box. "The ashes. They're in a traveling urn inside. Give her my best respects."

He went down to the hearse and Dillon closed the door. The Admiral had gone out to an early evening function at his club, but Jenny was in the kitchen. Dillon called to her and she came out.

"What is it?"

He held up the box. "Mr. Cox just left this for you," and turned and went into the study and put it on the table. She stood beside him, looking at it, then gently opened the lid and took out what was inside. It wasn't really an urn, just a square box in dark, patterned metal with a clasp holding the lid in place. The brass plate said: Henry Baker 1929–1992.

She put it down on the table and slumped into a chair. "That's what it all comes down to at the final end of things, five pounds of gray ash in a metal box."

She broke then and started to cry in total anguish. Dillon put his hands on her shoulders for a moment only. "Just let it come, it'll do you good. I'll make you a cup of coffee," and he turned and went along to the kitchen.

She sat there for a moment and it was as if she couldn't breathe. She had to get out, needed air. She got up, went into the hall, took the Admiral's old trenchcoat down from the stand and pulled it on. When she opened the door it had started to rain. She belted the coat and hurried along the pavement and Smith, sitting in the van with Johnson, saw her pass the entrance to the alley.

"Perfect," he said. "Let's get on with it," and he got out and went after her, Johnson at his heels.

Dillon went along the hall to the study, the cup of coffee in his hand, and was aware first of the silence. He went into the study, put down the cup and went back to the hall.

"Jenny?" he called and then noticed that the door was slightly ajar.

"For God's sake," he said, took down his flying jacket and went out, putting it on. There was no sign of her, the street deserted. He'd have to take a chance, turned left and ran along the pavement toward Great Peter Street.

It was raining very hard now and he paused on the corner for a moment, looking left and then right, and saw her at the far end where the street met Millbank. She was waiting for a gap in the traffic, saw her chance and darted across to Victoria Tower Gardens by the river, and Dillon also saw something else, Smith and Johnson crossing the road behind her. At that distance, he didn't actually recognize them, but it was enough. He swore savagely and started to run.

It was almost dark as Jenny crossed to the wall overlooking the Thames. There was a lamp about every twenty feet, rain slanting in a silver spray through a yellow light, and a seagoing freighter moved downstream, its red and green navigation lights plain. She took a few deep breaths to steady herself and felt better. It was at that moment she heard a movement behind her, turned and found Smith and Johnson standing there.

She knew she was in trouble at once. "What do you want?" she demanded and started to edge away.

"No need to panic, darling," Smith said. "A little conversation is all we need, a few answers."

She turned to run and Johnson was on her like a flash, pinning her arms and forcing her back against the wall. "Jenny, isn't it?" he asked and as she struggled desperately, he smiled. "I like that, do it some more."

"Leave off," Smith told him. "Can't you ever think of anything except what's in your pants?" Johnson eased away, but moved round to hold her from the rear and Smith said, "Now about this U-boat in the Virgin Islands. You don't really expect us to believe you don't know where it is?"

She tried to struggle and Johnson said, "Go on, answer the man or I'll give you a slapping."

A voice called, "Put her down. I mean, she doesn't know where you've been, does she? She might catch something."

Dillon's Zippo lighter flared as he lit the cigarette that dangled from the corner of his mouth. He walked forward and Smith went to meet him. "You want trouble, you've got it, you little squirt," and he swung a tremendous punch.

Dillon swayed to one side, reaching for the wrist, twisted it so that Smith cried out in agony, falling to one knee. Dillon's clenched fist swung down in a hammer blow of tremendous force across the extended arm, snapping the forearm. Smith cried out again, fell over on his side.

Johnson said, "You little bastard."

He threw Jenny to one side and took an automatic pistol from his left-hand raincoat pocket. Dillon moved in fast, blocking the arm to the side, so that the only shot Johnson got off went into the ground. At the same time the Irishman half-turned, throwing the other man across his extended leg, ramming his heel down so hard that he fractured two of Johnson's ribs.

Johnson writhed on the ground in agony and Dillon picked up the automatic. It was an old Italian Beretta, small caliber, somewhere close to a point-two-two.

"Woman's gun," Dillon said, "but it'll do the job." He crouched down beside Johnson. "Who do you work for, sonny?"

"Don't say a word," Smith called.

"Who said I was going to?" Johnson spat in Dillon's face. "Get fucked."

"Suit yourself."

Dillon rolled him over, put the muzzle of the gun against the back of his left knee and fired. Johnson gave a terrible cry and Dillon took a handful of his hair and pulled his head back.

"Do you want me to do the other one? I'll put you on sticks if you like."

"No," Johnson moaned. "We work for Santiago—Max Santiago."

"Really?" Dillon said. "And where would I find him?"

"He lives in Puerto Rico, but lately he's been in Paris."

"And you did the burglary at Lord North Street?"

"Yes."

"Good boy. See how easy it was?"

"You stupid bugger," Smith said to Johnson. "You've just dug your own grave."

Dillon tossed the Beretta over the wall into the Thames. "I'd say he's been very sensible. Westminster Hospital's not too far from here, first-class casualty department and free, even for animals like you, thanks to the National Health Service."

He turned and found Jenny staring at him in a daze and he took her arm. "Come on, love, let's go home."

As they walked away Smith called, "I'll get you for this, Dillon."

"No you won't," Dillon said. "You'll put it down to experience and hope that this Max Santiago feels the same way."

They emerged from the gardens and paused at the pavement edge, waiting for a gap in the traffic. Dillon said, "Are you all right?"

"My God!" she said wonderingly. "What kind of man are you, Sean Dillon, to do that?"

"They'd have done worse to you, my love."

He took her hand and ran with her across the road.

When they reached the house she went straight upstairs and Dillon went into the kitchen and put the kettle on, thinking about things as he waited for it to boil. Max Santiago? Progress indeed, something for Ferguson to get his teeth into there. He was aware of Jenny coming down the stairs and going into the study, made the coffee, put the cups on a tray. As he went to join her he realized she was on the phone.

"British Airways? What's the last flight to Paris tonight?" There was a pause. "Nine-thirty? Can you reserve me a seat? Grant—Jennifer Grant. Yes, I'll pick it up at reservations. Yes, Terminal Four, Heathrow."

She put the phone down and turned as Dillon entered. He put the tray on the desk. "Doing a runner are you?"

"I can't take it. I don't understand what's going on. Ferguson, you and now those men and that gun. I can't get it out of my mind. I was going away anyway, but I'm going to get out now while I can."

"To Paris?" he said. "I heard you on the phone."

"That's just a jumping-off point. There's someone I have to see, someone I want to take this to." She picked up the black metal box containing the ashes. "Henry's sister."

"Sister?" Dillon frowned.

"I'm probably about the only person left who knows he had one. There are special reasons for that so don't ask me and don't ask me where I'm going after Paris."

"I see."

She glanced at her watch. "Seven o'clock, Dillon, and the flight's at nine-thirty. I can make it, only don't tell Ferguson, not until I've gone. Help me, Dillon, please."

"Then don't waste time in talking about it," he said. "Go and get your bags now and I'll ring for a taxi."

"Will you, Dillon, honestly?"

"I'll go with you myself."

She turned and hurried out and Dillon sighed and said softly, "You daft bastard, what's getting into you?" and he picked up the phone.

It was very quiet in the waiting room of the small private nursing home in Farsley Street. Smith sat in an upright chair against the wall, his right forearm encased in plaster and held in a sling. The half hour after their encounter with Dillon had been a nightmare. They couldn't afford to go to a public hospital because that would have meant the police, so he'd had to go and get the van from the alley by Lord North Street from where he'd driven one-handed to Victoria Tower Gardens to retrieve Johnson. The trip to Farsley Street had been even worse. Dr. Shah emerged from the operating theater, a small, gray-haired Pakistani in green cap and gown, a mask hanging around his neck.

"How is he?" Smith asked.

"As well as can be expected with a split kneecap. He'll limp for the rest of his life."

"That fucking little Irish bastard," Smith said.

"You boys can never stay out of trouble, can you? Does Mr. Santiago know about it?"

"Why should he?" Smith was alarmed. "Nothing to do with him this one."

"I thought it might, that's all. He phoned me from Paris the other day on business so I knew he was around."

"No, not his bag this." Smith got up. "I'll get myself off home. I'll be in to see him tomorrow."

He went out of the glass front door. Shah watched him go, then walked past the reception desk, empty at that time of night, and went into his office. He always believed in covering himself. He picked up the phone and rang Santiago at the Ritz in Paris.

The traffic at that time in the evening was light and they were at Heathrow by eight o'clock. Jenny picked up her ticket at the reservation desk and went and booked in for the flight. She put her case through, but carried the traveling urn.

"Time for a drink?" Dillon suggested.

"Why not?"

She seemed in better spirits now and waited for him in the corner of the bar until he returned with an Irish whisky and a glass of white wine. "You're feeling better, I can tell," he said.

"It's good to be on the move again, to get away from it all. What will you tell Ferguson?"

"Nothing about you until the morning."

"You'll tell him I flew to Paris?"

"No point in not doing, he'd find that out in five minutes from a check on British Airways' passenger computer."

"That doesn't matter, I'll be well on my way by then. What about you?"

"St. John next stop. Tomorrow or the day after."

"See Bob Carney," she said. "Tell him I sent you, and introduce yourself to Billy and Mary Jones. They're running the cafe and bar for me while I'm away."

"What about you? When will you be back?"

"I don't honestly know. A few days, a week, I'll see how I feel. I'll look you up when I get back if you're still there."

"I don't know where I'll be staying."

"It's easy to find someone in St. John."

The flight was called and they finished their drinks, went down to the concourse and he accompanied her to the security entrance. "I'm sorry if I've made trouble for you with the Brigadier," she said.

"Entirely my pleasure," he assured her.

"You're quite a guy, Dillon." She kissed him on the cheek. "Frightening, mind you, but thank God you're on my side. I'll see you."

Dillon watched her go, then turned and made his way to the nearest row of telephones, took out a card with telephone numbers which Ferguson had given him and rang the Cavendish Square number. Kim answered the phone and informed him that the Brigadier was dining at the Garrick Club. Dillon thanked him, went out to the rank and took the first cab in the line.

"London," he said. "The Garrick Club. You know where that is?"

"Certainly, guv." The driver examined Dillon's open-necked shirt in the rear-view mirror. "Wasting your time there, guv, dressed like that. They won't let you in. Jacket-and-tie job. Members and their guests only."

"We'll have to see, won't we?" Dillon told him. "Just take me there."

When they reached the Garrick, the driver pulled in at the curb and turned. "Shall I wait, guv?"

"Why not? I'll be straight out again if what you say is true."

Dillon went up the steps and paused at the desk. The uniformed porter was civil enough. "Can I help you, sir?"

Dillon put on his finest public-school accent. "I'm looking for Brigadier Charles Ferguson. I was told he was dining here tonight. I need to see him most urgently."

"I'm afraid I can't allow you upstairs, sir. We do require a jacket and tie, but if you care to wait here I'll have a message sent to the Brigadier. What was the name, sir?"

"Dillon."

The porter picked up the telephone and spoke to someone. He put the phone down. "He'll be with you directly, sir."

Dillon moved forward into the hall, admiring the grand staircase, the oil paintings that covered the walls. After a while Ferguson appeared up there, looked over the rail at him and came down the stairs.

"What on earth do you want, Dillon? I'm halfway through my dinner."

"Oh, Jesus, Your Honor." Dillon stepped effortlessly into the Stage Irishman. "It's so good of you to see me, the grand man like yourself and this place so elegant."

The porter looked alarmed and Ferguson took Dillon by the arm and propelled him outside to the top of the steps. "Stop playing the fool, my steak will be quite ruined by now."

"Bad for you at your age, red meat." Dillon lit a cigarette, the Zippo flaring. "I've found out who the opposition is."

"Good God, who?"

"A name, that's all I have. Santiago—Max Santiago. He lives in Puerto Rico, but recently he's been in Paris. By the way, they also did the burglary."

"How did you find this out?"

"I had a run-in with our two friends from the coroner's court."

Ferguson nodded. "I see. I hope you didn't have to kill anyone?"

"Now would I do a thing like that? I'll leave it with you, Brigadier, I feel like an early night."

He went down the steps to the cab and got in. "I told you, guv," the cabby said.

"Oh, well," Dillon said. "You can't win them all. Take me to Lord North Street," and he leaned back and looked out at the London night scene.

Jack Lane, only recently divorced, lived alone in a flat in West End Lane on the edge of Hampstead. He was cooking a frozen pizza in his microwave oven when the phone rang and his heart sank.

"Jack? Ferguson here. Dillon had a run-in with those two suspicious characters who were at the coroner's court and the crematorium. They've been working for a Max Santiago, resident of Puerto Rico, recently in Paris."

"Is that all, sir?"

"It's enough. Get yourself down to the office. See if French Intelligence has anything on him, then try the CIA, the FBI, anybody you can think of. He must be on somebody's computer. Did you get anything on this Bob Carney fellow, the diver?"

"Yes, sir, an interesting man in more ways than one."

"Right, you can brief me in the morning, but get cracking on this Santiago thing now. Five hours earlier than us in the States, remember."

"I'll try to, sir."

Lane put the phone down with a groan, opened the microwave oven and looked with distaste at the pizza. What the hell, he'd nothing better to do and he could always pick up some fish and chips on the way to the Ministry.

At his flat, Smith was on his second large Scotch, his right forearm in plaster and held by a sling. He felt terrible and it was beginning to hurt a great deal. He was pouring another Scotch when the phone rang.

Santiago said, "Have you anything for me?"

"Not yet, Mr. Santiago." Smith searched wildly for something to say. "Maybe tomorrow."

"Shah has been on the phone. Johnson shot and you with a broken arm. 'Fucking little Irish bastard,' I believe that was the phrase you used. Presumably Dillon?"

"Well, yes, Mr. Santiago, we did have a run-in with him. We'd got the girl, see, and he managed to jump us. He had a gun."

"Did he really?" Santiago commented dryly. "And what did you say when he asked you who your employer was?"

Smith answered instinctively, "Not a bloody thing, it was Johnson who . . ."

He stopped dead and Santiago said, "Carry on, tell me the worst."

"All right, Mr. Santiago, the stupid bastard did give Dillon your name."

There was silence for a moment and then Santiago said, "I'm disappointed in you, my friend, most disappointed." The phone clicked and the line went dead.

Smith knew what that meant. More frightened than he had ever been in his life, he packed a suitcase one-handed, retrieved a thousand pounds mad money he kept in a sugar tin in the kitchen and left. Two minutes later he was behind the wheel of the van and driving away one-handed. He had an old girlfriend in Aberdeen who'd always had a weakness for him. Scotland, that was the place to go. As far away from Johnson as possible.

At the nursing home Shah sat behind his desk, the phone to his ear. After a while he put it down, sighed heavily and went out. He went into the small pharmacy at the side of the operating theater, fitted a syringe together and filled it from a phial he took from the medicine cupboard.

When he opened the door at the end of the corridor, Johnson was sleeping, linked to a drip. Shah stood looking down at him for a moment, then bared the left forearm and inserted the needle. Johnson sucked in air very deeply for about five times, then stopped altogether. Shah checked for vital signs, found none and went out. He paused at the reception desk, picked up the phone and dialed.

A voice said, "Deepdene Funeral Service. How may we serve you?"

"Shah here. I have a disposal for you."

"Ready now?"

"Yes."

"We'll be there in half an hour."

"Thank you."

Shah replaced the receiver and went back to his office, humming to himself.

It was almost eleven when Travers returned to Lord North Street and found Dillon sitting in the study reading a book. "Jennifer gone to bed?" Travers asked.

"More than an hour ago. She was very tired."

"Not surprising, been through a hell of a lot that girl. Fancy a nightcap, Dillon? Can't offer you Irish, but a good single malt perhaps?"

"Fine by me."

Travers poured it into two glasses, gave him one and sat opposite. "Cheers. What are you reading?"

"Epictetus." Dillon held the book up. "He was a Greek philosopher of the Stoic School."

"I know who he was, Dillon," Travers said patiently. "I'm just surprised that you do."

"He says here that a life not put to the test is not worth living. Would you agree to that, Admiral?"

"As long as it doesn't mean bombing the innocent in the name of some sacred cause or shooting people in the back, then I suppose I do."

"God forgive you, Admiral, but I never planted a bomb in the way you mean or shot anyone in the back in me life."

"God forgive me, indeed, Dillon, because for some obscure reason I'm inclined to believe you." Travers swallowed his whisky and got up. "Good night to you," he said and went out.

Things had gone better than Smith had expected and he soon had the hang of handling the wheel one-handed, just the fingers of his right hand touching the bottom of the wheel. The rain wasn't helping, of course, and beyond Watford he missed a turning for the motorway and found himself on a long dark road, no other vehicles in sight, and then headlights were switched on behind and a vehicle came up far too fast.

It started to overtake him, a large black truck, and Smith cursed, frightened to death, knowing what this was, and he frantically worked at the wheel. The truck swerved in, knocking him sideways, and with nowhere to go, the van spun off the road, smashed through a fence and turned over twice on its way down a seventy-foot bank. It came to a crumpled halt and Smith, still conscious as he lay on his side in the cab, could smell petrol as the fractured tank spilled its contents.

There was the noise of someone scrambling down the bank and footsteps approached. "Help me," Smith moaned, "I'm in here."

Someone struck a match. It was the last thing he remembered. One final moment of horror as it was flicked toward him through the darkness and the petrol fireballed.

SEVEN

In Paris at Charles de Gaulle Airport it was almost midnight by the time Jenny Grant had retrieved her suitcase and she walked out into the concourse quickly and found an Avis car rental desk.

"You're still open, thank goodness," she said as she got her passport and driving license out.

"But of course," the young woman on duty replied in English. "We always wait until the final arrival of the day, even when there is a delay. How long will you require the car for, mademoiselle?"

"Perhaps a week. I'm not certain, but I'll be returning here."

"That's fine." The girl busied herself with the paperwork and took a print from her charge card. "Follow me and I'll take you to the car."

Ten minutes later Jenny was driving out of the airport sitting behind the wheel of a Citroën saloon and headed west, Normandy the destination. The traveling urn was on the passenger seat beside her. She touched it briefly, then settled back to concentrate on her driving. She had a long way to go, would probably have to drive through the night, but that didn't matter because London and the terrible events of the last few days were behind her and she was free.

Dillon rose early, was in the kitchen cooking bacon and eggs at seven-thirty when Travers entered in his dressing gown.

"Smells good," the Admiral said. "Jenny about yet?"

"Well, to be honest with you, Admiral, she's not been about for some time." Dillon poured boiling water into a china teapot. "There you go, a nice cup of tea."

"Never mind that. What are you talking about?"

"Well, drink your tea like a good lad and I'll tell you. It began with her getting upset and going for a walk."

Dillon worked his way through his bacon and eggs while he related the events of the previous night. When he was finished the Admiral just sat there frowning. "You took too much on yourself, Dillon."

"She'd had enough, Admiral," Dillon told him. "It's as simple as that and I didn't see any reason to stop her."

"And she wouldn't tell you where she was going?"

"First stop Paris, that's all I know. After that, to some unknown destination to see Baker's sister. She's taking the ashes to her, that's obvious."

"Yes, I suppose so." Travers sighed wearily. "I'll have to tell Ferguson. He won't like it, won't like it one little bit."

"Well it's time he discovered what an unfair world it is," Dillon told him and opened the morning paper.

Travers sighed heavily again, gave up, went to his study and sat at the desk. Only then did he reluctantly reach for the phone.

It was just after nine when Jenny Grant braked to a halt outside the Convent of the Little Sisters of Pity in the village of Briac five miles outside Bayeux. She had driven through the night, was totally drained. Iron gates stood open, she drove inside and stopped in a graveled circular drive in front of the steps leading up to the door of the beautiful old building. A young novice, a white working smock over her robes, was raking the gravel.

Jenny got out holding the traveling urn. "I'd like to see the Mother Superior. It's most urgent. I've come a long way."

The young woman said in good English, "I believe she's in chapel, we'll see, shall we?"

She led the way through pleasant gardens to a small chapel, which stood separate from the main building. The door creaked when she opened it. It was a place of shadows, an image of the Virgin Mary floating in candlelight, and the smell of incense was overpowering. The young novice went and whispered to the nun who knelt in prayer at the altar rail, then returned.

"She'll be with you in a moment."

She went out and Jenny waited. After a while the Mother Superior crossed herself and stood up. She turned and came toward her, a tall woman in her fifties with a sweet, serene face. "I am the Mother Superior. How may I help you?"

"Sister Maria Baker?"

"That's right." She looked puzzled. "Do I know you, my dear?"

"I'm Jenny—Jenny Grant. Henry told me he'd spoken to you about me."

Sister Maria Baker smiled. "But of course, so you're Jenny." And then she looked concerned. "There's something wrong, I can tell. What is it?"

"Henry was killed in an accident in London the other day." Jenny held out the traveling urn. "I've brought you his ashes."

"Oh, my dear." There was pain on Sister Maria Baker's face and she crossed herself, then took the urn. "May he rest in peace. It was so kind of you to do this thing."

"Yes, but it wasn't just that. I don't know which way to turn. So many awful things have happened."

Jenny burst into tears and sat down in the nearest pew. Sister Maria Baker put a hand on her head. "What is it, my dear, tell me."

When Jenny was finished it seemed very quiet in the chapel. Sister Maria Baker said, "Mystery upon mystery here. Only one thing is certain. Henry's unfortunate discovery of that submarine is of critical importance to many people, but enough of that now."

"I know," Jenny said, "and I'll have to go back to St. John if only to help Sean Dillon. He's a bad man, sister, I know that, and yet so kind to me. Isn't that strange?"

"Not really, my dear." Sister Maria Baker drew her to her feet. "I suspect that Mr. Dillon is no longer so certain that what he longed for was right. But all that can wait. You need a few days of total rest, a time to reflect, and that's doctor's orders. I *am* a doctor, you know, we're a nursing order. Now let's find you a room," and they went out together, leaving the chapel to the quiet.

When Dillon and Travers were shown into the flat at Cavendish Square just before noon, Ferguson was sitting by the fire going over a file. Jack Lane was standing by the window looking out.

Dillon said, "God save all here."

Ferguson glanced up coldly. "Very amusing, Dillon."

"Well the correct reply is 'God save you kindly,' " Dillon said, "but we'll let it pass."

"What in the hell were you playing at?"

"She wanted to go, Brigadier, she'd had enough for the moment, it was as simple as that. The attack by those two apes in Victoria Tower Gardens finished her off."

"So you just decided to go along with her?"

"Not her, her needs, Brigadier." Dillon lit a cigarette. "She told me she wanted to see Baker's sister and begged me not to ask her where that would be. Said there were special reasons she didn't want to divulge."

"Would you be interested to know that Lane has run a check and can't find any mention of Baker having a sister?"

"Not at all. Jenny said she was probably the only person who knew he had one. Some dark family secret, perhaps."

"So, she flew to Paris and took off for God knows where?"

Lane cut in. "We did a check at Charles de Gaulle. She hired a car at the Avis desk."

"And after that, who the hell knows?" Ferguson was coldly angry.

Dillon said, "I told you, she'd had enough."

"But we need her, God dammit."

"She'll return to St. John when she's ready. In the meantime, we'll have to manage." Dillon shrugged. "You can't have everything in life, not even you."

Ferguson sat there glaring at him, thoroughly angry, then said, "At least we have some sort of a lead. Tell him, Jack."

Lane said, "Max Santiago. He's the driving force behind a hotel group in the States, home in Puerto Rico. Hotels in Florida, Vegas, various other places and a couple of casinos."

"Is that a fact?" Dillon said.

"Yes, my first break was with the FBI. Their highly illegal sensitive red information file. It's highly illegal because it lists people who can't be proved to have broken the law in any way."

"And why would Santiago be on that?"

"Suspicion of having contacts with the Colombian drug cartel."

"Really?" Dillon smiled. "The dog."

"It gets worse. Samson Cay Holding Company, registered in the U.S.A. and Switzerland, goes backwards through three other companies until you get to Santiago's name."

"Samson Cay?" Dillon leaned forward. "Now that is interesting. A direct link. But why?"

Lane said, "Santiago's sixty-three, old aristocratic family, born in Cuba, father a general and very involved with Batista. The family only got out by the skin of their teeth in nineteen fifty-nine when Castro took over. Given asylum in America and eventual citizenship, but according to the FBI file, the interesting thing is they had not much more than the clothes they stood up in."

"I see," Dillon said. "So how did good old Max develop a hotel chain that must be worth millions? The drug connection can't explain that. All that Colombian drug business is much more recent."

"The plain answer is nobody knows."

Travers had been sitting listening to all this, looking bewildered. "So what is the connection? To Samson Cay and U180, Martin Bormann, all that stuff?"

"Well, the FBI file took me to the CIA," Lane said. "They have him on their computer too, but for a different reason. Apparently Santiago's father was a great friend of General Franco in Spain, an absolutely rabid Fascist."

"Which could be the link with nineteen forty-five, the end of the war in Europe and Martin Bormann," Ferguson said.

Dillon nodded. "I see it now. The Kamaradenwerk, Action for Comrades."

"Could be." The Brigadier nodded. "More than likely. Just take one aspect. Santiago and his father reach America flat broke and yet mysteriously manage to get their hands on the very large funds necessary to go into business. We know for a fact that the Nazi Party salted away millions all over the world to enable their work to keep going." He shrugged. "All conjecture, but it makes sense."

"Except for one thing," Dillon said.

"And what's that?"

"How Santiago knew about Baker finding U180. I mean, how did he know about him coming to London, staying at Lord North Street with the Admiral, Jenny, me? He does seem singularly well-informed, Brigadier."

"I must say Dillon's got a point," Travers put in.

Ferguson said, "The point is well taken and we'll find the answer in time, but for the moment we'll just have to get on with it. You'll leave for the Caribbean tomorrow."

"Just as we planned?" Dillon said.

"Exactly. British Airways to Antigua, then onwards to St. John."

Dillon said, "Would you think it likely that Max Santiago will turn up there? He's had his fingers in everything else so far."

"We'll just have to see."

"As I said," Lane interrupted. "He has a home in Puerto Rico and that's very convenient for the Virgin Islands. Apparently he runs one of those multi-million-dollar motor yachts." He looked at his file. "It's called the *Maria Blanco*. Captain and a crew of six."

"If he turns up you'll just have to do the best you can," Ferguson said. "That's what you're going to be there for. You'll have your Platinum Card and traveler's checks for twenty-five thousand dollars. Your cover is quite simple. You're a wealthy Irishman."

"God save us, I didn't know there was such a thing."

"Don't be stupid, Dillon," Ferguson told him. "You're a wealthy Irishman with a company in Cork. General electronics, computers and so on. We've provided a nice touch for you. When you arrive in Antigua, there'll be a seaplane waiting. You *can* fly a seaplane, I presume?"

"I could fly a Jumbo if I had to, Brigadier, but then you knew that."

"So I did. What kind of plane did you say it was, Jack?"

"A Cessna 206, sir." Lane turned to Dillon. "Apparently it's got floats and wheels so you can land on sea or on land."

"I know the type," Dillon said. "I've flown planes like it."

"The center of things in St. John is a town called Cruz Bay," the Inspector carried on. "On occasions they've had a commercial seaplane service round there so there's a ramp in the harbor, facilities and so on."

Ferguson passed a folder across. "The documents department have done you proud. Two passports, Irish and British in your own name. Being born in Belfast, you're entitled to those. C.A.A. commercial pilot's license with a seaplane rating."

"They think of everything," Dillon said.

"You'll also find your tickets and traveler's checks in there. You'll be staying at Caneel Bay, one of the finest resorts in the world. Stayed there once myself some years ago. Paradise, Dillon, you're a lucky chap, paradise on a private peninsula not too far from Cruz Bay."

Dillon opened the file and leafed through some of the brochures. "Situated on its own private peninsula, seven beaches, three restaurants," he read aloud. "It sounds my kind of place."

"It's anyone's kind of place," Ferguson said. "The two best cottages are 7E and 7D. Ambassadors stay there, Dillon, film stars. I believe Kissinger was in 7E once. Also Harry Truman."

"I'm overwhelmed," Dillon said.

"It will all help with your image."

"One thing," Lane said. "It's an old tradition there that there are no telephones in the cottages. There are public telephones dotted around, but we've arranged for you to have a cellular portable phone. They'll give it to you when you check in."

Dillon nodded. "So I get there. Then what do I do?"

"That's really up to you," Ferguson said. "We hoped the girl would be there to assist, but thanks to your misplaced gallantry that isn't on for the moment. However, I would suggest you contact this diver she mentioned, this Bob Carney. He runs a firm called Paradise Watersports, based at Caneel Bay. There's a brochure there."

"Teaches tourists to dive," Lane said.

Dillon found the brochure and glanced through it. It was attractively set out with excellent underwater photos, but the most interesting one was of Captain Bob Carney himself seated at the wheel of a boat, good-looking, tanned and very fit.

"Jesus," Dillon said. "If you wanted an actor to play that fella you'd have trouble finding someone suitable at Central Casting."

Ferguson said, "An interesting man, this Carney chap. Tell him, Jack."

Lane opened another file.

"Born in Mississippi in nineteen forty-eight, but he spent most of his youth in Atlanta. Wife, Karye, a boy of eight, Walker, girl aged five named Wallis. He did a year at the University of Mississippi, then joined the Marines and went to Vietnam. Did two tours, in sixty-eight and sixty-nine."

"I always heard that was a bad time," Dillon said.

"Toward the end of his service he was with the 2nd Combined Action Group. He was wounded, received two Purple Hearts, the Vietnamese Cross of Valour and was recommended for a Bronze Star. That one got lost in channels."

"And afterwards he took to diving?"

"Not at first. He went to Georgia State University, courtesy of the Marine Corps, and did a bachelor's degree in Philosophy. Did a year in a graduate school in Oceanography."

"Is there anything else?"

Lane consulted the file. "He has a captain's ticket up to sixteen hundred tons, ran supply boats in the Mexican Gulf to the oil rigs, was a welder and diver in the oilfields. Went to St. John in seventy-nine." Lane closed the file.

"So there's your man," Ferguson said. "You've got to get him on our side, Dillon. Offer him anything, money no object, within reason, that is."

Dillon smiled. "I'm surprised at you, Brigadier. Money is never number one on the list to men like Carney."

"That's as may be." Ferguson got up. "That's it then, I'll see you again before you leave in the morning. What time is his plane, Jack?"

"Nine o'clock, sir, gets into Antigua just after two in the afternoon their time."

"Then I certainly won't see you." Ferguson sighed. "I suppose I must see you off in the right style. Bring him to the Garrick for dinner at seven-thirty, Garth, but now you must excuse me."

"He's all heart, isn't he?" Dillon said to the Admiral as they emerged onto the pavement.

"Never would have thought of describing him in quite that way," Travers said and raised his umbrella at a passing cab.

It was perhaps an hour later that Ferguson met Simon Carter in the snug of a public house called the St. George not too far from the Ministry of Defence.

He ordered a gin and tonic. "Thought I'd better bring you up to date," he said. "There's a lot happened."

"Tell me," Carter said.

So Ferguson did, the attack on Jenny by Smith and Johnson, Santiago, Jenny's flight, everything. When he finished, Carter sat there thinking about it.

"The Santiago thing—that's very interesting. Your chap Lane may have a point, the Fascist angle, General Franco and all that."

"It would certainly fit, but Dillon's right. None of it explains how Santiago seems to be so well informed."

"So what do you intend to do about him?"

"Nothing I *can* do officially," Ferguson said. "He's an American citizen, a multi-millionaire businessman and in the eyes of the world, highly respected. I mean, that stuff on the FBI and CIA files is confidential."

"And there is the fact that we don't want to involve the Americans in this in any way," Carter pointed out.

"Heaven forbid, the last thing we want."

"So we're in Dillon's hands," the Deputy Director said.

"I know and I don't like it one little bit." Ferguson stood up. "You'll let Pamer know where we're at."

"Of course," Carter told him. "Perhaps this Carney chap, the diver you mentioned, can give Dillon a lead."

"I'll keep you posted," Ferguson said and went out.

In Paris, Santiago, who was going to a black-tie dinner at the American Embassy, was adjusting his tie in the mirror when the phone rang. It was Pamer, and Santiago listened while he brought him up to date.

"So they know your name, Max." Pamer was very agitated. "And all thanks to those damned men who were working for you."

"Forget them," Santiago said. "They're yesterday's news."

"What's that supposed to mean?"

"Don't be stupid, Francis, you're a big boy now. Try to act like one." Pamer was horrified. "All right, Max, but what are we going to do?"

"They can't lay a finger on me, Francis, I'm an American citizen, and they won't want to include the American Government in this thing. In fact, Ferguson is acting quite illegally in sending Dillon to operate in another country's sovereign territory. The U-boat is in American waters, remember?"

"So what will you do?"

"I'll fly to Puerto Rico in the morning, then sail down to Samson Cay and operate from there. Dillon must stay at either the Hyatt or at Caneel Bay if he uses a hotel, and a simple phone call will confirm that. I suspect Caneel Bay if he wishes to cultivate the diver, this Carney."

"I suppose so."

"A pity about the girl. She'll turn up eventually though, and I still feel she could be the key to this thing. She could know more than she realizes."

"Let's hope so."

"For your sake particularly, I hope so too, Francis."

Dillon, suitably attired in his blazer and a Guards tie, followed Travers up the imposing stairway at the Garrick Club. "Jesus, they've got more portraits here than the National Gallery," he said and followed Travers through to the bar where Ferguson waited.

"Ah, there you are," he said. "I'm one ahead of you. Thought we'd have a spot of champagne, Dillon, just to wish you bon voyage. You prefer Krug as I recall."

They sat in the corner and the barman brought the bottle over in an ice bucket and opened it. He filled three glasses and retired. Ferguson thanked him, then took an envelope from his pocket and passed it across. "Just in case things get rough, there's the name of a contact of mine in Charlotte Amalie, that's the main town in St. Thomas. What you might call a dealer in hardware."

"Hardware?" Travers looked bewildered. "What on earth would he need with hardware?"

Dillon put the envelope in his pocket. "You're a lovely fella, Admiral, and long may you stay that way."

Ferguson toasted Dillon. "Good luck, my friend, you're going to need it." He emptied his glass. "Now let's eat."

There was something in his eyes, something that said there was more to this, much more, had to be, Dillon told himself, but he got up obediently and followed Travers and the Brigadier out of the bar.

And at Briac at the Convent of the Little Sisters of Pity, Jenny sat alone in the rear pew of the chapel, resting her arms on the backrest of the pew in front of her, gazing at the flickering candlelight at the altar and brooding. The door creaked open and Sister Maria Baker entered.

"There you are. You should be in bed."

"I know, Sister, but I was restless and wanted to think about things."

Sister Maria Baker sat down beside her. "Such as?"

"Dillon for one thing. He's done many terrible things. He was a member of the IRA, for example, and when those two men attacked me last night . . ." She shivered. "He was so coldly savage, so ruthless, and yet to me he was kindness itself and so understanding."

"So?"

Jenny turned to her. "I'm not a good Christian. In fact, when Henry found me, I was a very great sinner, but I do want to understand God, I really do."

"So what's the problem?"

"Why does God allow violence and killing to take place at all? Why does he allow the violence in Dillon?"

308 ——⌢——⌣—— JACK HIGGINS

"The simplest thing to answer, my child. What God does allow is free will. He gives us all a choice. You, me, and the Dillons of this world."

"I suppose so." Jenny sighed. "But I will have to go back to St. John and not just to help Dillon, but somehow for Henry too."

"Why do you feel so strongly?"

"Because Henry really didn't tell me where he discovered that U-boat, which means the secret must have died with him, and yet I have the oddest feeling that it didn't, that the information is back there in St. John, but I just can't think straight. It won't come, Sister."

She was distressed again and Sister Maria Baker took her hands. "That's enough, you need sleep. A few days' rest will work wonders. You'll remember then what you can't now, I promise you. Now let's have you in bed."

She took Jenny by the hand and led her out.

Ferguson's Daimler picked Dillon up at seven-thirty the following morning to take him to Gatwick and Travers insisted on accompanying him. The journey out of town at that time in the morning with all the heavy traffic going the other way was relatively quick, and Dillon was ready to go through passport control and security by eight-thirty.

"They've already called it, I see," Travers said.

"So it seems."

"Look here, Dillon," Travers said awkwardly. "We'll never see eye-to-eye, you and me, I mean the IRA and all that stuff, but I want to thank you for what you did for the girl. I liked her—liked her a lot."

"And so did I."

Travers shook Dillon's hand. "Take care, this Santiago sounds bad news."

"I'll try, Admiral."

"Another thing." Travers sounded more awkward than ever. "Charles Ferguson is a dear friend, but he's also the most devious old sod I've ever known in my life. Watch yourself in the clinches there too."

"I will, Admiral, I will," Dillon said, watched the Admiral walk away, then turned and went through.

A nice man, he thought as the Jumbo lifted off and climbed steadily, a decent man, but nobody's fool and he was right; there *was* more to all this than the surface of things, nothing was more certain than that, and Ferguson knew what it was. *Devious old sod.* An apt description.

"Ah, well, I can be just as devious," Dillon murmured and accepted the glass of champagne the stewardess offered.

EIGHT

The flight to Antigua took a little over eight hours thanks to a tailwind, and they arrived just after two o'clock local time. It was hot, really hot, very noticeable after London. Dillon felt quite cheered and strode ahead of everybody else toward the airport building, wearing black cord slacks and a denim shirt, his black flying jacket over one shoulder. When he reached the entrance a young black woman in a pale blue uniform was standing there with a board bearing his name.

Dillon paused. "I'm Dillon."

She smiled. "I'm Judy, Mr. Dillon. I'll see you through immigration and so on and then take you to your plane."

"You represent the handling agents?" he asked as they walked through.

"That's right. I need to see your pilot's license and there are a couple of forms to fill in for the aviation authority, but we can do that while we're waiting for the luggage to come through."

Twenty minutes later she was driving him out to the far side of the runway in a courtesy bus, an engineer called Tony in white overalls sitting beside her. The Cessna was parked beside a number of private planes, slightly incongruous because of its floats, with wheels protruding beneath.

"Shouldn't give you any problems," Tony said as he stowed Dillon's two suitcases. "Flies as sweet as a nut. Of course a lot of people are nervous about flying in the islands with a single engine, but the beauty about this baby is you can always come down in the water."

"Or something like that," Dillon said.

Tony laughed, reached into the cabin and pointed. "There's an air log listing all the islands and their airfields and charts. Our chief pilot has marked your course from here to Cruz Bay in St. John. Very straightforward. Around two hundred and fifty miles. Takes about an hour and a half." He glanced at his watch. "You should be there by four-thirty."

"It's American territory, but customs and immigration are expecting you. They'll be waiting at the ramp at Cruz Bay. When you're close enough, call in to St. Thomas and they'll let them know you're coming. Oh, and there will be a self-drive jeep waiting for you." Judy smiled. "I think that's about it."

"Thanks for everything." Dillon gave her that special smile of his with total charm and kissed her on the cheek. "Judy, you've been great." He shook Tony's hand. "Many thanks."

A moment later he was in the pilot's seat, closing the door. He strapped himself in, adjusted his earphones, then fired the engine and called the tower. There was a small plane landing and the tower told him to wait. They gave him the good word and he taxied to the end of the runway. There was a short pause, then the go signal and he boosted power, roared down the runway and pulled back the column at exactly the right moment, the Cessna climbing effortlessly out over the azure sea.

It was an hour later that Max Santiago flew into San Juan, where he was escorted through passport control and customs with a minimum of fuss by an airport official to where his chauffeur, Algaro, waited with the black Mercedes limousine.

"At your orders, Señor," he said in Spanish.

"Good to see you, Algaro," Santiago said. "Everything is arranged as I requested?"

"Oh yes, Señor. I've packed the usual clothes, took them down to the *Maria Blanco* myself this morning. Captain Serra is expecting you."

Algaro wasn't particularly large, five foot seven or eight, but immensely powerful, his hair cropped so short that he almost looked bald. A scar, running from the corner of the left eye to the mouth, combined to give him a sinister and threatening appearance in spite of the smart gray chauffeur's uniform he wore. He was totally devoted to Santiago, who had saved him from a life sentence for the stabbing to death of a young prostitute two years previously by the liberal dispensing of funds not only to lawyers but corrupt officials.

The luggage arrived at that moment and while the porters stowed it Santiago said, "Good, you needn't take me to the house. I'll go straight to the boat."

"As you say, Señor." They drove away, turned into the traffic of the main road and Algaro said, "Captain Serra said you asked for a couple of divers in the crew. It's taken care of."

"Excellent." Santiago picked up the local newspaper, which had been left on the seat for him, and opened it.

Algaro watched him in the mirror. "Is there a problem, Señor?"

Santiago laughed. "You're like an animal, Algaro, you always smell trouble."

"But that's what you employ me for, Señor."

"Quite right." Santiago folded the newspaper, selected a cigarette from an elegant gold case and lit it. "Yes, my friend, there is a problem, a problem called Dillon."

"May I know about him, Señor?"

"Why not? You'll probably have to, how shall I put it, take care of him for me, Algaro." Santiago smiled. "So listen carefully and learn all about him because this man is good, Algaro, very good indeed."

It was a perfect afternoon, the limitless blue sky with only the occasional cloud as Dillon drifted across the Caribbean at five thousand feet. It was pure pleasure, the sea constantly changing color below, green and blue, the occasional boat, the reefs and shoals clearly visible at that height.

He passed the islands of Nevis and St. Kitts, calling in to the local airport, moved on flying directly over the tiny Dutch island of Saba. He had a brisk tailwind and made good time, better than he had expected, found St. Croix on his port side on the horizon no more than an hour after leaving Antigua.

Soon after that, the main line of the Virgins lifted out of the heat haze to greet him, St. Thomas to port, the smaller bulk of St. John to starboard, Tortola beyond. He checked the chart and saw Peter Island below Tortola and east of St. John, Norman Island south of it, and south of there was Samson Cay.

Dillon called in to St. Thomas airport to notify them of his approach. The controller said, "Cleared for landing at Cruz Bay. Await customs and immigration officials there."

Dillon went down low, turning to starboard, found Samson Cay with no difficulty and crossed over at a thousand feet. There was a harbor dotted with yachts, a dock, cottages and a hotel block grouped around the beach amidst palm trees. The airstrip was to the north, no control tower, just an air sock on a pole. There were people lounging on the beach down there. Some stood up and waved. He waggled his wings and flew on, found Cruz Bay fifteen minutes later and drifted in for a perfect landing just outside the harbor.

He entered the harbor and found the ramp with little difficulty. There were several uniformed officials standing there and one or two other people, all black. He taxied forward, let the wheels down and ran up onto the ramp, killed the engine. One of the men in customs uniform held a couple of wedge-shaped blocks by a leather strap and he came and positioned them behind the wheels.

Dillon climbed out. "Lafayette, we are here."

Everyone laughed genially and the immigration people checked his passport, perfectly happy with the Irish one, while the customs men had a look at the luggage. Everything was sweetness and light and they all departed with mutual expressions of goodwill. As they walked away a young woman in uniform, rose pink this time, who had been waiting patiently at one side, came forward.

"I've got your jeep here as ordered, Mr. Dillon. If you could sign for me and show me your license, you can be on your way."

"That's very kind of you," Dillon said and carried the suitcases across and slung them on the backseat.

As he signed, she said, "I'm sorry we didn't have an automatic in at the moment. I could change it for you tomorrow. I've got one being returned."

"No, thanks, I prefer to be in charge myself." He smiled. "Can I drop you somewhere?"

"That's nice of you." She got in beside him and he drove away. About three hundred yards further on as he came to the road she said, "This is fine."

There was an extremely attractive looking development opposite. "What's that?" he asked.

"Mongoose Junction, our version of a shopping mall, but much nicer. There's also a super bar and a couple of great restaurants."

"I'll look it over sometime."

She got out. "Turn left, follow the main road. Caneel Bay's only a couple of miles out. There's a car park for residents. From there it's a short walk down to Reception."

"You've been very kind," Dillon told her and drove away.

The *Maria Blanco* had cost Santiago two million dollars and was his favorite toy. He preferred being on board to staying at his magnificent house above the city of San Juan, particularly since the death of his wife Maria from cancer ten years earlier. Dear Maria, his Maria Blanco, the one soft spot in his life. Of course, this was no ordinary boat, had every conceivable luxury, needed a captain and five or six crew members to man her.

Santiago sat at a table on the upper deck enjoying the sun and a cup of excellent coffee, Algaro standing behind him. The captain, Julian Serra, a burly, black-bearded man in uniform, sat opposite. He, like most of Santiago's employees, had been with him for years, had frequently taken part in activities of a highly questionable nature.

"So you see, my dear Serra, we have a problem on our hands here. The man Dillon will probably approach this diver, this Bob Carney, when he reaches St. John."

"Wrecks are notoriously difficult to find, Señor," Serra told him. "I've had experts tell me they've missed one by a few yards on occasions. It's not easy. There's a lot of sea out there."

"I agree," Santiago said. "I still think the girl must have some sort of an answer, but she may take her time returning. In the meantime, we'll surprise Mr. Dillon as much as possible." He smiled up at Algaro. "Think you can handle that, Algaro?"

"With pleasure, Señor," Algaro said.

"Good." Santiago turned back to Serra. "What about the crew?"

"Guerra, first mate. Solona and Mugica as usual, and I've brought in two men with good diving experience, Javier Noval and Vicente Pinto."

"And they're reliable?"

"Absolutely."

"And we're expected at Samson Cay?"

"Yes, Señor, I spoke to Prieto personally. You wish to stay there?"

"I think so. We could always drop anchor off Paradise Beach at Caneel, of course. I'll think about it." Santiago finished his coffee and stood up. "Right, let's get moving then."

Dillon took to Caneel from the moment he got there. He parked the jeep and, carrying his own bags, followed the obvious path. There was a magnificent restaurant on a bluff up above him, circular with open sides. Below it was the ruins of a sugar mill from the old plantation days. The vegetation was extremely lush, palm trees everywhere. He paused, noticing a gift shop on the left and set back. More important the smaller shop next to it said "Paradise Watersports," Carney's place. He remembered that from the brochure and went and had a look. As he would have expected, there were diving suits of various kinds on display, but the door was locked, so he carried on and came to the front desk lobby.

There were three or four people being dealt with at the desk before him so he dropped his bags and went back outside. There was a very large bar area, open at the sides, but under a huge barnlike roof, a vital necessity in a climate where instant heavy rain showers were common.

Beyond was Caneel Bay, he knew that from the brochure, boats of various kinds at anchor, a pleasant, palm-fringed beach beside another restaurant, people still taking their ease in the early evening sun, one or two windsurfers still out there. Dillon glanced at his watch. It was almost five-thirty and he started to turn away to go back to the front desk when he saw a boat coming in.

It was a 35-foot Sport Fisherman with a flying bridge, sleek and white, but what intrigued Dillon were the dozen or so airtanks stacked in their holders in the stern, and there were four people moving around on deck packing their gear into dive bags. Carney was on the flying bridge, handling the wheel, in jeans and bare feet, stripped to the waist, very tanned, the blond hair bleached by the sun. Dillon recognized him from the photo in the brochure.

The name of the boat was *Sea Raider*, he saw that as it got closer, moved to the end of the dock as Carney maneuvered it in. One of the dive students tossed a line, Dillon caught it and expertly tied up at the stern, then he moved along to the prow where the boat was bouncing against its fenders, reached over and got the other line.

Dillon lit a cigarette, his Zippo flashing, and Carney killed the engines and came down the ladder. "Thanks," he called.

Dillon said, "My pleasure, Captain Carney," and he turned and walked away along the dock.

One of the receptionists from the front desk took him out to his cottage in a small courtesy bus. The grounds were an absolute delight, not only sweeping grassland and palm trees, but every kind of tropical plant imaginable.

"The entire peninsula is private," she said as they followed a narrow road. "We have seven beaches and, as you'll notice, most of the cottages are grouped around them."

"I've only seen two restaurants so far," he commented.

"Yes, Sugar Mill and Beach Terrace. There's a third at the end of the peninsula, Turtle Bay, that's more formal. You know, collar and tie and so on. It's wonderful for an evening drink. You look out over the Windward Passage to dozens of little islands, Carval Rock, Whistling Cay. Of course a lot further away you'll see Jost Van Dyke and Tortola, but they're in the British Virgins."

"It sounds idyllic," he said.

She braked in a turned circle beside a two-storied, flat-roofed building surrounded by trees and bushes of every description. "Here we are, Cottage Seven."

There were steps up to the upper level. "It isn't all one then?" Dillon asked.

She opened the door into a little vestibule. "People do sometimes take it all, but up here it's divided into two units. Seven D and Seven E."

The doors faced each other, she unlocked 7D and led the way in. There was a superb shower room, a bar area with a spare icebox. The bedroom-cum-sitting room was enormous and very pleasantly furnished with tiled floor and comfortable chairs and a sofa, and there were venetian blinds at the windows, two enormous fans turning in the ceiling.

"Is this all right?" she asked.

"I should say so." Dillon nodded at the enormous bed. "Jesus, but a man would have to be a sprinter to catch his wife in that thing."

She laughed and opened the double doors to the terrace and led the way out. There was a large seating area and a narrow part round the corner that fronted the other windows. There was a grassy slope, trees and a small beach below, three or four large yachts of the ocean-going type at anchor some distance from shore.

"Paradise Beach," she said.

There was another beach way over to the right with a line of cottages behind it. "What's that?" he asked.

"Scott Beach and Turtle Bay is a little further on. You could walk there in fifteen minutes, although there *is* a courtesy bus service with stops dotted round the grounds."

There was a knock at the door, she went back inside and supervised the bellboy leaving the luggage. Dillon followed her. She turned. "I think that's everything."

"There was the question of a telephone," Dillon said. "You don't have them in the cottages, I understand."

"My, but I was forgetting that." She opened her carrying bag and took out a cellular telephone plus a spare battery and charger. She put it on the coffee table with a card. "Your number and instructions are there." She laughed. "Now I hope that really is everything."

Dillon opened the door for her. "You've been very kind."

"Oh, one more thing, our General Manager, Mr. Nicholson, asked me to apologize for not being here to greet you. He had business on St. Thomas."

"That's all right. I'm sure we'll catch up with each other later."

"I believe he's Irish too," she said and left.

Dillon opened the icebox under the bar unit, discovering every kind of drink one could imagine including two half-bottles of champagne. He opened one of them, poured a glass, then went out and stood on the terrace looking out over the water.

"Well, old son, this will do to take along," he said softly and drank the champagne with conscious pleasure.

In the end, of course, the sparkle on the water was too seductive and he went inside, unpacked, hanging his clothes in the ample wardrobe space, then undressed and found some swimming trunks. A moment later he was hurrying down the grass bank to the little beach, which for the moment he had entirely to himself. The water was incredibly warm and very clear. He waded forward and started to swim, there was a sudden swirl over on his right, an enormous turtle surfaced, looked at him curiously, then moved sedately away.

Dillon laughed aloud for pure pleasure, then swam lazily out to sea in the direction of the moored yachts, turning after some fifty yards to swim back. Behind him, the *Maria Blanco* came round the point from Caneel Bay and dropped anchor about three hundred yards away.

Santiago had changed his mind about Samson Cay only after Captain Serra had brought him a message from the radio room. An enquiry by ship-to-shore telephone had confirmed that Dillon had arrived at Caneel Bay.

"He's booked into Cottage Seven," Serra said.

"Interesting," Santiago told him. "That's the best accommodation in the resort." He thought about it, tapping his fingers on the table, and made his decision. "I know it well, it overlooks Paradise Beach. We'll anchor there, Serra, for tonight at least."

"As you say, Señor."

Serra went back to the bridge and Algaro, who had been standing by the stern rail, poured Santiago another cup of coffee.

Santiago said, "I want you to go ashore tonight. Take someone with you. There's the Land-Rover Serra leaves permanently in the car park at Mongoose Junction. He'll give you the keys."

"What do you require me to do, Señor?"

"Call in at Caneel, see what Dillon is up to. If he goes out, follow him."

"Do I give him a problem?" Algaro asked hopefully.

"A small one, Algaro," Santiago smiled. "Nothing too strenuous."

"My pleasure, Señor," Algaro said and poured him another cup of coffee.

Dillon didn't feel like anything too formal, wore only a soft white cotton shirt and cream linen slacks, both by Armani, as he walked through the evening darkness toward Caneel Beach. He carried a small torch in one pocket provided by the management for help with the dark spots. It was such a glorious night that he didn't need it. The Terrace Restaurant was already doing a fair amount of business, but then Americans liked to dine early, he knew that. He went to the front desk, cashed a traveler's check for five hundred dollars, then tried the bar.

He had never cared for the usual Caribbean liking for rum punches and fruit drinks, settled for an old fashioned vodka martini cocktail, which the genial black waitress brought for him quite rapidly. A group of musicians were setting up their instruments on the small bandstand and way out across the sea he could see the lights of St. Thomas. It really was very pleasant, too easy to forget he had a job to do. He finished his drink, signed for it and went along to the restaurant, where he introduced himself to the head waiter and was seated.

The menu was tempting enough. He ordered grilled sea scallops, a Caesar salad, followed by Caribbean lobster tail. No Krug but a very acceptable half-bottle of Veuve Clicquot completed the picture.

He was finished by nine o'clock and wandered down to reception. Algaro was sitting in one of the leather armchairs looking at the *New York Times*. The girl on duty was the one who'd taken Dillon to the cottage.

She smiled. "Everything okay, Mr. Dillon?"

"Perfect. Tell me, do you know a bar called Jenny's Place?"

"I sure do. It's on the front, just past Mongoose Junction on your way into town."

"They stay open late I presume?"

"Usually till around two in the morning."

"Many thanks."

He moved away and walked along the dock, lighting a cigarette. Behind him Algaro went out and hurried along the car park by Sugar Mill, laughter drifting down from the people dining up there. He moved past the taxis waiting for customers to where the Land-Rover waited. Felipe Guerra, the *Maria Blanco*'s mate, sat behind the wheel.

Algaro got in beside him and Guerra said, "Did you find him?"

"I was within touching distance. He was asking about that bar, Jenny's Place. You know it? On the front in Cruz Bay."

"Sure."

"Let's take a look. From the sound of it he intends to pay the place a visit."

"Maybe we can make it interesting for him," Guerra said and drove away.

Dillon drove past Mongoose Junction, located Jenny's Place, then turned and went back to the Junction car park. He walked along the front of the harbor through the warm night, went up the steps, glanced up at the red neon sign and entered. The cafe side of things was busy, Mary Jones taking orders while two waitresses, one white, the other black, worked themselves into a frenzy as they attempted to serve everybody. The bar was busy also although Billy Jones seemed to be having no difficulty in managing on his own.

Dillon found a vacant stool at the end of the bar and waited until Billy was free to deal with him. "Irish whisky, whatever you've got, and water."

He noticed Bob Carney seated at the other end of the long bar, a beer in front of him, talking to a couple of men who looked like seamen. Carney was smiling and then as he turned to reach for his beer, became aware of Dillon's scrutiny and frowned.

Billy brought the whisky and Dillon said, "You're Billy Jones?"

The other man looked wary. "And who might you be?"

"Dillon's the name—Sean Dillon. I'm staying at Caneel. Jenny told me to look you up and say hello."

"Jenny did?" Billy frowned. "When you see Miss Jenny?"

"In London. I went to Henry Baker's cremation with her."

"You did?" Billy turned and called to his wife. "Woman, get over here." She finished taking an order, then joined them. "This is my wife, Mary. Tell her what you just told me."

"I was with Jenny in London." Dillon held out his hand. "Sean Dillon. I was at Baker's funeral, not that there was much doing. She said he was an atheist, so all we did was attend the crematorium."

Mary crossed herself. "God rest him now, but he did think that way. And Jenny, what about her? Where is she?"

"She was upset," Dillon said. "She told me Baker had a sister."

Mary frowned and looked at her husband. "We never knew that. Are you sure, mister?"

"Oh, yes, he had a sister living in France. Jenny wouldn't say where, simply flew off to Paris from London. Wanted to take his ashes to the sister."

"And when is she coming back?"

"All she said was she needed a few days to come to terms with the death and so on. As I happened to be coming out here she asked me to say hello."

"Well I thank you for that," Mary said. "We've been so worried!" A customer called from one of the tables. "I'll have to go. I'll see you later."

She hurried away and Billy grinned. "I'm needed too, but hang around, man, hang around."

He went to serve three clamouring customers and Dillon savoured his whisky and looked around the room. Algaro and Guerra were drinking beer in a corner booth. They were not looking at him, apparently engaged in conversation. Dillon's eyes barely paused, passed on, and yet he recognized him from the reception at Caneel, the cropped hair, the brutal face, the scar from eye to the mouth.

"Judas Iscariot come to life," Dillon murmured. "And what's your game, son?" for he had learned the hard way over many years never to believe in coincidence.

The two men Carney had been talking to had moved on and he was sitting alone now, the stool next to him vacant. Dillon finished his drink, moved along the bar through the crowd. "Do you mind if I join you?"

Carney's eyes were very blue in the tanned face. "Should I?"

"Dillon, Sean Dillon." Dillon eased on to the stool. "I'm staying at Caneel. Cottage Seven. Jenny Grant told me to look you up."

"You know Jenny?"

"I was just with her in London," Dillon said. "Her friend, Henry Baker, was killed in an accident over there."

"I heard about that."

"Jenny was over for the inquest and the funeral." Dillon nodded to Billy Jones, who came over. "I'll have another Irish. Give Captain Carney whatever he wants."

"I'll have a beer," Carney said. "Did Jenny bury him in London?"

"No," Dillon told him. "Cremation. He had a sister in France."

"I never knew that."

"Jenny told me few people did. It seems he preferred it that way. Said she wanted to take the ashes to her. Last I saw of her she was flying to Paris. Said she'd be back here in a few days."

Billy brought the whisky and the beer and Carney said, "So you're here on vacation?"

"That's right. I got in this evening."

"Would you be the guy who came in the Cessna floatplane?"

"Flew up from Antigua." Dillon nodded.

"On vacation?"

"Something like that." Dillon lit a cigarette. "The thing is I'm interested in doing a little diving, and Jenny suggested I speak to you. Said you were the best."

"That's nice of her."

"She said you taught Henry."

"That's true." Carney nodded. "Henry was a good diver, foolish, but still pretty good."

"Why do you say foolish?"

"It never pays to dive on your own, you should always have a buddy with you. Henry would never listen. He would just up and go whenever he felt like it, and that's no good when you're diving regularly. Accidents can happen no matter how well you plan things." Carney drank some more beer and looked Dillon full in the face. "But then I'd say you're the kind of man who knows that, Mr. Dillon."

He had the slow, easy accent of the American southerner as if everything he said was carefully considered.

Dillon said, "Well in the end it was an accident that killed him in London. He looked the wrong way and stepped off the pavement in front of a London bus. He was dead in a second."

Carney said calmly, "You know the old Arab saying? 'Everybody has an appointment in Samarra.' You miss Death in one place, he'll get you in another. At least for Henry it was quick."

"That's a remarkably philosophical attitude," Dillon told him.

Carney smiled. "I'm a remarkably philosophical fellow, Mr. Dillon. I did two tours in Vietnam. Everything has been a bonus since. So you want to do some diving?"

"That's right."

"You any good?"

"I manage," Dillon told him. "But I'm always willing to learn."

"Okay. I'll see you at the dock at Caneel at nine o'clock in the morning."

"I'll need some gear."

"No problem, I'll open the shop for you."

"Fine." Dillon swallowed his whisky. "I'll see you then." He hesitated. "Tell me something. You see the two guys in the booth in the far corner? I particularly mean the ugly one with the scar. Do you happen to know who they are?"

"Sure," Carney said. "They work on a big motor yacht from Puerto Rico that calls in here now and then. It's owned by a man called Santiago. It's usually based at Samson Cay, that's over on the British side of things. The younger guy is the mate, Guerra, the other is a real mean son of a bitch called Algaro."

"Why do you say that?"

"He half-killed a fisherman outside one of the bars here about nine months ago. He was lucky to get away without doing some prison time. They laid a real hefty fine on him, but his boss paid it, so I heard. He's the kind of guy to step around."

"I'll certainly remember that." Dillon got up. "Tomorrow then," and he walked out through the crowd.

Billy came down the bar. "You want another beer, Bob?"

"What I need is something to eat, my wife being away and all," Carney said. "What did you make of him?"

"Dillon? He said he was in London with Jenny. Happened to be coming down here and she told him to look us up."

"Well that sure was a hell of a coincidence." Carney reached for his glass and noticed Algaro and Guerra get up and leave. He almost got up and went after them, but what the hell, it wasn't his problem, whatever it was, and in any case, Dillon was perfectly capable of looking after himself, he'd never been more certain of anything in his life.

Dillon drove out of Cruz Bay, changing down to climb the steep hill up from the town, thinking about Carney. He'd liked him straightaway, a calm, quiet man of enormous inner strength, but then, remembering his background, that made sense.

He breasted the hill, remembering that in St. John you kept on the left-hand side of the road just like England, was suddenly aware of the headlights coming up behind him very fast. He expected to be overtaken, wasn't, and as the vehicle behind moved right in on his tail knew he was in trouble. He recognized it as a Land-Rover in his rearview mirror an instant before it bumped him, put his foot down hard and pulled away, driving so fast that he went straight past the turning to Caneel Bay.

The Land-Rover had the edge and suddenly it swerved out to the right-hand side of the road and moved alongside. He caught a brief glimpse of Algaro's face, illuminated in the light from the dashboard as he gripped the wheel, and then the Land-Rover swerved in and Dillon spun off the road into the brush, bounced down a shallow slope and came to a halt.

Dillon rolled out of the jeep and got behind a tree. The Land-Rover had stopped and there was silence for a moment. Suddenly a shotgun roared, pellets scything through the branches overhead.

There was silence and then laughter. A voice called, "Welcome to St. John, Mr. Dillon," and the Land-Rover drove away.

Dillon waited until the sound had faded into the night, then he got back into the jeep, engaged four-wheel drive, reversed up the slope onto the road and drove back toward the Caneel turning.

In London it was three-thirty in the morning when the phone rang at the side of Charles Ferguson's bed in his flat at Cavendish Square. He came awake on the instant and reached for it.

"Ferguson here."

Dillon stood on the terrace, a drink in one hand, the cellular telephone in the other. "It's me," he said, "ringing you from the tranquil Virgin Islands, only they're not so tranquil."

"For God's sake, Dillon, do you know what time it is?"

"Yes, time for a few questions and hopefully some answers. A couple of goons just tried to run me off the road, old son, and guess who they were? Crewmen off Santiago's yacht, the *Maria Blanco*. They also loosed off a shotgun in my direction."

Ferguson was immediately alert, sat up and tossed the bedclothes aside. "Are you certain?"

"Of course I am." Dillon was not particularly angry, but made it sound as if he were. "Listen, you devious old sod, I want to know what's going on. I've only been in the damned place a few hours and yet they know me by name. I'd say they were expecting me, as they're here too, and how could that be, Brigadier?"

"I don't know," Ferguson told him. "That's all I can say for the moment. You're settled in all right?"

"Brigadier, I have an insane desire to laugh," Dillon told him. "But yes, I'm settled in, the cottage is fine, the view sublime and I'm diving with Bob Carney in the morning."

"Good, get on with it, then, and watch yourself."

"Watch myself?" Dillon said. "Is that the best you can do?"

"Stop whining, Dillon," Ferguson told him. "This sort of thing's exactly why I chose you for the job. You're still in one piece, right?"

"Just about."

"There you are then. They're trying to put the frighteners on you, that's all."

"That's all, he says."

"Leave it with me. I'll be in touch."

Ferguson put the phone down, switching off the light, and lay there thinking about it. After a while he drifted into sleep again.

Dillon went to the small bar. There were tea and coffee bags there. He boiled the water and opted for a cup of tea, taking it out on the terrace, looking out into the bay where there were lights on some of the boats. More to things than met the eye, he was more convinced than ever, and he hadn't liked the shotgun. It made him feel naked. There was an answer to that of course, a visit to the address Ferguson had given him in St. Thomas, the hardware specialist. That could come in the afternoon after he'd dived with Carney.

The moment he and Guerra were back on board Algaro reported to Santiago. When he was finished Santiago said, "You did well."

Algaro said, "He won't do anything about it, will he, Señor, the police I mean?"

"Of course not, he doesn't want the authorities to know why he's here, that's the beauty of it. That U-boat is in American waters, so legally it should be reported to the Coast Guard, but that's the last thing Dillon and this Brigadier Ferguson he works for want."

Algaro said, "I see."

"Go to bed now," Santiago told him.

Algaro departed and Santiago went to the rail. He could see a light in Cottage Seven. At that moment it went out. "Sleep well, Mr. Dillon," he said softly, turned and went below.

NINE

It was nine o'clock the following morning when Ferguson arrived at Downing Street. He had to wait for only five minutes before an aide took him upstairs and showed him into the study where the Prime Minister was seated at his desk, signing one document after another.

He looked up. "Ah, there you are, Brigadier."

"You asked to see me, Prime Minister?"

"Yes, I've had the Deputy Director of the Security Services and Sir Francis on my back about this Virgin Islands affair. Is it true what they tell me, that you've taken on this man Dillon to handle things?"

"Yes," Ferguson said calmly.

"A man with his record? Can you tell me why?"

"Because he's right for the job, sir. Believe me, I find nothing admirable in Dillon's past. His work some years ago for the IRA is known to us although nothing has ever been proven against him. The same applies to his activities on the international scene. He's a gun for hire, Prime Minister. Even the Israelis have used him when it suited them."

"I can't say I like it. I think Carter has a point of view."

"I can pull him out if that is what you wish."

"But you'd rather not?"

"I think he's the man for this particular job. To be frank, it's a dirty one and it has already become apparent since we last spoke that there are people he will have to deal with who play very dirty indeed."

"I see." The Prime Minister sighed. "Very well, Brigadier, I leave it to your own good judgment, but do try and make your peace with Carter."

"I will, Prime Minister," Ferguson said and withdrew.

Jack Lane was waiting in the Daimler. As it drove away he said, "And what was that all about?"

Ferguson told him. "He's got a point, of course."

"You know how I feel, sir, I was always against it. I wouldn't trust Dillon an inch."

"Interesting thing about Dillon," Ferguson said. "One of the things he's always been known for is a kind of twisted sense of honor. If he gives his word he sticks to it and expects others to do the same."

"I find that hard to believe, sir."

"Yes, I suppose most people would."

Ferguson picked up the car phone and rang through to Simon Carter's office. He wasn't there, he was meeting with Pamer at the House of Commons.

"Get a message through to him now," Ferguson told Carter's secretary. "Tell him I need to see them both urgently. I'll meet them on the Terrace at the House in fifteen minutes." He replaced the phone. "You can come with me, Jack, you've never been on the Terrace, have you?"

"What's going on, sir?"

"Wait and see, Jack, wait and see."

Rain drifted across the Thames in a fine spray, clearing the Terrace of people. Except for a few who stood under the awnings, drink in hand, everyone else had taken to the bars and cafes. Ferguson stood by the wall holding a large golfer's umbrella his chauffeur had given him, Lane sheltering with him.

"Doesn't it fill you with a sense of majesty and awe, Jack, the Mother of Parliaments and all that sort of thing?" Ferguson asked.

"Not with rain pouring down my neck, sir."

"Ah, there you are." They turned and saw Carter and Pamer standing in the main entrance to the Terrace. Carter was carrying a black umbrella, which he put up, and he and Pamer joined them.

Ferguson said, "Isn't this cozy?"

"I'm not in the mood for your feeble attempts at humor, Ferguson, now what do you want?" Carter demanded.

"I've just been to see the P.M. I understand you've been complaining again, old boy? Didn't do you any good. He's told me to carry on and use my judgment."

Carter was furious, but he managed to control himself and glanced at Lane. "Who's this?"

"My present assistant, Detective Inspector Jack Lane. I've borrowed him from Special Branch."

"That's against regulations, you can't do it."

"That's as may be, but I'm not a deckhand on your ship. I run my own and, as my time is limited, let's get down to facts. Dillon arrived in St. John around five o'clock in the evening their time yesterday. He was attacked by two crew members of Santiago's boat, the *Maria Blanco*, who ran him off the road in his jeep and fired a shotgun at him."

"My God!" Pamer said in horror.

Carter frowned. "Is he all right?"

"Oh, yes, a rubber ball our Dillon, always bounces back. Personally I think they were trying it on, hassling him. Of course the interesting thing is how come they knew who he was and knew he was there?"

"Now look here," Pamer began, "I trust you're not suggesting any lack of security on our part?"

Carter said, "Shut up, Francis, he's got a valid point. This Santiago man is far too well informed." He turned to Ferguson. "What are you going to do about it?"

"Actually, I was thinking of taking a brief holiday," Ferguson told him. "You know, sun, sea and sand, swaying palms? They tell me the Virgins are lovely at this time of the year."

Carter nodded. "You'll stay in touch?"

"Of course, dear old boy." Ferguson smiled and turned to Lane. "Let's go, Jack, we've lots to do."

On the way back to the Ministry Ferguson told his chauffeur to pull in beside a mobile sandwich bar on Victoria Embankment. "This man does the best cup of tea in London, Jack."

The owner greeted him as an old friend. "Rotten day, Brigadier."

"It was worse on the Hook, Fred," the Brigadier said and walked with his cup of tea to the wall overlooking the Thames.

As Lane received his cup of tea he said to Fred, "What did he mean, the Hook?"

"That was a really bad place that was, worst position in the whole of Korea. So many dead bodies that every time you dug another trench, arms and legs came out."

"You knew the Brigadier then?"

"Knew him? I was a platoon sergeant when he was a second lieutenant. He won his first Military Cross carrying me on his back under fire." Fred grinned. "That's why I never charge for the tea."

Lane, impressed, joined Ferguson and leaned on the parapet under the umbrella. "You've got a fan there, sir."

"Fred? Old soldier's tales. Don't listen. I'm going to need the Learjet. Direct flight to St. Thomas should be possible."

"I believe the work on those new tanks the RAF did has extended the range to at least four thousand miles, sir."

"There you are then." Ferguson glanced at his watch. "Just after ten. I want that Learjet ready to leave Gatwick no later than one o'clock, Jack. Top priority. Allowing for the time difference, I could be in St. Thomas somewhere between five or six o'clock their time."

"Do you want me with you, sir?"

"No, you'll have to hold the fort."

"You'll need accommodation, sir. I'll see to that."

Ferguson shook his head. "I've reserved it at this Caneel place where I booked Dillon in."

"You mean you were expecting what happened to happen?"

"Something like that."

"Look, sir," said Lane in exasperation, "exactly what is going on?"

"When you find out, tell me, Jack." Ferguson emptied his cup, went and put it on the counter. "Thanks, Fred." He turned to Lane. "Come on, Jack, must get moving, lots to do before I leave," and he got into the rear of the Daimler.

Santiago was up early, even went for a swim in the sea, and was seated at the table in the stern enjoying his breakfast in the early morning sunshine when Algaro brought him the telephone.

"It's Sir Francis," he said.

"A wonderful morning here," Santiago said. "How's London?"

"Cold and wet. I'm just about to have a sandwich lunch and then spend the whole afternoon in interminable Committee meetings. Look, Max, Carter saw the Prime Minister and tried to put the boot into Ferguson because he was employing Dillon."

"I didn't imagine Carter to be quite so stupid. Ferguson still got his way of course?"

"Yes, the P.M. backed him to the hilt. More worrying, he asked for another meeting with me and Carter, and told us Dillon had been attacked on his first night in St. John. What on earth was that about?"

"My people were just leaning on him a little, Francis. After all, and as you made clear, he knows of my existence."

"Yes, but what Ferguson's now interested in is how *you* knew who Dillon was, the fact that he was arriving in St. John and so on. He said you were far too well informed, and Carter agreed with him."

"Did he make any suggestion as to how he thought I was getting my information?"

"No, but he did say he thought he'd join Dillon in St. John for a few days."

"Did he now? That should prove interesting. I look forward to meeting him."

Pamer said, genuine despair in his words, "God dammit, Max, they know of your involvement. How long before they know about mine?"

"You're not on the boards of any of the companies, Francis, and neither was your father. No mention of the name Pamer anywhere, and the great thing about this whole affair is that it is a private war. As I've already told you, Ferguson won't want the American authorities in on this. We're rather like two dogs squabbling over the same bone."

"I'm still worried," Pamer told him. "Is there anything else I can do?"

"Keep the information flowing, Francis, and keep your nerve. Nothing else you can do."

Santiago put the phone down and Algaro said, "More coffee, Señor?"

Santiago nodded. "Brigadier Ferguson is coming."

"Here to Caneel?" Algaro smiled. "And what would you like me to do about him, Señor?"

"Oh, I'll think of something," Santiago said and drank his coffee. "In the meantime, let's find out what our friend Dillon is up to this morning."

Guerra went round to Caneel Beach in an inflatable, taking one of the divers with him, a young man called Javier Noval. They wore swimming shorts, tee-shirts and dark glasses, just another couple of tourists. They pulled in amongst other small craft at the dock, Guerra killed the outboard motor and Noval tied up. At that moment Dillon appeared at the end of the dock. He wore a black tracksuit and carried a couple of towels.

"That's him," Guerra told Noval. "Get going. I'll stay out of the way in case he remembers me from last night."

Bob Carney was manhandling dive tanks from a trolley on to the deck of a small twenty-five-foot dive boat, turned and saw Dillon. He waved and went along the dock to join him, passing Noval, who stopped to light a cigarette close enough to listen to them.

Carney said, "You're going to need a few things. Let's go up to the dive shop."

They moved away. Noval waited and then followed.

There was a wide range of excellent equipment. Dillon chose a three-quarter-length suit of black and green in padded nylon, nothing too heavy, a mask, fins and gloves.

"Have you tried one of these?" Carney opened a box. "A Marathon dive computer. The wonder of the age. Automatic readings on your depth, elapsed time under water, safe time remaining. Even tells you how long you should wait to fly."

"That's for me," Dillon told him. "I always was lousy at mental arithmetic."

Carney itemized the bill. "I'll put this on your hotel account."

Dillon signed it. "So what have you got planned?"

"Oh, nothing too strenuous, you'll see." Carney smiled. "Let's get going," and he led the way out.

Noval dropped down into the inflatable. "The other man is called Carney. He owns the diving concession here. Paradise Watersports."

"So they are going diving?" Guerra asked.

"They must be. Dillon was in the shop with him buying equipment." He glanced up. "Here they come now."

Dillon and Carney passed above them and got into the dive boat. After a moment Carney fired the engine and Dillon cast off. The boat moved out of the bay, weaving its way through various craft anchored there.

Guerra said, "There's no name on that boat."

"*Privateer*, that's what it's called," Noval told him. "I asked one of the beach guards. You know, I've done most of my diving around Puerto Rico, but I've heard of this Carney. He's big stuff."

Guerra nodded. "Okay, we'd better get back and let Señor Santiago know what's happening."

Noval cast off, Guerra started the outboard, and they moved away.

The *Privateer* was doing a steady twenty knots, the sea not as calm as it could have been. Dillon held on tight and managed to light a cigarette one-handed.

"Are you prone to sea sickness?" Carney asked.

"Not that I know of," Dillon shouted above the roar of the engine.

"Good, because it's going to get worse before it gets better. We've not too far to go though."

Waves swept in, long and steep, the *Privateer* riding up over them and plunging down, and Dillon hung on, taking in the incredible scenery, the peaks of the islands all around. And then they were very close to a smaller island, turned in toward it and moved into the calmer waters of a bay.

"Congo Cay," Carney said. "A nice dive." He went round to the prow, dropped the anchor and came back. "Not much to tell you. Twenty-five to ninety feet. Very little current. There's a ridge maybe three hundred feet long. If you want to limit your depth you could stay on top of that."

"Sounds the kind of place you'd bring novices," Dillon said, pulling on the black and green diving suit.

"All the time," Carney told him calmly.

Dillon got into his gear quickly and fastened a weight belt round his waist. Carney had already clamped tanks to their inflatable jackets and helped Dillon ease into his while sitting on the side of the boat. Dillon pulled on his gloves.

Carney said, "See you at the anchor."

Dillon nodded, pulled down his mask, checked that the air was flowing freely through his mouthpiece and went over backwards into the sea. He swam under the keel of the boat until he saw the anchor line and followed it down, pausing only to swallow a couple of times, a technique aimed at equalizing the pressure in his ears when they became uncomfortable.

He reached the ridge, paused with a hand on the anchor and looked at Carney descending to join him through a massive school of silversides. At that moment, an extraordinary thing happened. A black tip reef shark about nine feet in length shot out of the gloom scattering clouds of fish before it, swerved around Carney, then disappeared over the ridge as fast as it had come.

Carney made the okay sign with finger and thumb. Dillon replied in kind and followed him as he led the way along the reef. There were brilliant yellow tube sponges everywhere, and when they went over the edge there was lots of orange sponge attached to the rock faces. The coral outcroppings were multi-colored and very beautiful, and at one point Carney paused, pointing, and Dillon saw a huge eagle ray pass in the distance, wings flapping in slow motion.

It was a very calm, very enjoyable dive, but no big deal, and after about thirty minutes, Dillon realized they'd come full circle because the anchor line was ahead of them. He followed Carney up the line nice and slow, finally swam under the keel and surfaced at the stern. Carney, with practiced ease, was up over the stern pulling his gear behind him. Dillon unstrapped his jacket, slipped out of it and Carney reached down and pulled jacket and tank on board. Dillon joined him a moment later.

Carney busied himself clipping fresh tanks to the jackets and went and pulled in the anchor. Dillon put a towel over his shoulders and lit a cigarette. "The reef shark," he said. "Does that happen often?"

"Not really," Carney said.

"Enough to give some people a heart attack."

"I've been diving for years," Carney told him, "and I've never found sharks a problem."

"Not even a great white?"

"How often would you see one of those? No, nurse sharks in the main and they're no problem. Around here, reef sharks now and then or lemon sharks. Sure, they could be a problem, but hardly ever. We're big and they're big and they just want to keep out of the way. Having said that, did you enjoy the dive?"

"It was fine." Dillon shrugged.

"Which means you'd like a little more excitement." Carney started the engine. "Okay, let's go for one of my big boy dives," and he gunned the engine and took the *Privateer* out into open water.

They actually passed at some distance *Maria Blanco* still at anchor off Paradise Beach, and Guerra was in the deckhouse, scanning the area with binoculars. He recognized the boat and told Captain Serra, who examined the chart and then took a book on dive sites in the Virgin Islands from a drawer in the chart table.

"Keep watching," he told Guerra and leafed through.

"They've anchored," Guerra told him, "and run up the dive flag."

"Carval Rock," Serra said. "That's where they're diving."

At that moment Algaro came in and held the door open for Santiago, who was wearing a blue blazer and a Captain's cap, a gold rim to the peak. "What's happening?"

"Carney and Dillon are diving out there, Señor." Serra indicated the spot and gave Santiago the binoculars.

Santiago could just see the two men moving in the stern of *Privateer*. He said, "That couldn't be the site, could it?"

"No way, Señor," Serra told him. "It's a difficult place to dive, but hundreds of dives are made there every year."

"Never mind," Santiago said. "Put the launch in the water. We'll go and have a look. We'll see what these two divers of yours, Noval and Pinto, can do."

"Very well, Señor, I'll get things moving," and Serra went out followed by Guerra.

Algaro said, "You wish me to come too, Señor?"

"Why not?" Santiago said. "Even if Dillon sees you it doesn't matter. He knows you exist."

The rock was magnificent, rising up out of a very turbulent sea, birds of every kind perched up there on the ridge, gulls descending in slow motion in the heavy wind.

"Carval Rock," Carney said. "This is rated an advanced dive. Descends to about eighty or so feet. There's the wreck of a Cessna over on the other side that crashed a few years back. There are some nice ravines, fissures, one or two short tunnels and wonderful rock and coral cliffs. The problem is the current. Caused by tidal movement through the Pillsbury Sound."

"How strong?" Dillon asked as he fastened his weight belt.

"One or two knots is fairly common. Above two knots is unswimmable." He looked over and shook his head. "And I'd say it's three knots today."

Dillon lifted his jacket and tank on to the thwart and put it on himself. "Sounds as if it could be interesting."

"Your funeral."

Carney got his own gear on and Dillon turned to lean over and wash out his mask and saw a white launch approaching. "We're going to have company."

Carney turned to look. "I doubt it. No dive master I know would take his people down in this current today, he'd go somewhere easier."

The swells were huge now, the *Privateer* bucking up and down on the anchor line. Dillon went over, paused to check his air supply and started down to what looked like a dense forest below. He paused on the bottom, waiting until Carney had reached him, beckoned and turned toward the rock. Dillon followed, amazed at the strength of the current pushing against him, was aware of a stream of white bubbles over to his left and saw an anchor descend.

On the launch, Santiago sat in the wheelhouse while Serra went to the prow and dropped the anchor. Algaro was helping Noval and Pinto into their diving equipment.

Serra said finally, "They are ready to go, Señor, what are your orders?"

"Tell them to just have a look around," Santiago said. "No trouble. Leave Carney and Dillon alone."

"As you say, Señor."

The two divers were sitting together on the port side. Serra nodded and together they went over backwards into the water.

Dillon followed Carney with increasing difficulty because of the strength of the current up across rock and coral, following a deep channel that led through to the other side of the rocks. The force was quite tremendous and Carney was down on his belly pulling himself through with gloved hands, reaching for one handhold after another, and Dillon went after him, the other man's fins just three or four feet in front of him.

There was a kind of threshold. Carney was motionless for a while and then passed through, and Dillon had the same problem, faced with a kind of wall of pressure. He clawed at the rocks with agonizing slowness, foot by foot, and suddenly was through and into another world.

The surface was fifty feet above him and as he surged forward, he found himself in the middle of a school of tarpon at least four feet in length. There were yellow tail snappers, horse-eyed jacks, bonita, king mackerel and barracuda, some of them five feet long.

Carney plunged down to the other side, the rock face falling below, and Dillon followed him. They closed together and Dillon was aware of the current as they turned and saw Noval and Pinto trying to come through the cut. Noval almost made it, then lost his grip and was pushed into Pinto and they disappeared back to the other side.

Carney moved on and Dillon followed, down to seventy-five feet, and the current took them now in a fierce three-knot riptide that bounced them along the front of the wall in an upright position. They were surrounded by clouds of silversides, flying through space, the ultimate dream, and Dillon had never felt so excited. It seemed to go on forever, and then the current slackened and Carney was using his fins now and climbing.

Dillon followed through a deep ravine that led into another, waterlike black glass, checked his computer and was surprised to find that they had been under for twenty-five minutes. They moved away from the rock itself now, only three or four feet above the forest of the seabed, and came to a line and anchor. Carney paused to examine it, then turned and shook his head, moving on toward the left, finally arriving at their own anchor. They went up slowly, leaving the line at fifteen feet and swimming to one side of the boat, surfacing at the keel.

Carney reached down to take Dillon's tank and the Irishman got a foot in the tiny ladder and pulled himself up and over the stern. He felt totally exhilarated, unzipped his diving suit and pulled it off as Carney stowed their tanks.

"Bloody marvelous."

Carney smiled. "It wasn't bad, was it?"

He turned and looked across at the launch which was anchored over on the port side, swinging on its anchor chain in the heavy sea. Dillon said, "I wonder what happened to the two divers we saw trying to get through the cut?"

"They couldn't make it, I guess, that was rough duty down there." The launch swung round, exposing the stern. "That's the *Maria Blanco*'s launch," Carney added.

"Is that a fact?"

Dillon dried himself slowly with a towel and stood at the rail looking across. He recognized Algaro at once, standing in the stern with Serra, and then Santiago came out of the wheelhouse.

"Who's the guy in the blazer and cap?" Dillon enquired.

Carney looked across. "That's Max Santiago, the owner. I've seen him in St. John a time or two."

Santiago was looking across at them and on impulse, Dillon raised an arm and waved. Santiago waved back and at that moment Noval and Pinto surfaced.

"Time to go home," Carney said and he went round to the prow and heaved in the anchor.

On the way back Dillon said, "The *Maria Blanco*, where would it anchor when it's here, Caneel Bay?"

"More likely to be off Paradise Beach."

"Could we take a look?"

Carney glanced at him, then looked away. "Why not? It's your charter."

Dillon got the water bottle from the icebox, drank about a pint, then passed it to Carney and lit a cigarette. Carney drank a little and passed it back.

"You've dived before, Mr. Dillon."

"And that's a fact," Dillon agreed.

They were close to Paradise now and Carney throttled back the engine and the *Privateer* passed between two of the oceangoing yachts that were moored there and came to the *Maria Blanco*. "There she is," he said.

There were a couple of crewmen working on deck, who looked up casually as they passed. "Jesus," Dillon said, that thing must have made a dent in Santiago's wallet. A couple of million, I'd say."

"And then some."

Carney went up to full power and made for Caneel Beach. Dillon lit another cigarette and leaned against the wall of the deckhouse. "Do you get many interesting wrecks in this area?"

"Some," Carney said. "There's the *Cartanser Senior* off Buck Island over to St. Thomas, an old freighter that's a popular dive, and the *General Rodgers*. The Coast Guard sank her to get rid of her."

"No, I was thinking of something more interesting than that," Dillon said. "I mean you know this area like the back of your hand. Would it be possible for there to be a wreck on some reef out there that you'd never come across?"

Carney slowed as they entered the bay. "Anything's possible, it's a big ocean."

"So there could be something out there just waiting to be discovered?"

The *Privateer* coasted in beside the dock. Dillon got the stern line, went over and tied up. He did the same with the other line as Carney cut the engine, went back on board and pulled on his track suit.

Carney leaned by the wheel looking at him. "Mr. Dillon, I don't know what goes on here. All I know for certain is you are one hell of a diver, and that I admire. What all this talk of wrecks means I don't know and don't want to as I'm inclined to the quiet life, but I will give you one piece of advice. Your interest in Max Santiago?"

"Oh, yes?" Dillon said, continuing to put his diving equipment in a net diving bag.

"It could be unhealthy. I've heard things about him that aren't good, plenty of people could tell you the same. The way he makes his money, for example."

"A hotel keeper as I heard it." Dillon smiled.

"There's other ways that involve small planes or a fast boat by night to Florida, but what the hell, you're a grown man." Carney moved out on deck. "You want to dive with me again?"

"You can count on it. I've got business in St. Thomas this afternoon. How would I get there?"

Carney pointed to the other side of the dock where a very large launch was just casting off. "That's the resort ferry. They run back and forth during the day, but I figure you missed this one."

"Damn!" Dillon said.

"Mr. Dillon, you arrived at Cruz Bay in your own floatplane, and the front desk, who keep me informed of such things, tell me you pay with an American Express Platinum Card."

"What can I say, you've got me," Dillon told him amicably.

"Water taxis are expensive, but not to a man of your means. The front desk will order you one."

"Thanks." Dillon crossed to the dock and paused. "Maybe I could buy you a drink tonight. Will you be at Jenny's Place?"

"Hell, I'm there every night at the moment," Carney said, "otherwise I'd starve. My wife and kids are away on vacation."

"I'll see you then," Dillon said and turned and walked away along the dock toward the front desk.

The water taxi had seats for a dozen passengers, but he had it to himself. The only crew was a woman in a peaked cap and denims, who sat at the wheel and made for St. Thomas at a considerable rate of knots. It was noisy and there wasn't much chance to speak, which suited Dillon. He sat there smoking and thinking about the way things had gone so far, Algaro, Max Santiago and the *Maria Blanco*.

He knew about Santiago, but Santiago knew about him, that was a fact and yet to be explained. There had almost been a touch of comradeship in the way Santiago had waved back at him at Carval Rock. Carney, he liked. In fact, everything about him he liked. For one thing, the American knew his business, but there was power there and real authority. An outstanding example of a quiet man it wouldn't pay to push.

"Here we go," the water taxi driver shouted over her shoulder, and Dillon glanced up and saw that they were moving in toward the waterfront of Charlotte Amalie.

It was quite a place and bustling with activity, two enormous cruise liners berthed on the far side of the harbor. The waterfront was lined with buildings in white and pastel colors, shops and restaurants of every description. It had been a Danish colony, he knew that, and the influence still showed in some of the architecture.

He followed a narrow alley called Drake's Passage that was lined with colorful shops offering everything from designer clothes to gold and jewelry, for this was a free port, and came out into Main Street. He consulted the address Ferguson had given him and crossed to where some taxis waited.

"Can you take me to Cane Street?" he asked the first driver.

"I wouldn't take your money, man," the driver told him amiably. "Just take the next turning through to Back Street. Cane is the third on the left."

Dillon thanked him and moved on. It was hot, very hot, people crowding the pavements, traffic moving slowly in the narrow streets, but Cane Street, when he came to it, was quiet and shaded. The house he wanted was at the far end, clapboard, painted white with a red corrugated iron roof. There was a tiny garden in front of it and steps leading up to a porch on which an ageing black man with gray hair sat on a swing seat reading a newspaper.

He looked up as Dillon approached. "And what can I do for you?"

"I'm looking for Earl Stacey," Dillon told him.

The man peered at him over the top of reading glasses. "You ain't gonna spoil my day with no bills, are you?"

"Ferguson told me to look you up," Dillon said, "Brigadier Charles Ferguson. My name is Dillon."

The other man smiled and removed his glasses. "I've been expecting you. Come right this way," and he pushed open the door and led the way into the house.

I'm on my own since my wife died last year." Stacey opened a door, switched on a light and led the way down wooden steps to a cellar. There were wooden shelves up to the ceiling, pots of paint stacked there, cupboards below. He reached in and released some kind of catch and pulled it open like a door revealing another room. He switched on a light.

"Come into my parlor."

There was all kinds of weaponry, rifles, submachine guns, boxes of ammunition. "It looks like Christmas to me," Dillon told him.

"You just tell me what you want, man, and Ferguson picks up the tab, that was the arrangement."

"Rifle first," Dillon said. "Armalite perhaps. I like the folding stock."

"I can do better. I got an AK assault rifle here with a folding stock, fires automatic when you want, thirty-round magazine." He took the weapon from a stand and handed it over.

"Yes, this will do fine," Dillon told him. "I'll take it with two extra magazines. I need a handgun now, Walther PPK for preference, and a Carswell silencer. Two extra magazines for that as well."

"Can do."

Stacey opened a very large drawer under the bench which ran along one wall. Inside there was an assortment of handguns. He selected a Walther and passed it to Dillon for approval. "Anything else?"

There was a cheap-looking plastic holster with the butt of a pistol sticking out of it and Dillon was intrigued. "What's that?"

"It's an ace-in-the-hole." Stacey took it out. "That metal strip on the back is a magnet. Stick it underneath anywhere and as long as it's metal it'll hold fast. The gun don't look much, point-two-two Belgian, semi-automatic, seven-shot, but I've put hollow-nosed rounds in. They fragment bone."

"I'll take it," Dillon said. "One more thing. Would you happen to have any C4 explosive?"

"The kind salvage people use for underwater work?"

"Exactly."

"No, but I tell you what I do have, something just as good, Semtex. You heard of that stuff?"

"Oh, yes," Dillon said. "I think you could say I'm familiar with Semtex. One of Czechoslovakia's more successful products."

"The terrorist's favorite weapon." Stacey took a box down from the shelf. "The Palestinians, the IRA, all those cats use this stuff. You gonna use this underwater yourself?"

"Just to make a hole in a wreck."

"Then you need some detonation cord, a remote-control unit or I've got some chemical detonating pencils here. They work real good. You just break the cap. I got some timed for ten minutes and others for thirty." He pushed all the items together. "Is that it?"

"A night sight would be useful and a pair of binoculars."

"I can do them too." He opened another drawer. "There you go."

The night sight was small, but powerful, extending if needed like a telescope. The binoculars were by Zeiss and pocket size. "Excellent," Dillon said.

Stacey went and found an olive-green Army holdall, unzipped it, put the AK assault rifle in first and then the other things. He closed the zip, turned and led the way out, switching off the light and pushing the shelving back into place. Dillon followed him up the cellar stairs and out to the porch.

Stacey offered him the bag. "Mr. Dillon, I get the impression you intend to start World War Three."

"Maybe we can call a truce," Dillon said. "Who knows?"

"I wish you luck, my friend. I'll send my bill to Ferguson."

Stacey sat down, put on his reading glasses and picked up his newspaper, and Dillon walked out through the small garden and started back toward the waterfront.

He was walking along the side of the harbor to where the water taxis operated from when he saw that the Caneel ferry was in, a gangplank stretching down to the dock. The Captain was standing at the top as Dillon went up.

"You staying at Caneel, sir?"

"I certainly am."

"We'll be leaving soon. Just heard someone's on the way down from the airport."

Dillon went into the main cabin, put his bag on a seat and accepted a rum punch offered by one of the crew. He glanced out of the window and saw a large taxi bus draw up, a single passenger inside, went and sat down and drank some of his punch. One of the crew came in and put two suitcases in the corner, there was the sound of the gangplank being moved, the Captain went into the wheelhouse and started the engines. Dillon checked his watch. It was five-thirty. He put his plastic cup on the table, lit a cigarette and at the same time was aware of someone slumping down beside him.

"Fancy meeting you, dear boy," Charles Ferguson said. "Bloody hot, isn't it?"

TEN

Dillon had a quick swim off Paradise Beach, conscious that the *Maria Blanco* was still at anchor out there, then he went back up to the cottage, had a shower and changed into navy blue linen slacks and a short-sleeved white cotton shirt. He went out, crossed the vestibule and tapped on the door of 7E.

"Come," Ferguson called.

Dillon entered. The set-up was similar to his own, the bathroom marginally larger as was the other room. Ferguson, in gray flannel slacks and a white Turnbull and Asser shirt, stood in front of the mirror in the small dressing room easing the Guards tie into a neat Windsor knot at his neck.

"Ah, there you are," he said, took a double-breasted navy blue blazer and pulled it on. "How do I look, dear boy?"

"Like an advertisement for Gieves and Hawkes, the bloody English gentleman abroad."

"Just because you're Irish doesn't mean you have to feel inferior all the time," Ferguson told him. "Some very reasonable people were Irish, Dillon, my mother for instance, not to mention the Duke of Wellington."

"Who said that just because a man had been born in a stable didn't mean he was a horse," Dillon pointed out.

"Dear me, did he say that? Most unfortunate." Ferguson picked up a Panama hat and a Malacca cane with a silver handle.

"I never knew you needed a cane," Dillon said.

"Bought this during the Korean War. Strong as steel because it has a steel core weighted with lead at the tip. Oh, and here's a rather nice device."

He turned the silver handle to one side and pulled out a steel poniard about nine inches long.

"Very interesting," Dillon said.

"Yes, well we are in foreign parts. I call it my pig sticker." There was a click as Ferguson rammed the poniard home. "Now, are you going to offer me a quick drink before we go out or aren't you?"

Dillon had negotiated a supply of Krug from room service, had several half-bottles in one of the iceboxes. He filled two glasses and went out to Ferguson on the terrace, picking up the Zeiss field glasses on the way.

"That large white motor yacht out there is the *Maria Blanco*."

"Really?" Dillon passed him the Zeiss glasses and the Brigadier had a look. "A sort of minor floating palace I'd say."

"So it would appear."

Ferguson still held the glasses to his eyes. "As a young man I was a subaltern in the Korean War. One year of unmitigated hell. I did a tour of duty on a position called the Hook. Just like the First World War. Miles of trenches, barbed wire, mine fields and thousands of Chinese trying to get in. They used to watch us and we used to watch them. It was like a game, a particularly nasty game, which exploded into violence every so often." He sighed and lowered the glasses. "What on earth am I prattling on about, Dillon?"

"Oh, I'd say you're going the long way round to the pub to tell me that you suspect Santiago's watching too."

"Something like that. Tell me how far things have gone and don't leave anything out, not a single damn thing."

When Dillon was finished, he refilled the Brigadier's glass while Ferguson sat there thinking about it.

"What do you think the next move should be?" Dillon asked.

"Well, now you've gone and got yourself tooled up by Stacey I suppose you're eager for confrontation, a gunfight at the OK Corral?"

"I've taken precautions, that's all," Dillon said. "And I needed the Semtex to blast a way into the U-boat."

"If we find it," Ferguson said. "And not a murmur from the girl."

"She'll turn up eventually."

"And in the meantime?"

"I'd like to take things further with Carney. We really do need him on our side."

"I can see that, but it would be a question of how to approach him. Would a cash offer help?"

"Not really. If I'm right, Carney is the kind of man who'll only do a thing if he really wants to or if he thinks it right."

"Oh, dear." Ferguson sighed. "Heaven save me from the romantics of this world." He stood up and glanced at his watch. "Food, Dillon, that's what I need. Where shall we eat?"

"We could walk up to Turtle Bay Dining Room. That's more formal, I hear, but excellent. I've booked a table."

"Good, then let's get moving, and for heaven's sake put a jacket on. I don't want people to think I'm dining with a beachcomber."

Out in the gathering darkness of Caneel Bay, an inflatable from the *Maria Blanco* nosed in beside Carney's Sport Fisherman, *Sea Raider*, the only sound the muted throbbing of the outboard motor. Serra was at the helm and Algaro sat in the stern. As they bumped against the hull of *Sea Raider* he went up over the rail and into the wheelhouse, took a tiny electronic box from his pocket, reached under the instrument panel until he found metal and put it in place attached by its magnet.

A moment later he was back in the inflatable. "Now the small dive boat, *Privateer*," he said and Serra turned and moved toward it.

Max Santiago, wearing a white linen suit, was sitting in Caneel Bay Bar sipping a mint julep when Algaro came in. He wore a black tee-shirt and a loose-fitting baggy suit in black linen that made him look rather sinister.

"Did everything go well?" Santiago asked.

"Absolutely. I've put a bug on both of Carney's dive boats. That means we can follow wherever he goes without being observed. Ferguson booked in just after six. I checked with the reservations desk. Dillon has booked a table for two up at Turtle Bay Dining Room."

"Good," Santiago said. "It might be amusing to join him."

Captain Serra entered at that moment. "Have you any further orders, Señor?"

"If Dillon does as he did last night, he may probably visit this bar, Jenny's Place," Santiago said. "I'll probably look in there myself."

"So I'll take the launch round to Cruz Bay, Señor, to pick you up from there?"

Santiago smiled. "I've had a better idea. Go back to the *Maria Blanco*, pick up some of the crew and take them into Cruz. They can have a drink on me later, let off a little steam if you follow me."

"Perfectly, Señor." Serra smiled and went out.

It was just after midnight at the Convent of the Little Sisters of Pity and Jenny Grant, who had gone to bed early, was restless and unable to sleep. She got up, found her cigarettes, lit one and went and sat on the padded windowseat and peered out into driving rain. She could see the light still on in the window of Sister Maria Baker's office, but then, she never seemed to stop working. Strange how Henry had always kept her very existence a secret. It was as if he'd been somehow ashamed of her, the religious thing. He'd never been able to handle that.

Jenny felt much better than when she had arrived, infinitely more rested and yet restless at the same time. She wondered what was happening in St. John and how Dillon was getting on. She'd liked Dillon, that was the simple truth, in spite of everything in his background of which she thoroughly disapproved. On the other hand, you could only speak as you found, and to her he had been good, kind, considerate and understanding.

She went back to bed, switched off the light and dozed and had a dream of the half-waking sort, the U-boat in dark waters and Henry diving deep. Dear Henry. Such an idiot to have been down there in the first place and somewhere dangerous, somewhere unusual, somewhere people didn't normally go. It had to be.

She came awake in the instant and spoke out loud in the darkness. "Oh, my God, of course, and so simple."

She got out of bed and went to the window. The light was still on in the Mother Superior's office. She dressed quickly in jeans and sweater and hurried across the court-yard through the rain and knocked on the door.

When she entered, she found Sister Maria Baker seated behind her desk working. She glanced up in surprise. "Why, Jenny, what is it? Can't you sleep?"

"I'll be leaving tomorrow, Sister, I just wanted to let you know. I'm going back to St. John."

"So soon, Jenny? But why?"

"The location of the U-boat that Henry found and that Dillon is looking for? I think I can find it for him. It just came to me as I was falling asleep."

Ferguson sat on the terrace at Turtle Bay and looked out to the Sir Francis Drake Channel, islands like black cutouts against the dark sky streaked with orange as the sun descended.

"Really is quite extraordinary," the Brigadier said as they sipped a fruit punch.

" 'Sunsets exquisitely dying,' that's what the poet said," Dillon murmured.

The cicadas chirped ceaselessly, night birds calling to each other. He got up and moved to the edge of the terrace and Ferguson said, "Good heavens, I didn't realize you had a literary bent, dear boy."

Dillon lit a cigarette, the Zippo flaring. He grinned. "To be frank with you I'm a bloody literary genius, Brigadier. I did Hamlet at the Royal Academy. I can still remember most of the text." His voice changed suddenly into a remarkable impression of Marlon Brando. "I could have been somebody, I could have been a contender."

"Don't get maudlin on me at this stage in your life, Dillon, never pays to look back with regret because you can't change anything. And you've wasted too much time already on that damned cause of yours. I trust you realize that. Stay with the present. The main point which concerns me at the moment is how this wretched man Santiago comes to be so well informed."

"And wouldn't I like to know that myself?" Dillon said.

Santiago walked in through the arched gateway, Algaro at his shoulder. He looked around the terrace, saw Dillon and Ferguson and came over. "Mr. Dillon? Max Santiago."

"I know who you are, Señor," Dillon replied in excellent Spanish.

Santiago looked surprised. "I must congratulate you, Señor," he replied in the same language. "Such fluency in a foreigner is rare." He turned to Ferguson and added in English, "A pleasure to see you at Caneel Bay, Brigadier. Have a nice dinner, gentlemen," and he left followed by Algaro.

"He knew who you are and he knew you were here," Dillon said.

"So I noticed." Ferguson stood up. "Let's eat, I'm starving."

The service was good, the food excellent and Ferguson thoroughly enjoyed himself. They split a bottle of Louis Roederer Crystal Champagne and started with grilled sea scallops in a red pepper and saffron sauce, followed by a Caesar salad and then a pan-roasted pheasant. Ferguson, napkin tucked in his collar, devoured everything.

"To be honest, dear boy, I really prefer nursery food, but one must make an effort."

"An Englishman abroad again?" Dillon inquired.

"Ferguson, I need hardly point out, is the most Scots of Scottish names, Dillon, and as I told you, my mother was Irish."

"Yes, but Eton, Sandhurst and the Grenadier Guards got mixed up in that little lot somewhere."

Ferguson poured some more Crystal. "Lovely bottle. You can see right through it. Very unusual."

"Czar Nicholas designed it himself," Dillon told him. "Said he wanted to be able to see the champagne."

"Extraordinary. Never knew that."

"Didn't do him any good when the Bolsheviks murdered him."

"I'm glad you said murdered, Dillon, there's some hope for you still. What's friend Santiago doing?"

"Having dinner at the edge of the garden behind you. The ghoul with him, by the way, is called Algaro. He must be his minder. He's the one who ran me off the road and fired a shotgun."

"Oh, dear, we can't have that." Ferguson asked the waiter for tea instead of coffee. "What do you suggest our next move should be? Santiago is obviously pressing and intends we should know it."

"I think I need to speak to Carney. If anybody might have some ideas about where that U-boat is, it would be he."

"That's not only exquisitely grammatical, dear boy, it makes sense. Do you know where he might be?"

"Oh, yes."

"Excellent." Ferguson stood, picked up his Panama and Malacca cane. "Let's get moving then."

Dillon drove into the car park at Mongoose Junction and switched off. He took the holstered Belgian semi-automatic from his jacket pocket. "What on earth is that?" Ferguson demanded.

"An ace-in-the-hole. I'll leave it under the dashboard."

"Looks like a woman's gun to me."

"And like most women it gets the job done, Brigadier, so don't be sexist." Dillon clamped the holster under the dashboard. "Okay, let's go and see if we can find Carney."

They walked along the front from Mongoose Junction to Jenny's Place. It was about half-full when they went inside, Billy Jones working the bar, Mary and one waitress between them handling the dinner trade. There were only four tables taken and Carney sat at one.

Captain Serra and three of the crew from the *Maria Blanco* were at a booth table in the corner. Guerra, the mate, was one of them. Dillon recognized him from the first night, although the fact that Guerra said, "That's him," in Spanish and they all stopped talking was sufficient confirmation.

"Hello there." Mary Jones approached and Dillon smiled.

"We'll join Bob Carney. A bottle of champagne. Whatever you've got!"

"Two glasses." Ferguson raised his hat politely.

Mary took his arm, her teeth flashing in a delighted smile. "I like this man. Where did you find him? I love a gentleman."

Billy leaned over the bar. "You put him down, woman."

"It's not his fault," Dillon said. "He's a Brigadier. All that army training."

"A Brigadier General." Her eyes widened.

"Well, yes, that's true in your army," Ferguson said uncomfortably.

"Well, you go and join Bob Carney, honey. Mary's gonna take care of you right now."

Carney was just finishing an order of steak and french fries, a beer at his elbow, and looked up as they approached. "Mr. Dillon?" he said.

"This is a friend of mine, Brigadier Charles Ferguson," Dillon told him. "May we join you?"

Carney smiled. "I'm impressed, but I should warn you, Brigadier, all I made was corporal and that was in the Marines."

"Grenadier Guards," Ferguson told him, "hope you don't mind?"

"Hell, no, I guess we elite unit boys have got to stick together. Sit down." As they each pulled up a chair he went back to his steak and said to Dillon, "You ever in the army, Dillon?"

"Not exactly," Dillon told him.

"Hell, there's nothing exact about it, not that you hear about the Irish Army too much except that they seem to spend most of their time fighting for the United Nations in Beirut or Angola or someplace. Of course, there is the other lot, the IRA." He stopped cutting the last piece of steak for a moment, then carried on. "But no, that wouldn't be possible, would it, Dillon?"

He smiled and Ferguson said, "My dear chap, be reasonable, what on earth would the IRA be interested in here? What's more to the point, why would I be involved?"

"I don't know about that, Brigadier. What I do know is that Dillon here is a mystery to me and a mystery is like a crossword puzzle. I've just got to solve it."

Santiago came in followed by Algaro and the other four stood up. "We've got company," Dillon told Ferguson.

The Brigadier looked round. "Oh, dear," he said.

Bob Carney pushed his plate away. "Just to save you more questions, Santiago you know and that creep Algaro. The one with the beard is the captain of the *Maria Blanco*, Serra. The others will be crew."

Billy Jones brought a bottle of Pol Roget in a bucket, opened it for them, then went across to the booth to take Santiago's order. Dillon poured the champagne, raised his glass and spoke to Carney in Irish.

"Jesus," Carney said. "What in the hell are you saying, Dillon?"

"Irish, the language of kings. A very ancient toast. May the wind be always at your back. Appropriate for a ship's captain. I mean, you do have a master's ticket amongst other things?"

Carney frowned, then turned to Ferguson. "Let's see if I can put it together. He works for you?"

"In a manner of speaking."

At that moment, they heard a woman's voice say, "Please don't do that."

The waitress serving the drinks at Santiago's table was a small girl, rather pretty with her blonde hair in a plait bound up at the back. She was very young, very vulnerable. Algaro was running his hand over her buttocks and started to move down a leg.

"I hate to see that," Carney said and his face was hard.

Dillon said, "I couldn't agree more. To say he's in from the stable would be an insult to horses."

The girl pulled away, the crew laughing, and Santiago looked across, his eyes meeting Dillon's. He smiled, turned and whispered to Algaro, who nodded and got to his feet.

"Now let's keep our heads here," Ferguson said.

Algaro crossed to the bar and sat on a vacant stool. As the girl passed, he put an arm round her waist and whispered in her ear. She went red in the face, close to tears. "Leave me alone," she said and struggled to free herself.

Dillon glanced across. Santiago raised his glass and toasted him, a half-smile on his face, as Algaro slipped a hand up her skirt. Billy Jones was serving at the other end of the bar and he turned to see what was happening. Carney got to his feet, picked up his glass and walked to the bar. He put an arm around the girl's shoulders and eased her away, then he poured what was left of his beer into Algaro's crotch.

"Excuse me," he said, "I didn't see you there," and he turned and walked back to the table.

Everyone stopped talking and Dillon took the bottle from the ice bucket and refilled the Brigadier's glass. Algaro stood up and looked down at his trousers in disbelief. "Why, you little creep, I'm going to break your left arm for that."

He moved to the table fast, arms extended, and Carney turned, crouching to defend himself, but it was Dillon who struck first, reversed his grip on the champagne bottle and smashed it across the side of Algaro's skull not once but twice, the bottle splintering, champagne going everywhere. Algaro pulled himself up, hands on the edge of the table, and Dillon, still seated, kicked sideways at the kneecap. Algaro cried out and fell to one side. He lay there for a moment, then forced himself up on to one knee.

Dillon jumped up and raised a knee into the unprotected face. "You've never learned to lie down, have you?"

The other members of the crew of the *Maria Blanco* were on their feet, one of them picking up a chair, and Billy Jones came round the bar in a rush, a baseball bat in his hand. "Can it or I'll call the law. He asked for it, he got it. Just get him out of here."

They stopped dead, not so much because of Billy as Santiago, who said in Spanish, "No trouble. Just get him and leave."

Captain Serra nodded and Guerra, the mate, and Pinto went and helped Algaro to his feet. He appeared dazed, blood on his face, and they led him out followed by the others. Santiago stood up and raised his glass, emptied it and left.

Conversation resumed and Mary brought a brush and pan to sweep up the glass. Billy said to Dillon, "I couldn't get there fast enough. I thank you guys. How about another bottle of champagne on the house?"

"Include me out, Billy," Carney said. "Put the meal on my tab. I'm getting too old for this kind of excitement. I'm going home to bed." He stood up. "Brigadier, it's been interesting."

He started toward the door and Dillon called, "I'd like to dive in the morning. Does that suit you?"

"Nine-thirty," Carney told him. "Be at the dock," and he turned and went out.

His jeep was in the car park at Mongoose Junction. He walked along there, thinking about what had happened, was unlocking the door when a hand grabbed his shoulder and as he turned, Guerra punched him in the mouth.

"Now then you bastard, let's teach you some manners."

Serra stood a yard or two away supporting Algaro, Santiago beside them. Guerra and the other two crew members moved in fast. Carney ducked the first blow and punched the mate in the stomach, half-turning, giving Pinto a reverse elbow strike in the face and then they were all over him. They held him down, pinning his arms, and Algaro shuffled over.

"Now then," he said.

It was at that precise moment that Dillon and Ferguson, having taken a raincheck on the champagne, turned the corner. The Irishman went in on the run as Algaro raised a foot to stamp down on Carney's face, sent him staggering and punched the nearest man sideways in the jaw. Carney was already on his feet. Algaro was past it, but when Captain Serra moved in to help the other three it raised the odds and Dillon and Carney prepared to defend themselves, the jeep at their backs, arms raised, waiting. There was a sudden shot, the sound of it flat on the night air. Everyone stopped dead, turned and found Ferguson standing beside Dillon's jeep holding the Belgian semi-automatic in one hand.

"Now do let's stop playing silly buggers, shall we?" he said.

There was a pause and Santiago said in Spanish, "Back to the launch."

The crew shuffled away unwillingly, Serra and Guerra supporting Algaro, who still looked dazed.

"Another time, Brigadier," Santiago said in English and followed them.

Carney wiped a little blood from his mouth with a handkerchief. "Would somebody kindly tell me what in the hell is going on?"

"Yes, we do need to talk, Captain Carney," Ferguson said briskly, "and sooner rather than later."

"Okay, I give in." Carney smiled bleakly. "Follow me and we'll go to my place. It's not too far away."

Carney said, "It's the damnedest thing I ever heard of."

"But you accept it's true?" Ferguson asked. "I have a copy of the translation of the diary in my briefcase at Caneel, which I'd be happy for you to see."

"The U-boat thing is perfectly possible," Carney said. "They were in these waters during World War Two, that's a known fact, and there are locals who'll tell you stories about how they used to come ashore by night." He shook his head. "Hitler in the Bunker, Martin Bormann—I've read all those books, and it is an interesting thought that if Bormann landed on Samson Cay and didn't go down with the boat, it would explain all those sightings of him in South America in the years since the war."

"Good," Dillon said. "So you accept the existence of U180, but where would it be?"

"Let me get a chart." Carney went out and came back with one which he unrolled. It was the Virgin Islands chart for St. Thomas up to Virgin Gorda. "There's Samson Cay south of Norman Island in the British Virgins. If that hurricane twisted, which they sometimes do, and came in from an easterly direction, the U-boat would definitely be driven somewhere toward the west and south from St. John."

"Ending where?" Ferguson said.

"It wouldn't be anywhere usual. By that I mean somewhere people dive, however regularly, and I'll tell you something else. It would have to be within one hundred feet."

"What makes you say that?" Dillon asked.

"Henry was a recreational diver, that means no decompression is necessary if you follow the tables. One hundred and thirty feet is absolute maximum for that kind of sport diving, and at that depth he could only afford ten minutes bottom time before going back up to the surface. To examine the submarine and find the diary." Carney shook his head. "It just wouldn't be possible, and Henry was sixty-three years of age. He knew his limitations."

"So what are you saying?"

"To discover the wreck, enter it, hunt around and find that diary." Carney shrugged. "I'd say thirty minutes bottom time, so his depth would likely be eighty feet or so. Now dive masters take tourists to that kind of depth all the time, that's why I mean the location has got to be quite out of the ordinary."

He frowned and Ferguson said, "You must have some idea."

"The morning Henry made his discovery must have been the day after the hurricane blew itself out. He'd gone out so early that he was coming back in at around nine-thirty when I was taking a dive party out. We crossed each other and we spoke."

"What did he say?" Dillon asked.

"I asked him where he'd been. He said French Cap. Told me it was like a millpond out there."

"Then that's it," Ferguson said. "Surely?"

Carney shook his head. "I use French Cap a lot. The water is particularly clear. It's a great dive. In fact I took my clients out there after meeting Henry that morning and he was right, it was like a millpond. The visibility is spectacular." He shook his head. "No, if it was there it would have been found before now."

"Can you think of anywhere else?"

Carney frowned. "There's always South Drop, that's even further."

"You dive there?" Ferguson asked.

"Occasionally. Trouble is if the sea's rough, it's a long and uncomfortable trip, but it could be the sort of place. A long ridge running to a hundred and seventy or so on one side and two thousand on the other."

"Could we take a look at these places?" Ferguson asked.

Carney shook his head and examined the chart again. "I don't know."

Ferguson said, "I'd pay you well, Captain Carney."

"It isn't that," Carney said. "Strictly speaking, this thing is in United States territorial waters."

"Just listen, please," Ferguson said. "We're not doing anything wicked here. There are some documents on U180, or so we believe, which could give my government cause for concern. All we want to do is recover them as quickly as possible and no harm done."

"And Santiago, where does he fit in?"

"He's obviously after the same thing," Ferguson said. "Why, I don't know at this time, but I will, I promise you."

"You go to the movies, Carney," Dillon said. "Santiago and his bunch are the bad guys. Blackhats."

"And I'm a good guy?" Carney laughed out loud. "Get the hell out of here and let me get some sleep. I'll see you at the dock at nine-thirty."

Santiago, standing in the stern of the *Maria Blanco*, looked toward Cottage Seven and the lights which had just come on in both sections.

"So they are back," he said to Serra, who stood beside him.

"Now that they've made contact with Carney they may make their move sometime tomorrow," Serra said.

"You'll be able to follow them in the launch whichever boat they are in, thanks to the bugs, at a discreet distance of course."

"Shall I take the divers?"

"If you like, but I doubt that anything will come of it. Carney doesn't know where U180 is, Serra, I'm convinced of that. They've asked him for suggestions, that's all. Take the dive-site handbook for this area with you. If they dive somewhere that's mentioned in the book, you may take it from me it's a waste of time." Santiago shook his head. "Frankly, I'm inclined to think that the girl has the answer. We'll just have to wait for her return. By the way, if we ever did find the U-boat and needed to blast a way in, could Noval and Pinto cope?"

"Most assuredly, Señor, we have supplies of C4 explosive on board and all the necessary detonating equipment."

"Excellent," Santiago said. "I wish you luck tomorrow then. Good night, Captain."

Serra walked away and Algaro slipped out of the dark. "Can I go with the launch in the morning?"

"Ah, revenge, is it?" Santiago laughed. "And why not? Enjoy it while you can, Algaro," and he laughed as he went down to the salon.

ELEVEN

It was a beautiful morning when Dillon and Ferguson went down to the dock. *Sea Raider* was tied up, no sign of anyone around, and *Privateer* was moving out to sea with four people seated in the stern.

"Perhaps we got it wrong," Dillon observed.

"I doubt it," Ferguson said. "Not that sort of fellow."

At that moment Carney turned on to the end of the dock and came toward them pushing a trolley loaded with air tanks. "Morning," he called.

"Thought you'd left us," Dillon said, looking out toward *Privateer*.

"Hell, no, that's just one of my people taking some divers out to Little St. James. I thought we'd use *Sea Raider* today because we've a lot further to go." He turned to Ferguson. "You a good sailor, Brigadier?"

"My dear chap, I've just called in at the gift shop to obtain some sea-sickness pills of which I've taken not one but two."

He went on board and climbed the ladder to the flying bridge, where he sat in solitary splendor on one of the swivel seats while Dillon and Carney loaded the tanks. When they were finished Carney went up, joined Ferguson and switched on the engines. As they eased away from the dock, Dillon went into the deckhouse. He wasn't using his net dive bag, had put his diving gear into the olive-green army holdall Stacey had given him in St. Thomas. Underneath was the AK assault rifle, stock folded, and a thirty-round clip inserted ready for action plus an extra magazine. There was also his ace-in-the-hole. Belgian semi-automatic which he'd retrieved from the jeep. As with all Sport Fishermen, there was a wheel in the deckhouse as well as on the flying bridge so the boat could be steered from there in rough weather. Dillon felt under the instrument panel until he encountered a metal surface and clamped the holster and gun in place.

He went up the ladder and joined the others. "What's our course?"

"Pretty well due south through Pillsbury Sound, then south-west to French Cap." Carney grinned at Ferguson, who swung from side to side as the boat started to lift over waves to the open sea. "You okay, Brigadier?"

"I'll let you know. I presume you would anticipate our friends from the *Maria Blanco* following?"

"I've been looking, but I haven't seen anything yet. There's certainly no sign of the *Maria Blanco* herself, but then they'd use the white launch we saw at Carval Rock. That's a good boat. Good for twenty-five or -six knots. I don't get much more than twenty out of this." He said to Dillon, "There's some glasses in the locker if you want to keep a weather eye open."

Dillon got them out, focused and checked astern. There were a number of yachts and a small vehicle ferry with trucks on board crossing from St. Thomas, but no launch. "Not a sign," he said.

"Now I find that strange," Ferguson observed.

"You worry too much, Brigadier," Carney told him. "Now let's get out of here," and he pushed the throttle forward and took *Sea Raider* out to open water fast.

The launch was there, of course, but a good mile behind, Serra at the wheel, his eye occasionally going to the dark screen with the blob of light showing what was the *Sea Raider*. Algaro stood beside him and Noval and Pinto busied themselves with diving equipment in the stern. Algaro didn't look good. He had a black eye and his mouth was bruised and swollen.

"No chance of losing them?"

"No way," Serra said. "I'll show you." There was a steady and monotonous pinging sound coming from the screen. When he swung the wheel, turning to port, it raised its pitch, sounded frantic. "See, that tells us when we're off track." He turned back to starboard, straightening when he got the right sound again, checking the course reading.

"Good," Algaro said.

"How are you feeling?" Serra asked.

"Well, let's put it this way. I'll feel a whole lot better when I've sorted those bastards out," Algaro said, "particularly Dillon," and he turned and went and joined the others.

The water heaved in heavy, long swells as they drifted in to French Cap Cay. Dillon went to the prow to lower the anchor while Carney maneuvered the boat, leaning out under the blue awning of the flying bridge to give him instructions.

"There's what we call the Pinnacle under here," he said. "Its top is about forty-five feet down. That's what we're trying to catch the anchor on." After a while he nodded. "That's it," he called and cut the engines.

"What are we going to do?" Dillon asked as he zipped up his diving suit.

"Not much we can do," Carney told him as he fastened his weight belt. "It's around ninety-five feet at the most, ranging up to fifty. We can do a turn right round the rock base and general reef area. The visibility is incredible. You'll not find better anywhere. That's why I don't believe this is the right spot. That U-boat would have been spotted before now. By the way, I think you picked up my diving gloves by mistake yesterday and I've got yours." He rummaged in Dillon's holdall and found the rifle. "Dear God," he said, taking it out. "What's this?"

"Insurance," Dillon said as he pulled on his fins.

"An AK47 is considerably more than that." Carney unfolded the stock and checked it.

"I would remind you, Mr. Carney, that it was our friends who fired the first shot," Ferguson said. "You're familiar with that weapon?"

"I was in Vietnam, Brigadier. I've used one for real. They make a real ugly, distinctive sound. I never hope to hear one fired again."

Carney folded the stock, replaced the AK in the holdall and finished getting his diving gear on. He stepped awkwardly on to the diving platform at its rear and turned. "I'll see you down there," he said to Dillon, inserted his mouthpiece and tumbled backwards.

Serra watched them from about a quarter of a mile away through a pair of old binoculars. Noval and Pinto stood ready in their diving suits. Algaro said, "What are they doing?"

"They've anchored and Dillon and Carney have gone down. There's just the Brigadier on deck."

"What do you want us to do?" Noval asked.

"We'll go in very fast, but I won't anchor. We'll make it a drift dive, catch them by surprise, so be ready to go."

He pushed the launch up to twenty-five knots and as it surged forward, Noval and Pinto got the rest of their equipment on.

Carney hadn't exaggerated. There were all colors of coral, barrel and tube sponges, fish of every description, but it was the visibility that was so incredible, the water tinged with a deep blue stretching into a kind of infinity. There was a school of horse-eyed jacks overhead as Dillon followed Carney and a couple of manta rays flapped across the sandy slope to one side.

But Carney had also been right about the U-boat. No question that it could be on a site like this. Dillon followed him along the reef and the base of the rock until finally Carney turned and spread his arms. Dillon understood the gesture and swung round for the return to the boat and saw Noval and Pinto ahead of them and perhaps twenty feet higher. He and Carney hung suspended, watching them, and then the American gestured forward and led the way back to the anchor line. They paused there and looked up and saw the keel of the launch moving in a wide circle. Carney started up the line and Dillon followed him, finally surfacing at the stern.

"When did they arrive?" Dillon asked Ferguson as he shrugged off his jacket and tank.

"About ten minutes after you went down. Roared up at a hell of a speed, didn't put the anchor down, simply dropped two divers over the stern."

"We saw them." Dillon took his gear off and looked across at the launch. "There's Serra the captain and our old chum Algaro glowering away."

"They did a neat job of trailing us, I'll say that," Carney said. "Anyway, let's get moving."

"Are we still going to try this South Drop Place?" Dillon asked.

"I'm game if you are. Haul up the anchor."

Noval and Pinto surfaced beside the launch and heaved themselves in as Dillon went into the prow and started to pull in the anchor, only it wouldn't come. "I'll start the engine and try a little movement," Carney said.

It made no difference and Dillon looked up. "Stuck fast."

"Okay." Carney nodded. "One of us will have to go down and pull it free."

"Well that's me obviously." Dillon picked up his jacket and tank. "We need you to handle the boat."

Ferguson said, "Have you got enough air left in that thing?"

Dillon checked. "Five hundred. That's ample."

"Your turn, Brigadier," Carney said. "Get in the prow and haul that anchor up the moment it's free and try not to give yourself a hernia."

"I'll do my best, dear boy."

"One thing, Dillon," Carney called. "You won't have the line to come up on and there's a one- to two-knot current so you'll most probably surface well away from the boat. Just inflate your jacket and I'll come and get you."

As Dillon went in off the stern Algaro said, "What's happening?"

"Probably the anchor got stuck," Noval said.

Dillon had, in fact, reached it at that precise moment. It was firmly wedged in a deep crevasse. Above him Carney was working the boat on minimum engine power, and as the line slackened Dillon pulled the anchor free. It dragged over coral for a moment, then started up. He tried to follow, was aware of the current pushing him to one side and didn't fight it, simply drifted up slowly and surfaced. He was perhaps fifty yards away from *Sea Raider* and inflated his jacket, lifted high on the heavy swell.

The Brigadier had just about got the anchor in and Noval was the first one to spot Dillon. "There he is."

"Wonderful." Algaro shouldered Serra aside and took over the wheel. "I'll show him."

He gunned the engine, the launch bore down on Dillon, who frantically swam to one side, just managing to avoid it. Carney cried out a warning, swinging *Sea Raider* round from the prow, Ferguson almost falling into the sea. Dillon had his left hand raised, holding up the tube that allowed him to expel the air from his buoyancy jacket. The launch swerved in again, brushing him to one side. Algaro, laughing like a maniac, the sound clear across the water, was turning in a wide circle to come in again.

The Brigadier had the AK out of the holdall, was wrestling with it when Carney came down the ladder, his hands sliding on the guard rails. "I know how those things work, you don't, Brigadier."

He put it on full automatic, fired a burst over the launch. Serra was wrestling with Algaro now and Noval and Pinto had hit the deck. Carney fired another careful burst that ripped up some decking in the prow. By that time Dillon had disappeared and Serra had taken over the wheel. He turned in a wide circle and took off at full speed.

Ferguson surveyed the area anxiously. "Has he gone?"

Dillon surfaced some little distance away and Carney put down the AK, went into the lower wheelhouse and took the boat toward him. Dillon came in at the stern and Carney hurried back to relieve him of his jacket and tank.

"Jesus, but that was lively," Dillon said when he reached the deck. "What happened?"

"Algaro decided to run you down," the Brigadier told him.

Dillon reached for a towel and saw the AK. "I thought I heard a little gunfire." He looked up at Carney. "You?"

"Hell, they made me mad," Carney said. "You still want to try South Drop?"

"Why not?" Ferguson looked at the dwindling launch. "I don't think they'll be bothering us again."

"Not likely." Carney pointed south. "Rain squall rolling in and that's good because I know where I'm going and they don't," and he went up the ladder to the flying bridge.

The launch slowed half a mile away and Serra raised the glasses to his eyes and watched *Sea Raider* disappear into the curtain of rain and mist. He checked the screen. "They're moving south."

"Where are they going? Any ideas?" Algaro asked.

Serra took the dive-site handbook from a shelf, opened it and checked the map. "That was French Cap. The only one marked here further out is called South Drop." He riffled through the pages. "Here we are. There's a ridge at about seventy feet, around a hundred and sixty or seventy on one side, then it just drops on the other, all the way to the bottom. Maybe two thousand."

"Could that be it?"

"I doubt it. The very fact that it's in the handbook means it's dived reasonably frequently."

Noval said, "The way it works is simple. Dive masters only bring clients this far out in good weather. Any other kind and the trip is too long and rough, people get sick." He shrugged. "So a place like South Drop wouldn't get dived as often, but Captain Serra is right. The fact that it's in the handbook at all makes it very unlikely the U-boat is there. Somebody would have spotted it years ago."

"And that's a professional's opinion," Serra said. "I think Señor Santiago is right. Carney doesn't know anything. He's just taking them to one or two far-out places for want of something better to do. Señor Santiago thinks the girl is our only chance, so it's a question of waiting for her return."

"I'd still like to teach those swine a lesson," Algaro told him.

"And get shot at again."

"That was an AK Carney was firing, I recognized the sound. He could have knocked us all off." Algaro shrugged. "He didn't and he won't now."

Pinto was reading the section on South Drop in the site guide. "It sounds a good dive," he said to Noval, "except for one thing. It says here that black tip reef sharks have been noted."

"Are they dangerous?" Algaro demanded.

"Depends on the situation. If they get stirred up the wrong way, they can be a real threat."

Algaro's smile was unholy. "Have we still got any of that filthy stuff left you had in the bucket when you were fishing from the launch yesterday?" he asked Noval.

"You mean the bait we were using?" Noval turned to Pinto. "Is there any left?"

Pinto moved to the stern, found a large plastic bucket and took the lid off. The smell was appalling. There were all kinds of cut-up fish in there, mingled with intestines, rotting meat and oil.

"I bet the sharks would like that," Algaro said. "That would bring them in from miles around."

Noval looked horrified. "It would drive them crazy."

"Good, then this is what we do." Algaro turned to Serra. "Once they've stopped, we close in through the rain nice and quietly. We're bound to home in on them with that electronic gadget, am I right?"

Serra looked troubled. "Yes, but . . ."

"I don't want to hear any buts. We wait, give them time to go down, then we go in very fast, dump this shit over the side and get the hell out of it." There was a smile of pure joy on his face. "With any kind of luck Dillon could lose a leg."

The *Sea Raider* was at anchor, lifting in a heavy, rolling swell. Ferguson sat in the deckhouse watching as the other two got ready. Carney opened the deck locker and took out a long tube with a handle at one end.

"Is that what they call an underwater spear gun?" Ferguson asked.

"No, it's a power gun." Carney opened a box of ammunition. "What we call a power-head. Some people use a shotgun cartridge. Me, I prefer a .45ACP. Slide it on the rear chamber here, close her up nice and tight. There's a firing pin in the base. When I jab it against the target, the cartridge is fired, the bullet goes through but the gases blast a hole the size of your hand."

"And good night, Vienna." Dillon pulled on his jacket and tank. "You're going fishing this time?"

"Not exactly. When I was out here last there were reef sharks about and one of them got kind of heavy. I'm just being careful."

Dillon went in first, falling back off the diving platform, swam to the line and went down very quickly. He turned at the anchor and saw Carney following, the power-head in his left hand. He hovered about fifteen feet above Dillon, beckoned and started along the ridge, pausing on the edge of the drop.

The water was gin clear and Dillon could see a long way, the cliff vanishing way below. Carney beckoned again and turned to cross the reef to the shallower side. There was an eagle ray passing in slow motion in the far distance and suddenly a reef shark crossed its path and passed not too far from them. Carney turned, made a dismissive gesture and Dillon followed him to the other side.

Ferguson, aware of the rain in the wind, moved into the deckhouse, found the thermos flask that was full of hot coffee and poured himself a cup. He seemed to hear something, a muted throbbing, moved to the stern and stood there listening. There was a sudden roar as Serra pushed his engine up to full speed. The launch broke from the curtain of rain and cut across *Sea Raider*'s prow. Ferguson swore, dropped the thermos flask and started for the AK in the holdall in the deckhouse, aware of the men on the deck of the launch, the bucket emptying into the water. By the time he had the AK out they were gone, the sound of the engine rapidly disappearing into the rain.

Dillon was aware of something overhead, glanced up and saw the keel of the launch moving fast and then the bait drifting down into the water. He hovered there, watching as a barracuda went in like lightning, tearing at a piece of meat.

He was aware of a tug at his ankle, glanced down and saw Carney gesturing for him to descend. The American was flat on the bottom when Dillon reached him, and above them, there was a sudden turbulence in the water and a shark went in like a torpedo. Dillon lay on his back like Carney, looking up as another shark swerved in, jaws open. And then, to his horror, a third flashed in overhead. They seemed to be fighting amongst themselves and one of them snapped at the barracuda, taking its entire body, leaving only the head to float down.

Carney turned to Dillon, pointed across the ridge to the anchor line, motioned to keep low and led the way. Dillon followed, aware of the fierce turbulence, glanced back and saw them circling each other now and most of the bait had gone. He kept right behind Carney and so low that his stomach scraped the bottom, only starting to rise as they reached the anchor.

Something knocked him to one side with tremendous force, he bounced around as one of the sharks brushed past. It turned and started in again and Carney, above him, a hand on the line, jabbed the power-head. There was an explosion, the shark twisted away, leaving a trail of blood.

The other two sharks circled it, then one went in, jaws open. Carney tugged at Dillon's arm and started up the line. About halfway up Dillon looked down. The third shark had joined in now, tearing at the wounded one, blood in the water like a cloud. Dillon didn't look back after that, surfaced at the dive platform beside Carney and hauled himself on board, tank and all.

He sat on deck, laughing shakily. "Does that happen often?"

"There's a first time for everything." Carney took his tank off. "Nobody tried to do that to me before." He turned to Ferguson. "Presumably that was the launch? I expect the bastard came in on low power, then went up to full speed at the last minute."

"That's it exactly. By the time I got to the AK they were away," Ferguson said.

Carney dried himself and put on a tee-shirt. "I'd sure like to know how they managed to follow us though, especially in this rain and mist."

He went and hauled in the anchor and Dillon said, "I should have told you, Brigadier, I have my ace-in-the-hole stowed under here. Maybe you could have got to it faster."

He ran his hand under the instrument panel to find it and his fingers brushed against the bug. He detached it and held it out to Ferguson in the palm of his hand. "Well, now," Ferguson said, "we're into electronic wizardry, are we?"

"What in the hell have you got there?" Carney demanded as he came round from the prow.

Dillon held it out. "Stuck under the instrument panel on a magnet. We've been bugged, my old son, no wonder they were able to keep track of us so easily. They probably did the same thing to *Privateer* in case we used that."

"But she stayed close inshore this morning."

"Exactly, otherwise they might have got confused."

Carney shook his head. "You know I'm really going to have to do something about these people," and he went up the ladder to the flying bridge.

On the way back to St. John there was a break in the weather, another rain squall sweeping across the water. The launch was well ahead of it, pulled in beside the *Maria Blanco*, and Serra and Algaro went up the ladder and found Santiago in the stern under the awning.

"You look pleased with yourself," he said to Algaro. "Have you been killing people again?"

"I hope so." Algaro related the morning's events.

When he finished, Santiago shook his head. "I doubt whether Dillon sustained any lasting damage, this Carney man knows his business too well." He sighed. "We're wasting our time. There's nothing to be done until the girl returns. We'll run over to Samson Cay, I'm tired of this place. How long will it take, Serra?"

"Two hours, Señor, maybe less. There's a squall out there off Pillsbury Sound, but it's only temporary."

"Good, we'll leave at once. Let Prieto know we're coming." Serra turned away and Santiago said, "Oh, and by the way, phone up one of your fishermen friends in Cruz Bay. I want to know the instant that girl turns up."

The squall was quite ferocious, driving rain before it in a heavy curtain, but having a curious smoothing effect on the surface of the sea. Carney switched off the engines and came down the ladder and joined Ferguson and Dillon in the deckhouse.

"Best to ride this out. It won't last long." He grinned. "Normally I wouldn't carry alcohol, but this being a private charter."

He opened the plastic icebox and came up with three cans of beer. "Accepted gratefully." Ferguson pulled the tab and drank some down. "God, but that's good."

"There are times when an ice-cold beer is the only thing," Carney said. "Once in Vietnam I was in a unit that got mortared real bad. In fact, I've still got fragments in both arms and legs too small to be worth fishing out. I sat on a box in the rain, eating a sandwich while a Corpsman stitched me up and he was out of morphine. I was so glad to be alive I didn't feel a thing. Then someone gave me a can of beer, warm beer, mind you."

"But nothing ever tasted as good?" Dillon said.

"Until the smoke cleared and I saw a guy sitting against a tree with both legs gone." Carney shook his head. "God, how I came to hate that war. After my time I went to Georgia State on the Marines. When Nixon came and the police turned up to beat up the antiwar demonstrators all us veterans wore white tee-shirts with our medals pinned to them to shame them."

He laughed and Ferguson said, "The Hook in Korea was just like that. More bodies than you could count, absolute hell, and you ended up wondering what you were doing there."

"Heidegger once said that for authentic living what is necessary is the resolute confrontation of death," Dillon told them.

Carney laughed harshly. "I know the works of Heidegger, I took a Bachelor of Philosophy degree at Georgia State and I'll tell you this. I bet Heidegger was seated at his desk in the study when he wrote that."

Ferguson laughed. "Well said."

"Anyway, Dillon, what do you know about it? Which was your war?" Carney asked.

Dillon said calmly, "I've been at war all my life." He stood up, lit a cigarette and went up the ladder to the flying bridge.

Carney said, "Hey, wait a minute, Brigadier, that discussion we had about the Irish army last night at Jenny's Place when I made a remark about the IRA? Is that what he is, one of those gunmen you read about?"

"That's what he used to be, though they like to call themselves soldiers of the Irish Republican Army. His father was killed accidentally in crossfire by British soldiers in Belfast when he was quite young so he joined the glorious cause."

"And now?"

"I get the impression that his sympathy for the glorious cause of the IRA has dwindled somewhat. Let's be polite and say he's become a kind of mercenary and leave it at that."

"I'd say that's a waste of a good man."

"It's his life," Ferguson said.

"I suppose so." Carney stood up. "Clearing now. We'd better go."

He went up the ladder to the flying bridge. Dillon didn't say a word, simply sat there in the swivel chair smoking, and Carney switched on the engines and took the *Sea Raider* in toward St. John.

It was perhaps ten minutes later that Carney realized that the motor yacht bearing down on them was the *Maria Blanco*. "Well, damn me," he said. "Our dear old friend Santiago. They must be moving on to Samson Cay."

Ferguson climbed the ladder to the flying bridge to join them and Carney took the *Sea Raider* in so close that they could see Santiago in the stern with Algaro.

Carney leaned over the rail and called, "Have a nice day," and Ferguson lifted his Panama.

Santiago raised his glass to them and said to Algaro, "What did I tell you, you fool. The sharks probably came off worst."

At that moment Serra came along from the radio room and handed him the portable phone. "A call from London, Señor, Sir Francis."

"Francis," Santiago said. "How are you?"

"I was wondering if you'd had any breakthrough yet?"

"No, but there's no need to worry, everything is under control."

"One thing has just occurred to me. Can't imagine why I didn't think of it before. The caretakers of the old hotel at Samson Cay during the war, they were a black couple from Tortola, May and Joseph Jackson. She died years ago, but he's still around. About seventy-two, I think. Last time I saw him he was running a taxi on the Cay."

"I see," Santiago said.

"I mean, he was there when my mother arrived and then Bormann, you take my point. Sorry, I should have thought of it before."

"You should, Francis, but never mind. I'll attend to it." Santiago put the phone down and turned to Algaro. "Another job for you, but there's no rush. I'm going for a lie down. Call me when we get in."

Later in the afternoon Dillon was lying on a sun lounger on the terrace when Ferguson appeared.

"I've just had a thought," the Brigadier said. "This millionaire's retreat at Samson Cay. Might be rather fun to have dinner there. Beard the lion in his den."

"Sounds good to me," Dillon said. "We could fly over if you like. There's the airstrip. I passed over it on my way here and that Cessna of mine can put down on land as well as water."

"Perhaps we can persuade Carney to join us? Ring the front desk on your cellular phone, get the number and ask for the general manager's name."

Which Dillon did, writing the details down quickly. "There you go, Carlos Prieto."

Within two minutes Ferguson was speaking to the gentleman. "Mr. Prieto? Brigadier Charles Ferguson here, I'm staying at Caneel. One of my friends has a floatplane here and we thought it might be rather fun to fly over this evening and join you for dinner. It's a dual-purpose plane. We could put down on your airstrip. There would be three of us."

"I regret, Brigadier, but dining facilities are reserved for our residents."

"What a shame, I'd so hate to disappoint Mr. Santiago."

There was a slight pause. "Mr. Santiago was expecting you?"

"Check with him, do."

"A moment, Brigadier." Prieto phoned the *Maria Blanco*, for Santiago always preferred to stay on board when at Samson Cay. "I'm sorry to disturb you, Señor, but does the name Ferguson mean anything to you?"

"Brigadier Charles Ferguson?"

"He is on the telephone from Caneel. He wishes to fly over in a float-plane, three of them, for dinner."

Santiago laughed out loud. "Excellent, Prieto, marvelous, I wouldn't miss it for the world."

Prieto said, "We look forward to seeing you, Brigadier. At what time may we expect you?"

"Six-thirty or seven."

"Excellent."

Ferguson handed the cellular phone back to Dillon. "Get hold of Carney and tell him to meet us at Jenny's Place at six in his best bib and tucker. We'll have a cocktail and wing our way to Samson Cay. Should be a jolly evening," he said and went out.

TWELVE

It was seven o'clock in the evening when Jenny Grant reached Paris and Charles de Gaulle airport. She returned the hired car, went to the British Airways reservation desk and booked on the next flight to London. It was too late to connect with any flight to Antigua that day, but there was space the following morning on the nine A.M. flight from Gatwick arriving in Antigua just after two in the afternoon, and they even booked her on an onward flight to St. Thomas on one of the Liat inter-island service planes. With luck she would be in St. John by early evening.

She waited for her tickets, went and booked in for the London flight so that she could get rid of her luggage. She went to one of the bars and ordered a glass of wine. Best to stay overnight at Gatwick at one of the airport hotels. She felt good for the first time since she'd heard the news of Henry's death, excited as well, and couldn't wait to get back to St. John to see if she was right. She went and bought a phone card at one of the kiosks, found a telephone and rang Jenny's Place at Cruz Bay. It was Billy Jones who answered.

"Billy? It's me—Jenny."

"My goodness, Miss Jenny, where are you?"

"Paris. I'm at the airport. It's nearly seven-thirty in the evening here. I'm coming back tomorrow, Billy, by way of Antigua, then Liat up to St. Thomas. I'll see you around six."

"That's wonderful. Mary will be thrilled."

"Billy, has a man called Sean Dillon been in to see you? I told him to look you up."

"He sure has. He's been sailing around with Bob Carney, he and a Brigadier Ferguson. In fact, I just heard from Bob. He tells me they're meeting in here, the three of them, for a drink at six o'clock."

"Good. Give Dillon a message for me. Tell him I'm coming back because I think I might know where it is."

"Where what is?" Billy demanded.

"Never mind. Just you give him that message. It's very important."

She put the phone down, picked up her hand luggage and still full of excitement and elation, passed through security into the international lounge.

Ferguson and Dillon parked the jeep in the car park at Mongoose Junction and walked along to Jenny's Place. In blazer and Guards tie, the Panama at a suitable angle, the Brigadier looked extremely impressive. Dillon wore a navy blue silk suit, a white cotton shirt buttoned at the neck. When they entered Jenny's Place the bar was already half-full with the early evening trade. Bob Carney leaned on the bar wearing white linen slacks and a blue shirt, a blazer on the stool beside him.

He turned and whistled. "A regular fashion parade. Thank God I dressed."

"Well, we are meeting the Devil face to face, in a manner of speaking." Ferguson laid his Malacca cane on the bar. "Under the circumstances I think one should make an effort. Champagne, innkeeper," he said to Billy.

"I thought that might be what you'd want. I got a bottle of Pol Roget on ice right here." Billy produced it from beneath the bar and thumbed out the cork. "Now the surprise I've been saving."

"And what's that?" Carney asked.

"Miss Jenny was on the phone from Paris, France. She's coming home. Should be here right about this time tomorrow."

"That's wonderful," Carney said.

Billy filled three glasses. "And she gave me a special message for you, Mr. Dillon."

"Oh, and what would that be?" Dillon inquired.

"She said it was important. She said to tell you she's coming back because she thinks she might know where it is. Does that make any kind of sense to you, because it sure as hell doesn't to me?"

"All the sense in the world." Ferguson raised his glass and toasted the others. "To women in general, gentlemen, and Jenny Grant in particular.

Bloody marvelous." He emptied his glass. "Good, into battle," and he turned and led the way out.

Behind them, the bearded fisherman who had been sitting at the end of the bar listening, got up and left. He walked to a public phone just along the waterfront, took out the piece of paper Serra had given him and rang the *Maria Blanco*. Santiago was in his cabin getting ready for the evening when Serra hurried in carrying the phone.

"What on earth is it?" Santiago demanded.

"My informant in St. John. He just heard Dillon and his friends talking to Jones, the bartender at Jenny's Place. Apparently she was on the phone from Paris, will be in St. John tomorrow evening."

"Interesting," Santiago said.

"That's not all, Señor, she sent a message to Dillon to say she was coming back because she thinks she might know where it is."

Santiago's face was very pale and he snatched the phone. "Santiago here. Now repeat your story to me." He listened and finally said, "You've done well, my friend, you'll be taken care of. Continue to keep your eyes open."

He handed the portable phone to Serra. "You see, everything comes to he who waits," and he turned back to the mirror.

Ferguson, Dillon and Carney crossed from Mongoose and followed the trail to Lind Point toward the seaplane ramp. Ferguson said, "Rather convenient having a ramp here and so on."

"Actually we do have a regular seaplane service some of the time," Carney said. "When it's operating, you can fly to St. Thomas or St. Croix, even direct to San Juan on Puerto Rico."

They reached the Cessna and Dillon walked round checking it generally, then pulled the blocks away from the wheels. He opened the rear door. "Okay, my friends, in you go."

Ferguson went first, followed by Carney. Dillon opened the other door, climbed into the pilot's seat, slammed and locked the door behind him, strapping himself in. He released the brakes and the plane rolled down the ramp into the water and drifted outwards on the current.

Ferguson looked across the bay in the fading light. "Beautiful evening, but I've been thinking. We'll be flying back in darkness."

"No, it's a full moon tonight, Brigadier," Carney told him.

"I checked the weather forecast," Dillon added. "Clear, crisp night, perfect conditions. The flight shouldn't take more than fifteen minutes. Seat belts fastened, life jackets under the seat."

He switched on, the engine coughed into life, the propeller turned. He taxied out of harbor, checked to make sure there was no boat traffic and turned into the wind. They drifted up into the air and started to climb, leveling out at a thousand feet. They passed over part of the southern edge of St. John, then Reef Bay and finally Ram Head before striking out to sea toward Norman Island, Samson Cay perhaps four miles south of it. It was a flight totally without incident, and exactly fifteen minutes after leaving Cruz Bay he was making his first pass over the island. The *Maria Blanco* was lying in the harbor below, three hundred yards off-shore, and there were a number of yachts, still a few people on the beach in the fading light.

"A real rich folks' hideaway," Bob Carney said.

"Is that so?" Ferguson said, unimpressed. "Well I hope they do a decent meal, that's all I'm interested in."

Carlos Prieto came out of the entrance to reception and looked up as the Cessna passed overhead. There was an ancient Ford station wagon parked at the bottom of the steps, an ageing black man leaning against it.

Prieto said, "There they are, Joseph, get up to the airstrip and bring them in."

"Right away, sir." Joseph got behind the wheel and drove off.

As Prieto turned to go inside, Algaro emerged. "Ah, there you are, I've been looking for you. Do we have an old black somewhere around called Jackson, Joseph Jackson?"

"We certainly do. He was the driver of that station wagon that just drove off. He's gone to the airstrip to pick up Brigadier Ferguson and the others. Do you need him for anything important?"

"It can wait," Algaro told him and went back inside.

Dillon put the Cessna down for a perfect landing, taxied toward the other end of the airstrip, turning into the wind, and switched off. "Not bad, Dillon," Ferguson told him. "You can fly a plane, I'll grant you that."

"You've no idea how good that makes me feel," Dillon said.

They all got out and Joseph Jackson came to meet them. "Car waiting right over here, gents. I'll take you down to the restaurant. Joseph's the name, Joseph Jackson. Anything you want, just let me know. I've been around this island longer than anybody."

"Indeed?" Ferguson said. "I don't suppose you were here in the War? I understand it was unoccupied?"

"That ain't so," Jackson said. "There was an old hotel here, belonged to an American family, the Herberts. The hotel was unoccupied during the War, but me and my wife, May, we came over from Tortola to look after things."

They had reached the station wagon and Ferguson said, "Herbert, you say, they were the owners?"

"Miss Herbert's father, he gave it to her as a wedding present, then she married a Mr. Vail." Jackson opened the rear door for Ferguson to get in. "Then she had a daughter."

Dillon sat beside Ferguson and Carney took the front seat beside Jackson. The old boy was obviously enjoying himself.

"So, Miss Herbert became Mrs. Vail, who had a daughter called Miss Vail?" Dillon said.

Jackson started the engine and cackled out loud. "Only Miss Vail then became Lady Pamer, what do you think of that? A real English lady, just like the movies."

"Switch off that engine!" Ferguson ordered.

Jackson looked bewildered. "Did I say something?"

Bob Carney reached over and turned the key. Ferguson said, "Miss Vail became Lady Pamer, you're sure?"

"I knew her, didn't I? She came here at the end of the War with her baby, little Francis. That must have been in April forty-five."

There was a heavy silence. Dillon said, "Was anyone else here at the time?"

"German gent named Strasser. He just turned up one night. I think he got a fishing boat to drop him off from Tortola, but Lady Pamer, she was expecting him . . ."

"And Sir Joseph?"

"He came over from England in June. Mr. Strasser, he moved on. The Pamers left and went back to England after that. Sir Joseph, he used to come back, but that was years ago when the resort was first built."

"And Sir Francis Pamer?" Ferguson asked.

"Little Francis?" Jackson laughed. "He growed up real fine. I've seen him here many times. Can we go now, gents?"

"Of course," Ferguson said.

Jackson drove away, Dillon took out a cigarette and no one said a word until they reached the front entrance. Ferguson produced his wallet, extracted a ten-pound note and passed it to Jackson. "My thanks."

"And I thank you," Jackson told him. "I'll be ready for you gents when you want to go back."

The three of them paused at the bottom of the steps. Dillon said, "So now we know how Santiago comes to be so well informed."

"God in heaven," Ferguson said. "A Minister of the Crown and one of the oldest families in England."

"A lot of those people thought Hitler had the right ideas during the nineteen-thirties," Dillon said. "It fits, Brigadier, it all fits. What about Carter?"

"The British Secret Service was unfortunate enough to employ dear old Kim Philby, Burgess, MacLean, all of whom also worked for the KGB and sold us down the river to Communism without a moment's hesitation. Since then, there was Blunt, rumours of a fifth man, a sixth." Ferguson sighed. "In spite of the fact that I don't care a jot for Simon Carter, I must tell you that I believe he's an old-fashioned patriot and honest as the day is long."

Carlos Prieto appeared at the top of the steps. "Brigadier Ferguson, what a pleasure. Señor Santiago is waiting for you in the bar. He's just come over from the *Maria Blanco*. He prefers to stay on board while he's here."

The lounge bar was busy with the rich and the good as one would expect in such a place. People tended to be older rather than younger, the men especially, mostly American, being rather obviously close to the end of their working lives. There was a preponderance of trousers in fake Scottish plaid swelling over ample bellies, white tuxedos.

"God save me," Dillon said, "I've never seen so many men who resembled dance-band leaders in their prime."

Ferguson laughed out loud and Santiago, who was seated in a booth by the bar, Algaro bending over him, turned to look at them. He stood up and reached out a hand urbanely. "My dear Brigadier Ferguson, such a pleasure."

"Señor Santiago," Ferguson said formally. "I've long looked forward to this meeting." He pointed briefly at Algaro with his Malacca cane. "But do we really have to have this creature present? I mean couldn't he go and feed the fish or something?"

Algaro looked as if he would have liked to kill him on the spot, but Santiago laughed out loud. "Poor Algaro, an acquired taste, I fear."

"The little devil." Dillon wagged a finger at Algaro. "Now go and chew a bone or something, there's a good boy."

Santiago turned and said to Algaro in Spanish, "Your turn will come, go and do as I have told you."

Algaro went out and Ferguson said, "So, here we are. What now?"

"A little champagne perhaps, a pleasant dinner?" Santiago waved to Prieto, who snapped his fingers at a waiter and escorted him with a bottle of Krug in an ice bucket. "One can be civilized, can't one?"

"Isn't that a fact?" Dillon checked the label. "Eighty-three. Not bad, Señor."

"I bow to your judgment." The waiter filled the glasses and Santiago raised his. "To you, Brigadier Ferguson, to the playing fields of Eton and the continued success of Group Four."

"You *are* well informed," the Brigadier said.

"And you, Captain Carney, what a truly remarkable fellow you are. War hero, sea captain, diver of legendary proportions. Who on earth could they get to play you in the movie?"

"I suppose I'd just have to do it myself," Carney told him.

"And Mr. Dillon. What can I say to a man whose only rival in his chosen profession has been Carlos."

"So you know all about us," Ferguson said. "Very impressive. You must need what's in that U-boat very badly indeed."

"Let's lay our cards on the table, Brigadier. You want what should still be in the captain's quarters, Bormann's briefcase containing his personal authorization from the Führer, the Blue Book and the Windsor Protocol."

There was a pause and it was Carney who said, "Interesting, you didn't call him Hitler, you said the Führer."

Santiago's face was hard. "A great man, a very great man who had a vision of the world as it should be, not as it has turned out."

"Really?" Ferguson commented. "I'd always understood that if you counted Jews, Gypsies, Russians and war dead from various countries, around twenty-five million people died to prove him wrong."

"We both want the same thing, you and I," Santiago said. "The contents of that case. You don't want them to fall into the wrong hands. The old scandal affecting so many people, the Duke of Windsor, putting the Royal Family in the eye of the storm again. The media would have a field day. As I say, we both want the same thing. I don't want all that to come out either."

"So the work continues," Ferguson said. "The Kamaraden? How many names are on that list, famous names, old names who have prospered since the War in industry and business, all on the back of Nazi money?"

"Jesus," Dillon said. "It makes the Mafia look like small beer."

"Come now," Santiago told him. "Is any of this important after all these years?"

"It sure as hell must be, either to you or close friends," Carney said, "otherwise why would you go to such trouble?"

"But it is important, Mr. Carney," Ferguson said. "That's the point. If the network continues over the years, if sons become involved, grandsons, people in higher places, politicians, for example." He drank some more champagne. "Imagine, as I say, just for example, having someone high in Government. How useful that would be and then, after so many years, the kind of scandal that could bring everything down around your ears."

Santiago waved for the waiter to pour more champagne. "I thought you might be sensible, but I see not. I don't need you, Brigadier, or you, Mr. Carney. I have my own divers."

"Finding it is not enough." Carney said. "You've got to get into that tin can and that requires expertise."

"I have divers, Mr. Carney, an ample supply of C4, is that the name of the explosive? I only employ people who know what they are doing." He smiled. "But this is not getting us anywhere." He stood up. "At least we can eat like civilized men. Please, gentlemen, join me."

The Ford station wagon slowed to a halt at the side of the air strip, Algaro sitting in the rear behind Joseph Jackson. "Is this where you wanted, mister?"

"I guess so," Algaro said. "Those people you brought in from the plane, what were they like?"

"Nice gentlemen," Jackson said.

"No, what I mean is, were they curious? Did they ask questions?"

Jackson began to feel uncomfortable. "What kind of questions you mean, mister?"

"Let's put it this way," Algaro told him. "They talked and you talked. Now what about?"

"Well the English gentleman, he was interested in the old days. I told him how I was caretaker here in the Herbert place during the big War with my wife."

"And what else did you tell him?"

"Nothing, mister, I swear." Jackson was frightened now.

Algaro put a hand on the back of his neck and squeezed. "Tell me, damn you!"

"It was nothing much, mister." Jackson struggled to get away. "About the Pamers."

"The Pamers?"

"Yes, Lady Pamer and how she came here at the end of the War."

"Tell me," Algaro said. "Tell me everything." He patted him on the side of the face. "It's all right, just tell the truth."

Which Jackson did and when he was finished, Algaro said, "There, that wasn't too bad, was it?"

He slid an arm across Jackson's throat, put his other hand on top of his head and twisted, breaking the neck so cleanly that the old man was dead in a second. He went round, opened the door and pulled the body out. He positioned it with the head just under the car by the rear wheel, took out a flick knife, sprung it and stabbed the point into the rear off-side tire so that it deflated. He got the tool kit out, raised the car on the hydraulic jack, whistling as he pumped it up.

Very quickly, he undid the bolts and removed the tire. He stood back and kicked at the jack and the rear of the station wagon lurched to one side and descended on Jackson. He took out the spare tire and laid it beside the other one, then walked across to the Cessna and stood looking at it for quite some time.

The meal was excellent. West Indian chicken wings with blue cheese, conch chowder followed by baked red snapper. No one opted for dessert and Santiago said, "Coffee?"

"I'd prefer tea," Dillon told him.

"How very Irish of you."

"All I could afford as a boy."

"I'll join you," Ferguson said and at that moment Algaro appeared in the doorway.

"You must excuse me, gentlemen." Santiago got up and went and joined Algaro. "What is it?"

"I found out who the Jackson man was, the old fool driving that Ford taxi."

"So what happened?"

Algaro told him briefly and Santiago listened intently, watching as the waiter took tea and coffee to the table.

"But it means our friends now know that Sir Francis is involved in this business."

"It doesn't make any difference, Señor. We know the girl is returning tomorrow, we know she thinks she knows where the U-boat is. Who needs these people any more?"

"Algaro," Santiago said. "What have you done?"

As Santiago returned to the table, Ferguson finished his tea and stood up. "Excellent dinner, Santiago, but we really must be going."

"What a pity. It's been quite an experience."

"Hasn't it? By the way, a couple of presents for you." Ferguson took the two tracking bugs from his pocket and put them on the table. "Yours, I think. Give my regards to Sir Francis next time you're in touch, or I could give your regards to him."

"How well you put it," Santiago said and sat down.

They reached the front entrance to find Prieto standing at the top of the steps looking flustered. "I'm so sorry, gentlemen, but I've no idea what's happened to the taxi."

"It's of no consequence," Ferguson said. "We can walk there in five or six minutes. Good night to you. Excellent meal," and he went down the steps.

It was Carney who noticed the station wagon just as they reached the air-strip. "What's he doing over there?" he said and called, "Jackson?"

There was no reply. They walked across and saw the body at once. Dillon got down on his knees and got as close as he could. He stood up, brushing his clothes. "He's been dead for some time."

"The poor bastard," Carney said. "The jack must have toppled over."

"A remarkable coincidence," Ferguson said.

"Exactly." Dillon nodded. "He tells us all about Francis Pamer and bingo, he's dead."

"Just a minute," Carney put in. "I mean, if Santiago knew about the old boy's existence, why leave it till now? I'd have thought he'd have got rid of him a lot earlier than this."

"But not if he didn't realize he existed," Ferguson said.

Dillon nodded. "Until somebody told him, somebody who's been feeding all the other information he needed."

"You mean, this guy Pamer?" Carney asked.

"Yes, isn't it perfectly dreadful," Ferguson said. "Just shows you you can't trust anyone these days. Now let's get out of here."

He and Carney got in the rear seats and strapped themselves in. Dillon got a torch from the map compartment and did an external inspection. He came back, climbed into the pilot's seat and closed the door. "Everything looks all right."

"I don't think he'll want to kill us yet," Ferguson said. "All the other little pranks have been aggravation, but he still needs us to hopefully lead him to that U-boat, so let's get moving, there's a good fellow, Dillon."

Dillon switched on, the engine roared into life, the propeller turned. He carefully checked the illuminated dials on the instrument panel. "Fuel, oil pressure." He recited the litany. "Looks good to me. Here we go."

He took the Cessna down the runway and lifted into the night, turning out to sea.

It was a magnificent night, stars glittering in the sky, the sea and the islands below bathed in the hard white light of the full moon. St. John loomed before them. They crossed Ram Head, moving along the southern coast, and it happened, the engine missed a beat, coughed and spluttered.

"What is it?" Ferguson demanded.

"I don't know," Dillon said and then checked the instruments and saw what had happened to the oil pressure.

"We've got problems," he said. "Get your life jackets on."

Carney got the Brigadier's out and helped him into it. "But surely the whole point of these things is that you don't have to crash, you can land on the sea," Ferguson said.

"That's the theory," Dillon told him and the engine died totally and the propeller stopped.

They were at nine hundred feet and he took the plane down in a steep dive. "Reef Bay dead ahead," Carney said.

"Right, now this is how it goes," Dillon told them. "If we're lucky, we'll simply glide down and land on the water. If the waves are too much we might start to tip, so bail out straightaway. How deep is it down there, Carney?"

"Around seven fathoms close in."

"Right, there's a third alternative, Brigadier, and that's going straight under."

"You've just made my night," Ferguson told him.

"If that happens, trust Carney, he'll see to you, but on no account waste time trying to open the door on your way down. It'll just stay closed until we've settled and enough water finds its way inside and equalizes the pressure."

"Thanks very much," Ferguson said.

"Right, here we go."

The surface of the bay was very close now and it didn't look too rough. Dillon dropped the Cessna in for what seemed like a perfect landing and something went wrong straightaway. The plane lurched forward sluggishly, not handling at all, then tipped and plunged beneath the surface nose-down.

The water was like black glass, they were already totally submerged and descending, still plenty of air in the cabin, the lights gleaming on the instrument panel. Dillon felt the water rising up over his ankles and suddenly it was waist deep and the instrument panel lights went out.

"Christ almighty!" Ferguson cried.

Carney said, "I've unbuckled your belt. Be ready to go any second now."

The Cessna, still nose-down, touched at that moment a patch of clear sand at the bottom of the bay, lifted a little, then settled to one side, the tip of the port wing braced against a coral ridge. The rays of the full moon drifting down through the water created an astonishing amount of light and Dillon, looking out through the cockpit window as the water level reached his neck, was surprised at how far he could see.

He heard Carney say, "Big breath, Brigadier, I'm opening the door now. Just slide out through and we'll go up together."

Dillon took a deep breath himself and as the water passed over his head, opened his door, reached for the wing strut and pulled himself out. He turned, still hanging on the strut, saw Carney clutching at the Brigadier's sleeve, kicking away from the wing, and then they started up.

It was usually argued that if you went up too fast and didn't expel air slowly on the way there was a danger of rupturing the lungs, but in a situation like this there was no time for niceties and Dillon floated up, the rays of moonlight filtering down through the clear water, aware of Carney and the Brigadier to the left and above him. It all seemed to happen in slow motion, curiously dreamlike, and then he broke through to the surface and took a deep lungful of salt air.

Carney and Ferguson floated a few yards away. Dillon swam toward them. "Are you all right?"

"Dillon." Ferguson was gasping for breath. "I owe you dinner. I owe you both a dinner."

"I'll hold you to that," Dillon said. "You can take me to the Garrick again."

"Anywhere you want. Now do you think it's possible we could get the hell out of here?"

They turned and swam toward the beach, Carney and Dillon on either side of the older man. They staggered out of the water together and sat on the sand recovering.

Carney said, "There's a house not too far from here. I know the people well. They'll run us into town."

"And the plane?" Ferguson asked.

"There's a good salvage outfit in St. Thomas. I'll phone the boss at home tonight. They'll probably get over first thing in the morning. They've got a recovery boat with a crane that'll lift that baby straight off the bottom." He turned to Dillon. "What went wrong?"

"The oil pressure went haywire and that killed the engine."

"I must say your landing left much to be desired," Ferguson said and stood up wearily.

"It was a good landing," Dillon said. "Things only went sour at the very last moment and there has to be a reason for that. I mean, one thing going wrong is unfortunate, two is highly suspicious."

"It'll be interesting to see what those salvage people find," Carney commented.

As they started across the beach, Dillon said, "Remember when I was checking the plane back at Samson, Brigadier, and you said you didn't think he'd want to kill us yet?"

"So?" Ferguson said. "What's your point?"

"Well I think he just tried."

The man Carney knew at the house nearby got his truck out and ran them down to Mongoose, where they went their separate ways, Carney promising to handle the salvaging of the plane and to report back to them in the morning.

Back at the cottage at Caneel Dillon had a hot shower, standing under it for quite some time thinking about things. Finally, he poured himself a glass of champagne and went and stood on the terrace in the warm night.

He heard his door open and Ferguson came in. "Ah, there you are." He too wore a robe, but also had a towel around his neck. "I'll take a glass of that, dear boy, and also the phone. What time is it?"

"Just coming up to midnight."

"Five o'clock in the morning in London. Time to get up," and Ferguson dialed the number of Detective Inspector Jack Lane's flat.

Lane came awake with a groan, switched on the bedside lamp and picked up the phone. "Lane here."

"It's me, Jack," Ferguson told him. "Still in bed, are we?"

"For God's sake, sir, it's only five o'clock in the morning."

"What's that got to do with it? I've got work for you, Jack. I've discovered how our friend Santiago has managed to stay so well informed."

"Really, sir?" Lane was coming awake now.

"Would you believe Sir Francis Pamer?"

"Good God!" Lane flung the bedclothes to one side and sat up. "But why?"

Ferguson gave him a brief account of what had happened, culminating in old Joseph Jackson's revelations and the plane crash.

Lane said, "It's difficult to believe."

"Isn't it? Anyway, give the Pamer family the works, Jack. Where did old Sir Joseph's money come from, how does Sir Francis manage to live like a prince? Use all the usual sources."

"What about the Deputy Director, sir, do I inform him in any way?"

"Simon Carter?" Ferguson laughed out loud. "He'd go through the roof. It would be at least a week before he could bring himself to believe it."

"Very well, sir. I'll get moving on things right away."

Ferguson said, "So, that's taken care of."

"I've been thinking," Dillon said. "You were right when you said earlier that you didn't think Santiago was ready to kill us yet because he needed us. So, assuming the crash was no accident, I wonder what made him change his mind?"

"I've no idea, dear boy, but I'm sure we'll find out." Ferguson punched the numbers on the cellular phone again. "Ah, Samson Cay Resort? Mr. Prieto, if you please."

A moment later a voice said, "Prieto here."

"Charles Ferguson calling from Caneel. Wonderful evening, excellent meal. Do thank Mr. Santiago for me."

"But of course, Brigadier, it was kind of you to call."

Ferguson replaced the phone. "That will give the bastard pause for thought. Give me another drop of champagne, dear boy, then I'm off to my bed."

Dillon filled his glass. "Not before you tell me something."

Ferguson swallowed half the champagne. "And what would that be?"

"You knew you'd be coming to St. John from the beginning, booked your accommodation at the same time you booked mine and that was before I got here, before it became apparent that Santiago knew my name and who I was and why I was here."

"Which means what?"

Dillon said, "You knew Pamer was up to no good before I left London."

"True," Ferguson said. "I just didn't have any proof."

"But how did you know?"

"Process of elimination, dear boy. After all, who knew about the affair at all? Henry Baker, the girl, Admiral Travers, myself, Jack Lane, you, Dillon, the Prime Minister. Every one of you could be instantly discarded."

"Which only left Carter and Pamer."

"Sounds like an old-fashioned variety act, doesn't it? Carter, as I told you earlier and based on my past experience of the man, is totally honest."

"Which left the good Sir Francis?"

"Exactly and that seemed absurd. As I've said before, a baronet, one of England's oldest families, a Government Minister." He finished his champagne and put the glass down. "But then, as I think the great Sherlock Holmes once said, when you've exhausted all the possibilities, then the impossible must be the answer." He smiled. "Goodnight, dear boy, I'll see you in the morning."

THIRTEEN

The following morning Santiago went for a swim in the sea, then sat in the stern under the awnings, had coffee and toast and a few grapes while he thought about things. Algaro waited by the rail patiently, saying nothing.

"I wonder what went wrong," Santiago said. "After all, it would be unusual for you to make a mistake, Algaro."

"I know my business, I did what was necessary, Señor, believe me."

At that moment Captain Serra presented himself. "I've just had a call from my man in Cruz Bay, Señor. It appears the Cessna crashed in Reef Bay last night, that's on the south coast of St. John. It finished up forty feet down on the bottom. Ferguson, Carney and Dillon all survived.

"Damn them to hell!" Algaro said angrily.

"Soon enough." Santiago sat there, frowning.

Serra said, "Have you any order, Señor?"

"Yes." Santiago turned to Algaro. "After lunch, you take Guerra and go to St. John in the launch. The girl should arrive at around six in the evening."

"You wish us to bring her to you, Señor?"

"That won't be necessary. Just find out what she knows, I'm sure that's not beyond your capability."

Algaro's smile was quite evil. "At your orders, Señor," and he withdrew.

Serra waited patiently while Santiago poured more coffee. "How long will the launch take to make the run to Cruz Bay?" Santiago asked.

"Depending on the weather, two to two and a half hours, Señor."

"About the same time as the *Maria Blanco* would take?"

"Yes, Señor."

Santiago nodded. "I may want to return to our mooring at Paradise some time tonight. I'm not sure. It depends on events. In any case, get me Sir Francis in London."

It took twenty minutes for Serra to run Pamer to earth and he finally located him at a function at the Dorchester. He sounded rather irritated when he came to the phone. "Who is this? I hope it's important, I've got a speech to make."

"Oh, I'm sure you'll do marvelously, Francis."

There was a pause and Pamer said, "Oh, it's you, Max, how are things?"

"We succeeded in locating the old man you mentioned, Jackson. What a mind. Quite remarkable. Remembered everything about nineteen forty-five in sharpest detail."

"Oh, my God," said Pamer.

Santiago, who had never seen any point in not facing up to the facts of any situation, carried on, "Luckily for you, he had an accident when changing a wheel on his car and has gone to a better place."

"Please, Max, I don't want to know this."

"Don't be silly, Francis, this is hold-on-to-your-nerves time, particularly as the old boy told everything he knew to Ferguson before my man helped him on his way. Unfortunate that."

"Ferguson knows?" Pamer felt as if he were about to choke and tore at his tie. "About my mother and father, Samson Cay, Martin Bormann?"

"I'm afraid so."

"But what are we going to do?"

"Get rid of Ferguson obviously, Dillon as well, and Carney. The girl arrives this evening and my information is that she knows where the U-boat is. She'll be of no further use after that, of course."

"For God's sake, no," Pamer implored and suddenly turned quite cold. "I've just thought of something. My secretary asked me if there was anything wrong with my financial affairs this morning. When I asked her why, she told me she'd noticed a trace being run through the computer. I didn't think anything of it. I mean, when you're a Minister, they keep these various checks going for your own protection."

"Right," Santiago said. "Have the source checked at once and report back to me."

He handed the phone to Serra. "You know, Serra," he said, "it's a constant source of amazement to me, the frequency with which I become involved with stupid people."

When Ferguson, Dillon and Carney drove down to Reef Bay in Carney's jeep, they could see the Cessna suspended on the end of the crane at the stern of the salvage boat, clear of the water. There were three men on deck in diving suits and one in a peaked cap, denim shirt and jeans. Carney whistled, the man turned, waved then, dropped into an inflatable at the side of the boat, started the outboard and aimed for shore.

He came up the beach holding Ferguson's Malacca cane, and said to Carney, "This belong to somebody?"

Ferguson reached for it. "I'm deeply indebted to you. Means a great deal to me."

Carney introduced them. "What's the verdict, or haven't you had time yet?"

"Hell, it's open and shut," the salvage captain said and turned to Dillon. "Bo tells me your oil pressure gauge went wild?"

"That's true."

"Not surprising. The filler cap was blown off. That kind of pressure is usually only generated when there's a substantial amount of water in the oil. As the engine heats up, the water turns to steam and there you go."

"Wouldn't you say it was kind of strange to have that much water in the oil?" Carney asked.

"Not for me to say. What is certain is some vandal or other intended you harm. Somebody went to work on the bottom of the floats with what looks like a fire axe, that's why your landing was fouled. The moment you hit the water, it poured into those floats." He shrugged. "The rest, you know. Anyway, we'll haul her back to St. Thomas. I'll arrange repairs and keep you posted." He shook his head. "You guys were real lucky," and he went back to the inflatable and returned to the salvage boat.

They sat in a booth at Jenny's Place and Mary Jones brought them chowder and hunks of French bread. Billy supplied the beer, ice-cold, and shook his head. "You gents must live right. I mean, you shouldn't be here."

He walked away and Dillon said, "So you were wrong, Brigadier, he did try to have us killed. Why?"

"Maybe it had something to do with what that old guy Jackson said," Carney put in.

"Yes, that would be part of it, but I'm still surprised," Ferguson said. "I still thought we had our uses."

"Well, we sure will have when Jenny gets in," Carney told him.

"Let's hope so." The Brigadier raised his arm. "Let's have some more beer, innkeeper, it really is quite excellent."

When Pamer called Santiago back it was six o'clock in the evening in London.

"It couldn't be worse," he said. "That computer trace has been authorized by Detective Inspector Lane, he's Ferguson's assistant at the moment, on temporary loan from Special Branch. It's a check on my family's financial background, Max, searching way back. I'm finished."

"Don't be a fool. Just stay cool. Just think of the time scale. If you consider when Ferguson found out about you, he can only have had time to speak to this Lane and tell him to start digging."

"But what if he's spoken to Simon Carter or the P.M.?"

"If he had, you'd know by now, and why should he? Ferguson's played this whole thing very close to his chest and that's the way he'll continue."

"But what about Lane?"

"I'll have him taken care of."

"For God's sake no," Pamer moaned. "I can't take any more killing."

"Do try to act like a man occasionally," Santiago said. "And you do have one consolation. Once we have the Bormann documents in our hands, the Windsor Protocol should prove a very useful tool to have in your possession, and there must be people whose fathers or grandfathers appear in the Blue Book who'd give anything to prevent that fact coming out." He laughed. "Don't worry, Francis, we'll have lots of fun with this one."

He replaced the phone, thought about it, then picked it up again and dialed another London number. He spoke in Spanish. "Santiago. I have a major elimination for you which must be carried out tonight. A Detective Inspector Jack Lane, Special Branch. I'm sure you can find the address." He handed the phone back to Algaro. "And now, my friend, I think it's time you and Guerra departed for St. John."

It was half-past five when Jenny came in on the ferry to Cruz Bay. It was only a few hundred yards along the front to Jenny's Place and when she went in there were already a few people at the bar, Billy Jones standing behind. He came round to meet her.

"Why, Miss Jenny, it's so good to see you."

"Is Mary here?"

"She sure is. In the kitchen getting things right for this evening. Just go through."

"I will in a moment. Did you speak to Dillon? Did you give him my message?"

"I did. He and that friend of his and Bob Carney have been as thick as thieves these past few days. I don't know what's going on, but something sure is."

"So Dillon and Brigadier Ferguson are still at Caneel?"

"They sure are. You want to get in touch with him?"

"As soon as possible."

"Well you know they don't have telephones in the cottages at Caneel, but Dillon has a cellular phone. He gave me the number." He went behind the bar, opened the cash register drawer and took out a piece of paper. "Here it is."

Mary came through the kitchen door at that moment and came to a dead halt. "Jenny, you're back." She kissed her on the cheek, then held her at arm's length. "You look terrible, honey, what you been doing?"

"Nothing much." Jenny gave her a tired smile. "Just driving halfway across France, then catching a plane to London, another to Antigua, a third to St. Thomas. I've never felt so tired in my life."

"What you need is food, a hot bath and a night's sleep."

"That's a great idea, Mary, but I've things to do. A cup of coffee would be fine. Let me have it in the office, I want to make a telephone call."

Algaro and Guerra had obtained the address of the house at Gallows Point from the fisherman who was Captain Serra's contact in Cruz Bay. They had already paid the place a visit, although Algaro had decided against a forced entry at that time. They went back to the waterfront, watched the ferry come in from St. Thomas and the passengers disembark. Out of the twenty or so passengers only five were white and three of those were men. As the other woman was at least sixty, there was little doubt who the younger one with the suitcase was. They followed her at a discreet distance and saw her go up the steps to the cafe.

"What do we do now?" Guerra asked.

"Wait," Algaro told him. "She'll go to the house sooner or later."

Guerra shrugged, took out a cigarette and lit it and they went and sat on a bench.

Dillon was actually swimming off Paradise Beach, had left the cellular phone with his towel on a recliner on the beach. He heard the phone and swam as fast as he could to the shore.

"Dillon here."

"It's Jenny."

"Where are you?"

"At the bar, I just got in. How have things been?"

"Well, let's say it's been lively and leave it at that. There were people waiting for me the moment I got here, Jenny, the wrong sort of people. There's a man called Santiago, who was responsible for the break-in at Lord North Street, and those two thugs who tried to jump you by the Thames. He's been hanging around here in a motor yacht called the *Maria Blanco* causing us as much trouble as possible."

"Why?"

"He wants Bormann's briefcase, it's as simple as that."

"But how did he know about the U-boat's existence?"

"There was a leak at the London end of things, someone connected with Intelligence. You were right about Bob Carney. Quite a guy, but he's not been able to come up with a solution. Do you really think you can help, Jenny?"

"It's just an idea, so simple that I'm afraid to tell you, so let's leave it until we meet." She glanced at her watch. "Six o'clock. I could do with a hot bath and all the trimmings. Let's say we'll meet here at seven-thirty, and bring Bob."

"Fine by me."

Dillon put the phone down, toweled himself dry, then he picked it up and tried Carney's house at Chocolate Hole. It was a while before he answered. "Dillon here."

"I was in the shower."

"We're in business, Jenny's just phoned me from the bar. She just got in."

"Has she told you where it is?"

"No, she's still being mysterious. She wants to see us at the bar at seven-thirty."

"I'll be there."

Dillon rang off, then hurried back up the slope to the cottage to report to Ferguson.

When Jenny came out of the office Mary was standing at the end of the bar talking to her husband. "You still look like a bad weekend, honey," she said.

"I know. I'm going to walk up to the house, have a shower and put on some fresh clothes, then I'm coming back. I've arranged to meet Dillon, Brigadier Ferguson and Bob Carney at seven-thirty."

"You ain't walking anywhere, honey. Billy, you take her up in the jeep, check out the house. Make sure everything's in order, then bring her back when she's ready. I'll get young Annie from the kitchen to tend bar while you're gone."

"No need for that, Mary," Jenny told her.

"It's settled. Don't give me no argument, girl. Now on your way."

When Jenny emerged from the bar, Billy Jones was at her side carrying the suitcase. Algaro and Guerra followed them at a distance, saw them get in the jeep in the car park at Mongoose Junction and drive away.

"He's taking her up to the house, I bet you," Guerra said.

Algaro nodded. "We'll walk up, it's not far. He'll have left by the time we get there. We'll get her then."

Guerra said, "No sign of Dillon or the other two. That means she hasn't had a chance to speak to them yet."

"And maybe she never will," Algaro told him.

Guerra paused and licked his lips nervously. "Now look, I don't want to get in anything like that, not with any woman. That's bad luck."

"Shut your mouth and do as you're told," Algaro told him. "Now let's get moving."

At the Ministry of Defence, just before midnight, the light still shone from the windows of Ferguson's office overlooking Horse Guards Avenue. Jack Lane finished his preliminary reading of the first facts to emerge from the computer concerning the Pamer family and very interesting reading they made. But he'd done enough for one night. He put them in his briefcase, placed it in the secure drawer of his desk, got his raincoat, switched off the lights and left.

He came out of the Horse Guards Avenue entrance and walked along the pavement. The young man sitting behind the wheel of the stolen Jaguar on the opposite side of the road checked the photo on the seat beside him with a torch, just to make sure, then slipped it into a pocket. He wore glasses and a raincoat over a neat blue suit, looked totally ordinary.

He started the engine, watched Lane cross the road and start along Whitehall Court. Lane was tired and still thinking of the Pamer affair, glanced casually to the right, was aware of the Jaguar, but had plenty of time to cross the road. There was the sudden roar of the engine, he half-turned, too late, the Jaguar hit him with such force that he was flung violently to one side. Lane lay there, trying to push himself up, was aware that the Jaguar was reversing. The rear bumper fractured his skull, killing him instantly, and the car bumped over his body.

The young man got out and walked forward to check that the Inspector was dead. The street was quite empty, only the rain falling as he got back into the Jaguar, swerved around Lane's body and drove away. Five minutes later he dumped the Jaguar in a side street off the Strand and walked rapidly away.

At Gallows Point, Jenny had a long hot shower and washed her hair while downstairs Billy opened shutters to air the rooms, got a broom and swept the front porch. Algaro and Guerra watched from the bushes nearby.

"Damn him, why doesn't he go?" Algaro said.

"I don't know, but I wouldn't advise trying anything with that one," Guerra said. "They tell me he used to be heavyweight boxing champion of the Caribbean."

"I'm frightened to death," Algaro said.

After a while, Jenny came out on the porch and joined Billy. She wore white linen trousers, a short-sleeved blouse, looked fresh and relaxed.

"Now that's better," Billy said.

"Yes, I actually feel human again," she said. "We'll go back now, Billy."

They got in the jeep and drove away and the two men emerged onto the dirt road. "Now what?" Guerra demanded.

"No problem," Algaro said. "We'll get her later. For now, we'll go back to the bar," and they set off down the road.

It was almost dark when Bob Carney went into Jenny's Place and found her serving behind the bar with Billy. She came round and greeted him warmly with a kiss and drew him over to a booth.

"It's good to see you, Jenny." He put a hand on hers. "I was real sorry about Henry. I know what he meant to you."

"He was a good man, Bob, a decent, kind man."

"I saw him on that last morning," Carney told her, "coming in as I was leaving with a dive party. He must have gone out real early. I asked him where he'd been, and he told me French Cap." He shook his head. "Not true, Jenny. Dillon and I checked out French Cap, even had a look at South Drop."

"But they're sites people go to anyway, Bob. That U-boat couldn't have just sat there all those years without someone having seen it."

It was at that moment that Dillon and Ferguson entered. They saw Carney and Jenny at once and came over. Ferguson raised his Panama. "Miss Grant."

She held out a hand to Dillon, he took it for a moment and there was an awkwardness between them. "Did things work out all right?"

"Oh, yes, I saw Henry's sister. Sorry I was so mysterious. The truth is she's a nun, Little Sisters of Pity. In fact she's the Mother Superior."

"I never knew that," Carney said.

"No, Henry never talked about her, he was an atheist, you see. He felt she was burying herself away to no purpose. It led to a rift between them."

Billy came up at that moment. "Can I get you folks some drinks?"

"Later, Billy," she said. "We have business to discuss here."

He went away and Ferguson said, "Yes, we're all ears. Hopefully you're going to tell us the location of U180."

"Yes, Jenny." Bob Carney was excited now. "Where is it?"

"I don't know is the short answer," she said simply.

There was consternation on Ferguson's face. "You don't know? But I was led to believe you did."

Dillon put a restraining hand on the Brigadier's arm. "Give her a chance."

"Let me put it this way," Jenny said. "I think I might know where that information may be found, but it's so absurdly simple." She took a deep breath. "Oh, let's get on with it." She turned to Carney. "Bob, the *Rhoda* is still moored there in the harbor. Will you take us out there?"

"Sure, Jenny."

Carney stood up and Ferguson said, "The *Rhoda*?"

Carney explained. "Henry's boat, the one he was out in that day. Come on, let's go."

They went down the steps to the road and went along the waterfront to the dock, and Algaro and Guerra watched them descend to an inflatable. Carney sat in the stern, started the outboard and they moved out into the harbor.

"Now what?" Guerra asked.

"We'll just have to wait and see," Algaro replied.

Carney switched on the light in the deckhouse and they all crowded in. "Well, Miss Grant," Ferguson said. "We're all here, so what have you got to tell us?"

"It's just an idea." She turned to Carney. "Bob, what do a lot of divers do after a dive?"

"You mean, check their equipment . . ."

She broke in. "Something much more basic. What I'm thinking of is the details of the dive."

Carney said, "Of course."

"What on earth is she getting at?" Ferguson demanded.

"I think I see," Dillon said. "Just like pilots, many divers keep logs. They enter details of each dive they make. It's common practice."

"Henry was meticulous about it," she said. "Usually the first thing he did after getting back on board and drying himself. He usually kept it in here." She opened the small locker by the wheel, reached inside and found it at once. It had a red cover, Baker's name stamped on it in gold. She held it out to Dillon. "I'm afraid I might be wrong. You read it."

Dillon paused, then turned the pages and read the last one. "It says here he made an eighty- to ninety-foot dive at a place called Thunder Point."

"Thunder Point?" Carney said. "I'd never have thought it. No one would."

"His final entry reads: Horse-eyed jacks in quantity, yellow-tail snappers, angel and parrot fish and one type VII German Submarine, U180, on ledge on east face."

"Thank God," Jenny Grant said. "I was right."

There was a profound silence as Dillon closed the log and Ferguson said, "And now I really could do with that drink."

Algaro and Guerra watched them return. Algaro said, "She's told them something, I'm sure of it. You stay here and keep an eye on things while I go down to the public phone and report in."

Inside, they sat at the same booth and when Billy came over Ferguson said. "This time champagne is very definitely in order." He rubbed his hands. "Now we can really get down to brass tacks."

Dillon said to Carney, "You seemed surprised, I mean about the location, this Thunder Point. Why?"

"It's maybe twelve miles out. That's close to the edge of things. I've never dived there. No one dives there. It's the most dangerous reef in this part of the world. If the sea is at all rough, it's a hell of a haul to get there and when you do, the current is fierce, can take you every which way."

"How do you know this if you've never dived it?" Dillon asked.

"There was an old diver here a few years back, old Tom Poole. He's dead now. He dived it on his own years back. He told me he happened to be that far out by chance and realized it was calmer than usual. From what he said it's a bit like South Drop. A reef around seventy feet, about a hundred and eighty feet on one side and two thousand on the other. In spite of the weather being not too bad, the old boy nearly lost his life. He never tried again."

"Why didn't he see the U-boat?" Ferguson demanded.

"Maybe he just didn't get that far, maybe it's moved position since his time. The one thing we know for sure is it's there because Henry found it," Carney told him.

"I just wonder why he even attempted such a dive," Jenny said.

"You know what Henry was like," Carney told her. "Always diving on his own when he shouldn't, and that morning, after the hurricane, the sea was calmer than I've ever seen it. I figure he was just sailing out there for the pure joy of it, realized where he was and saw that conditions were exceptional. In those circumstances he would have dropped his hook on that reef and been over the side in no time at all."

"Well, according to Rear Admiral Travers," Dillon said, "and he talked extensively to Baker, Bormann was using the captain's cabin except that it wasn't really a cabin. It just had a curtain across. It's on the port side opposite the radio and sound room, that's in the forward part of the boat. The idea of having it there was so the captain had instant access to the control room."

"That seems reasonably straightforward to me," Carney said.

"Yes, but the only access from the control room is by the forward watertight hatch and Baker told Travers it was corroded to hell, really solid."

"Okay," Carney said, "so we'll have to blow it. C4 is the thing, the stuff Santiago was going on about when we were at Samson."

"I'm ahead of you there," Dillon told him. "I couldn't get hold of any C4, but I thought Semtex would be an acceptable substitute. I've also got chemical detonating pencils."

"Is there anything you forgot?" Carney asked ironically.

"I hope not."

"So when do we go?" Ferguson demanded.

Dillon said, "I'd say that's up to Carney here, he's the expert."

Carney nodded, slightly abstracted. "I'm thinking about it." He nodded again. "The way I see it, we want to be in and out before Santiago even knows what's going on."

"That makes sense," Ferguson agreed.

"They can't track us any longer because we got rid of the bugs in both boats. We could capitalize on that by leaving around midnight, making the trip under cover of darkness. Dawn at five to five-thirty. We could go down at first light."

"Sounds good to me," Dillon said.

"Right, I left *Sea Raider* at Caneel Bay this evening so we'll leave from there. You'll need to pick up that Semtex you mentioned. Any extras we need I can get from the dive shop."

"But not right now," Ferguson told him. "Now we eat. All this excitement has given me quite an appetite."

It started to rain a little and Algaro and Guerra sheltered under a tree. "Mother of God, is this going to take all night?" Guerra demanded.

"It takes as long as is needed," Algaro told him.

Inside, they had dined well on Mary's best chowder and grilled snapper, were at the coffee stage when Dillon's cellular phone rang. He answered it, then handed it across to Ferguson. "It's for you. Somebody from Special Branch in London."

The Brigadier took the phone. "Ferguson here." He listened and suddenly turned very pale and his shoulders sagged. "Just a moment," he said wearily and got up. "Excuse me. I'll be back," and he went out.

"What in the hell is that all about?" Carney asked.

"Well, it's not good, whatever it is," Dillon said. Ferguson returned at that moment and sat down.

"Jack Lane, my assistant, is dead."

"Oh, no," Jenny said.

"Hit-and-run accident round about midnight. He'd been working late, you see. The police have found the car dumped in a side street off the Strand. Blood all over it. Stolen of course."

"Another remarkable coincidence," Dillon said. "You tell him to check up on Pamer and in no time he's lying dead in a London side street."

It was the first time he'd seen real anger in Ferguson's face. Something flared in the Brigadier's eyes. "That hadn't escaped me, Dillon. The bill will be paid in full, believe me."

He took a deep breath and stood up. "Right, let's get going. Are you coming with us, my dear?"

"I don't think so," Jenny told him. "That kind of boat ride is the last thing I need after what I've been through, but I'll come and see you off. I'll follow you in my jeep. You carry on, I'll catch you up, I just want a word with Mary."

She went into the kitchen and Dillon beckoned Billy to the end of the bar. "Do you think you and Mary could spend the night at Jenny's house?"

"You think there could be a problem?"

"We've had too many for comfort," Ferguson told him.

Dillon took the Belgian semi-automatic from his pocket. "Take this."

"That bad?" Billy inquired.

"That bad."

"Then this is better." Billy took a Colt .45 automatic from under the counter.

"Fine." Dillon slipped the Belgian semi-automatic back in his pocket. "Take care. We'll see you in the morning."

In the kitchen Mary was working hard at the stove. "What you doing now, girl?"

"I've got to go up to Caneel, Mary, Bob Carney is taking the Brigadier and Mr. Dillon on a special dive. I want to see them off."

"You should be in bed."

"I know. I'll go soon."

She went out through the bar and hurried down the steps. Algaro said, "There she is. Let's get after her."

But Jenny started to run, catching Ferguson, Dillon and Carney at Mongoose Junction. Algaro and Guerra watched as their quarry got into her jeep, Carney at her side, and followed Dillon and Ferguson out of the car park.

"All right," Algaro said. "Let's get after them," and they ran toward their own vehicle.

At the cottage, Dillon got the olive-green army holdall, took everything out, the Semtex and fuses, the AK, and the Walther and its silencer. Ferguson came in as he was finishing, wearing cord slacks, suede desert boots and a heavy sweater.

"Are we going to war again?" he asked.

Dillon stowed everything back in the holdall. "I hope not. Carney and I are going to have enough on our plate just making the dive, but you know where everything is if you need it."

"You think you can pull it off?"

"We'll see." Dillon found his tracksuit top. "I'm sorry about Lane, Brigadier."

"So am I."

Ferguson looked bleak. "But our turn will come, Dillon, I promise you. Now let's get on with it."

As they made for the door, Dillon paused and opened the bar cupboard. He took out half a bottle of brandy and dropped it into the holdall. "Purely medicinal," he said and held the door open. "It's going to be bloody cold down there at that time of the morning."

Carney had brought the *Sea Raider* in to the end of the dock at Caneel. Jenny was sitting on a bench looking down at the boat as he checked the air tanks. A three-piece band was playing in the bar, music and laughter drifting over the water on the night air. Ferguson and Dillon walked along the front, passed the Beach Terrace Restaurant and came along the dock. Ferguson stepped on board and Dillon passed him the holdall.

He turned to Jenny. "Are you all right?"

"Fine," she said.

"Not long now," Dillon told her. "As some poet put it, 'all doubts resolved, all passion spent.'"

"And then what will you do?" she asked.

Dillon kissed her briefly on the cheek. "Jesus, girl, will you give a man a chance to draw breath?"

He took the Belgian semi-automatic out of his pocket. "Put that in your purse and don't tell me you don't know what to do with it. Just pull the slider, point and fire."

She took it reluctantly. "You think this is necessary?"

"You never can tell. Santiago has been ahead of us too many times. When you get back to the bar you'll find that Billy and Mary intend to spend the night with you."

"You think of everything, don't you?"

"I try to. It would take a good man to mess with Billy."

He stepped on board and Carney looked down at them from the flying bridge. "Cast off for us, Jenny."

He switched on the engines, she untied the stern line and handed it to Dillon, went and did the same with the other. The boat drifted out, then started to turn away.

"Take care, my dear," Ferguson called.

She raised an arm as *Sea Raider* moved out to sea. Dillon looked back at her, standing there under the light at the end of the dock, and then she turned and walked away.

She went past the bar and the shop, and started up the path past the Sugar Mill Restaurant to the car park where the taxis waited. Algaro and Guerra had watched the departure from the shadows and now they followed her.

"What shall we do?" Guerra whispered.

"She's bound to go home sooner or later," Algaro said. "The best place to deal with her, all nice and quiet and we don't even need to follow her."

Jenny got into her jeep and started the engine and they waited until she was driving away before moving toward their own vehicle.

There were still a few people in the bar when she went in and Mary was helping one of the waitresses to clear the tables. She came to the end of the bar and Billy joined them.

"They got off all right then?" Billy asked.

"That's right."

"Are we going to be told what they're up to, Miss Jenny? Everyone is sure acting mighty mysterious."

"Maybe one of these days, Billy, but not right now."

She yawned, feeling very tired, and Mary said, "Don't you hold her up with any damn fool questions, she needs her sleep." She turned to Jenny. "Mr. Dillon asked us to spend the night with you and that's what we're going to do."

"All right," Jenny said. "I'll go on up to the house."

"Maybe you should wait for us, Miss Jenny," Billy told her. "It will only take us five minutes to close."

She opened her purse and took out the Belgian semi-automatic. "I've got this, Billy, and I know how to use it. I'll be fine. I'll see you soon."

She'd parked the jeep right outside at the bottom of the steps and she slid behind the wheel, turned on the engine and drove away, so tired that for a moment she forgot to switch on the lights. The streets were reasonably quiet now as she drove out toward Gallows Point and she was at the house in five minutes. She parked in the driveway, went up the steps, found her key and unlocked the front door. She switched on the porch light, then went in.

God, but she was tired, more tired than she had ever been, and she mounted the stairs wearily, opened her bedroom door and switched on the light. It was hot, very hot in spite of the ceiling fan, and she crossed to the French windows leading to the balcony and opened them. There were a few heavy spots of rain and then a sudden rush, the kind of thing that happened at night at that time of year. She stood there for a moment enjoying the coolness, then turned and found Algaro and Guerra standing just inside the room.

It was as if she was dreaming, but that terrible face told her otherwise, the cropped hair, the scar from the eye to the mouth. He laughed suddenly and said to Guerra in Spanish, "This could prove interesting."

And Jenny, in spite of her tiredness, surprised even herself by darting forward and around them to the door, almost made it, and it was Guerra who caught her right wrist and swung her around. Algaro struck her heavily across the face, then hurled her back on the bed. She tried to pull the gun from her purse. He took it from her, turned her on her face, pulling her left arm up, twisted and applied some special kind of leverage. The pain was terrible and she cried out.

"You like that, eh?" Algaro was enjoying himself and tossed the gun across the room. "Let's try some more."

And this time, the pain was the worst thing she'd ever known and she screamed at the top of her voice. He turned her over, slapped her heavily again and took a flick knife from his pocket. When he jumped the blade she saw that it was razor sharp. He grabbed a handful of her hair.

"Now I'm going to ask you some questions." He stroked the blade across her cheek and pricked it gently with the needle point so that blood came. "If you refuse to answer, I'll slit your nose and that's just for starters."

She was only human and terrified out of her mind. "Anything," she pleaded.

"Right. Where would we find the wreck of U180?"

"Thunder Point," she gasped.

"And where would that be?"

"It's on the chart. About ten or twelve miles south of St. John. That's all I know."

"Dillon, the Brigadier and Carney, we saw them leave from the dock at Caneel Bay. They've gone to Thunder Point to dive on the U-boat, is that right?" She hesitated and he slapped her again. "Is that right?"

"Yes," she said. "They're diving at first light."

He patted her face, closed the knife and turned to Guerra. "Lock the door."

Guerra seemed bewildered. "Why?"

"I said lock the door, idiot." Algaro walked past him and swung it shut, turning the key. He turned and his smile was the cruellest thing Jenny had ever seen in her life. "You did say you'd do anything?" and he started to take his jacket off.

She screamed again, totally hysterical now, jumped to her feet, turned and ran headlong through the open French windows on to the balcony in total panic, hit the railings and went over, plunging down through the heavy rain to the garden below.

Guerra knelt beside her in the rain and felt for a pulse. He shook his head. "She looks dead to me."

"Right, leave her there," Algaro said. "That way it looks like an accident. Now let's get out of here."

The sound of their jeep's engine faded into the night and Jenny lay there, rain falling on her face. It was only five minutes later that Billy and Mary Jones turned into the drive in their jeep and found her at once, lying half across a path, half on grass. "My God." Mary dropped to her knees and touched Jenny's face. "She's cold as ice."

"Looks like she fell from the balcony," Billy said.

At that moment Jenny groaned and moved her head slightly. Mary said, "Thank God, she's alive. You carry her inside and I'll phone for the doctor," and she ran up the steps into the house.

FOURTEEN

lgaro spoke to Santiago from a public telephone on the waterfront. Santiago listened intently to what he had to say. "So, the girl is dead? That's unfortunate."

"No sweat," Algaro told him. "Just an accident, that's how it will look. What happens now?"

"Stay where you are and phone me back in five minutes."

Santiago put the phone down and turned to Serra. "Thunder Point, about ten or twelve miles south of St. John."

"We'll have a look on the chart, Señor." Santiago followed him along to the bridge and Serra switched on the light over the chart table. "Ah, yes, here we are."

Santiago had a look, frowning slightly. "Dillon and company are on their way there now. They intend to dive at first light. Is there any way we could beat them to it if we left now?"

"I doubt it, Señor, and that's open sea out there. They'd see the *Maria Blanco* coming for miles."

"I take your point," Santiago said, "and, as we learned the other day, they're armed." He examined the chart again and nodded. "No, I think we'll let them do all the work for us. If they succeed, it will make them feel good. They'll sail back to St. John happy, maybe even slightly off-guard because they will think they have won the game."

"And then, Señor?"

"We'll descend on them when they return to Caneel, possibly at the cottage. We'll see."

"So, what are your orders?"

"We'll sail back to St. John and anchor off Paradise Beach again." The phone was ringing in the radio room. "That will be Algaro calling back," and Santiago went to answer it.

Algaro replaced the phone and turned to Guerra. "They intend to let those bastards get on with it and do all the work. We'll hit them when they get back."

"What, just you and me?"

"No, stupid, the *Maria Blanco* will be back off Paradise Beach in the morning. We'll rendezvous with her then. In the meantime, we'll go back to the launch and try to catch a little shut-eye."

Jenny's head, resting on the pillow, was turned to one side. She looked very pale, made no movement even as the doctor gave her an injection. Mary said, "What do you think, Doctor?"

He shook his head. "Not possible to make a proper diagnosis at this stage. The fact that she's not regained consciousness is not necessarily bad. No overt signs of broken bones, but hairline fractures are always possible. We'll see how she is in the morning. Hopefully she'll have regained consciousness by then." He shook his head. "That was a long fall. I'll have her transferred to St. Thomas Hospital. She can have a scan there. You'll stay with her tonight?"

"Me and Billy won't move an inch," Mary told him.

"Good." The doctor closed his bag. "The slightest change, call me."

Billy saw him out, then came back up to the bedroom. "Can I get you anything, honey?"

"No, you go and lie down, Billy, I'll just sit here with her," Mary said.

"As you say."

Billy went out and Mary put a chair by the bed, sat down and held Jenny's hand. "You'll be fine, baby," she said softly. "Just fine. Mary's here."

At three o'clock they ran into a heavy squall, rain driving in under the canopy over the flying bridge, stinging like bullets. Carney switched off the engine. "We'll be better off below for a while."

Dillon followed him down the ladder and they went into the deckhouse where Ferguson lay stretched out on one of the benches, his head propped up against the holdall. He yawned and sat up. "Is there a problem?"

Sea Raider swung to port, buffeted by the wind and rain. "Only a squall," Carney said. "It'll blow itself out in half an hour. I could do with a coffee break anyway."

"A splendid idea."

Dillon found the thermos and some mugs and Carney produced a plastic box containing ham and cheese sandwiches. They sat in companionable silence for a while eating them, the rain drumming against the roof.

"It's maybe time we discussed how we're going to do this thing," Carney said to Dillon. "For a no-decompression dive at eighty feet, we're good for forty minutes."

"So a second dive would be the problem?"

Ferguson said, "I don't understand the technicalities, would someone explain?"

"The air we breathe is part oxygen, part nitrogen," Carney told him. "When you dive, the pressure causes nitrogen to be absorbed by the body tissues. The deeper you go, the increase in pressure causes more nitrogen to be absorbed. If you're down too long or come up too quickly, it can form bubbles in your blood vessels and tissues, just like shaking a bottle of club soda. The end result is decompression sickness."

"And how can you avoid that?"

"First of all by limiting the time we're down there, particularly on the first dive. Second time around, we might need a safety stop at fifteen feet."

"And what does that entail?" Ferguson asked.

"We rise to that depth and just stay there for a while, decompressing slowly."

"How long for?"

"That depends."

Dillon lit a cigarette, the Zippo flaring in the gloom. "What we're really going to have to do is find that submarine fast."

"And lay the charge on the first dive down," Carney said.

"Baker did say it was lying on a ledge on the east face."

Carney nodded. "I figure that to be the big drop side so we won't waste time going anywhere else." He swallowed his coffee and got up. "If we had the luck, went straight down, got in the control room and laid that Semtex . . ." He grinned. "Hell, we could be in like Flynn and out and back up top in twenty minutes."

"That would make a big difference to the second dive," Dillon said.

"It surely would." The rain had stopped, the sea was calm again now and Carney glanced at his watch. "Time to get moving, gents," and he went back up the ladder to the flying bridge.

———

In London it was nine o'clock in the morning and Francis Pamer was just finishing a delicious breakfast of scrambled eggs and bacon which his housekeeper had prepared when the phone rang. He picked it up. "Pamer here."

"Simon Carter."

"Morning, Simon," Pamer said, "any word from Ferguson?"

"No, but something rather shocking which affects Ferguson has happened."

"What would that be?"

"You know his assistant, the one he borrowed from Special Branch, Detective Inspector Lane?"

Pamer almost choked on the piece of toast he was eating. "Yes, of course I do," he managed to say.

"Killed last night when he was leaving the Ministry of Defence around midnight. Hit and run. Stolen car apparently, which the police have recovered."

"How terrible."

"Thing is, Special Branch aren't too happy about it. It seems the preliminary medical report indicates that he was hit twice. Of course, that could simply mean the driver panicked and reversed or something. On the other hand, Lane sent a lot of men to prison. There must be many who bore him a grudge."

"I see," Pamer said. "So Special Branch are investigating?"

"Oh, yes, you know what the police are like when one of their own gets hit. Free for lunch, Francis?"

"Yes," Pamer said. "But it would have to be at the House. I'm taking part in the debate on the crisis in Croatia."

"That's all right. I'll see you on the Terrace at twelve-thirty."

Pamer put the phone down, his hand shaking, and looked at his watch. No sense in ringing Santiago now, it would be four in the morning over there. It would have to wait. He pushed his plate with the rest of his breakfast on it away from him, suddenly revolted, bile rising in his throat. The truth was he had never been so frightened in his life.

Way over toward the east the sun was rising as *Sea Raider* crept in toward Thunder Point, Carney checking the fathometer. "There it is," he said as he saw the yellow ridged lines on the black screen. "You get to the anchor," he told Dillon. "I'll have to do some maneuvering so you can hit that ridge at seventy feet."

There was a heavy swell, the boat, with the engines throttled back, just about holding her own. Dillon felt the anchor bite satisfactorily, called up to Carney on the flying bridge and the American switched off the engines.

Carney came down the ladder and looked over the side. "There's a rough old current running here. Could be three knots at least."

Ferguson said, "I must say the water seems exceptionally clear. I can see right down to the reef."

"That's because we're so far from the mainland," Carney said. "It means there is very little particulate matter in the water. In fact, it gives me an idea."

"What's that?" Dillon asked.

Carney took off his jeans and tee-shirt. "This water is so clear, I'm going to go trolling. That means I'll stay at less than ten feet, work my way across and locate the edge of the cliff. If I'm lucky and the water down there is as clear as it looks, I might manage to pinpoint the U-boat."

He zipped up his diving suit and Dillon helped him into his tank. "Do you want a line?"

Carney shook his head. "I don't think so."

He pulled on his mask, sat on the high thwart, waited for the swell to rise high and went over backwards. The water was so clear that they could mark his progress for a while.

"What's the point of all this?" Ferguson asked.

"Well, by staying at such a shallow depth, it will have no effect on the diving later. It could save time, and time is crucial on this one, Brigadier. If we use too much of it, we just wouldn't be able to dive again, perhaps for many hours."

Carney surfaced a hundred yards away and waved his arms. Ferguson got out the old binoculars and focused them. "He's beckoning."

Carney's voice echoed faintly. "Over here."

Dillon switched on the engines by the deckhouse wheel and throttled down. "Try and get the anchor up, Brigadier, I'll do my best to give you a bit of movement."

Ferguson went round to the prow and got to work, while Dillon tried to give him some slack. Finally, it worked, the Brigadier shouted in triumph and hauled in. Dillon throttled down and coasted toward Carney.

When they came alongside, the American called, "Drop the hook right here."

Ferguson complied, Dillon switched off the engine, Carney swam around to the dive platform, slipped off his jacket and climbed aboard.

"Clearest I've ever seen," he said. "We're right on the edge of the cliff. There's been a lot of coral damage recently, maybe because of the hurricane, but I swear I can see something sticking out over a ledge."

"You're sure?" Ferguson demanded.

"Hell, nothing's certain in this life, Brigadier, but if it is the U-boat, we can go straight down and be inside in a matter of minutes. Could make all the difference. Now let's see what you've got in the bag, Dillon."

Dillon produced the Semtex. "It'll work better if it's rolled into a rope and placed around the outer circle of the hatch."

"You would know, would you?" Carney asked.

"I've used the stuff before."

"Okay, let's have a look at those chemical detonating fuses." Dillon passed them to him and Carney examined them. "These are good. I've used them before. Ten- or thirty-minute delay. We'll use a ten."

Dillon was already into his diving suit and now he sliced a large section off the block of Semtex and first kneaded it, then rolled it between his hands into several long sausages. He put it into his dive bag with the detonating fuses.

"I'm ready when you are."

Carney helped him on with his gear, then handed him an underwater spot lamp. "I'll see you at the anchor and remember, Dillon, speed is everything, and be prepared for that current."

Dillon nodded and did what Carney had done, simply sat on the thwart, waited until the swell lifted and went in backwards.

The water was astonishingly clear and very blue, the ridge below covered with elkhorn coral and large basket sponges in muted shades of orange. As he waited at the anchor, a school of barracuda-like fish called sennet moved past him and when he looked up, there were a number of large jacks overhead.

The current was strong, so fierce that when he held on to the anchor chain his body was extended to one side. He glanced up again and Carney came down toward him, paused for a moment, already drifting sideways, and gestured. Dillon went after him, checking his dive computer, noting that he was at sixty-five feet, followed Carney over the edge of the cliff, looking down into the blue infinity below and saw, to the left, the great scar where the coral had broken away, the bulk of U180, the prow sticking out from the ledge.

They descended to the conning tower, held on to the top of the bridge rail, dropped down from the high gun platform to the ragged fifteen-foot gash in the hull below the conning tower. Dillon hovered as Carney went inside, checked his dive computer and saw that it was seven minutes since leaving *Sea Raider*. He switched his spot lamp on and went after the American.

It was dark and gloomy, a confusion of twisted metal in spite of the illumination from Carney's lamp. He was crouched beside the forward hatch, trying to turn the unlocking wheel with no success.

Dillon opened his dive bag, took out the Semtex and handed a coil to Carney. They worked together, Dillon taking the top of the hatch, Carney the bottom, pressing the plastic of the explosive in place until they had completed a full circle. They finished, Carney turned and held out a gloved hand. Dillon passed him two of the chemical detonating pencils. Carney paused, broke the first one and pushed it onto the Semtex at the top of the circular hatch. A small spiral of bubbles appeared at once. Carney did the same at the bottom of the circle with the other.

Dillon glanced at his computer. Seventeen minutes. Carney nodded and Dillon turned and went out through the rent, rose to the edge of the cliff, went straight to the anchor and started up the line, holding on with one hand, Carney just behind him. As they left the line at fifteen feet and moved under the keel of the stern, he checked the computer again. Twenty-one minutes. He broke through to the surface, slipped out of his jacket and climbed on to the diving platform.

You found it?" Ferguson demanded.

"Just like Carney said," Dillon told him. "In like Flynn and out again. Twenty minutes, that's all. Just twenty bloody minutes."

Carney was changing the tanks for fresh ones. "Sweet Jesus, I've never seen such a sight. I've been diving twenty years or more and I've got to tell you, I've never seen anything to beat that."

Dillon lit a cigarette with his Zippo. "Santiago, eat your heart out."

"I'd like to take him down, weight him with lead and leave him inside," Carney said, "except it would be an insult to brave sailors who died down there."

The surface of the sea lifted, spray scattering, foam appeared, moved outwards in concentric circles over the swell. They stood at the rail watching until the activity dwindled.

Finally Carney said, "That's it. Let's get moving."

They got their diving gear on again. Dillon said, "What happens now? I mean, how long?"

"If we're lucky and we find what we want straightaway, then there's no problem. The whole forward part of the boat has been sealed all these years." Carney tightened his weight belt. "That should mean no silt, very little detritus. Human remains will have dissolved years ago except for a few bones. In other words, it should be relatively clear." He sat on the thwart and pulled on his fins. "If I think we should stop on the way back, I'll just signal and hang in there."

Dillon followed him down, aware of motion in the water, some sort of current like shockwaves that hadn't been there before. Carney hovered over the edge of the cliff and when Dillon joined him, he saw the problem at once. The force of the explosion had caused the U-boat to move, the stern had lifted, the prow, stretching out over that 2,000-feet drop, was already dipping.

They held on to the bridge rail beside the gun and Dillon could actually feel the boat move. He looked at Carney and the American shook his head. He was right, of course, another few feet higher at the stern and U180 would slide straight over into oblivion, and Dillon couldn't accept that.

He turned to go down, was aware of Carney's restraining hand, managed to pull free and jack-knifed, heading for the rent in the hull, pulling himself into the control room. Everything was stirring with the effects from the explosion, the movement of the boat. He switched on his spot lamp and moved forward and saw the great ragged hole where the hatch cover had been.

It was dark in there, far murkier than he had expected, again from the effects of the explosion. He shone his spotlight inside and as he pulled himself through was aware of a strange, eerie noise as if some living creature was groaning in pain, was aware of the boat moving, lurching a little. Too late to retreat now and his own stubbornness refused to let him.

The radio and sound room was on the right, the captain's quarters opposite to his left, no curtain left now, long since decayed over the years. There was a metal locker, a door hanging off, the skeleton of a bunk. He splayed the beam of the torch around and saw it lying in the corner, coated with filth, a metal briefcase with a handle, just like the one Baker had taken to London.

He ran a hand across it, silver gleamed dully, and then the floor tilted at an alarming angle and everything seemed to be moving. He bounced against the bulkhead, dropping the case, grabbed it again, turned and started through the hatch. His jacket snagged and he stopped dead, struggling frantically, aware of the boat tilting farther. And then Carney was in front of him, reaching through to release him.

The American turned and made for that gash in the hull and Dillon went after him, the whole boat tilting now, sliding, the strange, groaning noises, metal scraping across the edge, and Carney was through, drifting up, and Dillon rose to join him, hovering on the edge of the cliff, and as they turned to look down, the great whalelike shape of U180 slid over the edge and plunged into the void.

Carney made the okay sign, Dillon responded, then followed him across the ridge to the anchor line. He checked his computer. Another twenty minutes, which was fine, and he followed up the line slowly, but Carney was taking no chances. At fifteen feet he stopped and looked down. Dillon nodded, moved up beside him and raised the briefcase in his right hand. He could tell that Carney was smiling.

They stayed there for five minutes, then surfaced at the stern to find Ferguson leaning over anxiously. "Dear God. I thought the end of the world had come," he said.

They stowed the gear, made everything shipshape. Carney pulled on jeans and a tee-shirt, Dillon his tracksuit. Ferguson got the thermos, poured coffee and added brandy from the half-bottle.

"The whole bloody sea erupted," he said. "Never seen anything like it. Sort of boiled over. What happened?"

"She was lying on a ledge, Brigadier, you knew that," Carney said. "Already sticking right out, and the force of the explosion made her start to move."

"Good God!"

Carney drank some of the coffee. "Christ, that's good. Anyway, this idiot here decided he was going to go inside anyway."

"Always suspected you were a fool, Dillon," Ferguson told him.

"I got the briefcase, didn't I? It was in the corner of the captain's quarters on the floor, and then the whole damn boat started to go, taking me with it because I got snagged trying to get back out of the hatch."

"What happened?"

"A mad, impetuous fool called Bob Carney who'd decided to follow me and pulled me through."

Carney went and looked over the side, still drinking his coffee. "A long, long way down. That's the last anyone will ever see of U180. It's as if she never existed."

"Oh, yes, she did," Ferguson said. "And we have this to prove it," and he held up the briefcase.

There wasn't much encrusting. Carney got a small wire brush from the tool kit and an old towel. The surface cleaned up surprisingly well, the Kriegsmarine insignia clearly etched into the right-hand corner. Carney unfastened the two clips and tried to raise the lid. It refused to move.

"Shall I force it, Brigadier?"

"Get on with it," Ferguson told him, his face pale with excitement.

Carney pushed a thin-bladed knife under the edge by the lock, exerted pressure. There was a cracking sound and the lid moved. At that moment it started to rain. Ferguson took the briefcase into the deckhouse, sat down with it on his knees and opened it.

The documents were in sealed envelopes. Ferguson opened the first one, took out a letter and unfolded it. He passed it to Dillon. "My German is a little rusty, you're the language expert."

Dillon read it aloud. "From the Leader and Chancellor of the State. Reichsleiter Martin Bormann is acting under my personal orders in a matter of the utmost importance to the State. He is answerable only to me. All personnel, military or civil, without distinction of rank, will assist him in any way he sees fit." Dillon handed it back. "It's signed Adolf Hitler."

"Really?" Ferguson folded it again and put it back in its envelope. "That would fetch a few thousand at auction at Christie's." He passed another, larger envelope over. "Try that."

Dillon opened it and took out a bulky file. He leafed through several pages. "This must be the Blue Book, alphabetical list of names, addresses, a paragraph under each, a sort of thumbnail sketch of the individual."

"See if Pamer is there."

Dillon checked quickly. "Yes, Major, Sir Joseph Pamer, Military Cross, Member of Parliament, Hatherley Court, Hampshire. There's an address in Mayfair. The remarks say he's an associate of Sir Oswald Mosley, politically sound and totally committed to the cause of National Socialism."

"Really?" Ferguson said dryly.

Dillon looked through several more pages and whistled softly. "Jesus, Brigadier, I know I'm just a little Irish peasant, but some of the names in here, you wouldn't believe. Some of England's finest. A few of America's also."

Ferguson took the file from him, glanced at a couple of pages, his face grave. "Who would have thought it?" He put the file back in its envelope and passed another. "Try that."

There were several documents inside and Dillon looked them over briefly. "These are details of numbered bank accounts in Switzerland, various South American countries and the United States." He handed them back. "Anything else?"

"Just this." Ferguson passed the envelope to him. "And we know what that must be, the Windsor Protocol."

Dillon took the letter out and unfolded it. It was written on paper of superb quality, almost like parchment, and was in English. He read it quickly, then passed it over. "Written at a villa in Estoril in Portugal in July 1940, addressed to Hitler and the signature at the bottom seems to be that of the Duke of Windsor."

"And what does it say?" Carney asked.

"Simple enough. The Duke says too many have already died on both sides, the war is pointless and should be ended as soon as possible. He agrees to take over the throne in the event of a successful German invasion."

"My God!" Carney said. "If that's genuine, it's dynamite."

"Exactly." Ferguson folded the letter and replaced it in its envelope. "If it *is* genuine. The Nazis were past masters at forgery." But his face was sad as he closed the case.

"Now what?" Carney asked.

"We return to St. John where Dillon and I will pack and make our way back to London. I have a Learjet awaiting my orders at St. Thomas." He held up the case and smiled bleakly. "The Prime Minister is a man who likes to hear bad news as quickly as possible."

The *Maria Blanco* had dropped anchor off Paradise Beach mid-morning and Algaro and Guerra, in the launch, had made contact at once. Santiago, sitting at his massive desk in the salon, listened as they went over the events of the previous night, then turned to Serra, who was standing beside him.

"Tell me about the situation as you see it, Captain."

"A long run out there, Señor, perhaps two and a half hours to come back because they'll be sailing into the wind all the way. I'd say they'll be back quite soon, probably just before noon."

"So what do we do, hit them tonight?" Algaro asked.

"No." Santiago shook his head. "I'd anticipate Ferguson making a move back to London as soon as possible. According to our information he has a Learjet on standby at St. Thomas airport." He shook his head. "No, we make our move on the instant."

"So what are your orders?" Algaro demanded.

"The simple approach is the best. You and Guerra will go ashore in one of the inflatables dressed as tourists. Leave the inflatable on Paradise below Cottage Seven, where Ferguson and Dillon are staying. Serra will give you each a walkie-talkie so you can keep in touch with each other and the ship. You, Algaro, will stay in the general vicinity of the cottage. Read a book on the beach, enjoy the sun, try to look normal if that's possible."

"And me, Señor?" Guerra asked.

"You go down to Caneel Beach and wait. When Carney's boat arrives, notify Algaro. Ferguson and Dillon must return to the cottage to change clothes and pack. That's when you strike. Once you have the Bormann briefcase, you return in the inflatable and we'll get out of here. Remember, the briefcase is distinctive. It's made of aluminium and is silver in appearance."

"Do we return to San Juan, Señor?" Serra asked.

"No." Santiago shook his head. "Samson Cay. I want time to consider my next move. The contents of that case will be more than interesting, Serra, they could give my life a whole new meaning." He opened a drawer at his right hand. There were a number of handguns in there. He selected a Browning Hi Power and pushed it across to Algaro. "Don't fail me."

"I won't," Algaro said. "If they have that briefcase, we'll get it for you."

"Oh, they'll have it all right." Santiago smiled. "I have every faith in our friend Dillon. His luck is good."

When *Sea Raider* moved in through all the moored yachts to the dock at Caneel Bay, the sun was high in the heavens. There were people windsurfing out in the bay and the beach was crowded with sun worshippers. Guerra was one of them, sitting on a deck chair in flowered shirt and Bermuda shorts, dark glasses shading his eyes. He saw Dillon step on to the dock to tie up. He returned on board, then came back, the olive-green holdall in one hand. Ferguson followed him carrying the briefcase, Carney walking at his side.

Guerra pulled on a white floppy sunhat that, with the brim down, partially concealed his features, adjusted the dark glasses and moved off the beach along the front of the restaurant to where the path from the dock emerged. He reached it almost at the same time as the three men, and at that moment a young black receptionist hurried out of the front desk lobby.

"Oh, Captain Carney, I saw you coming in. There was an urgent message for you."

"And what was it?" Carney demanded.

"It was Billy Jones. He said to tell you Jenny Grant had an accident last night. Fell from a balcony at her house up at Gallows Point. She's there now. They're moving her over to St. Thomas Hospital real soon."

"My God!" Carney said and nodded to the girl. "That's okay, honey, I'll handle it."

"Another bloody accident," Dillon said bitterly and handed the holdall to Ferguson. "I'm going to see her."

"Yes, of course, dear boy," Ferguson replied. "I'll go back to the cottage, have a shower, get packed and so on."

"I'll see you later." Dillon turned to Carney. "Are you coming?"

"I sure as hell am," Carney told him, and they hurried off toward the car park together.

With the holdall in his right hand and the briefcase in his left, Ferguson set off, following the path that led past the cottages fronting Caneel Bay. Guerra paused in the shelter of some bushes and using the walkie-talkie called up Algaro, who, sitting on the beach at Paradise, answered at once.

"Yes, I hear you."

"Ferguson is on his way and alone. The others have gone to see the girl."

"They've what?" Algaro was thrown, but quickly pulled himself together. "All right, meet me on the downside of the cottage."

Guerra switched off and turned. He could see Ferguson a couple of hundred yards further on and hurried after him.

Ferguson put the briefcase on the bed, then pulled off his sweater. He should have felt exhilarated, he told himself looking down at the case, but then too much had happened. Joseph Jackson at Samson Cay, a poor old man who had never done anyone harm in his life, and Jack. He sighed, opened the door to the bar cupboard and found a whisky miniature. He poured it into a glass, added water and drank it slowly. Jack Lane, the best damn copper he had ever worked with. And now Jenny Grant. Her so-called accident was beyond coincidence. Santiago had much to answer for. He took the briefcase from the bed and stood it at the side of the small desk, checked that the front door was locked, then went into the bathroom and turned on the shower.

Guerra and Algaro went up the steps and entered the lobby. Very gently, Guerra tried the door. He shook his head. "Locked."

Algaro beckoned and led the way out, back down the steps. It was very quiet, no one about, and the garden surrounding the cottage was very luxuriant, shielding a great deal of it from view. Above their heads, a large terrace jutted out, there was a path, some steps, a low wall, a small tree beside it.

"Easy," Algaro said. "Stand on the wall, brace yourself on the tree and I'll make a step up for you with my hands. You can reach the terrace rail. I'll wait at the door." He handed him the Browning. "Take this."

Guerra was on the terrace in a matter of seconds. The venetian blinds were down at the windows, but he managed to peer inside through narrow slats. There was no sign of Ferguson. Very gently he tried the handle to the terrace door which opened to his touch. He took out the Browning, aware of the sound of the shower, glanced around the room, saw no immediate sign of the briefcase and went to the outside door and opened it.

Algaro moved in and took the Browning from him. "In the shower, is he?"

"Yes, but I can't see the briefcase," Guerra whispered.

But Algaro did, moved quickly to the desk and picked it up triumphantly. "This is it. Let's go."

As they turned to the door, Ferguson emerged from the bathroom tying the belt of a terry toweling robe. The dismay on his face was instant, but he didn't waste breath on words, simply flung himself at them. Algaro struck him across the side of the head with the barrel of the Browning and when Ferguson fell to one knee stamped him sideways into the wall.

"Come on!" Algaro cried to Guerra, pulled open the door and hurried down the steps.

Ferguson managed to get to his feet, dizzy, his head hurting like hell. He staggered across the room, got the terrace door open and went out in time to see Algaro and Guerra running down to the little beach at the bottom of the grass slope. They pushed the inflatable into the water, started the outboard and moved out from the shore. It was only then that Ferguson, looking up, realized that the *Maria Blanco* was anchored off there.

He never felt so impotent in his life, never so full of rage. He went into the bathroom, got a damp flannel for his head, found the field glasses and focused them on the yacht. He saw Algaro and Guerra go up the ladder and hurry along the stern to where Santiago sat under the awning, Captain Serra beside him. Algaro placed the briefcase on the table. Santiago placed his hands on it, then turned and spoke to Serra. The captain moved away and went on the bridge. A moment later, they started to haul up the anchor and the *Maria Blanco* began to move.

And then a strange thing happened. As if realizing he was being observed, Santiago raised the briefcase in one hand, waved with the other and went into the salon.

It was Billy who opened the front door to admit Dillon and Bob Carney at the house at Gallows Point. "I'm real glad to see you," he said.

"How is she?" Carney demanded.

"Not too good. Seems like she fell from the balcony outside her bedroom. When me and Mary found her, she was lying there in the rain."

"He wants her—the doctor—over to St. Thomas Hospital for a scan. They're coming to pick her up in an hour," Mary said.

"Can she speak?" Dillon asked as they went upstairs.

"Came to around an hour ago. It was you she asked for, Mr. Dillon."

"Did she tell you how it happened?"

"No. In fact, she ain't said much at all. Listen, I'll go and make coffee while you stay with her. Come on, Billy," she told her husband and they went out.

Carney said, "Her face is real bad."

"I know," Dillon said grimly, "and she didn't get that from any accident. If she'd fallen on her face from such a height it would have been smashed completely."

He took her hand and she opened her eyes. "Dillon?"

"That's right, Jenny."

"I'm sorry, Dillon, sorry I let you down."

"You didn't let us down, Jenny. We found the U-boat. Carney and I went down together."

"Sure, Jenny." Carney leaned over. "We blew a hole in her and we found Bormann's briefcase."

She didn't really know what she was saying, of course, but carried on. "I told him, Dillon, I told him you had gone to Thunder Point."

"Told who, Jenny?"

"The man with the scar, the big scar from his eye to his mouth."

"Algaro," Carney said.

She gripped Dillon's hand lightly. "He hurt me, Dillon, he really hurt me. Nobody ever hurt me like that," and she closed her eyes and drifted off again.

When Dillon turned, the rage on his face was a living thing. "He's a dead man walking, Algaro, I give you my word," and he brushed past Carney and went downstairs.

The front door was open, Billy sitting on the porch, and Mary was pouring coffee. "You gonna have some?"

"Just a quick one," Dillon said.

"How is she?"

"Drifted off again," Carney told her as he came out on the porch.

Dillon nodded to him and moved to the other end of the porch. "Let's examine the situation. It was probably round about midnight Algaro put the screws on Jenny and found out that we'd gone to Thunder Point."

"So?"

"No sign of the opposition turning up, either there or on the way back. Does Max Santiago seem the kind of man who'd just give up at this point?"

"No way," Carney said.

"I agree. I think it much more likely he decided to try and relieve us of Bormann's briefcase at the earliest opportunity."

"Exactly what I was thinking."

"Good." Dillon swallowed his black coffee and put the cup down. "Let's get back to Caneel fast. You check around the general area of Caneel Beach, the bar, the dock and I'll find Ferguson. We'll meet up in the bar later."

They went back to Mary and Billy. "You boys going?" Mary asked.

"Got to," Dillon said. "What about you?"

"Billy will run things down at the bar, but me, I'm going to St. Thomas with Jenny."

"Tell her I'll be in to see her," Dillon said. "Don't forget now," and he hurried down the steps followed by Carney.

When Dillon hammered on the door of 7E it was opened by Ferguson holding a flannel loaded with ice cubes to his head.

"What happened?" Dillon demanded.

"Algaro happened. I was in the shower and the door was locked. God knows how he got in, but I walked out of the bathroom and there he was with one of the other men. I did my best, Dillon, but the bastard had a Browning. Clouted me across the head."

"Let me see." Dillon examined it. "It could be worse."

"They had an inflatable on the beach and took off for *Maria Blanco*. It was anchored out there."

Dillon pulled up the venetian blinds in one of the windows. "Well it isn't now."

"I wonder where he's gone, back to San Juan perhaps." Ferguson scowled. "I saw him in the stern through those field glasses, saw Algaro give him the briefcase. He seemed to know I was watching. He raised the case in one hand and waved with the other." Ferguson scowled. "Cheeky bastard."

"I told Carney we'd see him in the bar," Dillon said. "Come on, we'd better go and break the bad news and decide what we're going to do."

In the darkest corner of the bar, Ferguson and Dillon shared a table. The Brigadier was enjoying a large Scotch tinkling with ice while Dillon had contented himself with Evian water and a cigarette. Carney came in quickly to join them and called to the waitress, "Just a cold beer."

"What happened?"

"I checked with a friend who was out fishing. They passed him heading south-east, which means they must be going to Samson Cay."

Dillon actually laughed. "Right, you bastard, I've got you now."

"What on earth do you mean?" Ferguson demanded.

"The *Maria Blanco* will be anchored off Samson tonight, and if you remember, the general manager, Prieto, told us that Santiago always stays on board when he's there. It's simple. We'll go in under cover of darkness and I'll get the briefcase back, if Carney will run us down there in *Sea Raider* of course."

"Try stopping me," Carney told him.

Ferguson shook his head. "You don't give up easily, do you, Dillon."

"I could never see the point." Dillon poured more Evian water and raised his glass.

FIFTEEN

It was toward evening as Dillon and Ferguson waited on the dock at Caneel Bay, sitting on the bench, the Irishman smoking a cigarette, the olive-green military holdall on the ground between them.

"I think that's him now," Ferguson said and pointed and Dillon saw *Sea Raider* coming in from the sea, slowly to negotiate the moored yachts. There were still people on the beach, some of them swimming in the evening sun, laughter drifting across the water.

Ferguson said, "From what I know of Santiago, I should think he'd be ready to repel boarders. Do you really think you can pull this off?"

"Anything's possible, Brigadier." Dillon shrugged. "You don't need to come, you know. I'd understand."

"I'll overlook the insult this time," Ferguson said coldly, "but don't ever say something like that to me again, Dillon."

Dillon smiled. "Cheer up, Brigadier. I've no intention of dying at a place called Samson Cay. After all, I've got a dinner at the Garrick Club to look forward to again with you."

He got up and moved to the edge of the dock as *Sea Raider* drifted in. He waved up to Carney, jumped across the gap, got the fenders over, then threw a line to the Brigadier. Carney killed the engines and came down the ladder as they finished tying up.

"I've refuelled so everything's shipshape. We can leave any time you like."

Ferguson passed the holdall to Dillon and stepped across as Dillon took it into the deckhouse and put it on one of the benches.

At that moment the receptionist who'd given them the news about Jenny when they'd come in earlier came along the dock. "I've just taken a phone call from Mary Jones at St. Thomas Hospital, Mr. Dillon. She'd like for you to call her back."

Carney said, "I'll come with you."

The Brigadier nodded. "I'll wait here and keep my fingers crossed."

Dillon stepped over the side and turned along the dock, Carney at his side.

Mary said, "She's going to be fine, but a good job she had that scan. There's what they call a hairline fracture in the skull, but the specialist he say nothing that care and good treatment won't cure."

"Fine," Dillon said. "Don't forget to tell her I'll be in to see her."

Carney was leaning at the entrance of the telephone booth, his face anxious. "Hairline fracture of the skull," Dillon told him as he hung up. "But she's going to be okay."

"Well that's good," Carney said as they walked back to the dock.

"That's one way of putting it," Dillon said. "Another is that Santiago and Algaro have got a lot to answer for, not to mention that bastard Pamer."

Ferguson got up and came out of the deckhouse as they arrived. "Good news?"

"It could be worse," Dillon said and told him.

"Thank God!" Ferguson took a deep breath. "All right, I suppose we'd better get going."

Carney said, "Sure, but I'd like to know how we're going to handle this thing. Even in the dark, there's a limit to how close we can get in *Sea Raider* without being spotted."

"It seems to me the smart way would be an approach underwater," Dillon said. "Only there's no *we* about it, Carney. I once told you you were one of the good guys. Santiago and his people, they're the bad guys and that's what I am. I'm a bad guy, too. Ask the Brigadier, he'll tell you. That's why he hired me for this job in the first place. This is where I earn my keep and it's a one-man affair."

"Now look," Carney said. "I can hold up my end."

"I know that and you've got the medals to prove it. The Brigadier showed me your record, but Vietnam was different. You were stuck in a lousy war that wasn't really any of your business. I suppose you were just trying to stay alive."

"And I made it. I'm here, aren't I?"

"Remember when you and the Brigadier were swapping war stories about Vietnam and Korea and you asked me what I knew about war and I told you I'd been at war all my life?"

"So?"

"At an age when I should have been taking girls out to dances I was fighting the kind of war where the battlefield was rooftops and back alleys, leading British paratroopers a dance through the sewers of the Falls Road in Belfast, being chased by the SAS through South Armagh and they're the best."

"What are you trying to say to me?" Carney asked.

"That when I go over the rail of the *Maria Blanco* to recover that briefcase I'll kill anyone who tries to get in my way." Dillon shrugged. "Like I said, I can do that without a moment's hesitation because I'm a bad guy. I don't think you can, and thank God for it."

There was silence. Carney turned to Ferguson, who nodded. "He's right, I'm afraid."

"Okay," Carney said reluctantly. "This is the way it goes. I'll go as close to the *Maria Blanco* as we dare and drop anchor, then I'll take you the rest of the way in an inflatable." Dillon tried to speak and Carney cut him off. "No buts, that's the way it's going to be. I've got an inflatable moored out there on the buoy with *Privateer*. We'll pick it up on the way."

"All right," Dillon said. "Have it your way."

"And I come in, Dillon, if anything goes wrong, I come in."

"On horseback, bugles blowing?" Dillon laughed. "The South shall rise again? You people never could come to terms with losing the Civil War."

"There was no Civil War." Carney went up to the flying bridge. "You must be referring to the war for the independence of the Confederacy. Now let's get moving."

He switched on the engines, Dillon stepped over to the dock and untied the lines. A moment later and they were moving out into the bay.

The *Maria Blanco* was anchored in the bay at Samson Cay and Santiago sat in the salon, reading the documents in Bormann's briefcase for the third time. He'd never been so fascinated in his life. He examined the personal order from Hitler, the signature, then reread the Windsor Protocol. It was the Blue Book which was the most interesting though. All those names, Members of Parliament, Peers of the Realm, people at the highest levels of society who had supported, however secretly, the cause of National Socialism, but then it was hardly surprising. In the England of the great depression with something like four million people out of work, many would have looked at Germany and thought that Hitler had the right idea.

He got up, went to the bar and poured a glass of dry sherry, then returned to the desk, picked up the telephone and called the radio room. "Get me Sir Francis Pamer in London."

Pamer was sitting alone at the desk in his office at the House of Commons when the phone rang.

"Francis? Max here."

Pamer was immediately all attention. "Has anything happened?"

"You could say that. I've got it, Francis, right here on my desk, Bormann's briefcase, and Korvettenkapitän Paul Friemel was right. The Reichsleiter wasn't just shooting his mouth off while drunk. It's all here, Francis. Hitler's order to him, details of numbered bank accounts, the Windsor Protocol. Now there's an impressive-looking document. If they forged it, I can only say they did a good job."

"My God!" Pamer said.

"And the Blue Book, Francis, absolutely fascinating stuff. Such famous names and a neat little background paragraph for each. Here's an interesting one. I'll read it to you. Major, Sir Joseph Pamer, Military Cross, Member of Parliament, Hatherley Court, Hampshire, an associate of Sir Oswald Mosley, politically sound, totally committed to the cause of National Socialism."

"No." Pamer groaned and there was sudden sweat on his face. "I can't believe it."

"I wonder what your local Conservative Association would make of that? Still, all's well that ends well, as they say. A good thing I've got it and no one else."

"You'll destroy it of course?" Pamer said. "I mean, you'll destroy the whole bloody lot?"

"Leave it to me, Francis, I'll see to everything," Santiago said. "Just like I always do. I'll be in touch soon."

He put down the phone and started to laugh, was still laughing when Captain Serra came in. "Have you any orders, Señor?"

Santiago looked at his watch. It was just after seven. "Yes, I'll go ashore for a couple of hours and eat at the restaurant."

"Very well, Señor."

"And make sure the deck is patrolled tonight, Serra, just in case our friends decide to pay us a visit."

"I don't think we need worry, Señor, they'd have trouble getting close to us without being spotted, but we'll take every precaution."

"Good, make the launch ready, I'll be with you in a moment," and Santiago went into the bedroom, taking the briefcase with him.

S*ea Raider* crept to the west side of Samson Cay, round the point from the resort and the main anchorage. Carney switched off the engines, came down the ladder as Dillon went in to the prow and dropped the anchor.

"Shunt Bay they call this," Carney said. "I've been here before, a long time ago. Only four or five fathoms, clear sand bottom. You can't get down to it because of the cliffs so when guests want to swim here they bring them round from the resort by boat. We'll be safe here at this time of night."

Ferguson checked his watch. "Ten o'clock. What time will you go?"

"Maybe another hour. I'll see." Dillon went into the deck-house, opened the holdall and took out the AK47 assault rifle and passed it to Ferguson. "Just in case."

"Let's hope not." Ferguson put it on the bench.

Dillon took the Walther from the holdall, checked it and put it in the dive bag with the Carswell silencer. Then he put in what was left of the Semtex and a couple of detonating fuses, the thirty-minute ones.

"You really are going to war," Ferguson said.

"You better believe it." Dillon slipped the night sight into the bag also.

Carney said, "I'll take you as close as I can in the inflatable, and hope to see you on the way back."

"Fine." Dillon smiled. "Break out the thermos, Brigadier, and we'll have some coffee and then it's action stations."

S antiago had enjoyed an excellent meal, starting with caviar, followed by grilled filet mignon with artichoke hearts, washed down by a bottle of Chateau Palmer 1966. Deliberate self-indulgence because he felt on top of the world. He liked things to go well and the Bormann affair had gone very well indeed. It was like a wonderful game. The information contained in the documents was so startling that the possibilities were endless.

He asked for a cigar, Cuban, of course, just like the old days before that madman Castro had ruined everything. Prieto brought him a Romeo and Julietta, trimmed the end and warmed it for him.

"The meal, it was satisfactory, Señor Santiago?"

"The meal, it was bloody marvelous, Prieto." Santiago patted him on the shoulder. "I'll see you tomorrow." He stood up, picked up the Bormann briefcase from the floor beside the table and walked to the door where Algaro was waiting. "We'll go back to the ship now, Algaro."

"As you say, Señor."

Santiago went down the steps and walked along the dock to the launch, savouring the night, the scent of his cigar. Yes, life could really be very good.

Carney took the inflatable round the point, the outboard motor throttled down, the noise of it a murmur in the night. There were yachts in the bay scattered here and there and a few smaller craft. *Maria Blanco*, anchored three hundred yards out, was by far the largest.

Carney killed the engine, took a couple of short wooden oars from the bottom of the boat and fitted them into the rowlocks. "Manpower the rest of the way," he said. "The way I see it and with those other boats around, I can get you maybe fifty yards away without being spotted."

"That's fine."

Dillon was already wearing his jacket and tank and a black nylon diving cowl Carney had found him. He took the Walther from his dive bag, screwed the Carswell silencer into place and slipped the weapon inside his jacket.

"You'd better pray you don't get a misfire," Carney said as he rowed. "Water does funny things to guns. I learned that in Vietnam in those damn paddy fields."

"No problem with a Walther, it's a Rolls-Royce," Dillon said.

They couldn't see each other, their faces a pale blur in the darkness. Carney said, "You actually enjoy this kind of thing?"

"I'm not too sure if enjoy is the right word exactly."

"I knew guys in Vietnam like that, Special Forces mainly. They kept drawing these hard assignments and then a strange thing happened. They ended up wanting more. Couldn't get enough. Is that how you feel, Dillon?"

"There's a poem by Browning," Dillon told him. "Something about our interest being on the dangerous edge of things. When I was young and foolish in those early days with the IRA and the SAS chasing the hell out of me all over South Armagh, I also discovered a funny thing. I loved it more than anything I'd ever known. I lived more in a day, really lived, than in a year back in London."

"I understand that," Carney said. "It's like being on some sort of drug, but it can only end one way. On your back in the gutter in some Belfast street."

"Oh, you've no need to worry about that," Dillon told him. "Those days are over. I'll never go back to that."

Carney paused, sniffing. "I think I can smell cigar smoke."

They floated there in the darkness and the launch emerged on the other side of a couple of yachts and moved to the bottom of the *Maria Blanco*'s steel stairway under the light. Serra was on deck looking over. Guerra hurried down to take the line and tied up and Santiago went up to the deck followed by Algaro.

"Looks like he's carrying the briefcase with him," Carney said.

Dillon got the night sight from his dive bag and focused it. "You're right. He's probably afraid to let it out of his sight."

"What now?" Carney said.

"We'll hang on for a little while, give them a chance to settle down."

Santiago and Serra descended from the bridge to the main deck. Guerra and Solona stood at the bottom of the ladder, each armed with an M16 rifle. Algaro stood by the rail.

"Two hours on and four off. We'll rotate during the night and we'll leave the security lights on."

"That seems more than adequate. We might as well turn in now," Santiago said. "Good night, Captain."

He went along to the salon and Algaro followed him. "Do you need me any more tonight, Señor?"

"I don't think so, Algaro, you can go to bed."

Algaro withdrew, Santiago put the briefcase on the desk, then he took off his jacket and went and poured a cognac. He returned to the desk, sat down and leaned back, sipping his cognac and just looking at the briefcase. Finally, as he knew he would, he opened it and started to go through the documents again.

Dillon focused the night sight. He picked out Solona in the shadows by a lifeboat in the prow. Guerra, in the stern, had made no attempt to hide, sat on one of the chairs under the awning smoking a cigarette, his rifle on the table.

Dillon handed Carney the night sight. "All yours. I'm on my way."

He dropped back over the side of the inflatable, descended to ten feet and approached the ship. He surfaced at the stern of the launch, which was tied up at the bottom of the steel stairway. Suddenly, Solona appeared up above on the platform. Dillon eased under the water, aware of footsteps descending. Solona paused halfway down and lit a cigarette, the match flaring in cupped hands. Dillon surfaced gently at the stern of the launch, took the Walther from inside his jacket and extended his arm.

"Over here," he whispered in Spanish.

Solona glanced up, the match still flaring, and the silenced Walther coughed as Dillon shot him between the eyes. Solona fell back and to one side, slid over the rail and dropped ten feet into the water.

It didn't make too much of a splash, but Guerra noticed it and got to his feet. "Hey, Solona, is that you?"

"Yes," Dillon called softly in Spanish. "No problem."

He could hear Guerra walking along the deck above, went under and swam to the anchor. He opened his jacket, unzipped his diving suit and forced the Walther inside. Then he slipped out of the jacket and tank, clipped them to the anchor line and hauled himself up the chain, sliding in through the port.

Algaro, lying on his bunk, was only wearing a pair of boxer shorts because of the oppressive heat. For that reason, he had the porthole open and heard Guerra calling to Solona; he also heard Dillon's reply. He frowned, went to the porthole and listened.

Guerra called softly again, "Where are you, Solona?"

Algaro picked up the revolver on his bedside locker and went out.

Guerra called again, "Where are you, Solona?" and moved to the forward deck, the M16 ready.

"Over here, *amigo*," Dillon said and as Guerra turned, shot him twice in the heart, driving him back against the bulkhead.

Dillon went forward cautiously, leaned over to check that he was dead. There was no sound behind, for Algaro was bare-footed, but Dillon was suddenly aware of the barrel of the revolver against his neck.

"Now then, you bastard, I've got you." Algaro reached over and took the Walther. "So, a real professional's weapon? I like that. In fact I like it so much I'm going to keep it." He tossed the revolver over the rail into the sea. "Now turn round. I'm going to give you two in the belly so you take a long time."

Bob Carney, watching events through the night sight, had seen Algaro's approach, had never been so frustrated in his life at his inability to do something about it, was never totally certain what happened afterwards because everything moved so fast.

Dillon turned, his left arm sweeping Algaro's right to the side, the Walther discharging into the deck. Dillon closed with him. "If you're going to do it, do it, don't talk about it." They struggled for a moment, feeling each other's strength. "Why don't you call for help?"

"Because I'll kill you myself with my own hands," Algaro told him through clenched teeth. "For my own pleasure."

"You're good at beating up girls, aren't you?" Dillon said. "How are you with a man?"

Algaro twisted round, exerting all his strength, and pushed Dillon back against the rail at the prow. It was his last mistake, for Dillon let himself go straight over, taking Algaro with him, and the sea was Dillon's territory, not his.

Algaro dropped the Walther as they went under the water and started to struggle and Dillon held on, pulling him down, aware of the anchor chain against his back. He grabbed for it with one hand and got a forearm across Algaro's throat. At first he struggled very hard indeed, feet kicking, but quickly weakened. Finally, he was still. Dillon, his own lungs nearly bursting, reached one-handed and unbuckled his weight belt. He passed it around Algaro's neck and fastened the buckle again, binding him to the anchor chain.

He surfaced, taking in great lungfuls of air. It occurred to him then that Carney would be watching events through the night sight and he turned and raised an arm, then hauled himself back up the anchor chain.

He kept to the shadows, moving along the deck until he came to the main salon. He glanced in a porthole and saw Santiago sitting at the desk, the briefcase open, reading. Dillon crouched down, thinking about it, then made his decision. He took what was left of the Semtex from his dive bag, inserted the two thirty-minute detonator fuses, went and dropped it down one of the engine room air vents, then returned and peered through the porthole again.

Santiago was sitting at the desk, but now he replaced the documents in his briefcase, closed it, yawned and got up and went into the bedroom. Dillon didn't hesitate. He moved into the companionway, opened the salon door and darted across to the desk, and as he picked up the briefcase, Santiago came back into the room.

The cry that erupted from his mouth was like a howl of anguish. "No!" he cried and Dillon turned and ran for the door. Santiago got the desk drawer open, grabbed a Smith & Wesson and fired blindly.

Dillon was already into the companionway and making for the deck. By now, the ship was aroused and Serra appeared from his cabin at the rear of the bridge, a gun in his hand.

"What's going on?" he demanded.

"Stop him!" Santiago cried. "It's Dillon."

Dillon didn't hesitate, but kept to the shadows, running to the stern and jumped over the rail. He went under as deep as he could, but the case made things awkward. He surfaced, aware that they were firing at him, and struck out for the darkness as fast as possible. In the end, it was Carney who saved him, roaring out of the night and tossing him a line.

"Hang on and let's get the hell out of here," he called, boosted speed and took them away into the friendly dark.

Serra said, "Guerra's dead, his body is still here, but no sign of Solona and Algaro."

"Never mind that," Santiago told him. "Dillon and Carney didn't come all the way in that inflatable from St. John. Carney's Sport Fisherman must be nearby."

"True," Serra said, "and they'll up anchor and start back straightaway."

"And the moment they move, you'll see them on your radar, right? I mean, there's no other boat moving out to sea from Samson Cay tonight."

"True, Señor."

"Then get the anchor up."

Serra pressed the bridge button for the electric hoist. The motor started to whine. Santiago said, "What now?"

The three remaining members of the crew, Pinto, Noval and Mugica, were down on the forward deck and Serra leaned over the bridge rail. "The anchor line is jamming. Check it."

Mugica leaned over the prow, then turned. "It's Algaro. He's tied to the chain."

Santiago and Serra went down the ladder and hurried to the prow and looked over. Algaro hung there from the anchor chain, the weight belt around his throat. "Mother of God!" Santiago said. "Pull him up, damn you!" He turned to Serra. "Now let's get moving."

"Don't worry, Señor," Serra told him. "We're faster than they are. There's no way they can get back to St. John without us overtaking them," and he turned to the ladder and went up to the bridge as Noval and Mugica hauled Algaro's body in through the chain port.

At Shunt Bay, Ferguson leaned anxiously over the stern of *Sea Raider* as the inflatable coasted in out of the darkness.

"What happened?" he demanded.

Dillon passed the Bormann briefcase up to him. "That's what happened. Now let's get out of here."

He stepped on to the diving platform and Carney passed him the inflatable line and Dillon tied it securely, then went to the deckhouse and worked his way round to the prow and started to pull in the anchor. It came free of the sandy bottom with no difficulty. Behind him, Carney had already gone up to the flying bridge and was starting the engines.

Ferguson joined him. "How did it go?"

"He doesn't take prisoners, I'll say that for him," Carney said. "But let's get out of here. We don't have any kind of time to hang about."

Sea Raider plowed forward into the night, the wind freshening four to five. Ferguson sat in the swivel chair and Dillon leaned against the rail beside Carney.

"They're faster than we are, you know that," Carney said. "And he's going to keep coming."

"I know," Dillon told him. "He doesn't like to lose."

"Well, I sure as hell can't go any faster, we're doing twenty-two knots and that's tops."

It was Ferguson who saw the *Maria Blanco* first. "There's a light back there, I'm sure there is."

Carney glanced round. "That's them all right, couldn't be anyone else."

Dillon raised the night sight.

"Yes, it's the *Maria Blanco*."

"He's got good radar on that thing, must have," Carney said. "No way I can lose him."

"Oh, yes there is," Dillon said. "Just keep going."

Serra, on the bridge of the *Maria Blanco*, held a pair of night glasses to his eyes. "Got it," he said and passed the glasses to Santiago.

Santiago focused them and saw the outline of *Sea Raider*. "Right, you bastards." He leaned over the bridge rail and looked down at Mugica, Noval and Pinto, who all waited on the forward deck, holding M16 rifles. "We've seen them. Get yourselves ready."

Serra increased speed, the *Maria Blanco* raced forward over the waves and Santiago raised the glasses again, saw the outline of *Sea Raider* and smiled. "Now, Dillon, now," he murmured.

The explosion, when it came, was instantaneous, tearing the bottom out of the ship. What happened was so catastrophic that neither Santiago, Captain Serra nor the three remaining crew members had time to take it in as their world disintegrated and the *Maria Blanco* lifted, then plunged beneath the waves.

On the flying bridge of *Sea Raider* what they saw first was a brilliant flash of orange fire and then, a second or two later, the explosion boomed across the water. And then the fire disappeared, extinguished, only darkness remaining. Bob Carney killed the engine instantly.

It was very quiet. Ferguson said, "A long way down."

Dillon looked back through the night sight. "U180 went further." He put the night sight in the locker under the instrument panel. "He did say they were carrying explosives, remember?"

Carney said, "We should go back, perhaps there are survivors."

"You really think so after that?" Dillon said gently. "St. John's that way."

Carney switched on the engines, and as they plowed forward into the night Dillon went down the ladder to the deckhouse. He took off his diving suit, pulled on his tracksuit, found a pack of cigarettes, went to the rail.

Ferguson came down the ladder and joined him. "My God!" he said softly.

"I don't think he had much to do with it, Brigadier," Dillon said and he lit a cigarette, the Zippo flaring.

It was just after ten the following morning when a nurse showed the three of them into the private room at the St. Thomas Hospital. Dillon was wearing the black cord slacks, the denim shirt and the black flying jacket he'd arrived in on the first day, Ferguson supremely elegant as usual in his Panama, blazer and Guards tie. Jenny was propped up against pillows, her head swathed in white bandages.

Mary, sitting beside her, knitting, got up. "I'll leave you to it, but don't you gentlemen overtire her."

She went out and Jenny managed a weak smile. "My three musketeers."

"Now that's kind of fanciful." Bob Carney took her hand. "How are you?"

"I don't feel I'm here half the time."

"That will pass, my dear," Ferguson said. "I've had a word with the Superintendent. Anything you want, any treatment you need, you get. It's all taken care of."

"Thank you, Brigadier."

She turned to Dillon, looked up at him without speaking. Bob Carney said, "I'll be back, honey, you take care."

He turned to Ferguson, who nodded, and they went out.

Dillon sat on the bed and took her hand. "You look terrible."

"I know. How are you?"

"I'm fine."

"How did it all go?"

"We've got the Bormann briefcase. The Brigadier has his Learjet waiting at the airport. We're taking it back to London."

"The way you put it, you make it sound as if it was easy."

"It could have been worse. Don't go on about it, Jenny, there's no point. Santiago and his friends, that animal, Algaro, they'll never bother you again."

"Can you be certain of that?"

"As a coffin lid closing," he said bleakly.

There was a kind of pain on her face. She closed her eyes briefly, opened them again. "People don't really change, do they?"

"I am what I am, Jenny," he said simply. "But then you knew that."

"Will I see you again?"

"I don't think that's likely." He kissed her hand, got up, went to the door and opened it.

"Dillon," she called.

He turned. "Yes, Jenny?"

"God bless and take care of yourself."

The door closed softly, she closed her eyes and drifted into sleep.

They allowed Carney to walk out across the tarmac to the Lear with them, a porter pushing a trolley with the luggage. One of the two pilots met them and helped the porter stow the luggage while Dillon, Ferguson and Carney stood at the bottom of the steps.

The Brigadier held up the briefcase. "Thanks for this, Captain Carney. If you ever need help or I can do you a good turn." He shook hands. "Take care, my friend," and he went up the steps.

Carney said, "What happens now, in London, I mean?"

"That's up to the Prime Minister," Dillon said. "Depends what he wants to do with those documents."

"It was a long time ago," Carney said.

"A legitimate point of view."

Carney hesitated, then said, "This Pamer guy, what about him?"

"I hadn't really thought about it," Dillon said calmly.

"Oh, yes you have." Carney shook his head. "God help you, Dillon, because you'll never change," and he turned and walked away across the tarmac.

Dillon joined Ferguson inside and strapped himself in. "A good man that," Ferguson said.

Dillon nodded. "The best."

The second pilot pulled up the steps and closed the door, went and joined his colleague in the cockpit. After a while, the the engines fired and they moved forward. A few moments later, they were climbing high and out over the sea.

Ferguson looked out. "St. John over there."

"Yes," Dillon said.

Ferguson sighed. "I suppose we should discuss what happens when we get back."

"Not now, Brigadier." Dillon closed his eyes. "I'm tired. Let's leave it till later."

The house at Chocolate Hole had never seemed so empty when Bob Carney entered it. He walked slightly aimlessly from room to room, then went in the kitchen and got a beer from the icebox. As he went to the living room the phone rang.

It was his wife, Karye. "Hi, honey, how are you?"

"I'm fine, just fine. How about the kids?"

"Oh, lively as usual. They miss you. This is an impulse call. We're at a gas station near Orlando. I just stopped to fill up."

"I'm sure looking forward to you coming back."

"It won't be long now," she said. "I know it's been lonely for you. Anything interesting happened?"

A slow smile spread across Carney's face and he took a deep breath. "Not that I can think of. Same old routine."

"Bye, honey, I'll have to go."

He put the phone down, drank some of his beer, went out on the porch. It was a fine, clear afternoon and he could see the islands on the other side of Pillsbury Sound and beyond. A long way, but not as far as Max Santiago had gone.

SIXTEEN

It was just before six o'clock the following evening in Ferguson's office at the Ministry of Defence and Simon Carter sat on the other side of the desk, white-faced and shaken as Ferguson finished talking.

"So what's to be done about the good Sir Francis?" Ferguson asked. "A Minister of the Crown, behaving not only dishonourably but in what can only be described as a criminal way."

Dillon, standing by the window in a blue Burberry trenchcoat, lit a cigarette and Carter said, "Does *he* have to be here?"

"Nobody knows more of this affair than Dillon, can't keep him out of it now."

Carter picked up the Blue Book file, hesitated, then put it down and unfolded the Windsor Protocol to read it again. "I can't believe this is genuine."

"Perhaps not, but the rest of it is." Ferguson reached across for the documents, replaced them in the briefcase and closed it. "The Prime Minister will see us at Downing Street at eight. Naturally I haven't invited Sir Francis. I'll meet you there."

Carter got up. "Very well."

He went to the door, was reaching for the handle when Ferguson said, "Oh, and Carter."

"Yes?"

"Don't do anything stupid like phoning Pamer. I'd stay well clear of this if I were you."

Carter's face sagged, he turned wearily and went out.

It was ten minutes later and Sir Francis Pamer was clearing his desk at the House of Commons before leaving for the evening when his phone rang. "Pamer here," he said.

"Charles Ferguson."

"Ah, you're back, Brigadier," Pamer said warily.

"We need to meet," Ferguson told him.

"Quite impossible tonight, I have a most important function, dinner with the Lord Mayor of London. Can't miss that."

"Max Santiago is dead," Ferguson said, "and I have here, on my desk, the Bormann briefcase. The Blue Book makes very interesting reading. Your father is featured prominently on page eighteen."

"Oh, dear God!" Pamer slumped down on his chair.

"I wouldn't speak to Simon Carter about this if I were you," Ferguson said. "That wouldn't really be to your advantage."

"Of course not, anything you say." Pamer hesitated. "You haven't spoken to the Prime Minister then?"

"No, I thought it best to see you first."

"I'm very grateful, Brigadier, I'm sure we can work something out."

"You know Charing Cross Pier?"

"Of course."

"One of the river boats, the *Queen of Denmark*, leaves there at six forty-five. I'll meet you on board. You'll need an umbrella, by the way, it's raining rather hard."

Ferguson put down the phone and turned to Dillon, who was still standing by the window. "That's it then."

"How did he sound?" Dillon asked.

"Terrified." Ferguson got up, went to the old-fashioned hall stand he kept in the corner and took down his overcoat, the type known to Guards officers as a British warm, and pulled it on. "But then, he would be, poor sod."

"Don't expect me to have any sympathy for him." Dillon picked up the briefcase from the desk. "Come on, let's get on with it," and he opened the door and led the way out.

When Pamer arrived at Charing Cross Pier the fog was so thick that he could hardly see across the Thames. He bought his ticket from a steward at the head of the gangplank. The *Queen of Denmark* was scheduled to call in at Westminster Pier and eventually Cadogan Pier at Chelsea Embankment. A popular run on a fine summer evening, but on a night like this, there were few passengers.

Pamer had a look in the lower saloon where there were half-a-dozen passengers and a companionway to the upper saloon where he encountered only two ageing ladies talking to each other in whispers. He opened a glass door and went outside, and looked down. There was someone standing at the rail in the stern holding an umbrella over his head. He went back inside, descended the companionway and went out on deck, opening his umbrella against the driving rain.

"That you, Ferguson?"

He went forward hesitantly, his hand on the butt of the pistol in his right-hand raincoat pocket. It was a very rare weapon from the exclusive collection of World War Two handguns his father had left him, a Volka specially designed for use by the Hungarian Secret Service and as silenced as a pistol could be. He'd kept it in his desk at the Commons for years. The *Queen of Denmark* was moving away from the pier now and starting her passage upriver. Fog swirled up from the surface of the water, the light from the saloon above was yellow and sickly. There were no rear windows to the lower saloon. They were alone in their own private space.

Ferguson turned from the rail. "Ah, there you are." He held up the briefcase. "Well, there it is. The Prime Minister's having a look at eight o'clock."

"Please, Ferguson," Pamer pleaded. "Don't do this to me. It's not my fault that my father was a Fascist."

"Quite right. It's also not your fault that your father's immense fortune in post-war years came from his association with the Nazi movement, the Kamaradenwerk. I can even excuse as simply weakness of character the way you've been happy over the years to accept a large, continuing income from Samson Cay Holdings, mostly money produced by Max Santiago's more dubious enterprises. The drug business, for example."

"Now look here," Pamer began.

"Don't bother to deny it. I'd asked Jack Lane to investigate your family's financial background, not realizing I was sentencing him to death, of course. He'd really made progress before he was killed, or should I say murdered? I found his findings in his desk earlier today."

"It wasn't my fault, any of it," Pamer said wildly. "All my father and his bloody love affair with Hitler. I had my family name to think of, Ferguson, my position in the Government."

"Oh, yes," Ferguson conceded. "Rather selfish of you, but understandable. What I can't forgive is the fact that you acted as Santiago's lap dog from the very beginning, fed him every piece of information you could. You sold me out, you sold out Dillon, putting us in danger of our very lives. It was your actions that resulted in Jennifer Grant being attacked twice, once in London where God knows what would have happened if Dillon hadn't intervened. The second time in St. John, where she was severely injured and almost died. She's in a hospital now."

"I knew none of this, I swear."

"Oh, everything was arranged by Santiago, I grant you that. What I'm talking about is responsibility. On Samson Cay, a poor old man called Joseph Jackson who gave me my first clue to the truth behind the whole affair, the man who was caretaker at the old Herbert Hotel in 1945, was brutally murdered just after talking to me. Now that was obviously the work of Santiago's people, but how did he know of the existence of the old man in the first place? Because you told him."

"You can't prove that, you can't prove any of it."

"True, just as I can't prove exactly what happened to Jack Lane, but I'll make an educated guess. Those were computer printouts I found in his desk. That means he was doing a computer sweep on your family affairs. I presume one of your staff noticed. Normally, you wouldn't have been concerned, it happens to Crown Ministers all the time, but in the light of recent events, you panicked, feared the worst, and phoned Santiago, who took care of it for you." Ferguson sighed. "I often think the direct dialing system a curse. In the old days it would have taken the international operator at least four hours to connect you to a place like the Virgins. These days all you do is punch a rather long series of numbers."

Pamer took a deep breath and squared his shoulders. "As regards my family's business interests, that was my father's affair, not mine. I'll plead ignorance if you persist with this thing. I know the law, Ferguson, and you seem to have forgotten that I was a working barrister for a short while."

"Actually I had," Ferguson said.

"Santiago being dead, the only thing you have left is my father's inclusion in the Blue Book. Hardly my fault." He seemed to have recovered his nerve. "You can't prove a thing. I'll tough it out, Ferguson."

Ferguson turned and looked at the river. "As I said, I could understand your panic, an ancient name tarnished, your political career threatened, but the attacks on that girl, the death of that old man, the cold-blooded murder of Inspector Lane—on those charges you are every bit as culpable as the men who carried them out."

"Prove it," Pamer said, clutching his umbrella in both hands.

"Goodbye, Sir Francis," Charles Ferguson said and turned and walked away.

Pamer was trembling, and he'd totally forgotten about the Volka in his pocket. Too late now for any wild ideas like relieving Ferguson of the briefcase at gunpoint. He took a deep breath and coughed as the fog bit at the back of his throat. He fumbled for his cigarette case, got one to his mouth and tried to find his lighter.

There was the softest of footfalls and Dillon's Zippo flared. "There you go."

Pamer's eyes widened in fear. "Dillon, what do you want?"

"A word only." Dillon put his right arm around Pamer's shoulders under the umbrella and drew him against the stern rail. "The first time I met you and Simon Carter on the Terrace at the House of Commons I made a joke about security and the river and you said you couldn't swim. Is that true?"

"Well, yes." Pamer's eyes widened as he understood. He pulled the Volka from his raincoat pocket, but Dillon, in close, swept the arm wide. The weapon gave a muted cough, the bullet thudded into the bulkhead.

The Irishman grabbed for the right wrist, slamming it on the rail so that Pamer cried out and dropped the pistol in the river.

"Thanks, old son," Dillon said. "You've just made it easier for me."

He swung Pamer round and pushed hard between the shoulder blades so that he sagged across the stern rail, reached down, grabbed him by the ankles and heaved him over. The umbrella floated upside down, Pamer surfaced, raised an arm. There was a strangled cry as he went under again and the fog swirled across the surface of the Thames, covering everything.

Five minutes later the *Queen of Denmark* pulled in at Westminster Pier next to the bridge. Ferguson was first down the gangway and waited under a tree for Dillon to join him. "Taken care of?"

"I think you could say that," Dillon told him.

"Good. I've got my appointment at Downing Street now. I can walk there from here. I'll see you at my flat in Cavendish Square, let you know what happened."

Dillon watched him go, then moved away himself in the opposite direction, fading into the fog and rain.

Ferguson was admitted to Downing Street some fifteen minutes early for his appointment. Someone took his coat and umbrella and one of the Prime Minister's aides came down the stairs at that moment. "Ah, there you are, Brigadier."

"A trifle early, I fear."

"No problem. The Prime Minister would welcome the opportunity to consider the material in question himself. Is that it?"

"Yes." Ferguson handed him the briefcase.

"Please make yourself comfortable. I'm sure he won't keep you long."

Ferguson took a seat in the hall, feeling rather cold. He shivered and the porter by the door said, "No central heating, Brigadier. The workmen moved in today to install the new security systems."

"Ah, so they've finally started?"

"Yes, but it's bleeding cold of an evening. We had to light a fire in the Prime Minister's study. First time in years."

"Is that so?"

A few moments later there was a knock at the door, the porter opened it and admitted Carter. "Brigadier," Carter said formally.

The porter took his coat and umbrella and at that moment, the aide reappeared. "Please come this way, gentlemen."

The Prime Minister sat at his desk, the briefcase open at one side. He was reading through the Blue Book and glanced up briefly. "Sit down, gentlemen, I'll be with you directly."

The fire burned brightly in the grate of the Victorian fireplace. It was very quiet, only sudden flurries of rain hammering against the window.

Finally, the Prime Minister sat back and looked at them. "Some of the names on this Blue Book list are really quite incredible. Sir Joseph Pamer, for example, on page eighteen. I presume this is why you didn't ask Sir Francis to join us, Brigadier?"

"I felt his presence would be inappropriate in the circumstances, Prime Minister, and Sir Francis agreed."

Carter turned and glanced at him sharply. The Prime Minister said, "You have informed him of his father's presence in the Blue Book then?"

"Yes, sir, I have."

"I appreciate Sir Francis's delicacy in the matter. On the other hand, the fact that his father was a Fascist all those years ago is hardly his fault. We don't visit the sins of the fathers on the children." The Prime Minister glanced at the Blue Book again, then looked up. "Unless you have anything else to tell me, Brigadier?" There was a strange set look on his face, as if he was somehow challenging Ferguson.

Carter glanced at Ferguson puzzled, his face pale, and Ferguson said firmly, "No, Prime Minister."

"Good. Now we come to the Windsor Protocol." The Prime Minister unfolded it. "Do you gentlemen consider this to be genuine?"

"One can't be certain," Carter said. "The Nazis did produce some remarkable forgeries during the War, there is no doubt about that."

"It is a known fact that the Duke hoped for a speedy end to the War," Ferguson said. "This is in no way to suggest that he was disloyal, but he deeply regretted the loss of life on both sides and wanted it to end."

"Be that as it may, the tabloid press would have a field day with this and the effect on the Royal Family would be catastrophic, and I wouldn't want that," the Prime Minister said. "You've brought me the original of Korvettenkapitän Friemel's diary as I asked and the translation. Are these all the copies?"

"Everything," Ferguson assured him.

"Good." The Prime Minister piled the documents together, got up and went to the fire. He put the Windsor Protocol on top of the blazing coals first. "An old story, gentlemen, a long time ago."

The Protocol flared, curled into ash. He followed it with the Hitler Order, the bank lists, the Blue Book and finally Paul Friemel's diary.

He turned. "It never happened, gentlemen, not any of it."

Carter stood up and managed a feeble smile. "A wise decision, Prime Minister."

"Having said that, it would appear this business of using the services of the man Dillon worked out, Brigadier?"

"We only reached a successful conclusion because of Dillon's efforts, sir."

The Prime Minister came round the desk to shake hands and smiled. "I'm sure it's an interesting story. You must tell me sometime, Brigadier, but for now, you must excuse me."

By some mystery, the door opened smoothly behind them and the aide appeared to usher them out.

In the hall the porter helped them on with their coats. "A satisfactory conclusion all round, I'd say," Carter remarked.

"You think so, do you?" Ferguson said.

The porter opened the door and at that moment, the aide hurried in from the rear office. "A moment, gentlemen, we've just had a most distressing call from the River Police. They recovered the body of Sir Francis Pamer from the Thames a short time ago. I'm about to inform the Prime Minister."

Carter was struck dumb and Ferguson said, "Very sad. Thank you for letting us know," and he stepped out past the policeman on the step, put up his umbrella and started to walk along Downing Street to Whitehall.

He walked very fast, was almost at the security gates before Carter caught up with him and grabbed his arm. "What was it you said to him, Ferguson, I want to know."

"I gave him all the facts," Ferguson said. "You are aware of the part he played from the beginning in this affair. I reminded him of that. I can only imagine he decided to do the decent thing."

"Very convenient."

"Yes, isn't it." They were on the pavement of Whitehall now. "Do you want to share a cab?"

"Damn you to hell, Ferguson!" Simon Carter told him and walked away.

Ferguson stood there for a moment, rain bouncing from his umbrella, and a black cab swerved into the curb. The driver peered out, a cap down over his eyes and asked in perfect cockney, "You want a cab, guvnor?"

"Thank you." Ferguson climbed in and the cab pulled away.

Dillon removed his cap and smiled at Ferguson in the rearview mirror. "How did it go?"

Ferguson said, "Did you steal this thing?"

"No, it belongs to a good friend of mine."

"London-Irish, no doubt?"

"Of course. Actually it's not registered as a working cab, but as everyone assumes it is, it's great for parking. Now what about the Prime Minister?"

"He put everything on the fire, said it was an old story, was even charitable about Francis Pamer."

"Did you put him straight there?"

"I couldn't see the point."

"And how did Carter take it?"

"Rather badly. Just as we were leaving, the Prime Minister's office received a report from the River Police. They recovered Pamer's body."

"And Carter thinks he did it because of pressure from you?"

"I don't know what he thinks, or care. The only thing I worry about is Carter's competence. He dislikes me so much that it clouded his judgment. For example, he was so taken up with the mention of Sir Joseph Pamer in the Blue Book on page eighteen that he missed the gentleman on page fifty-one."

"And who would that be?"

"An army sergeant from the First World War, badly wounded on the Somme, no pension, out of work in the twenties and understandably angry with the Establishment, another associate of Sir Oswald Mosley, who entered politics and became General Secretary of a major trade union. He died about ten years ago."

"And who are we talking about?"

"The Prime Minister's uncle on his mother's side."

"Mother of God!" Dillon said. "And you think he knew, the Prime Minister I mean?"

"That I knew? Oh, yes." Ferguson nodded. "But as he said, an old story and the evidence has just gone up in smoke anyway. Which is why I can afford to tell you, Dillon. After all your efforts in this affair I think you're entitled to know."

"Very convenient, I must say," Dillon observed.

"No, the Prime Minister was right, we can't visit the sins of the fathers on the children. Pamer was different. Where are we going, by the way?"

"Your place, I suppose," Dillon said.

Ferguson opened the window a little and let the rain blow in. "I've been thinking, Dillon, my department's under severe pressure at the moment. Besides the usual things we've got the Yugoslavian business and all this Neo-Nazi stuff in Berlin and East Germany. Losing Jack Lane leaves me in rather a hole."

"I see," Dillon said.

Ferguson leaned forward. "Right up your street, the sort of thing I have in mind. Think about it, Dillon."

Dillon swung the wheel, did a U-turn and started back the other way.

Ferguson was flung back in his seat. "What are you doing, for God's sake?"

Dillon smiled in the rearview mirror. "You did mention dinner at the Garrick Club, didn't you?"

On Dangerous Ground

For Sally Palmer with love

Prologue

The pilot, Flight Lieutenant Joe Caine of RAF Transport Command, was tired, frozen to the bone, his hands clamped to the control column. He eased it forward and took the plane down, emerging from low cloud at three thousand feet into driving rain.

The aircraft ploughing its way through heavy cloud and thunderstorm was a Douglas DC3, the famous Dakota, as much a workhorse for the American Air Force as the RAF, who together operated them out of the Assam Airfields of North India, flying supplies to Chiang Kai-shek's Chinese army. On their way, they negotiated the infamous Hump, as it was known to Allied aircrews, the Himalayan mountains, trying to survive in some of the worst flying conditions in the world.

"There she is, Skipper," the second pilot said. "Dead ahead. Three miles."

"And the usual lousy blackout," Caine said, which was true enough. The inhabitants of Chungking were notoriously lazy in that respect and there were lights all over the place.

"Well, here we go," he said.

"Message from control tower," the wireless operator called from behind.

Caine switched on to VHF and called the tower. "Sugar Nan here. Is there a problem?"

"Priority traffic coming in. Please go round," a neutral voice said.

"For God's sake," Caine replied angrily, "I've just clocked 1,000 miles over the Hump. We're tired, cold, and almost out of fuel."

"VIP traffic to starboard and below you. Go 'round. Please acknowledge." The voice was firm.

The second pilot looked out of the side, then turned. "About five hundred feet below, Skipper. Another Dakota. A Yank from the look of it."

"All right," Caine said wearily and banked to port.

The man who stood on the porch of the Station Commander's office staring up into the rain, listening to the sound of the first Dakota coming in, wore the uniform of a Vice-Admiral of the British Navy, a trenchcoat over his shoulders. His name was Lord Louis Mountbatten and he was cousin to the King of England. A highly decorated war hero, he was also Supreme Allied Commander South East Asia.

The burly American General in steel-rimmed spectacles who emerged behind him, pausing to light a cigarette, was General Vinegar Joe Stillwell, his deputy and also Chief of Staff to Chiang Kai-shek. The greatest expert on China of anyone in the Allied Forces, he was also fluent in Cantonese.

He perched on the rail. "Well, here he comes, the great Chairman Mao."

"What happened to Chiang Kai-shek?" Mountbatten asked.

"Found an excuse to go up-country. It's no use, Louis, Mao and Chiang will never get together. They both want the same thing."

"China?" Mountbatten said.

"Exactly."

"Yes, well I'd like to remind you this isn't the Pacific, Joe. Twenty-five Jap divisions in China, and since the start of their April offensive they've been winning. No one knows that better than you. We need Mao and his Communist Army. It's as simple as that."

They watched the Dakota land. Stillwell said, "The Washington viewpoint is simple. We've given enough lend-lease to Chiang."

"And what have we got for it?" Mountbatten asked. "He sits on his backside doing nothing, saving his ammunition and equipment for the civil war with the Communists when the Japs are beaten."

"A civil war he'll probably win," Stillwell said.

"Do you really think so?" Mountbatten shook his head. "You know, in the West Mao and his people are looked upon as agrarian revolutionaries, that all they want is land for the peasants."

"And you don't agree?"

"Frankly, I think they're more Communist than the Russians. I think they could well drive Chiang Kai-shek out of mainland China and take over after the war."

"An interesting thought," Stillwell told him, "but if you're talking about making friends and influencing people, that's up to you. Washington won't play. Fresh supplies of arms and ammunition must come from your people, not American sources. We'll have a big enough problem handling Japan after the war. China is your baby."

The Dakota came toward them and stopped. A couple of waiting ground crew wheeled steps forward and waited for the door to open.

"So you don't think I'm asking dear old Chairman Mao too much?"

"Hell, no!" Stillwell laughed. "To be honest, Louis, if he agrees, I don't see how you'll be getting very much in return for all that aid you intend to give him."

"Better than nothing, old sport, especially if he agrees."

The door swung open, a young Chinese officer emerged. A moment later Mao Tse-tung appeared. He paused for a moment looking toward them, wearing only a simple uniform and cap with the red star, then he started down the steps.

Mao Tse-tung, Chairman of the Chinese Communist Party, was at that time fifty-one, a brilliant politician, a master of guerilla warfare, and a soldier of genius. He was also the implacable foe of Chiang Kai-shek, and the two sides had been engaged in open warfare instead of taking on the Japanese together.

In the office, he sat behind the Station Commander's desk, the young officer behind him. To one side of Mountbatten and Stillwell stood a British Army Major. His left eye was covered by a black eye patch and the badge in his cap was that of the Highland Light Infantry. A Corporal wearing the bonnet of the same regiment stood against the wall behind him, a cardboard office file under his left arm.

Stillwell said in fluent Cantonese, "I'll be happy to translate for these proceedings, Chairman Mao."

Mao sat facing him, face enigmatic, then said in excellent English, an ability he seldom advertised, "General, my time is limited." Stillwell stared at him in astonishment and Mao said to Mountbatten, "Who is this officer and the man with him?"

Mountbatten said, "Major Ian Campbell, Chairman, one of my aides. The Corporal is his batman. Their regiment is the Highland Light Infantry."

"Batman?" Mao enquired.

"A soldier servant," Mountbatten explained.

"Ah, I see." Mao nodded enigmatically and turned to Campbell. "The Highlands of Scotland, am I right? A strange people. The English put you to the sword, turned your people off their land, and yet you go to war for them."

Ian Campbell said, "I am a Highlander, flesh and bone, a thousand years behind me, Laird of Loch Dhu Castle and all around like my father and his before me, and if the English need a helping hand now and then, why not?"

Mao actually smiled and turned to Mountbatten. "I like this man. You should lend him to me."

"Not possible, Chairman."

Mao shrugged. "Then to business. I have little time. I must make the return journey in no more than thirty minutes. What do you offer me?"

Mountbatten glanced at Stillwell, who shrugged, and the Admiral said to Mao, "Our American friends are not able to offer arms and ammunition to you and your forces."

"But everything the Generallisimo needs they will supply?" Mao asked.

He stayed surprisingly calm and Mountbatten said, "I believe I have a solution. What if the RAF flew in ten thousand tons a month over the Hump to Kunming, assorted weapons, ammunition, and so forth?"

Mao selected a cigarette from an old silver case and the young officer lit it for him. The Chairman blew out a long plume of smoke. "And what would I have to do for such munificence?"

"Something," Mountbatten said. "I mean, we have to have something. That's only fair."

"And what would you have in mind?"

Mountbatten lit a cigarette himself, walked to the open door, and looked out at the rain. He turned. "The Hong Kong Treaty, the lease to Britain. It expires July first, nineteen ninety-seven."

"So?"

"I'd like you to extend it by one hundred years."

There was a long silence. Mao leaned back and blew smoke to the ceiling. "My friend, I think the rains have driven you a little crazy. Generallisimo Chiang Kai-shek rules China, the Japanese permitting, of course."

"But the Japanese will go," Mountbatten said.

"And then?"

The room was very quiet. Mountbatten turned and nodded. The Corporal clicked his heels and passed the file to Major Campbell, who opened it and took out a document which he passed across the desk to the Chairman.

"This is not a treaty but a covenant," Mountbatten said. "The Chungking Covenant, I call it. If you will read it and approve it with your signature above mine, you will agree to extend, if you ever control China, the Hong Kong treaty by a hundred years. In exchange, His Majesty's Government will supply you with all your military needs."

Mao Tse-tung examined the document, then glanced up. "Have you a pen, Lord Mountbatten?"

It was the Corporal who supplied one, moving in quickly. Mao signed the document. Major Campbell produced three more copies and laid them on the table. Mao signed each one, Mountbatten countersigned.

He handed the pen back to the Corporal and stood up. "A good night's work," he said to Mountbatten, "but now I must go."

He started for the door and Mountbatten said, "A moment, Mr. Chairman, you're forgetting your copy of the covenant."

Mao turned. "Later," he said. "When it has been countersigned by Churchill."

Mountbatten stared at him. "Churchill?"

"But of course. Naturally this should not delay the flow of arms, but I do look forward to receiving my copy signed by the man himself. Is there a problem?"

"No." Mountbatten pulled himself together. "No, of course not."

"Good. And now I must go. There is work to do, gentlemen."

He went out and down the steps followed by the young officer, crossed to the Dakota, and went in. The door was closed, the steps wheeled away, the plane started to taxi, and Stillwell burst into laughter.

"God help me, that's the weirdest thing I've seen in years. He certainly is a character. What are you going to do?"

"Send the damn thing to London for Churchill's signature, of course." Mountbatten turned back in the entrance and said to Major Campbell, "Ian, I'm going to give you a chance to have dinner at the Savoy. I want you on your way to London as soon as possible with a dispatch from me for the Prime Minister. Did I hear another plane land?"

"Yes, sir, a Dakota from Assam."

"Good. Give orders for it to be refueled and turned around." Mountbatten glanced at the Corporal. "You can take Tanner with you."

"Fine, sir."

Campbell shuffled the papers to put them in the file and Mountbatten said, "Three copies. One for Mao, another for the Prime Minister, and the third for President Roosevelt. Didn't I sign four?"

"I took the liberty of making an extra copy, sir, just in case of accidents," Campbell said.

"Good man, Ian," Mountbatten nodded. "On your way then. Only one night out at the Savoy, then straight back."

"Of course, sir."

Campbell saluted and went out followed by Tanner. Stillwell lit a cigarette. "He's a strange one, Campbell."

"Lost his eye at Dunkirk," Mountbatten said. "Got a well-earned Military Cross. Best aide I ever had."

"What's all this Laird of Loch Dhu crap?" Stillwell said. "You English are really crazy."

"Ah, but Campbell isn't English, he's Scots, and more than that, he's a Highlander. As Laird of Loch Dhu he heads a sect of Clan Campbell and that, Joe, is a tradition that existed before the Vikings sailed to America."

He walked to the door and stared out at the driving rain. Stillwell joined him. "Are we going to win, Louis?"

"Oh, yes," Mountbatten nodded. "It's what will come after that bothers me."

In Campbell's quarters, Tanner packed the Major's hold-all with military thoroughness while Campbell shaved. They had been together since boyhood, for Tanner's father had been a gamekeeper on the Loch Dhu estate, and together they endured the shattering experience of Dunkirk. When Campbell had first worked for Mountbatten at Combined Operations Headquarters in London he had taken the Corporal with him as his batman. The move to South East Asia Command had followed that. But to Jack Tanner, good soldier with a Military Medal for bravery in the field to prove it, Campbell would never be anything else but the Laird.

The Major came out of the bathroom drying his hands. He adjusted the black eye patch and smoothed his hair, then pulled on his tunic. "Got the briefcase, Jack?"

Tanner held it up. "The papers are inside, Laird."

He always gave Campbell the title when they were alone. Campbell said, "Open it. Take out the fourth copy, the extra copy."

Tanner did as he was told and passed it to him. The single sheet of paper was headed "Supreme Allied Commander South East Asia Command." Mao had signed it, not only in English but in Chinese, with Mountbatten countersigning.

"There you are, Jack," Campbell said as he folded it. "Piece of history here. If Mao wins, Hong Kong will stay British until July first, twenty ninety-seven."

"You think it will happen, Laird?"

"Who knows. We've got to win the war first. Pass me my Bible, will you?"

Tanner went to the dresser where the Major's toilet articles were laid out. The Bible was about six inches by four with a cover of embossed silver, a Celtic cross standing out clearly. It was very old. A Campbell had carried it to war for many centuries. It had been found in the pocket of the Major's ancestor who had died fighting for Bonnie Prince Charlie at Culloden. It had been recovered from the body of his uncle, killed on the Somme in 1916. Campbell took it everywhere.

Tanner opened it. The inside of the Bible's cover was also silver. He felt carefully with his nail; it sprang open revealing a small hidden compartment. Campbell folded the sheet of paper to the appropriate size and fitted it in, closing the lid.

"Top secret, Jack, only you and I know it's there. Your Highland oath on it."

"You have it, Laird. Shall I put it in the hold-all, Laird?"

"No, I'll carry it in my map pocket." There was a knock at the door, Tanner went to open it and Flight Lieutenant Caine stepped in. He was carrying heavy flying jackets and sheepskin boots.

"You'll need these, sir. We'll probably have to go as high as twenty thousand over part of the Hump. Bloody freezing up there."

The young man looked tired, dark circles under his eyes. Campbell said, "I'm sorry about this. I know you've only just got in."

"That's all right, sir. I carry a co-pilot, Pilot Officer Giffard. We can spell each other. We also have a navigator and wireless operator. We'll make out." He smiled. "One can hardly say no to Lord Mountbatten. All the way to Delhi on this one, I see."

"That's right. Then onwards to London."

"Wish I was doing that leg of the trip." Caine opened the door and looked out at the rain. "Never stops, does it? What a bloody country. I'll see you at the plane, sir."

He went out. Campbell said, "Right, Jack, let's get moving."

They pulled on the flying boots, the heavy sheepskin jackets. Finally ready, Tanner picked up his hold-all and the Major's.

"On your way, Jack."

Tanner moved out. Campbell glanced around the room, reached for his cap and put it on, then he picked up the Bible, put it in the map pocket of his flying jacket, and fastened the flap. Strange, but he felt more than tired. It was as if he had reached the end of something. His Highland blood speaking again. He shrugged the feeling off, turned, and went out into the rain, following Tanner to the Dakota.

To Kunming from Chungking was four hundred and fifty miles. They took the opportunity to refuel and then pressed on to the most hazardous section of the trip, the five hundred and fifty miles over the Hump to the Assam airfields.

Conditions were appalling, heavy rain and thunderstorms, and the kind of turbulence that threatened to break the plane up. Several hundred aircrew had died making this run over the past couple of years, Campbell knew that. It was probably the most hazardous flying duty in the RAF or the USAF. He wondered what persuaded men to volunteer for such work and while thinking about it, actually managed some sleep, only surfacing as they came into their Assam destination to refuel.

The onward trip to Delhi was another eleven hundred miles and a completely different proposition. Blue skies, considerable heat, and no wind to speak of. The Dakota coasted along at ten thousand feet and Caine, leaving the flying to Giffard, came back and tried to get a couple of hours' sleep.

Campbell dozed again and came awake to find the wireless operator shaking Caine by the shoulder. "Delhi in fifteen minutes, Skipper."

Caine got up, yawning. He grinned at Campbell. "Piece of cake this leg, isn't it?"

As he turned away there was an explosion. Pieces of metal flew off the port engine, there was thick black smoke, and as the propeller stopped turning, the Dakota banked and dived steeply, throwing Caine off his feet.

Campbell was hurled against the bulkhead behind with such force that he was almost knocked senseless. The result was that he couldn't really take in what was happening. There was a kind of nightmare as if the world was breaking up around him, the impact of the crash, the smell of burning and someone screaming.

He was aware of being in water, managed to focus his eyes, and found himself being dragged through a paddy field by a wild-eyed Tanner, blood on his face. The Corporal heaved him onto a dyke, then turned and hurried back, knee-deep in water, to the Dakota which was burning fiercely now. When he was halfway there, it blew up with a tremendous explosion.

Debris cascaded everywhere and Tanner turned and came back wearily. He eased the Major higher on the dyke and found a tin of cigarettes. His hand shook as he lit one.

"Are we hit?" Campbell managed to croak.

"So it would appear, Laird."

"Dear God." Campbell's hands moved over his chest. "The Bible," he whispered.

"Dinna fash yourself, Laird, I'll hold it safe for you."

Tanner took it from the map pocket and then all sounds faded for Campbell, all color, nothing now but quiet darkness.

In Chungking, Mountbatten and Stillwell were examining on the map the relentless progress of the advancing Japanese, who had already overrun most of the Allied airfields in eastern China.

"I thought we were supposed to be winning the war," Stillwell said.

Mountbatten smiled ruefully. "So did I."

Behind him, the door opened and an aide entered with a signal flimsy. "Sorry to bother you, sir, but this is from Delhi—marked urgent."

Mountbatten read it then swore softly. "All right, you can go."

The aide went out. Stillwell said, "Bad news."

"The Dakota Campbell was traveling in lost an engine and crashed just outside Delhi. It fireballed after landing. By all accounts, the documents and my dispatches went with it."

"Is Campbell dead?"

"No, that Corporal of his managed to get him out. All the crew were killed. It seems Campbell received a serious head injury. He's in a coma."

"Let's hope he hangs in there," Stillwell said. "Anyway, something of a setback for you, your Chungking Covenant going up in flames. What will you do? Try to get Mao to sign another one?"

"I doubt if I'll ever get close enough to him again. It was always an anything-is-better-than-nothing situation. I didn't really expect much to come out of it. Anyway, in my experience, Chinese seldom give you a second bite at the cherry."

"I agree," Stillwell said. "In any case, the wily old bastard is probably already regretting putting his signature to that thing. But what about his supplies?"

"Oh, we'll see he gets those because I want him actively on our side taking on the Japanese. The Hong Kong business was never serious, Joe. I thought we ought to get something out of the deal if we could, and the Hong Kong thing was all that the Prime Minister and I could come up with. Not that it matters now, we've got far more serious things to consider." He walked back to the wall map. "Now show me exactly where those Japanese forward units are."

1993

LONDON

ONE

Norah Bell got out of the taxi close to St. James's Stairs on Wapping High Street. She paid off the cab driver and walked away, a small, hippy, dark haired girl in leather jacket, tight black mini skirt, and high-heeled ankle boots. She walked well with a sort of total movement of the whole body. The cab driver watched her put up her umbrella against the heavy rain, sighed deeply, and drove away.

She paused on the first corner and bought an *Evening Standard*. The front page was concerned with only one thing, the arrival of the American President in London that day to meet with both the Israeli and British Prime Ministers, to discuss developments in the Palestinian situation. She folded the newspaper, put it under her left arm, and turned the corner of the next street, walking down toward the Thames.

The youth standing in a doorway opposite was perhaps eighteen and wore lace-up boots, jeans, and shabby bomber jacket. With the ring in his left nostril and the swastika tattooed on his forehead, he was typical of a certain type of gang animal that roamed the city streets in search of prey. She looked easy meat and he went after her quickly, only running in at the last minute to grab her from behind, one hand over her mouth. She didn't struggle, went completely still which should have told him something, but by then he was beyond reason, charged with the wrong kind of sexual excitement.

"Just do as you're told," he said, "and I won't hurt you."

He urged her into the porch of a long-disused warehouse, pushing against her. She said, "No need to be rough."

To his amazement she kissed him, her tongue flickering in his mouth. He couldn't believe his luck and, still clutching her umbrella, she moved her other hand down between them, brushing against his hardness.

"Jesus," he moaned and kissed her again, aware that her hand seemed to be easing up her skirt.

She found what she was looking for, the flick knife tucked into the top of her right stocking. It came up, the blade jumped, and she sliced open the left side of his face from the corner of the eye to the chin.

He screamed, falling back. She said calmly, putting the point under his chin, "Do you want some more?"

He was more afraid than he had ever been in his life. "No, for God's sake, no!"

She wiped the blade on his jacket. "Then go away."

He moved out into the rain, then turned, holding a handkerchief to his face. "Bitch! I'll get you for this."

"No you won't." Her accent was unmistakably Ulster Irish. "You'll find the nearest casualty department as fast as you can, get yourself stitched up, and put the whole thing down to experience."

She watched him go, closed the knife, slipping it back in the top of the stocking, then she turned and continued down toward the Thames, moving along the waterfront, finally pausing at an old warehouse.

There was a Judas gate in the main entrance, she opened it and went in. It was a place of shadows, but at the far end there was a glass office with a light in it. It was reached by a flight of wooden stairs. As she moved toward it, a young, dark-skinned man moved out of the darkness, a Browning Hi-Power in one hand.

"And who might you be?" she asked.

The door of the office was opened and a small man with dark tousled hair wearing a reefer jacket appeared. "Is that you, Norah?"

"And who else?" she replied. "Who's your friend?"

"Ali Halabi, meet Norah Bell. Come away up."

"I'm sorry," the Arab said.

She ignored him and went up the stairs and he followed, noting with approval the way her skirt tightened over her hips.

When she went into the office the man in the reefer coat put his hands on her shoulders. "God help me, but you look good enough to eat," and he kissed her lightly on the lips.

"Save the blarney." She put her umbrella on the desk, opened her handbag, and took out a packet of cigarettes. "Anything in a skirt, Michael Ahern. I've known you too long."

She put a cigarette in her mouth and the Arab hurriedly took out a lighter and lit it for her. He turned to Ahern. "The lady is part of your organization?"

"Well I'm not with the bloody IRA," she said. "We're Prods, mister, if you know what that means."

"Norah and I were in the Ulster Volunteer Force together and then the Red Hand of Ulster," Ahern said "Until we had to move on."

Norah laughed harshly. "Until they threw us out. A bunch of old women, that lot. We were killing too many Catholics for their liking."

"I see," Ali Halabi said. "Is it Catholics who are you target or the IRA?"

"The same difference," she said. "I'm from Belfast Mr. Halabi. My father was an Army sergeant, killed the Falklands War. My mother, my kid sister, my old granddad, all the family I had in the world, were killed in a street bomb planted by the IRA back in eighty-six. You might say I've been taking my revenge ever since."

"But we are open to offers," Ahern said amiably. "Any revolutionary organization needs money."

The door banged below. Ali took the gun from his pocket and Ahern moved to the door. "Is that you Billy?"

"As ever was."

"Would that be Billy Quigley?" Norah asked.

"Who else?" Ahern turned to Ali. "Another one the Red Hand threw out. Billy and I did some time together in the Maze prison."

Quigley was a small, wiry man in an old raincoat. He had faded blond hair and a careworn face that was old beyond his years.

"Jesus, is that you, Norah?"

"Hello, Billy."

"You got my message?" Ahern said.

"Yes, I drop in to the William of Orange in Kilburn most nights."

Ahern said to Ali, "Kilburn is what you might call the Irish quarter of London. Plenty of good Irish pubs there, Catholic and Protestant. This, by the way, is Ali Halabi from Iran."

"So what's it all about?" Quigley demanded.

"This." Ahern held up the *Evening Standard* with the headline about the American President. "Ali, here, represents a group of fundamentalists in Iran called the Army of God. They, shall we say, deeply deplore Arafat's deal with Israel over the new status of Palestine. They are even more unhappy with the American President presiding over that meeting at the White House and giving it his blessing."

"So?" Quigley said.

"They'd like me to blow him up for them while he's in London, me having a certain reputation in that field."

"For five million pounds," Ali Halabi said, "don't let us forget that."

"Half of which is already on deposit in Geneva." Ahern smiled. "By God, Billy, couldn't we give the IRA a run for their money with a million pounds to spend on arms?"

Quigley's face was pale. "The American President? You wouldn't dare, not even you."

Norah laughed that distinctive harsh laugh, "Oh, yes he would."

Ahern turned to her. "Are you with me, girl?"

"I wouldn't miss it for the world."

"And you, Billy?" Quigley licked dry lips and hesitated. Ahern put a hand on his shoulder. "In or out, Billy?"

Quigley smiled suddenly. "Why not. A man can only die once. How do we do it?"

"Come down below and I'll show you."

Ahern led the way down the steps and switched on a light at the bottom. There was a vehicle parked in a corner covered by a dust sheet which he pulled away revealing a British Telecom truck.

"Where in the hell did you get that?" Quigley demanded.

"Someone knocked it off for me months ago. I was going to leave it outside one of those Catholic pubs in Kilburn with five hundred pounds of Semtex inside and blow the hell out of some Sinn Fein bastards, but I decided to hang on to it until something really important turned up." Ahern smiled cheerfully. "And now it has."

"But how do you intend to pull it off?" Ali demanded.

"Hundreds of these things all over London. They can park anywhere without being interfered with because they usually have a manhole cover up while the engineers do what they have to do."

"So?" Quigley said.

"Don't ask me how, but I have access through sources to the President's schedule. Tomorrow he leaves the American Embassy in Grosvenor Square at ten o'clock in the morning to go to Number Ten Downing Street. They take the Park Lane route turning into Constitution Hill beside Green Park."

"Can you be sure of that?" Norah asked.

"They always do, love, believe me." He turned to Quigley and Ali. "You two, dressed in Telecom overalls which are inside the van, will park halfway along Constitution Hill. There's a huge beech tree. You can't miss it. As I say, you park, lift the manhole cover, put up your signs and so on. You'll be there at nine-thirty. At nine-forty-five you walk away through Green Park to Piccadilly. There are some men's toilets. You can get rid of your overalls there."

"And then what?" Ali demanded.

"I'll be in a car waiting with Norah for the golden moment. As the

President's cavalcade reaches the Telecom truck, I'll detonate by remote control." He smiled. "It'll work, I promise you. We'll probably kill everyone in the cavalcade."

There was silence, a kind of awe on Quigley's face, and Norah was excited, face pale. "You bastard," she said.

"You think it will work?"

"Oh, yes."

He turned to Ali. "And you? You're willing to take part?"

"An honor, Mr. Ahern."

"And you, Billy?" Ahern turned to him.

"They'll be singing about us for years," Quigley said.

"Good man yourself, Billy." Ahern looked at his watch. "Seven o'clock. I could do with a bite to eat. How about you, Norah?"

"Fine," she said.

"Good. I'm taking the Telecom van away now. I shan't be returning to this place. I'll pick you two up in the Mall at nine o'clock in the morning. You'll arrive separately and wait at the park gates across from Marlborough Road. Norah will be behind me in a car. You two will take over and we'll follow. Any questions?"

Ali Halabi was incredibly excited. "I can't wait."

"Good, off you go now. We'll leave separately." The Arab went out and Ahern turned to Quigley and held out his hand. "A big one this, eh, Billy?"

"The biggest, Michael."

"Right, Norah and I will go now. Come and open the main gate for us. I'll leave you to put out the lights and follow on."

They went downstairs. Norah climbed into the passenger seat, but Ahern shook his head. "Move into the rear out of sight and pass me one of those orange jackets. We've got to look right. If a copper sees you he might get curious."

It said "British Telecom" across the back of the jacket. "It'll never catch on," she told him.

He laughed and drove out into the street, waving at Quigley, who closed the gate behind them. He traveled only a few yards, then swung into a yard and switched off the engine.

"What is it?" she demanded.

"You'll see. Follow me and keep your mouth shut."

He opened the Judas gate gently and stepped in. Quigley was in the office, they could hear his voice and when they reached the bottom of the stairs, they could even hear what he was saying.

"Yes, Brigadier Ferguson. Most urgent." There was a pause. "Then patch me through, you silly bugger, this is life or death."

Ahern took a Walther from his pocket and screwed on a silencer as he went up, Norah behind him. The door was open and Quigley sat on the edge of the desk.

"Brigadier Ferguson?" he said suddenly. "It's Billy Quigley. You said only to call you when it was big. Well this couldn't be bigger. Michael Ahern and that bitch Norah Bell and some Iranian named Ali Halabi are going to try to blow up the American President tomorrow." There was a pause. "Yes, I'm supposed to be in on it. Well this is the way of it."

"Billy boy," Ahern said, "that's really naughty of you." As Quigley turned he shot him between the eyes.

Quigley went back over the desk and Ahern picked up the phone. "Are you there, Brigadier? Michael Ahern here. You'll need a new man." He replaced the receiver, turned off the office light, and turned to Norah. "Let's go, my love."

"You knew he was an informer?" she said.

"Oh, yes, I think that's why they let him out of the Maze prison early. He was serving life, remember. They must have offered him a deal."

"The dirty bastard," she said. "And now he's screwed everything up."

"Not at all," Ahern said. "You see, Norah, it's all worked out exactly as I planned." He opened the van door and handed her in. "We'll go and get a bite to eat and then I'll tell you how we're really going to hit the President."

In 1972, aware of the growing problem of terrorism, the British Prime Minister of the day ordered the setting up of a small elite intelligence unit which became known rather bitterly in intelligence circles as the Prime Minister's private army, as it owed allegiance only to that office.

Brigadier Charles Ferguson had headed the unit since its inception, had served many Prime Ministers, but had no political allegiance whatsoever. His office was on the third floor of the Ministry of Defence overlooking Horse Guards Avenue. He had been working late when Quigley's call was patched through. He was a rather untidy-looking man in a Guards tie and tweed suit and was standing looking out of his window when there was a knock at the door.

The woman who entered was in her late twenties and wore a fawn trouser suit of excellent cut and black horn-rimmed glasses that contrasted with close-cropped red hair. She could have been a top secretary or P.A. She was, in fact, a Detective Chief Inspector of Police from Special Branch at Scotland Yard borrowed by Ferguson as his assistant after the untimely death in the line of duty of her predecessor. Her name was Hannah Bernstein.

"Was there something, Brigadier?"

"You could say so. When you worked with antiterrorism at Scotland Yard, did you ever come across a Michael Ahern?"

"Irish terrorist, Orange Protestant variety. Wasn't he Red Hand of Ulster?"

"And Norah Bell?"

"Oh, yes," Hannah Bernstein said. "A very bleak prospect, that one."

"I had an informer, Billy Quigley, in deep cover. He just phoned me to say that Ahern was masterminding a plot to blow up the American President tomorrow. He'd recruited Quigley. Bell is involved and an Iranian named Ali Halabi."

"Excuse me, sir, but I know who Halabi is. He belongs to the Army of God. That's an extreme fundamentalist group very much opposed to the Israeli-Palestine accord."

"Really?" Ferguson said. "That is interesting. Even more interesting is that Quigley was shot dead while filling me in. Ahern actually had the cheek to pick up the phone and speak to me. Told me it was him. Said I'd need a new man."

"A cool bastard, sir."

"Oh, he's that all right. Anyway, notify everyone. Scotland Yard antiterrorist unit, MI Five, and security at the American Embassy. Obviously the Secret Servicemen guarding the President will have a keen interest."

"Right, sir."

She turned to the door and he said, "One more thing. I need Dillon on this."

She turned. "Dillon, sir?"

"Sean Dillon. Don't pretend you don't know who I mean."

"The only Sean Dillon I know, sir, was the most feared enforcer the IRA ever had, and if I'm right, he tried to blow up the Prime Minister and the War Cabinet in February, nineteen ninety-one during the Gulf War."

"And nearly succeeded," Ferguson said, "but he works for this Department now, Chief Inspector, so get used to it. He only recently completed a most difficult assignment on the Prime Minister's orders that saved the Royal Family considerable grief. I need Dillon, so find him. Now on your way."

Ahern had a studio flat in what had been a warehouse beside the canal in Camden. He parked the Telecom van in the garage, then took Norah up in what had been the old freight hoist. The studio was simply furnished, the wooden floor sanded and varnished, a rug here and there, two or three large sofas. The paintings on the wall were very modern.

"Nice," she said, "but it doesn't seem you."

"It isn't. I'm on a six months' lease."

He opened the drinks cabinet, found a bottle of Jameson Irish Whiskey, and poured some into two glasses. He offered her one, then opened a window and stepped out onto a small platform overlooking the canal.

"What's going on, Michael?" she said. "I mean, we don't really stand much of a chance of blowing up the President on Constitution Hill, not now."

"I never thought for a moment that I could. You should remember, Norah, that I never let my left hand know what my right hand is doing."

"Explain," she said.

"Because of Quigley's phone call, wherever the President goes tomorrow they'll be on tenterhooks. Now follow my reasoning. If there is an abortive explosion on his intended route to Number Ten Downing Street, everyone heaves a sigh of relief, especially if they find what's left of Halabi there."

"Go on."

"They won't expect another attempt the same day in an entirely different context."

"My God," she said. "You planned this all along, you used Quigley."

"Poor sod." Ahern brushed past her and helped himself to more whiskey. "Once they have their explosion, they'll think that's it, but it won't be. You see, tomorrow night at seven-thirty, the American President, the Prime Minister, and selected guests board the river boat *Jersey Lily* at Cadogan Pier on the Chelsea Embankment for an evening of frivolity and cocktails, cruising the Thames past the Houses of Parliament, ending up at Westminster Pier. The catering is in the hands of Orsini and Co. of whom you and I are employed as waiters." He opened a drawer and took out two security cards. "My name is Harry Smith, nice and innocuous. You'll note the false moustache and horn-rimmed glasses. I'll add those later."

"Mary Hunt," Norah said. "That does sound prim. Where did you get my photo?"

"An old one I had. I got a photographer friend to touch it up and add the spectacles. They intend a cocktail party on the forward deck, weather permitting."

"What about weapons? How would we get through security?"

"Taken care of. An associate of mine was working as a crew member until yesterday. He's left two silenced Walthers wrapped in cling film at the bottom of the sand in a fire bucket in one of the men's restrooms, and that was after the security people did their checks."

"Very clever."

"I'm no kamikaze, Norah, I intend to survive this. We hit from the upper decks. With silenced weapons, he'll go down as if he's having a heart attack."

"And what happens to us?"

"The ship has an inflatable tender on a line at the stern. My associate checked it out. It has an outboard motor. In the confusion, we'll drop in and head for the other side of the river."

"As long as the confusion is confusion enough."

"Nothing's perfect in this life. Are you with me?"

"Oh, yes," she said. "To the final end, Michael, whatever comes."

"Good girl." He put an arm round her and squeezed. "Now could we go and get something to eat? I'm starving."

TWO

"A strange man, Sean Dillon," Ferguson said.

"I'd say that was an understatement, sir," Hannah Bernstein told him.

They were sitting in the rear of Ferguson's Daimler threading their way through the West End traffic.

"He was born in Belfast, but his mother died in childbirth. His father came to work in London, so the boy went to school here. Incredible talent for acting. He did a year at the Royal Academy of Dramatic Art and one or two roles at the National Theatre. He also has a flair for languages, everything from Irish to Russian."

"All very impressive, sir, but he still ended up shooting people for the Provisional IRA."

"Yes, well that was because his father, on a trip home to Belfast, got caught in some crossfire and was killed by a British Army patrol. Dillon took the oath, did a fast course on weaponry in Libya, and never looked back."

"Why the switch from the IRA to the international scene?"

"Disenchantment with the glorious cause. Dillon is a thoroughly ruthless man when he has to be. He's killed many times in his career, but the random bomb that kills women and children? Let's say that's not his style."

"Are you trying to tell me he actually has some notion of morality?"

Ferguson laughed. "Well he certainly never played favorites. Worked for the PLO, but also as an underwater specialist for the Israelis."

"For money, of course."

"Naturally. Our Sean does like the good things in life. The attempt to blow up Downing Street, that was for money. Saddam Hussein was behind that. And yet eighteen months later he flies a light plane loaded with medical supplies for children into Bosnia and no payment involved."

"What happened, did God speak down through the clouds to him or something?"

"Does it matter? The Serbs had him, and his prospects, to put it mildly, looked bleak. I did a deal with them which saved him from a firing squad. In return he came to work for me, slate wiped clean."

"Excuse me, sir, but that's a slate that will never wipe clean."

"My dear Chief Inspector, there are many occasions in this line of work when it's useful to be able to set a thief to catch one. If you are to continue to work for me, you'll have to get used to the idea." He peered out as they turned into Grafton Street. "Are you sure he's at this place?"

"So they tell me, sir. His favorite restaurant."

"Excellent," Ferguson said. "I could do with a bite to eat myself."

Sean Dillon sat in the upstairs bar of Mulligan's Irish Restaurant and worked his way through a dozen oysters and half a bottle of Krug champagne to help things along as he read the evening paper. He was a small man, no more than five-feet-five, with hair so fair that it was almost white. He wore dark cord jeans, an old black leather flying jacket, a white scarf at his throat. The eyes were his strangest feature, like water over a stone, clear, no color, and there was a permanent, slight ironic quirk to the corner of his mouth, the look of a man who no longer took life too seriously.

"So there you are," Charles Ferguson said and Dillon glanced up and groaned. "No place to hide, not tonight. I'll have a dozen of those and a pint of Guinness."

A young waitress standing by had heard. Dillon said to her in Irish, "A fine lordly Englishman, *a colleen*, but his mother, God rest her, was Irish, so give him what he wants."

The girl gave him a smile of true devotion and went away. Ferguson sat down and Dillon looked up at Hannah Bernstein. "And who might you be, girl?"

"This is Detective Chief Inspector Hannah Bernstein, Special Branch, my new assistant, and I don't want you corrupting her. Now where's my Guinness?"

It was then that she received her first shock, for as Dillon stood, he smiled, and it was like no smile she had ever seen before, warm and immensely charming, changing his personality completely. She had come here wanting to dislike this man, but now . . .

He took her hand. "And what would a nice Jewish girl like you be doing in such bad company? Will you have a glass of champagne?"

"I don't think so, I'm on duty." She was slightly uncertain now and took a seat.

Dillon went to the bar, returned with another glass, and poured Krug into it. "When you're tired of champagne, you're tired of life."

"What a load of cobblers," she said, but took the glass.

Ferguson roared with laughter. "Beware this one, Dillon. She ran across a hoodlum emerging from a supermarket with a sawed-off shotgun last year. Unfortunately for him she was working the American Embassy detail that week and had a Smith and Wesson in her handbag."

"So you convinced him of his wicked ways?" Dillon said.

She nodded. "Something like that."

Ferguson's Guinness and oysters appeared. "We've got trouble, Dillon, bad trouble. Tell him, Chief Inspector."

Which she did in a few brief sentences. When she was finished, Dillon took a cigarette from a silver case and lit it with an old-fashioned Zippo lighter.

"So what do you think?" she asked.

"Well, all we know for certain is that Billy Quigley is dead."

"But he did manage to speak to the Brigadier," Hannah said. "Which surely means Ahern will abort the mission."

"Why should he?" Dillon said. "You've got nothing except the word that he intends to try and blow up the President sometime tomorrow. Where? When? Have you even the slightest idea, and I'll bet his schedule is extensive!"

"It certainly is," Ferguson said. "Downing Street in the morning with the P.M. and the Israeli Prime Minister. Cocktail party on a river steamer tomorrow night and most things in between."

"None of which he's willing to cancel?"

"I'm afraid not." Ferguson shook his head. "I've already had a call from Downing Street. The President refuses to change a thing."

Hannah Bernstein said, "Do you know Ahern personally?"

"Oh, yes," Dillon told her. "He tried to kill me a couple of times and then we met for face-to-face negotiations during a truce in Derry."

"And his girlfriend?"

Dillon shook his head. "Whatever else Norah Bell is, she isn't that. Sex isn't her bag. She was just an ordinary working-class girl until her family was obliterated by an IRA bomb. These days she'd kill the Pope if she could."

"And Ahern?"

"He's a strange one. It's always been like a game to him. He's a brilliant manipulator. I recall his favorite saying. That he didn't like his left hand to know what his right hand was doing."

"And what's that supposed to mean?" Ferguson demanded.

"Just that nothing's ever what it seems with Ahern."

There was a small silence, then Ferguson said, "Everyone is on this case. We've got them pumping out a not very good photo of the man himself."

"And an even more inferior one of the girl," Hannah Bernstein said.

Ferguson swallowed an oyster. "Any ideas on finding him?"

"As a matter of fact, I have," Dillon said. "There's a Protestant pub in Kilburn, the William of Orange. I could have words there."

"Then what are we waiting for?" Ferguson swallowed his last oyster and stood up. "Let's go."

The William of Orange in Kilburn had a surprising look of Belfast about it with the fresco of King William victorious at the Battle of the Boyne on the white-washed wall at one side. It could have been any Orange pub in the Shankhill.

"You wouldn't exactly fit in at the bar, you two," Dillon said as he sat in the back of the Daimler. "I need to speak to a man called Paddy Driscoll."

"What is he, UVF?" Ferguson asked.

"Let's say he's a fund-raiser. Wait here. I'm going 'round the back."

"Go with him, Chief Inspector," Ferguson ordered.

Dillon sighed. "All right, Brigadier, but I'm in charge."

Ferguson nodded. "Do as he says."

Dillon got out and started along the pavement. "Are you carrying?" he asked.

"Of course."

"Good. You never know what will happen next in this wicked old world."

He paused in the entrance to a yard, took a Walther from his waistband at the rear, produced a Carswell silencer and screwed it into place, then he slipped it inside his flying jacket. They crossed the cobbled yard through the rain, aware of music from the bar area where some loyalist band thumped out "The Sash My Father Wore." Through the rear window was a view of an extensive kitchen, a small, gray-haired man seated at a table doing accounts.

"That's Driscoll," Dillon whispered. "In we go." Driscoll, at the table, was aware of some of his papers fluttering in a sudden draft of wind, looked up, and found Dillon entering the room, Hannah Bernstein behind him.

"God bless all here," Dillon said, "and the best of the night yet to come, Paddy, me old son."

"Dear God, Sean Dillon." There was naked fear on Driscoll's face.

"Plus your very own Detective Chief Inspector. We *are* treating you well tonight."

"What do you want?"

Hannah leaned against the door and Dillon pulled a chair over and sat across the table from Driscoll. He took out a cigarette and lit it. "Michael Ahern. Where might he be?"

"Jesus, Sean, I haven't seen that one in years."

"Billy Quigley? Don't tell me you haven't seen Billy because I happen to know he drinks here regularly."

Driscoll tried to tough it out. "Sure, Billy comes in all the time, but as for Ahern . . ." He shrugged. "He's bad news that one, Sean."

"Yes, but I'm worse." In one swift movement Dillon pulled the Walther from inside his flying jacket, leveled it, and fired. There was a dull thud, the lower half of Driscoll's left ear disintegrated and he moaned, a hand to the ear, blood spurting.

"Dillon, for God's sake!" Hannah cried.

"I don't think He's got much to do with it." Dillon raised the Walther. "Now the other one."

"No, I'll tell you," Driscoll moaned. "Ahern did phone here yesterday. He left a message for Billy. I gave it to him around five o'clock when he came in for a drink."

"What was it?"

"He was to meet him at a place off Wapping High Street, a warehouse called Olivers. Brick Wharf."

Driscoll fumbled for a handkerchief, sobbing with pain. Dillon slipped the gun inside his flying jacket and got up. "There you are," he said. "That didn't take long."

"You're a bastard, Dillon," Hannah Bernstein said as she opened the door.

"It's been said before." Dillon turned in the doorway. "One more thing, Paddy, Michael Ahern killed Billy Quigley earlier tonight. We know that for a fact."

"Dear God!" Driscoll said.

"That's right. I'd stay out of it if I were you," Dillon said and closed the door gently.

Shall I call for backup, sir?" Hannah Bernstein said as the Daimler eased into Brick Wharf beside the Thames.

Ferguson put his window down and looked out. "I shouldn't think it matters, Chief Inspector, if he was here, he's long gone. Let's go and see."

It was Dillon who led the way in, the Walther ready in his left hand, stepping through the Judas gate, feeling for the switch on the wall, flooding the place with light. At the bottom of the steps he found the office switch and led the way up. Billy Quigley lay on his back on the other side of the desk. Dillon stood to one side, shoving the Walther back inside his flying jacket, and Ferguson and Hannah Bernstein moved forward.

"Is that him, sir?" she asked.

"I'm afraid so." Ferguson sighed. "Take care of it, Chief Inspector."

She started to call in on her mobile phone and he turned and went down the stairs followed by Dillon. He went out into the street and stood by a rail overlooking the Thames. As Dillon joined him, Hannah Bernstein appeared. Ferguson said, "Well, what do you think?"

"I can't believe he didn't know that Billy was an informer," Dillon said.

Ferguson turned to Hannah. "Which means?"

"If Dillon's right, sir, Ahern is playing some sort of game with us."

"But what?" Ferguson demanded.

"There are times for waiting, Brigadier, and this is one of them," Dillon said. "If you want my thoughts on the matter, it's simple. We're in Ahern's hands. There will be a move tomorrow, sooner rather than later. Based on that, I might have some thoughts, but not before."

Dillon lit a cigarette with his old Zippo, turned, and walked back to the Daimler.

It was just before nine the following morning when Ahern drove the Telecom van along the Mall, stopping at the park gates opposite Marlborough Road. Norah followed him in a Toyota sedan. Ali Halabi was standing by the gates dressed in a green anorak and jeans. He hurried forward.

"No sign of Quigley."

"Get in." The Arab did as he was told, and Ahern passed him one of the orange Telecom jackets. "He's ill. Suffers from chronic asthma and the stress has brought on an attack." He shrugged. "Not that it matters. All you have to do is drive the van. Norah and I will lead you to your position. Just get out, lift the manhole cover, then walk away through the park. Are you still on?"

"Absolutely," Halabi said.

"Good. Then follow us and everything will be all right."

Ahern got out. Halabi slid behind the wheel. "God is great."

"He certainly is, my old son," Ahern said and he turned and walked back to Norah parked at the curb in the Toyota.

Norah went all the way 'round passing Buckingham Palace, turning up Grosvenor Place, and back along Constitution Hill by the park. On Ahern's instructions she pulled in at the curb opposite the beech tree and paused.

Ahern put his arm out of the window and raised a thumb. As they moved away, the Telecom van eased into the curb. There was a steady flow of traffic. Ahern let her drive about fifty yards, then told her to pull in. They could see Halabi get out. He went 'round to the back of the van and opened the doors. He returned with a clamp, leaned down, and prised up the manhole cover.

"He's working well, is the boy," Ahern said.

He took a small plastic remote control unit from his pocket and pressed a button. Behind them the van fire-balled and two cars passing it, caught in the blast, were blown across the road.

"That's what dedication gets for you." Ahern tapped Norah on the shoulder. "Right, girl dear. Billy told them they'd get an explosion and they've got one."

"An expensive gesture. With Halabi gone we won't get the other half of the money."

"Two and a half million pounds on deposit in Switzerland, Norah, not a bad pay day, so don't be greedy. Now let's get out of here."

It was late in the afternoon with Ferguson still at his desk at the Ministry of Defence when Hannah Bernstein came in.

"Anything new?" he asked.

"Not a thing, sir. Improbable though it sounds, there was enough of Halabi left to identify, his fingerprints anyway. It seems he must have been on the pavement, not in the van."

"And the others?"

"Two cars caught in the blast. Driver of the front one was a woman doctor, killed instantly. The man and woman in the other were going to a sales conference. They're both in intensive care." She put the report on his desk. "Quigley was right, but at least Ahern's shot his bolt."

"You think so?"

"Sir, you've seen the President's schedule. He was due to pass along Constitution Hill at about ten o'clock on the way to Downing Street. Ahern must have known that."

"And the explosion?"

"Premature. That kind of thing happens all the time, you know that, sir. Halabi was just an amateur. I've looked at his file in depth. He had an accountancy degree from the London School of Economics."

"Yes, it all makes sense—at least to me."

"But not to Dillon. Where is he?"

"Out and about. Nosing around."

"He wouldn't trust his own grandmother, that one."

"I suppose that's why he's still alive," Ferguson told her. "Help yourself to coffee, Chief Inspector."

At the studio flat in Camden, Ahern stood in front of the bathroom mirror and rubbed brilliantine into his hair. He combed it back leaving a center parting, then carefully glued a dark moustache and fixed it in place. He picked up a pair of horn-rimmed spectacles and put them on, then compared himself with the face on the security pass. As he turned, Norah came in the room. She wore a neat, black skirt and white blouse. Her hair was drawn back in a tight bun. Like him she wore spectacles, rather large ones with black rims. She looked totally different.

"How do I look?" she said.

"Bloody marvelous," he told her. "What about me?"

"Great, Michael. First class."

"Good." He led the way out of the bathroom and crossed to a drinks cabinet. He produced a bottle of Bushmills and two glasses. "It's not champagne, Norah Bell, but it's good Irish whiskey." He poured and raised his glass. "Our country too."

"Our country too," she replied, giving him that most ancient of loyalist toasts.

He emptied his glass. "Good. All I need is our box of cutlery and we'll be on our way."

It was around six-thirty when Ferguson left the Ministry of Defence with Hannah Bernstein and told his driver to take him to his flat in Cavendish Square. The door was opened by Kim, the ex-Ghurka Corporal who had been his manservant for years.

"Mr. Dillon has been waiting for you, Brigadier."

"Thanks," Ferguson said.

When they went into the living room Dillon was standing by the open French window, a glass in his hand. He turned. "Helped myself. Hope you don't mind."

"Where have you been?" Ferguson demanded.

"Checking my usual sources. You can discount the IRA on this one. It really is Ahern, and that's what bothers me."

"Can I ask why?" Hannah Bernstein said.

Dillon said, "Michael Ahern is one of the most brilliant organizers I ever knew. Very clever, very subtle, and very, very devious. As I told you, he doesn't let his left hand know what his right is doing."

"So you don't think he's simply shot his bolt on this one?" Ferguson said.

"Too easy. It may sound complicated to you, but I think everything from Quigley's betrayal and death to the so-called accidental explosion of the Telecom van on the President's route was meant to happen."

"Are you serious?" Hannah demanded.

"Oh, yes. The attempt failed so we can all take it easy. Let me look at the President's schedule."

Hannah passed a copy across and Ferguson poured himself a drink. "For once I really do hope you're wrong, Dillon."

"Here it is," Dillon said. "Cocktail party on the Thames riverboat *Jersey Lily*. The Prime Minister, the President and the Prime Minister of Israel. That's where he'll strike, that's where he always intended; the rest was a smokescreen."

"You're mad, Dillon," Ferguson said. "You must be," and then he turned and saw Hannah Bernstein's face. "Oh, my God," he said.

She glanced at her watch. "Six-thirty, sir."

"Right," he said, "let's get moving. We don't have much time."

At the same moment, Ahern and Norah were parking the Toyota in a side street off Cheyne Walk. They got out and walked down toward Cadogan Pier. There were police cars by the dozen, uniformed men all over the place, and at the boarding point a portable electronic arch that everyone had to pass through. Beside it were two large young men in blue suits.

Ahern said, "Secret Service, the President's bodyguard. I think they get their suits from the same shop."

He and Norah wore their identity cards on their lapels and he grinned and passed a plastic box to one of the Secret Servicemen as they reached the arch. "Sorry to be a nuisance, but there's two hundred knives, spoons, and forks in there. It might blow a fuse on that thing."

"Give it to me and you go through," the Secret Serviceman said.

They negotiated the arch, and he opened the plastic box and riffled the cutlery with his hand. At that moment, several limousines drew up.

"For Christ's sake, man, it's the Israeli Prime Minister," his colleague called.

The Secret Serviceman said to Ahern, "You'll have to leave this box. On your way."

"Suit yourself." Ahern went up the gangplank followed by Norah. At the top he simply slipped through a door and, following a plan of the ship he had memorized, led the way to a toilet area.

"Wait here," he told Norah and went into the men's restroom marked number four.

There was a man washing his hands. Ahern started to wash his hands also. The moment the man left, he went to the red fire bucket in the corner, scrabbled in the sand, and found two Walthers wrapped in cling film, each with a silencer on the end. He slipped one into the waistband of his trousers at the rear and concealed the other inside his uniform blazer. When he went outside he checked that no one was around for the moment and passed the second Walther to Norah, who slipped it into the inside breast pocket of her blazer under the left armpit.

"Here we go," he said.

At that moment a voice with a heavy Italian accent called. "You two, what are you doing?" When they turned, a gray-haired man in black coat and striped trousers was coming along the corridor. "Who sent you?"

Ahern, already sure of his facts, said, "Signor Orsini. We were supposed to be at the buffet at the French Embassy, but he told us to come here at the last minute. He thought you might be shorthanded."

"And he's right." The Head Waiter turned to Norah. "Canapés for you. And wine for you," he added to Ahern. "Up the stairs on the left. Now get moving," and he turned and hurried away.

The Prime Minister and the President had already boarded and the crew were about to slip the gangway when Ferguson, Dillon, and Hannah drew up in the Daimler. Ferguson led the way, hurrying up the gangway, and two Secret Servicemen moved to intercept him.

"Brigadier Ferguson. Is Colonel Candy here?"

A large, gray-haired man in a black suit and striped tie hurried along the deck. "It's all right. Is there a problem, Brigadier?"

"These are aides of mine, Dillon and Chief Inspector Bernstein." Behind him the gangway went down as the crew cast off and the *Jersey Lily* started to edge out into the Thames. "I'm afraid there could be. The explosion this morning? We now believe it to be a subterfuge. You've had a photo of this man Ahern. Please alert all your men. He could well be on the boat."

"Right." Candy didn't argue and turned to the two Secret Servicemen. "Jack, you take the stern, George, go up front. I'll handle the President. Alert everybody."

They all turned and hurried away. Ferguson said, "Right, let's try to be useful in our own small way, shall we?"

There was music on the night air provided by a jazz quartet up in the prow, people crowding around, mainly politicians and staff from the London Embassies, the President, the Prime Minister, and the Israeli Prime Minister moving among them, waiters and waitresses offering wine and canapés to everyone.

"It's a nightmare," Ferguson said.

Candy appeared, running down a companionway. "The big three will all say a few words in about ten minutes. After that we continue down past the Houses of Parliament and disembark at Westminster Pier."

"Fine." Ferguson turned to Dillon as the American hurried away. "This is hopeless."

"Maybe he's not here," Hannah said. "Perhaps you're wrong, Dillon."

It was as if he wasn't listening to her. "He'd have to have a way out." He turned to Ferguson. "The stern, let's look at the stern."

He led the way to the rear of the ship quickly., pushing people out of the way, and leaned over the stern rail. After a moment, he turned. "He's here."

"How do you know?" Ferguson demanded.

Dillon reached over and hauled in a line, and an inflatable with an outboard motor came into view. "That's his way out," he said. "Or it was." He reached over, opened the snap link that held the line, and the inflatable vanished into the darkness.

"Now what?" Hannah demanded.

At that moment, a voice over the tannoy system said, "Ladies and Gentlemen, the Prime Minister."

Dillon said, "He isn't the kind to commit suicide, so he wouldn't walk up to him in the crowd." He looked up at the wheelhouse perched on top of the ship, three levels of decks below it. "That's it. It has to be."

He ran for the steps leading up, Hannah at his heels, Ferguson struggling behind. He looked along the first deck which was deserted and started up the steps to the next. As he reached it, the Prime Minister said over the tannoy, "I'm proud to present to you the President of the United States."

At the same moment as Dillon reached the deck he saw a waiter open the saloon door at the far end and enter followed by a waitress carrying a tray covered by a white napkin.

The saloon was deserted. Ahern moved forward and looked down through the windows to the forward deck where the President stood at the microphone, the British and Israeli Prime Ministers beside him. Ahern eased one of the windows open and took out his gun.

The door opened gently behind him and Dillon moved in, his Walther ready. "Jesus, Michael, but you never give up, do you."

Ahern turned, the gun against his thigh. "Sean Dillon, you old bastard," and then his hand swung up.

Dillon shot him twice in the heart, a double thud of the silenced pistol that drove him back against the bulkhead. Norah Bell stood there, frozen, clutching the tray.

Dillon said, "Now if there was a pistol under that napkin and you were thinking about reaching for it, I'd have to kill you, Norah, and neither of us would like that, you being a decent Irish girl. Just put the tray down."

Very slowly, Norah Bell did as she was told and placed the tray on the nearest table. Dillon turned, the Walther swinging from his right hand, and said to Ferguson and Hannah, "There you go, all's well that ends well."

Behind him Norah hitched up her skirt, pulled the flick knife from her stocking and sprang the blade, plunging it into his back. Dillon reared up in agony and dropped his Walther.

"Bastard!" Norah cried, pulled out the knife, and thrust it into him again.

Dillon lurched against the table and hung there for a moment. Norah raised the knife to strike a third blow and Hannah Bernstein dropped to one knee, picked up Dillon's Walther and shot her in the center of the forehead. At the same moment, Dillon slipped from the table and rolled onto his back.

It was around midnight at the London Clinic, one of the world's greatest hospitals, and Hannah Bernstein sat in the first floor reception area close to Dillon's room. She was tired which, under the circumstances, was hardly surprising, but a diet of black coffee and cigarettes had kept her going. The door at the end of the corridor swung open, and to her astonishment Ferguson entered followed by the President and Colonel Candy.

"The President was returning to the American Embassy," Ferguson told her.

"But under the circumstances I felt I should look in. You're Chief Inspector Bernstein, I understand." The President took her hand. "I'm eternally grateful."

"You owe more to Dillon, sir. He was the one who thought it through, he was the one who knew they were on board."

The President moved to the window and peered in. Dillon, festooned with wires, lay on a hospital bed, a nurse beside him.

"How is he?"

"Intensive care, sir," she said. "A four-hour operation. She stabbed him twice."

"I brought in Professor Henry Bellamy of Guy's Hospital, Mr. President," Ferguson said. "The best surgeon in London."

"Good." The President nodded. "I owe you and your people for this, Brigadier, I'll never forget."

He walked away and Colonel Candy said, "Thank God it worked out the way it did, that way we can keep it under wraps."

"I know," Ferguson said. "It never happened."

Candy walked away and Hannah Bernstein said, "I saw Professor Bellamy half an hour ago. He came to check on him."

"And what did he say?" Ferguson frowned. "He's going to be all right, isn't he?"

"Oh, he'll live, sir, if that's what you mean. The trouble is Bellamy doesn't think he'll ever be the same again. She almost gutted him."

Ferguson put an arm around her shoulder. "Are you all right, my dear?"

"You mean, am I upset because I killed someone tonight? Not at all, Brigadier. I'm really not the nice Jewish girl Dillon imagines. I'm a rather Old Testament Jewish girl. She was a murderous bitch. She deserved to die." She took out a cigarette and lit it. "No, it's Dillon I'm sorry for. He did a good job. He deserved better."

"I thought you didn't like him," Ferguson said.

"Then you were wrong, Brigadier." She looked in through the window at Dillon. "The trouble is I liked him too much and that never pays in our line of work."

She turned and walked away. Ferguson hesitated, glanced once more at Dillon, then went after her.

THREE

And two months later in another hospital, Our Lady of Mercy in New York on the other side of the Atlantic, young Tony Jackson clocked in for night duty as darkness fell. He was a tall, handsome man of twenty-three who had qualified as a doctor at Harvard Medical School the year before. Our Lady of Mercy, a charity hospital mainly staffed by nuns, was not many young doctors' idea of the ideal place to be an intern.

But Tony Jackson was an idealist. He wanted to practice real medicine and he could certainly do that at Our Lady of Mercy, which could not believe their luck at getting their hands on such a brilliant young man. He loved the nuns, found the vast range of patients fascinating. The money was poor, but in his case money was no object. His father, a successful Manhattan attorney, had died far too early from cancer, but he had left the family well provided for. In any case, his mother, Rosa, was from the Little Italy district of New York with a doting father big in the construction business.

Tony liked the night shift, that atmosphere peculiar to hospitals all over the world, and it gave him the opportunity to be in charge. For the first part of the evening he worked on the casualty shift, dealing with a variety of patients, stitching slashed faces, handling as best he could junkies who were coming apart because they couldn't afford a fix. It was all pretty demanding, but slackened off after midnight.

He was alone in the small canteen having coffee and a sandwich when the door opened and a young priest looked in. "I'm Father O'Brien from

St. Marks. I had a call to come and see a Mr. Tanner, a Scottish gentleman. I understand he needs the last rites."

"Sorry, Father, I only came on tonight, I wouldn't know. Let me look at the schedule." He checked it briefly, then nodded. "Jack Tanner, that must be him. Admitted this afternoon. Age seventy-five, British citizen. Collapsed at his daughter's house in Queens. He's in a private room on level three, number eight."

"Thank you," the priest said and disappeared.

Jackson finished his coffee and idly glanced through the *New York Times*. There wasn't much news: an IRA bomb in London in the city's financial center, an item about Hong Kong, the British Colony in China which was to revert to Chinese control on the first of July, nineteen ninety-seven. It seemed that the British governor of the colony was introducing a thoroughly democratic voting system while he had the chance and the Chinese government in Peking was annoyed, which didn't look good for Hong Kong when the change took place.

He threw the paper down, bored and restless, got up and went outside. The elevator doors opened and Father O'Brien emerged. "Ah, there you are, Doctor. I've done what I could for the poor man, but he's not long for this world. He's from the Highlands of Scotland, would you believe? His daughter is married to an American."

"That's interesting," said Jackson. "I always imagined the Scots as Protestant."

"My dear lad, not in the Highlands," Father O'Brien told him. "The Catholic tradition is very strong." He smiled. "Well, I'll be on my way. Good night to you."

Jackson watched him go, then got in the elevator and rose to the third level. As he emerged, he saw Sister Agnes, the night duty nurse, come out of room eight and go to her desk.

Jackson said, "I've just seen Father O'Brien. He tells me this Mr. Tanner doesn't look good."

"There's his chart, Doctor. Chronic bronchitis and severe emphysema."

Jackson examined the notes. "Lung capacity only twelve percent and the blood pressure is unbelievable."

"I just checked his heart, Doctor. Very irregular."

"Let's take a look at him."

Jack Tanner's face was drawn and wasted, the sparse hair snow-white. His eyes were closed as he breathed in short gasps, a rattling sound in his throat at intervals.

"Oxygen?" Jackson asked.

"Administered an hour ago. I gave it to him myself."

"Aye, but she wouldn't give me a cigarette." Jack Tanner opened his eyes. "Is that no the terrible thing, Doctor?"

"Now, Mr. Tanner," Sister Agnes reproved him gently. "You know that's not allowed."

Jackson leaned over to check the tube connections and noticed the scar on the right side of the chest. "Would that have been a bullet wound?" he asked.

"Aye, it was so. Shot in the lung while I was serving in the Highland Light Infantry. That was before Dunkirk in nineteen-forty. I'd have died if the Laird hadn't got me out, and him wounded so bad he lost an eye."

"The Laird, you say?" Jackson was suddenly interested, but Tanner started to cough so harshly that he almost had a convulsion. Jackson grabbed for the oxygen mask. "Breathe nice and slowly. That's it." He removed it after a while and Tanner smiled weakly. "I'll be back," Jackson told him and went out.

"You said the daughter lives in Queens?"

"That's right, Doctor."

"Don't let's waste time. Send a cab for her now and put it on my account. I don't think he's got long. I'll go back and sit with him."

Jackson pulled a chair forward. "Now, what were you saying about the Laird?"

"That was Major Ian Campbell, Military Cross and Bar, the bravest man I ever knew. Laird of Loch Dhu Castle in the Western Highlands of Scotland as his ancestors had been for centuries before him."

"Loch Dhu?"

"That's Gaelic. The black loch. To us who grew up there it was always the Place of Dark Waters."

"So you knew the Laird as a boy?"

"We were boys together. Learned to shoot grouse, deer, and the fishing was the best in the world, and then the war came. We'd both served in the reserve before it all started, so we went out to France straight away."

"That must have been exciting stuff?"

"Nearly the end of us, but afterwards they gave the Laird the staff job working for Mountbatten. You've heard of him?"

"Earl Mountbatten, the one the IRA blew up?"

"The bastards, and after all he did in the war. He was Supreme Commander in South East Asia with the Laird as one of his aides and he took me with him."

"That must have been interesting."

Tanner managed a smile. "Isn't it customary to offer a condemned man a cigarette?"

"That's true."

"And I am condemned, aren't I?"

Jackson hesitated, then took out a pack of cigarettes. "Just as we all are, Mr. Tanner."

"I'll tell you what," Tanner said. "Give me one of those and I'll tell you about the Chungking Covenant. All those years ago I gave the Laird my oath, but it doesn't seem to matter now."

"The what?" Jackson asked.

"Just one, Doc, it's a good story."

Jackson turned off the oxygen, lit a cigarette, and held it to his lips. The old man inhaled, coughed, then inhaled again. "Christ, that's wonderful." He lay back. "Now let's see, when did it all start?"

Tanner lay with his eyes closed, very weak now. "What happened after the crash?" Jackson asked.

The old man opened his eyes. "The Laird was hurt bad. The brain, you see. He was in a coma in a Delhi hospital for three months, and I stayed with him as his batman. They sent us back to London by sea, and by then the end of the war was in sight. He spent months in the brain-damage unit for servicemen at Guy's Hospital, but he never really recovered, and he had burns from the crash as well and almost total loss of memory. He came so close to death early in forty-six that I packed his things and sent them home to Castle Dhu."

"And did he die?"

"Not for another twenty years. Back home we went to the estate. He wandered the place like a child. I tended his every want."

"What about family?"

"Oh, he never married. He was engaged to a lassie who was killed in the London blitz in forty. There was his sister, Lady Rose. Although everybody calls her Lady Katherine. Her husband was a baronet killed in the desert campaign. She ran the estate then and still does though she's eighty now. She lives in the gate lodge. Sometimes rents the big house for the shooting season to rich Yanks or Arabs."

"And the Chungking Covenant?"

"Nothing came of that. Lord Louis and Mao never managed to get together again."

"But the fourth copy in the Laird's Bible, you saved that. Wasn't it handed over to the authorities?"

"It stayed where it was in his Bible. The Laird's affair, after all, and he not up to telling anyone much of anything." He shrugged. "And then the years had rolled by and it didn't seem to matter."

"Did Lady Katherine ever come to know of it?"

"I never told her. I never spoke of it to anyone and he was not capable and, as I said, it didn't seem to matter any longer."

"But you've told me?"

Tanner smiled weakly. "That's because you're a nice boy who talked to me and gave me a cigarette. A long time ago, Chungking in the rain and Mountbatten and your General Stillwell."

"And the Bible?" Jackson asked.

"Like I told you, I sent all his belongings home when I thought he was going to die."

"So the Bible went back to Loch Dhu?"

"You could say that." For some reason Tanner started to laugh and that led to him choking again.

Jackson got the oxygen mask and the door opened and Sister Agnes ushered in a middle-aged couple. "Mr. and Mrs. Grant."

The woman hurried forward to take Tanner's hand. He managed a smile, breathing deeply, and she started to talk to him in a low voice and in a language totally unfamiliar to Jackson.

He turned to her husband, a large, amiable-looking man. "It's Gaelic, Doctor, they always spoke Gaelic together. He was on a visit. His wife died of cancer last year back in Scotland."

At that moment Tanner stopped breathing. His daughter cried out and Jackson passed her gently to her husband and bent over the patient. After a while he turned to face them. "I'm sorry, but he's gone," he said simply.

There it might have ended except for the fact that having read the article in the *New York Times* on Hong Kong and its relations with China, Tony Jackson was struck by the coincidence of Tanner's story. This became doubly important because Tanner had died in the early years hours of Sunday morning and Jackson always had Sunday lunch, his hospital shifts permitting, at his grandfather's home in Little Italy where his mother, since the death of his grandmother, kept house for her father in some style.

Jackson's grandfather, after whom he had been named, was called Antonio Mori and he had been born by only a whisker in America because his pregnant mother had arrived from Palermo in Sicily just in time to produce her baby at Ellis Island. Twenty-four hours only, but good enough and little Antonio was American born.

His father had friends of the right sort, friends in the Mafia. Antonio had worked briefly as a laborer until these friends had put him into first the olive oil and then the restaurant business. He had kept his mouth shut and always done as he was told, finally achieving wealth and prominence in the construction industry.

His daughter hadn't married a Sicilian. He accepted that, just as he accepted the death of his wife from leukemia. His son-in-law, a rich Anglo-Saxon attorney, gave the family respectability. His death was a convenience. It brought Mori and his beloved daughter together again plus his fine grandson, so brilliant that he had gone to Harvard. No matter that he was a saint and chose medicine. Mori could make enough money for all of them because he was Mafia, an important member of the Luca family whose leader, Don Giovanni Luca, in spite of having returned to Sicily, was *Capo di tutti Capi*. Boss of all the Bosses in the whole of the Mafia. The respect that earned for Mori couldn't be paid for.

When Jackson arrived at his grandfather's house, his mother Rosa was in the kitchen supervising the meal with the maid, Maria. She turned, still handsome in spite of gray in her dark hair, kissed him on both cheeks, then held him off.

"You look terrible. Shadows under the eyes."

"Mamma, I did the night shift. I lay on my bed three hours, then I showered and came here because I didn't want to disappoint you."

"You're a good boy. Go and see your grandfather."

Jackson went into the sitting room where he found Mori reading the Sunday paper. He leaned down to kiss his grandfather on the cheek and Mori said, "I heard your mother and she's right. You do good and kill yourself at the same time. Here, have a glass of red wine."

Jackson accepted it and drank some with pleasure. "That's good."

"You had an interesting night?" Mori was genuinely interested in his grandson's doings. In fact, he bored his friends with his praises of the young man.

Jackson, aware that his grandfather indulged him, went to the French window, opened it, and lit a cigarette. He turned. "Remember the Solazzo wedding last month?"

"Yes."

"You were talking with Carl Morgan, you'd just introduced me."

"Mr. Morgan was impressed by you, he said so." There was pride in Mori's voice.

"Yes, well, you and he were talking business."

"Nonsense, what business could we have in common?"

"For God's sake, grandfather, I'm not a fool and I love you, but do you think I could have reached this stage in my life and not realized the business you were in?"

Mori nodded slowly and picked up the bottle. "More wine? Now tell me where this is leading."

"You and Mr. Morgan were talking about Hong Kong. He mentioned huge investments in skyscrapers, hotels, and so on and the worry about what would happen when the Chinese Communists take over."

"That's simple. Billions of dollars down the toilet," Mori said.

"There was an article in *The Times* yesterday about Peking being angry because the British are introducing a democratic political system before they go in ninety-seven."

"So where is this leading?" Mori asked.

"So I am right in assuming that you and your associates have business interests in Hong Kong?"

His grandfather stared at him thoughtfully. "You could say that, but where is this leading?"

Jackson said, "What if I told you that in nineteen forty-four Mao Tse-tung signed a thing called the Chungking Covenant with Lord Louis Mount-batten under the terms of which he agreed that if he ever came to power in China he would extend the Hong Kong Treaty by one hundred years in return for aid from the British to fight the Japanese?"

His grandfather sat there staring at him, then got up, closed the door, and returned to his seat.

"Explain," he said.

Jackson did, and when he was finished his grandfather sat thinking about it. He got up and went to his desk and came back with a small tape recorder. "Go through it again," he said. "Everything he told you. Omit nothing."

At that moment, Rosa opened the door. "Lunch is almost ready."

"Fifteen minutes, *cara*," her father said. "This is important, believe me."

She frowned but went out, closing the door. He turned to his grandson. "As I said, everything," and he switched on the recorder.

When Mori reached the Glendale Polo ground later that afternoon it was raining. There was still a reasonable crowd huddled beneath umbrellas or the trees because Carl Morgan was playing and Morgan was good, a handicap of ten goals indicating that he was a player of the first rank. He was fifty years of age, a magnificent-looking man, six feet in height with broad shoulders and hair swept back over his ears.

His hair was jet black, a legacy of his mother, niece of Don Giovanni, who had married his father, a young army officer, during the Second World War. His father had served gallantly and well in both the Korean and Vietnam wars, retiring as a Brigadier General to Florida, where they enjoyed a comfortable retirement thanks to their son.

All very respectable, all a very proper front for the son who had walked out of Yale in nineteen sixty-five and volunteered as a paratrooper during the Vietnam War, emerging with two Purple Hearts, a Silver Star, and a Vietnamese Cross of Valour. A war hero whose credentials had taken him to Wall Street and then the hotel industry and the construction business, a billionaire at the end of things, accepted at every social level from London to New York.

There are six chukkas in a polo game lasting seven minutes each, four players on each side. Morgan played forward because it gave the most opportunity for total aggression and that was what he liked.

The game was into the final chukka as Mori got out of the car and his chauffeur came round to hold an umbrella over him. Some yards away, a vividly pretty young woman stood beside an estate car, a Burberry trench-coat hanging from her shoulders. She was about five-foot-seven with long blond hair to her shoulders, high cheekbones, green eyes.

"She sure is a beautiful young lady, Mr. Morgan's daughter," the chauffeur said.

"Stepdaughter, Johnny," Mori reminded him.

"Sure, I was forgetting, but with her taking his name and all. That was a real bad thing, her mother dying like that. Asta, that's kind of a funny name."

"It's Swedish," Mori told him.

Asta Morgan jumped up and down excitedly. "Come on, Carl, murder them."

Carl Morgan glanced sideways as he went by, his teeth flashed, and he went barreling into the young forward for the opposing team, slamming his left foot under the boy's stirrup and lifting him, quite illegally, out of the saddle. A second later, he had thundered through and scored.

The game was won, he cantered across to Asta through the rain, and stepped out of the saddle. A groom took his pony, Asta handed him a towel, then lit a cigarette and passed it to him. She looked up, smiling, an intimacy between them that excluded everyone around.

"He sure likes that girl," Johnny said.

Mori nodded. "So it would appear."

Morgan turned and saw him and waved, and Mori went forward. "Carl, nice to see you. And you, Asta." He touched his hat.

"What can I do for you?" Morgan asked.

"Business, Carl, something came up last night that might interest you."

Morgan said, "Nothing you can't talk about in front of Asta, surely?"

Mori hesitated. "No, of course not." He took the small tape recorder from his pocket. "My grandson, Tony, had a man die on him at Our Lady of Mercy Hospital last night. He told Tony a hell of a story, Carl. I think you could be interested."

"Okay, let's get in out of the rain." Morgan handed Asta into the estate car and followed her.

Mori joined them. "Here we go." He switched on the tape recorder.

Morgan sat there after it had finished, a cigarette drooping from the corner of his mouth, his face set.

Asta said, "What a truly astonishing story." Her voice was low and pleasant, more English than American.

"You can say that again." Morgan turned to Mori. "I'll keep this. I'll have my secretary transcribe it and send it to Don Giovanni in Palermo by coded fax."

"I did the right thing?"

"You did well, Antonio." Morgan took his hand.

"No, it was Tony, Carl, not me. What am I going to do with him? Harvard Medical School, the Mayo Clinic, a brilliant student, yet he works with the nuns at Our Lady of Mercy for peanuts."

"You leave him," Morgan said. "He'll find his way. I went to Vietnam, Antonio. No one can take that away from me. You can't argue with it, the rich boy going into hell when he didn't need to. It says something. He won't be there forever, but the fact that he was will make people see him as someone to look up to for the rest of his life. He's a fine boy." He put a hand on Mori's shoulder. "Heh, I hope I don't sound too calculating."

"No," Mori protested. "Not at all. He's someone to be proud of. Thank you, Carl, thank you. I'll leave you now. Asta." He nodded to her and walked away.

"That was nice," Asta told Morgan. "What you said about Tony."

"It's true. He's brilliant, that boy. He'll end up in Park Avenue, only unlike the other brilliant doctors there he'll always be the one who worked downtown for the nuns of Our Lady of Mercy, and that you can't pay for."

"You're such a cynic," she said.

"No, sweetheart, a realist. Now let's get going. I'm famished. I'll take you out to dinner."

They had finished their meal at The Four Seasons, were at the coffee stage when one of the waiters brought a phone over. "An overseas call for you, sir. Sicily. The gentleman said it was urgent."

The voice over the phone was harsh and unmistakable. "Carl. This is Giovanni."

Morgan straightened in his seat. "Uncle?" He dropped into Italian. "What a marvelous surprise. How's business?"

"Everything looks good, particularly after reading your fax."

"I was right to let you know about this business then?"

"So right that I want you out of there on the next plane. This is serious business, Carl, very serious."

"Fine, Uncle. I'll be there tomorrow. Asta's with me. Do you want to say hello?"

"I'd rather look at her, so you'd better bring her with you. I look forward to it, Carl."

The phone clicked off, the waiter came forward and took it from him. "What was all that about?" Asta said.

"Business. Apparently Giovanni takes this Chungking Covenant thing very seriously indeed. He wants me in Palermo tomorrow. You too, my love. It's time you visited Sicily," and he waved for the head waiter.

They took a direct flight to Rome the following morning where Morgan had a Citation private jet standing by for the flight to Punta Raisi Airport twenty miles outside Palermo. There was a Mercedes limousine waiting with a chauffeur and a hard-looking individual in a blue nylon raincoat with heavy cheekbones and the flattened nose of the prize fighter. There was a feeling of real power there, although he looked more Slav than Italian.

"My uncle's top enforcer," Morgan whispered to Asta, "Marco Russo." He smiled and held out his hand. "Marco, it's been a long time. My daughter, Asta."

Marco managed a fractional smile. "A pleasure. Welcome to Sicily, Signorina, and nice to see you again, Signore. The Don isn't at the town house, he's at the Villa."

"Good, let's get moving then."

Luca's villa was outside a village at the foot of Monte Pellegrino, which towers into the sky three miles north of Palermo.

"During the Punic Wars the Carthaginians held out against the Romans on that mountain for three years," Morgan told Asta.

"It looks a fascinating place," she said.

"Soaked in blood for generations." He held up the local paper, which Marco had given him. "Three soldiers blown up by a car bomb last night, a priest shot in the back of the neck this morning because he was suspected of being an informer."

"At least you're on the right side."

He took her hand. "Everything I do is strictly legitimate, Asta, that's the whole point. My business interests and those of my associates are pure as driven snow."

"I know, darling," she said. "You must be the greatest front man ever.

Granddad Morgan a General, you a war hero, billionaire, philanthropist, and one of the best polo players in the world. Why, last time we were in London, Prince Charles asked you to play for him."

"He wants me next month." She laughed and he added, "But never forget one thing, Asta. The true power doesn't come from New York. It lies in the hands of the old man we're going to see now."

At that moment they turned in through electronic gates set in ancient, fifteen-foot walls and drove through a semitropical garden toward the great Moorish villa.

The main reception room was enormous, black-and-white-tiled floor scattered with rugs, seventeenth-century furniture from Italy in dark oak, a log fire blazing in the open hearth, and French windows open to the garden. Luca sat in a high-backed sofa, a cigar in his mouth, hands clasped over the silver handle of a walking stick. He was large, at least sixteen stone, his gray beard trimmed, the air of a Roman Emperor about him.

"Come here, child," he said to Asta and when she went to him, kissed her on both cheeks. "You're more beautiful than ever. Eighteen months since I saw you in New York. I was desolated by your mother's unfortunate death last year."

"These things happen," she said.

"I know. Jack Kennedy once said, anyone who believes there is fairness in this life is seriously misinformed. Here, sit beside me." She did as she was told and he looked up at Morgan. "You seem well, Carlo." He'd always insisted on calling him that.

"And you, Uncle, look wonderful."

Luca held out his hand and Morgan kissed it. "I like it when your Sicilian half floats to the surface. You were wise to contact me on this Chungking business and Mori showed good judgment in speaking to you."

"We owe it to his grandson," Morgan said.

"Yes, of course. Young Tony is a good boy, an idealist, and that's good. We need our saints, Carlo, they make us rather more acceptable to the rest of the world." He snapped a finger and a white-coated houseboy came forward.

"Zibibbo, Alfredo."

"At once, Don Giovanni."

"You will like this, Asta. A wine from the island Pantelleria, flavored with anise." He turned to Morgan. "Marco took me for a run into the country the other day, to that farmhouse of yours at Valdini."

"How was it?"

"The caretaker and his wife seemed to be behaving themselves. Very peaceful. You should do something with it."

"Grandfather was born there, Uncle, it's a piece of the real Sicily. How could I change that?"

"You're a good boy, Carlo, you may be half American, but you have a Sicilian heart."

As Alfredo opened the bottle, Morgan said, "So, to the Chungking Covenant. What do you think?"

"We have billions invested in Hong Kong in hotels and casinos and our holdings will be severely damaged when the Communists take over in ninety-seven. Anything that could delay that would be marvelous."

"But would the production of such a document really have an effect?" Asta asked.

He accepted one of the glasses of Zibibbo from Alfredo. "The Chinese have taken great care to handle the proposed changes in the status of Hong Kong through the United Nations. These days they want everything from international respectability to the Olympic Games. If the document surfaced with the holy name of Mao Tse-tung attached to it, who knows what the outcome would be."

"That's true," Morgan agreed. "All right, they'd scream forgery."

"Yes," Asta put in, "but there is one important point. It isn't a forgery, it's the real thing, we know that and any experts brought in will have to agree."

"She's smart, this girl." Luca patted her knee. "We've nothing to lose, Carlo. With that document on show we can at least hold the whole proceedings up if nothing else. Even if we still lose millions, I'd like to mess it up for the Chinese and particularly for the Brits. It's their fault they didn't sort the whole mess out years ago."

"Strange you should say that," Asta told him. "I'd have thought that was exactly what Mountbatten was trying to do back in forty-four."

He roared with laughter and raised his glass. "More wine, Alfredo."

"What do you suggest?" Morgan asked.

"Find this silver Bible. When you have that, you have the Covenant."

"And that must be somewhere at the Castle at Loch Dhu according to what Tanner said," Asta put in.

"Exactly. There's a problem. I had my London lawyer check on the situation at the house the moment I received your fax. It's rented out at the moment to a Sheik from Trucial Oman, a Prince of the Royal Family, so there's nothing to be done there. He's in residence and he won't be leaving for another month. My lawyer has leased it in your name for three months from then."

"Fine," Morgan said. "That gives me plenty of time to clear the decks where business is concerned. That Bible must be there somewhere."

"I instructed my lawyer to get straight up there and see this Lady Katherine Rose, the sister, to do the lease personally. He raised the question of the Bible, told her he'd heard the legend of how all the Lairds carried it into battle. When he phoned me he said she's old and a bit confused and told him she hadn't seen the thing in years."

"There is one thing," Asta said. "According to Tony Jackson, he said to Tanner, 'So the Bible went back to Loch Dhu?' "

Morgan cut in, "And Tanner replied, 'You could say that.' "

Asta nodded. "And then Tony said he started to laugh. I'd say that's rather strange."

"Strange or not, that Bible must be there somewhere," Luca said. "You'll find it, Carlo." He stood up. "Now we eat."

Marco Russo was standing by the door in the hall and as they passed him, Luca said, "You can take Marco with you in case you need a little muscle." He patted Marco's face. "The Highlands of Scotland, Marco, you'll have to wrap up."

"Whatever you say, Capo."

Marco opened the dining room door where two waiters were in attendance. Back in the reception room Alfredo cleared the wine bottle and glasses and took them into the kitchen, putting them beside the sink for the maid to wash later. He said to the cook, "I'm going now," went out, lit a cigarette, and walked down through the gardens to the staff quarters. Alfredo Ponti was an excellent waiter, but an even better policeman, one of the new dedicated breed imported from mainland Italy. He'd managed to obtain the job with Luca three months previously.

Usually he phoned from outside when he wanted to contact his superiors, but the other two houseboys, the cook, and the maid were working, so for the moment he was alone. In any case, what he had overheard seemed important so he decided to take a chance, lifted the receiver on the wall phone at the end of the corridor, and dialed a number in Palermo. It was answered at once.

"Gagini, it's me, Ponti. I've got something. Carl Morgan appeared tonight with his stepdaughter. I overheard them tell a most curious story to Luca. Have you ever heard of the Chungking Covenant?"

Paolo Gagini, who was a Major in the Italian Secret Intelligence Service from Rome posing as a business man in Palermo, said, "That's a new one. Let me put the tape recorder on. Thank God for that photographic memory of yours. Right, start talking. Tell me everything."

Which Alfredo did in some detail. When he had finished, Gagini said,

"Good work, though I can't see it helping us much. I'll be in touch. Take care."

Alfredo replaced the receiver and went to bed.

Gagini, in his apartment in Palermo, sat thinking. He could let them know in Rome, not that anyone would be very interested. Everyone knew what Carl Morgan was, but he was also very legitimate. In any case, anything he did in Scotland was the responsibility of the British authorities, which made him think of his oldest friend in British intelligence. Gagini smiled. He loved this one. He got out his code book and found the number of the Ministry of Defence in London.

When the operator answered he said, "Give me Brigadier Charles Ferguson, Priority One, please."

It was perhaps two hours later when Morgan and Asta had retired that Alfredo was shaken awake to find Marco bending over him.

"The Capo wants you."

"What is it?"

Marco shrugged. "Search me. He's on the terrace."

He went out and Alfredo dressed quickly and went after him. He was aware of no particular apprehension. Things had gone so well for three months now and he'd always been so careful, but as a precaution, he placed a small automatic in his waistband.

He found Luca sitting in a cane chair, Marco leaning against a pillar. The old man said, "You made a phone call earlier."

Alfredo's mouth went dry. "Yes, my cousin in Palermo."

"You're lying," Marco said. "We have an electronic tracking machine. It registered the no return bar code so the number can't be traced."

"And that only applies to the security services," Luca said.

Alfredo turned and ran through the garden for the fence and Marco drew a silenced pistol.

"Don't kill him," Luca cried.

Marco shot him in the leg and the young man went down but turned on the ground, pulling the automatic from his waistband. Marco, with little choice in the matter, shot him between the eyes.

Luca went forward, leaning on his cane. "Poor boy, so young. They will keep trying. Get rid of him, Marco."

He turned and walked away.

FOUR

Ferguson was at his desk when Hannah Bernstein came in and put a file on his desk. "Everything there is on Carl Morgan."

Ferguson sat back. "Tell me."

"His father is a retired Brigadier General, but his mother is the niece of Giovanni Luca which means that, in spite of Yale and all the war hero stuff in Vietnam and his hotels and construction business, he's fronting for the Mafia."

"Some people would say he was the new, legitimate face of the Mafia."

"With the greatest respect, Brigadier, that's a load of crap."

"Why, Chief Inspector, you said a rude word. How encouraging."

"A thug is a thug even if he does wear suits by Brioni and plays polo with Prince Charles."

"I couldn't agree more. Have you checked on Loch Dhu Castle and the situation there?"

"Yes, sir, it's at present leased to Prince Ali ben Yusef from the Oman. He'll be there for another month."

"Not much joy there. Arab royal families are always the very devil to deal with."

"Something else, sir. Carl Morgan has already taken a lease on the place for three months when the Prince leaves."

"Now why would he do that?" Ferguson frowned and then nodded. "The Bible. It's got to be."

"You mean he needs to search for it, sir?"

"Something like that. What else can you tell me about the estate?"

"It's owned by a Lady Rose, Campbell's sister. He was never married. She lives in the gate lodge. She's eighty years of age and in poor health." Hannah looked in the file. "I see there's also a small hunting lodge to rent. Ardmurchan Lodge it's called. About ten miles from the main house in the deer forest."

Ferguson nodded. "Look, let's try the simple approach. Book the Lear out of Gatwick as soon as you like and fly up there and descend on Lady Katherine. Express an interest in the shooting lodge on my behalf. Tell her you've always had an interest in the area because your grandfather served with Campbell in the war. Then raise the question of the Bible. For all we know it could be lying on a coffee table."

"All right, sir, I'll do as you say." The phone went on his desk and she picked it up, listened, and put it down again. "Dillon is having his final check at the hospital."

"I know," Ferguson said.

"About the Bible, sir? Do you really think it could be just lying around?"

"Somehow I don't think so. Luca and Morgan would have thought of that. The fact that they are going ahead with a lease on the place would seem to indicate that they know damn well it isn't."

"That's logical." She put another file on his desk. "Dillon's medical report. Not good."

"Yes. Professor Bellamy spoke to me about it. That's why he's giving him a final examination this morning, then Dillon is coming round to see me."

"Is he finished, sir?"

"Looks like it, but that's not your worry, it's mine, so off you go to Scotland and see what you can find. In the meantime, I'll speak to the Prime Minister. A phone call at this stage will be enough, but I do think he should know what's going on sooner rather than later."

You can dress now, Sean," Bellamy told him. "I'll see you in my office."

Dillon got off the operating table on which the professor had examined him. The flesh seemed to have shrunk on his bones, there were what appeared to be bruises under his eyes. When he glanced over his shoulder he could see, in the mirror, the angry raised weal of the scars left by the two operations that had saved his life after Norah Bell had gutted him.

He dressed slowly, feeling unaccountably weak, and when he put on his jacket the Walther in the special left pocket seemed to weigh a ton. He went out to the office where Bellamy sat behind his desk.

"How do you feel generally?"

Dillon slumped down. "Bloody awful. Weak, no energy, and then there's the pain." He shook his head. "How long does this go on?"

"It takes time," Bellamy said. "She chipped your spine, damaged the stomach, kidneys, bladder. Have you any idea how close to death you were?"

"I know, I know," Dillon said. "But what do I do?"

"A holiday, a long one, preferably in the sun. Ferguson will take care of it. As for the pain"—he pushed a pill bottle forward—"I've increased your morphine dose to a quarter grain."

"Thanks very much, I'll be a junkie before you know it." Dillon got up slowly. "I'll be on my way. Better see Ferguson and get it over with."

As he got to the door Bellamy said, "I'm always here, Sean."

Hannah, due at Gatwick in an hour, was checking the final details of her trip in the outer office. Loch Dhu was situated in a place called Moidart on the northwest coast of Scotland and not far from the sea, about a hundred and twenty square miles of mountain and moorland with few inhabitants. One good thing. Only five miles from Loch Dhu was an old abandoned airstrip called Ardmurchan used by the RAF as an air-sea rescue base during the war. It could comfortably accommodate the Lear. Four hundred and fifty miles, so the trip would take, say, an hour and a half. Then she would need transport to the Castle. She found the telephone number of the gate lodge and called Lady Katherine Rose.

The first person to answer was a woman with a robust Scottish voice, but after a while her mistress replaced her. Her voice was different, tired somehow and a slight quaver in it. "Katherine Rose here."

"Lady Rose? I wonder if I could come and see you on behalf of a client of mine?" and she went on to explain.

"Certainly, my dear, I'll send my gardener, Angus, to pick you up. I look forward to seeing you. By the way, just call me Lady Katherine. It's customary here."

Hannah put down the receiver and pulled on her coat. The door opened and Dillon entered. He looked dreadful and her heart sank.

"Why, Dillon, it's good to see you."

"I doubt that, girl dear. On the other hand, I must say you look good enough to eat. Is the great man in?"

"He's expecting you. Listen, I'll have to dash, the Lear's waiting for me at Gatwick and I've a fast trip to make to Scotland."

"Then I won't detain you. Happy landings," and he knocked on Ferguson's door and went in.

God save all here," Dillon said.

Ferguson glanced up. "You look bloody awful."

" 'God save you kindly' was the reply to that one," Dillon told him. "And as I see the brandy over there I'll help myself."

He did, taking it down in one swallow, then lit a cigarette. Ferguson said, "Remarkably bad habits for a sick man."

"Don't let's waste time. Are you putting me out to grass?"

"I'm afraid so. Your appointment was never exactly official, you see. That makes things awkward."

"Ah, well, all good things come to an end."

He helped himself to more brandy and Ferguson said, "Normally there would have been a pension, but in your circumstances I'm afraid not."

Dillon smiled. "Remember Michael Aroun, the bastard I did away with in Brittany in ninety-one after the Downing Street affair? He was supposed to put two million into my bank account and screwed me."

"I remember," Ferguson said.

"I cleaned out his safe before I left. Assorted currencies, but it came to around six hundred thousand pounds. I'll be all right." He finished the brandy. "Well, working with you has been a sincere sensation, I'll say that, but I'd better be on my way."

As he put his hand to the door, Ferguson said formally, "One more thing, Dillon, I presume you're carrying the usual Walther. I'd be obliged if you'd leave it on my desk."

"Screw you, Brigadier," Sean Dillon said and went out.

The flight to Moidart was spectacular, straight over the English Lake District at thirty thousand feet, then Scotland and the Firth of Forth, the Grampian Mountains on the right, and soon the islands, Eigg and Rhum, and the Isle of Skye to the north. The Lear turned east toward the great shining expanse of Loch Shiel, but before it was the deer forest, Loch Dhu Castle and the loch itself, black and forbidding. The copilot was navigating and he pointed as they descended and there was the airfield, decaying Nissan huts, two hangars, and an old control tower.

"Ardmurchan field. Air-sea rescue during the big war."

It was on the far side of the loch from the Castle, and as they turned to land Hannah saw an old station wagon approaching. The Lear rolled to a halt. Both the pilots, who were RAF on secondment, got out with her to stretch their legs. The skipper, a Flight Lieutenant Lacey, said, "Back of beyond this, Chief Inspector, and no mistake."

"Better get used to it, Flight Lieutenant. I suspect we'll be up here again," she said and walked toward the station wagon.

The driver was a man in tweed cap and jacket with a red face, blotched from too much whiskey drinking. "Angus, Miss, her ladyship sent me to find you."

"My name's Bernstein," she said and got into the passenger seat. As they drove away she said, "You've no idea how excited I am to be here."

"Why would that be, Miss?" he inquired.

"Oh, my grandfather knew the old Laird during the war, Major Campbell. They served in the Far East together with Lord Mountbatten."

"Ah, well I wouldn't know about that, Miss. I'm only sixty-four, so all I did was National Service and that was in nineteen forty-eight."

"I see. I remember my grandfather saying the Laird had a batman from the estate, a Corporal Tanner. Did you know him?"

"Indeed I did, Miss, he was estate manager here for years. Went on a visit to his daughter in New York and died there. Only the other day that happened."

"What a shame."

"Death comes to us all," he intoned.

It was like a line from a bad play, especially when delivered in that Highland Scots accent, and she lapsed into silence as he turned the station wagon into huge, old-fashioned iron gates and stopped beside the lodge.

Lady Katherine Rose was old and tired and it showed on her wizened face as she sat there in the wing-backed chair, a rug over her knees. The drawing room in which she greeted Hannah was pleasantly furnished, most of the stuff obviously antique. There was a fire in the hearth, but she had a French window open.

"I hope you don't mind, my dear," she said to Hannah, "I need the air, you see. My chest isn't what it used to be."

A pleasant, rather overweight woman in her fifties bustled in with tea and scones on a tray, which she placed on a mahogany table. "Shall I pour?" she said, and like Angus her accent was Highland.

"Don't fuss, Jean, I'm sure Miss Bernstein is quite capable. Off you go."

Jean smiled, picked up a shawl which had slipped to the floor, and put it around the old woman's shoulders. Hannah went and poured the tea.

"So," Lady Katherine said, "your employer is Brigadier Charles Ferguson, is that what you said?"

"Yes. He was wondering whether there might be a chance of renting Ardmurchan Lodge for the shooting. I did contact your agents in London but was given to understand that the big house was leased."

"Indeed it is, an Arab Prince no less, a dear man with several children who keep descending on me. Far too generous. He sends me food I can't eat and bottles of Dom Perignon I can't drink."

Hannah put her cup of tea on a side table. "Yes. I heard he was in residence for another month and after that an American gentleman."

"Yes, a Mr. Morgan. Scandalously wealthy. I've seen his picture in the *Tatler* magazine playing polo with Prince Charles. His lawyer flew up to see me just like you in a jet plane. He's taken the place for three months." She didn't bother with the tea. "There are some cigarettes in the silver box. Get one for me, there's a dear, and help yourself, if you indulge." She held it in a hand that shook slightly. "That's better," she said as she inhaled. "Clears my chest. Anyway, to business. Ardmurchan Lodge is free and has full sporting rights. Deer, grouse next month, then fishing. There are two bathrooms, five bedrooms. I could arrange servants."

"No need for that. The Brigadier has a manservant who also cooks."

"How very convenient. And you'd come too?"

"Some of the time at least."

"The Brigadier must be as wealthy as this American, what with private airplanes and so forth. What does he do?"

"Various things on the international scene." Hannah hurried on. "I was telling your gardener what a thrill it was for me to be here. I first heard of Loch Dhu when I was a young girl from my mother's father. He was an army officer during the Second World War and served on Lord Louis Mountbatten's staff in the Far East." She was making it up as she went along. "Gort was his name, Colonel Edward Gort. Perhaps your brother spoke of him?"

"I'm afraid not, my dear. You see, Ian was involved in a dreadful air crash in India in forty-four. He was only saved by the courage of his batman, Jack Tanner, a man who'd grown up with him on the estate here. My brother was hospitalized on and off for years. Brain damage, you see. He was never the same. He never talked about the war. To be frank, the poor dear never talked much about anything. He wasn't capable."

"How tragic," Hannah said. "My grandfather never mentioned that. I believe the last time he saw him was in China."

"That must have been before the crash."

Hannah got up and poured more tea into her cup. "Can I get you anything?"

"Another cigarette, my dear, my only vice and at my age, what does it matter?"

Hannah did as she was told, then walked to the French window and looked out from the terrace at the great house in the distance. "It looks wonderful. Battlements and turrets, just as I imagined it would be." She turned. "I'm a hopeless romantic. It was the idea of the Laird of the Clan, as my grandfather described it, that intrigued me. Bagpipes and kilts and all that sort of thing." She came back. "Oh, and there was another rather romantic side to it. He told me that Major Campbell always carried a silver Bible with him that was a family heirloom. He'd had it at Dunkirk, but the story was that all the Campbells had carried it into battle for centuries."

"You're right," she said. "It was certainly in Rory Campbell's pocket when he died at the Battle of Culloden fighting for Bonnie Prince Charlie. It's interesting that you should mention it. I haven't thought about that Bible in years. I suppose it must have been lost in the plane crash."

"I see," Hannah said carefully.

"Certainly nothing survived except poor Ian and Jack Tanner, of course." She sighed. "I just heard the other day that Jack died in New York on a visit to see his daughter. A good man. He ran things on the estate for me for years. The new man, Murdoch, is a pain. You know the kind. College degree in estate management so he thinks he knows everything."

Hannah nodded and got up. "So, we can have Ardmurchan Lodge?"

"Whenever you like. Leave me the details and I'll have Murdoch send you a contract."

Hannah was already prepared for that and took an envelope from her handbag, which she placed on the table. "There you are. The Brigadier's office is in Cavendish Square. I'll find Angus, shall I, and get him to run me back to the plane?"

"You'll find him in the garden."

Hannah went and took her hand, which was cool and weightless. "Goodbye, Lady Katherine."

"Goodbye, my dear, you're a very lovely young woman."

"Thank you."

She turned to the French window and Lady Katherine said, "A strange coincidence. When that lawyer was here he asked about the Bible, too. Said Mr. Morgan had mentioned reading about it in an article on Highland legends in some American magazine. Isn't that extraordinary?"

"It certainly is," Hannah said. "He must have been disappointed it wasn't on show."

"That was the impression I received." The old woman smiled. "Goodbye, my dear."

Hannah found Angus digging in the garden. "Ready to go, Miss?"

"That's right," she said.

As they walked round to the front, a Range Rover drew up and a tall, saturnine young man in a hunting jacket and a deerstalker cap got out. He looked at her inquiringly.

"This is Miss Bernstein," Angus told him. "She's been seeing the Mistress."

"On behalf of my employer, Brigadier Charles Ferguson," she said. "Lady Katherine has agreed to rent the Ardmurchan Lodge to us."

He frowned. "She didn't mention anything to me about it." He hesitated, then put out his hand. "Stewart Murdoch. I'm the estate factor."

"I only spoke to her this morning."

"Then that explains it. I've been at Fort William for two days."

"I've left her full details and look forward to receiving the contract." She smiled and got into the station wagon. "I must rush, there's a Lear waiting for me at Ardmurchan. We'll meet again, I'm sure."

Angus got behind the wheel and drove away. Murdoch watched them go, frowning, then went inside.

The Lear took off, climbing steeply, rising to thirty thousand feet rapidly. Hannah checked her watch. It was only just after two. With luck she'd be at Gatwick by three-thirty, sooner with a tailwind. Another hour to reach the Ministry of Defence. She picked up the phone and told the co-pilot to patch her in to Ferguson.

His voice was clear and sharp. "Had a good trip?"

"Excellent, sir, and the lease on Ardmurchan Lodge is in the bag. No luck with the Bible. The lady hasn't seen it in years. Always presumed it was lost in the plane crash."

"Yes, well we know it wasn't, don't we?"

"Looks like we're in for a sort of country house weekend treasure hunt, sir."

"You mean Morgan is, Chief Inspector."

"So how do we handle it?"

"I don't know, I'll think of something. Come home, Chief Inspector, I'll look for you at the office."

She put down the phone, made herself a cup of instant coffee, and settled back to read a magazine.

When she reached the Ministry she found Ferguson pacing up and down in his office. "Ah, there you are, I was beginning to despair," he said unreasonably. "And don't bother to take your coat off, we can't keep the Prime Minister waiting."

He took down his coat from the stand, picked up his Malacca cane, and went out and she hurried after him, slightly bewildered.

"But what's going on, sir?"

"I spoke to the Prime Minister earlier and he told me he wished to see us the moment you got back, so let's get cracking."

The Daimler was admitted at the security gates at the end of Downing Street with no delay. In fact, the most famous door in the world opened the second they got out of the car, and an aide took their coats and ushered them up the stairs past all the portraits of previous Prime Ministers and along the corridor, knocking gently on the door of the great man's study.

They went in, the door closed behind them, the Prime Minister looked up from his desk. "Brigadier."

"May I introduce Detective Chief Inspector Hannah Bernstein, Prime Minister, my assistant?"

"Chief Inspector." The Prime Minister nodded. "I was naturally more than intrigued by your telephone call this morning. Now tell me everything you've discovered about this affair so far."

So Ferguson told him, leaving nothing out.

When he was finished, the Prime Minister turned to Hannah. "Tell me about your visit to this place."

"Of course, Prime Minister."

As she ended, he said, "No question that Lady Katherine could be wrong?"

"Absolutely not, Prime Minister, she was adamant that she hadn't seen it, the Bible I mean, in years."

There was silence while the Prime Minister brooded. Ferguson said, "What would you like us to do?"

"Find the damn thing before they do, Brigadier, we've had enough trouble with Hong Kong. It's over, we're coming out, and that's it, so if this thing exists, you find it and burn it. And I don't want the Chinese involved. There would be hell to pay, and keep our American cousins out of it too."

It was Hannah who had the temerity to cut in. "You really think all this is true, Prime Minister, that it exists?"

"I'm afraid I do. After the Brigadier phoned me this morning I spoke with a certain very distinguished gentleman, now in his nineties, who was once a power at the Colonial Office during the war. He tells me that many years ago, he recalls rumours about this Chungking Covenant. Apparently it was always dismissed as a myth."

"So what do you wish us to do, Prime Minister?"

"We can hardly ask Prince Ali ben Yusef for permission to ransack the house and we can hardly send the burglars in."

"He leaves in four weeks and Morgan moves straight in," Hannah said.

"Well, he would, wouldn't he? Once he's in he can take his time and do anything he wants." The Prime Minister looked up at Ferguson. "But you'll be there at this Ardmurchan Lodge to keep an eye on things. What do you intend to do?"

"Improvise, sir." Ferguson smiled.

The Prime Minister smiled back. "You're usually rather good at that. See to it, Brigadier, don't let me down. Now you must excuse me."

As they settled in the back of the Daimler, Hannah said, "What now?"

"We'll go up to Ardmurchan Lodge just before Morgan in three to four weeks. In the meantime, I want a check on him. Use all international police contacts. I want to know where he goes and what he does."

"Fine."

"Good, now let me give you dinner. Blooms, I think, in Whitechapel. You can't say no to that, Chief Inspector, the finest Jewish restaurant in London."

After leaving the Ministry of Defence, Dillon had simply caught a taxi to Stable Mews not far from Ferguson's flat in Cavendish Square. He had a two-bedroom cottage there at the end of the cobbled yard. By the time he reached it the pain had come again quite badly, so he took one of the morphine capsules Bellamy had prescribed and went and lay down on the bed.

It obviously knocked him out and when he came awake quite suddenly it was dark. He got up, visited the toilet, and splashed water over his face. In the mirror he looked truly awful and he shuddered and went downstairs. He checked his watch. It was seven-thirty. He really needed something to eat, he knew that, and yet the prospect of food was repugnant to him.

Perhaps a walk would clear his head and then he could find a cafe. He opened the front door. Rain fell gently in a fine mist through the light of the street lamp on the corner. He pulled on his jacket, aware of the weight of the Walther, and paused, wondering whether to leave it, but the damn thing had been a part of him for so long. He found an old Burberry trench-coat and a black umbrella and ventured out.

He walked from street to street, pausing only once to go into a corner pub where he had a large brandy and a pork pie, which was so disgusting that just one bite made him want to throw up.

He continued to walk aimlessly. There was a certain amount of fog now, crouching at the end of the street, and it gave a closed-in feeling to things as if he was in his own private world. He felt a vague sense of alarm, probably drug paranoia, and somewhere in the distance Big Ben struck eleven, the sound curiously muffled by the fog. There was silence now, and then the unmistakable sound of a ship's foghorn as it moved down river, and he realized the Thames was close at hand.

He turned into another street and found himself beside the river. There was a corner shop still open. He went in and bought a packet of cigarettes and was served by a young Pakistani youth.

"Would there be a cafe anywhere near at hand?" Dillon asked.

"Plenty up on High Street, but if you like Chinese, there's the Red Dragon round the corner on China Wharf."

"An interesting name," Dillon said, lighting a cigarette, hand shaking.

"The tea clippers used to dock there in the old days of the China run." The youth hesitated. "Are you all right?"

"Nothing to worry about, just out of hospital," Dillon said, "but it's kind of you to ask."

He walked along the street past towering warehouses. It was raining heavily now, and then he turned the corner and saw a ten-foot dragon in red neon shining through the rain. He put down his umbrella, opened the door, and went in.

It was a long, narrow room with dark paneled walls, a bar of polished mahogany, and a couple of dozen tables each covered with a neat white linen cloth. There were a number of artifacts on display and Chinese watercolors on the wall.

There was only one customer, a Chinese of at least sixty with a bald head and round, enigmatic face. He was no more than five feet tall and very fat, and in spite of his tan gabardine suit bore a striking resemblance to a bronze statue of Buddha, which stood in one corner. He was eating a dish of cuttlefish and chopped vegetables with a very Western fork and ignored Dillon completely.

There was a Chinese girl behind the bar. She had a flower in her hair and wore a *cheongsam* in black silk, embroidered with a red dragon which was twin to the one outside.

"I'm sorry," she said in perfect English. "We've just closed."

"Any chance of a quick drink?" Dillon asked.

"I'm afraid we only have a table license."

She was very beautiful with her black hair and pale skin, dark, watchful eyes and high cheekbones, and Dillon felt like reaching out to touch her and then the red dragon on her dark dress seemed to come alive, undulating, and he closed his eyes and clutched at the bar.

Once in the Mediterranean on a diving job for the Israelis that had involved taking out two PLO high-speed boats that had been involved in landing terrorists by night in Israel, he had run out of air at fifty feet. Surfacing half-dead he'd had the same sensation as now of drifting up from the dark places into light.

The fat man had him in a grip of surprising strength and put him into a chair. Dillon took several deep breaths and smiled. "Sorry about this. I've been ill for some time and I probably walked too far tonight."

The expression on the fat man's face did not alter, and the girl said in Cantonese, "I'll handle this, Uncle, finish your meal."

Dillon, who spoke Cantonese rather well, listened with interest as the man replied, "Do you think they will still come, niece?"

"Who knows? The worst kind of foreign devils, pus from an infected wound. Still, I'll leave the door open a little longer." She smiled at Dillon. "Please excuse us. My uncle speaks very little English."

"That's fine. If I could just sit here for a moment."

"Coffee," the girl said. "Very black and with a large brandy."

"God save us, the brandy is fine, but would you happen to have a cup of tea, love? It's what I was raised on."

"Something we have in common."

She smiled and went behind the bar and took down a bottle of brandy and a glass. At that moment a car drew up outside. She paused, then moved to the end of the bar and peered out through the window.

"They are here, Uncle."

As she came round the end of the bar, the door opened and four men entered. The leader was six feet tall with a hard, raw-boned face. He wore a cavalry twill car coat that looked very expensive.

He smiled quite pleasantly. "Here we are again then," he said. "Have you got it for me?"

The accent was unmistakably Belfast. The girl said, "A waste of your time, Mr. McGuire, there is nothing for you here."

Two of his companions were black, the fourth an albino with lashes so fair they were almost transparent. He said, "Don't give us any trouble, darlin', we've been good to you. A grand a week for a place like this? I'd say you were getting off lightly."

She shook her head. "Not a penny."

McGuire sighed, plucked the bottle of brandy from her hand, and threw it into the bar mirror, splintering the glass. "That's just for openers. Now you, Terry."

The albino moved fast, his right hand finding the high neck of the silk dress, ripping it to the waist, baring one of her breasts. He pulled her close, cupping the breast in one hand.

"Now then, what have we here?"

The fat man was on his feet and Dillon kicked a chair across to block his way. "Stay out of this, Uncle, I'll handle it," he called in Cantonese.

The four men turned quickly to face Dillon and McGuire was still smiling. "What have we got here then, a hero?"

"Let her go," Dillon said.

Terry smiled and pulled the girl closer. "No, I like it too much." All the frustration, the anger and the pain of the last few weeks rose like bile in Dillon's mouth and he pulled out the Walther and fired blindly, finishing off the bar mirror.

Terry sent the girl staggering. "Look at his hand," he whispered, "he's shaking all over the place."

McGuire showed no sign of fear. "The accent makes me feel at home," he said.

"I mind yours too, old son," Dillon told him. "The Shankhill or the Falls Road, it's no difference to me. Now toss your wallet across."

McGuire didn't even hesitate and threw it on the table. It was stuffed with notes. "I see you've been on your rounds," Dillon said. "It should take care of the damage."

"Here, there's nearly two grand there," Terry said.

"Anything over can go to the widows and orphans." Dillon glanced at the girl. "No police, right?"

"No police."

Behind her the kitchen door opened and two waiters and a chef emerged. The waiters carried butchers' knives, the chef a meat cleaver.

"I'd go if I were you," Dillon said. "These people have rather violent ways when roused."

McGuire smiled. "I'll remember you, friend. Come on, boys," and he turned and went out.

They heard the car start up and drive away. What little strength Dillon had left him. He sagged back in the chair and replaced the Walther. "I could do with that brandy now."

And she was angry, that was the strange thing. She turned on her heel and pushed past the waiters into the kitchen.

"What did I do wrong?" Dillon asked as the staff followed her through.

"It is nothing," the fat man said. "She is upset. Let me get you your brandy."

He went to the bar, got a fresh bottle and two glasses, came back, and sat down. "You spoke to me in Cantonese. You have visited China often?"

"A few times, but not often. Hong Kong mainly."

"Fascinating. I am from Hong Kong and so is my niece. My name is Yuan Tao."

"Sean Dillon."

"You're Irish and visit Hong Kong only now and then and yet your Cantonese is excellent. How can this be?"

"Well, it's like this. Some people can do complicated mathematics in their head quicker than a computer."

"So?"

"I'm like that with languages. I just soak them up." Dillon drank a little brandy. "I presume that lot have been here before?"

"I understand so. I only flew in yesterday. I believe they have been pressing their demands here and elsewhere for some weeks."

The girl returned wearing slacks and a sweater. She was still angry and ignored her uncle, glaring at Dillon. "What do you want here?"

Yuan Tao cut in. "We owe Mr. Dillon a great deal."

"We owe him nothing and he has ruined everything. Is it just coincidence that he walks in here?"

"Strangely enough, it was," Dillon said. "Girl dear, life's full of them."

"And what kind of man carries a gun in London? Another criminal."

"Jesus," Dillon told Yuan Tao, "the logic on her. I could be a copper or the last of the vigilantes doing a Charles Bronson eradicating the evildoers." The brandy had gone to his head and he got up. "I'll be on my way. It's been fun," and he got up and was out of the door before they could stop him.

FIVE

Dillon was tired, very tired, and the pavement seemed to move beneath his feet. He followed the road and it brought him alongside the Thames. He stood at some railings staring into the fog, aware of another ship moving out there. He was confused, things happening in slow motion, not aware that someone was behind him until an arm slipped around his neck, cutting off his air. A hand slipped inside his jacket and found the Walther. Dillon was shoved into the railings, stayed there for a moment, then turned and moved forward.

The albino, Terry, stood there holding the Walther. "Here we are again then."

A black limousine pulled into the curb. Dillon was aware of someone else at his back, took a deep breath, and brought up all his resources. He swung his right foot up, caught Terry's hand, and the Walther soared over the railings into the Thames. He jerked his head back, crunching the nose of the man behind, then ran along the pavement. He turned the corner and found himself on a deserted wharf blocked by high gates securely padlocked.

As he turned, the limousine arrived and they all seemed to come at him together. The first man with an iron bar which clanged against the gate as Dillon lost his footing and fell, rolling desperately to avoid the swinging kicks. And then they had him up, pinning him against the gates.

McGuire, lighting a cigarette, stood by the limousine. He said, "You asked for this, friend, you really did. Okay, Terry, slice him up."

Terry's hand came out of his pocket holding an old-fashioned, cut-throat razor which he opened as he came forward. He was quite calm and the blade of the razor flashed dully in the light of a street lamp and somewhere a cry echoed flatly on the damp air. Terry and McGuire swung round and Yuan Tao came walking out of the rain.

The jacket of his gabardine suit was soaked and somehow he was different, moving with a kind of strange relentlessness as if nothing could ever stop him, and McGuire said, "For God's sake, put him out of his misery."

The man with the iron bar darted round the limousine and ran at Yuan Tao, the bar swinging, and the Chinese actually took the blow on his left forearm with no apparent effect. In the same moment his right fist jabbed in a short screwing motion that landed under the man's breast bone. He went down like a stone without a sound.

Yuan Tao leaned over him for a second and McGuire ran round the limousine and kicked out at him. The older man caught the foot with effortless ease and twisted so that Dillon could have sworn he heard bone crack, then he lifted, hurling McGuire across the bonnet of the car. He lay on the pavement, moaning. Yuan Tao came round the limousine, his face very calm, and the man holding Dillon from the rear released him and ran away.

Terry held up the razor. "All right, fatty, let's be having you."

"What about me then, you bastard?" Dillon said, and as Terry turned, gave him a punch in the mouth, summoning all his remaining strength.

Terry lay on the pavement, cursing, blood on his mouth, and Yuan Tao stamped on his hand and kicked the razor away. A van turned into the street and braked to a halt. As the chef got out, the two waiters came 'round the corner holding the man who had run away.

"I'd tell them to leave him in one piece," Dillon said in Cantonese. "You'll need him to drive this lot away."

"An excellent point," Yuan Tao said. "At least you are still in one piece."

"Only just. I'm beginning to see why your niece was annoyed. Presumably you were actually hoping McGuire would show up?"

"I flew in especially from Hong Kong for the pleasure. Su Yin, my niece, cabled for my help. A matter of family. It was difficult for me to get away. I was at a retreat at one of our monasteries."

"Monasteries?" Dillon asked.

"I should explain, Mr. Dillon, I am a Shaolin monk, if you know what that is."

Dillon laughed shakily. "I certainly do. If only McGuire had. It means, I suspect, that you're an expert in kung fu?"

"Darkmaster, Mr. Dillon, our most extreme grade. I have studied all my life. I think I shall stay for two or three weeks to make sure there is no more trouble."

"I shouldn't worry, I think they'll have got the point."

McGuire, Terry, and one of the blacks still lay on the pavement and the chef and two waiters brought the fourth man forward. Yuan Tao went and spoke to them in Cantonese and then returned. "They'll deal with things here. Su Yin is waiting in her car at the restaurant."

They walked back, turned the corner, and found a dark sedan parked under the Red Dragon. As they approached she got out and, ignoring her uncle, said to Dillon in Cantonese, "Are you all right?"

"I am now."

"I am sorry for my behavior." She bowed. "I deserve punishment as my honorable uncle pointed out. Please forgive me."

"There's nothing to forgive," Dillon told her and from the direction of the river a scream sounded.

She turned to her uncle. "What was that?"

"The little worm with the white hair, the one who shamed you before us, I told them to cut off his right ear."

Su Yin's face didn't alter. "I thank you, Uncle." She bowed again, then turned to Dillon. "You will come with us now, Mr. Dillon," and this time she spoke in English.

"Girl dear, I wouldn't miss it for the world," he said and got in the back of the car.

If you have studied judo or karate you will have heard of kiai, the power that makes a man perform miracles of strength and force. Only the greatest of masters acquire this and only after years of training and discipline, both mental and physical."

"Well you certainly have it," Dillon said. "I can still see that steel bar bounce off your arm."

He was immersed to his neck in a bath of water so hot that sweat ran down his face. Yuan Tao squatted against the wall in an old robe and peered at him through the steam.

Dillon carried on, "Once in Japan I was taken to see an old man of eighty, a Zen priest with arms like sticks. I think he might have weighed seven stone. He remained seated while two karate black belts repeatedly attacked him."

"And?"

"He threw them effortlessly. I was told later that his power sprang from what they called the *tanden*, or second brain."

"Which can only be developed by years of meditation. All this is a development of the ancient Chinese art of Shaolin Temple Boxing. It came from India in the sixth century with Zen Buddhism and was developed by the monks of Shaolin Temple in Hohan province."

"Isn't that a rough game for priests? I mean, I had an uncle, a Catholic priest, who taught me bare-knuckle boxing as a boy and him a prize fighter as a younger man, but this . . . ."

"We have a saying. A man avoids warfare only by being prepared for it. The monks learned that lesson. Centuries ago members of my family learned the art and passed it down. Over the centuries my ancestors fought evildoers on behalf of the poor, even the forces of the Emperor when necessary. We served our society."

"Are you talking of the Triad Society here?" Dillon asked. "I thought they were simply a kind of Chinese version of the Mafia."

"Like the Mafia, they started as secret societies to protect the poor against the rich landowners and like the Mafia they have become corrupted over the years, but not all."

"I've read something about this," Dillon said. "Are you telling me you are a Triad?"

"Like my forefathers before me I am a member of the Secret Breath, the oldest of all, founded in Hohan in the sixteenth century. Unlike others, my society has not been corrupted. I am a Shaolin monk, I also have business interests, there is nothing wrong in that, but I will stand aside for no man."

"So all this and your fighting ability has been handed down?"

"Of course. There are many methods, many schools, but without *ch'i* they are nothing."

"And what would that be?"

"A special energy. When accumulated just below the navel, it has an elemental force which is infinitely greater than physical force alone. It means that a fist is simply a focusing agent. There is no need for the tremendous punches used by Western boxers. I strike from only a few inches away, screwing my fist on impact. The result may be a ruptured spleen or broke bones."

"I can believe that, but deflecting that steel bar with your arm. How do you do that?"

"Practice, Mr. Dillon, fifty years of practice."

"I haven't got that long." Dillon stood up and Yuan Tao passed him a towel.

"One may accomplish miracles in a matter of weeks with discipline and application, and with a man like you I doubt whether one would be starting from scratch. There are scars from knife wounds in your back and that is an old bullet wound in the left shoulder and then there was the gun." He shrugged. "No ordinary man."

"I was stabbed in the back fairly recently," Dillon told him. "They saved me with two operations, but it poisoned my system."

"And your occupation?"

"I worked for British Intelligence. They threw me out this morning, said I wasn't up to it anymore."

"Then they are wrong."

There was a pause and Dillon said, "Are you saying you'll take me on?"

"I owe you a debt, Mr. Dillon."

"Come off it, you didn't need me. I interfered."

"But you didn't know you were interfering and that makes a difference. It is a man's intentions which are important." Yuan Tao smiled. "Wouldn't you like to prove your people wrong?"

"By God and I would so," Dillon said, and then he hesitated as Yuan Tao handed him a robe. "I'd prefer honesty between us from the beginning."

"So?"

Dillon stood up and pulled on the robe. "I was for years a member of the Provisional IRA and high on the most wanted list of the Royal Ulster Constabulary and British Intelligence."

"And yet worked for the British."

"Yes, well, I didn't have much choice at first."

"But now something has changed inside your head?"

Dillon grinned. "Is there nothing you don't know? Anyway, does it make a difference?"

"Why should it? From the way you struck one of those men tonight, I think you have studied karate."

"Some, but no big deal. Brown belt and working for black, then I ran out of time."

"This is good. I think we can accomplish a great deal. But now we will eat. Flesh on your bones again."

He led the way along a corridor to a sitting room furnished in a mixture of European and Chinese styles. Su Yin sat by the fire reading a book and wearing a black silk trouser suit.

"I have news, niece," Yuan Tao said as she got up. "Mr. Dillon is to spend three weeks as our guest. This will not inconvenience you?"

"Of course not, Uncle, I will get the supper now."

She moved to the door, opened it, and glanced back at Dillon over her shoulder, and for the first time since they had met she smiled.

It was the morning of the Fourth of July that Morgan and Asta flew into London. They were picked up at Heathrow by a Rolls laid on by his London head office.

"The Berkeley?" she said.

"Where else, the best hotel in town. I've got us the Wellington Suite up on the roof with the two bedrooms and that wonderful conservatory."

"And so convenient for Harrods," she said.

He squeezed her hand. "When did I ever tell you not to spend my money? I'll just drop you off, I've business at the office, but I'll be back. Don't forget we have the Fourth of July party at the American Embassy tonight. Wear something really nice."

"I'll knock their eyes out."

"You always do, sweetheart, your mother would have been real proud of you," and he took her hand as the Rolls moved away.

Hannah Bernstein knocked and went into Ferguson's office and found him working hard at his desk. "Paper and even more paper." He sat back. "What is it?"

"I've had a phone call from Kim at Ardmurchan Lodge. He arrived there safely last night in the Range Rover you appropriated. He said the journey was very strenuous, that the mountains reminded him of Nepal, but that the lodge is very nice. Apparently Lady Katherine's cook, Jeannie, appeared with a meat and potato pie to make sure he was all right."

Kim, once a Corporal in the Ghurkas, had been Ferguson's body servant, cook, and general man-about-the-house since army days.

"Good, and Morgan?"

"The Prince moves out on Sunday morning. He has slots arranged from Air Traffic Control from Ardmurchan Airfield. I've checked and Morgan has booked a slot to fly in that lunchtime in his company Citation. No time for breaking and entering, I'm afraid."

"And where is he now?"

"Arrived at Heathrow an hour ago with his step-daughter, booked into the Wellington Suite at the Berkeley."

"Good God, the Duke must be turning in his grave."

"Appearance at the American Embassy tonight, sir."

"Which means I'll have to skip that Fourth of July junket. Never mind. Is the other business in hand?"

"Yes, sir."

"Excellent. I'll see you later then."

He returned to his work and she went out.

Dillon came awake early from a deep sleep aware at once of pale evening light filtering in through the curtained window. He was alone. He turned to look at the pillow beside him, at the indentation where her head had been, and then he got up, walked to the window, and looked out through the half-drawn curtains to the cobbled street of Stable Mews.

It was a fine evening and he turned and went to the wardrobe feeling relaxed and alive, but more important, whole again. His eyes were calm, his head clear, and the ache in his stomach was honest hunger. He stood in front of the mirror and examined himself. He looked younger, fitter in every way. When he turned to examine his back in the mirror, the angry weal of the operation scars from the knife wounds were already fading into white lines. It was extraordinary. Barely four weeks since that night in Wapping. What Yuan Tao had achieved was a miracle. He pulled on a track suit, then followed the sound of running water to the bathroom. When he opened the door, Su Yin was in the shower.

"It's me," he called. "Are we having dinner tonight?"

"I have a business to run," she called. "You keep forgetting."

"We could eat late."

"All right, we'll see, now go and do your exercises."

He closed the door and returned to the bedroom. It was cool in there and quiet, only the faint traffic sounds in the distance. He could almost hear the silence, and he stood there, relaxing completely, remembering the lines of the ancient Taoist verse that Yuan Tao had taught him.

In motion, be like water,
At rest, like a mirror,
Respond, like the echo,
Be subtle as though non-existent.

The ability to relax completely, the most important gift of all, a faculty retained by all other animals except man. Cultivated, it could provide a power that could be positively superhuman, created by vigorous discipline and a system of training at least a thousand years old. Out of it sprang the intrinsic energy *ch'i,* the life force which in repose gave a man the pliability of a child and in action the power of the tiger.

He sat on the floor cross-legged, relaxing totally; breathing in through his nose and out through his mouth. He closed his eyes and covered his left ear with his right hand. He varied this after five minutes by covering his right ear with his left hand, still breathing deeply and steadily. Then he covered both ears, arms crossed.

Darkness enfolded him and when he finally opened his eyes, his mouth was sharply cool. He took a long, shuddering breath and when he got to his feet, his limbs seemed to be filled with power. He wondered how Bellamy would react, and yet the results were there for all to see. A hand that no longer trembled, a clear eye and a strength he would never have believed possible.

Su Yin came in at that moment wearing cream slacks and a Spanish shirt in vivid orange. She was combing her hair. "You look pleased with yourself."

"And why wouldn't I? I've spent the afternoon in bed with a supremely beautiful woman and I still feel like Samson."

She laughed. "You're hopeless, Sean. Get me a taxi."

He phoned the usual number, then turned. "What about tonight? We could eat late at the Ritz and catch the cabaret."

"It's not possible." She put a hand to her face. "I know how good you feel these days, but you can't have everything in this life." She hesitated. "You miss Yuan Tao, don't you?"

"Very much, which is strange considering he only left five days ago."

"Would you miss me as much?"

"Of course. Why do you ask?"

"I'm going home, Sean. My sister and her husband are opening a new night club in Hong Kong. My uncle phoned me last night. They need me."

"And the Red Dragon?"

"Will continue quite happily with my head waiter promoted to manager."

"And me?" he said. "What about me?"

"Are you trying to say you love me?" He hesitated before replying and it was enough. "No, Sean, we've had as good a time together as any two people could hope for in this life, but everything passes and it's time for me to go home."

"How soon?"

"Probably the weekend." As the doorbell went, she picked up her briefcase. "There's my taxi. I must go. I've lots to do."

He went with her to the door and opened it. The taxi was waiting, engine running. She paused on the step. "This isn't the end, Sean. You'll call me?"

He kissed her lightly on both cheeks. "Of course."

But he wouldn't, he knew that and she knew it too, he could tell that by the way she paused before getting into the taxi, glancing back as if aware that it was the last time, and then the door slammed and she was gone.

He was in the shower for a good fifteen minutes, thinking about it, when the front door bell rang. Perhaps she'd come back? He found a bathrobe and went out, drying his hair with a towel. When he opened the door a man in brown overalls stood there, a clipboard in his hand, a British Telecom van parked behind him.

"Sorry to bother you, sir, we've had four telephone breakdowns already this morning in the mews. Could I check your box?" He held up a British Telecom identity pass with his photo on it above the name J. Smith.

"Sure and why not?" Dillon turned and led the way along the corridor. "The junction box is under the stairs. I'll just go and change."

He went upstairs, finished drying his hair, combed it and pulled on an old track suit and trainers, then went downstairs. The telephone engineer was under the stairs.

"Everything all right?" Dillon asked.

"I think so, sir."

Dillon turned to go through the living room to the kitchen and saw a large laundry basket in the middle of the room. "What in the hell is this?" he demanded.

"Oh, that's for you."

A second telephone engineer in the same uniform overalls stepped from behind the door holding an Italian Beretta automatic pistol. He was getting on a little and had a wrinkled and kindly face.

"Jesus, son, there's no need for that thing, just tell me what you want," Dillon said and moved to the wide Victorian fireplace and stood with his hand on the mantelpiece.

"I wouldn't try to grab for the Walther you keep hanging from a nail just into the chimney, sir, we've already removed it," the older man said. "So just lie on the floor, hands behind your neck."

Dillon did as he was told as Smith joined them. "Steady does it, Mr. Dillon," he said and Dillon was aware of a needle jabbing into his right buttock.

Whatever it was, it was good. One moment he was there, the next he was gone, it was as simple as that.

He came back to life as quickly as he had left it. It was night now and the only illumination in the room was from a kind of night light on the locker beside the single bed on which he lay. He still wore his track suit; they hadn't even taken off his trainers. He swung his legs to the floor, took a couple of deep breaths, then heard voices and a key rattled in the lock. He hurriedly lay back and closed his eyes.

"Still out. Is that all right, Doc?" It was Smith speaking, Dillon recognized his voice.

Someone else said, "Let me see." A finger checked his pulse on the right wrist and then his track suit top was unzipped and a stethoscope applied. "Pulse fine, heart fine," the doctor said and rolled back Dillon's eyelids one after the other and probed with a light. He was a tall, cadaverous Indian in a white coat, and Dillon, by an act of supreme will, stayed rigid, staring. "No, he'll be awake soon. One cannot be certain of the time element with these drug dosages. There are individual variations in response. We'll come back in an hour."

The door closed, the key turned. Two bolts were also rammed home. Dillon was on his feet now, moved to the door and stood there listening. There was little point in wasting time on the door, that was obvious. He moved to the window and drew the curtain and was immediately presented with solid bars. He peered out. Rain fell steadily, dripping through a leak from the gutter which was just above his head. There was a garden outside, a high wall about fifty yards away.

If the gutter was where it was that meant there was only roof space above him. It could be an attic, but there was only one way to find out.

There was a small wooden table and a chair against the wall. He dragged the table into the corner by the window and climbed into it. The plaster of the ceiling was so old and soft that when he put his elbow into it, it broke at once, shards of plaster crumbling, dropping into the room. He enlarged the hole quickly, tearing wooden lathing away with his bare hands. When it was large enough, he got down, placed the chair on the table, then clambered up on it, pulling himself up to find a dark, echoing roof space, a chink of light drifting through a crack here and there.

He moved cautiously, walking on beams. The roof space was extensive and obviously covered the whole house, a rabbit warren of half-walls and eaves. He finally came to a trapdoor which he opened cautiously. Below was a small landing in darkness, stairs leading down to where there was diffused light.

Dillon dropped to the landing, paused to listen, and then went down the stairs. He found himself at one end of a long corridor which was fully lit. He hesitated, and at that moment, a door opened on his left and Smith and the Indian doctor walked out. And Smith was fast, Dillon had to give him that, pulling a Walther from his pocket even as Dillon moved in, smashing a fist into his stomach and raising a knee into the man's face as he keeled over. Smith dropped the Walther as he fell and Dillon picked it up.

"All right, old son," he said to the doctor. "Answers. Where am I?"

The Indian was hugely alarmed. "St. Mark's Nursing Home, Holland Park, Mr. Dillon. Please." His hands fluttered. "I loathe guns."

"You'll loathe them even more when I've finished with you. What's going on here? Who am I up against?"

"Please, Mr. Dillon." The man was pleading now. "I just work here."

There was a sudden shout and Dillon turned to see the second of his kidnappers standing at the end of the corridor. He drew his Beretta, Dillon took a quick snap-shot with the Walther, the man went over backwards. Dillon shoved the Indian into the room, turned, and went headlong down the stairs. Before he reached the bottom a shrill alarm bell sounded monotonously over and over again. Dillon didn't hesitate, reaching the corridor on the ground floor in seconds, running straight for the door at the far end. He unlocked it hurriedly and plunged out into the garden.

It was raining hard. He seemed to be at the rear of the house and somewhere on the other side he heard voices calling and the bark of a dog. He ran across a piece of lawn and carried on through bushes, a hand raised to protect his face from flailing branches, until he reached the wall. It was about fifteen feet high, festooned with barbed wire. Possible to climb a nearby tree, perhaps, and leap across, but the black wire strung at that level looked ominous. He picked up a large branch lying on the ground and reached up. When he touched the wire there was an immediate flash.

He turned and ran on, parallel to the wall. There was more than one dog barking now, but the rain would help kill his scent, and then he came to the edge of trees and the drive to the gates leading to the outside world. They were closed and two men stood there wearing berets and camouflage uniforms and holding assault rifles.

A Land-Rover drew up and someone got out to speak to them, a man in civilian clothes. Dillon turned and hurried back toward the house. The alarm stopped abruptly. He paused by the rear entrance he had exited from earlier, then opened it. The corridor was silent and he moved along it cautiously and stood at the bottom of the stairs.

There were voices in the distance. He listened for a moment, then went cautiously back up the stairs. The last place they'd look for him, or so he hoped. He reached the corridor on the top floor. Smith and the other man had gone, but as Dillon paused there, considering his next move, the door opened on his right, and for the second time that night the Indian doctor emerged.

His distress was almost comical. "Oh, my God, Mr. Dillon, I thought you well away by now."

"I've returned to haunt you," Dillon told him. "You didn't tell me your name."

"Chowdray—Dr. Emas Chowdray."

"Good. I'll tell you what we're going to do. Somewhere in this place is the person in charge. You're going to take me to where he is. If you don't"— he tucked Chowdray under the chin with the Walther—"you'll loathe guns even more."

"No need for this violence, I assure you, Mr. Dillon, I will comply."

He led the way down the stairs, turning along a corridor on the first floor, reaching a carpeted landing. A curving Regency staircase led to a magnificent hall. The dogs were still barking in the garden outside, but it was so quiet in the hall they could hear the ticking of the grandfather clock in the corner.

"Where are we going?" Dillon whispered.

"Down there, the mahogany door," Chowdray told him.

"Down we go then."

They descended the carpeted stairs, moved across the hall to the door. "The library, Mr. Dillon."

"Nice and easy," Dillon said. "Open it."

Chowdray did so and Dillon pushed him inside. The walls were lined with books, a fire burned brightly in an Adam fireplace. Detective Chief Inspector Hannah Bernstein stood by the fire talking to the two fake telephone engineers.

She turned and smiled. "Come in, Mr. Dillon, do. You've just won me five pounds. I told these two this is exactly where you would end up."

SIX

The car which dropped Dillon at his cottage in Stable Mews waited while he went in. He changed into gray slacks, a silk navy blue polo neck sweater, and a Donegal tweed jacket. He got his wallet, cigarette case, and lighter and was outside and into the car again in a matter of minutes. It was not long afterwards that they reached Cavendish Square and he rang the bell of Ferguson's flat. It was Hannah Bernstein who answered.

"Do you handle the domestic chores as well now?" he asked. "Where's Kim?"

"In Scotland," she told him. "You'll find out why. He's waiting."

She led the way along the corridor into the sitting room where they found Ferguson sitting beside the fire reading the evening paper. He looked up calmly. "There you are, Dillon. I must say you look remarkably fit."

"More bloody games," Dillon said.

"A practical test which I thought would save me a great deal of time and indicate just how true the reports I've been getting on you were." He looked at Hannah. "You've got it all on video?"

"Yes, sir."

He returned to Dillon. "You certainly gave poor old Smith a working over, and as for his colleague, it's a good job you only had blanks in that Walther." He shook his head. "My God, Dillon, you really are a bastard when you get going."

"God bless your honor for the pat on the head," Dillon said. "And is there just the slightest chance you could be telling me what in the hell this is all about?"

"Certainly," Ferguson said. "There's a bottle of Bushmills on the sideboard. You get the file out, Chief Inspector."

"Thank you," Dillon said with irony and went and helped himself.

Ferguson said, "If I hadn't seen it with my own eyes I wouldn't have believed it. Remarkable fellow this Yuan Tao. Wish he could work for me."

"I suppose you could always try to buy him," Dillon said.

"Not really," Ferguson said. "He owns three factories in Hong Kong and one of the largest shipping lines in the Far East, besides a number of minor interests, restaurants, that sort of thing. Didn't he tell you?"

"No," Dillon said and then he smiled. "He wouldn't have. He's not that sort of bloke, Brigadier."

"His niece seems an attractive girl."

"She is. She's also returning to Hong Kong this weekend. I bet you didn't know that."

"What a pity. We'll have to find another way of filling your time."

"I'm sure you won't have the slightest difficulty," Dillon told him.

"As usual, you've hit the nail on the head. I obviously wanted you back anyway, but as it happens something special has come up, something that I think requires the Dillon touch. For one thing, there's a rather attractive young lady involved, but we'll come to that later. Chief Inspector, the file."

"Here, sir," she said and handed it to him.

"Have you heard of a man called Carl Morgan?"

"Billionaire hotel owner, financier amongst other things," Dillon said. "Never out of the society pages in the magazines. He's also closely linked with the Mafia. His uncle is a man called Don Giovanni Luca. In Sicily he's *Capo di tutti Capi*, Boss of all the bosses."

Ferguson was genuinely impressed. "How on earth do you know all this?"

"Oh, about a thousand years ago when I worked with a certain illegal organization called the IRA, the Sicilian Mafia was one of the sources from which we obtained arms."

"Really," Hannah Bernstein said dryly. "It might be useful to have you sit down and commit everything you remember about how that worked to paper."

"It's a thought," Dillon told her.

She handed him a file. "Have a look at that."

"Delighted."

"I'll make some tea, sir."

She went out and Dillon sat on the windowseat, smoking a cigarette. As he finished, she returned with a tray and he joined them by the fire.

"Fascinating stuff this Chungking Covenant business." There were some photos clipped to the back of the file, one of them of Morgan in polo kit. "The man himself. Looks like an advert for some manly aftershaves."

"He's a dangerous man," Hannah said as she poured tea. "Don't kid yourself."

"I know, girl dear," he said. There were other photos, some showing Morgan with the great and good and a couple with Luca. "He certainly knows everybody."

"You could say that."

"And this?" Dillon asked.

The last photo showed Morgan on his yacht at Cannes Harbor, reclining in a deck chair, a glass of champagne in hand, gazing up at a young girl who leaned on the rail. She looked about sixteen and wore a bikini, blond hair to her shoulders.

"His stepdaughter, Asta, though she uses his name," Hannah told him.

"Swedish?"

"Yes. Taken more than four years ago. She's twenty-one in three weeks or so. We have a photo of her in *Tatler* somewhere taken with Morgan at Goodwood races. Very, very attractive."

"I'd say Morgan would agree with you, to judge from the way he's looking at her in that picture."

"Why do you say that particularly?" Ferguson asked.

"He smiles a lot usually, he's smiling on all the other photos, but not on this one. It's as if he's saying, 'I take you seriously.' Where does the mother fit in? You haven't indicated her on any photos."

"She was drowned a year ago while diving off a Greek island called Hydra."

"An accident?"

"Faulty air tank, that's what the autopsy said, but there's a copy of an investigation mounted by the Athens police here." Hannah produced it from the file. "The Brigadier tells me you're an expert diver. You'll find it interesting."

Dillon read it quickly, then looked up frowning. "No accident this. That valve must have been tampered with. Did it end at that?"

"The police didn't even raise the matter with Morgan. I got this from their dead file courtesy of a friend in Greek Intelligence," Ferguson told him. "Morgan has huge interests in Greek shipping, casinos, hotels. There was an order from the top to kill the investigation."

"They'd never have got anywhere," Hannah said. "Not with the kind of money he has and all that power and influence."

"But what we're saying is he killed his wife or arranged to have it done," Dillon said. "Why would he do that? Was she wealthy?"

"Yes, but nothing like as rich as he is," Ferguson said. "My hunch is that perhaps she'd got to know too much."

"And that's your opinion?" Dillon asked Hannah Bernstein.

"Possibly." She picked up the photo taken on the yacht. "But maybe it was something else. Perhaps he wanted Asta."

Dillon nodded. "That's what I was thinking." He turned to Ferguson. "So what are we going to do on this one?"

Ferguson nodded to Hannah, who took charge. "The house at Loch Dhu, Morgan goes in this coming Monday. The Brigadier and I are going up on Friday, flying to this old RAF station at Ardmurchan, and we move into Ardmurchan Lodge where Kim is already in residence."

"And what about me?"

"You're my nephew," Ferguson said. "My mother was Irish, remember? You'll join us a few days later."

"Why?"

"Our information is that Asta isn't going with Morgan. She's attending a ball at the Dorchester, which is being given by the Brazilian Embassy on Monday night. Morgan was supposed to go and she's standing in for him," Hannah said. "We've discovered that she flies to Glasgow on Tuesday and then intends to take the train to Fort William and from there to Arisaig, where she'll be picked up by car."

"How do you know this?" Dillon asked.

"Oh, let's say we have a friend on the staff at the Berkeley," she said.

"Why take the train from Glasgow when she could fly direct to Ardmurchan on Morgan's Citation?"

"God knows," Ferguson said. "Perhaps she fancies the scenic route. That train goes through some of the most spectacular scenery in Europe."

"So what am I supposed to do?"

"The Chief Inspector has a gold-edged invitation for one Sean Dillon to attend the Brazilian Embassy Ball on Monday night," Ferguson told him. "It's black tie for you, Dillon, you do have one?"

"Sure and don't I need it for those spare nights I'm a waiter at the Savoy? And what do I do when I'm there?"

For the first time Hannah Bernstein looked unsure. "Well, try and get to know her."

"Pick her up, you mean? Won't that look something of a coincidence when I turn up at Ardmurchan Lodge later?"

"Quite deliberate on my part, dear boy. Remember our little adventure in the American Virgins?" Ferguson turned to Hannah. "I'm sure you've read the file, Chief Inspector. The late lamented Señor Santiago and his motley crew knew who we were just as we knew who they were and what

they were up to. It was what I call a we know that you know that you know
that we know situation."

"So?" Dillon said.

"Morgan at Loch Dhu for nefarious purposes, an isolated estate miles
from anywhere in the Highlands of Scotland, discovers he's got neighbors
up for the shooting staying on the other side of the Loch at Ardmurchan
Lodge. He'll be checking us out the minute he knows we're there, dear boy,
and don't tell me we could all use false names. With the kind of company
he keeps, especially his Mafia contacts in London, he'll not have the
slightest difficulty in sorting us out."

"All right, point taken, but I know you, you old bugger, and there's
more to it."

"Hasn't he an elegant turn of phrase, Chief Inspector?" Ferguson
smiled. "Yes, of course there is. As I've indicated, I want him to know we're
there, I want him to know we're breathing down his bloody neck. Of course
I'll also see that the story, Morgan taking Loch Dhu and Asta standing in for
him at the Brazilian Embassy affair, is leaked to the *Daily Mail*'s gossip column. You could always say later that you read that, were intrigued because
you were going to the same spot, so you went out of your way to meet her. It
won't make the slightest difference. Morgan will still smell stinking fish."

"Won't that be dangerous, Brigadier?" Hannah Bernstein commented.

"Yes it will, Chief Inspector, that's why we have Dillon." He smiled
and stood up. "It's getting late and dinner is indicated. You must be famished, both of you. I'll take you to the River Room at the Savoy. Excellent
dance band, Chief Inspector, you can have a turn round the floor with the
desperado here. He may surprise you."

When Monday night came Dillon arrived early at the Dorchester. He wore
a dark blue Burberry trenchcoat, which he left at the cloakroom. His dinner
jacket was a totally conventional piece of immaculate tailoring by Armani,
single breasted with lapels of raw silk, black studs vivid against the white
shirt. He was really rather pleased with his general appearance and hoped
that Asta Morgan would feel the same. He fortified himself with a glass of
champagne in the Piano Bar and went down to the grand ballroom where
he presented his card and was admitted to discover the Brazilian Ambassador and his wife greeting their guests.

His name was called and he went forward. "Mr. Dillon?" the Ambassador said, a slight query in his voice.

"Ministry of Defence," Dillon said. "So good of you to invite me." He
turned to the Ambassador's wife and kissed her hand gallantly. "My compliments on the dress, most becoming."

She flushed with pleasure and as he walked away he heard her say in Portuguese to her husband, "What a charming man."

The ballroom was already busy, a dance band playing, exquisitely gowned women, most men in black tie, although there was a sprinkling of military dress uniforms and here and there a church dignitary. With the crystal chandeliers, the mirrors, it was really quite a splendid scene and he took a glass of champagne from a passing waiter and worked his way through the crowd looking for Asta Morgan and seeing no sign of her. Finally he went back to the entrance, lit a cigarette, and waited.

It was almost an hour later that he heard her name called. She wore her hair up revealing the entire face, the high Scandinavian cheek bones, and the kind of arrogance that seemed to say that she didn't give a damn about anyone or anything, for that matter. She wore an absurdly simple dress of black silk, banded at the waist, the hem well above the knee, black stockings, and carried an evening purse in a sort of black chain mail. Heads turned to watch as she stood talking to the Ambassador and his wife for quite some time.

"Probably making Morgan's excuses," Dillon said softly.

Finally she came down the stairs, pausing to open her purse. She took out a gold cigarette case, selected one, then searched for a lighter. "Damn!" she said.

Dillon stepped forward, the Zippo flaring in his right hand. "Sure and nothing's ever there when you want it, isn't that the truth?"

She looked him over calmly, then held his wrist and took the light. "Thank you."

As she turned to go, Dillon said cheerfully, "Six inches at least those heels, mind how you go, dear girl, a plaster cast wouldn't go well with that slip of a dress."

Her eyes widened in astonishment, then she laughed and walked away.

She seemed to know a vast number of people, working her way from group to group, occasionally posing for society photographers, and she was certainly popular. Dillon stayed close enough to observe her and simply waited to see what the night would bring.

She danced on a number of occasions, with a variety of men including the Ambassador himself and two Government ministers and an actor or two. Dillon's opportunity came about an hour later when he saw her dancing with a Member of Parliament notorious for his womanizing. As the dance finished he kept his arm round her waist as they left the floor. They were standing by the buffet and she was trying to get away, but he had her by the wrist now.

Dillon moved in fast. "Jesus, Asta, I'm sorry I'm so late. Business." The other man released her, frowning, and Dillon kissed her on the mouth. "Sean Dillon," he murmured.

She pushed him away and said petulantly, "You really are a swine, Sean, nothing but excuses. Business. Is that the best you can do?"

Dillon took her hand, totally ignoring the MP. "Well, I'll think of something. Let's take a turn round the floor."

The band played a foxtrot and she was light in his arms. "By God, girl, but you do this well," he said.

"I learned at boarding school. Twice a week we had ballroom dancing in the hall. Girls dancing together, of course. Always a row over who was to lead."

"I can imagine. You know when I was a boy back home in Belfast we used to club together so one of the crowd could pay to get in at the dancehall, then he'd open a fire door so the rest got in for free."

"You dogs," she said.

"Well at sixteen you didn't have the cash, but once in, it was fantasy time. All those girls in cotton frocks smelling of talcum powder." She grinned. "We lived in a very working class area. Perfume was far too expensive."

"And that's where you perfected your performance?"

"And what performance would that be?"

"Oh, come off it," she said. "The smooth act you pulled back there. Now I'm supposed to be grateful, isn't that how it goes?"

"You mean we vanish into the night so that I can have my wicked way with you?" He smiled. "I'm sorry, my love, but I've other things planned and I'm sure you do." He stopped on the edge of the floor and kissed her hand. "It's been fun, but try and keep better company."

He turned and walked away and Asta Morgan watched him go, a look of astonishment on her face.

The pianist in the Piano Bar at the Dorchester was Dillon's personal favorite in the whole of London. When the Irishman appeared, he waved and Dillon joined him, leaning on the piano.

"Heh, you look great, man, something special tonight?"

"Ball for the Brazilian Embassy, the great and the good sometimes making fools of themselves."

"Takes all sorts. You want to fill in? I could do with a visit to the men's room."

"My pleasure."

Dillon slipped behind the piano and sat down as the pianist stood. A waitress approached, smiling. "The usual, Mr. Dillon?"

"Krug, my love, non-vintage." Dillon took a cigarette from his old silver case, lit it, and moved into "A Foggy Day in London Town," a personal favorite.

He sat there, the cigarette dangling from the side of his mouth, smoke drifting up, immersed in the music and yet still perfectly aware of Asta Morgan's approach.

"A man of talent, I see."

"As an old enemy of mine once said, a passable bar-room piano, that's all, fruits of a misspent youth."

"Enemy you say?"

"We supported the same cause, but had different attitudes on how to go about it, let's put it that way."

"A cause, Mr. Dillon? That sounds serious."

"A heavy burden." The waitress arrived with the Krug in a bucket and he nodded. "A glass for the lady, we'll sit in the booth over there."

"I was a stranger in the city," she said, giving him some of the verse.

"Out of town were the people I knew," he replied. "Thank the Gershwins for it, George and Ira. They must have loved this old town. Wrote it for a movie called *A Damsel in Distress*. Fred Astaire sang it."

"I hear he could dance a little too," she said.

The black pianist returned at that moment. "Heh, man, that's nice."

"But not as good as you. Take over." Dillon got out of the way as the pianist sat beside him.

They sat in the booth and Dillon lit a cigarette for her and gave her a glass of champagne.

"I'd judge you to be a man of accomplishment and high standards and yet you drink non-vintage," she said as she sampled the Krug.

"The greatest champagne of all, the non-vintage," he said. "It's quite unique. It's the grape mix, and not many people know that. They go by what's printed on the label, the surface of things."

"A philosopher too. What do you do, Mr. Dillon?"

"As little as possible."

"Don't we all? You spoke of a cause, not a job or a profession, a cause. Now that I do find interesting."

"Jesus, Asta Morgan, here we are in the best bar in London drinking Krug champagne and you're turning serious on me."

"How do you know my name?"

"Well the *Tatler* knows it and *Hello* and all those other society magazines you keep appearing in. Hardly a secret, you and your father keeping such high-class company. Why, they even had you in the Royal Enclosure at Ascot last month with the Queen Mother, God save her, and me just a poor Irish peasant boy with his nose to the window."

"I was in the Enclosure because my father had a horse running, and I doubt whether you've ever put your nose to a window in your life, Mr. Dillon. I've a strong suspicion you'd be much more likely to kick it in." She stood up. "My turn to leave now. It's been nice and I'm grateful for you intervening back there. Hamish Hunt is a pig when he's been drinking."

"A girl like you, my love, would tempt a cardinal from Rome and no drink taken," Dillon told her.

For a moment she changed, the hard edge gone, flushed, looking slightly uncertain. "Why, Mr. Dillon, compliments and at this time of night? Whatever next?"

Dillon watched her go, then got up and followed. He paid his check quickly, retrieved his Burberry and pulled it on, walking out into the magnificent foyer of the Dorchester. There was no sign of her at the entrance and the doorman approached.

"Cab, sir?"

"I was looking for Miss Asta Morgan," Dillon told him. "But I seem to have missed her."

"I know Miss Morgan well, sir. She's been at the ball tonight. I'd say her driver will be picking her up at the side entrance."

"Thanks."

Dillon walked round and followed the pavement, the Park Lane traffic flashing by. There were a number of limousines parked, waiting for their passengers, and as he approached, Asta Morgan emerged wearing a rather dramatic black cloak, the hood pulled up. She paused, looking up and down the line of limousines, obviously not finding what she was looking for and started along the pavement. At the same moment the MP, Hamish Hunt, emerged from the hotel and went after her.

Dillon moved in fast, but Hunt had her by the arm and up against the wall, his hands under her cloak. His voice was loud, slurred with the drink. "Come on, Asta, just a kiss."

She turned her face away and Dillon tapped him on the shoulder. Hunt turned in surprise and Dillon ran a foot down his shin, stamping hard on Hunt's instep, then head-butted him sharply and savagely and with total economy. Hunt staggered back and slid down the wall.

"Drunk again," Dillon said. "I wonder what the voters will say," and he took Asta's hand and pulled her away.

A Mercedes limousine slid up to the curb and a uniformed chauffeur jumped out. "I hope I haven't kept you waiting, Miss Asta, the police were moving us on earlier, I had to go round."

"That's all right, Henry."

A uniformed police officer moved along the pavement toward Hunt, who was sitting against the wall, and Asta opened the rear door of the Mercedes and pulled Dillon by the hand.

"Come on, we'd better get out of here."

He followed her in, the chauffeur got behind the wheel and eased into the traffic. "Jesus, ma'am, the grand car you've got here and me just a poor Irish boy up from the country and hoping to make a pound or two."

She laughed out loud. "Poor Irish boy, Mr. Dillon, I've never heard such rot. If you are, it's the first one I've heard of who wears clothes by Armani."

"Ah, you noticed?"

"If there's one thing I'm an expert on it's fashion. That's *my* fruits of a misspent youth."

"Sure and it's the terrible old woman you are already, Asta Morgan."

"All right," she said. "Where can we take you?"

"Anywhere?"

"The least I can do."

He pressed the button that lowered the glass window separating them from the chauffeur. "Take us to the Embankment, driver," he said and raised the window again.

"The Embankment?" she said. "What for?"

He offered her a cigarette. "Didn't you ever see those old movies where the fella and his girl walked along the pavement by the Embankment overlooking the Thames?"

"Before my time, Mr. Dillon," she said and leaned forward for a light, "but I'm willing to try anything once."

When they reached the Embankment, it was raining. "Would you look at that now," Dillon said.

She put the partition window down. "We're going to walk, Henry. Pick us up at Lambeth Bridge. Have you an umbrella?"

"Certainly, Miss Asta."

He got out to open the doors and put up a large black umbrella, which Dillon took. Asta slipped a hand in his arm and they started to walk. "Is this romantic enough for you?" he demanded.

"I wouldn't have thought you the romantic type," she said. "But if you mean do I like it, yes. I love the rain, the city by night, the feeling that anything could be waiting just up around the next corner."

"Probably a mugger these days."

"Now I know you're not a romantic."

He paused to get out his cigarettes and gave her one. "No, I take your point. When I was young and foolish a thousand years ago life seemed to have an infinite possibility to things."

"And what happened?"

"Life." He laughed.

"You don't mess about, do you? I mean, back there with that creep Hamish Hunt, you went in hard."

"And what does that tell you?"

"That you can take care of yourself, and that's unusual in a man who wears an evening suit that cost at least fifteen hundred pounds. What do you do?"

"Well now, let's see. I went to the Royal Academy of Dramatic Art, but that was a long time ago. I played Lyngstrand in Ibsen's *Lady from the Sea* at the National Theatre. He was the one who coughed a lot."

"And afterwards? I mean you obviously gave up acting or I'd have heard of you."

"Not entirely. You might say I took a considerable interest in what might be termed the theater of the street back home in the old country."

"Strange," she said. "If I had to guess I'd say you'd been a soldier."

"And who's the clever girl then?"

"Damn you, Dillon," she said. "Mystery piles on mystery with you."

"You'll just have to unpeel me layer by layer like an onion, but that would take time."

"And that's exactly what I don't have," she said. "I'm going up to Scotland tomorrow."

"I know," Dillon said. "There was a mention in Nigel Dempster's gossip column in the *Mail* this morning. 'Carl Morgan takes the lease on a Highland Estate for the shooting,' that was the byline. It also said you were standing in for him tonight at the Brazilian Embassy Ball."

"You *are* well informed."

They had reached Lambeth Bridge by now and found the Mercedes waiting. Dillon handed her in. "I enjoyed that."

"I'll drop you off," she said.

"No need."

"Don't be silly, I'm curious to see where you live."

"Anything to oblige." He got in beside her. "Stable Mews, Henry, that's close to Cavendish Square. I'll show you where when we get there."

When they turned into the cobbled street, it was still raining. He got out and closed the door. Asta put the window down and looked out at the cottage.

"All in darkness. No lady friend, Dillon?"

"Alas no, but you can come in for a cup of tea if you like."

She laughed. "Oh, no, I've had enough excitement for one night."

"Another time perhaps."

"I don't think so. In fact, I doubt whether we'll ever see each other again."

"Ships that pass in the night?"

"Something like that. Home, Henry," and as she put up the window the Mercedes pulled away.

Dillon watched it go, and as he turned to open the door he was smiling.

SEVEN

It was peaceful in the small railway station by the lochside and Dillon peered out of the rear compartment keeping out of sight. Following her had been easy. The Lear had taken him to Glasgow Airport at breakfast time and he had waited until Asta had arrived on the morning shuttle from London, had followed her down to the central railway station. Keeping out of the way from Glasgow to Fort William had been easy, for the train was busy with many tourists here to see Loch Lomond and afterwards the spectacular mountain scenery of the Highlands.

The smaller, local train from Fort William to Arisaig had been more difficult, for there were only a handful of passengers and he'd kept out of sight, only leaping into the rear compartment at the last moment. The station they had stopped at now was named Shiel according to the board at one side of the ticket office. They seemed to be standing there for quite some time. It was very pleasant, a mountain above them rearing three thousand feet into the clear blue sky, sunlight glinting on a waterfall that spilled over granite into birch trees.

Asta Morgan suddenly stepped onto the platform. She wore a leather jacket and linen slacks and leather brogues. She made an attractive sight in the quiet setting. She moved across to the ticket collector who stood at the barrier. There was some conversation, a burst of laughter, and she went through the barrier.

The ticket collector moved to join the guard, who was standing by the open door beside Dillon. "You've lost a passenger, Tom."

"Do you tell me?"

"A bonny lass, a Miss Morgan, hair of corn and a face to thank God for. Her father is yon fella Morgan that's just leased Loch Dhu Castle. She's away over the mountain. You'll put her luggage down at Arisaig and leave a message."

Dillon grabbed his Burberry trenchcoat and brushed past the guard. "Do you mean there's a shortcut over the mountain?"

"Well that would depend where you want to be."

"Ardmurchan Lodge."

The guard nodded. "Over the top of Ben Breac and a twelve-mile walk to the other side. You'll be staying with Brigadier Ferguson, the new tenant?"

"My uncle, he'll be waiting at Arisaig. Perhaps you could tell him where I am and give him my luggage." Dillon slipped a five-pound note into his hand.

"Leave it to me, sir."

The guard blew his whistle and boarded the train. Dillon turned to the ticket collector. "Where do I go?"

"Through the village and over the bridge. There's a path through the birches, hard going, but you can't miss the cairns that mark the way. Once over the top the track is plain to the glen below."

"Will the weather hold?"

The man looked up at the mountain. "A touch of mist and rain in the evening. I'd keep going, don't waste time on top." He smiled. "I'd tell the young lady that, sir, no place for a lassie to be on her own."

Dillon smiled. "I'll do that, a pity to see her get wet."

"A thousand pities, sir."

At the small village store he purchased two packs of cigarettes and two half-pound bars of milk chocolate for sustenance. Twelve miles on the other side of the mountain and that didn't count the miles that stood up on end. Something told him he could be hungry before he reached Ardmurchan.

He marched down the street and crossed the bridge. The track snaked up through the birch trees, lifting steeply, bracken pressing in on either side. It was cool and dark and remote from the world, and Dillon, thanks to his renewed energy, was enjoying every moment of it. There was no sign of Asta, which suited him for now.

The trees grew sparser and he emerged onto a bracken-covered slope. Occasionally grouse or plover lifted out of the heather disturbed by his presence and finally he came to a boulder-strewn plain that stretched to the lower slopes of Ben Breac. He saw Asta then, six or seven hundred feet up on the shoulder of the mountain.

She turned to look down and he dropped into the bracken. When he glanced up a few moments later, she had disappeared round the shoulder of the mountain. She was certainly moving fast, but then she was young and healthy and the track was plainly visible.

There was another way, of course, though only a fool would try that, which was straight up the breast of the mountain and the granite cliffs beyond to the summit. He took out an Ordnance Survey map of Moidart and had a look at the situation. Dillon glanced up. What the hell, strong nerves were all that was needed here, and with luck he might actually get ahead of her. He tied his Burberry around his waist and started up.

The lower slopes were easy going with his new-found strength, but after a half hour he came to a great cascading bank of scree and loose stones that moved beneath his feet alarmingly. He went to his left, found the waterfall he'd noted from the station, and followed its trail upwards, moving from boulder to boulder.

Finally, he reached the plateau and the final cliffs were before him and they were not quite as intimidating as they'd looked from the station, fissured with gullies and channels reaching to the top. He looked, checking his route, ate half a bar of chocolate, then made sure his raincoat was secure and started up, climbing strongly, testing each handhold. He looked down once and saw the railway station in the valley below like a child's toy. The next time he looked it had disappeared, blanked out by mist, and a sudden breeze touched him coldly.

He came over the granite edge to the summit a few minutes later to find himself cocooned in mist and he'd spent enough time in hill country in the past to know that there was only one thing to do in such conditions. Stay put. He did just that, lighting a cigarette, wondering how Asta Morgan was getting on. It was a good hour later when a sudden current of air dissolved the curtain of the mist, and down there the valleys lay dark and quiet in the evening sunlight.

In the distance was a cairn of stones marking the ultimate peak, but there was no Asta. He cut across the track and followed it back until he reached a point where he could look down almost three thousand feet to the railway line, and there was no sign of her. So she had beaten him to the summit, hardly surprising, for with the track to follow the mist would have been no problem.

He turned back, following the track to descend on the other side and paused suddenly as he stared down at the incredible sight before him. The sea in the distance was calm, the islands of Rum and Eigg like cardboard cutouts, and on the dark horizon, the Isle of Skye, the final barrier to the

Atlantic. It was one of the most beautiful sights he had ever seen and he started down.

Asta was tired and her right ankle was beginning to ache, legacy of an old skiing accident. It had been harder crossing Ben Breac than she had imagined and now she was faced with a twelve-mile hike. What had originally started as an amusing idea was now becoming rather a bore.

The track along the glen was dry and dusty and hard on her feet, and after a while she came to a five-barred gate with a sign that said LOCH DHU ESTATE—KEEP OUT. It was padlocked and she pulled herself over and limped on. And then she rounded a curve and saw a small hunting lodge by the burn. The door was locked, but when she went round to the rear a window stood ajar. She hauled herself through and found herself in a small kitchen area.

It was gloomy now, darkness falling, but there was an oil lamp and kitchen matches. She lit the lamp and went into the other room. It was adequately furnished with whitewashed walls and a wooden floor and a fire was laid in the hearth. She put a match to it and sat in one of the wing-backed chairs, suddenly tired. The warmth from the fire felt good, and her ankle didn't hurt now. She added pine logs to the fire and heard a vehicle drive up outside. A key rattled in the lock and the front door opened.

The man who stood there was of medium height with a weak, sullen face and badly needed a shave. He wore a shabby tweed suit and cap, his yellow hair shoulder-length, and he carried a double-barreled shotgun.

"Would you look at that now?" he said.

Asta said calmly, "What do you want?"

"That's a good one," he said, "and you trespassing. How in the hell did you get in here?"

"Through the kitchen window."

"I don't think my boss would like that. He's new. Just took over the estate yesterday did Mr. Morgan, but I know a hard man when I see one. I mean, if he knew about this he might make it a police matter."

"Don't be stupid. I turned my ankle coming over Ben Breac. I needed a rest, that's all. Now that you're here, you can give me a lift."

He moved closer and his hand was shaking as he put it on her shoulder. "That depends, doesn't it?"

His blotched face, the stink of whiskey on his breath was suddenly repulsive to her. "What's your name?"

"That's more friendly. It's Fergus—Fergus Munro."

She pulled away and sent him staggering with a vigorous push. "Then don't be stupid, Fergus Munro."

He reached angrily, dropping the shotgun. "You bitch, I'll teach you." He grabbed at her, catching the blouse beneath the leather coat, the thin material ripping from her left shoulder to the breast.

She gave a cry of rage, striking out at him, her nails gouging his right cheek, and then beyond him she saw a man materialize from the darkness into the doorway.

Dillon punched him in the kidneys very hard and hauled him back by the scruff of the neck and hurled him across the room. Munro hit the wall and fell to one knee. He reached for the shotgun which Dillon kicked out of the way, grabbing for his right wrist, twisting it up, taut and straight, ramming Munro headfirst into the wall. He scrambled up, blood on his face, and plunged through the open door.

As Dillon went after him Asta cried, "Let him go!"

Dillon paused, a hand on each side of the door frame, then he closed it and turned. "Are you all right?"

Outside an engine burst into life. "Yes, fine, what was that?"

"He had a Shogun."

She eased herself back in the chair. "I was really beginning to despair, Dillon, I thought you were never going to catch up with me. What on earth are you doing here?"

"Confession time," he said. "I've an uncle, Brigadier Charles Ferguson, who rented a place called Ardmurchan Lodge not far from here for the shooting, which it shares with the Loch Dhu Estate."

"Really? My father will be surprised. He never likes to share anything with anyone."

"Yes, well, when I read that item in the gossip column in the *Daily Mail*, saw your photo, I couldn't resist wangling myself an invitation to the Brazilian Embassy to meet you."

"Just like that?"

"I'm terribly well connected. You'd be surprised."

"Nothing would surprise me about you, and for what it's worth, I don't believe a word of it." She put down her right foot and winced. "Damn!"

"Trouble?"

"An old injury, that's all."

She pulled up the right leg of her slacks and he eased off the shoe and sock. "I'd have thought you would have caught up with me."

"I tried the short route straight up and it proved longer. I had to sit down in the mist."

"I just kept on walking. I noticed you at the station in Glasgow. I was coming out of the toilets and saw you buying a map at the bookstall. I waited till you boarded the train before getting on board myself. Most intriguing, especially when you changed trains as I did at Fort William."

"So, you left the train to draw me on?"

"Of course."

"Damn you, Asta, I should put you over my knee."

"Is that a promise? We Swedes are reputed to be terribly oversexed."

He laughed out loud. "I'd better get on with this foot while Fergus Munro hotfoots it to Loch Dhu Castle with his tale of woe. I should think we can expect company soon."

"I should hope so. I haven't the slightest intention of walking any further."

Dillon raised her foot. There was a faint puffiness at the ankle and a jagged scar.

"How did you get that?"

"Skiing. There was a time when I was an Olympic possibility."

"Too bad. I'll take the lamp for a minute."

He went into the kitchen, checked the drawers, and found some kitchen towels. He soaked one in cold water and returned to the living room.

"A cold compress will help." He bandaged the ankle expertly. "Tired?"

"Not too much. Hungry though."

He got one of the half-pound blocks of chocolate from his Burberry pocket. "Bad for your figure, but sustaining."

"You're a magician, Dillon." She ate the chocolate greedily and he lit a cigarette and sat by the fire. She suddenly paused. "What about you?"

"I had some." He stretched. "The grand place this. Fish in the burn, deer in the forest, a roof over your head, and a fine, strong girl like yourself to help on the land."

"Thanks very much. An arid sort of life, I should have thought."

"Haven't you heard the old Italian saying? One can live well on bread and kisses."

"Or chocolate." She held up what was left of the bar and they both laughed.

Dillon got up, went and opened the door. There was a full moon and the only sound was the burn as its waters ran by.

"We could be the last two people left on earth," she said.

"Not for long, there's a vehicle coming." He moved out of the porch and stood there waiting.

Two Shoguns braked to a halt. Fergus Munro was driving the first one and Murdoch was sitting next to him. As Munro got out, the factor came round from the other side clutching a shotgun. Carl Morgan was at the wheel of the second one and got out, an enormously powerful-looking figure in his sheepskin coat.

Murdoch said something to Munro and clicked back the hammers on the shotgun. Munro opened the door of the Shogun and Murdoch whistled softly. There was a sudden scramble inside and a black shadow materialized from the darkness to stand beside him.

"Flush him out, boy."

As the dog came forward with a rush, Dillon saw that it was a Doberman pinscher, one of the most deadly fighting dogs in the world. He went forward to meet it.

"Good boy," he said and extended a hand.

The dog froze, a growl starting somewhere at the back of the throat, and Munro said, "That's him, Mr. Morgan. That's the bastard who attacked me and his fancy woman still inside, no doubt."

Morgan said, "Private property, my friend, you should have stayed out."

The dog growled again, full of menace, and Dillon whistled softly, and eerie sound that set the teeth on edge. The dog's ears went back and Dillon fondled his muzzle and stroked him.

"Good God!" Murdoch said.

"Easy when you know how," Dillon told him. "I learned that from a man who was once my friend." He smiled. "Later, he regretted teaching me anything, but that's life."

Morgan said calmly, "Who in the hell are you?"

It was then that Asta joined the scene. "Carl, is that you? Thank God you're here."

She stumbled from the doorway and Morgan, astonishment on his face, moved fast to catch her in his arms. "Asta, for God's sake, what is this?"

He helped her inside and Fergus Munro said to Murdoch, "Asta? Who in the hell is Asta?"

"Something tells me you're in for a very unpleasant surprise, my old son," Dillon told him, and he turned and followed them in, the Doberman at his heels.

Asta was back in the chair and Morgan knelt beside her, holding a hand. "It was horrible, Carl. I left the train at Lochailort and came over the mountain, turned my ankle and was feeling absolutely foul when I found the lodge and got in through the kitchen window. And then this man came, the man out there. He was horrible."

Morgan stood up. "The man out there?" he said and his face was very pale.

"Yes, Carl, he threatened me." Her hand went to the torn blouse. "In fact, he was thoroughly unpleasant, and then Mr. Dillon here came and there was a struggle and he threw him out."

Morgan had murder in his eyes. He turned to Murdoch, who stood in the doorway. "Do you realize who this is? My daughter Asta. Where's that bastard who brought us here, Fergus?"

The roar of an engine breaking into life answered him and he pushed Murdoch to one side and ran out to see one of the Shoguns drive away.

"Shall I go after him?" Murdoch said.

"No." Morgan shook his head, hands unclenching. "We'll deal with him later." He turned to Dillon and held out a hand. "I'm Carl Morgan and I would seem to be considerably in your debt."

"Dillon—Sean Dillon."

Morgan turned to Asta. "Are you trying to tell me you walked over that damn mountain this afternoon?"

"It seemed like a good idea at the time. I thought I'd just walk in on you. Surprise you."

Morgan turned to Dillon, who, lighting a cigarette, forestalled him. "I'm on my way to join my uncle, Brigadier Charles Ferguson, for the shooting. He's leased a place called Ardmurchan Lodge."

There was something in Morgan's eyes straight away, but he simply said, "That makes us neighbors then. I presume you also thought it was a good idea to walk over the mountain?"

"Not at all. I thought it was a lousy idea and so did the ticket collector when she left the train. To be frank, I'd noticed her destination from her luggage labels. I got out to stretch my legs and saw her make off. When I asked the ticket collector what was going on, he told me she was going to walk over the mountain. As I said, he didn't think much of the idea and neither did I, so I decided to follow. Unfortunately I chose another route and was delayed by the mist, so I didn't catch up with her until she reached the lodge."

Asta said weakly, "I'm afraid I've made something of a fool of myself. Could we go now, Carl?"

She was acting up to the hilt and Dillon, an actor himself, saw that, but not Morgan, who put an arm round her, instant concern there. "Of course we will." He glanced at Dillon. "We'll drop you off on the way."

"That would be fine," Dillon said.

Murdoch took the wheel on the way down the glen and Dillon and Morgan sat on the large bench seat, Asta between them, the Doberman on the floor at their feet. Dillon fondled its ears.

"Guard dog, they said." Morgan shook his head. "With you he's more like a big pussy cat."

"An emotional thing between me and him, Mr. Morgan. He likes me."

"Loves you, more like," Asta said. "I've never seen anything like it."

"I still wouldn't like to be the intruder who comes over the wall and finds him there."

"So Brigadier Ferguson is your uncle?" Morgan said. "I haven't had the pleasure yet, but then I only arrived at Loch Dhu Castle myself yesterday."

"Yes," Dillon said, "so I understand."

"Is the Brigadier retired or in business or what?"

"Oh, he was in the army for years, but now he's a consultant to a number of businesses worldwide."

"And you?"

"I help out. A sort of middleman, you might say. I've got this thing for languages, so he finds me useful."

"I'm sure he does."

Murdoch changed down and swung in through gates following a narrow drive to the house beyond, lights at the window. He braked to a halt. "Ardmurchan Lodge."

It was raining again, rattling against the windscreen. Morgan said, "It does that a lot, six days out of seven, driving in from the Atlantic."

"Just think," Asta said, "we could be in Barbados."

"Oh, it has its points, I'm sure," Dillon said.

She took his hand. "I hope to get a chance to thank you properly. Perhaps tomorrow?"

Morgan said, "Plenty of time for that, I'll fix something up. You both need a chance to settle in."

As Dillon got out, Morgan followed him. "I'll see you to the door."

At that moment it opened and Ferguson appeared. "Good God, Sean, is that you? We got your message at Arisaig, but I was beginning to get worried. What happened?"

"A long story, I'll tell you later. Can I introduce our neighbor, Carl Morgan?"

"What a pleasure." Ferguson took Morgan's hand. "Your reputation precedes you. Will you have a drink before you go?"

"No, I must get my daughter home," Morgan said. "Another time."

"I believe we'll be sharing the shooting," Ferguson said genially.

"Yes, they didn't tell me that when I took the lease," Morgan told him.

"Dear me, I trust there won't be a problem."

"Oh, I don't see why there should be as long as we're not shooting from opposite sides." Morgan smiled. "Good night." He got back in the Shogun and it drove away.

"He knows," Dillon said.

"Of course he does," Ferguson told him. "Now come in out of this appalling rain and tell me what you've been up to."

When the Shogun arrived at Loch Dhu Castle, Morgan helped Asta out and said to Murdoch, "You come too, we need to talk."

"Very well, Mr. Morgan."

The great iron-banded oak door was opened by Marco Russo wearing a black alpaca jacket and striped trousers. "My God, Marco," Asta said. "I can't believe it, a butler now?"

She was probably the only human being he ever smiled for, and he did now. "A short engagement only, Miss Asta."

"Tell the maid to run a bath," Morgan said and turned to Murdoch. "You wait in the study."

He took Asta through the magnificent baronial hall and placed her in the great oak chair beside the log fire that crackled in the open hearth.

"Right," he said, "Dillon. He followed you over the mountain. Why?"

"He told you."

"That's a load of tripe."

"Well, he knew who I was and where I was going, but not because of my luggage labels."

"Explain."

Which she did—the Brazilian Embassy Ball, the write-up in the *Daily Mail*'s social column, everything.

"I might have known," Morgan said when she finished.

"Why do you say that?"

"As soon as I heard about the new tenant at Ardmurchan Lodge I had him checked. Brigadier Charles Ferguson, Asta, is head of a very elite section of British Intelligence, usually involved with anti-terrorism and responsible to the Prime Minister only."

"But I don't understand."

"They know," he said. "The Chungking Covenant."

"My God!" she said. "And Dillon works for him?" She nodded. "It makes sense now."

"What does?"

"Well, I told you Dillon saved me from that beast Hamish Hunt at the ball. What I didn't tell you was that Hunt grabbed me in Park Lane afterwards. He was terribly drunk, Carl, and pretty foul."

His face was pale again. "And?"

"Dillon appeared and beat him up. I've never seen anything like it. He was so economical."

"He would be, a real pro. I thought so." Morgan smiled. "So I owe him not once, but twice." He helped her up. "Off you go and get your bath, we'll have some supper later." As he walked away, he called, "Marco?"

528 ━━◡◡◠◠ JACK HIGGINS

The Sicilian appeared from the shadows. "Signore?"

"Listen to this." Very quickly Morgan gave him a résumé of events in Italian.

When he was finished, Marco said, "He sounds hot stuff, this Dillon."

"Get on to London now. I want answers and they've only got an hour, make that clear."

"As you say, Signore."

He walked away and Morgan went and opened the study door. It was a pleasant room, lined with books, French windows to a terrace, and as in the hall, a fire burned on the hearth. Murdoch was standing staring down into it and smoking a cigarette.

Morgan sat at the desk, opened a drawer, and took out a check book. "Over here."

"Yes, Mr. Morgan." Murdoch crossed the room and Morgan wrote a check and handed it to him. The factor looked at it in astonishment. "Twenty-five thousand pounds. But what's this for, Mr. Morgan?"

"Loyalty, Murdoch, I like greedy people and I've formed the opinion that that's what you are."

Murdoch was stunned. "If you say so, sir."

"Oh, but I do, and here's the good news, Murdoch. When I leave, you get the same amount, for services rendered, naturally."

Murdoch had control of himself now, a slight smile on his face. "Of course, sir, anything you say."

Morgan said, "For several hundred years the Lairds of Loch Dhu took a silver Bible into battle. It was always recovered, even when they died. It was with the old Laird when his plane crashed in India in nineteen forty-four. I've reason to believe it was returned to the castle, but where is it, Murdoch, that's the thing?"

"Lady Katherine, sir . . ."

"Knows nothing, hasn't seen it in years. It's here, Murdoch, tucked away somewhere, and we're going to find it. Understand?"

"Yes, sir."

"Discuss it with the servants. Just tell them it's a valuable family heirloom and there's a reward for whoever finds it."

"I will, sir."

"You can go now." Murdoch had the door open when Morgan called, "And Murdoch?"

"Yes, sir?"

"Brigadier Ferguson and Dillon, they're not on our side."

"I understand, sir."

"Good and don't forget. I want to know where that bastard Fergus Munro is to be found, preferably tonight."

"Yes, sir."

"One more thing. Is there anyone on the estate staff who works at Ardmurchan Lodge?"

"Ferguson has his own man, sir, this Ghurka body servant. There's Lady Katherine's gardener, Angus. He sees to the garden and the daily wood supply."

"Can he be bought?"

Murdoch nodded. "I'd say so."

"Good. Eyes and ears is what I want. See to it, and find Fergus."

"I will, sir." Murdoch went out, closing the door.

Morgan sat there for a while, then noticed a library ladder. On impulse he got up, pushed it to one end of the shelves on one of the walls, and mounted. He climbed to the top and started to remove the books a few at a time, peering behind.

EIGHT

Dillon, having bathed and changed into a comfortable track suit, sprawled in front of the fire, Hannah Bernstein in the chair opposite. He had just finished his account of the day's events and Ferguson was pouring drinks at the cabinet in the corner.

"Anything for you, Chief Inspector?"

"No thank you, sir."

"Well, the boy here could do with a brandy, I'm sure."

"It was rather a long walk," Dillon said and accepted the glass. "What do you think?"

"About Morgan? Oh, he knows, that was totally apparent from our little exchange."

"So what will his next move be?" Hannah asked.

"I'm not sure, we'll see what tomorrow brings." Ferguson sat down. "It's an interesting situation, by the way, the shooting rights and the fishing. Kim tells me he was fishing in Loch Dhu on the day before we arrived when some damn rascals who work for this Murdoch fellow as keepers turned up and suggested he leave and not too pleasantly."

"Who are they?"

"I've made inquiries. Tinkers—the last remnants of a broken clan. You know, a touch of all that Scottish romantic nonsense. They've wandered the Highlands since Culloden and all that sort of tosh. Old Hector Munro and his brood. I saw them in Ardmurchan Village yesterday and there's nothing romantic about them. Bunch of ragged, foul-smelling rogues. There's old Hector, Fergus . . ."

"He'll be the one I had the run-in with."

"Then there's the other brother, Rory, big, rough-looking lout, hair tied in a pony tail. I mean, why do they do that, Dillon? Earrings as well. After all, it's not the seventeenth century."

Hannah burst out laughing and Dillon said, "They broke the mould with you, Brigadier. And you say they ran Kim off the place?"

"Yes, I sent him round to the castle with a stiff letter of complaint to this Murdoch chap, the factor, told him I was considering laying a complaint with the Chief Constable of the county."

"What happened?"

"Murdoch was round like a shot, full of apologies. Said he'd keep them in line. Gave me some cock-and-bull story about arctic tern nesting near Loch Dhu and not wanting to disturb them. Apologized for the Munros. Said he'd kick their backsides and so on."

Dillon went and helped himself to another brandy. He came back to the fire. "We're entitled to be here, to shoot deer in the forest, to fish in the loch?"

"Of course we are," Ferguson said. "Mind you, Morgan doesn't like it, I mean, he made that clear on the doorstep, didn't he?"

"Let's draw his teeth then. I'll put my head in the jaws of the tiger tomorrow. You've got all we need for the fishing?"

"And the shooting."

"Good, I'll try Loch Dhu in the morning, plenty of trout, I suppose?"

"Masses, dear boy. Quarter-pounders—or occasional pounders."

"Good, I'll take a rod down there after breakfast."

Hannah said, "The Munros could prove unpleasant if they catch you, especially after your bout with Fergus. I was with the Brigadier when we saw them in Ardmurchan Village. They really are a fearsome-looking clan. I'd say they are the sort who don't take kindly to being beaten."

"And neither do I." Dillon finished his drink. "I'll see you at breakfast," and he went up to bed.

At the same moment, Asta was sitting opposite Morgan by the fire in the great hall at the castle when Marco came in, a piece of paper in his hand.

"Fax from London, Signore."

Morgan read it quickly, then laughed out loud. "Dear God, listen to this. The Bernstein woman is a Detective Chief Inspector, Special Branch, at Scotland Yard, but it's Dillon who takes the biscuit. Sean Dillon, once an actor, RADA and the National Theatre, superb linguist, speaks many languages. First-class pilot, expert diver. Good God, he worked for the Israelis in Beirut."

"But what was he doing there?"

"Sinking PLO boats, apparently. Not choosy, our Mr. Dillon. He's worked for just about everyone you've ever heard of and that includes the KGB in the old days."

"You mean he's some kind of mercenary?" Asta asked.

"That's one way of putting it, but before that he was for some years with the Provisional IRA, one of their most feared enforcers. There's even a suggestion he was behind the attack on Downing Street during the Gulf War."

"Then why would he be working for Ferguson?"

"I suppose the Brits were the only people he hadn't worked for and you know how unscrupulous they are. They'd use anybody to suit their purposes."

"A thoroughly dangerous man," Asta said. "How exciting."

Morgan handed the fax to Marco. "Oh, we've handled thoroughly dangerous men before, haven't we, Marco."

"Many times, Signore, will there be anything else?"

"Yes, bring me some coffee and tell Murdoch I'll see him now."

Asta got up. "I'm for bed. Can we ride tomorrow?"

"Why not?" He took her hand. "Sleep well."

She kissed him on the forehead and went away up the great staircase. Morgan reached for a cigar, clipped it and lit it, and Murdoch entered, his oilskin coat wet.

"Well?" Morgan asked.

"No luck, I'm afraid, that old bastard Hector Munro was immovable. He said Fergus had gone off on his evening rounds and they hadn't seen him since. He's lying, of course."

"What did you do?"

"Searched their stinking caravans, which he didn't like, but I insisted."

"I want Fergus," Morgan said. "I want him where I can deal with him personally. He put his filthy hands on my daughter and no man does that and gets away with it. Try again tomorrow."

"Yes, Mr. Morgan, good night, sir."

Murdoch went out and Marco came in with the coffee. As he poured it, Morgan said in Italian, "What do you think of him?"

"Murdoch? A piece of dung, Signore, no honor, only money counts there."

"That's what I thought, keep an eye on him. You can go to bed now."

Marco went out and Morgan sat there brooding, drinking his coffee and gazing into the fire.

He was sitting in the study at the desk at eight the following morning working his way through various business papers when there was a knock at the door and Murdoch looked in.

"I have Angus here, sir."

"Bring him in."

Angus entered, took off his tweed cap and rolled it between his hands. "Mr. Morgan, sir."

Morgan looked him over. "You look like a practical man to me, would I be right?"

"I hope so, sir."

Morgan opened a drawer and took out a bundle of notes, which he tossed across. Angus picked it up. "Five hundred pounds. Anything unusual happens at Ardmurchan Lodge you phone Murdoch."

"I will, sir." he was sweating slightly.

"Have you been there this morning?"

"To do the wood supply, sir."

"And what's happening?"

"Mr. Dillon was having an early breakfast before going for the fishing on Loch Dhu. He asked my advice."

Morgan nodded. "Good. On your way."

Angus left and Murdoch said, "If the Munros come across him, he could be in trouble."

"Exactly what I was thinking." Morgan smiled and at that moment Asta came in wearing a hacking jacket and jodhpurs.

"There you are," she told him. "You said we could go riding."

"And why not?" He glanced at Murdoch. "Get the horses ready, you can come with us." He smiled. "We could have a look at the loch."

The waters of Loch Dhu were darker than even the name suggested, still and calm in the gray morning and yet dappled by falling rain. Dillon wore waders, an old rainhat, and an Australian drover's waterproof with caped shoulders, both of which he had found at the lodge.

He lit a cigarette and took his time over putting his rod together. Behind him the heather was waist deep, a line of trees above, and a plover lifted into the morning. A wind stirred the surface of the loch and suddenly a trout came out of the water beyond the sandbar, a good foot in the air, and disappeared again.

Suddenly Dillon forgot everything, remembering only his uncle's sheep farm in County Down and the lessons he'd given his young nephew in the great art. He tied the fly Ferguson had recommended, apparently one of his own manufacture, and went to work.

His first dozen casts were poor and inexpert, but gradually, as some of the old skill returned, he had better luck and hooked two quarter-pounders. The rain still fell relentlessly. He let out another couple of yards of line, lifted his tip, and cast out beyond the sandbar to where a black fin sliced through the water. His cast was the most accurate he'd ever made, the fly skimming the surface, the rod bent over and his line went taut.

Two pounds if it was an ounce. His reel whined as the hooked trout made for deep water and he moved along the sandbank, playing it carefully. The line went slack and he thought he'd lost it, but the trout was only resting and a moment later the line tightened again. He played it for a good ten minutes before turning to reach for his net. He lifted the floundering fish, removed the hook, and turned back to shore.

A harsh voice said, "Well and good, me bucko, a fine dinner for us."

The man who had spoken was old, at least seventy. He wore a tweed suit that had seen better days and white hair showed beneath his Glengarry bonnet. His face was weatherbeaten and wrinkled and covered with a heavy stubble and he had a shotgun crooked in his right arm.

Behind him, two men stood up in the heather. One was large and raw-boned with a perpetual smile, and that would be Rory, Dillon told himself. The other was Fergus, a livid bruise down one side of his face, his mouth swollen.

"That's him, Da, that's the bastard who attacked me," and he raised his shotgun waist high.

Rory knocked it to one side and it discharged into the ground. "Try not to play the fool as usual, little brother," he said in Gaelic.

Dillon, an Irish speaker, had no difficulty in understanding, especially when Hector said, "He doesn't look much to me," and swung a punch.

Dillon ducked, avoiding it, but his foot slipped and he fell into the shallows. He scrambled up and the old man raised his shotgun. "Not now, my brave wee man," he said in English. "You'll get your chance. Slow and easy. Walk on."

As Dillon moved forward, Fergus said, "Wait till I've done with you," and swung the butt of his shotgun. Dillon avoided it easily and Fergus went down on one knee.

Rory lifted him by the scruff of his neck. "Will you listen or must I kick your arse?" he demanded in Gaelic and pushed him ahead.

"God help him but he never will learn that one," Dillon told him in Irish. "Some men stay children all their lives."

Rory's mouth went slack with astonishment. "By God, Da, did you hear that, the strangest Gaelic I ever heard."

"That's because it's Irish, the language of kings," Dillon said. "But close enough that we can understand each other," and he walked on ahead of them.

There was smoke beyond the trees, the sound of children's voices, so they were not taking him to Morgan and he realized he had made something of a miscalculation. They moved down into a hollow containing the camp. The three wagons were old with canvas tilts and patched many times, far removed from the romantic idea of a caravan. There was an air of poverty to everything from the shabby clothes worn by the women who squatted by the fire drinking tea to the bare feet of the children who played in the grass beside several bony horses.

Fergus gave Dillon a push that sent him staggering forward and the women scattered. The children paused in their play and came to watch. Hector Munro sat himself on an old box vacated by one of the women, placed his shotgun across his knees, and took out a pipe. Fergus and Rory stood slightly behind Dillon.

"An attack on one of us is an attack on all, Mr. Dillon, or whatever your name is. The great pity you weren't knowing that." He stuffed tobacco into his pipe. "Rory." Rory moved fast, pulling Dillon's arms behind him, and the old man said, "Enjoy yourself, Fergus."

Fergus moved in fast and punched Dillon in the stomach right and left handed. Dillon made no move except to tense his muscles, and Fergus drove a fist into his ribs on the right side. "Now for that pretty face of yours," he said. "Hold his head up, Rory."

In taking a handful of Dillon's hair, Rory had to release one of his arms. Dillon flicked a foot forward catching Fergus in the crutch, half-turned delivering a reverse elbow strike to the edge of Rory's jaw. The big man released him, staggering back, and Dillon ran for it and stumbled headlong as one of the women stuck out a foot.

He rolled desperately as they all kicked at him, even the children, and then there was the drumming of horses, and a voice called, "Stop that, damn you!" and a shotgun was fired.

The women and children broke and ran and Dillon got up to find Murdoch on horseback, a shotgun braced against his thigh. Behind him Carl Morgan and Asta rode down into the hollow. Dillon was aware of Fergus slipping under one of the wagons.

"Stay there, you silly bastard," Rory hissed in Gaelic, then glanced at Dillon in alarm, realizing he had heard.

Carl Morgan urged his mount down into the hollow. The hooves of his horse scattered the fire, and he pulled on the right rein so that the animal turned, its hind quarters catching Hector Munro a blow that sent him staggering.

He reined in. "Tell them who I am," he ordered.

"This is Mr. Carl Morgan, new tenant of Loch Dhu Castle," Murdoch said, "and your employer."

"Is that so?" Hector Munro said.

"So bare your head, you mannerless dog," Murdoch told him, leaned down from his horse, and plucked the old man's bonnet from his head and threw it down.

Rory took a step forward and Dillon said in Irish, "Easy boy, there's a time and a place for everything."

Rory turned, frowning, and his father said, "The man Dillon was fishing in the loch, we were only doing our duty."

"Don't lie to me, Munro," Murdoch told him. "Mr. Dillon is nephew to Brigadier Ferguson, tenant at Ardmurchan Lodge, and don't tell me you didn't know that. You scoundrels know everything that goes on in the district before it bloody well happens."

"Enough of this," Morgan said and looked down at Munro. "You wish to continue to work for the estate?"

"Why yes, sir," the old man said.

"Then you know how to behave in future."

"Yes, sir." Munro picked up his bonnet and put it on.

"And now that son of yours, Fergus. He assaulted my daughter. I want him."

"And we have not seen him, sir, as I told Mr. Murdoch. If he gave offense to the young lady I'm sorry, but the great one for wandering is Fergus."

"Away for days sometimes," Rory said. "Who could be knowing where he might be?" He glanced at Dillon briefly, but Dillon said nothing.

Morgan said, "I can wait. We'll go now, Mr. Dillon."

"I'll be fine," Dillon said. "I want to get my fishing tackle. I can walk back." He moved to Asta's stirrup and looked up at her.

"Are you all right?" she asked.

"Just fine," Dillon said. "I do this kind of thing most mornings, it gives me an appetite for lunch."

Morgan said, "I'll be in touch, Dillon. Come on, Asta," and he cantered away.

Dillon turned to look down into the hollow at the Munros. Fergus crawled out from under the wagon and Dillon called in Irish. "So there you are, you little rascal. I'd take care if I were you."

He went down to the shore and retrieved his rod and fishing basket.

As he turned to go, Rory Munro moved out of the trees. "Now why would you do a thing like that for Fergus, and you and he bad friends?" he asked in Gaelic.

"True, but then I dislike Morgan even more. Mind you, the girl is different. If Fergus touches her again I'll break both his arms."

Rory laughed. "Oh, the hard one are you, small man?"

"You could always try me," Dillon told him.

Rory stared at him, frowning, and then a slow smile appeared. "And perhaps that time will come," he said, turned, and walked back into the trees.

Dillon drank tea by the fire at Ardmurchan Lodge while he detailed the events of the morning to Ferguson and Hannah Bernstein.

"So the plot thickens," Ferguson said.

"Lucky for you that Morgan turned up when he did," Hannah said. "You might have been a hospital case by now."

"Yes, a useful coincidence," Ferguson said.

"And you know how much I believe in those," Dillon told him.

Hannah frowned. "You think Morgan was behind the whole thing?"

"I'm not sure about that, but I believe he expected it. That's why he turned up."

"Very possibly." Ferguson nodded. "Which raises the question of how he knew you were going to go fishing this morning."

"I know, life's just one big mystery," Dillon said. "What happens now?"

"Lunch, dear boy, I thought we might venture into Ardmurchan Village and sample the delights of the local pub. They must offer food of some sort."

"Pub grub, Brigadier, you?" Hannah Bernstein said.

"And you, Chief Inspector, although I hardly expect it will be kosher."

"I'll find out," she said. "I think that chap Angus is working in the garden." She opened the French windows and went out, returning a few moments later. "He says the Campbell Arms does do food. Shepherd's pie, things like that."

"Real food," Ferguson said. "How wonderful. Let's get going then."

Morgan was standing on the terrace at the top of the steps with Asta when Murdoch joined them. "I've just had a phone call from Angus. Our friends are going to the Campbell Arms for lunch."

"Really?" Morgan said.

"It could lead to an interesting situation. The day after tomorrow is the local fair and Highland Games. There are tinkers around, horse traders, and so on. The Munros will probably be there."

"Is that so?" Morgan smiled and turned to Asta. "We couldn't possibly miss that, could we?" He raised his voice and called, "Marco!" Russo appeared in the open windows. "Bring the estate car round, we're going to the village for a drink and you drive. I've a feeling we might need you."

The Campbell Arms was very old, built of gray granite, but the sign that hung above the door was freshly painted. Dillon parked across the street and he and Hannah and Ferguson got out and crossed, pausing as a young gypsy rode by bareback on a pony leading three others behind. There was a poster on the wall advertising the Ardmurchan Fair and Games.

"That looks like fun," Ferguson said and opened the door and led the way in.

There was an old-fashioned snug bar, the type that in the old days was for women only. This was empty, but a further door gave access to a large saloon, beams in the ceiling. There was a long bar with a marble top, scores of bottles behind ranged against a great mirror. There was a peat fire on an open hearth, tables, chairs, booths with high-backed wooden settles. It was not exactly shoulder-to-shoulder, but perhaps a crowd of thirty or more, some obviously gypsies to do with the fair, others more local, old men wearing cloth caps and leggings, or in some cases Highland bonnets and plaids like Hector Munro, who stood at one end of the bar with Rory and Fergus.

There was a buzz of conversation that stopped abruptly as Ferguson stepped in, the others at his shoulder. The woman behind the bar came round wiping her hands on a cloth. She wore an old hand-knitted jumper and slacks. "You are welcome in this place, Brigadier," she said in a Highland accent and took his hand. "My name is Molly."

"Good to be here, my dear," he said. "I hear your food is excellent."

"Over here." She led them to one of the booths by the fire and turned to the room. "Get on with your drinking while I handle the damned English," she told them in Gaelic.

Sean Dillon said in Irish, "A bad mistake you make in my case, woman of the house, but I'll forgive you if you can find me a Bushmills whiskey."

She turned, her mouth open in surprise, then put a hand to his face. "Irish is it? Good lad yourself and I might surprise you." They settled down and she added in English, "Fish pie is what there is today if you have a mind to eat. Fresh cod, onions, and potatoes."

"Which sounds incredible to me," Ferguson told her. "I'll have a Guinness, lager beer for the lady, and whatever you and my friend here have decided."

"A man after my own heart and a good Scots name to you."

She went off and as the conversation flowed again Dillon lit a cigarette. "The old man with the granite face and the bonnet at the end of the bar is

Hector Munro, the damaged one is Fergus, and the bit of rough with the good shoulders that's looking at you so admiringly, Hannah, my love, is Rory."

She flushed. "Not my type."

Dillon turned and nodded to the Munros. "Oh, I don't know, with a couple of drinks in you at the shank of the night, who knows?"

"You are a bastard, Dillon."

"I know, it's been said before."

Hector Munro wiped his mouth with the back of his hand and came over, shouldering men aside. "Mr. Dillon, you did my son a service," he said in English, "and for that I thank you. Maybe we got off on the wrong foot."

"This is my uncle, Brigadier Ferguson," Dillon said.

"I ken the name Ferguson," Munro said. "There are a few not many miles from here Tomentoul way, they were on our left flank at Culloden fighting King George's bloody Germans."

"You do have a lengthy memory," Ferguson said. "Almost two hundred and fifty years long. Yes, my ancestors did fight at Culloden for Prince Charles."

"Good man yourself." Munro pumped his hand and went back to the bar.

"My goodness, we are trapped in memory lane," Ferguson said as Molly brought the drinks. She put them on the table and the door opened and Morgan and Asta walked in, Murdoch and Marco behind them.

There was another silence, Morgan surveying the room, and then he came forward with Asta. Behind him Marco stayed at the bar and Murdoch approached Molly. Morgan and Asta sat on the settle opposite Ferguson and his party.

"Brigadier, what a pleasure. I didn't have a chance to introduce you to my daughter last night. Asta—Brigadier Ferguson."

"A pleasure, my dear," Ferguson told her. "You know my nephew. This charming lady, by the way, is my secretary, Miss Hannah Bernstein."

Murdoch came from the bar with glasses and a bottle of white wine. "Not much choice, sir, it's a Chablis."

"As long as they didn't make it in the back yard it will be fine," Morgan said. "What about the food?"

"Fish and potato pie, old boy," Ferguson said. "They only have one dish a day."

"Then fish and potato pie it is," Morgan told him. "We're hardly having lunch at the Caprice."

"Indeed not," Ferguson said. "Very different waters."

"Exactly." Murdoch poured the wine and Morgan raised his glass. "What shall we drink to?"

"Confusion to our enemies," Dillon said. "A good Irish toast."

"How very apt."

Asta drank a little wine and said, "How nice to meet you, Miss Bernstein. Strange, but in the time we were together, Dillon never mentioned you. Having met you, of course, I understand why."

"Try and behave yourself, why don't you," Dillon told her.

Her eyes widened in outrage and Morgan frowned, and then Murdoch leaned over and whispered in his ear and Morgan turned and looked toward the bar. At that moment Fergus was sliding toward the door.

Morgan called in Italian, "Stop him, Marco, that's the one I want."

Marco put a hand to Fergus's chest and pushed him back and Hector Munro and Rory took a step forward. "Leave my son be or you answer to me," the old man said.

Morgan called, "Munro, I asked for your son earlier and you claimed no knowledge as to his whereabouts. As your employer, I expected better."

"My son is my business. What touches him touches us all."

"Please spare me that kind of peasant claptrap. He assaulted my daughter and for that he must pay."

And Fergus was frightened now, his face white and desperate. He tried to dodge around Marco, who caught him with ease, grabbing him by the neck, turning him, sending him to his knees before Morgan.

The bar was totally silent. "Now then, you animal," Morgan said.

Rory came in on the run. "Here's for you," he cried and swung a punch into the base of Marco's spine. The Sicilian shrugged it off, turned, blocking Rory's next punch, and gave him a right that landed high on the left cheek, sending Rory staggering back against the bar.

Fergus, cowering in fear on the floor, saw his chance, got up to make for the door. Marco, turning, was already moving to block him off when Hannah Bernstein stuck out a foot and tripped him. Marco went sprawling and Fergus was out of the door like a weasel.

"Dreadful, isn't it," Ferguson said to Morgan. "I can't take her anywhere."

As Marco got up, Rory moved in from the bar and Dillon jumped in between them. "This dog is mine," he said in Irish to Rory. "Now drink your beer like a good lad and let be."

Rory stared at him, rage in his eyes, then took a deep breath. "As you say, Irishman, but if he lays a hand on me again, he is my meat," and he turned and went back to the bar.

"Strange," Ferguson said to Morgan, "but since meeting you life's taken on an entirely new meaning."

"Hasn't it?" Morgan said amiably, and at that moment Molly arrived with a huge tray containing plates of her fish and potato pie.

"My word that does smell good." Ferguson beamed. "Let's tuck in, I'm sure we're going to need all our strength."

Afterwards, standing in the street outside, Morgan said, "I wondered about dinner tomorrow night perhaps. I thought it might be nice to invite Lady Katherine."

"Excellent thought," Ferguson said. "Delighted to accept."

Asta said, "Do you ride, Dillon?"

"It's been known."

"Perhaps you could join us tomorrow morning. We could mount you with no trouble."

"Ah, well there you have me," he said. "My uncle promised to take me deer stalking tomorrow. Have you ever tried it?"

"Deer stalking? That sounds absolutely wonderful." She turned. "Carl? I'd love to go."

"Not my style and I've business to take care of tomorrow."

Ferguson said amiably, "We'd be delighted to have you join us, my dear, that is if you have no objection, Morgan?"

"Why should I, an excellent idea."

"We'll pick you up," Ferguson said. "Nine-thirty." He raised his tweed hat. "Goodbye for now," and turned and led the way back to the Range Rover.

"Right, let's go," Morgan said, and Asta led the way to the parked station wagon.

Murdoch murmured, "A word, sir, I've an idea where Fergus might have gone."

"Is that so?" Morgan said. "All right, we'll take Miss Asta home and then you can show me."

At Ardmurchan Lodge Ferguson shrugged off his coat and went and stood with his back to the fire. "And what do you make of that?"

"The heavy blocking the door, sir, is his present minder, one Marco Russo," Hannah Bernstein said. "I checked with Immigration. He came in with Morgan. Information from the Italian police indicates he's a known Mafia enforcer and member of the Luca family."

"A thoroughly nasty bit of work if you ask me," Ferguson said and turned to Dillon. "What's all this deer stalking nonsense then?"

"You've never stalked deer, Brigadier?" Dillon shook his head. "You've never lived, and you a member of the upper classes."

"Of course I've stalked deer," Ferguson told him. "And kindly keep your fatuous comments to yourself. What I want to know is why are we taking the girl tomorrow? You obviously wanted it, which is why I asked her."

"I'm not sure," Dillon said. "I'd like to get to know her a little better. It might lead somewhere."

Hannah Bernstein said, "Dillon, get one thing straight, that is one tough, capable, and intelligent young lady. If you think she doesn't know exactly how Morgan makes his money you're fooling yourself. Observe them, use your eyes. They're a very intimate couple. I'd give you odds she knows exactly what they're doing up here."

Dillon said, "Which is exactly why I want to cultivate her."

"I agree," Ferguson said. "So we go as planned in the morning. Kim can be a gun bearer, you'll stay here and hold the fort, Chief Inspector."

"As you say, sir."

Ferguson turned to Dillon. "Anything else?"

"Yes, I've decided to pay a visit to the castle tonight. Check things out, see what's going on. Any objections?"

"Not at all. Come to think of it, it's rather a good idea." Ferguson smiled. "Strange, but Morgan's actually quite civilized when you meet him, don't you agree?"

"Not really, sir," Hannah Bernstein said. "As far as I'm concerned he's just another gangster in a good suit."

NINE

Fergus squatted on a truckle bed in the old hunting bothy at the west end of Loch Dhu and drank from a bottle of whiskey. He was no longer afraid now, the events at the pub behind him, but he was angry, particularly when he thought of Asta.

"You bitch," he said to himself. "All your fault." He drank some more whiskey. "Just wait. If I ever get my hands on you again."

There was a sudden creak, the door swung open, and Murdoch slipped in. "Here he is, sir," he said, and Morgan moved through the door behind him, a riding crop in his hand, Marco at his side.

"Now then, you piece of dirt," Morgan said.

Fergus was terrified. He got up, the bottle of whiskey in one hand. "Now look, there's no need for this, it was a mistake, I didn't know who she was."

"Mistake?" Morgan said. "Oh, yes, your mistake, you little swine." He turned. "Marco."

Marco was pulling on a pair of leather gloves. Fergus suddenly smashed the whiskey bottle, spraying the bed with its contents, and held up the jagged glass threateningly. "I'll do for you, I swear I will."

As Marco advanced, Fergus swung the bottle. The Sicilian blocked his arm to one side and punched him with sickening force under the ribs. Fergus dropped the bottle and staggered back on the bed.

Morgan said, "Leave him."

Marco stood back and Morgan went forward. "You put your filthy hands on my daughter."

He slashed Fergus across the face with his riding crop again and again, and Fergus, screaming, tried to protect himself with his raised arms. Morgan rained blow after blow, then stood back and Marco moved in again, punching Fergus in the face, sending him to the floor, kicking him with brutal efficiency.

"Enough." Marco stepped back and Fergus lay moaning on the floor. Morgan turned and found Murdoch in the doorway looking as frightened as Fergus had done. "Do you have a problem?" Morgan asked.

"No, Mr. Morgan."

"Good. Let's get going then."

He led the way outside and they got in the station wagon, Marco behind the wheel, and drove away.

It was some time later, evening falling, when Fergus appeared in the doorway. He looked dreadful, blood on his face. He stood there swaying a little and then staggered down the slope to the loch. He waded into the shallows and dropped to his knees, scooping water over his face and head. The pain in his head was terrible, the worst thing he'd ever known. It was really a merciful release when everything went dark and he fell forward into the water.

It was eleven o'clock and raining hard as Hannah Bernstein turned the Range Rover in beside the wall of Loch Dhu Castle. "My God," she said, "it's a miracle when it does stop raining here."

"That's bonny Scotland for you," Dillon said. He was all in black, sweater, jeans, running shoes, and now he pulled a black ski mask over his head, only his eyes and mouth showing.

"You certainly look the part," she said.

"That's the idea." He pulled on thin black leather gloves and took a Walther from the glove compartment and fitted the new short Harley silencer to it.

"For God's sake, Dillon, you aren't going to war."

"That's what you think, my lovely." He slipped the gun into his waistband and his teeth flashed in the opening of the ski mask as he smiled. "Here we go then, give me an hour," and he opened the door and was away.

The wall was only twelve feet high and simple enough to negotiate. A crumbling edge or two for footholds and he was over and dropping into damp grass. He moved through trees, came out into an area of open grass, and jogged toward the castle, finally halting in another clump of trees, looking across smooth lawn toward the lighted windows of the castle.

The rain fell relentlessly. He stood there sheltered slightly by a tree and the great oaken front door opened and Marco Russo appeared there, the Doberman at his side. Marco gave the dog a shove with his foot, obviously putting it out for the purposes of nature, then went inside. The dog stood there, sniffing the rain, then lifted a leg. Dillon gave the low, curious whistle he had used at the hunting lodge, the Doberman's ears went up, then it came bounding toward him.

He crouched, stroking its ears, allowing it to lick his hands. "Good boy," he said softly. "Now do as you're told and keep quiet."

He moved across the lawn and peered in through French windows and found Asta in the study reading a book by the fire. She made an appealing figure in a pair of black silk lounging pajamas. He moved away, the dog at his heels, looked in through a long narrow window and saw the empty hall.

He moved round to the far side and heard voices and noticed a French window standing ajar. Curtains were partly drawn, and when he peered cautiously inside, he saw Morgan and Murdoch in a large drawing room. There were several bookcases against the wall and Morgan was replacing books in one of them.

"I've been through every inch in this room, taken down every book, searched every drawer, every cupboard, and the same in the study. Not a bloody sign. What about the staff?"

"They've all got their instructions, sir, every one of them is eager to win the thousand-pound reward you promised, but nothing as yet."

"It's got to be here somewhere, tell them to renew their efforts."

The Doberman whined, slipped in through the window, and rushed up to Morgan, who rather surprisingly greeted it with some pleasure. "You big lump, where have you been?" He leaned down to pat the animal. "My God, he's soaking, he could catch pneumonia. Take him to the kitchen, Murdoch, and towel him of. I'm going to bed."

Murdoch went out, his hand on the Doberman's collar, and Morgan turned and walked to the window. He stood there, looking at the night for a moment, then crossed to the door and went out, switching off the light.

Dillon slipped in through the window, went to the door, and stood listening for a moment, then he opened the door a crack, aware of voices, Asta's and Morgan's. The study door was open and he heard Morgan say, "I'm for bed. What about you?"

"I suppose so," Asta said. "If I'm out on the moors tomorrow stalking deer I'll need all my energy."

"And wits," he said. "Listen to everything Ferguson and Dillon say, store it up and remember it."

"Yes, oh master."

She laughed and when they came out, Morgan had an arm about her waist. "You're a great girl, Asta, one of a kind."

Strange, but watching them go up the great staircase together was something of a surprise to Dillon, no suggestion of the wrong kind of intimacy at all, and at the top of the stairs, Morgan only kissed her on the forehead. "Good night, my love," he said and he went one way and she the other.

"Well, I'll be damned," Dillon said softly.

He stayed there for a while, thinking. There was little point in going any further. He'd picked up one useful piece of intelligence, that they hadn't got anywhere as regards finding the Bible. That was a good enough night's work and the truth was what he'd done had been more for the hell of it than anything else.

On the other hand, again just for the hell of it, he could do with a drink and he'd noticed through the French windows the drinks cabinet in the study. He opened the door and hurried across the great hall to the study door. As he got it open, the Doberman arrived, skidding on the tiles as it tried to brake, sliding past him into the study.

Dillon closed the door and switched on a lamp on one of the tables. "You great eejit," he said to the dog and fondled its ears.

He went to the drinks cabinet and found no Irish whiskey so made do with Scotch. He went and stood looking down into the fire, taking his time, and behind him the door opened. As he turned, drawing the Walther, Asta came in. She didn't notice him at first, closed the door and turned.

And she didn't show any sign of fear, stood there looking at him calmly, and then said, "That couldn't be you, could it, Dillon?"

Dillon laughed softly. "Jesus, girl, you really are on Morgan's side, aren't you?"

He slipped the Walther back in his waistband at the rear and pulled off his ski mask.

"Why shouldn't I be? He's my father, isn't he?"

"Stepfather." Dillon helped himself to a cigarette from a silver box on a coffee table and lit it with his ever-present Zippo. "Mafia stepfather."

"Father as far as I'm concerned, the only decent one I've ever known, the first version was a rat, the kind of man who sniffed around everything in a skirt. He made my mother's life hell. It was a blessing when his car ran off the road one day and he was burned to death in the crash."

"That must have been rough."

"A blessing, Dillon, and then after a year or two my mother met Carl, the best man in the world."

"Really?"

She took a cigarette from the box. "Look, Dillon, I know all about you, all about the IRA, all that stuff, and I know who decent old Ferguson really is, Carl told me."

"I bet he tells you everything. I suppose you could give me chapter and verse on the Chungking Covenant."

"Of course I could, Carl tells me everything."

"I wonder. I mean there's the Carl Morgan of the social pages, the polo player, Man of the Year, billionaire, and then back there in the shadows is the same old Mafia sources of cash flow, drugs, prostitution, gambling, extortion."

She moved to the French windows, opened one, and looked out at the rain. "Don't be tiresome, Dillon, after all, you can talk. What about all those years with the Provisional IRA? How many soldiers did you kill, how many women and kids did you blow up?"

"I hate to disappoint you, but I never blew up a woman or a child in my life. Soldiers, yes, I've killed a few of those, but as far as I'm concerned, that was war. Come to think of it, I did blow up a couple of PLO boats in Beirut harbor, but they were due to land terrorists on the Israeli coast with the deliberate intention of blowing up women and kids."

"All right, point taken. What are you doing here anyway?"

"Just curious, that's all. I wondered if you were getting anywhere, but I overheard Morgan discussing things with Murdoch, and of the Bible, there is no sign."

"It must be here," she said. "Tanner said it came back." She frowned. "I'm not giving anything away, am I? I mean you and Ferguson wouldn't be here if you didn't know."

"That's right," he said. "Lord Louis Mountbatten, the Laird, Ian Campbell, the Dakota crash in India."

"You needn't go on. Carl would love to know how you found out, but I don't suppose you'll tell me."

"Classified information." He finished his drink and there was a noise in the hall. "On my way." He pulled on his ski mask and as he slipped out of the French window, said, "See you in the morning."

The door opened and Morgan came in. He looked surprised. "Good God, Asta, you startled me. I thought you'd gone to bed."

"I decided to come down for my book and guess what, Dillon was here." Morgan's eyes narrowed. "Really?"

"He looked terribly dramatic. All in black with a ski mask. Looked like Carlos the Jackal on a bad Saturday night in Beirut. He's just gone."

"What was he after?"

"Just prowling around to see what was happening. Apparently he overheard you and Murdoch discussing your lack of success at finding the Bible." Morgan poured a brandy and came over to stand beside her at the French windows. "They know everything, Carl, Mountbatten, Corporal Tanner, the Laird, everything," she said.

"You got that much out of him?"

"Easy, Carl, he likes me and he wasn't giving anything away. He wouldn't tell me how they found out, and you said yourself it was obvious they knew otherwise why would a man like Ferguson be here."

He nodded. "And they don't care that we know. Interesting tactics." He swallowed some brandy. "Are they still picking you up in the morning?"

"Yes."

"Good." He emptied his glass and closed the window. "Bed then, and this time let's mean it."

So the decks really are cleared for action now," Ferguson said.

"You did say you wanted him to know we were breathing down his neck," Dillon reminded him.

"Yes, it's a good tactic, don't you agree, Chief Inspector?"

He turned to Hannah Bernstein, who was leaning against his desk. "I suppose so, sir, if we're playing games, that is."

"So that's what you think we're doing?"

"I'm sorry, sir, it's just that I don't feel we're really getting to grips with this thing. We know what Morgan is up to and he knows what we are, I'm not sure it makes sense."

"It will, my dear, when that Bible turns up."

"Will it? Let's say he suddenly found it at the back of a drawer tonight, Brigadier. They could be into his Citation and flying out of the country in the morning and nothing we could do about it."

"Well, we'll just have to see, won't we." Kim came in with tea on a tray. Ferguson shook his head. "It's bed for me, I'll see you in the morning."

He went out and Kim poured the tea and retired. Hannah said to Dillon, "What do you think?"

"You could be right, but I've a hunch it isn't so." He moved to the window, opened it, and looked at the rain bouncing on the flagged terrace. "I don't think that Bible is tucked away in some casual spot so that a maid might find it while she's dusting." He turned. "Remember what Tanner said when the doctor asked him if the Bible had been returned to Loch Dhu?"

"Yes, his answer was: 'You could say that.' "

"And then he laughed. Now why would he do that?"

Hannah shrugged. "Some private joke?"

"Exactly. Quite a mystery, and I came across another tonight."

"What was that?"

Dillon said, "When I was snooping around earlier at the castle I saw Morgan and Asta going up to bed."

"So?"

"It wasn't what I expected, not a hint of a sexual relationship. At the top of the stairs he kissed her forehead and they went their separate ways."

"Now that *is* interesting," Hannah Bernstein told him.

"It is if you consider any theory that says his motive for killing the mother was because he had designs on Asta." Dillon finished his tea and grinned. "You can put that fine Special Branch mind to work on that one, my love, but as for me, I'm for bed," and he left her there.

The following morning it had stopped raining for the first time in two days. As the Range Rover drove up to Loch Dhu Castle, Kim at the wheel, Asta and Morgan came out and stood waiting. She wore a Glengarry bonnet, leather jacket, and a plaid skirt.

"Very ethnic," Dillon said as he got out.

"Morning," Ferguson boomed. "A good day's sport with any luck. I'm glad this damn rain's stopped."

"So am I," Morgan said. "Did you have a good night, Brigadier?"

"Certainly. Slept like a top. It's the Highland air."

Morgan turned to Dillon. "And you?"

"I'm like a cat, I only nap."

"That must be useful." Morgan turned back to the Brigadier. "Dinner tonight? Seven o'clock suit you?"

"Excellent," Ferguson said. "Black tie?"

"Of course, and bring that secretary of yours and I'll try and persuade Lady Katherine to join us."

"Couldn't look forward to it more. We'll see you this evening then," and Morgan ushered Asta down the steps into the Shogun.

As the sun came up and the morning advanced, Dillon almost forgot why he had come to this wild and lonely place as they proceeded on foot, climbing up and away from the glen. He and Asta forged ahead, leaving Ferguson and Kim to follow at their own pace.

Dillon was aware of a kind of lazy content. The truth was that he was enjoying the girl's company. He'd never had much time for women, the exigencies of his calling he used to say, and no time for relationships, but there was something elemental about this one that touched him deep inside. They didn't talk much, simply concentrated on climbing, and finally came up over an edge of rock and stood there, the glen below purple with heather and the sea in the distance calm, islands scattered across it.

"I don't think I've ever seen anything more beautiful," Asta said.

"I have," Dillon told her.

The wind folded her skirt about her legs, outlining her thighs, and when she pulled off her Glengarry and shook her head, her near-white hair shimmered in the sun. She fitted the scene perfectly, a golden girl on a golden day.

"Your hair and mine are almost the same color, Dillon." She sat down on a rock. "We could be related."

"Jesus, girl, don't wish that on me." He lit two cigarettes, hands cupped against the wind, gave her one, then lay on the ground beside her. "Lots of fair hair in Ireland. A thousand years ago Dublin was a Viking capital."

"I didn't know that."

"Did you tell Morgan about my visit last night?"

"Of course I did. In fact, you almost came face-to-face. The noise you heard in the hall was Carl."

"And what did he have to say?"

"My goodness, Dillon, you do expect a lot for your cigarette." She laughed. "All right, I told him everything you told me, the Chungking Covenant and so on, but that was because you wanted me to, didn't you?"

"That's right."

"Carl said he didn't mind. He checked on Ferguson the moment he discovered he was at the lodge, knew who he was in a matter of hours and you. He knew you must have been aware of what was going on, otherwise why would you be here. He's no fool, Dillon, he would hardly be where he is today if he was that."

"You really think a great deal of him, don't you?"

"As I said last night, I know all about you, Dillon, so don't waste time telling me what a bad man Carl is. It would be the pot calling the kettle black, don't you agree?"

"A nice turn of phrase you have."

"I had an excellent education," she said. "A good Church of England boarding school for young ladies. St. Michael's and St. Hugh's College, Oxford, afterwards."

"Is that so? I bet you didn't get calluses on your knees from praying."

"You are a bastard," she said amiably, and at that moment Ferguson came over the rise, Kim following with the gun case, a pair of old-fashioned Zeiss binoculars around his neck.

"There you are." Ferguson slumped down. "Getting old. Coffee, Kim."

The Ghurka put down the gun case, opened the haversack that hung at his side, took out a thermos flask and several paper cups which he filled and passed round.

"This is nice," Asta said. "I haven't been on a picnic in years."

"You can forget that notion, young lady," Ferguson told her. "This is a serious expedition, the object of which is to expose you to the finer points of deer stalking. Now drink up and we'll get on."

And so, tramping through the heather in the sunshine, he kept up a running commentary stressing first a deer's incredible sense of smell so that any successful approach could only be made downwind.

"You can shoot, I suppose?" he asked her.

"Of course, Carl trained me, clay pigeon shooting mostly. I've been out with him after grouse during the season many times."

"Well that's something."

They had been on the go for a good hour when Kim suddenly pointed. "There, Sahib."

"Down, everybody," Ferguson told them, and Kim passed him the binoculars.

"Excellent." Ferguson handed them to Dillon. "Three hundred yards. Two hinds and a Royal Stag. Quite magnificent antlers."

Dillon had a look. "My God, yes," he said and passed the binoculars to Asta.

When she focused them, the stag and the hinds jumped clearly into view. "How marvelous," she breathed and turned to Ferguson. "We couldn't possibly shoot such wonderful creatures, could we?"

"Just like a bloody woman," Ferguson said. "I might have known."

Dillon said, "The fun is in the stalking, Asta, it's like a game. They're well able to look after themselves, believe me. We'll be lucky to get within a hundred yards."

Kim wet a finger and raised it. "Downwind, Sahib, okay now." He looked up at the sky where clouds were forming. "I think wind change direction soon."

"Then we move fast," Ferguson said. "Pass me the rifle."

It was an old Jackson and Whitney bolt action. He loaded it carefully and said, "They're downhill from us, remember."

"I know," Dillon said. "Shoot low. Let's get going."

Asta found the next hour one of the most exhilarating she'd ever known. They moved through gulleys, crouching low, Kim leading the way.

"He certainly knows his stuff," she said to Dillon at one point.

"He should do," Ferguson told her. "The best tracker on a tiger shoot I ever knew in India in the old days."

Finally, they took to the heather and crawled in single file until Kim called a halt and paused in a small hollow. He peered over the top cautiously. The deer browsed contentedly no more than seventy-five yards away.

"No closer, Sahib." He glanced up. "Wind changing already."

"Right." Ferguson moved the bolt and rammed a round into the breech. "Your honor, my dear."

"Really?" Asta was flushed with excitement, took the rifle from him gingerly, then settled herself on her elbows, the stock firmly into her shoulder.

"Don't pull, just squeeze gently," Dillon told her.

"I know that."

"And aim low," Ferguson added.

"All right." What seemed like rather a long time passed and suddenly she rolled over and thrust the rifle at him. "I can't do it, Brigadier, that stag is too beautiful to die."

"Well we all bloody-well die sometime," Ferguson said, and at that moment, the stag raised its head.

"Wind change, Sahib, he has our scent," Kim said, and in an instant the stag and the two hinds were leaping away through the bracken at an incredible speed.

Dillon rolled over, laughing, and Ferguson said, "Damn!" And then he scowled. "Not funny, Dillon, not funny at all." He handed the rifle to Kim. "All right, put it away and break out the sandwiches."

On the way back some time later they paused for a rest on a crest that gave an excellent view of the glen below the castle above Loch Dhu and Ardmurchan Lodge on the other side. Dillon noticed something he hadn't appreciated before. There was a landing stage below the castle, a boat moored beside it.

"Give me the binoculars," he said to Kim and focused them, closing in on a twenty-five-foot motor launch with a deckhouse. "I didn't know that was there," he said, passing the binoculars to Ferguson.

"The boat, you mean?" Asta said. "It goes with the castle. It's called the *Katrina*."

"Have you been out in it yet?" Dillon asked.

"No reason. Carl isn't interested in fishing."

"Better than ours." Ferguson swung the binoculars to the rickety pier below Ardmurchan Lodge on the other side of the loch and the boat tied up there, an old whaler with an outboard motor, and a rowboat beside it. He handed the binoculars to Kim. "All right, let's move on."

"Frankly I'm getting bored with this track," Asta said. "Can't we just go straight down, Dillon?"

He turned to Ferguson, who shrugged. "Rather you than me, but if that's what you want. Come on, Kim," and he continued along the track.

Dillon took Asta by the hand. "Here we go and watch yourself, we don't want you turning that ankle again," and they started down the slope.

It was reasonably strenuous going for most of the way, the whole side of the mountain flowing down to the loch below. He led the way, picking his way carefully for something like a thousand feet and then, as things became easier, he took her hand and they scrambled on down together until suddenly she lost her balance, laughing out loud and fell, dragging Dillon with her. They rolled over a couple of times and came to rest in a soft cushion of heather in a hollow. She lay on her back, breathless, and Dillon pushed himself up on one elbow to look at her.

Her laughter faded, she reached up and touched his face, and for a moment he forgot everything except the color of her hair, the scent of her perfume. When they kissed, her body was soft and yielding, everything a man could hope for in this world.

He rolled onto his back and she sat up. "I wondered when you would, Dillon. Very satisfactory."

He got a couple of cigarettes from his case, lit them, and passed one to her. "Put it down to the altitude. I'm sorry."

"I'm not."

"You should be. I've got twenty years on you."

"That must be some Irish thing," she said. "All that rain. Is it supposed to have a dampening effect on love?"

"What's love got to do with it?"

She blew out cigarette smoke and lay back, a hand behind her head. "Now there's romantic for you."

He sat up. "Stop indulging in flights of fantasy, Asta, you aren't in love with me."

She turned to look at him. "You said it yourself. What's love got to do with it?"

"Morgan wouldn't think very much of the idea."

She sat up and shrugged. "He doesn't control my life."

"Really? I'd have thought that's exactly what he does do."

"Damn you, Dillon!" She was angry and stubbed her cigarette out on a rock. "You've just ruined a lovely day. Can we go now?"

She got up and started down the hill, and after a while, he stood himself and followed her.

They reached the edge of the loch about thirty minutes later and started to follow the shoreline. They hadn't spoken since the incident in the hollow and now Dillon said, "Are we speaking again or what?"

She laughed and took his arm. "You're a pig, Dillon, but I like you."

"All part of my irresistible charm," he said and paused suddenly.

They were close to the west end of the loch, the old hunting bothy where Morgan and Marco had dealt with Fergus on their left. He was still lying down on the shoreline, face in the shallows.

Asta said, "My God, isn't that a body?"

"That's what it looks like."

They hurried down the slope and reached the sand-bar. She stood there while Dillon waded in and turned Fergus over. Asta gave a sudden exclamation. "Fergus."

"Yes." Dillon waded back. "I'd say he was given a thorough beating. Wait here." He went up to the hunting bothy. She watched him go in. A moment later, he returned. "From the state of things, that's where the fight was. After they'd gone he must have come down to the shore to revive himself and fell in. Something like that."

"An accident," she said and there was a strange calmness on her face. "That was it."

"You could describe it that way," Dillon said. "I'm sure Carl Morgan would."

"Leave it, Dillon." She reached out and grabbed his lapel. "Do this for me, just leave it, I'll handle it."

There was a fierceness to her that was something new. He said, "I'm beginning to wonder if I really know you at all, Asta. All right, I'll leave Morgan to stew in it."

She nodded. "Thank you, I'll get back now." She walked away, paused, and turned. "I'll see you tonight."

He nodded. "I wouldn't miss it for anything."

She hurried away. He looked out again at the body by the sandbar, then climbed up the slope and reached the road. He had walked along it for perhaps five minutes when a horn sounded and he turned and found the Range Rover bearing down on him.

Ferguson opened the door. "Where's the girl?"

"She's cut across to the castle on her own."

Dillon climbed in and Kim drove on. "I must say you look thoughtful, dear boy."

"So would you," Dillon said, lit a cigarette, and brought him up to date.

Morgan was in the study when she went in, sitting at his desk and talking to Marco. He turned and smiled. "Had a nice day?"

"It was until things went sour."

He stopped smiling and said to Marco, "You can go."

"No, let him stay. You found Fergus, didn't you, you beat him up?"

Morgan reached for a cigar and clipped it. "He had it coming, Asta. Anyway, how do you know?"

"Dillon and I just found his body. He was lying in the shallows down there in the loch just below that old hunting lodge. He must have fallen in and drowned."

Morgan glanced at Marco, then put the cigar down. "What did Dillon do?"

"Nothing. I begged him to leave it to me."

"And he agreed?"

She nodded. "He said he'd leave you to stew in it."

"Yes, that's exactly how he would play it." Morgan nodded. "And so would Ferguson. It wouldn't suit the dear old Brigadier to have a police investigation, not at the moment." He glanced at Marco. "And it wouldn't get anywhere without a body, would it?"

"No, Signore."

Morgan stood up. "All right, let's take care of it. You stay here, Asta," and he went out followed by Marco.

In the trees that fringed the loch below Ardmurchan Lodge just above the small jetty, Ferguson and Dillon waited, the Irishman holding the Zeiss binoculars. The light was fading, but visibility was still good enough for him to see the motor launch *Katrina* moving along the shoreline on the other side.

"There they go," he said and focused the binoculars.

Morgan was in the wheelhouse and he reversed the launch toward the shore, Marco in the stern. Marco jumped over into the water and Morgan went to help him. A moment later Fergus came over the rail. Morgan went back into the wheelhouse and turned out toward the middle of the loch. Dillon passed the binoculars to Ferguson.

The Brigadier said, "It looks to me as if Marco is wrapping a length of chain around the body." He shook his head. "How very naughty."

He passed the binoculars back to Dillon, who focused them again in time to see Marco slide the body over the side. It went straight under and a moment later the *Katrina* got under way and turned back toward the castle.

"So that's it," Dillon said and turned to Ferguson. "You're happy to leave it that way?"

"I think so. A crime has undoubtedly been committed, but that's a police matter, and frankly I don't want the local constabulary swarming all over Loch Dhu Castle. We've bigger fish to fry here, Dillon."

"I doubt whether the good Chief Inspector Bernstein would agree," Dillon said. "A great one for the letter of the law, that lady."

"Which is why we don't say a word about this to her."

Dillon lit another cigarette. "One thing we can count on, he won't be missed, ould Fergus, not for a few days. The Munros will think he's just keeping out of the way."

"Which will be what Morgan is counting on. I would imagine he's hoping to be out of here quite quickly." Ferguson stood up. "Let's get moving, we've got dinner to look forward to. It should prove an interesting evening."

TEN

They arrived at the castle only a few minutes after seven, Dillon at the wheel of the old estate car that went with Ardmurchan Lodge. He and Ferguson were in dinner jackets and Hannah Bernstein wore a cream trouser suit in silk crepe. The door was opened by Marco wearing his alpaca jacket and striped trousers and he ushered them in, his face expressionless, to where Morgan stood by the fire in the hall, Asta in a green silk dress on the sofa beside Lady Katherine Rose.

"Ah, there you are," Morgan said genially. "Come in. I think you've met Brigadier Ferguson, Lady Katherine?"

"Indeed, yes. He called and took tea with me, he and this charming young gel."

Hannah looked amused and Ferguson took her hand. "Lovely to see you again. I don't think you've met my nephew, Sean Dillon."

"Mr. Dillon."

Dillon took the cool, dry hand, liking her immediately. "A great pleasure."

"Irish?" she said. "I like the Irish, charming rogues, the lot of them, but nice. Do you smoke, young man?"

"My one vice."

"What a liar you are. Give me one, will you."

"Lady Katherine, I'm so sorry." Morgan picked up a silver cigarette box and came forward. "I'd no idea."

She took one and accepted a light from Dillon. "I've been smoking all my life, Mr. Morgan, no point in stopping now."

Marco appeared with a bottle of Crystal in a bucket and six glasses on a tray. He placed it on a side table and said in heavily accented English, "Shall I open the champagne, sir?"

"Not for me," Lady Katherine said. "It doesn't go down well these days. A vodka martini very dry would be just the ticket. That's what got me through the war, that and cigarettes."

"I'll get it," Asta said and went to the drinks cabinet as Marco uncorked the champagne bottle.

"You served in the war then, Lady Katherine?" Ferguson asked her.

"By God I did. All this nonsense about young gels being allowed to fly in the RAF these days." She snorted. "All old hat. I was a pilot from nineteen-forty with the old Air Transport Auxiliary. They used to call us the Attagirls."

Asta brought the martini and sat beside her, fascinated. "But what did you do?"

The old lady sampled the drink. "Excellent, my dear. We ferried warplanes between factories and RAF Stations to free pilots for combat. I flew everything, we all did. Spitfires and Hurricanes and once a Lancaster bomber. The ground crew at the RAF Station I delivered it to couldn't believe it when I took off my flying helmet and they saw my hair."

"But all in all, it must have been extremely dangerous," Hannah said.

"I crash-landed once in a Hurricane, wheels up. Not my fault, engine failure. Another time an old Gloucester Gladiator, they were biplanes, started to fall apart on me in midair so I had to bail out."

"Good God!" Morgan said. "That's amazing."

"Oh, it was hard going," she said. "Out of the women in my unit sixteen were killed, but then we had to win the war, didn't we, Brigadier?"

"We certainly did, Lady Katherine."

She held up her empty glass. "Another one, somebody, and then I'll love you and leave you."

Asta went to get it and Morgan said, "Lady Katherine doesn't feel up to dinner, I'm afraid."

"Only eat enough for a sparrow these days." She accepted the drink Asta brought and looked up at Morgan. "Well, have you found the Bible yet?"

He was momentarily thrown. "The Bible?"

"Oh, come on, Mr. Morgan, I know you've had the servants turning the place upside down. Why is it so important?"

He was in command again now. "A legend, Lady Katherine, of great importance to your family. I just thought it would be nice to find it and give it to you."

"Indeed." She turned to Hannah and there was something in her eyes. "Amazing the interest in the Bible all of a sudden and I can't help. Haven't seen it in years. I still think it was lost in the air crash that injured my brother so badly."

Morgan glanced at Ferguson, who was smiling, and made a determined effort to change the subject. "Tell me, just how old is the castle, Lady Katherine?"

Asta got up and moved to the French windows at the end of the hall and opened them and Dillon went to join her, moving out onto the terrace as she did, the murmur of voices behind them.

The beech trees above the loch were cut out of black cardboard against a sky that was streaked with vivid orange above the mountains. She took his arm and they strolled across the lawn, Dillon lighting a cigarette.

"Do you want one?"

"No, I'll share yours," which she did, handing it back to him after a moment. "It's peaceful here and old, the roots go deep. Everyone needs roots, don't you agree, Dillon?"

"Maybe it's people, not places," he said. "Take you, for instance. Perhaps your roots are Morgan."

"It's a thought, but you, Dillon, what about you? Where are your roots?"

"Maybe nowhere, love, nowhere at all. Oh, there's the odd aunt or uncle and a few cousins here and there in Ulster, but no one who'd dare come near. The price of fame."

"Infamy, more like."

"I know, I'm the original bad guy. That's why Ferguson recruited me."

"You know I like you, Dillon, I feel as if I've known you a long time, but what am I going to do with you?"

"Take your time, girl dear, I'm sure something will occur to you."

Morgan appeared on the terrace and called, "Asta, are you there?"

"Here we are, Carl." They walked back and went up the steps to the terrace. "What is it?"

"Lady Katherine's ready to leave."

"What a pity. I wish she would stay, she's wonderful."

"One of a kind," Morgan said. "But there it is. I'll run her down to the lodge."

"No you won't," Asta told him. "I'll see to it. You've got guests, Carl. We mustn't forget our manners."

"Shall I come with you?" Dillon asked.

"It's only three hundred yards down the drive for heaven's sake," she said. "I'll be back in no time."

They went inside and Lady Katherine said, "There you are. Thought we'd lost you."

She pushed herself up on her stick and Asta put an arm around her. "No chance, I'm taking you home now."

"What a lovely girl." Lady Katherine turned to them all. "Such a delight. Do come and see me any time. Good night all."

Morgan had a hand on her elbow and he and Asta took her out of the front door. A moment later the castle's station wagon engine started up and Morgan returned.

He snapped his fingers at Marco. "More champagne."

Marco replenished the glasses and Ferguson looked around the great hall, the weapons on the wall, the trophies, the armour. "Quite an amazing collection, all this. Fascinating."

"I agree," Hannah said. "If you're into death, that is."

"Aren't you being a little harsh?" Morgan said.

She sipped some of her champagne. "If it was a museum exhibition they'd probably call it 'In Praise of War.' I mean look at those great swords crossed under the shields. Their only purpose was to slice somebody's arm off."

"You're wrong," Dillon said amiably. "The back-stroke was intended to remove heads. Those swords are Highland Claymores and the shield was called a Targ. That's where the word *target* comes from."

"Actually, the particular one you're looking at up there was carried at the Battle of Culloden by the Campbell of the day," Morgan said. "He died fighting for Bonnie Prince Charlie."

"Well I don't consider that much of an ambition."

"Haven't you any sense of history?" Ferguson demanded.

"I can't afford one, I'm Jewish, remember, Brigadier. My people have always had enough on to simply survive in the present."

There was a silence and Dillon said, "Well that's a showstopper if ever I've heard one."

As he spoke the door opened and Asta came in. "That's done. I've left her in the hands of the redoubtable Jeannie. Can we eat now? I'm starving."

"Only waiting for you, my love," Morgan said and he gave her his arm and led the way in.

The dining room was quite splendid, the walls lined with oak paneling, the table decorated with the finest crystal and silver, candles in great silver sticks flaring. Marco served the meal aided by two young housemaids in black dresses and white aprons.

"We've kept the meal relatively simple as I wasn't sure what everyone would like," Morgan said.

His idea of simplicity was extraordinary. Beluga caviar and smoked salmon followed by roast pheasant with the usual trimmings, all washed down with vintage Chateau Palmer.

"Absolutely wonderful," Ferguson said as he tucked into his pheasant. "You must have an extraordinary cook here."

"Oh, she's all right for the simple things, but it's Marco who roasted the pheasant."

"A man of many talents." Ferguson glanced up as Marco, face imperturbable, refilled the glasses.

"Yes, you could say that," Morgan agreed.

Marco disappeared shortly afterwards, Dillon noticed that as the two maids cleared the plates. Asta said, "And what delight do you have for the climax?"

"Hard act to follow with a simple pudding," Ferguson observed.

"Nothing simple about this, Brigadier, something Marco specializes in," Morgan told him.

Marco entered the room at that moment with a large silver chafing dish, the maids behind him. He removed the lid and a most delicious smell became apparent.

"Cannolo," Asta said in delight.

"Yes, the most famous sweet in Sicily and so simple," Morgan said. "A tube of flour and egg filled with cream."

Ferguson tried a spoonful and shook his head. "Nothing simple about this. The man's a genius. Where on earth did he learn to do such cooking?"

"His father had a small restaurant in Palermo. As a boy, he was raised to it."

"Amongst other things," Dillon said.

"Yes, my friend," Morgan told him calmly. "I suspect you and Marco would have a great deal in common."

"Now then, Dillon, let's concentrate on the meal," Ferguson said. "There's a good chap."

Which they did, returning to sit round the great fireplace in the hall for the coffee, which was Yemeni mocha, the finest in the world.

Ferguson accepted a cigar. "Well I must tell you this, Morgan, that was the best simple meal I've ever had in my life."

"We aim to please."

"A most pleasant evening," the Brigadier replied.

Dillon felt like laughing out loud at the insanity of it, the pretense of this amazing game they were all playing, the urbanity of the Brigadier's exchanges with a man who only a few hours earlier he had seen dispose of Fergus Munro's body.

"Well now," he said. "If we're going to play patty fingers here I'll use mine on the piano if you don't mind."

"Be my guest," Morgan told him.

Dillon moved to the grand piano and raised the lid. It was very old, a Schiedmayer, but the tone wasn't too bad when he tried a few chords. He lit a cigarette and sat there with it drooping from the corner of his mouth and started to work his way through a few standards.

Hannah came and leaned on the piano, sipping her coffee. "You consistently surprise me, Dillon."

"The secret of my fatal charm. Any requests?"

Asta was watching, a slight frown on her face, and Hannah murmured, "Now that's interesting, I do believe she's jealous. What have you been up to, Dillon?"

"You should be ashamed, you and your bad thoughts," Dillon told her.

Behind them Morgan said, "Asta tells me you had an excellent day with the deer."

"Yes," Ferguson said, "only when we got close enough to a King Stag to see the damned eyes and I lined her up with my gun, she wouldn't pull the trigger. She said she couldn't kill such a magnificent creature."

Hannah turned. "Good for you," she said to Asta.

"Well it *was* magnificent," Asta said.

"Still a damn silly attitude," Ferguson told her.

"No, I think the Chief Inspector has a point," Morgan told him. "The deer can't fight back. At least in the ring the bull has a chance of sticking his horn in."

There was silence and Dillon said, "Sure and you put your foot in it there, old son."

"Dear me, so I did." Morgan smiled at Hannah. "So sorry, Chief Inspector, I wasn't supposed to know, was I?"

"Oh, I wouldn't say that," Ferguson told him.

"All out in the open, so we all know where we are," Dillon said.

"And on that note we'll say goodnight." Ferguson stood up. "Whatever else, you're an excellent host, Morgan. You must allow me to do the same for you sometime."

"I'll look forward to it."

Marco opened the door and they moved out onto the steps. The sky was dotted with clouds and yet undulated with strange, shimmering lights.

"What's that?" Hannah demanded.

"The aurora borealis," Dillon told her, "the northern lights."

"It's the most beautiful thing I've ever seen," Asta said. "What a night for a drive. Can we, Carl?"

"Asta, be reasonable. It's late."

"Oh, you're no fun, you." She turned to Ferguson. "Can I come with you, Brigadier? You could have that wonderful Ghurka of yours bring me back."

"Of course, my dear, if you'd like that."

"It's settled then." She ran indoors.

Dillon said to Morgan, "Don't worry, I'll bring her back myself."

"Now that I am worried about," Morgan said and Asta reappeared wearing a blue mink coat.

"I'm ready when you are." She kissed Morgan on the cheek. "I won't be long." Then she got in the rear of the estate car with Hannah.

Dillon got behind the wheel, Ferguson joined him in front, and they drove away.

The drive along the side of the loch was pleasantly eerie, the northern lights reflected in the dark water so that they seemed to sparkle with a kind of strange silver fire.

"Wonderful," Asta said, "I'm so glad I came."

Dillon changed down to climb the hill up through the trees as they rounded the eastern end of the loch. The old estate car responded well; they went over the crest and started down. It was very steep with a bend or two below. As their speed increased, Dillon put his foot on the brake pedal. There was no response and the pedal went right down to the floor.

"Damn!" he said.

"What is it?" Ferguson demanded.

"The brakes have failed."

"Good God, man, how? They worked perfectly well on the way here."

"Since when we've been parked outside Loch Dhu Castle," Dillon told him and desperately tried to change down.

They were going very fast indeed now. There was a grinding of gears as he wrestled with the stick and then he did manage to force it into third as they came to the first bend.

"Hang on!" Ferguson called as Dillon worked the wheel and just managed to scrape round.

"For God's sake, stop it, Dillon!" Asta cried.

Not that he had any choice and the estate car hurtled down the straight, another considerable bend waiting for them. Again he worked the wheel hard, trying the old racing driver's technique of driving into the bend and almost made it and then they scraped against a granite wall on the left and bounced away. And it was that which saved them, for Dillon got control again as they went down another slope into a hollow and started up a gentle incline. Gradually the speed slowed, he changed down to bottom gear, and applied the handbrake.

There was silence and Ferguson said, "Now that could have been very nasty indeed."

"Let's take a look," Dillon said.

He found a torch in the dashboard locker and went and raised the estate car's bonnet, Ferguson at his side. A moment later, Hannah and Asta joined them.

Dillon peered into the engine and nodded. "There you are."

"What is it?" Hannah asked.

"See that kind of canister there? It holds brake fluid, only it doesn't any longer. The valve's been ripped off at the top, probably with a screwdriver. No fluid, no brakes. It's a hydraulic system."

"We could have been killed," Hannah said, "all of us, but why?"

"I think Asta knows why," Dillon said.

Asta pulled the collar of her mink around her throat and shivered. "But why would Carl do that?"

"More important, why would he do it to you, my dear?" Ferguson asked her. "After all, he made no attempt to stop you coming with us." And to that she had no reply. He turned to Dillon. "Will it still work?"

"Oh, yes, it's a straight road to the lodge on the other side of this hill and I'll stay in bottom gear."

"Good. Let's get moving then," and Ferguson ushered the two women back into the estate car.

I think you could probably do with this," Ferguson said to Asta, who was sitting by the fire in the sitting room at the lodge, still hugging her mink around her.

It was brandy he was holding out and she took the large crystal tumbler in both hands, staring into it, then swallowed the brandy down. She sat there, still holding the glass, and Dillon took it from her gently and turned to Ferguson.

"She's a little in shock," he said.

She stood up then, took off her mink, and tossed it over a chair. "Shock be damned. I'm angry, Dillon, bloody angry."

At that moment, Hannah came in from the kitchen with Kim, who started pouring coffee. The Chief Inspector took a cup to Asta. "Just sit down, Asta, and take it easy."

Asta took the cup of coffee and did as she was told. "The rest of you would make some kind of sense, but why me? I don't understand."

"I think you will if you pause and think about it, Asta," Dillon said.

"His connection with Mafia and all that stuff? You mean I know too much? But I always have."

"Yes, but something more important than that has cropped up, you know that."

Hannah Bernstein looked puzzled and Ferguson said, "You signed the Official Secrets Act when you joined me which means anything which takes place during your duties with me is sacrosanct. Am I correct?"

"Of course, sir."

"Dillon?" he said.

"I found Fergus Munro's body earlier today in the shallows by Loch Dhu. Asta was with me. By my observation he'd been given a severe beating. I'd say he'd collapsed in the water afterwards and drowned."

"My God!" Hannah said.

Dillon turned to Asta, who said, "I asked Dillon to let it go."

"Why?" Hannah said.

"Because in a way it was my fault. It was because of me Carl wanted to teach him a lesson."

"I see." Hannah turned to Ferguson. "On the face of it, you've condoned a criminal offense, sir, manslaughter at the very least."

"Absolutely right, Chief Inspector. If you want the sordid details, Dillon and I observed Morgan and the man Marco recover the body in the motor launch *Katrina*. They then disposed of it wrapped in a length of chain in the middle of the loch."

She said, "You've stood by and let him get away with it?"

"You've got it wrong, girl dear," Dillon said. "Retribution can come later."

"Exactly," Ferguson told her. "More important things to consider." He took her hand, sat on the couch, and pulled her down beside him. "I chose you to assist me in my work because you're one of the most astute brains at Scotland Yard."

"Now it's flattery, Brigadier?"

"Nonsense. Look at your background. Your grandfather is a highly respected Rabbi, your father a brilliant Professor of Medicine. You have a Cambridge M.A. in Psychology. You could have been anything. You chose to be a policewoman on the beat in Brixton and have risen because of your own abilities. I need you and I want you, but this isn't normal police work. This is a rather complicated game, our kind of work. We only have the end in view."

"Because the end justifies the means?"

It was Dillon who leaned down, took her hands, and pulled her up. "God save us, girl, but he's right, sometimes it does. It's called the greater good."

He actually put an arm round her and she leaned against him. Then she straightened and managed a faint smile. "They must have loved you at the National Theatre, Dillon, you'd have ended up with a Knighthood. Instead you chose the IRA." She turned to Ferguson. "No problem, sir, anything I can do?"

He inclined his head toward Asta, and Hannah sat beside her and took her hand. "When you told Morgan you wanted to come with us he didn't say no. Am I right?"

"I suppose so," Asta said.

"Let's be logical. He was after us, hadn't counted on you being involved, but when the chance came, when you said what you did, he didn't say no."

Asta sat there staring at her mutely. She moistened her lips. "Why? He loves me."

"His account with you was full, Asta. Oh, you knew all about the Mafia background and so on, and what you don't realize is that was always a liability. But Fergus." Hannah Bernstein shook her head. "Even if he drowned because of the beating, the charge would be manslaughter that would get Carl Morgan seven years at the Old Bailey, and Mafia lawyers don't enjoy the same kind of success in court in England as they do in America. Seven years, Asta. Seven years for a billionaire polo player used to the good things of life. There was no way he could take that chance. You knew too much."

Asta jumped up and paced across the room and turned. "He's always been so good to me. I can't believe this."

Ferguson turned to Dillon. "Would you say it's time?"

"I think so."

Ferguson said to Hannah, "The Greek file, Chief Inspector." Hannah went to the desk and he carried on. "You take over, Dillon."

Dillon took Asta's hand and brought her back to the sofa by the fire and sat down with her. "What we've got to show you now is bad, Asta, as bad as anything could be. It's to do with Hydra and your mother's accident scuba diving."

She frowned. "I don't understand."

"You will, my dear." Ferguson took the file from Hannah Bernstein and passed it to her. "Read that."

Asta put the file to one side and sat there, her hands clenched. "It doesn't seem possible."

"You've seen the file," Ferguson told her. "The technical details are beyond dispute. Someone interfered with your mother's equipment."

"An accident?" she said desperately.

"No accident." Dillon sat down beside her and took her hand. "I'm an expert diver, Asta. Believe me, what was done to your mother's gear was deliberate. Now you tell me who was responsible. Can you think of anyone who wished your mother harm?" He shook his head. "Only Carl, Asta. We think she knew too much and that's the truth of it."

She closed her eyes and took a deep breath and when she opened them again she was remarkably in control. "I can't let him get away with that— not that. What can I do?"

"You could help us," Ferguson said. "Keep us informed of the situation up there at the castle. Most important thing of all, you could let us know the moment he finds the Bible."

She nodded. "Right. I'll do it." She took another deep breath. "Could I have another brandy?"

"Of course, my dear." Ferguson nodded to Dillon, who got up and went to the drinks cabinet. He returned with the brandy and Asta took it from him.

Hannah sat beside her. "Look, Asta, are you sure you can go through with this? I mean, you've got to go back and smile in his face and act as if nothing's changed."

Asta said, "We buried my mother back home in Sweden, flew her body there from Athens, and do you know something? He stood at the side of my mother's grave and he cried." She emptied the brandy glass with a single swallow. "I'll see him pay for that if it's the last thing I do." She placed the brandy glass on the coffee table and got up. "I think I should go back now."

"I'll take you," Dillon said.

She walked toward the door, picking up her mink and pulling it on. She turned. "All right. So far, the search for the Bible isn't getting very far in spite of the fact that Carl has offered a substantial reward for anyone who finds it."

"Thank you for that," Ferguson said.

"As regards future moves, we're supposed to put in an appearance at the Ardmurchan Fair and Games tomorrow. I don't think there's anything else."

Dillon said, "I'll take you now, Asta."

She turned at the door. "I've just remembered, Angus the gardener, he's on Carl's payroll now."

"We'll bear that in mind," Ferguson said.

She went out and Dillon followed her.

On the way back to the castle in the Range Rover she sat beside him, clutching the collar of her mink coat around her neck, saying nothing.

"Are you all right?" he asked as they neared the gates.

"Oh, yes." She nodded. "Don't worry about me, Dillon. I'll play my part."

They drove along the drive and he braked to a halt at the steps. Before they could get out, the front door opened and Morgan appeared.

"I was beginning to get worried," he said as Dillon went round and opened the door for Asta.

"Sorry, Carl," she said as she went up the steps. "But we nearly had a nasty accident."

He was immediately all concern. "What happened?"

"The brakes failed on the estate car," Dillon said. "Some sort of rupture in the canister, so we lost the hydraulic fluid. It's been around a few years, that car."

"Dillon was wonderful," she said. "Drove like Nigel Mansell going down the hill. I really thought we'd had it."

"My God!" He gave her a squeeze. "How can I thank you, Dillon?"

"Self-preservation," Dillon told him. "I always struggle to survive, Mr. Morgan."

Asta said, "I'll go in, Carl. I think I'll go to bed."

She went inside and Morgan turned as Dillon got in the Range Rover. "Thanks again. Will you be at the fair tomorrow?"

"I should imagine so."

"Good, we'll see you then." He went in and closed the door.

"And I'll see you, you bastard," Dillon said as he drove away.

ELEVEN

The following day was a local holiday, Ardmurchan Village awash with people from the surrounding district and others who had driven many miles to see the fair and take part in the games. And there were the tinkers and the gypsies with their ponies and horses to trade. Ferguson, Dillon, and Hannah arrived just before lunch, parked the Range Rover at the church, and walked down to the Campbell Arms.

"A little bracer, I think, then all the fun of the fair," Ferguson said.

"Ten minutes short of noon, Brigadier," Hannah reminded him. "That counts as morning drinking."

"If the booze was going to get me, Chief Inspector, it would have done so long ago, the Korean War to be exact as a twenty-year-old subaltern. I sat in a trench in the snow, twenty degrees below, with the Chinese attacking ten thousand at a time. Only the rum kept me going."

He pushed open the door and led the way in. The saloon bar was packed, nowhere to sit, but he shouldered his way through cheerfully to the bar where Molly worked feverishly with four local women to aid her.

"Guinness," Ferguson called, "three." He turned to Hannah. "Extremely nourishing."

Molly served them herself. "Were you hoping to eat, Brigadier?"

"It's an idea," he said.

"Nothing fancy today, just hot Cornish pasties."

"A unique thought as we're in Scotland, but why not? We'll have one each."

"Right. There's someone moving from the settle by the fire right now. You sit yourselves down and I'll bring them."

She was right, three men getting up at that moment and moving off, and Ferguson pushed through the crowd to secure the places. He sat down and rubbed his hands. "Nothing like a day out in the country."

"Shouldn't we have more important things to do, sir?" Hannah asked.

"Nonsense, Chief Inspector, everyone needs a break now and then."

Molly brought the Guinness and the three pasties, which were enormous. "If that isn't enough for you there's the refreshment tent," she said as Ferguson paid her. "Up at the fair."

"We'll bear it in mind, my dear."

Ferguson sampled his drink and then tried the pasty. "My goodness, this is good."

Hannah said, "All right, sir, but what happens now?"

"What would you like to happen?" Dillon asked her.

"I don't know. In fact, all I do know is that Morgan took care of Fergus rather permanently and then tried to kill the lot of us last night. I'd say that amounts to open warfare."

"Yes, but now we've got Asta on our side," Ferguson told her, and at that moment Asta came in followed by Morgan and Marco.

She saw them at once and came straight over. She was wearing the bonnet she had worn when deer stalking and and the plaid skirt, and there wasn't a man in the room who didn't look her way.

She smiled. "There you are."

Dillon stood up to let her sit. "You're looking particularly fragrant this morning."

"Well that's how I feel. Fighting fit, Dillon. It seems to me that's the way I need to be."

Behind her Morgan spoke to Marco, who went to the bar, and Morgan crossed to join them. "How are you? Asta was describing what happened last night. That's terrible."

"Exciting to say the least," Ferguson told him, "but the boy here kept his head and drove like Stirling Moss in his prime." He smiled. "A long time ago, but still the only British racing driver worth his salt, as far as I'm concerned."

Marco brought two lagers, gave one to Morgan and the other to Asta, and retired to the door. Asta said, "All the fun of the fair. I'm looking forward to it."

The door opened again and Hector Munro entered with Rory. On seeing them by the fire he paused and put a finger to his forehead. "Ladies," he said courteously and started to the bar.

"No sign of that son of yours, I suppose," Morgan said.

"Ah, well Fergus is away to see relatives, Mr. Morgan," Hector told him. "I doubt he'll be back for a while."

He moved off to the bar and Ferguson finished his drink. "Right, let's get moving." He stood up. "See you later, Morgan," and he led the way out.

There was a refreshment tent, two or three roundabouts for children, and a primitive boxing ring, which for the moment was empty. The main event taking place when they arrived was the horse sale and they stood on the edge of the crowd and watched the gypsy boys running up and down, clutching the horses' bridles as they showed their paces. Dillon noticed Hector Munro and Rory at one point, inspecting a couple of ponies.

He strolled over, lighting a cigarette, and said in Irish, "Dog meat only, those two."

"Do I need telling?" Hector replied in Gaelic.

Rory grinned. "Expert are you?"

"I spent enough time on my uncle's farm in County Down as a boy to know rubbish when I see it."

Dillon smiled amiably and returned to the others. "Games just starting," Ferguson said. "Come on."

There were fifty-yard dashes and sack races for the younger children, but the adult sports were more interesting. Large men tossed the caber, an object resembling a telegraph pole. There was hammer throwing and the long jump, even Scottish reels danced to the skirl of the bagpipes.

Morgan and Asta, Marco behind them, appeared on the other side of the crowd. She saw Dillon and waved. He waved back and then turned to watch as the wrestling began. Brawny men in kilts with thighs like tree trunks grappled with the power and striking force of sumo wrestlers, the crowd urging them on.

"Rather jolly all this." Ferguson produced a hip flask. He unscrewed the top and took a swallow. "Just like Samson. Didn't he smite the Philistines hip and thigh, Chief Inspector?"

"I believe he did, sir, but frankly, it isn't my cup of tea."

"No, I don't suppose it would be."

And then the crowd moved away toward the boxing ring, carrying them with it. Dillon said, "Now this looks more like it."

"What is it?" Hannah demanded.

"Old style prize fighting, I'd say. Let's see what happens."

A middle-aged man in boxing boots and shorts slipped under the ropes into the ring. He had the flattened nose of the professional fighter, scar tissue around his eyes. On the back of his old nylon robe was the legend "Tiger Grant."

"By God, he's seen a few fights," Ferguson said.

"A hard one," Dillon nodded in agreement.

At that moment Asta joined them, Marco forcing a way through for her and Morgan. The Sicilian looked up at Tiger Grant, his expression enigmatic.

Dillon said, "From the look of his face, Marco here has done a bit himself."

"Light heavyweight champion of Sicily in his day," Morgan said. "Twenty-two fights."

"How many did he win?"

"All of them. Three decisions on points, twelve knockouts, seven where the referee stopped the fight."

"Is that a fact?" Dillon said. "I must remember to avoid him on a dark night."

Marco turned to look at him, something in his eyes, but at that moment a small man in tweed suit and cap climbed through the ropes clutching a pair of boxing gloves and turned, waving for silence.

"Now there must be a few sporting gentlemen here, so I'll give you a chance of some real money." He took a wad of bank notes from his inside pocket. "Fifty pounds, my friends, to any man who can last three rounds with Tiger Grant. Fifty pounds."

He didn't have to wait long. Dillon saw two burly young men on the other side of the ring talking to the Munros. One took off his jacket and gave it to Rory and slipped between the ropes.

"I'm on," he said and the crowd cheered.

The small man helped him into the boxing gloves while Tiger Grant tossed his robe to someone acting as his second in the corner. The small man got out of the ring, took a stopwatch from one pocket and a handbell from the other.

"Each round three minutes, let battle commence."

The young man moved in on Grant aggressively, the crowd cheering and Asta clutching Dillon's arm. "This is exciting."

"Butchery would be a better description," Hannah Bernstein observed.

And she was right, for Grant, easily evading the wild punches, moved in fast and gave his opponent a short and powerful punch in the stomach that put him down, writhing in agony. The crowd roared as the second and the small man helped the unfortunate youth from the ring.

The small man returned. "Any more takers?" But already the other one who had been standing with the Munros was climbing into the ring. "I'll have you, that was my brother."

Grant remained imperturbable and when the bell went and the youth rushed him, stepped from side-to-side, blocking wild punches, eventually putting him down as he had the brother.

The crowd groaned and Hannah said, "This is terrible."

"It could be worse," Dillon said. "Grant could have made mincemeat of those two and didn't. He's all right."

He was suddenly aware of Morgan saying something to Marco. He couldn't hear what it was because of the noise of the crowd, but the Sicilian stripped off his jacket and was under the ropes and into the ring, beating Rory Munro by a second.

"Another sportsman," the small man called although his smile slipped a little as he tied Marco's boxing gloves on.

"Oh, dear, he's not so sure now," Ferguson observed.

"Care to have a side bet, Brigadier?" Morgan asked. "Let's say a hundred pounds."

"You'll lose your money," Dillon said to Ferguson.

"I don't need you to tell me that, dear boy. Sorry, Morgan."

The bell jangled, Marco stood, arms at his side, and for some reason the crowd went silent. Grant crouched, feinted, then moved in fast. Marco swayed with amazing speed to one side, pivoted and punched him in the ribs twice, the sound echoing over the crowd. Grant's head went up in agony and Marco punched him on the jaw, the blow traveling hardly any distance at all. Grant went down like a sack of coal and lay there and there was a gasp of astonishment from the crowd.

The small man was on one knee trying to revive him helped by the second, and Marco paced about like a nervous animal. "My money, where's my money?" he demanded and pulled off his right glove and lifted the small man up. He, in his turn, looked terrified, took the notes from his pocket, and passed them over.

Marco moved round each side of the ring, waving the money over his head. "Anyone else?" he called.

There were boos and catcalls as the small man and the second got Grant out of the ring and then a voice called, "I'm for you, you bastard," and Rory Munro climbed into the ring.

Marco kicked the spare gloves over to him and Dillon said, "A good lad in a pub brawl, but this could be the death of him."

Rory went in hard and actually took Marco's first punch, slipping one in himself that landed high on the Sicilian's right cheek. Marco feinted, then punched him again in the side, but again, Rory rode the punch and hit him again on the right cheek, splitting the skin. Marco stepped back, touched his glove to his cheek, and saw the blood. There was rage in his eyes now as he came on, head down, and punched Rory in the ribs, once, twice, and then a third time.

"He'll break bones before he's through," Dillon said.

Ferguson nodded. "And that young fool won't lie down."

Rory swayed, obviously in real pain, and Marco punched him in the face several times, holding his head with one gloved hand. The crowd roared their disapproval at such illegality and Marco, contemptuous of them, stepped back and measured Rory for a final punch as he stood there swaying and defenseless.

"Oh, God, no!" Hannah cried.

Dillon slipped through the ropes, stepped between Marco and Rory, and held his hand out palm first to the Sicilian. "He's had enough."

He turned, took Rory's weight, and helped him to his corner, taking off his gloves and easing him down through the ropes to his father and willing hands. "If I was thirty years younger I'd do for that bastard myself," Munro said in Gaelic.

"Well you're not."

Dillon turned and found Marco standing looking at him, gloved hands on hips. "You fancy some too, you Irish dog?" he said in Italian.

"That could be arranged," Dillon replied in the same language.

"Then get your gloves on."

"Who needs them." Dillon kicked them out of the ring. "With gloves I can't hurt you."

It was deliberate baiting and Marco fell for it. "Delighted to oblige."

"No, Dillon, no!" Asta called. "He'll kill you."

In motion be like water, that's what Yuan Tao had taught him. Total calm, complete control. This was no longer a boxing match and Marco had made a bad error.

The Sicilian came in fast and swung a punch, Dillon swayed to one side, stamping at the left kneecap, pivoted, and struck Marco in the side, screwing the punch as Yuan Tao had shown him. Marco cried out in agony and Dillon struck him again in the same manner and then turned his back, delivering a reverse elbow strike, smashing Marco's mouth.

The crowd roared and Dillon walked away, and Marco, with amazing resilience, went after him like a wild man and as Dillon turned, punched him under the left cheek. Dillon was flung back by the assault, bounced off the ropes and fell over, and Marco kicked him in the ribs.

The crowd was going wild now and Dillon rolled away rapidly and got to his feet. "Jesus, son, this is getting to be a bore," he said, and as Marco swung another punch, he grabbed the Sicilian's right wrist, swung it round until the elbow locked, and ran him headfirst through the ropes and out of the ring to fall on his face in front of Ferguson, Morgan, and the two women.

As Marco rolled onto his back, Dillon vaulted the ropes and put a foot on his neck. "You lie still now, like a good dog, or I'll break it."

Morgan said in Italian, "Leave it, Marco, I order you." He held out the man's jacket and turned to Dillon. "You are a remarkable man, my friend."

"A hero." Asta clutched his arm.

"No he's not, he's a bloody fool," Ferguson said. "Now let's go to the refreshment tent, Dillon, I really think we've earned a drink after that little lot," and he turned and led the way through the crowd of well-wishers, all eager to pat Dillon on the back.

It was reasonably quiet in the marquee, most people preferring to take advantage of the good weather. Ferguson went to the bar, which was laid out on a large trestle table. Dillon and Hannah sat at another of the tables and she took out her handkerchief and soaked it in the jug of water on the table. "Dillon, it's split. I think you're going to need stitches."

"We'll see. I can't feel a thing at the moment."

"Well, hold that handkerchief to it for a while."

"Better to let it dry up." He lit a cigarette.

"And you're slowly killing yourself with those things."

"A Fascist, that's what you are. It'll be booze you're banning next, then sex." He grinned. "Nothing left."

"I always thought you had a death wish," she told him, but she was smiling.

Ferguson came back with drinks on a tray. "Scotch for us, gin and tonic for you, Chief Inspector."

"I'd rather have tea, sir, and it wouldn't do Dillon any harm either," and she got up and went to the refreshment bar.

"I knew it," Ferguson said. "When that girl marries she'll be one of those Jewish mothers you read about, the kind who rules her husband with a rod of iron and tells everybody what to do."

"Jesus, Brigadier, but you must be getting old. I've news for you. There's many a man would happily join the queue to be ruled with a rod of iron by Hannah Bernstein."

At that moment, Asta appeared in the entrance, looked around, saw them, and came over. "There you are."

She sat down and Dillon said, "Where's Morgan?"

"Taking Marco down to the local hospital at Arisaig. He thinks you may have broken a rib. I said I'd make my own way back to the castle."

"What perfectly splendid news," Ferguson said.

Hannah joined them with a tray piled with cups and two teapots. "I saw you coming," she told Asta. "Help yourself."

Asta laid the cups and saucers out on the table as Hannah poured. "Wasn't Dillon wonderful?"

"I suppose it depends on your point of view."

"Oh, come now, Chief Inspector, that wretched man had it coming, deserved every minute of it."

Hector Munro came in and went to the bar. As they watched he purchased half a bottle of whiskey and turned to leave. He saw them sitting there, hesitated, and came over.

"Ladies," he said politely and then to Dillon in Gaelic, "You'll be expecting my thanks, I'm thinking?"

"Not really," Dillon said in Irish. "How is he?"

"The hard head, that one, but that bastard hurt him." He grinned suddenly. "Mind you, you're a bit of a bastard yourself, Mr. Dillon."

He walked away and Asta said, "Was that Gaelic?"

"That's right and I used Irish. They're very similar."

"Was he thanking you for saving his son?" Hannah asked.

Dillon smiled. "He never thanked anyone in his life, that one."

Someone called, "There you are," and as they turned, Lady Katherine came through the crowd, leaning on her stick, Jeannie holding her other arm.

"My dear lady." Ferguson got up. "I'm amazed to see you and in all this crowd of people."

Jeannie helped her into a seat and Lady Katherine said, "I have to put in an appearance, they expect it, you know." She turned to Dillon. "I saw you from a distance over the heads of the crowd. Rather a nasty business and hardly sporting. My goodness, he made a mess of your face."

"True, ma'am, but he looks worse," Dillon said.

She smiled and turned to Ferguson. "I really must go, can't afford to overdo it, but I've been thinking."

"Thinking, Lady Katherine?"

"Yes, the Bible. I've had a thought. Why don't you drop in on your way home? I'll discuss it with you." She pushed herself up. "Come on, Jeannie, let's make a move. Goodbye all."

She moved away through the crowd leaning on Jeannie's arm and Hannah said, "Now there's a turn-up for the book."

"It certainly is," Ferguson said. "Frankly I can't wait to hear what she's got to say. What do you think, Dillon?"

Dillon lit a cigarette, frowning. "Whatever it is, it's going to be special. I don't think she's going to say look at the back of the third drawer down in the writing desk in the study or anything like that." He nodded slowly. "No, something we haven't even thought of."

"And neither has Carl." Asta turned to Ferguson. "Can I come too, Brigadier? I'd love to see you steal a march on him."

Ferguson smiled. "Of course, my dear, why not? After all, you are on our side now."

Dillon drove the Range Rover on the way to Loch Dhu Castle. Before leaving the fair he'd visited the first-aid tent, and now sticking plaster adorned his right cheek, although the lady on duty from the St. John's Ambulance Brigade had advised him to seek proper medical attention.

"Are you all right, my boy?" Ferguson asked as they got out in front of the gate lodge.

"I'm fine, just forget it," Dillon grinned. "It's all in the mind."

Ferguson knocked on the door and Jeannie opened it after a few moments. "Her ladyship is in the drawing room."

Ferguson led the way in. Lady Katherine sat in a chair by the fire, a rug over her knees. "Ah, there you are. Come in, sit down. Tea and biscuits, Jeannie, and open the French windows. It's far too close in here."

"Certainly, your ladyship." Jeannie did as she was told.

Everyone settled down, Dillon leaned on the piano and lit a cigarette. "This is nice," he said.

"You can give me one of those cancer sticks, young man, and pass around that photo in the silver frame on the end of the piano."

"Certainly, ma'am." He did as he was told, lit the cigarette, and went and got the photo. It showed a young woman in an RAF flying jacket and helmet of Second World War vintage standing beside a Spitfire. It was quite obviously Lady Katherine.

"You look like some film star in one of those old war films," he said and passed it to Ferguson.

The Brigadier smiled. "Amazing, Lady Katherine, truly amazing," and he handed it to Hannah and Asta, who were sitting together on the couch.

"Yes, those were the days. They gave me the M.B.E., you know. Telling you about it at dinner last night brought it all back. I started thinking about it all in the early hours today, couldn't sleep, you see. So many amazing incidents, all those brave women who died, and I suddenly recalled a rather strange affair. A wonderful flier called Betty Keith-Jopp was piloting a Barracuda over Scotland when she ran into bad weather. Landed in the Firth of Forth and sank forty feet. She got out and made the surface all right. Was picked up by a fishing boat."

"Amazing," Ferguson said, "but what has that to do with the Bible?"

She said patiently, "Because thinking of that reminded me of the Lysander that crashed into Loch Dhu while trying to land at Ardmurchan RAF base. You see I've remembered now, that was the plane carrying my brother's belongings."

It was nineteen forty-six, March as I recall. I should tell you that besides the injury to his brain in that terrible crash in India, my brother sustained some quite severe burns to his right arm and hand so when he was thought fit enough he was transferred to a place called East Grinstead."

"Now that I do know about," Ferguson said. "It was the unit pioneered by Archibald McIndoe. He specialized in plastic surgery for aircrew who'd suffered severe burns."

"A wonderful man," she said. "His patients weren't always RAF. My brother, for instance."

"What happened?" Dillon asked her.

"Ian suffered a serious relapse that needed further brain surgery. Jack Tanner was with him still acting as his batman. Anyway, they gave up on him, expecting him to die at any time."

"So?" Ferguson said.

"At that time he had a visitor, an RAF officer who'd been a fellow patient for some months, but was now returned to duty, a Wing Commander Smith—Keith Smith. I believe he rose to some very senior rank later. It turned out that he had been given command of the RAF station on the Island of Stornaway in the Outer Hebrides and was due to fly up there in a Lysander, piloting himself."

"A Lysander?" Asta asked. "What kind of plane was that?"

"It was a high, wing-braced monoplane, a wheels-down job. Flew them myself many times. Room for a pilot and a couple of passengers. They could take off or land on quite a small field."

Ferguson managed to restrain his impatience. "I see, but where does Wing Commander Smith fit in?"

"Well if he was flying to Stornaway his course would take him right over here, you see, and Ardmurchan RAF base was still operational. As it seemed as if my brother was about to die, he told Jack Tanner that if he gathered all Ian's belongings together, he'd take them with him, land at Ardmurchan, and drop them off. He would then refuel and fly on to Stornaway."

"My God," Hannah Bernstein sighed. "I see it all now."

Lady Katherine carried on. "I was at home at the time on leave. The weather was very bad, a thunderstorm and low cloud. I didn't see it happen, I mean it was all so quick. He lost his engine on the final approach across the loch and ditched. It went down like a stone, but he just managed to get out with his dinghy."

There was silence and it was Asta who spoke. "It makes sense now. When Tanner was talking to Tony Jackson at Our Lady of Mercy Hospital he told Jackson that he sent all the Laird's belongings home because he thought he was going to die."

"And Jackson asked him if the Bible had gone back to Loch Dhu," Dillon put in.

"And Tanner said, 'You could say that,' and then according to Jackson he started to laugh." Hannah nodded slowly. "I always did wonder about that."

"Well all is certainly revealed now." Ferguson turned to Lady Katherine. "No attempt at recovery?"

"They didn't have the equipment. Keith Smith came to see me, of course, lovely man. Strange thing about him. He hadn't been in fighters or bombers. He joked about being a transport pilot, but he had a DSO and two DFCs. I often wondered about that. No, as I say, they left the Lysander down there. Checked out its position and so forth, or so he told me." She smiled. "So there you go. Poor old Ian's Bible is down there at the bottom of the loch in one of his suitcases, if there's anything left, of course. Now let's have some more tea."

"We've taken up enough of your time, dear lady," Ferguson told her.

"Nonsense, I insist." She rang the bell for Jeannie.

Ferguson nodded to Dillon and walked to the French windows and Dillon followed him. As they moved out onto the terrace, Ferguson said, "We've got to move fast now. I'll call in the Lear and I want you and the Chief Inspector to get down to London and check this out with RAF records."

Dillon put a hand on his arm, frowning, and Ferguson turned to find Angus close to the wall, ivy on the ground at his feet, pruning shears in his hand.

"Why, Angus, it's you," Ferguson said. "Have you been there long?"

"Just doing some pruning, sir. I'm finished now." He hurriedly bundled the clippings up, dumped them in his barrow, and wheeled it away.

Hannah appeared in the open window, Asta at her shoulder. "Do you think we were overheard?" Hannah asked.

"Of course we were," Dillon told her. "That's what the bastard was doing there. He'll go straight to Morgan."

"Undoubtedly." Ferguson turned to Asta. "When you see Morgan you must cover yourself by telling him everything, it will strengthen your position. Do you understand?"

"Yes," she nodded.

"Good." He looked at his watch. "Three o'clock. If I contact the office now they'll have the standby Lear take off at once. Priority with air traffic control, so no delays." He shrugged. "Should be here by five at the latest. Immediate turnaround and back to London."

"And then?" Dillon said.

"Check RAF records and try to establish details of the Lysander's position and procure the right equipment for a search." He smiled. "It looks as if you're going diving again, Dillon."

"So it would seem," Dillon said.

Ferguson turned and went inside and they heard him say, "I was wondering, dear lady, if I might use your telephone?"

TWELVE

It was a good two hours later that Asta saw the Shogun draw up in front of the house and Morgan and Marco got out. One side of the Sicilian's face was covered by a dressing and tape. Angus was lurking near the house and he hurried forward as Morgan and Marco started up the steps. They talked for quite a long time and then Morgan took out his wallet and passed several notes across. He started up the steps again with Marco, and Asta eased back into the study and sat by the fire.

The moment the door opened and Morgan entered, she jumped up and ran to him. "Thank God, you're back. Is Marco all right?"

"They took an X ray. A couple of cracked ribs, but they're only hairline and he's had stitches in his face."

"Dillon needs stitches too," she said.

"You saw him?"

"All of them, Carl. Lady Katherine invited us back for tea and came up with some sensational news."

"Really?" he said and reached for a cigar. "Tell me."

When she was finished he paced across to the window and back again. "That's it, it's got to be."

"So what are you going to do?"

"Wait, my love, let them do all the work, Dillon's a master diver, remember. If they can position that plane, he'll go down and bring up what's inside."

"And then?"

"We'll take it from there. I'll have the Citation standing by at Ard-murchan so we can get out of here fast."

"And you think Dillon and Ferguson will just stand by and let you take it?"

"I'll handle it, Asta."

There was the sound of a plane taking off on the other side of the loch and they went to the terrace in time to see the Lear in the distance lifting into the early evening sky.

"There they go." He smiled and put an arm about her shoulders. "I feel good about this, Asta, it's going to work."

"Of course, the document could have rotted away by now," she said, "down there in the water."

"True," he said, "but hidden in that Bible I don't think so." He smiled. "Trust me."

In the Lear, Dillon sat on one side of the aisle facing Hannah, who sat on the other. "Exciting, isn't it?" he said. "Never a moment's peace."

"It's worse than Scotland Yard," she said.

He reached for the bar box and found a miniature of whiskey, which he poured into a plastic cup and added water. "All the comforts of home."

"The water on its own would be better for you, especially at this height in an airplane, Dillon."

"Isn't it terrible," he said. "I never could do the right thing."

She settled back. "So what happens now?"

"We find out what we can about the crash of that Lysander and so on."

"RAF records from those days may be hard to uncover."

"Yes, well it was Air Ministry in those days and now it's Ministry of Defence where you work yourself, so if you can't trace them, who can?" He grinned. "Power, Hannah Bernstein, that's what it's all about. Better get on the phone and start them moving at the Information Centre."

"No, that comes second," she said, and reached for the phone. "First we get your face fixed."

"God help me," Dillon said. "The mother I never had," and he folded his arms and closed his eyes.

They had a tailwind so strong that they made Gatwick in an hour and twenty minutes and it was only an hour after that at approximately seven-thirty that Dillon found himself lying on his back in a small theater at the London Clinic while Professor Henry Bellamy sat beside him and stitched the split in the left cheek.

"Doesn't hurt?" he asked.

"Can't feel a thing," Dillon said.

"Well you damn well ought to." Bellamy dropped the needles into the pan the nurse held out to him. "Major surgery at the highest level, I do some of my best work, even wrote a paper on your case. They published it in the *Lancet*."

"Marvelous," Dillon said. "I'm immortalized for posterity."

"Don't be silly." Bellamy swabbed the line of stitches, then put a length of plaster along them. "I put you together again and then you go off and try to commit suicide."

Dillon swung his legs to the floor, stood and reached for his jacket. "I'm fine now. You're a bloody medical genius, so you are."

"Flattery will get you nowhere, just pay your bill and if you feel like telling me the secret of your remarkable recovery sometime, I'd love to know."

They went out into the corridor where Hannah Bernstein waited. "Six stitches, Chief Inspector, that'll spoil his beauty."

"You think that would bother this one?" Dillon asked.

Hannah pulled down the collar of his jacket, which was standing up. "He drinks whiskey of the Irish variety and smokes far too many cigarettes, Professor, what am I to do with him?"

"She didn't tell you I also play cards," Dillon said.

Bellamy laughed out loud. "Go on, get out of here, you rogue, I have work to do," and he walked away.

The night duty clerk at the Information Centre at the Ministry of Defence usually had little to do. She was a widow called Tina Gaunt, a motherly-looking lady of fifty whose husband, an army sergeant, had died in the Gulf War. She was rather sweet on Dillon, had seen his confidential report, and while horrified at his IRA background had also been secretly rather thrilled.

"Second World War RAF records and the National Service period after the war are still available in the Hurlingham Cellars, as we call them, but they're out in Sussex. We do have a microfiche availability on the computer, of course, but it's usually more of an outline than anything else. I may not be able to help."

"Sure and I can't believe that of a darling woman like yourself," Dillon told her.

"Isn't he terrible, Chief Inspector?" Tina Gaunt said.

"The worst man in the world," Hannah told her. "Let's start with this service record. Wing Commander Keith Smith."

"Right, here goes." Her fingers went to work nimbly on the keys and she watched the screen, then paused, frowning. "Wing Commander Smith, D.S.O., D.F.C. and Bar, Legion of Honour. My goodness, a real ace." She shook her head. "I don't understand. My father was a Lancaster bomber pilot during the war. It's always been a bit of a hobby of mine, all those Battle of Britain pilots, the great aces, but I've never heard of this one."

"Isn't that strange?" Hannah said.

Tina Gaunt tried again. She sat back a moment later. "Even stranger, there's a security block. Just his rank and his decoration, but no service record."

Hannah glanced at Dillon. "What do you think?"

"You're the copper, do something about it."

She sighed. "All right, I'll telephone the Brigadier," and she went out.

Tina Gaunt stood with the phone to her ear and nodded. "All right, Brigadier, I'll do it, but you see my back's covered." She put the phone down. "The Brigadier's assured me that he'll have a grade-one warrant on my desk signed by the Secretary of State for Defence tomorrow. Under the circumstances, I've agreed to cut corners."

"Fine," Dillon said, "let's get moving then."

She started on the keyboard again and once again sat back frowning. "I'm now cross-referenced to SOE."

"SOE? What's that?" Hannah demanded.

"Special Operations Executive," Dillon told her. "Set up by British Intelligence on Churchill's orders to coordinate resistance and the underground movement in Europe."

"Set Europe ablaze, that's what he said," Tina Gaunt told them and tapped the keys again. "Ah, it's all explained."

"Tell us," Dillon said.

"There was a squadron at Tempsford, one-three-eight Special Duties. It was known as the Moonlight Squadron, all highly secret. Even the pilots' wives thought their husbands just flew transports."

"And what did they do?" Hannah asked.

"Well they used to fly Halifax bombers painted black to France and drop agents by parachute. They also flew them in in Lysanders."

"You mean landed and took off again in occupied territory?" Hannah said.

"Oh, yes, real heroes."

"So now we know how Wing Commander Keith Smith won all those medals," Dillon said. "When did he die?"

She checked her screen again. "There's no date for that here. He was born in nineteen-twenty. Entered the RAF in nineteen thirty-eight aged eighteen. Retired as an Air Marshal in nineteen seventy-two. Knighted."

"Jesus," Dillon said. "Have you an address for him?"

She tried again and sat back. "No home address and, as I said, the information on the fiche is limited. If you wanted more, you'd have to try the Hurlingham Cellars tomorrow."

"Damn," Dillon said. "More time to waste." He smiled. "Never mind, you've done well, my love, God bless you."

He turned to the door and Hannah said, "I've had a thought, Tina, do you know about this place they had in East Grinstead during the war for burns patients?"

"But they still do, Chief Inspector, the Queen Victoria Hospital. Some of their wartime patients go back every year for checkups and further treatment. Why?"

"Smith was a patient there. Burned hands."

"Well I can certainly give you the number." Tina checked the computer, then wrote a number on her notepad, tore it off, and passed it across.

"Bless you," Hannah said and followed Dillon out.

In Ferguson's office, it was quiet and she sat on the edge of his desk, the phone to her ear, and waited. Finally she got her answer.

"I see. Air Marshal Sir Keith Smith," an anonymous voice said. "Yes, the Air Marshal was here for his annual check in June."

"Good, and you have his home address?" Hannah started to write. "Many thanks." She turned to Dillon. "Hampstead Village, would you believe that?"

"Everything comes full circle." Dillon glanced at his watch. "Nearly half-ten. We can't bother the ould lad tonight. We'll catch him in the morning. Let's go and get a snack."

They sat in the Piano Bar at the Dorchester drinking champagne and a waitress brought scrambled eggs and smoked salmon.

"This is your idea of a snack?" Hannah said.

"What's wrong with having the best if you can afford it? That thought used to sustain me when I was being chased through side streets and the sewers of the Bogside in Belfast by British Paratroopers."

"Don't start all that again, Dillon, I don't want to know." She ate some of her smoked salmon. "How do you think we'll fare with the good Air Marshal?"

"I would imagine rather well. Anyone who could win all those medals and rise to the rank he did has got to be hot stuff. My bet is he's never forgotten a thing."

"Well, we'll find out in the morning." The waitress brought coffee and Hannah took out her notebook. "You'd better give me a list of the diving equipment you're going to need and I'll get them started on it at the office first thing."

"All right, here goes. The suppliers will know what everything is. A mask, nylon diving suit, medium, with a hood because it'll be cold. Gloves, fins, four weight belts with twelve pounds in the pockets, a regulator, buoyancy control device, and half a dozen empty air tanks."

"Empty?" she said.

"Yes, we're flying rather high. You'll also get a portable Jackson Compressor, the electric type. I'll fill the tanks using that and an Orca dive computer."

"Anything else?"

"Three hundred feet of nylon rope, snap links, a couple of underwater lamps, and a big knife. That should take care of it. Oh, and a couple of Sterling submachine guns, the silenced variety." He smiled. "To repel boarders."

She put the notebook in her handbag. "Good, can I go now? We've got a big day tomorrow."

"Of course." They moved to the door and he paused to pay the bill. As they went out into the foyer, he said, "You wouldn't consider stopping at Stable Mews on the way?"

"No, Dillon, what I'd really like to do is surprise my mother."

Ferguson's driver eased the Daimler into the curb, the Head Porter opening the door for her. "I think that's marvelous," Dillon said. "It shows such an affectionate nature."

"Stuff you, Dillon," she said and the Daimler drew away.

"Taxi, sir?" the porter asked.

"No, thanks, I'll walk," Dillon said and he lit a cigarette and strode away.

The house was in a quiet backwater not far from Hampstead Heath. It was just nine-thirty the following morning when Dillon and Hannah arrived in Ferguson's Daimler. The chauffeur parked it in the street and they went in through a small gate in a high wall and walked through a small garden to the front door of a Victorian cottage. It was raining slightly.

"This is nice," Hannah said as she rang the bell.

After a while it was opened by a middle-aged black woman. "Yes, what can I do for you?" she asked in a West Indian accent.

"We're from the Ministry of Defence," Hannah told her. "I know it's early, but we'd very much like to see Sir Keith if that's possible."

"Not too early for him." She smiled. "He's been in the garden an hour already."

"In this rain?" Dillon asked.

"Nothing keeps him out of that garden. Here, I'll show you." She took them along a flagged path and round the corner to the back garden. "Sir Keith, you've got visitors."

She left them there and Hannah and Dillon walked to a small terrace with open French windows to the house. On the other side of the lawn they saw a small man in a rainproof anorak and an old Panama hat. He was pruning roses. He turned to look at them, his eyes sharp and blue in a tanned face that was still handsome.

He came forward. "Good morning, what can I do for you?"

Hannah got her ID out and showed it to him. "I'm Detective Chief Inspector Hannah Bernstein, assistant to Brigadier Charles Ferguson of the Ministry of Defence."

"And my name is Dillon, Sean Dillon." The Irishman held out his hand. "I work for the same department."

"I see." The Air Marshal nodded. "I'm familiar with Brigadier Ferguson's work. I served on the three services joint security committee for five years after I retired. Am I to assume this is a security matter?"

"It is indeed, Sir Keith," she said.

"But it goes back a long way," Dillon told him. "To when you crashed a Lysander into Loch Dhu in the Scottish Highlands back in nineteen forty-six."

The old man said in astonishment, "That *is* going back a bit. You'd better come inside and I'll get Mary to make some tea and we can talk about it," and he led the way in through the French windows.

That was so long ago," Sir Keith said. His housekeeper brought tea in on a tray. "That's all right, Mary," he told her. "We'll manage."

"I'll pour, if I may," Hannah said.

"Of course, my dear. Now what is it you want exactly?"

"You met a Major Ian Campbell at the East Grinstead burns unit," Dillon said.

"I certainly did." Sir Keith held up his hands. The skin was light and shiny and the middle finger was missing on the left one. "That was from a run-in with an ME262, that was the jet fighter the Germans did so well with at the end of things. February, nineteen forty-five. Blew me out of the sky over Northern France. I was in a Lysander you see, no contest."

"Yes, we checked your records at the Ministry of Defence," Dillon said. "Found out about your work for SOE. We had to pull strings for that. You're still classified."

"Am I, by God." He took the cup of tea Hannah offered and laughed.

"We got onto you through Ian Campbell's sister," Hannah said. "Lady Katherine Rose."

"Good Lord, is she still alive? Was an ATA pilot in the war. Wonderful woman."

"Yes, she still lives up there on the Loch Dhu estate," Dillon said. "It was she who told us about you coming down in the loch in a Lysander."

"That's right, March of forty-six, I was on my way to a new command at Stornaway, tried to land in damn bad weather at Ardmurchan and lost my engine on the approach. I was lucky to get out. The plane sank almost at once." He spooned sugar into his tea. "But why are you interested in that?"

"Do you remember calling in at East Grinstead and finding Ian Campbell on the point of death?" Hannah asked.

"That's right, though I heard he recovered later."

"You told his batman you were flying to Stornaway and offered to take his Laird's belongings and drop in at Ardmurchan."

"That's right, two suitcases, that was the reason I was going to land there anyway." He looked slightly bewildered. "But what's that got to do with it?"

"There was something of vital importance in one of those suitcases," she said. "Something of national importance."

"Good heavens, what on earth could it be?"

She hesitated. "Well actually, Sir Keith, the matter is classified. We're acting on the Prime Minister's instructions."

"Well you would be if Ferguson's involved."

Dillon turned to her. "Jesus, girl, he was decorated from here to Christmas, knighted by the Queen, and ended up an Air Marshal. If he can't keep a secret, who can?"

"Yes, you're right," she said. "Of course you are." She turned back to Sir Keith. "Strictly in confidence."

"My word on it."

So she told him about the Chungking Covenant, everything.

Sir Keith searched in the bottom drawer of a bureau, found an old cardboard file and a folded map which he brought across to the dining table.

"The file is a copy of the original accident report. There had to be a hearing, always is, but I was completely exonerated." He held up his hands. "The state of these never stopped me flying."

"And the map?" Dillon asked.

"See for yourself, Ordnance Survey map of the area. Large scale as you can see." He unfolded it. There was Loch Dhu, the castle, and Ardmurchan Lodge. "I was meticulous in noting my exact position when the Lysander went down. See the red line from the little jetty at Ardmurchan Lodge? That's where I landed."

Dillon ran a finger along the line. "That seems clear enough."

"One hundred and twenty yards south from the jetty. X marks the spot and I know I'm right because the boys from the base dragged for her with a grappling hook on a line and brought up a piece of fuselage."

"How deep?" Dillon asked.

"About ninety feet. The Air Ministry decided it wasn't worth trying to recover her. It would have meant sending up special equipment, and the war, after all, was over. They were scrapping aircraft, so why bother? Different thing if there had been something of value down there."

"Which there was, only nobody knew about it," Hannah said.

"Yes, there's irony for you." He turned to Dillon. "You intend some sort of recovery, I presume?"

"Yes, I'm an experienced diver. I'll go down and see what I can find."

"I shouldn't expect too much, not after all these years. Would you like the map?"

"I certainly would. I'll see you get it back."

Hannah said, "We've taken up enough of your time. You've really been more than helpful."

"I certainly hope I have. I'll see you out." He took them to the front door and opened it. "Forgive an old buffer like me, my dear, but I must say the police have improved since my day."

On impulse, she kissed him on the cheek. "It's been an honor to meet you."

"Good luck, the both of you, with this Morgan fellow. Make sure he goes down, Dillon, and give Ferguson my regards."

"I will," Dillon said and they went down the path.

"Oh, and Dillon?" Sir Keith called as they reached the gate.

They turned and Dillon said, "What is it?"

"If they're still there, you won't find two suitcases down there, there should be three and one of them's mine. Can't expect much after forty-seven years, but it would be fun to have it back."

"I'll see that you do," Dillon said and they went out.

They got in the back of the Daimler and Hannah said, "What an absolutely smashing man."

"Yes, they don't make them like that anymore," Dillon said. "Now what?"

"A place called Underseas Supplies located in Lambeth. They've got the order for those things you wanted. The manager said he'd have them ready by noon. He'd like you to check them out before he rushes them to Gatwick."

"And the two Sterlings I asked for?"

"In the boot. I got them from the armourer at the Ministry before I picked you up this morning."

"What a girl," Dillon said. "Let's get moving then."

The warehouse in Lambeth was crammed with diving equipment of every kind. The manager, a man called Speke, handled things himself and he and Dillon went through the list, checking each item off as they did so.

"There seems an awful lot," Hannah said. "Do you really need all this? I mean what's this thing?"

She held up a yellow colored Orca and Dillon said, "That's my lifeline, girl dear, a diving computer that tells me how deep it is, how long I've been down there, how long I've got to go. It even warns me if I'm coming up too fast."

"I see."

"I need it just like I need this." He picked up the heavy nylon diving suit in orange and green. "It's going to be very cold down there and very dark. It isn't the Caribbean."

"About the visibility, Mr. Dillon," Speke said. "The two lamps you asked for. I've given you the new Royal Navy halogen type. Twice the power."

"Excellent," Dillon said. "That's it then. Get this lot up to Gatwick as soon as you can."

"It'll take at least two hours, sir, maybe three."

"Just do your best," Hannah said.

As they got into the Daimler, Dillon said, "What kind of time do you think we'll get off?"

"Three o'clock," she said.

"Good." He took her hand. "You and I can take a little time off. What about Mulligan's for oysters and Guinness? After all, tomorrow I'll be diving down to God knows what."

"Dammit, Dillon, why not?" She laughed. "We've earned it. Oysters and Guinness at Mulligan's it is."

THIRTEEN

The flight from London Gatwick was reasonably smooth until the final stages when the weather deteriorated into low cloud and heavy rain. As they made their approach over the loch, Flight Lieutenant Lacey said over the loud speaker, "Headquarters have notified the Brigadier of our arrival time. He's on his way."

They dropped in for the touchdown and as they rolled along the runway they saw the Citation standing inside one of the hangars.

"Now what's that doing here?" Hannah said.

"I'd say it was on standby for a quick move out," Dillon said. "It makes sense. That's what I'd do."

As he opened the door for them Flight Lieutenant Lacey said, "You've got company, Chief Inspector."

"That's the personal plane of Mr. Carl Morgan presently of Loch Dhu Castle," Dillon told him.

"The polo player?"

"Jesus, son," Dillon laughed. "And isn't that the grand way to describe him?"

The Range Rover was crossing the decaying tarmac toward them, Kim at the wheel, Ferguson beside him. It stopped and the Brigadier got out. "Everything go well?"

"Couldn't be better," Dillon told him. "I've got a map of the loch with the exact location. By the way, guess who the pilot of that Lysander turned out to be?"

"Surprise me?"

"Air Marshal Sir Keith Smith," Hannah told him.

Ferguson looked genuinely astonished. "Of course! I didn't make the connection when Lady Katherine told us his name. I mean, nineteen forty-six, a wing commander."

Lacey said, "We'll get all this stuff in the back of the Range Rover, Brigadier, if your man could lend a hand."

"Of course." Ferguson nodded to Kim, then took a large golfing umbrella from inside the Range Rover and put it up against the rain.

"Morgan's plane seems to have taken up permanent residence," Hannah said.

"Yes, the bastard's there himself keeping an eye on us. I saw their Shogun parked in the hangar beside the Citation. Probably got their field glasses turned our way right now."

"Let's give them something to see then," Dillon said. "Pass me those two Sterling submachine guns, Flight Lieutenant."

Lacey handed them over and Ferguson smiled. "What a happy thought. Hold the umbrella for me, Chief Inspector." He checked one of the Sterlings expertly and then said, "Right, let's move out into the open so they can see what we've got."

Which he and Dillon did, standing in the rain for a few moments and then turning back to the Range Rover.

"That should do it," Dillon said and put the Sterlings on the backseat.

"You looked like a couple of little boys then playing gangsters in the school yard," Hannah said.

"Ah, if it were only so, Chief Inspector, but the time approaches when this whole thing becomes serious business. I've just, in a manner of speaking, given Morgan fair warning, but let's make certain. We'll take a walk."

He moved directly toward the hangar and the Citation and they moved with him, all three sheltered by the huge golfing umbrella. As they got close, they saw the Shogun, Marco and Morgan leaning against it. Two men in flying overalls were hanging around on the other side of the plane. Hannah slipped her right hand inside her handbag, which hung from a shoulder strap low on her thigh.

"No need for that, Chief Inspector," Ferguson murmured. "He isn't about to declare war just yet." He raised his voice. "Ah, there you are, Morgan. Good day to you."

"And a good day to you, Brigadier." Morgan came forward followed by Marco with his battered face, who stood there glaring at Dillon.

"Successful trip, Chief Inspector?" Morgan asked.

"Couldn't have been better," she told him.

"Who would have thought it?" He turned and looked out across the loch, quiet in the rain. "Down there on the bottom for all these years. Place of Dark Waters, isn't that what the locals call it in Gaelic? Aptly named, Dillon. I should think you'll have problems down there."

"Who knows?" Dillon told him.

"I see you've got your plane on standby," Ferguson said.

"Yes, leaving at the crack of dawn. We've got an eight o'clock start. Let's face it, Brigadier, you've won and I've certainly had enough of the delights of Loch Dhu Castle and this eternal bloody rain."

"Really?" Ferguson said. "Carl Morgan giving up? I find that difficult to believe."

"Oh, he's just being a good sport, aren't you, Morgan?" Dillon said.

"But of course," Morgan said calmly.

"Well, give our best to Asta as we probably shan't be seeing her again," Ferguson told him.

"I will."

"Good, we'll be off now."

As they walked back to the plane, Hannah said, "I don't believe a word of it. He isn't going anywhere."

"Or if he is he intends to come back," Dillon said. "I'm not sure how, but that's what he'll do."

"Of course he will," Ferguson said. "We're back with the kind of game playing that's characterized this affair from the beginning. We know that he intends to return and he knows that we know." He shook his head. "Inconceivable that he'd give up now. It's against his nature. Have you ever seen him boot an opponent out of the saddle in a polo match? Well that's Carl Morgan. He's always got to win whatever it costs."

"I'd say this is a situation Asta could help with, sir," Hannah said.

"Yes, well we'll see."

They reached the Lear and Lacey said, "All in, Brigadier, is there anything else we can do?"

"Not at the moment, Flight Lieutenant, except return to Gatwick. As usual, I require a twenty-four-hour standby."

"I'll see to it, Brigadier."

"Good, on your way then." He turned. "Come on, you lot. Let's move out."

They got into the Range Rover, Kim behind the wheel, and as they drove away, the Lear was already starting up behind them.

Morgan went into the study and poured himself a brandy, then moved to the fire. He sipped the brandy slowly, savouring it, and the door opened and Asta came in.

"They arrived back then, I heard the plane."

He nodded. "They unloaded a quantity of diving equipment and Ferguson and Dillon rather ostentatiously displayed a couple of Sterling submachine guns, all for my benefit. We had a nice chat."

"And?"

"I told Ferguson I was retiring from the fray, flying out at eight in the morning."

"And they believed you?"

He smiled. "Of course not. Ferguson knows damn well I'll return in some way. Of course, the important thing is that I know that he expects that, so it's all a question of timing."

"How do you mean?"

He smiled. "There's a bottle of champagne over there in the bucket, my love. Go and open it and I'll tell you."

At Ardmurchan Lodge, the light was on in the garage, the diving equipment arranged neatly on the floor. There was a steady hum from the compressor as Dillon showed Kim how to fill the first air tank.

Hannah came in and stood watching, arms folded. "Does he know what he's doing?"

"Kim?" Dillon laughed. "I've just shown him, haven't I, and you only show a Ghurka something once." He said to Kim, "All six."

"Yes, Sahib, I'll take care of it."

Dillon followed Hannah in through the side door and through the kitchen to the sitting room, where they found Ferguson sitting at the desk.

He glanced up. "All in order?"

"So far," Dillon said.

"Good, so the plan is simple. As soon as Morgan leaves in the Citation, we get to work. You hold the fort in the house, Chief Inspector, while Kim and myself go out with Dillon in the whale boat."

"Dillon, I'm totally ignorant about diving," she said, "so forgive my questions that seem stupid. Just how difficult will it be and just how long will it take?"

"Well, to start with, I'll go down very fast, my weight belt helps with that. If Sir Keith's positioning is accurate I could be onto the plane in minutes, but it's going to be dark down there and there's no way of knowing what the bottom's like. There could be ten feet of sludge. Another thing, the depth is important. The deeper you go the more air you use. It's astonishing how much ten or fifteen feet reduces your bottom line. Ideally, I'd like to do this dive within sport-diving limits, because if I can't, I'll have to decompress on the way up and that takes time."

"Why, exactly?"

"The deeper you go and the longer you're there, the more nitrogen you get in your bloodstream. It's like fizz in a bottle of champagne wanting to burst out. It can give you the bends, cripple you, and sometimes kill you." He smiled. "Here endeth the lesson."

"I must say it all sounds rather heavy to me."

"I'll be all right." He went and helped himself to a Bushmills. "I've had a thought though, Brigadier."

"What's that?"

"Have Kim up at the airstrip in the morning with a pair of field glasses. I mean, we'll hear that plane leave, but let's make sure it just doesn't have the pilots on board."

"Good idea," Ferguson said. He glanced at his watch. "Eleven o'clock. I've had an even better idea, Dillon, another of your little night forays up at the castle. See if you can have a word with Asta."

"I'm surprised we haven't heard from her," Hannah said.

"I'm not, too damn dangerous for the girl to use the phone, unless she's absolutely certain Morgan isn't around," Ferguson told her. "No, you take Dillon up there like you did the other night, Chief Inspector, and we'll see what happens."

It was still raining as Hannah turned in at the side of Loch Dhu Castle and switched off the engine. As on the previous occasion, Dillon wore black. He took out his Walther and tested it, then put it back into his waistband at the rear.

"Seems to me we've done this before."

"I know," Hannah smiled. "You'll have to think of a variation."

He pulled the sinister ski mask on, leaving only his eyes and lips visible. "I could always give you a kiss."

"While you're wearing that thing? Don't be disgusting, Dillon. Go on, on your way."

The door closed gently and he disappeared into the darkness in a second.

He negotiated the wall in the same way as before and made his way through the grounds to the lawn and paused in the trees, looking across at the lights of the castle. After a while, the French windows to the study opened and Morgan appeared smoking a cigar, followed by Asta wearing a sweater and slacks, an umbrella in her hand.

"What are you going to do?" Morgan demanded.

"Walk the dog. You can come too, Carl."

"In this rain? You must be crazy. Don't be too long," he told her and turned back inside.

She put the umbrella up and moved down the steps of the terrace.

"Come on, boy," she called and the Doberman came out of the study in a flash and hurried across the lawn.

There was a small summer house and Dillon moved to stand to one side of it. The dog stopped dead and whined. Dillon gave that peculiar low whistle and the dog bounded to his side and licked his hand gently.

"Where are you, boy?" Asta said.

"Over here," Dillon said softly.

"It's you, Dillon." She hurried forward and stood there, clutching the umbrella. "What are you up to this time?"

"Oh, I didn't want to let you go without a word," he said. "You are leaving in the morning, that's right, isn't it?" He pulled off his ski mask.

"Eight o'clock," she said.

"Yes, that's what Morgan told us at the airfield. So graceful in defeat he was. So bloody graceful that we didn't believe a word of it. He's coming back, isn't he, Asta?"

She nodded. "He didn't expect you to believe him, that's what he told me. He said you'd expect him to return so the only thing to get right was the timing."

"All right, tell me."

"We leave at eight in the Citation. Carl said he would anticipate you making the dive the moment we're on our way."

"Then what?"

"You know how far Arisaig is?"

"About twenty miles."

"Exactly. There's another ex-RAF airstrip there like Ardmurchan. He and Marco took the estate car down there and came back in the Shogun. The Citation will land there after leaving Ardmurchan. We'll come back by road in the estate car. The pilots will give it an hour, then fly back to Ardmurchan."

"Where we'll have been caught with our pants down?" Dillon said.

"Exactly."

"Oh, well, we'll have to see what we can come up with." He put a hand on her shoulder. "You're managing, are you?"

"Yes," she said, "I'm managing just fine."

"Good for you." He pulled on the ski mask. "Keep the faith," and he disappeared into the darkness.

Carl Morgan appeared on the terrace. "Are you there, Asta?"

"Yes, Carl, I'm coming," she said and went across the lawn, the umbrella raised, her hand in the dog's collar.

Kim was at the airstrip by eleven-thirty. He hadn't taken the car in case he was seen and lay on the edge of a small copse with a pair of field glasses and observed the Citation in the hangar. He could see the two pilots walking around doing their checks, and after a while, the Shogun appeared. It stopped just outside the hangar and Morgan and Asta got out. The two pilots came forward, there was a brief conversation, and they got the luggage out. As Morgan and Asta went into the hangar, Marco drove the Shogun inside.

Kim waited. After a while the engines fired and the Citation moved out into the open and taxied to the end of the runway, turning into the wind. He watched it race to the end of the runway and lift into the gray sky, then got up and ran back to the lodge.

Dillon had his diving suit on and was already pushing a wheelbarrow loaded with four air tanks down to the little jetty, where Hannah and Ferguson waited in the whaler. It was raining unmercifully and yet in spite of it there was a cloud of mist ten or twelve feet high rolling across the water, reducing visibility considerably. Ferguson wore an anorak and a rain hat, Hannah was wearing an old raincoat and trilby she had found in the cloakroom. There was a smaller rowing boat, several inches of water swishing around inside it.

As Hannah got out of the whaler to meet him he said, "Pull that one out of the way."

She did as he said, and as he started to pass the air tanks down to Ferguson there was the sound of the plane taking off. "There they go," Ferguson said.

"Right," Dillon told him. "I'll make do with the four tanks. With any kind of luck I won't need all of them. I'll get the rest of my gear."

He pushed the wheelbarrow back up to the lodge, loaded it with everything else including the two Sterlings. As he started back down to the jetty, Kim came out of the trees on the run. He caught up with Dillon just before he reached the whaler.

"You saw them go?" Ferguson demanded.

"Yes, Sahib, they arrived in the Shogun. I saw Morgan and the lady get out and go inside to the plane. The man, Marco, was there too. He drove the Shogun into the hangar. The plane came out and took off very quickly."

"You mean they got on inside the hangar?" Dillon said.

"Yes, Sahib."

Dillon frowned, pausing as he handed the rest of the gear down and Ferguson said, "You're worried."

"For some reason, yes."

"I can't see why. He himself told us he was going. We expected him to try and work a flanker on us and Asta told us exactly what he planned. And Kim did see them leave."

"He saw the plane leave," Dillon said. "But what the hell, let's get moving."

Kim jumped down into the whaler and Dillon passed everything down. Ferguson put the two Sterlings on the stern seat. "One thing is certain, dear boy, anyone who tried to take us on when we've got those things to repel boarders would have to be crazy."

"Let's hope so." Dillon handed Hannah up. "Now you take care."

She took a Walther from her pocket. "Don't worry, I've got this."

"Well I do worry, that's how I've lasted as long as I have."

He dropped into the boat, went to the stern, and started the outboard motor. Hannah unfastened the line and tossed it into the boat. "Good luck," she called as they eased away.

"Like I said, take care, the foolish one you can be on occasions, though lovable with it," Dillon called and took the whaler round in a broad curve.

Hannah watched them go, then turned and walked back up to the lodge. She went in the front door, took off the raincoat and the old trilby hat. She was cold and her feet were damp. She shivered, and decided to make a cup of coffee and went into the kitchen. She started to fill the kettle at the sink. There was a slight eerie creaking behind her. The larder door swung open and Hector Munro stepped out, a sawed-off shotgun in his hands.

And her Walther was in the raincoat. Ah God, Dillon, she thought, you're right, I am a fool. She turned and darted to the open kitchen door, straight into Rory Munro. Like his father he carried a sawed-off and he held her easily in one arm.

His face looked terrible, raw and bruised, but he smiled for all that. "And where would you be going, darling?"

He pushed her gently back into the room where Hector sat on the edge of the table filling his pipe. "Now be a good lassie and you'll come to no harm. There's a nice dry cellar for you, we've already checked."

"No windows to break out of, mind you," Rory said, "and an oak door with double bolts that you'd need a fire axe to break through."

"Aye," Munro told her. "You'll do well enough, not even a need to tie your wrists."

"See how lucky you are?" Rory said.

She stepped away from him and went to the other side of the kitchen to face them. "You're working for Morgan, aren't you? But why?" She gestured to Rory. "Remember what happened in the boxing ring. Look at what that animal Marco did to your son's face."

"But Mr. Morgan wasn't responsible for that, a bit of sport surely. My lad can take his knocks." The old man put a match to his pipe. "And then there is the question of the ten thousand pounds we're getting for helping him."

"What does he intend to do?"

"Ah well, you'll have to wait and see, won't you?" Hector Munro told her.

She took a deep breath. "I'm a police officer, did you know that?"

Rory laughed out loud and Munro said, "What bloody nonsense are you trying now, girl? Everybody knows you're secretary to the Brigadier."

"I can show you my ID, let me get it. I'm a Detective Chief Inspector at Scotland Yard."

"Detective Chief Inspector?" Munro shook his head sadly. "Events have turned her wits, Rory." He got up, walked to the cellar door and opened it. "Down with her."

Rory shoved her through, the door closed, the bolts rammed home. She lost her balance and slipped several steps, banging a knee painfully. And then she remembered the one thing she should have said, the one thing that might have had an effect.

Fergus.

She went up the steps, found the switch and turned it on, and light came on down in the cellar. She hammered on the door with clenched fists.

"Let me out," she called. "I've got something to tell you. He killed your son, he killed Fergus."

But by that time there was no one there to answer her.

Hector Munro and his son walked down toward the jetty in the rain. They could hear the whaler's outboard but couldn't see the boat itself because of the mist. They went along the jetty and paused beside the rowing boat.

"Dammit, there's nine inches of water in the bottom," Rory said.

"And a bucket under the seat for you to bale her out with, so get on with it." Hector took out an old silver watch on a chain and consulted it. "Not that we're in a hurry. We've got thirty minutes to wait, by my reckoning."

Rory had laid down the shotgun and got into the rowing boat, cursing as water slopped over his boots. He looked up into the rain. "By God, it's to be hoped Fergus has a roof of some sort over his head wherever he is."

"Never mind, he won't need to keep out of the way much longer, they'll all be away out of it," Hector Munro told him. "Now get on with it, boy."

Rory picked up the bucket and started to bale.

Ferguson took over the tiller while Dillon consulted the map. After a while the Irishman said, "It's got to be about here." He turned and could just see the chimneys of the lodge above the mist, the wood behind. "Yes, that's the line according to Sir Keith's notation on this map. Kill the engine." They almost stopped, drifting slowly, and he turned to Kim to find the Ghurka already putting the anchor over.

Dillon had cut the great coil of nylon rope into two lengths of one hundred feet with snap links on the ends. He tied a weight belt to each of them and turned to Kim, who was securing them round the center seat.

"Over we go," Dillon said and the Ghurka slipped them over.

Dillon pulled up the cowl of his diving suit, strapped the knife in its orange sheath to his leg. Then he assembled his equipment, clamping a tank to his inflatable. The Orca computer went out on the line of his air pressure gauge, then Kim helped him into the jacket, taking the weight of the tank until Dillon had strapped the Velcro wrappers across his chest. He fastened the weight belt around his waist, then pulled on his gloves. He sat down to get his fins on. It was all very awkward because of the size and shape of the boat, but that couldn't be helped. He got one of the lamps and looped it around his left wrist. He spat in his mask, leaned over and swilled it in the water, and pulled it on. Then he sat on the thwart, checked that the air was flowing freely through his mouth piece, waved at Ferguson, and went over backwards.

He swam under the keel of the boat until he found the anchor line, which, adopting the usual procedure, he followed down, pausing a couple of times to equalize the pressure in his ears by swallowing hard. To his surprise, the water was quite clear, dark, but rather like black glass.

He went feet first, hauling himself down the anchor line, aware of the other two lines they had put down close at hand. He checked his Orca computer. Forty, then suddenly sixty, seventy, seventy-five. It was darker there and he switched on the powerful lamp and there was the bottom.

It wasn't as he had expected, nothing like the silt he had looked for. Instead, large patches of sand in between a kind of seagrass, great fronds waving to and fro in the current at least six feet in length.

He hovered, checking the computer to see how long he had, then moved away from the anchor line, the beam of the halogen light splayed out in front of him, and there it was, a dark shadow at first, tilted up on its nose, tail high.

The Bristol Perseus engine was quite visible due to fuselage corrosion and the triple propeller was still there. The canopy had been pushed back, obviously when Sir Keith had got out fast after hitting the surface of the loch. There was a corrugated metal ladder leading up to the passenger section and beside it, the outline of RAF roundels.

Dillon went into the pilot's section headfirst. It was all still intact in a kind of skeleton form, the instrument panel, the control column. He turned and pressed into the passenger section. There were two seats, only the tubular construction remaining, leather and cloth long since rotted away.

The suitcases were there, as for some strange reason he had always known they would be. One was metal, the other two leather, and when he touched one of those, it started to crumble. He ran his hand across the metal one and the faint etching of a name appeared. There were three words. The first two were hopelessly faded, but when he rubbed with his gloved hand, the lamp held close, the name Campbell was plain.

He backed out, pulling the metal case out first, depositing it on the sand beside the Lysander, then he went back for the other two. The first one stayed reasonably intact, but the second seemed to come apart in his hand. When it burst open, he caught a brief glimpse of decaying clothes, some corroded toilet articles, what was left of an RAF sidecap, and the remnants of a tunic with RAF pilot's wings above medal ribbons. Keith Smith's case obviously. Dillon scrabbled in the detritus and came up with a blackened silver cigarette case. Something to take back to the old boy at least. He stuffed it into one of the pockets in his inflatable, then swam back to where the two down lines from the whaler dangled to the bottom. He fastened the case to one of the line's snap links, then returned to the metal case, brought it back with him, and fastened it to the end of the other line.

He paused, making sure that everything was in order, then started up, one foot a second.

Ferguson and Kim, waiting in the heavy rain, suddenly became aware of the sound of an engine. Quickly Ferguson picked up one of the Sterlings, handed it to Kim, and reached for the other himself. He cocked it quickly.

"Don't hesitate," he said to Kim. "If it's Morgan and the man, Marco, they'll kill us without the slightest hesitation."

"Have no fear, Sahib, I have killed many times as the Sahib well knows."

A voice called high and clear, "Is that you, Brigadier? It's Asta."

Ferguson hesitated and said to Kim, "Stay ready."

The Loch Dhu Castle boat, the *Katrina*, drifted out of the mist, Asta at the wheel in the deck house. She wore rubber boots, a white sweater, and jeans.

"It's only me, Brigadier, can I come alongside?"

"What on earth's going on?" Ferguson said. "Kim saw you leaving in the Citation."

"Oh, no," she said. "That was Carl and Marco. He told me to go back to the castle in the Shogun and wait for him. Did you see me go into the hangar, Kim?"

"Oh, yes, Memsahib."

"It was Morgan and Marco who boarded the plane. I drove back in the Shogun afterwards."

Kim turned to Ferguson and said awkwardly, "I am sorry, Brigadier Sahib, I left as the plane took off. I did not see the Memsahib drive away."

"Never mind that now." Ferguson put down the Sterling. "Take the line from the Memsahib and tie her boat alongside."

She switched off the engine and came to the rail. "Is Dillon down there now?"

"Yes, dropped in about fifteen minutes ago."

"How very convenient." The door to the saloon opened and Carl Morgan emerged, a Browning Hi-Power in his hand and Marco behind him holding an Israeli Uzi submachine gun.

FOURTEEN

At that precise moment Dillon broke through to the surface and floated there, looking up at them all. He raised his mask.

"Asta, what is this?"

"It means we've been had, I'm afraid," Ferguson said.

Dillon looked straight up at her. "You're on his side in spite of what he did to your mother?"

Morgan's face turned dark with anger. "I'll take pleasure in making you pay for that filthy lie. Asta told me all about it. I loved my wife, Dillon, more than anything in this life. She gave me the daughter I'd never had and you think I could have killed her?"

There was silence, only the sound of the rain hissing into the loch. Dillon said, "I'd say you're well suited to each other."

Morgan put an arm around her. "She did her work well telling you about my plan to fly to Arisaig, omitting the fact that we didn't actually intend to get on the plane. I knew one of you would be waiting, probably that man of yours, Ferguson, so we just stayed in the hangar until he'd gone. I saw him running off through the trees through my field glasses. Then all that was needed was Asta to pilot the boat while Marco and I stayed below and the poor old Brigadier fell for it, Dillon. Strange how I always get my way, isn't it?"

"Yes," Ferguson said, "I must say you have excellent connections. Probably with the Devil."

"But of course," Morgan raised his voice. "Are you there, Munro?"

"On our way in," Munro called and the rowboat appeared, Rory at the oars.

"What about the woman?"

"Locked her in the cellar."

They bumped against the hull of the motor cruiser and climbed on board.

Morgan looked down at Dillon. "So here we are at the final end of things. Did you find the plane?"

Dillon just floated there, staring up at him, and Morgan said, "Don't fuck with me, Dillon, if you do I'll blow the Brigadier's head off and that would be a pity because I've got plans for him."

"Really?" Ferguson said.

"Yes, you're going to love this. I'll take you back to Palermo with me and then we'll sell you to one of the more extreme Arab fundamentalist groups in Iran. You should fetch a rather high price. They'd love to get their hands on a British Intelligence officer as senior as you, and you know what those people are like, Ferguson, they'll take the skin off you inch by inch. Before they've finished you'll be singing like a bird."

"What a vivid imagination you have," Ferguson said.

Morgan nodded to Marco, who fired a burst from the Uzi into the water close to Dillon. "Now don't mess with me, Dillon, or I swear the next burst takes your boss apart."

"All right, I get the picture." Dillon put in his mouthpiece, pulled down his mask, and let himself sink.

He didn't bother with the anchor line, simply jack-knifed halfway down and continued headfirst, reaching the bottom to the left of the Lysander above a forest of waving fronds. When he turned on his lamp, the first thing he saw was Fergus Munro on his back, a length of chain wrapped around his body. His face was swollen and bloated, the eyes staring, but he was completely recognizable. Dillon hovered, looking down at him, then pulled out his knife and cut the rope that held the chain. The body bounced from the bottom and he got a grip on Fergus's jacket and towed the corpse back to the downlines.

He left it on the sandy bottom, untied the flimsier case and went and clipped it beside the metal case on the other line. Then he went back to the body, towed it across to the second downline and tied it on, winding the rope round the waist and fastening it with the snap link. Then he pulled on the line that secured the cases and started up.

Kim and Ferguson were still hauling the line in when Dillon surfaced. He floated beside the cases, untied the leather one, and passed it up to Kim. It was already falling apart and broke in the Ghurka's hands, spilling a mass of rotting clothes onto the deck.

"That's no bloody good," Morgan said, leaning over the rail and looking down into the whaler. "The other one, Dillon, the other."

Dillon pushed the metal suitcase against the hull and Ferguson and Kim reached over to get it. Dillon murmured, "If you get a chance to jump, I can give you air under the surface, but only one of you. In a minute I'll be going down again and I want you to haul in the other line, Kim, it's vital."

"Thanks for the offer," Ferguson whispered. "But I've never even liked swimming. What you suggest is a quite appalling prospect. Kim might feel differently."

"Hurry it up!" Morgan called.

They got the suitcase over and into the bottom of the whaler. The metal was blackened and streaked with green seaweed.

"Get it open," Morgan ordered.

Ferguson tried the clasps on the locks, but they were rigid. "Damn thing's corroded, won't budge."

"Well try harder."

Dillon pulled the knife from his leg sheath and handed it up to Kim, who forced it behind the two clasps in turn and ripped them off, then he worked the point of the knife under the edge of the lid and prised. Quite suddenly, the lid lifted. There were clothes inside, mildewed but in surprisingly good condition. There was a uniform tunic on top, still recognizable with Major's crowns on the epaulettes.

"Come on, damn you!" Morgan was intensely excited as he leaned over the rail. "Empty it out!"

Kim turned the case over, spilling its contents into the bottom of the whaler, and found it at once, a book-size package wrapped in yellow oilskin.

"Open it, man, open it!" Morgan ordered.

It was Ferguson who unwrapped the oilskin, layer by layer, until he held in his hand the Bible, its silver blackened by the years.

"It would seem to be what we've all been looking for," he said.

"Go on, get it open, see if it's still there."

Ferguson took the knife from Kim and ran its point along the inside of the front cover. The secret compartment flicked open, the folded document inside, immediately apparent. Ferguson unfolded it, read it, then he looked up, face calm.

"Yes, this would appear to be the fourth copy of the Chungking Covenant."

"Give it to me," and Morgan reached down. Ferguson hesitated and Marco raised the Uzi threateningly. "You can die now," Morgan said. "It's your choice."

"Very well." Ferguson passed up the document.

"Now get up here yourself," Morgan told him and turned. "As for you, Dillon . . ."

But Dillon had gone, dropping under the surface. Marco fired a futile burst into the water and Kim ducked and kept hauling on the line and suddenly Fergus Munro's body surfaced, a totally macabre sight.

"God help me, it's Fergus!" Hector Munro called, leaning over the rail. Rory joined him, staring down into the water. "What happened to him, Da?"

"Ask your friend Morgan. He and his henchman here beat him to death," Ferguson said.

"You bastards!" Hector Munro cried and he and Rory turned, their shotguns coming up too late as Marco raked both of them with a long burst from the Uzi, driving them over the rail into the water.

"Get out of it, Kim!" Ferguson cried and the Ghurka dived headfirst from the whaler into the dark water, pulling himself down with powerful strokes as Marco sprayed the water behind him.

There is a technique known as buddy breathing to any experienced diver by which, if there is no alternate source of air available, it is possible to share your air supply with a companion by passing the regulator back and forth between you.

Dillon, at twelve feet, reached up and caught Kim by the foot, pulled him close, took out his mouthpiece and passed it across. The hardy little warrior, a veteran of thirty years of campaigning, understood at once, took in a supply of air, then passed it back.

Dillon started to kick with his fins, making for the shore, pulling Kim along beside him and sharing the air supply as they went. After a while, he raised his thumb and started up, surfacing into a cocoon of mist, no sign of the boats at all. A moment later, Kim came up beside him, coughing.

Dillon said, "What happened after I dived?"

"When the body surfaced, the Munros went crazy. Marco shot both of them with the Uzi."

"And the Brigadier?"

"Cried to me to jump, Sahib."

Dillon could hear the motor cruiser moving away at high speed, but not across the loch in the direction of the castle.

"Where in the hell are they going?" he said.

"There is that old concrete jetty the RAF used just below the airstrip, Sahib," Kim told him. "Perhaps they're making for that."

"And a quick departure," Dillon said and at that moment there was a thunder of engines overhead as Morgan's Citation made its approaches.

Dillon said, "Right, we can't be far from the jetty, so let's get moving," and he made for the shore.

They landed ten minutes later. Dillon stripped off his equipment and ran toward the house, still wearing his diving suit, Kim jogging at his heels. The Irishman flung open the front door, ran into the study and opened the top drawer in the desk. There was a Browning in there. As he checked it, Kim came in.

"Sahib?"

"I'm going up to the airstrip. You get the Memsahib from the cellar and tell her what's happened."

He ran outside and cut across the back lawn. No point in taking the Range Rover, he'd be quicker on foot and the rubber and nylon diving socks he wore protected his feet. He ran into the wood, weaving in and out amongst the trees, aware that the engines of the Citation hadn't stopped. As he emerged from the wood, he could see it taxiing to the end of the runway and turning into the wind. At the same moment, Morgan and Asta, Marco holding the Uzi against Ferguson's back, came round the corner of the main hangar and started toward the Citation. Dillon stopped running and watched helplessly as they boarded. A moment later the Citation roared along the runway and lifted into the sky.

When Dillon arrived back at Ardmurchan Lodge and went in the door Hannah rushed to meet him. "What happened? I heard the plane taking off."

"Exactly. Morgan had it all worked out. He didn't even go back to the castle. Not a minute wasted. I arrived in time to see them boarding, he and Asta, Marco and the Brigadier. They took off straight away."

"I've been onto headquarters. I've asked them to check the flight plan they filed."

"Good. Get straight onto them again and order Lacey to get up here in the Lear like it was yesterday."

"I've ordered that too, Dillon," she said.

"Nothing like Scotland Yard training. I'm going to change."

When he returned he was wearing black jeans, a white polo neck sweater, and his old black flying jacket. Hannah was in the sitting room at Ferguson's desk, the telephone at her ear. Kim came in with a jug of coffee and two cups.

She put the phone down. "They were routed to Oslo."

"That makes sense. He wanted to be out of our air space fast. Then what?"

"Refueling, then onwards to Palermo."

"Well, that's what he said his intended destination was. He's taking the Covenant to Luca."

"And the Brigadier?"

"Didn't Kim tell you? He's going to sell him to some Arab fanatics or other in Iran."

"Can't we stop him in Oslo?"

Dillon looked at his watch. "The rate that thing goes he'll be just about landing. Can you imagine how long it would take to go through Foreign Office channels to the Norwegian Government? No chance, Hannah, he's long gone."

"Then that leaves the Italian Government, Palermo."

Dillon lit a cigarette. "The best joke I've heard in a long time. This is Don Giovanni Luca we're talking about, the most powerful man in Sicily. He has judges killed to order."

She was upset now and it showed, her face very pale. "We can't let them get away with it, Dillon, Morgan and that conniving little bitch."

"Yes, she was good, wasn't she?" He smiled bleakly. "She certainly fooled me."

"Oh, to hell with your damned male ego, it's the Brigadier I'm thinking of."

"And so am I, girl dear. You get back to headquarters and tell them you want to contact Major Paolo Gagini of the Italian Secret Intelligence Service in Palermo. He should be more than interested. After all, he's the one who brought the story of the Covenant to Ferguson in the first place. He's also the expert on Luca, according to the file you showed me. Let's see what he can come up with."

"Right, good thinking." She picked up the phone and got to work, and Dillon walked out to the terrace, lit a cigarette, and looked out into the rain, wondering about it.

He was aware of Hannah's voice on the phone, but was somewhere else, thinking of Ferguson and what would happen to him in Iran and that was too awful to contemplate. Strange, but it was only now in a situation like this that he realized he actually had a certain affection for the Brigadier. He also thought about Morgan with a kind of cold, killing rage, and as for Asta . . .

Hannah came to the open French windows. "I've got Gagini on the phone from Palermo. I've filled him in on the situation and he wants to speak to you."

Dillon went in and picked up the phone. "Gagini, I've heard good things about you," he said in Italian. "What can we do in this thing?"

"I've heard of you too, Dillon. Look, you know what the situation is like here. Mafia everywhere. If I get a court order, which would be difficult, it would take time."

"What about Immigration and Customs at the airport?"

"Half of them have Mafia connections, just like the police. Any move I make at an official level Luca will know about within fifteen minutes."

"There must be something you can do."

"Leave it with me. I'll phone back in an hour."

Dillon put the phone down and turned to Hannah. "He's calling back in an hour. He's going to see what he can do."

"This is nonsense," she said. "All they have to do is meet the damn plane with a police squad."

"Have you ever been to Sicily?"

"No."

"I have. It's another world. The minute Gagini makes an official request for the police to meet that plane, someone will reach for a phone to inform Luca."

"Even from police headquarters?"

"Especially from police headquarters, the Mafia's fingers reach everywhere. Scotland Yard it's not, Hannah. If Luca thought there was a problem he'd contact Morgan and tell him to go elsewhere, perhaps even tell him to fly direct to Teheran and that's the last thing we want."

"So what do we do?"

"We wait for Gagini to phone back," he said, turned, and went outside again.

And when Gagini did phone just under an hour later he sounded excited. "My sources tell me the Citation isn't booked to land at Palermo."

"They must have a flight plan even in Sicily," Dillon said.

"Of course, my friend, just listen. Carl Morgan has an old farmhouse inland from Palermo at a place called Valdini. He doesn't use it much. There's just a caretaker and his wife in residence. It's an old family property."

"So?" Dillon glanced at Hannah, who was listening on the extension.

"The thing is, Morgan had an airstrip laid out there the other year, probably to be used for drug deliveries. It's grass, but open meadow about a mile long, so it's perfectly adequate for the Citation to land."

"Are you saying that's what he intends to do?"

"That's what the flight plan says."

"But what about Customs and Immigration?" Hannah broke in.

"All taken care of by Luca, Chief Inspector."

Dillon said, "Can we get in?"

"I doubt it. That's real Mafia country. You couldn't pass through a village without being noted, every shepherd boy on a hill with his flock is like a sentry. Troop movements, as with the police, are an impossibility."

"I see," Dillon said.

There was a sudden roar as the Lear from Gatwick passed overhead to make its landing.

"What do you want me to do, my friend?"

"Let me think about it. Our plane has just arrived. I'll let you know. The only certain thing is that we'll be coming to Palermo."

He replaced the phone as did Hannah. "It doesn't sound too good, does it?" she said.

"We'll see. Now let's get out of here."

Lacey came along from the cockpit and crouched down. "An hour to Gatwick. We'll refuel and get straight off to Palermo."

"Good," Dillon said. "Speed is of the essence on this one, Flight Lieutenant."

Kim lay back in one of the rear seats, eyes closed. Hannah glanced back at the little Ghurka. "What about him?"

"We'll drop him at Gatwick. Nothing for him to do where I'm going."

"And where would that be?"

"Valdini obviously."

"But Gagini has just told us that would be impossible."

"Nothing's impossible in this life, Hannah, there's always a way." He reached for the bar box, found a half bottle of Scotch, poured himself a shot into a plastic cup, and sat there brooding.

About twenty minutes before they reached Gatwick, Lacey patched a call through which Dillon took. It was Gagini.

"An interesting development. I've got one of my undercover men working at the local garage near Luca's place. His driver came in to fill up the tank. Told the owner they were taking a run out to Valdini."

"That makes sense," Dillon said. "Everything coming together."

"So, my friend, have you had any thoughts on how to handle this?"

"Yes, what about flying in?"

"But they would be alerted the moment you tried to land."

"I'm thinking of something different. A story Ferguson told me once. He had a fella called Egan working for him and he needed to get down fast in a similar sort of situation. That was in Sicily too, about ten years ago."

"Of course, I remember the case, he parachuted in."

"That's right."

"But he was an expert at that kind of thing. He jumped at eight hundred feet, my friend."

"Well he would, wouldn't he, but I can do that. I've jumped before. I know my stuff, believe me. Can you lay on a plane, parachute, weapons, and so on?"

"That shouldn't be a problem."

"We'll see you at the airport then," Dillon said and put the phone down.

"What was all that about?" Hannah demanded, but at that moment the seat belt signs went on and they started to descend toward Gatwick.

"I'll tell you later," Dillon told her. "Now be a good girl and fasten your belt."

The stopover at Gatwick took only an hour. Hannah took Kim across to the small office the Special Flying Unit used and arranged a taxi.

"I would rather come with you, Memsahib."

"No, Kim, you go back to Cavendish Square and make things nice for the Brigadier."

"He will come back, Memsahib, you swear it?"

She took a deep breath and, against every conviction, lied to him. "He'll be back, Kim, I promise you."

He smiled. "Blessings on you, Memsahib," and he crossed to his taxi.

She found Dillon in the waiting room feeding coins into a sandwich machine. "Plastic food, but what can you do? Would you like something? Personally, I'm starving."

"I suppose so. Anything there is."

"Well, you won't want the ham so we'll make it tomato and boiled egg. There's tea and coffee on board. Come on."

As they walked out to the Lear, the fuel truck was just moving away. Lacey stood waiting, the co-pilot already on board.

"Ready when you are," the Flight Lieutenant said.

"We'll get moving then," Dillon told him and went up the steps behind Hannah.

They settled in their seats and a few minutes later the Lear started to taxi.

Dillon waited until they leveled off at thirty thousand feet, then made tea in the plastic cups. He sat there eating the sandwiches without saying anything.

Finally Hannah said, "You were going to tell me what you were going to do?"

"There was a fella called Egan worked for Ferguson a few years back, ex-SAS. He had a similar problem about getting somewhere fast and that was in Sicily too."

"How did he solve it?"

"Parachuted in from eight hundred feet from a small aircraft. At that height, you hit the ground in thirty seconds."

There was genuine horror on her face. "You must be mad."

"Not at all. As far as they're concerned it will be just a plane passing overhead, a bit low perhaps, but they won't be expecting what I have in mind, and it will be dark by then."

"And Major Gagini has agreed to this?"

"Oh, yes, he's arranging a suitable plane, equipment, weapons, everything. All I have to do is jump out of the plane. You can follow on and land in the Lear, say thirty minutes later."

He drank some of his tea and she sat there staring at him and then a curious expression appeared on her face. "When you were talking to Gagini I heard you say you'd jumped before. I wondered what you were talking about. It makes sense now."

"Well it would, wouldn't it."

"Except that for some strange reason I think you were lying to him. I don't think you've ever made a parachute jump in your life, Dillon."

He gave her his best smile and lit a cigarette. "True, but there's always a first time for everything, and you be a good girl now and don't speak a word about this to Gagini. I wouldn't want him changing his mind."

"It's madness, Dillon. Anything might happen. You could break your bloody neck, for one thing."

"Would you listen to the language, and you the decent girl?" He shook his head. "Can you think of an alternative? You have all the facts."

She sat there quiet for a moment, then sighed. "When you come right down to it, no."

"It's simple, my love, forget the Chungking Covenant and just think of Ferguson. Never tell him this, but I actually like the old sod, and I won't stand by and see him go to hell if I can prevent it." He leaned across and put a hand on hers and smiled, that special smile, nothing but warmth there and immense charm. "Now then, could you do with another cup of tea?"

They came in over the sea, Palermo on the port side, evening falling fast and already lights twinkled in the city. There were a few cumulus clouds in a sky that was otherwise clear and a half moon. They landed at Punta Raisi a few minutes later and Lacey, obeying orders from the tower, taxied to a remote area at the far end of the airport, where a number of private planes were parked.

The truck which had shown them the way drove off and Lacey killed the engines. There was a small man in a cloth cap and old flying jacket standing in front of the hangar and as Dillon and Hannah went down the steps, he came forward.

"Chief Inspector Bernstein? Paolo Gagini." He held out his hand. "Mr. Dillon, it's a real pleasure. Come this way. We believe Morgan landed at Valdini two hours ago, by the way. His Citation put down here a little while ago. It's over there being refueled, but it isn't going anywhere tonight. I saw the pilots leave the airport."

Dillon turned as Lacey and the co-pilot came down the ladder. "You'd better come too."

They went into the hangar and Gagini led them to a large, glass-walled office. "Here you are, my friend. Everything I could think of." There was a parachute, a Celeste silenced machine pistol, a Beretta pistol in a shoulder holster, a Walther and a bulletproof vest in dark blue, and a pair of infrared night glasses.

"Everything but the kitchen sink," Lacey said. "Are you going to war, Mr. Dillon?"

"You could say that."

"There's a camouflaged suit for you over here," Gagini told him, "and some Army jump boots. I hope to God they're the right size."

"Fine, I'll go and get changed," Dillon said. "If you'll point me to the men's room." He turned to Hannah. "You fill in the Flight Lieutenant and his friend while I'm gone," and he followed Gagini out.

And at that same moment at Valdini Luca's Mercedes sedan turned in through the gates in the wall and went up the gravel drive to park at the bottom of the steps leading up to the front door. As the driver helped Luca out, the front door opened and Morgan appeared and hurried down the steps.

"Don Giovanni."

They embraced. The old man said, "So you got it, Carlo, against all the odds? I'm proud of you. I can't wait to see it."

"Come, let's go in, Uncle," Morgan said and turned to the driver. "You stay here. I'll have them bring you something from the kitchen."

He helped Luca up the steps and into the house. Asta came out of the living room and put her arms around Luca at once and he kissed both her cheeks.

"Carl did it, Don Giovanni, isn't he clever?"

"Don't listen to her," Morgan said. "She played more than her part this time, believe me."

"Good, you must tell me about it."

He led the way into the living room where Ferguson sat by the log fire, Marco standing behind him, Uzi in hand.

"So, this is the redoubtable Brigadier Ferguson," Luca said, leaning on his stick. "A great pleasure."

"For you perhaps, but not for me," Ferguson told him.

"Yes, that's understandable." Luca eased himself down into a large chair opposite Ferguson and held out his hand. "Where is it, Carlo?"

Morgan took the document from his inside pocket, unfolded it, and passed it over. "The Chungking Covenant, Uncle."

Luca read it slowly, then looked up and laughed. "Incredible, isn't it?" He looked at Ferguson. "Think of the mischief I'll be able to make with this, Brigadier."

"Actually, I'd rather not," Ferguson told him.

"Come, Brigadier." Luca folded the Covenant and put it in his inside pocket. "Don't be a spoilsport. You've lost and we've won. I know you face an uncertain future, but surely we can be civilized about it." He smiled up at Morgan. "A nice dinner and a bottle of wine, Carlo. I'm sure we can make the Brigadier a happier man."

Dillon returned in the camouflage uniform and jump boots, picked up the bulletproof vest, and pulled it on. He checked the Walther and slipped it under the waistband at the back under the tunic, then tried the Celeste. Gagini had some large blow-up photos on the table which he was showing to the two RAF pilots and Hannah.

"What's this?" Dillon asked.

"Pictures of the farmhouse at Valdini taken from the air. I got them from drug squad files."

"Would you anticipate any problems landing there?" Dillon asked Lacey.

"Not really. That strip across the meadow is one hell of a length and that half-moon will help."

"Good." Dillon turned to Gagini. "What about a plane?"

"Navajo Chieftain waiting outside ready to go."

"And a good pilot who knows what he's doing?"

"The best." Gagini spread his arms wide. "Me, Dillon, didn't I tell you I was in the Air Force before I transferred to Intelligence work?"

"Well that's convenient. How long to get there?"

"With the Navajo's speed no more than fifteen minutes."

Dillon nodded. "Right. I need half an hour on the ground."

"Understood," Gagini nodded. "I'll come straight back here and join the others in the Lear. By the time we're landing at Valdini it should be just about right. I'll go and get the engines fired up."

Dillon said to Lacey, "I'll leave you that Beretta in the shoulder holster, just in case." He picked up the parachute. "Now show me how to put this on."

Lacey looked shocked. "You mean you don't know?"

"Don't let's argue about it, Flight Lieutenant, just show me."

Lacey helped him buckle the straps, pulling them tight. "Are you really sure about this?"

"Just show me what to pull," Dillon said.

"The ring there and don't mess about, not at eight hundred feet. The Navajo has an Airstair door. Just go down it, fall off, and pull on that ring straight away."

"If you say so." Dillon picked up the Celeste machine pistol and slung it across his chest and hung the night glasses around his neck. He turned to Hannah. "Well, are you going to kiss me goodbye?"

"Get out of here, Dillon," she said.

"Yes, ma'am."

He gave her a mock salute, turned, and went out and across the tarmac to the Navajo where Gagini sat in the cockpit, propellers turning. Dillon went up the steps and turned. Hannah had a last glimpse of him pulling up the Airstair door and then the Navajo moved away.

FIFTEEN

The night sky was clear to the horizon and alive with stars and in the light of the half moon the countryside below was perfectly visible. They were flying at two thousand feet along a deep valley, mountains rising on either side, and when Dillon looked out of one of the windows he could see the white line of a road winding along the valley bottom.

It was all very quick. Gagini climbed to two and a half thousand to negotiate a kind of hump at the end of the valley and beyond was a great sloping plateau and he started down.

Five minutes later he leveled off at eight hundred, turned and called over his shoulder, "Drop the Airstair door. It's any minute now and I don't want to have to go round again, it could alert them. Go when I tell you, and good luck, my friend."

Dillon moved back to the door, awkwardly because of the parachute. He rotated the handle, the door fell out into space, the steps unfolded. There was a roar of air and he held onto the fuselage buffeted by the wind and looked down, and way over on his left was the farmhouse looking just like the photo.

"Now!" Gagini cried.

Dillon took two steps down holding the handrail and then allowed himself to fall, headfirst, turning over once in the plane's slipstream, pulling the ring of the rip cord at the same moment. He looked up, saw the plane climbing steeply over on his left, the noise of the engine already fading.

In the dining room of the farmhouse they had just finished the first course of the dinner and Marco, acting as butler again, was clearing them away when they heard the plane.

"What in the hell is that?" Morgan demanded and he got up and moved out on the terrace, Marco behind him.

The noise of the plane was fading over to the right. Asta came out at that moment. "Are you worried about something?"

"The plane. It seemed so low that for a wild moment I thought it might intend to land."

"Dillon?" She shook her head. "Even he wouldn't be crazy enough to try that."

"No, of course not." He smiled and they went back inside. "Just a passing plane," he said to Luca and he turned to the Brigadier and shrugged. "No cavalry riding to the rescue this time."

"What a pity," Ferguson said.

"Yes, isn't it? We'll continue with the meal, shall we? I'll be back in a moment." He nodded to Marco and went out into the hall with him.

"What is it?" Marco demanded.

"I don't know. That plane made no attempt to land, but it was certainly low when it made its pass."

"Someone sniffing out the lay of the land perhaps," Marco suggested.

"Exactly, then if someone was approaching by road, they could let them know how the situation looked by radio."

Marco shook his head. "No one could get within twenty miles of here by road without us being informed, believe me."

"Yes, perhaps I'm being overcautious, but who have we got?"

"There's the caretaker, Guido. I put him on the gate, and the two shepherds, the Tognolis, Franco and Vito. They've both killed for the Society, they're good men."

"Get them out in the garden and you see to things. I just want to be sure." He laughed and put a hand on Marco's shoulder. "It's my Sicilian half talking."

He returned to the dining room and Marco went to the kitchen where he found Rosa, the caretaker's wife, busy at the stove and the Tognoli brothers seated at one end of the table eating stew.

"You can finish that later," he said. "Right now you get out into the garden just in case. Signore Morgan was unhappy about the plane that passed over."

"At your orders," Franco Togloni said, wiping his mouth with the back of a hand, and he unslung, from the back of his chair, his *Lupara*, the sawed-off shotgun that was the traditional weapon of the Mafia since time immemorial. "Come on," he told his brother. "We've got work to do," and they went out.

Marco picked up a glass of red wine that stood on the table. "You'll have to serve the food yourself, Rosa," he said, emptied the glass at a single swallow, then took a Beretta from his shoulder holster and checked it as he went out.

The silence was extraordinary. Dillon felt no particular exhilaration. It was a strange black-and-white world in the moonlight, rather like one of those dreams in which you dreamed you were flying and time seemed to stand still, and then suddenly the ground was rushing up at him and he hit with a thump and rolled over in long meadow grass.

He lay there for a moment to get his breath, then punched the quick release clip and stepped out of the parachute harness. The farmhouse was two hundred yards to the left beyond an olive grove on a slight rise. He started to run quite fast until he reached the grove, got down in the shelter of trees on the other side and found himself approximately seventy-five yards from the crumbling white wall of the farmhouse.

He focused the night glasses on the gate which stood open and saw Guido the caretaker at the gate straight away in cloth cap and shooting jacket, a shotgun over his shoulder, and yet he wasn't the problem. What was, was the large, old-fashioned bell hanging above the gate, rope dangling. One pull on that and the whole place would be roused.

There was a break on the ground to his right, a gully stretching toward the wall perhaps two feet deep. He crawled along it cautiously and finally reached the wall. The grass was long and overgrown at that point and he unslung the silenced Celeste machine pistol and moved cautiously along the wall, keeping to the grass, but it petered out when he was still twenty yards away.

Guido was smoking a cigarette, his back to Dillon, looking up at the stars, and Dillon stood up and moved quickly, out in the open now. When he was ten yards away, Guido turned, saw him at once, his mouth opening in dismay. He reached up for the bellrope and Dillon fired a short burst that lifted him off his feet, killing him instantly.

It was amazing how little noise the Celeste had made, but there was no time to lose. Dillon dragged Guido's body into the shelter of the wall and dashed through the gate. He immediately left the drive and moved into the shelter of the lush, overgrown semitropical garden. Here too the grass badly needed cutting. He moved cautiously through it between the olive trees toward the house. Quite suddenly, it started to rain, one of those sudden showers common to the region at that time of year and he crouched there, aware of the terrace, the open windows, and the sound of voices.

Marco, on his way down the drive, cursed as the rain started to fall, pulled up his collar, and continued to the gate. It was apparent at once that Guido wasn't there. Marco pulled out his Beretta, moved outside, and saw the body lying at the foot of the wall. He reached for the rope, rang the bell furiously for a few moments, then ran inside the gate.

"Someone's here," he called. "Watch yourselves," then he moved into the bushes, crouching.

In the dining room there was immediate upheaval. "What's happening?" Luca demanded.

"The alarm bell," Morgan said. "Something's up."

"Well, now, who would have thought it?" Ferguson said.

"You shut your mouth." Morgan went to a bureau, opened a drawer to reveal several handguns. He selected a Browning and handed Asta a Walther. "Just in case," he said and at that moment a shotgun blasted outside.

It was Vito Togloni who, panicking, made the mistake of calling to his brother, "Franco, where are you? What's happening?"

Dillon fired a long burst in the direction of the voice. Vito gave a strangled cry and pitched out of the bushes on his face.

Dillon crouched in the rain, waiting, and after a while heard a rustle in the bushes and Franco's voice low, "Hey, Vito, I'm here."

A second later, he moved out of the bushes and paused under an olive tree. Dillon didn't hesitate, driving him back against the tree with another burst from the Celeste. Franco fell, discharging his shotgun, and lay very still. Dillon moved forward, looking down at him, and behind there was the click of a hammer going back.

Marco said, "I've got you now, you bastard. Put that thing down and turn around."

Dillon laid the Celeste on the ground and turned calmly. "Ah, so it's you, Marco, my old son, I wondered where you'd be hiding."

"God knows how you got here, but that doesn't matter now. The only important thing is you're here and I get the pleasure of killing you myself."

He picked up Franco's shotgun with one hand and holstered the Beretta, then he called out, "It's Dillon, Signore Morgan, I've got him here."

"Have you now?" Dillon said.

"This is the *Lupara*, always used by Mafia for a ritual killing."

"Yes, I had heard that," Dillon said. "The only trouble is, old son, it's only double-barreled and it discharged when Franco went down."

There was one single second when Marco took in what he had said and realized it was true. He dropped the shotgun, his hand went inside his coat to the holstered Beretta.

Dillon said, "Goodbye, me old son." His hand found the silenced Walther in his waistband under the tunic at his back, it swung up and he fired twice, each bullet striking Marco in the heart and driving him back.

Dillon stood there looking down at him, then he replaced the Walther in his waistband, reached down and picked up the Celeste. He took a step forward, looking out through the bushes at the terrace, then fired a long burst, raking the wall beside the window.

"It's Dillon," he called. "I'm here, Morgan."

Morgan in the drawing room stood by the dining table, Luca on one side, Asta on the other holding the Walther in her hand.

"Dillon?" he called. "Can you hear me?"

Dillon called back. "Yes."

Morgan went round the table and got Ferguson by the collar. "On your feet," he said. "Or I'll kill you now."

He pushed the Brigadier around the table toward the open windows and the terrace. "Listen to me, Dillon, I've got your boss here. I'll blow his brains all over the room unless you do as I say. After all, he's what you've come for."

There was a marked silence, only the rain falling, and then incredibly Dillon appeared, coming up the steps to the terrace, the Celeste in his hands. He reached the terrace himself and stood there, the rain beating down.

"Now what?" he said.

Morgan, the muzzle of his Browning against Ferguson's temple, pulled him back, step-by-step, until he stood at the end of the table, Luca still sitting on one side of him, Asta on the other, her right hand clutching the Walther against her thigh.

Dillon moved into the entrance, a supremely menacing figure in the camouflaged uniform, his hair plastered to his skull. He spoke in Irish and then smiled.

"That means God bless all here."

Morgan said, "Don't make the wrong move."

"Now why would I?" Dillon moved to one side of the table and nodded to Asta. "Is that a gun in your hand, girl? I hope you know how to use it."

"I know," she said and her eyes were like dark holes, her face very pale.

"Then move to one side." She hesitated and he said, his voice harsh, "Do it, Asta."

She stepped back and Morgan said, "Don't worry. If he fires that thing he takes all of us and that includes the Brigadier, isn't that so, Dillon?"

"True," Dillon said. "I presume the overweight gentleman is your uncle, Giovanni Luca. It would include him too. A great loss to this Honoured Society of yours."

"There is a time for all things, Dillon," the old man said. "I'm not afraid."

Dillon nodded. "I respect that, but you're living in the past, Capo, you've been Lord of Life and Death too long."

"Everything comes to an end sometime, Mr. Dillon," Luca said and there was a strange look in his eyes.

Morgan said, "To hell with this, put the machine pistol on the table, Dillon, or I'll spread Ferguson's brains over the cutlery, I swear it."

Dillon stood there, holding the Celeste comfortably, and Ferguson said, "I abhor bad language, dear boy, but you have my permission to shoot the fucking lot of them."

Dillon smiled suddenly, that deeply personal smile of total charm. "God save you, Brigadier, but I came to take you home and I didn't intend in a coffin."

He moved to the table, placed the Celeste down, and pushed it along to the end where it came to a halt in front of Luca.

There was a kind of relief on Morgan's face and he pushed Ferguson away from him. "So, here we are, Dillon. You're a remarkable man, I'll give you that."

"Oh, don't flatter me, old son."

"Marco?" Morgan asked.

"He's gone the way of all flesh plus two fellas in cloth caps I found prowling in the garden." Dillon smiled. "Sure and I was forgetting the one at the gate. That makes four, Morgan. I'm nearly as good as that tailor in the fairy tale by the Brothers Grimm. He boasted six at one blow, but they were flies on the jam and bread."

"You bastard," Morgan said. "I'm going to enjoy killing you."

Dillon turned to Asta. "Are you taking all this in? It's fun, isn't it? Right up your street!"

She said, "Talk all you want, Dillon, you're finished."

"Not yet, Asta, things to be said." He smiled at Morgan. "A strange one, the girl here. She looks like she's off page fifty-two in *Vogue* magazine, but there's another side to her. She likes the violence. Gets off on it."

"Shut your mouth!" Asta said in a low voice.

"And why should I do that, girl, especially if he's going to blow me away? A few words only. The condemned man's entitled to that."

Morgan said, "You're talking yourself into the grave."

"Yes, well, that's waiting for all of us, the one sure thing, the only difference is how you get there. Now take your wife, for instance, a strange business that."

The Browning seemed suddenly heavy in Morgan's hand. It came down and he held it against his thigh. "What are you talking about, Dillon?"

"She died scuba diving off Hydra in the Aegean Sea, am I right? An unfortunate accident."

"That's right."

"Ferguson got a copy of the report compiled by the Athens police. There were you and your wife, Asta, and a divemaster on board."

"So?"

"She ran out of air and the police report indicates that was no accident. The valve system in her equipment had been interfered with. Difficult to prove anything, especially with a man as powerful as the great Carl Morgan, so they put that report on file."

"You're lying," Morgan said.

"No, I've seen the report. Now who would want to kill her? Hardly the divemaster, so we can eliminate him. We thought it was you and told Asta as much, but you said on the boat it was a filthy lie and seemed to mean it." Dillon shrugged. "That only seems to leave one person."

Asta screamed, "You bastard, Dillon!"

Morgan stilled her with one raised hand. "That's nonsense, it can't be."

"All right, so you're going to kill me, so just answer one question. The night of the dinner party, the brakes were interfered with on our estate car. Now if that was you it would imply you wanted Asta dead because you let her take a ride back to the lodge with us."

"But that's nonsense," Morgan said, "I'd never do anything to harm Asta. It was an accident."

There was a silence and Dillon turned to Asta. When she smiled, it was the most terrible thing he'd ever seen in his life. "You really are a clever one, aren't you?" she said and her hand came up with the Walther.

"You screwed up the braking system and yet you came with us?" he said.

"Oh, I had every confidence in you, Dillon, it seemed likely we'd survive with you at the wheel, but I knew you'd blame Carl and that would strengthen my position with you." She turned to Morgan. "It was all for you, Carl, so I could find out every move they were likely to make."

"And your mother?" Ferguson said. "Was that also for Morgan?"

"My mother?" She stared at them, a strangely blank look on her face, and she turned to Morgan again. "That was different. She was in the way, trying to take you away from me, and she shouldn't have done that. I saved her, saved her from my father." She smiled. "He interfered with our lives once too often." She smiled again. "He liked fast women and he liked fast cars, so I made sure he ran off the road in one."

Morgan looked at her, horror on his face. "Asta, what are you saying?"

"Please, Carl, you must understand. I love you, I always have. No one else has ever loved you as I have, just like you love me."

The look on her face was that of the truly mad and Morgan seemed to come apart. "Love you? There was only one woman I loved and you killed her."

The Browning swung up, but already Dillon's hand was on the butt of the Walther in his waistband at the rear. He shot Morgan twice in the heart. Morgan went down and Luca reached for the Celeste. Dillon turned, his arm extended, and shot him between the eyes and the Capo went back over the chair.

In the same moment Asta screamed, "No!" She shot Dillon twice in the back, driving him facedown across the table, then she turned and ran out through the French windows.

Dillon, having difficulty breathing, almost unconscious, was aware of Ferguson calling his name, distress in his voice. His hands found the edge of the table, he levered himself up and lurched to the nearest chair. He sat there, gasping for breath, then reached for the Velcro tabs on the bulletproof waistcoat, opened them, and took it off. When he examined it, the two bullets she had fired were embedded in the material.

"Would you look at that now?" he said to Ferguson. "Thank God for modern technology."

"Dillon, I thought I'd lost you. Here, have a drink." Ferguson poured red wine into one of the glasses on the table. "I could do with one myself."

Dillon took it down. "Jesus, that's better. Are you all right, you old sod?"

"Never better. How in the hell did you get here?"

"Gagini flew me in and I parachuted."

Ferguson looked shocked. "I didn't know you could do that."

"There's always a first time." Dillon reached for the bottle and poured another glass.

Ferguson toasted him. "You're a remarkable man."

"To be honest with you, Brigadier, there's those who might think me a bit of a bloody genius, but that could be a subject for debate. What happened to the Covenant?"

Ferguson went to Luca, dropped to one knee, and felt in his inside pocket. He stood up, turned and unfolded the document. "The Chungking Covenant, that's what it was all about."

"And this is how it ends," Dillon said. "Do you have a match and we'll burn the damn thing?"

"No, I don't think so." Ferguson folded it carefully, took out his wallet, and put it inside. "I think we'll leave that to the Prime Minister."

"You old bastard," Dillon said. "It's a Knighthood you're after so it is."

He got up, lit a cigarette, and went out to the terrace and Ferguson joined him. "I wonder where she is? I heard some sort of car leave when I was trying to revive you."

"Long gone, Brigadier," Dillon said.

There was a roar of engines overhead, a dark shadow swooping down to the meadow. "Good God, what's that?" Ferguson said.

"Hannah Bernstein coming to pick up the pieces plus the good Major Gagini. He's been more than helpful on this. You owe him one."

"I shan't forget," Ferguson said.

Hannah Bernstein stood just inside the dining room, Gagini at her side, and surveyed the scene. "Oh, my God," she said, "a butcher's shop."

"Do you have a problem with this, Chief Inspector?" Ferguson asked. "Let me tell you what happened here." Which he did.

She took a deep breath when he was finished, and on impulse went and kissed him on the cheek. "I'm glad to see you in one piece."

"Thanks to Dillon."

"Yes." She looked again at Morgan and Luca. "He doesn't take prisoners, does he?"

"Four more in the grounds, my dear."

She shuddered and Dillon came in through the French windows with Gagini. The Italian stood looking down at Luca and shook his head. "I never thought to see the day. They won't believe he's gone in Palermo."

"You should put him in an open coffin in a shop window like they used to do with outlaws in the Wild West," Dillon told him.

"Dillon, for God's sake," Hannah said.

"You think I was bad, Hannah?" Dillon shrugged. "An animal, this one, who grew fat not only off gambling but on drugs and prostitution. He was responsible for the corruption of thousands. To hell with him," and he turned and walked out.

At Punta Raisi it was raining as they waited in the office. Lacey looked in the door. "Ready when you are."

Gagini came through the hangar with them and walked across the apron. "Strange how it all worked out, Brigadier, I thought I was doing you a favor when I got in touch with you about the Chungking Covenant, and in the end you do me the biggest favor of all. You got rid of Luca for me."

"Ah, but that was Dillon's doing, not mine."

Dillon said sourly, "Don't get too worked up, Major, there'll be someone to take his place by tomorrow morning."

"True," Gagini said. "But some sort of victory." He held out his hand. "Thank you, my friend. Anything I can ever do you only have to ask."

"I'll remember that."

Dillon shook hands, went up the steps into the Lear, and settled in one of the rear seats. Ferguson sat opposite him on the other side and Hannah took the seat behind him. They strapped themselves in and the engines turned over. A few moments later they were moving along the runway and lifting into the air. They climbed steadily until they reached thirty thousand and started to cruise.

Hannah sat there, face grave, and Dillon said belligerently, "What's wrong with you?"

"I'm tired, it's been a long day and I can still smell the cordite and the blood, Dillon, is that so strange? I don't like it." She exploded suddenly, "My God, you just killed six people, six, Dillon. Doesn't that bother you?"

"What am I hearing?" he said. "Some sort of fine interpretation on this? The kind of morality that says let your enemy do it unto you, but don't do it unto him?"

"All right, so I don't know what I mean." There was no doubt that she was genuinely upset.

Dillon said, "Then maybe you're in the wrong job. I'd think about that if I were you."

"And how do you see yourself, as some sort of public executioner?"

"Enough, both of you." Ferguson opened the bar box, took out a half bottle of Scotch, poured some into a plastic cup and handed it to her. "Drink that, it's an order."

She took a deep breath and reached for it. "Thank you, sir."

Ferguson poured a generous measure into another cup and passed it to Dillon. "Try that." Dillon nodded and drank deep and the Brigadier poured himself one.

"It's the business we're in, Chief Inspector, try to remember that. Of course, if you're unhappy and wish to return to normal duty?"

"No, sir," she said. "That won't be necessary."

Dillon reached for the bottle and poured another and Ferguson said, "I wonder what happened to that wretched young woman?"

"God knows," Dillon said.

"Mad as a hatter," Ferguson said, "so much is obvious, but that isn't our problem," and he closed his eyes and lay back in the seat.

It was at about the same time that Asta arrived at the gate of Luca's Villa. She kept her hand on the horn and the guard appeared on the other side. He took one look and hurriedly opened the gate and she drove through and up to the house. When she got out of the station wagon, the door opened at the top of the steps and Luca's houseboy, Giorgio, appeared.

"Signorina. You are alone? The Capo and Signore Morgan come later?"

She could have told him the truth, yet for some reason hesitated and at the same time realized why. If Luca was still alive she could still use his power and she wanted that power.

"Yes," she said, "the Capo and Signore Morgan are staying at Valdini on business. You will get in touch with the chief pilot of the Lear. What is his name?"

"Ruffolo, Signorina."

"Yes, that's right. Find where he is and tell him to get out here as fast as possible and get in touch with our contact at the airport. There is a Lear from England there. It may have already left, but get all the information you can."

"Of course, Signorina." He bowed, ushering her into the house, closed the door, and went to the phone.

She went and poured herself a drink and stood sipping it, staring out across the terrace, and was surprised at how quickly Giorgio returned. "I've found Ruffolo, he is on his way and you were right, Signorina. The English Lear has departed. There were two pilots and three passengers."

She stared at him. "Three, are you sure?"

"Yes, a woman, a stout ageing man, and a small man with very fair hair. Our contact didn't get the names, but saw them boarding."

"I see. Good work, Giorgio. Call me when Ruffolo gets here."

Asta stripped and stood under a hot shower. It was like a bad dream, so difficult to believe that Dillon was still alive. Carl, her beloved Carl, and Luca and it was all Dillon's fault. How could she have ever liked him? Dillon and Ferguson, but especially Dillon. They'd ruined everything and for that they had to pay.

She got out of the shower, toweled herself down, then oiled her body, thinking about it. Finally, she pulled on a robe and started to comb her hair. The phone rang. When she lifted it up it was Giorgio.

"Signorina. Captain Ruffolo is here."

"Good, I'll be right down."

Ruffolo was in an open-necked shirt, blazer, and slacks when she went in the sitting room. He came to greet her, kissing her hand.

"Forgive me, Signorina, I'd gone out for a meal, but Giorgio managed to trace me. How can I serve you?"

"Please, sit down." She waved him to a chair, went and started to open a bottle of Bollinger champagne Giorgio had left in an ice bucket. "You'll take a glass, Captain."

"My pleasure, Signorina." His eyes fastened on the ripe curves of her young body and he sat up straight.

Asta poured champagne into two crystal glasses and handed one to him. "This is a delicate matter, Captain. The Capo has given me a special task. I am to go to England tomorrow, but not officially, if you understand me."

Ruffolo sampled a little of the champagne. "Excellent, Signorina. What you mean is you would like to land in England illegally, no trace that you are there, am I right?"

"Exactly, Captain."

"There is no problem on this. There is a private airfield in Sussex we can use. I've done this before. There is so much traffic in the London approaches that if I go in from the sea at six hundred feet there is no trace. Is it London you wish to go to?"

"Yes," she said.

"Only thirty miles away by road. No problem."

"Wonderful," she said, got up and went back to the champagne bucket. "The Capo will be pleased. Now let me give you another glass of champagne."

SIXTEEN

It was just before six the following evening when the Daimler was admitted through the security gates at Downing Street. Dillon, Ferguson, and Hannah Bernstein sat in the back and when the chauffeur opened the door for them it was only Ferguson and Hannah who got out.

Ferguson turned. "Sorry about this but you'll have to wait for us, Dillon. I don't expect we'll be long."

"I know." Dillon smiled. "I embarrass the man."

They went to the door where the duty policeman, recognizing Ferguson, saluted. It opened at once and they passed inside, where an aide took their coats and Ferguson's Malacca cane. They followed him upstairs and along the corridor. A second later and he was admitting them to the study where they found the Prime Minister sitting behind his desk working his way through a mass of papers.

He glanced up and sat back. "Brigadier, Chief Inspector. Do sit down."

"Thank you, Prime Minister," Ferguson said and they pulled chairs forward.

The Prime Minister reached for a file and opened it. "I've read your report. An absolutely first-class job. Dillon seems to have acted with his usual rather ruthless efficiency."

"Yes, Prime Minister."

"On the other hand, without him we'd have lost you, Brigadier, and I wouldn't have liked that at all, a disaster for all of us, wouldn't you agree, Chief Inspector?"

"Absolutely, Prime Minister."

"Where is Dillon now, by the way?"

"Waiting outside in my Daimler, Prime Minister," Ferguson told him. "I feel it the sensible thing to do considering Dillon's rather unusual background."

"Of course." The Prime Minister nodded and then smiled. "Which leaves us with the Chungking Covenant." He took it from the file. "Remarkable document. It raises such infinite possibilities, but as I said at the first meeting we had about this affair, we've had enough trouble with Hong Kong. We're getting out and that's it, which is why I told you to find the damn thing and burn it."

"I rather thought you'd like to do that yourself, Prime Minister."

The Prime Minister smiled. "Very thoughtful of you, Brigadier."

There was a fire burning brightly in the grate of the Victorian fireplace. He got up, went to it, and placed the document on top. The edges curled in the heat, then it burst into flame. A moment later it was simply gray ash already dissolving.

The Prime Minister turned, came round his desk. "I'd like to thank you both." He shook hands with them. "And thank Dillon for me, Brigadier."

"I will, Prime Minister."

"And now you must excuse me, I'm due at the House of Commons. An extra Prime Minister's question time. We must let members have their moment of fun."

"I understand, Prime Minister," Ferguson said.

Behind them, by the usual mysterious alchemy, the door opened and the aide reappeared to show them out.

It went well then?" Dillon said as the Daimler turned out through the security gates into Whitehall.

"You could say that. He enjoyed the pleasure of putting the Chungking Covenant on the fire himself."

"Well that was nice for the man."

"He did ask the Brigadier to thank you, Dillon," Hannah said.

"Did he now?" Dillon turned to Ferguson, who sat with his hands folded over the silver handle of his Malacca cane. "You didn't mention that."

"Didn't want it to go to your head, dear boy." He opened the partition window. "Cavendish Square." He sat back. "I thought we'd all have a drink at my place."

"Oh, Jesus, your honor," Dillon said. "It's so kind of you to ask us, the grand man like yourself."

"Stop playing the stage Irishman, Dillon, it doesn't suit you."

"Terribly sorry, sir." Dillon was all public school English now. "But the fact is I'd take it as a real honor if you and the Chief Inspector would have a drink with me at my place." He opened the partition window again. "Change of venue, driver, make it Stable Mews."

As Dillon closed the window Ferguson sighed and said to Hannah, "You'll have to excuse him, he used to be an actor, you see."

The Daimler turned into the cobbled yard of Stable Mews and stopped outside Dillon's cottage. "Wait for us," Ferguson told his driver as the Irishman unlocked the front door and Hannah followed him in. Ferguson joined them, closing the door.

"This is really rather nice," he said.

"Come in the sitting room." Dillon led the way in, feeling for the switch and when the light came on, Asta Morgan was sitting in the wing-backed chair by the fireplace. She wore a jump suit in black crushed velvet and a black beret. More important, she held a Walther in her lap, a silencer screwed to the end of the barrel.

"Well this is nice, here I was waiting for you, Dillon, and I get all three." Her eyes glittered, her face was very pale, dark shadows under her eyes.

"Now don't be a silly girl," Ferguson told her.

"Oh, but I've been a very *clever* girl, Brigadier. I'm not even supposed to be in the country and when I've finished here, my plane's waiting on a quiet little airstrip in Sussex to fly me out again."

"What do you want, Asta?" Dillon said.

"Turn round and lean on the table. As I remember, you favor a gun in the waistband at the back. That's how you killed Carl." There was nothing there. She checked his armpits. "No gun, Dillon. That's rather careless."

"We've been to Downing Street, you see," Ferguson said. "Most sophisticated alarm system in the world there. Try passing through the security gates with any kind of gun and all hell would break loose."

"Yes, well you can bend over too." Ferguson did as he was told and when she was finished she turned to Hannah. "Empty your handbag on the floor."

Hannah did as she was told and a compact, gold lipstick, wallet, comb, and car keys scattered on the floor. "See, no gun, the Brigadier was telling the truth."

"Stand over there," Asta ordered, "and you move to the right, Brigadier." Dillon still had his back to her. "I thought I'd killed you back there at the farm, Dillon. I'd like to know how I failed."

"Bulletproof vest," he said. "They're all the rage these days."

"Oh, you're good with the one-liners," she said, "but you ruined everything for me, Dillon, took Carl from me and for that you pay."

"And what would you suggest?" Dillon said, easing his feet apart ever so slightly.

"Two in the stomach, that should make you squirm."

Hannah Bernstein reached for a small Greek statue that stood on the coffee table next to her and threw it at her. Asta ducked and fired wildly, catching Hannah in the left shoulder and knocking her back across the sofa. Dillon made his move, but she turned, the barrel of the Walther pushing out toward him.

"Goodbye, Dillon."

Behind her there was a click as Charles Ferguson turned the silver handle of his Malacca cane to one side, the nine-inch poniard it contained flashed out, and he plunged it into her back, penetrating her heart, the point emerging through the front of the jump suit.

She didn't even have time to cry out, the Walther falling from a nerveless hand, and she lurched forward, Dillon's hands catching each arm. Ferguson withdrew the poniard. She glanced down at her chest in a kind of amazement, looked at Dillon once more as if she didn't believe what was happening, and then her knees gave way and she went down, rolling on her back.

Dillon let her go and crossed to Hannah, who lay back against the sofa, a hand to her shoulder, blood oozing between her fingers. He got his handkerchief out and put it in her hand. "Hold this against it hard. You'll be all right, I promise you."

He turned to find Ferguson on the telephone. "Yes, Professor Henry Bellamy for Brigadier Charles Ferguson. An emergency." He stood there waiting, the bloodstained poniard in his hand, the cane on the floor. "Henry? Charles here. Gunshot wound in the left shoulder, Chief Inspector Bernstein. I'll have Dillon bring her round to the London Clinic now. I'll see you later."

He put the phone down and turned. "Right, Dillon, into the Daimler and round to the clinic fast. Bellamy will be there as soon as you are."

Dillon helped Hannah up and glanced at Asta. "What about her?"

"Quite dead, but I'll see to it. Now get moving."

He followed them along the hall, opened the door, and saw them into the Daimler, then he went back. He had laid the poniard on the desk and now he picked it up, took his handkerchief from his breast pocket, and wiped the blade carefully. He replaced it in the Malacca cane, stood looking down at her, then picked up the phone and dialed a number.

A calm, detached voice said, "Yes?"

"Ferguson. I have a disposal for you. Absolutely top priority. I'm at Stable Mews round the corner from Cavendish Square."

"Dillon's place?"

"That's right. I'll wait for you."

"Twenty minutes, Brigadier."

Ferguson replaced the receiver, stepped over Asta's body, went to Dillon's drinks cabinet and poured a Scotch.

Dillon was sitting in the corridor outside the operating theater an hour later when Ferguson joined him. "How are things?" the Brigadier said as he sat down.

"We'll know soon. Bellamy said a simple extraction job. He didn't anticipate any problems." Dillon lit a cigarette. "You moved fast back there, Brigadier, I really thought I was on the way out."

"Well you weren't."

"What have you done about it?"

"Called in the disposal unit. I waited for them. She'll be processed through a certain crematorium in North London that we find rather useful. Six pounds of gray ash by tomorrow morning and as far as I'm concerned they can do what they like with it. We won't tell the Chief Inspector until she's back on her feet."

"I know," Dillon said. "That fine Hassidic conscience of hers."

The theater door opened and Bellamy emerged, mask down. They got up. "How is she?" Ferguson demanded.

"Fine. Nice clean wound. A week in the hospital, that's all. She'll be on the mend in no time. Here she comes now."

A nurse pushed out Hannah Bernstein on a trolley. Her face was drawn and pale under a white skullcap. The nurse paused for them to look down and Hannah's eyelids flickered, then opened.

"Dillon, is that you?"

"As ever was, girl dear."

"I'm glad you're all right. You are a bastard, but for some strange reason I like you."

Her eyes closed again. "Take her away, nurse," Bellamy said and turned to Ferguson. "I'll get off now, Charles, see you tomorrow," and he walked away.

Ferguson put a hand on Dillon's shoulder. "I think we should go too, dear boy, it's been a hell of a day. I think a drink is in order."

Now where shall we go?" Ferguson said as the Daimler pulled away.

Dillon slid back the glass partition. "The Embankment, Lambeth Bridge end will do fine."

Ferguson said, "Any particular reason?"

"The night of the Brazilian Embassy Ball, Asta Morgan and I walked along the Embankment in the rain."

"I see," Ferguson said and sat back without another word.

Ten minutes later, the Daimler pulled in by the bridge. It was raining hard and Dillon got out and walked to the parapet beside the river. Ferguson joined him a moment later holding an umbrella.

"As I said, she was as mad as a hatter, not your problem, dear boy."

"Don't worry, Brigadier, just exorcising the ghost." Dillon took out a cigarette and lit it. "Actually, she can rot in hell as far as I'm concerned. Now let's go and get that drink," and he turned and went back to the car.